THE FANS DEMAND A SEQUEL!

JACK, QUINT, JUNE, and **DIRK** are basking in the success of their very first graphic novel collab—the Heroes of Apocalyptia is an instant hit! But being bestselling authors isn't all fun and games. Now the kids must get to work on the sequel, and like all sequels, it must be **BIGGER, BETTER,** and **PACKED WITH EVEN MORE NEAT STUFF!**

So the kids put their heads together to plot another action-packed adventure for their superhero alter egos.

After succeeding Z-Man in becoming the new protectors of Apocalyptia, Doc Baker, Boy Lightning, Moonstar, and the Savage Aloner make a startling discovery: super-villains do *not* come up with their own evil plans! The shocking truth? Every super-villain scheme comes from the mind of a single, mysterious bad guy.

With new villains popping up in every corner of Apocalyptia, our superheroes are sent on a mad-dash, puzzle-filled mission to stop the **BIGGEST EVIL PLAN IN HISTORY!** Will they triumph once more? Or be crushed by the power of *too many villains*?!?

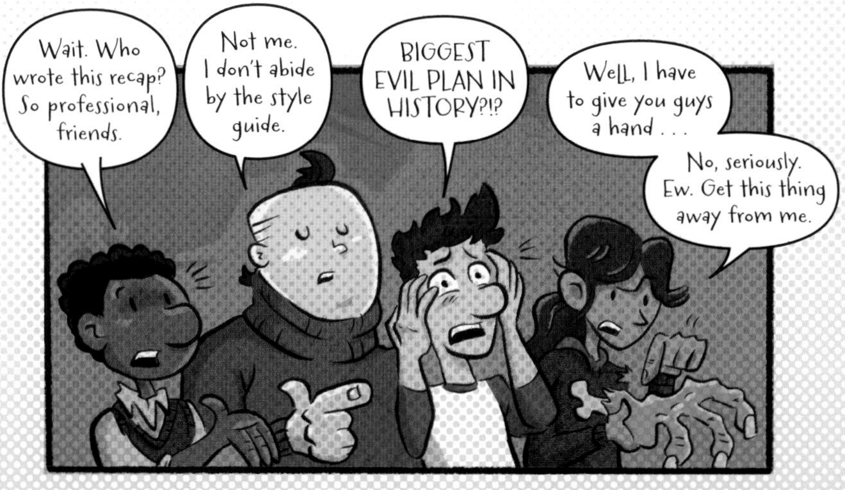
Wait. Who wrote this recap? So professional, friends.
Not me. I don't abide by the style guide.
BIGGEST EVIL PLAN IN HISTORY?!?
Well, I have to give you guys a hand . . .
No, seriously. Ew. Get this thing away from me.

A STILL-SORTA-NEW DAWN FOR THE LAST KIDS ON EARTH CONTINUES TO BEGIN!

THE LAST ~~KIDS~~ COMICS ON EARTH

TOO MANY VILLAINS!

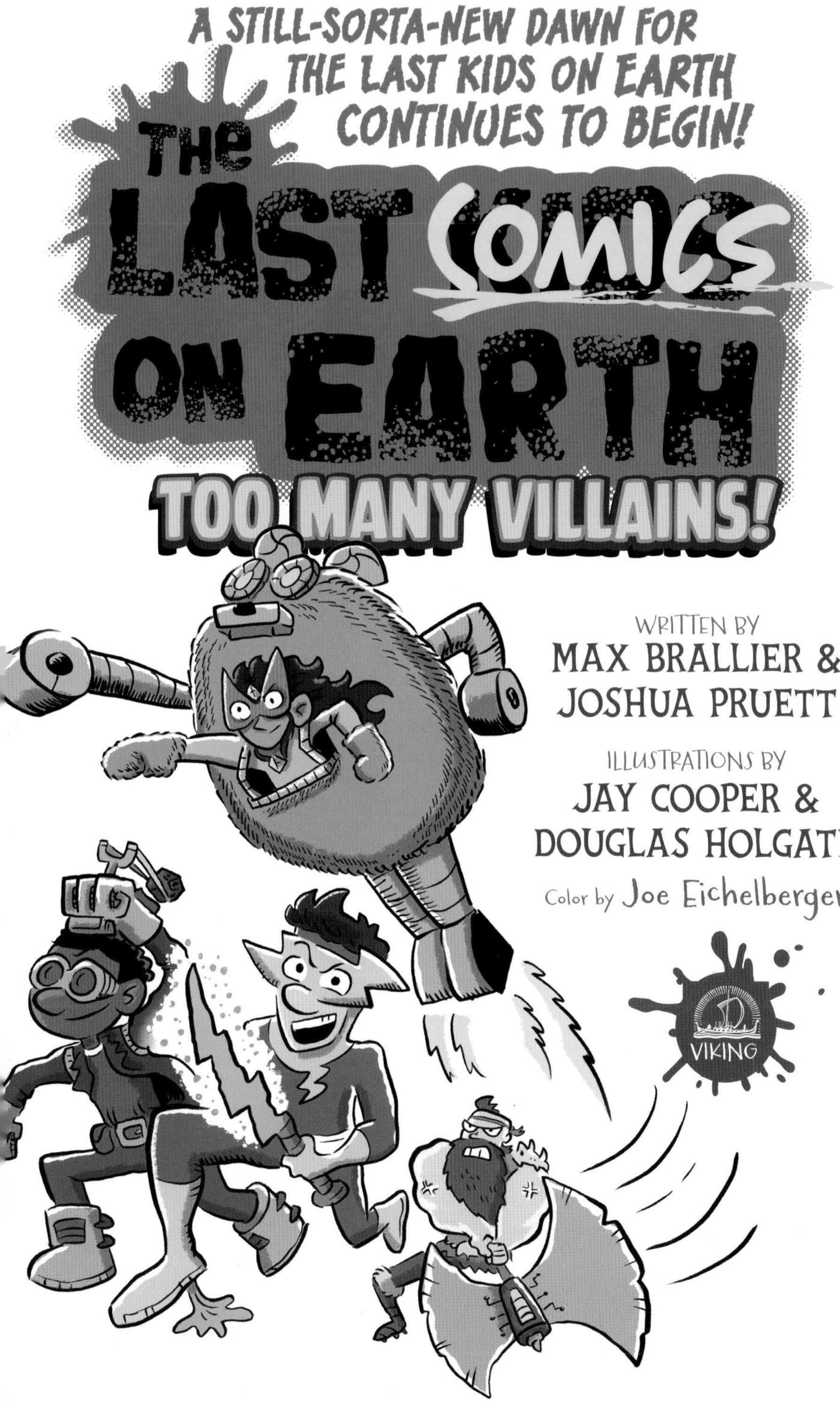

WRITTEN BY

MAX BRALLIER & JOSHUA PRUETT

ILLUSTRATIONS BY

JAY COOPER & DOUGLAS HOLGATE

Color by Joe Eichelberger

VIKING

VIKING
An imprint of Penguin Random House LLC, New York

First published in the United States of America by Viking,
an imprint of Penguin Random House LLC, 2024

Text copyright © 2024 by Max Brallier
Illustrations pages 6–12, 174–177, 236–239 copyright © 2024 by Douglas Holgate
Illustrations page 244 from *The Last Kids on Earth: Thrilling Tales from the
Tree House* copyright © 2021 by Penguin Random House LLC
All other illustrations, unless otherwise marked, copyright © 2024
  by Penguin Random House LLC
Clock image on page 69 courtesy of iStock

Visit us online at PenguinRandomHouse.com.

Library of Congress Cataloging-in-Publication Data is available.

ISBN 9780593526798

10   9   8   7   6   5   4   3   2   1

TOPL

Manufactured in China

Book design by Jim Hoover and Chris Dickey   Color by Joe Eichelberger

For Alyse and Lila.

—M. B.

For Amanda, who laughs at most of my jokes,
and Catie and Zach, who laugh at the rest of them.
And to Myself, who laughs at *all* of my jokes.

—J. P.

For Vinny,
my favorite (occasionally evil) genius.
I miss you.

—J. C.

CHAPTER ONE A SEQUEL SHALL RISE

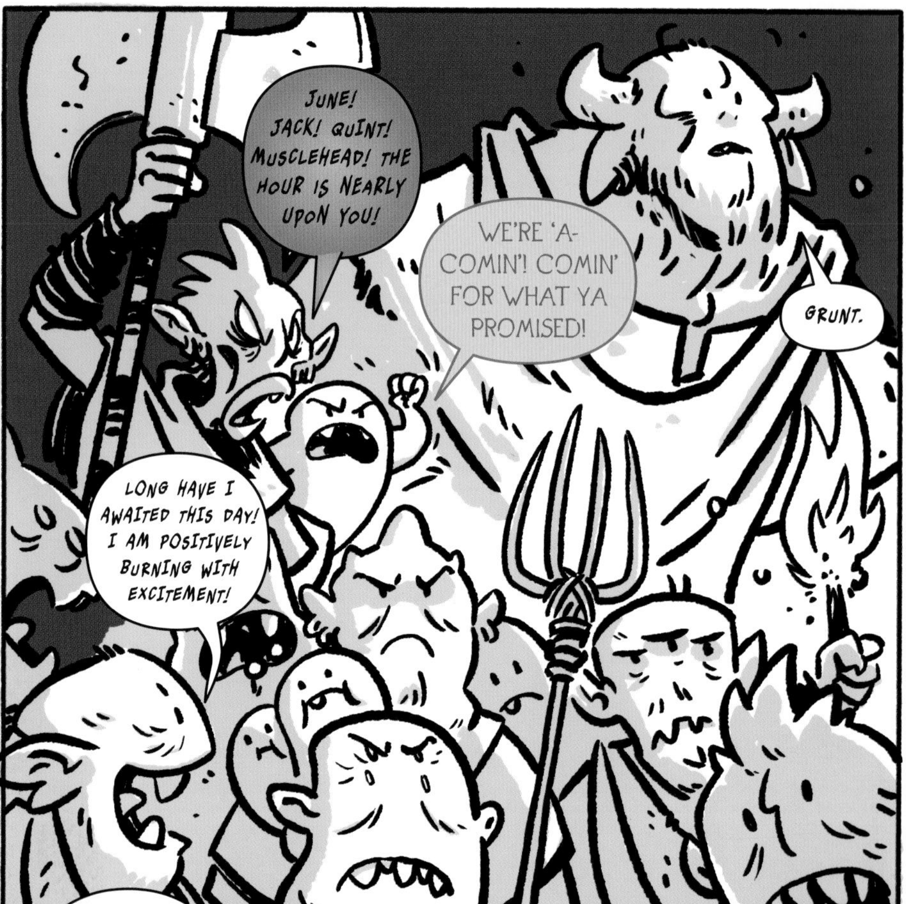

JUNE! JACK! QUINT! MUSCLEHEAD! THE HOUR IS NEARLY UPON YOU!
WE'RE 'A-COMIN'! COMIN' FOR WHAT YA PROMISED!
GRUNT.
LONG HAVE I AWAITED THIS DAY! I AM POSITIVELY BURNING WITH EXCITEMENT!

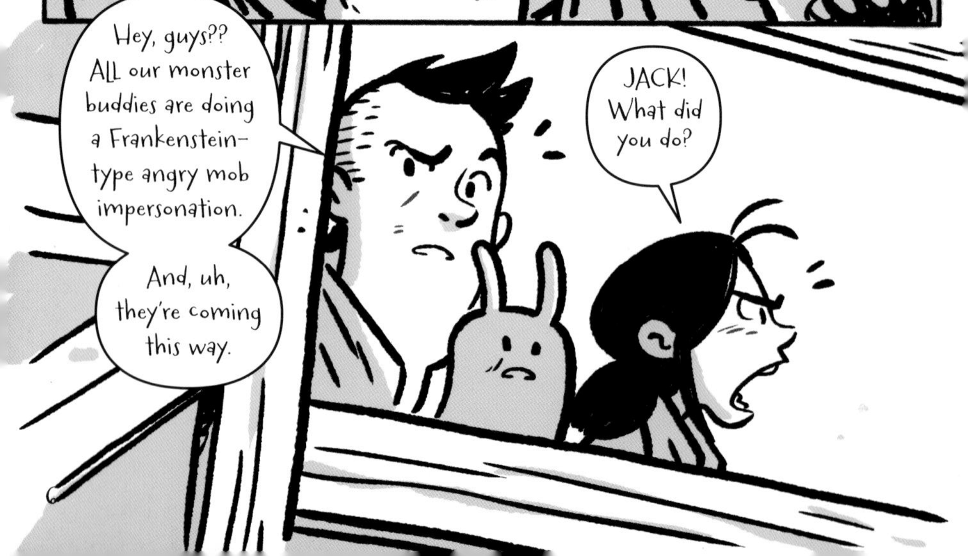

Hey, guys?? ALL our monster buddies are doing a Frankenstein-type angry mob impersonation.
And, uh, they're coming this way.
JACK! What did you do?

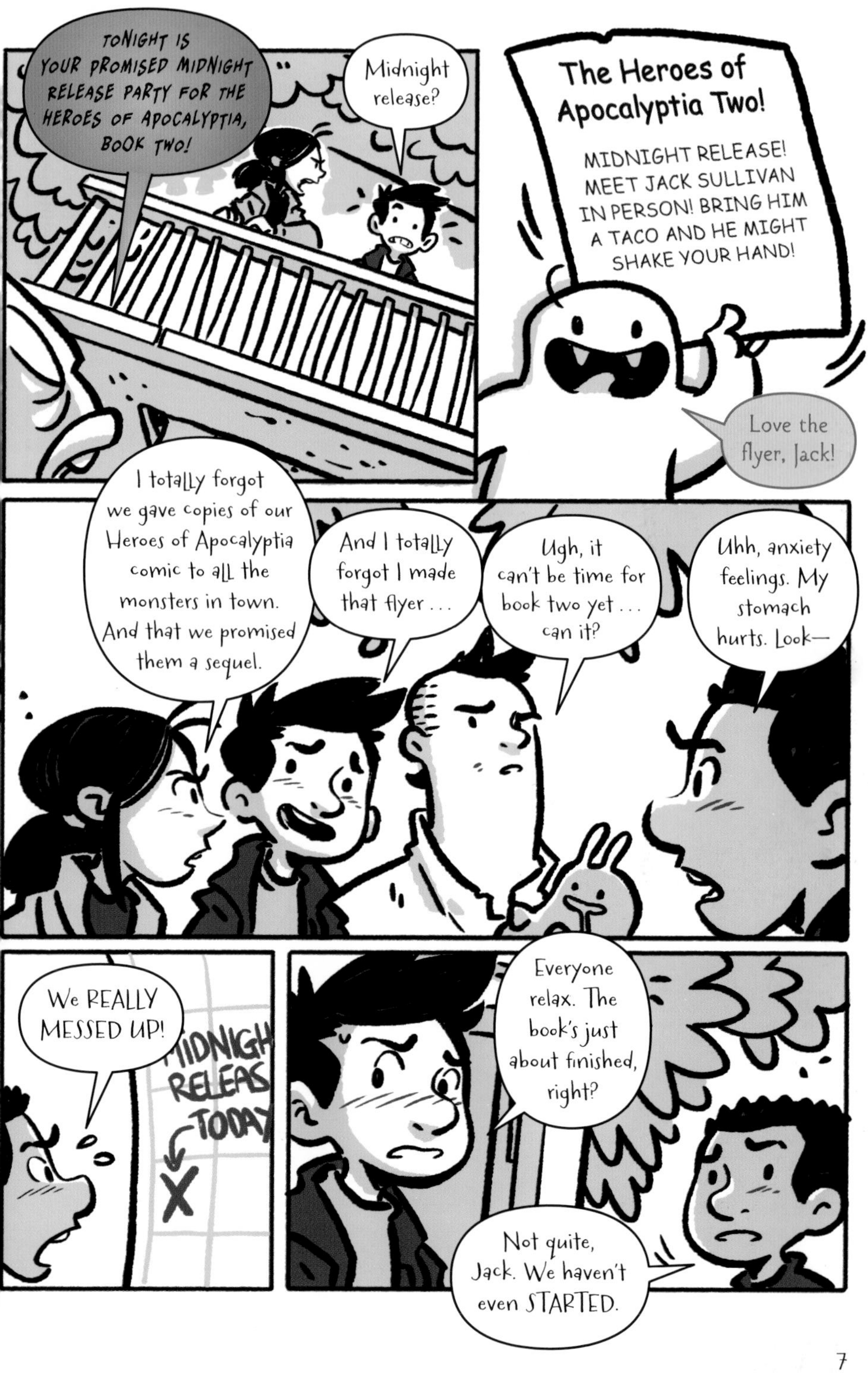
TONIGHT IS YOUR PROMISED MIDNIGHT RELEASE PARTY FOR THE HEROES OF APOCALYPTIA, BOOK TWO!
Midnight release?
The Heroes of Apocalyptia Two!
MIDNIGHT RELEASE! MEET JACK SULLIVAN IN PERSON! BRING HIM A TACO AND HE MIGHT SHAKE YOUR HAND!
Love the flyer, Jack!
I totally forgot we gave copies of our Heroes of Apocalyptia comic to all the monsters in town. And that we promised them a sequel.
And I totally forgot I made that flyer . . .
Ugh, it can't be time for book two yet . . . can it?
Uhh, anxiety feelings. My stomach hurts. Look—
We REALLY MESSED UP!
MIDNIGH
RELEAS
TODAY
X
Everyone relax. The book's just about finished, right?
Not quite, Jack. We haven't even STARTED.

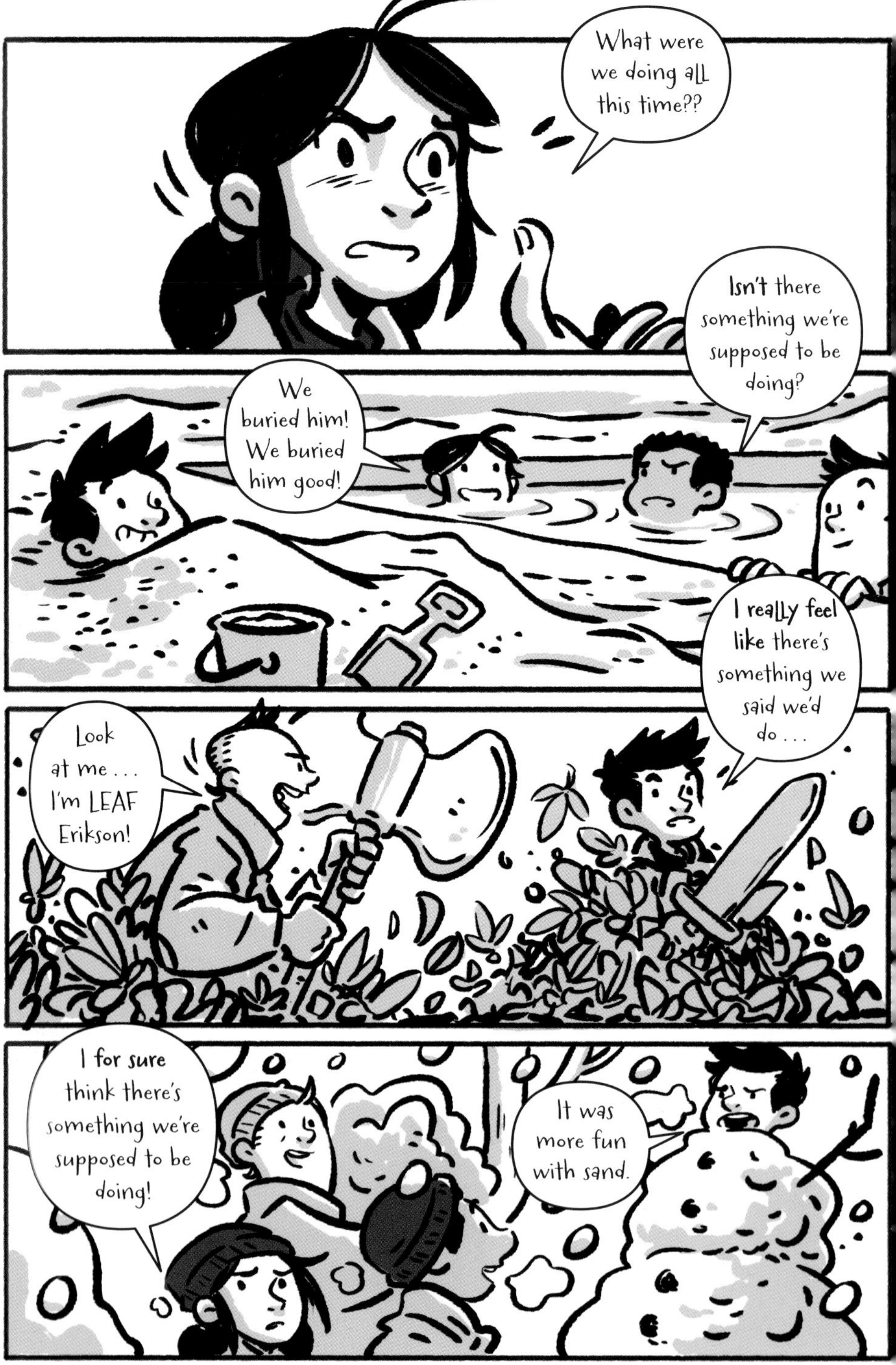
What were we doing aLL this time??
We buried him! We buried him good!
Isn't there something we're supposed to be doing?
Look at me . . . I'm LEAF Erikson!
I really feel like there's something we said we'd do . . .
I for sure think there's something we're supposed to be doing!
It was more fun with sand.

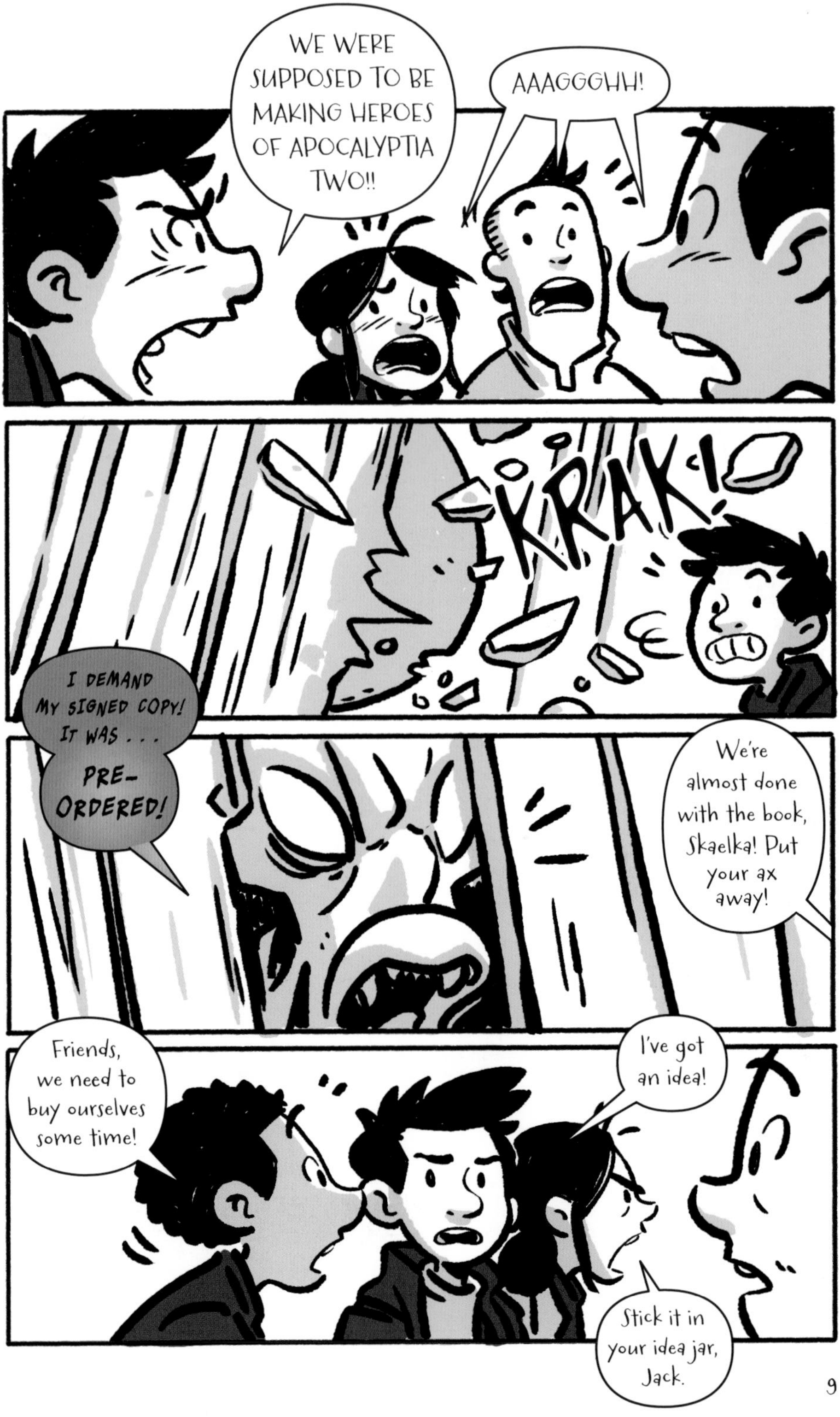
WE WERE SUPPOSED TO BE MAKING HEROES OF APOCALYPTIA TWO!!
AAAGGGHH!
KRAK!
I DEMAND MY SIGNED COPY! IT WAS . . .
PRE-ORDERED!
We're almost done with the book, Skaelka! Put your ax away!
Friends, we need to buy ourselves some time!
I've got an idea!
Stick it in your idea jar, Jack.

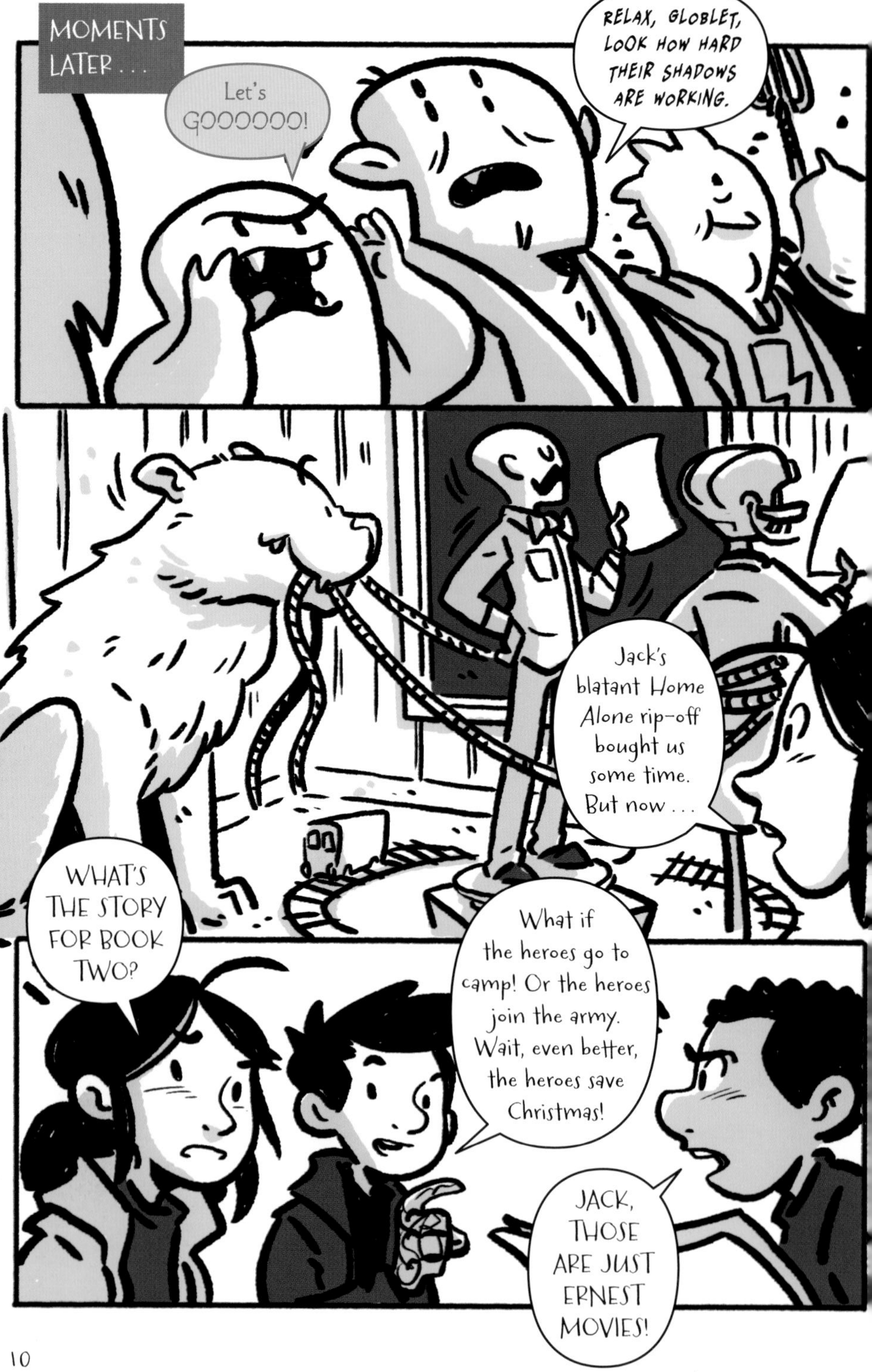
MOMENTS LATER . . .
Let's GOOOOOO!
RELAX, GLOBLET, LOOK HOW HARD THEIR SHADOWS ARE WORKING.
Jack's blatant Home Alone rip-off bought us some time. But now . . .
WHAT'S THE STORY FOR BOOK TWO?
What if the heroes go to camp! Or the heroes join the army. Wait, even better, the heroes save Christmas!
JACK, THOSE ARE JUST ERNEST MOVIES!

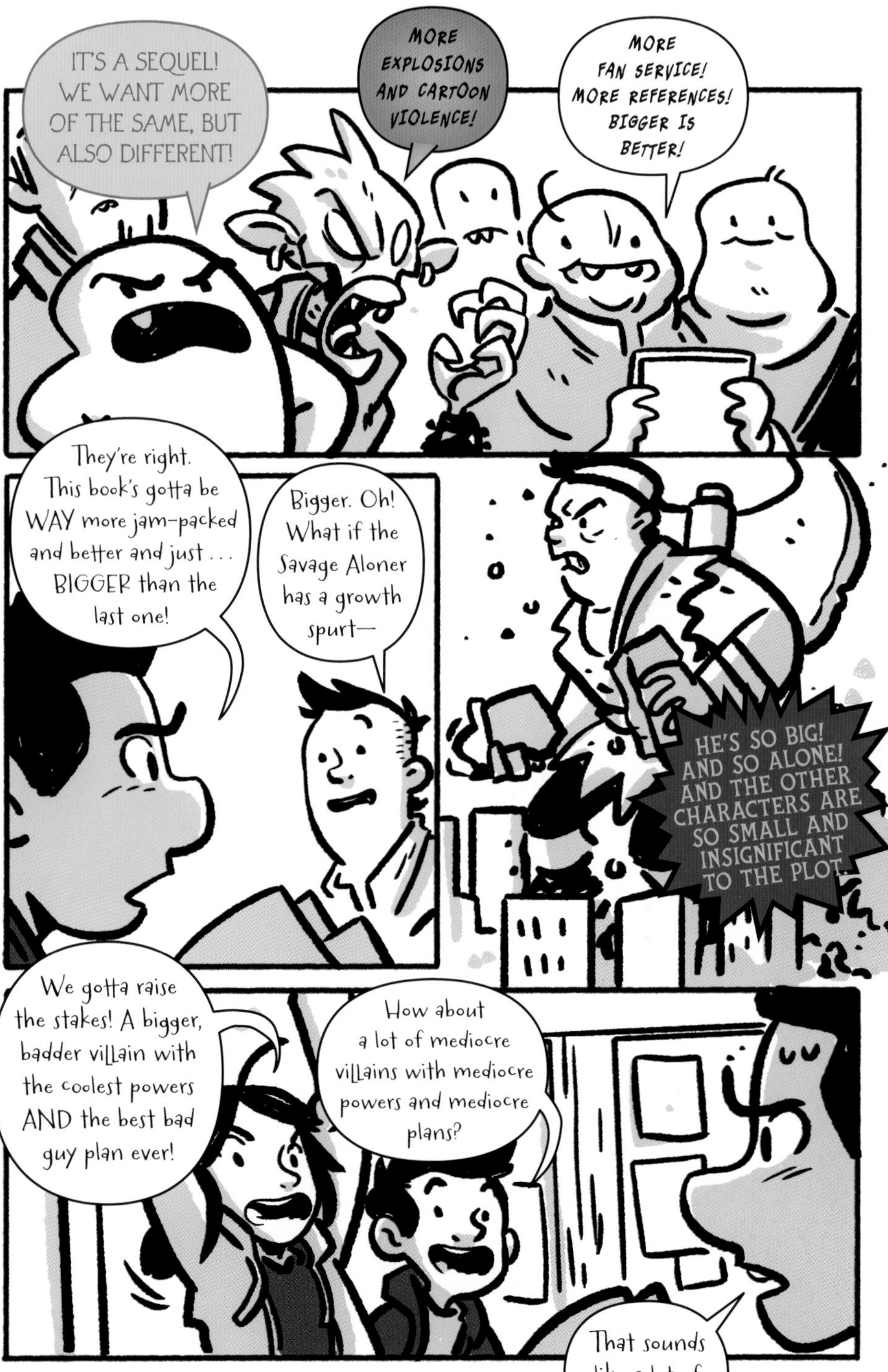
IT'S A SEQUEL! WE WANT MORE OF THE SAME, BUT ALSO DIFFERENT!
MORE EXPLOSIONS AND CARTOON VIOLENCE!
MORE FAN SERVICE! MORE REFERENCES! BIGGER IS BETTER!
They're right. This book's gotta be WAY more jam-packed and better and just . . . BIGGER than the last one!
Bigger. Oh! What if the Savage Aloner has a growth spurt—
HE'S SO BIG! AND SO ALONE! AND THE OTHER CHARACTERS ARE SO SMALL AND INSIGNIFICANT TO THE PLOT.
We gotta raise the stakes! A bigger, badder villain with the coolest powers AND the best bad guy plan ever!
How about a lot of mediocre villains with mediocre powers and mediocre plans?
That sounds like a lot of drawing.

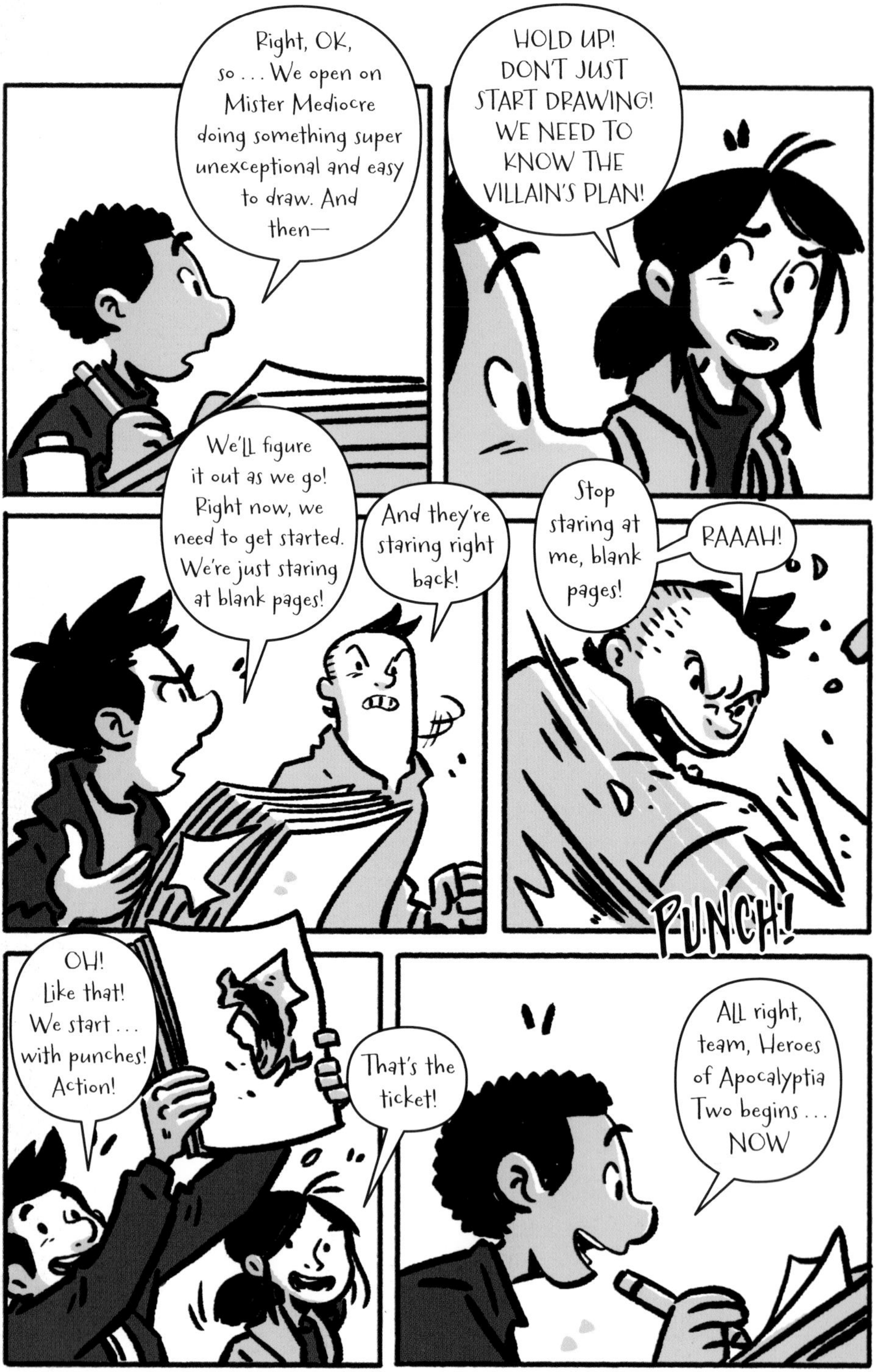
Right, OK, so . . . We open on Mister Mediocre doing something super unexceptional and easy to draw. And then—
HOLD UP! DON'T JUST START DRAWING! WE NEED TO KNOW THE VILLAIN'S PLAN!
We'll figure it out as we go! Right now, we need to get started. We're just staring at blank pages!
And they're staring right back!
Stop staring at me, blank pages!
RAAAH!
PUNCH!
OH! Like that! We start . . . with punches! Action!
That's the ticket!
All right, team, Heroes of Apocalyptia Two begins . . . NOW

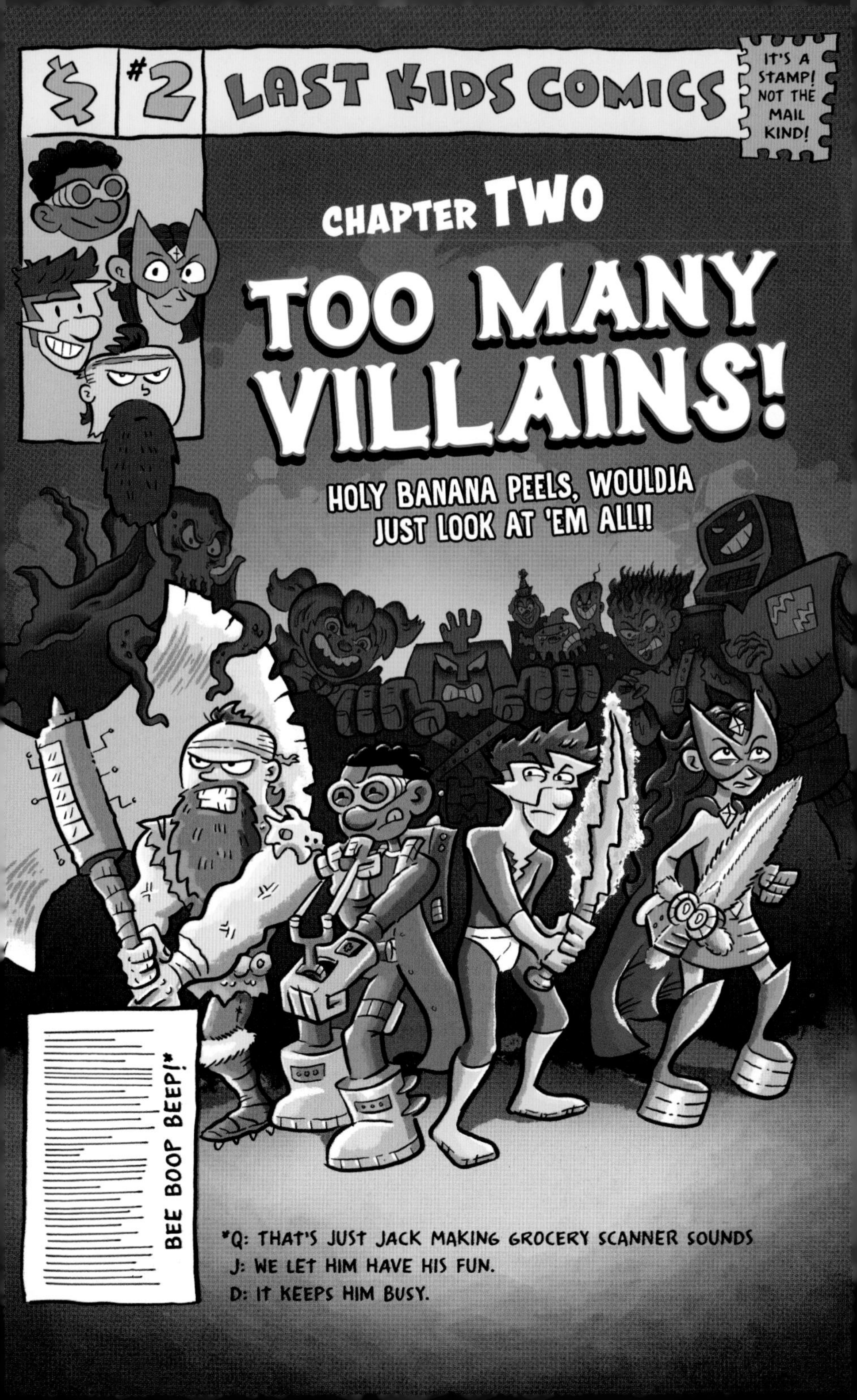
$ #2 LAST KIDS COMICS
IT'S A STAMP! NOT THE MAIL KIND!
CHAPTER TWO
TOO MANY VILLAINS!
HOLY BANANA PEELS, WOULDJA JUST LOOK AT 'EM ALL!!
BEE BOOP BEEP!*
*Q: THAT'S JUST JACK MAKING GROCERY SCANNER SOUNDS
J: WE LET HIM HAVE HIS FUN.
D: IT KEEPS HIM BUSY.

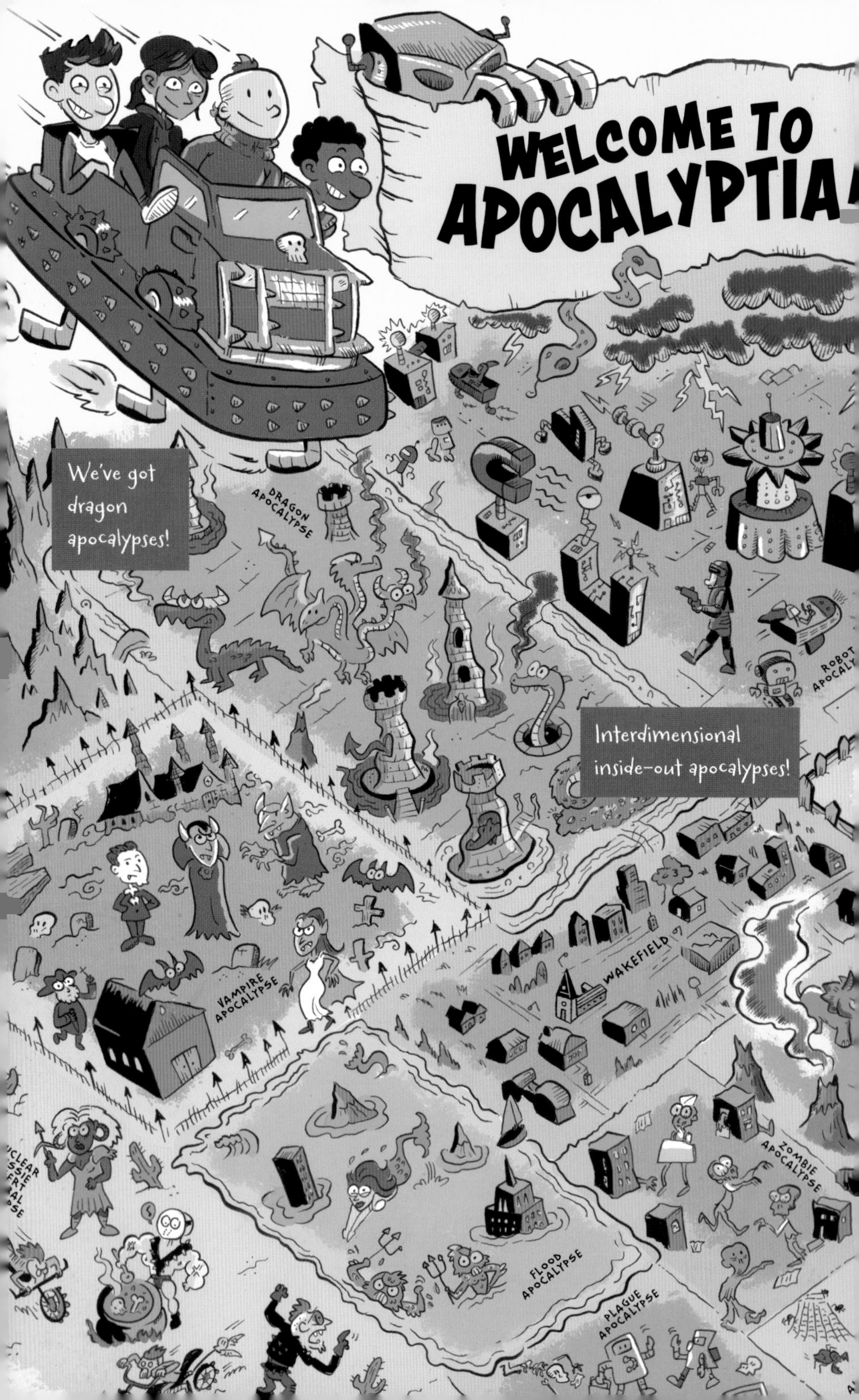
WELCOME TO
APOCALYPTIA!
We've got dragon apocalypses!
DRAGON APOCALYPSE
Interdimensional inside-out apocalypses!
ROBOT
VAMPIRE APOCALYPSE
WAKEFIELD
ZOMBIE APOCALYPSE
FLOOD APOCALYPSE
PLAGUE APOCALYPSE

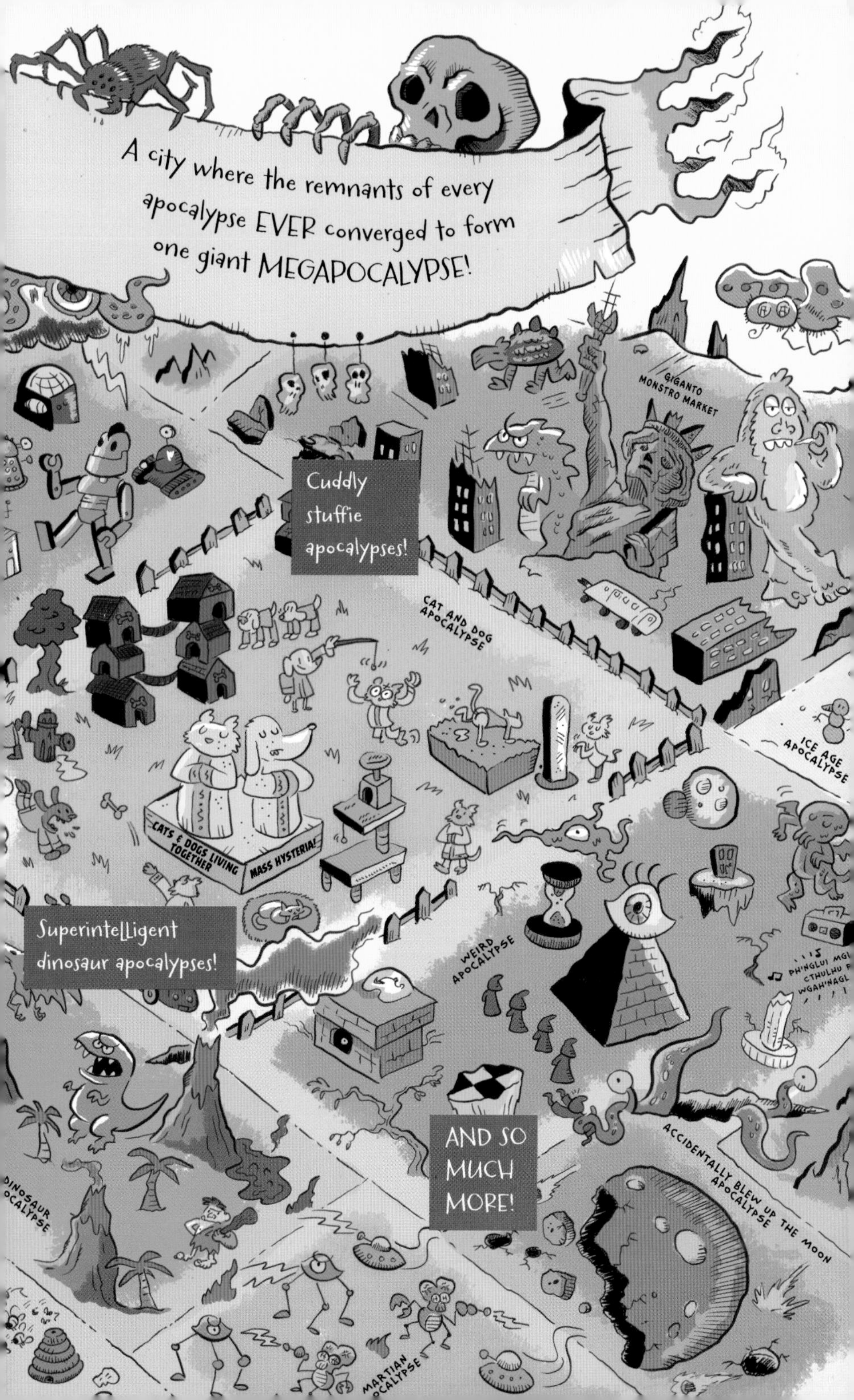
A city where the remnants of every apocalypse EVER converged to form one giant MEGAPOCALYPSE!
GIGANTO MONSTRO MARKET
Cuddly stuffie apocalypses!
CAT AND DOG APOCALYPSE
ICE AGE APOCALYPSE
CATS & DOGS LIVING TOGETHER
MASS HYSTERIA!
Superintelligent dinosaur apocalypses!
WEIRD APOCALYPSE
PH'NGLUI MGL
CTHULHU R
WGAH'NAGL
AND SO MUCH MORE!
ACCIDENTALLY BLEW UP THE MOON APOCALYPSE
DINOSAUR
MARTIAN

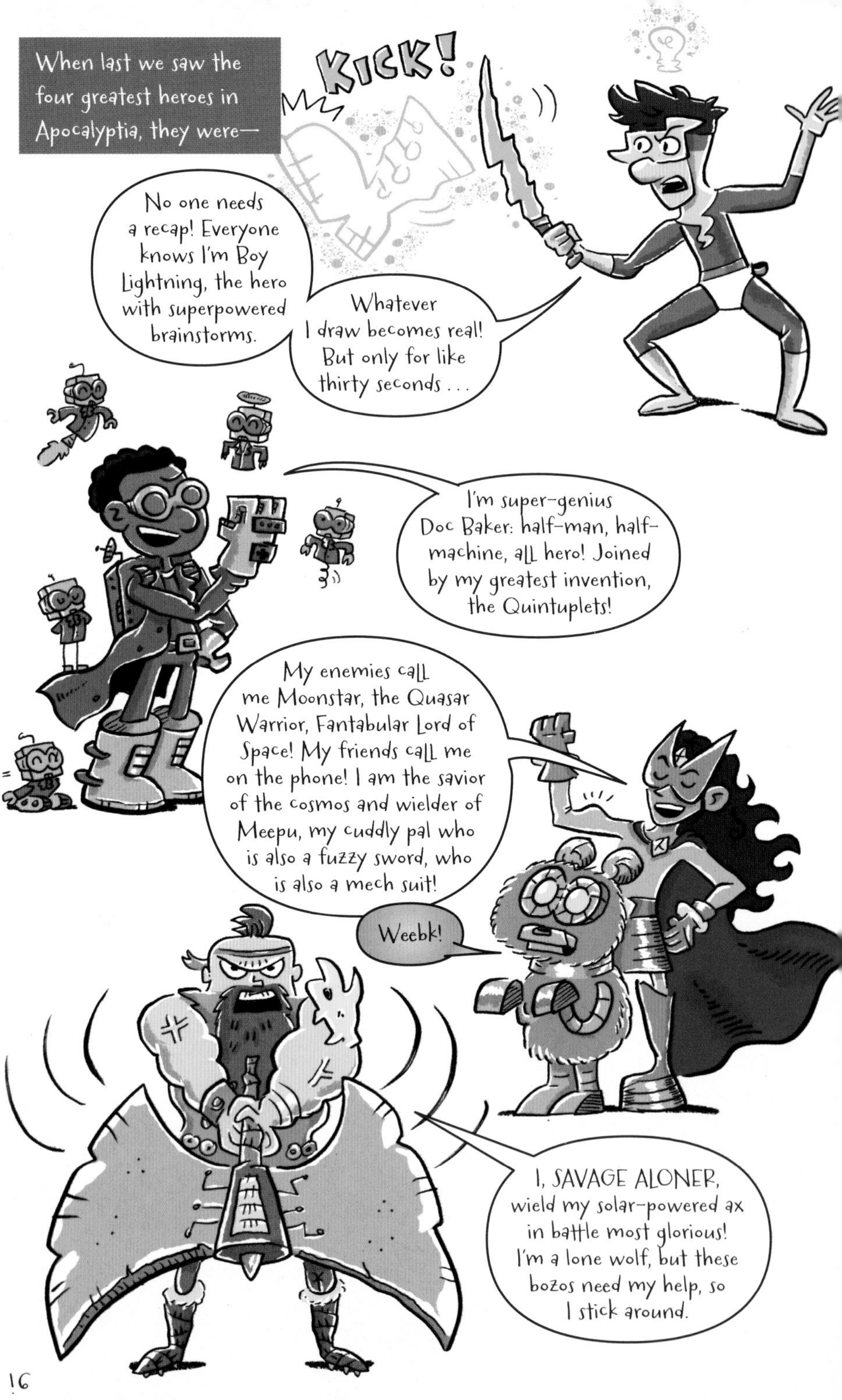
When last we saw the four greatest heroes in Apocalyptia, they were—
KICK!
No one needs a recap! Everyone knows I'm Boy Lightning, the hero with superpowered brainstorms.
Whatever I draw becomes real! But only for like thirty seconds . . .
I'm super-genius Doc Baker: half-man, half-machine, all hero! Joined by my greatest invention, the Quintuplets!
My enemies call me Moonstar, the Quasar Warrior, Fantabular Lord of Space! My friends call me on the phone! I am the savior of the cosmos and wielder of Meepu, my cuddly pal who is also a fuzzy sword, who is also a mech suit!
Weebk!
I, SAVAGE ALONER, wield my solar-powered ax in battle most glorious! I'm a lone wolf, but these bozos need my help, so I stick around.

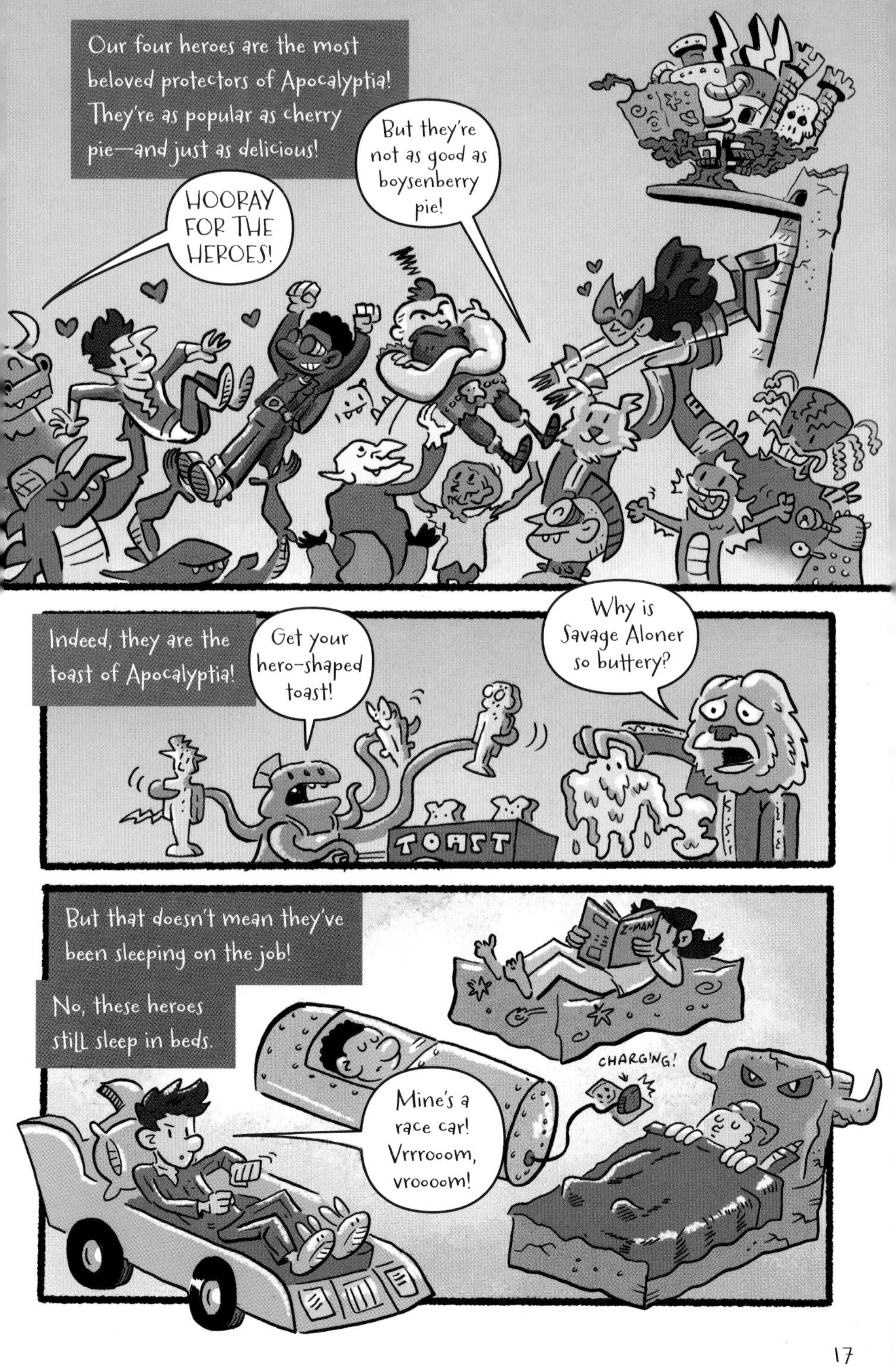
Our four heroes are the most beloved protectors of Apocalyptia! They're as popular as cherry pie—and just as delicious!
HOORAY FOR THE HEROES!
But they're not as good as boysenberry pie!
Indeed, they are the toast of Apocalyptia!
Get your hero-shaped toast!
TOAST
Why is Savage Aloner so buttery?
But that doesn't mean they've been sleeping on the job!
No, these heroes still sleep in beds.
Z-MAN
CHARGING!
Mine's a race car! Vrrrooom, vroooom!

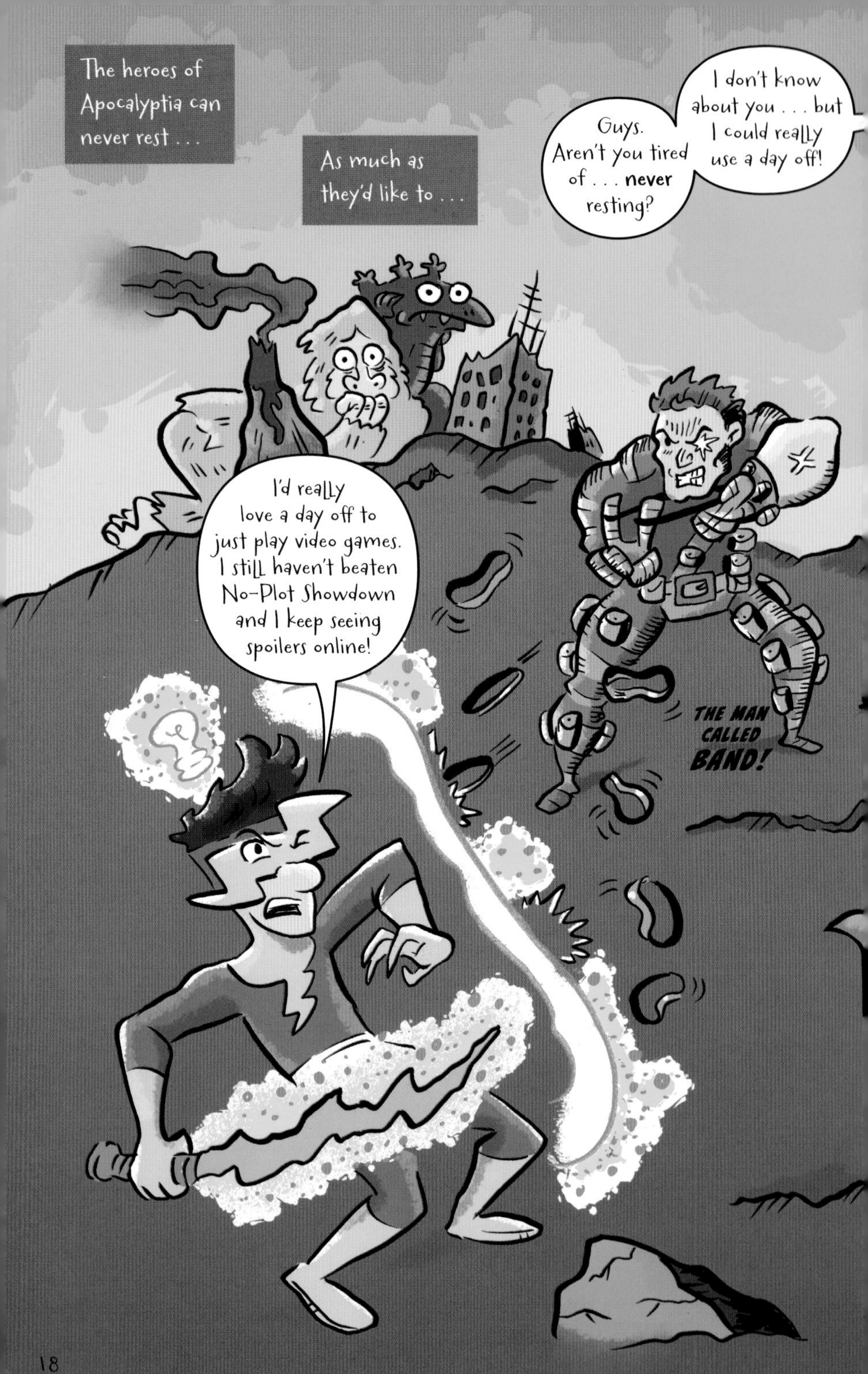

The heroes of Apocalyptia can never rest . . .
As much as they'd like to . . .
Guys. Aren't you tired of . . . **never** resting?
I don't know about you . . . but I could really use a day off!
I'd really love a day off to just play video games. I still haven't beaten No-Plot Showdown and I keep seeing spoilers online!
THE MAN CALLED BAND!

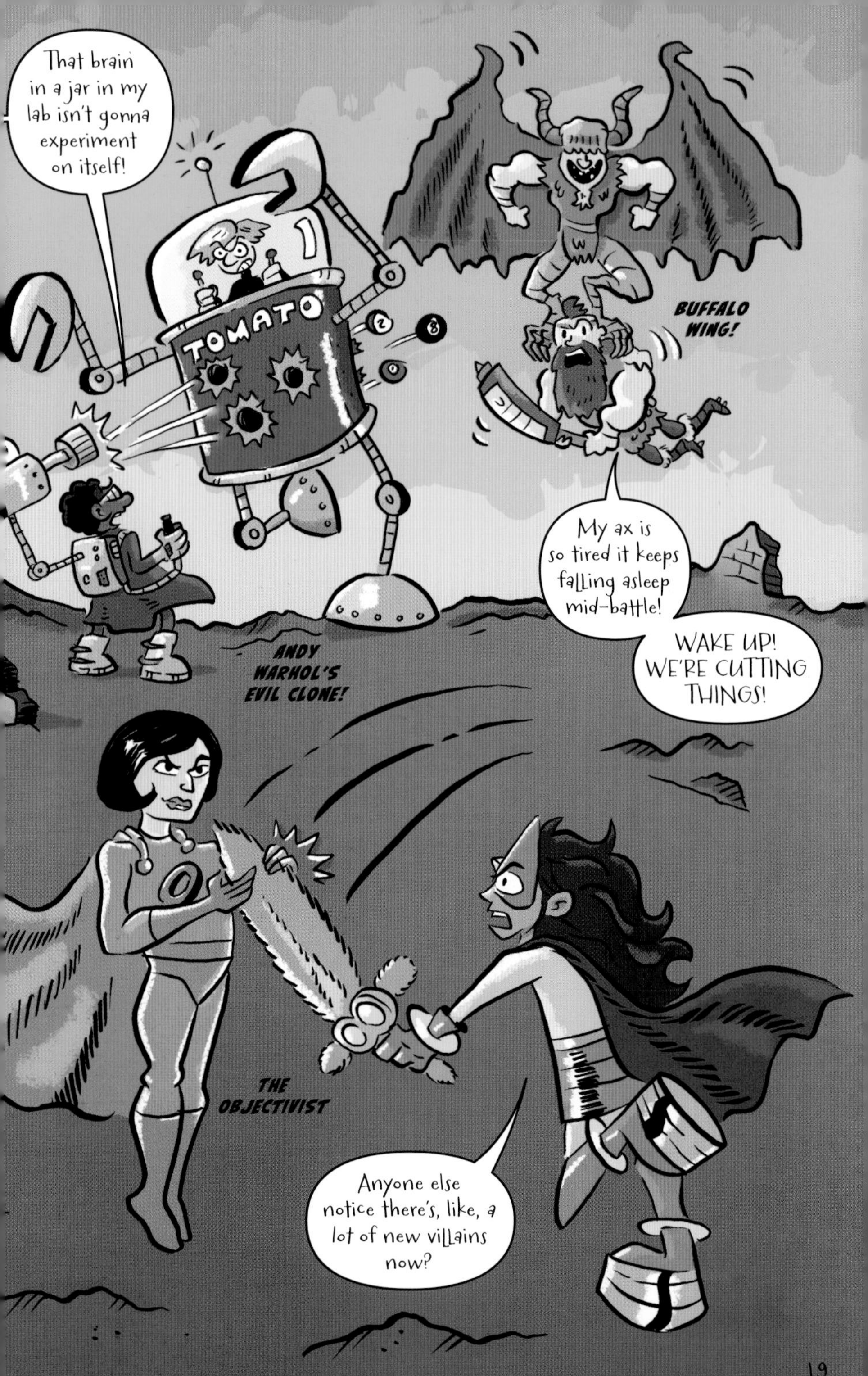
That brain in a jar in my lab isn't gonna experiment on itself!
TOMATO
BUFFALO WING!
My ax is so tired it keeps falling asleep mid-battle!
WAKE UP! WE'RE CUTTING THINGS!
ANDY WARHOL'S EVIL CLONE!
THE OBJECTIVIST
Anyone else notice there's, like, a lot of new villains now?

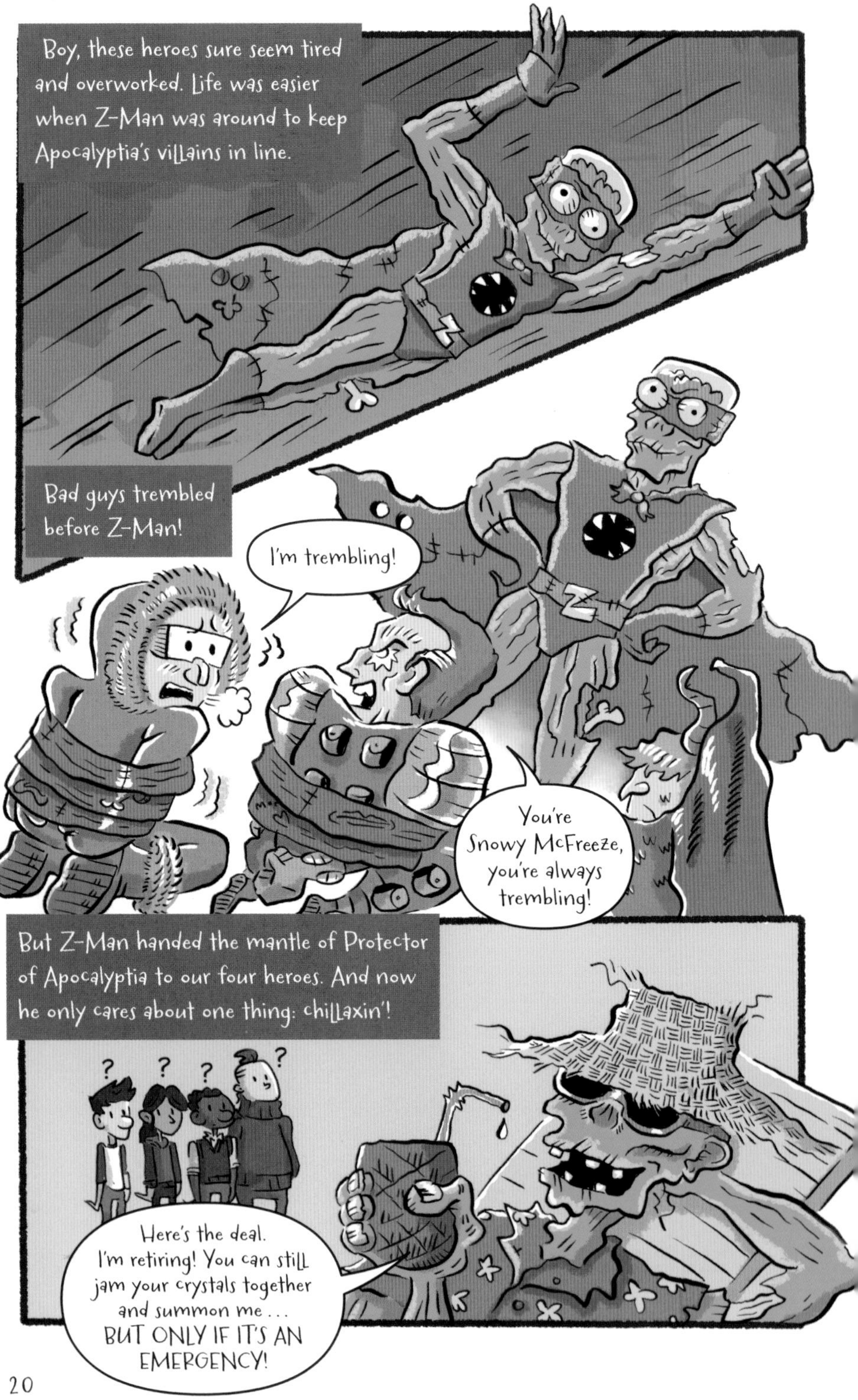
Boy, these heroes sure seem tired and overworked. Life was easier when Z-Man was around to keep Apocalyptia's villains in line.
Bad guys trembled before Z-Man!
I'm trembling!
You're Snowy McFreeze, you're always trembling!
But Z-Man handed the mantle of Protector of Apocalyptia to our four heroes. And now he only cares about one thing: chillaxin'!
? ? ? ?
Here's the deal. I'm retiring! You can still jam your crystals together and summon me . . . BUT ONLY IF IT'S AN EMERGENCY!

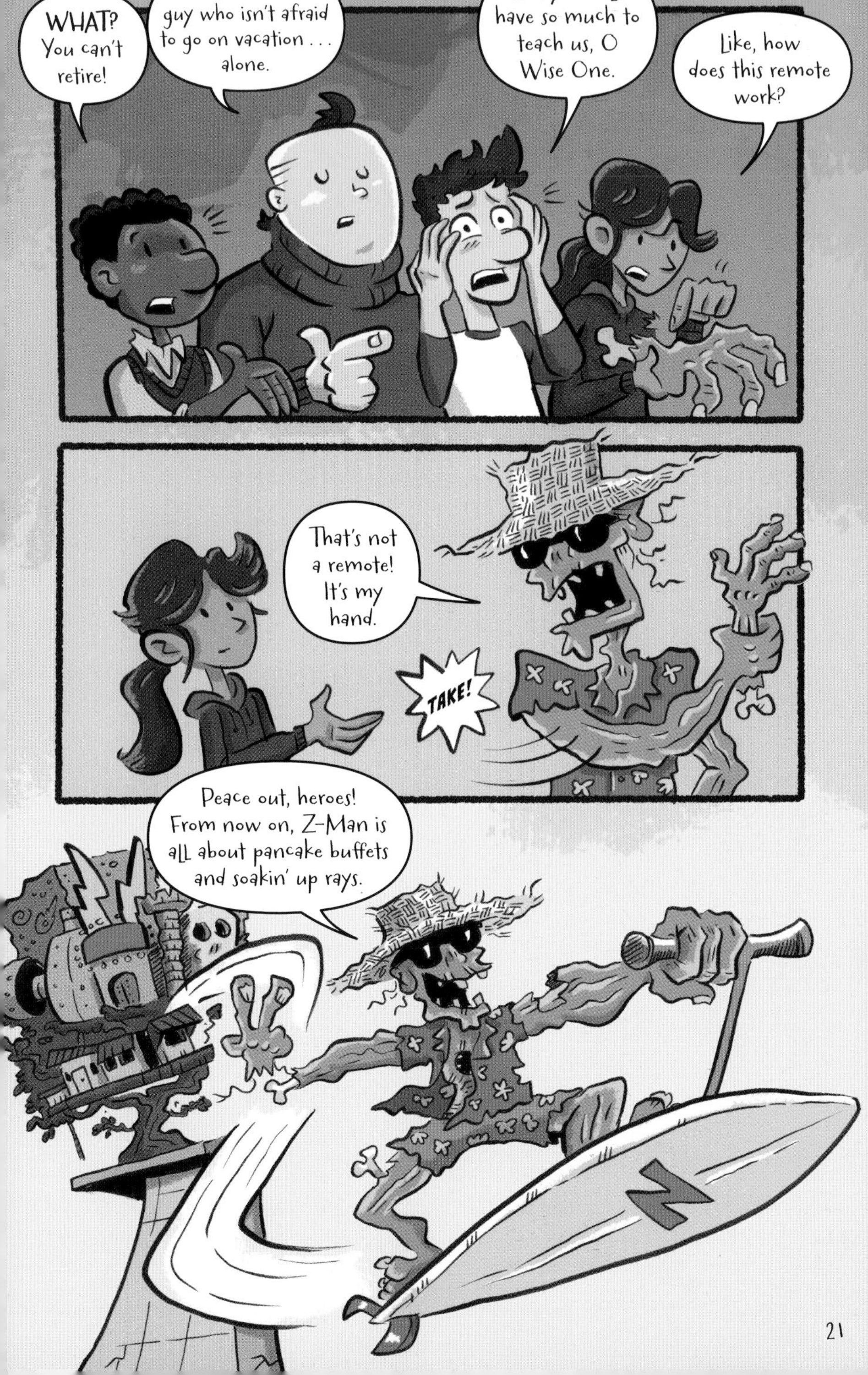
WHAT? You can't retire!
I admire a guy who isn't afraid to go on vacation . . . alone.
But you still have so much to teach us, O Wise One.
Like, how does this remote work?
That's not a remote! It's my hand.
TAKE!
Peace out, heroes! From now on, Z-Man is all about pancake buffets and soakin' up rays.

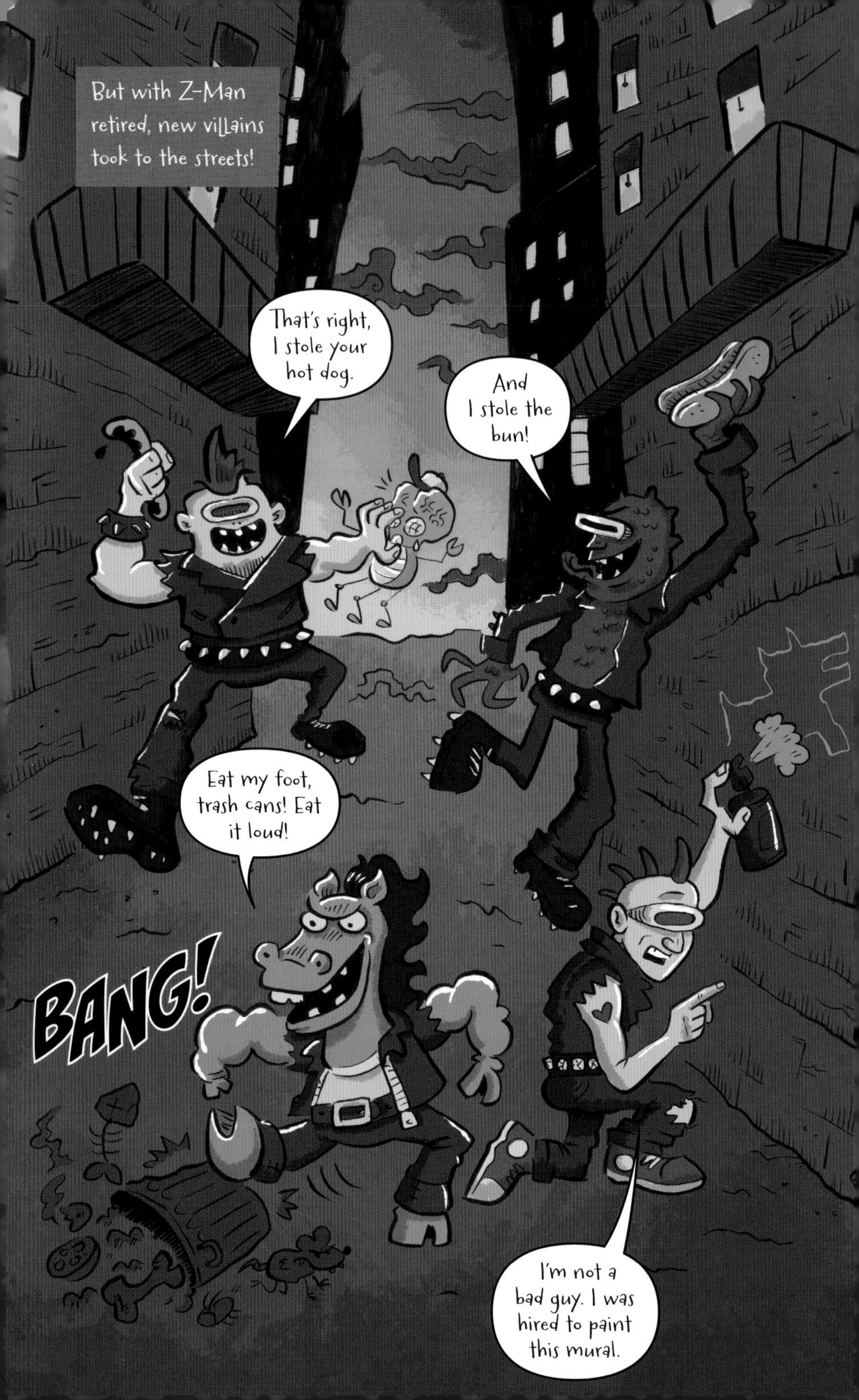
But with Z-Man retired, new villains took to the streets!
That's right, I stole your hot dog.
And I stole the bun!
Eat my foot, trash cans! Eat it loud!
BANG!
I'm not a bad guy. I was hired to paint this mural.

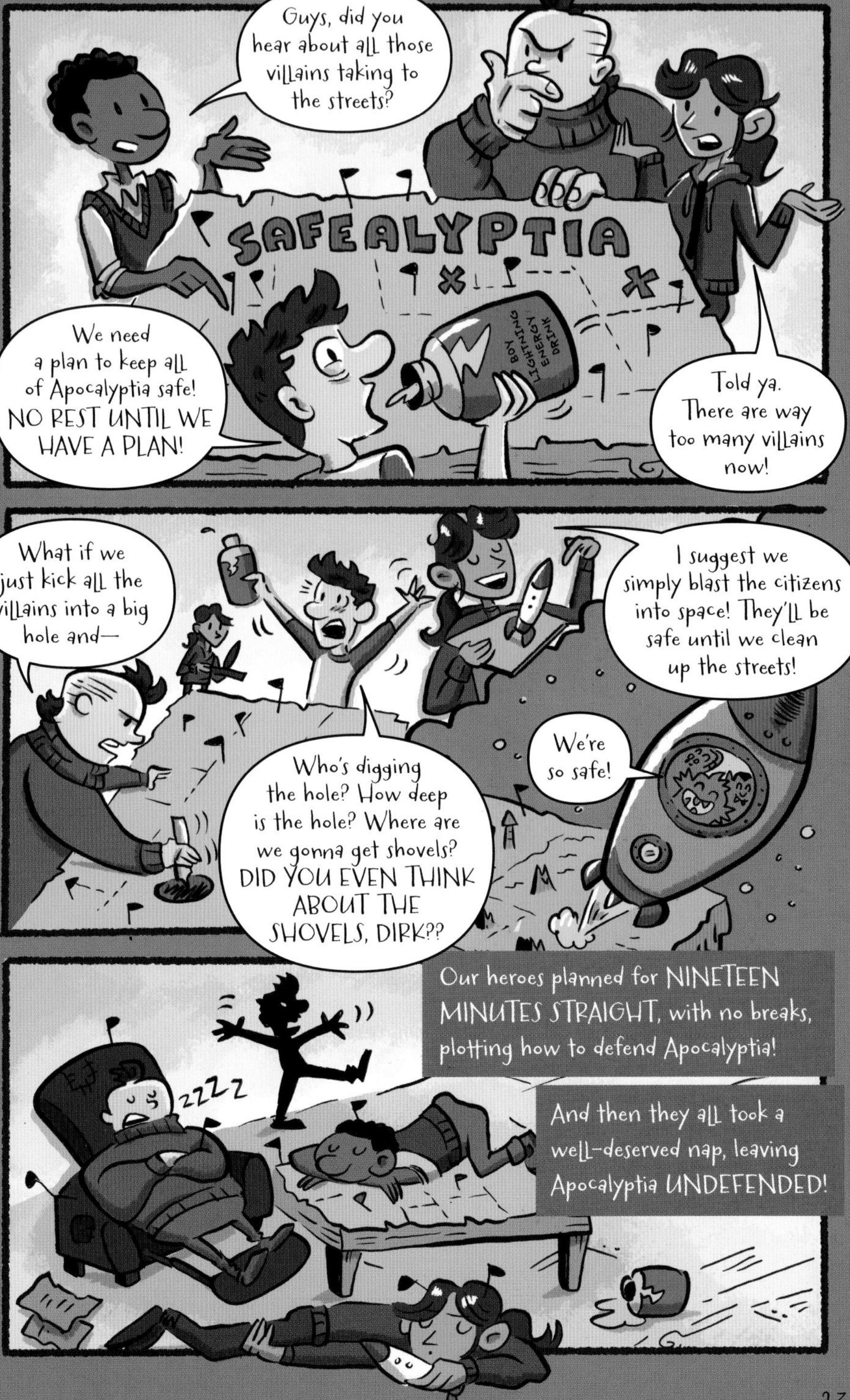
Guys, did you hear about all those villains taking to the streets?
SAFEALYPTIA
BOY LIGHTNING ENERGY DRINK
We need a plan to keep all of Apocalyptia safe! NO REST UNTIL WE HAVE A PLAN!
Told ya. There are way too many villains now!
What if we just kick all the villains into a big hole and—
I suggest we simply blast the citizens into space! They'll be safe until we clean up the streets!
We're so safe!
Who's digging the hole? How deep is the hole? Where are we gonna get shovels? DID YOU EVEN THINK ABOUT THE SHOVELS, DIRK??
Our heroes planned for NINETEEN MINUTES STRAIGHT, with no breaks, plotting how to defend Apocalyptia!
ZZZZ
And then they all took a well-deserved nap, leaving Apocalyptia UNDEFENDED!

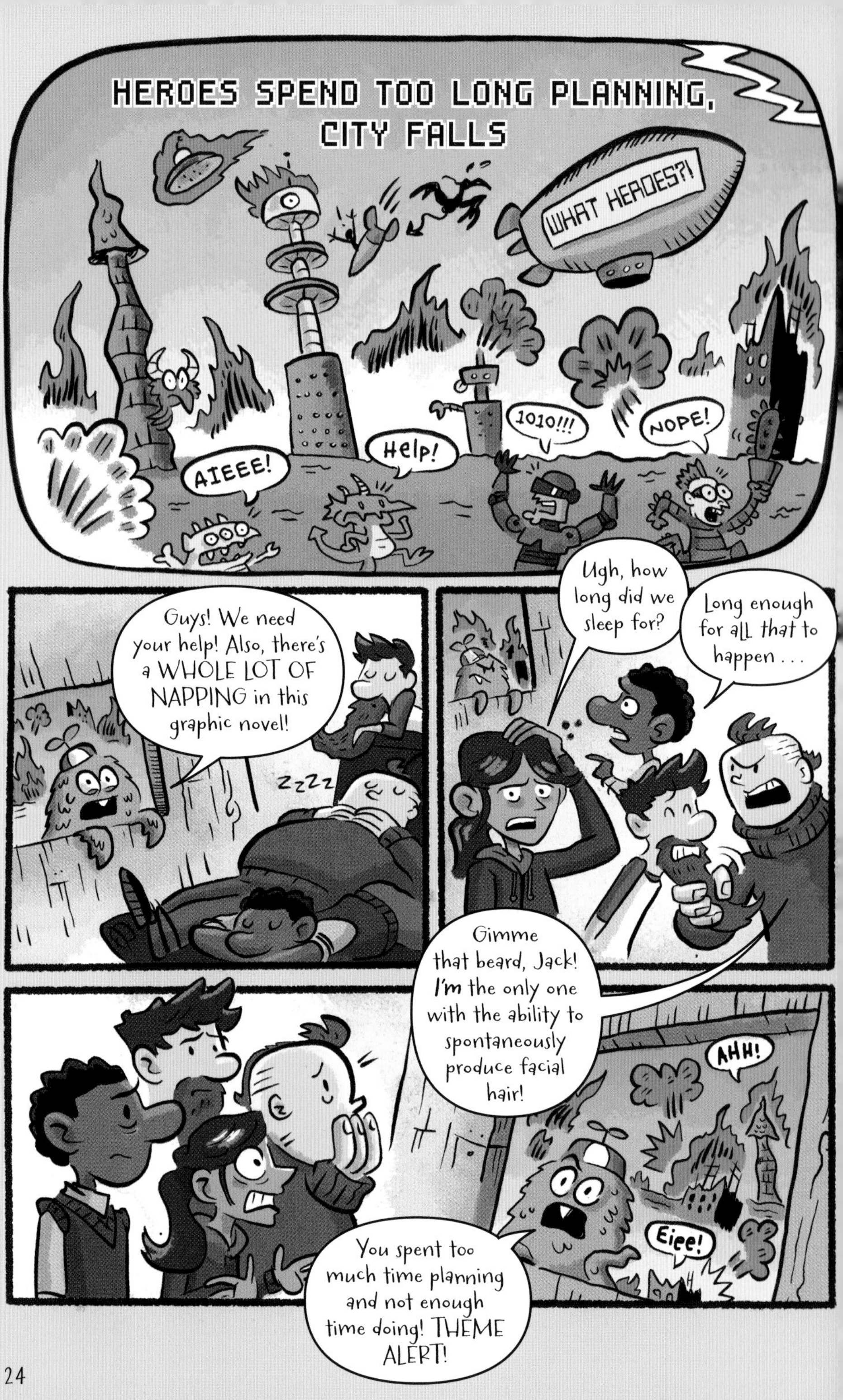
HEROES SPEND TOO LONG PLANNING, CITY FALLS
WHAT HEROES?!
AIEEE!
Help!
1010!!!
NOPE!
Guys! We need your help! Also, there's a WHOLE LOT OF NAPPING in this graphic novel!
ZZZZ
Ugh, how long did we sleep for?
Long enough for all that to happen . . .
Gimme that beard, Jack! I'm the only one with the ability to spontaneously produce facial hair!
AHH!
Eiee!
You spent too much time planning and not enough time doing! THEME ALERT!

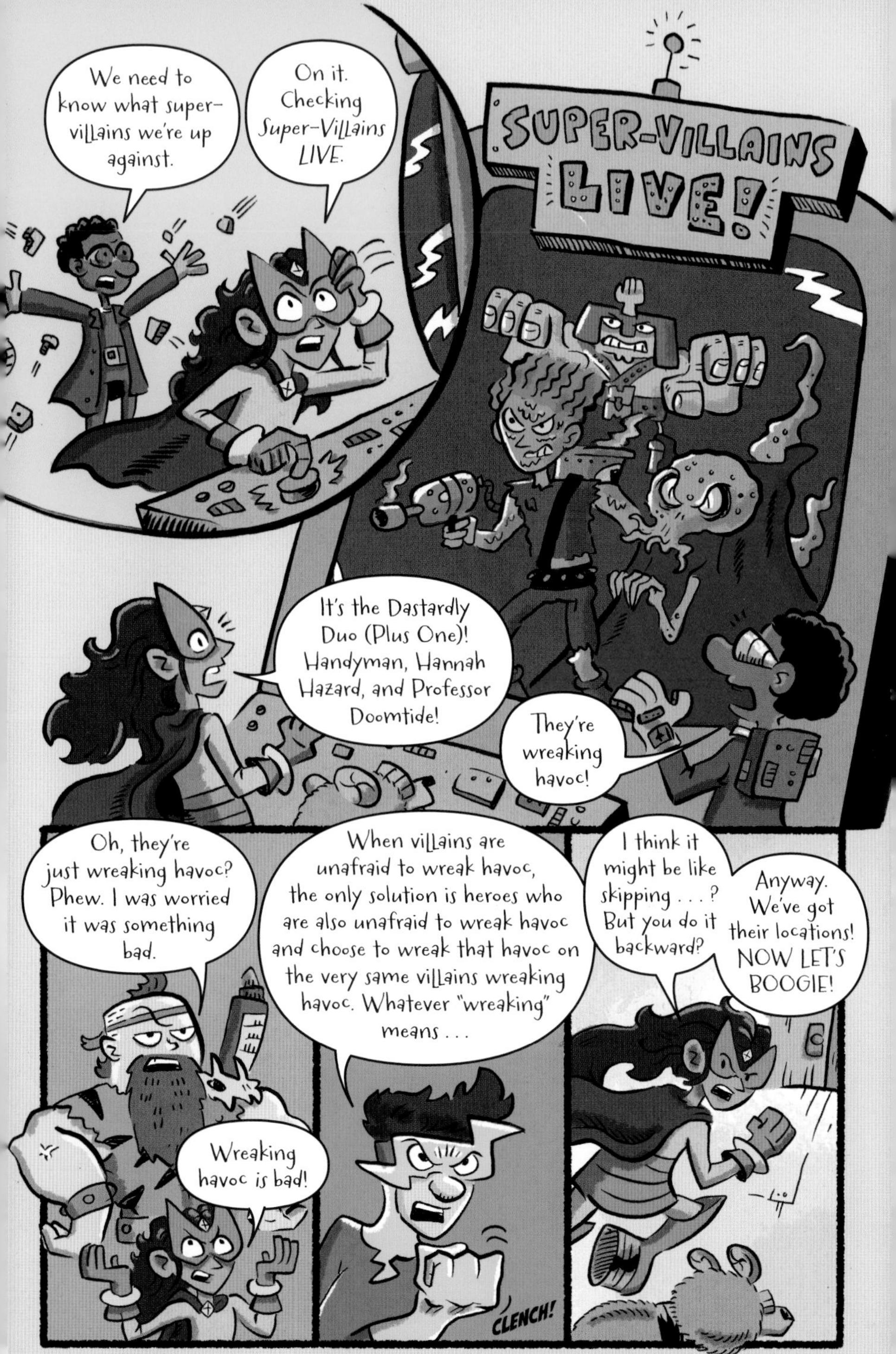
We need to know what super-villains we're up against.
On it. Checking Super-Villains LIVE.
SUPER-VILLAINS LIVE!
It's the Dastardly Duo (Plus One)! Handyman, Hannah Hazard, and Professor Doomtide!
They're wreaking havoc!
Oh, they're just wreaking havoc? Phew. I was worried it was something bad.
Wreaking havoc is bad!
When villains are unafraid to wreak havoc, the only solution is heroes who are also unafraid to wreak havoc and choose to wreak that havoc on the very same villains wreaking havoc. Whatever "wreaking" means . . .
CLENCH!
I think it might be like skipping . . . ? But you do it backward?
Anyway. We've got their locations! NOW LET'S BOOGIE!

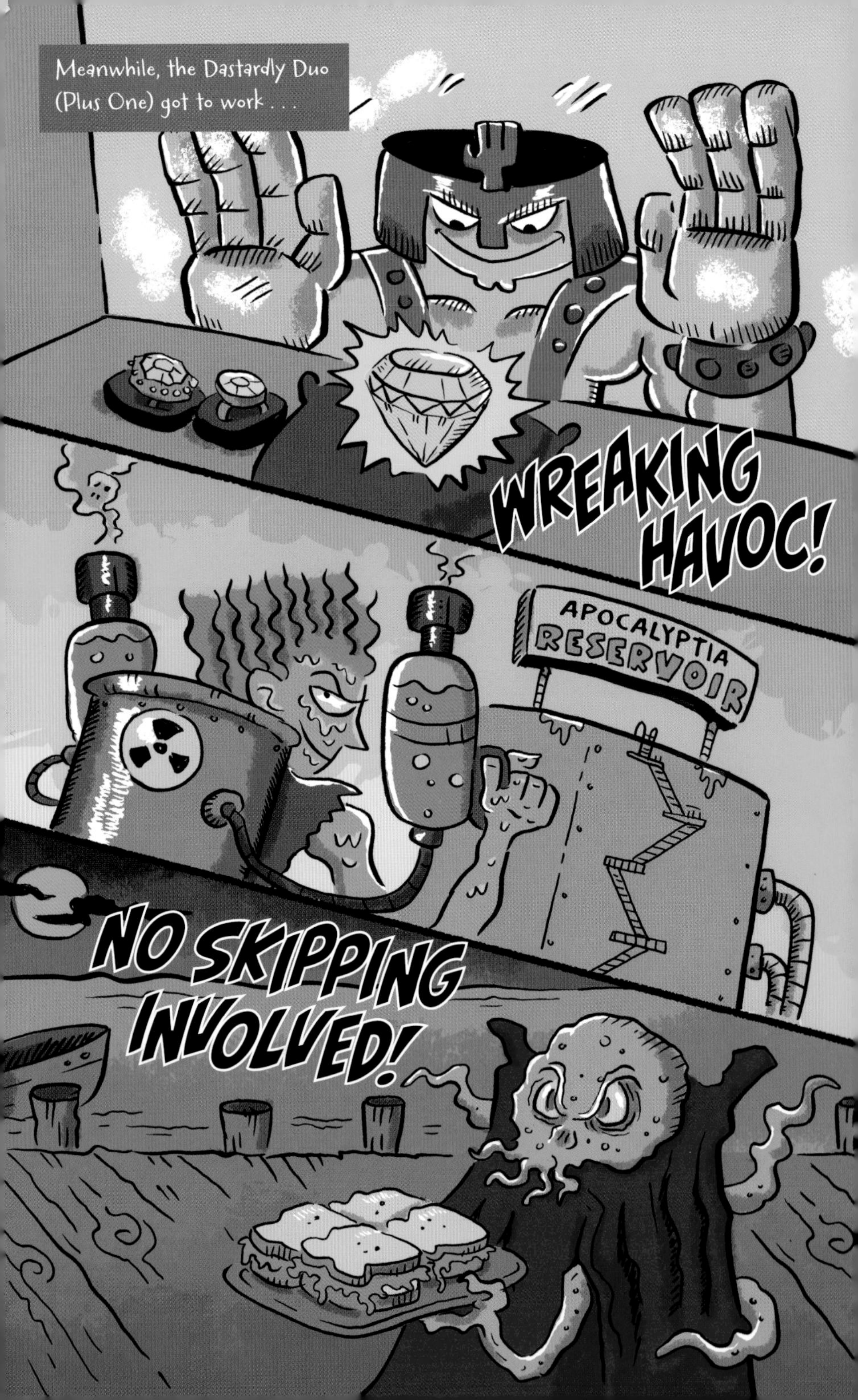
Meanwhile, the Dastardly Duo (Plus One) got to work . . .
WREAKING HAVOC!
APOCALYPTIA RESERVOIR
NO SKIPPING INVOLVED!

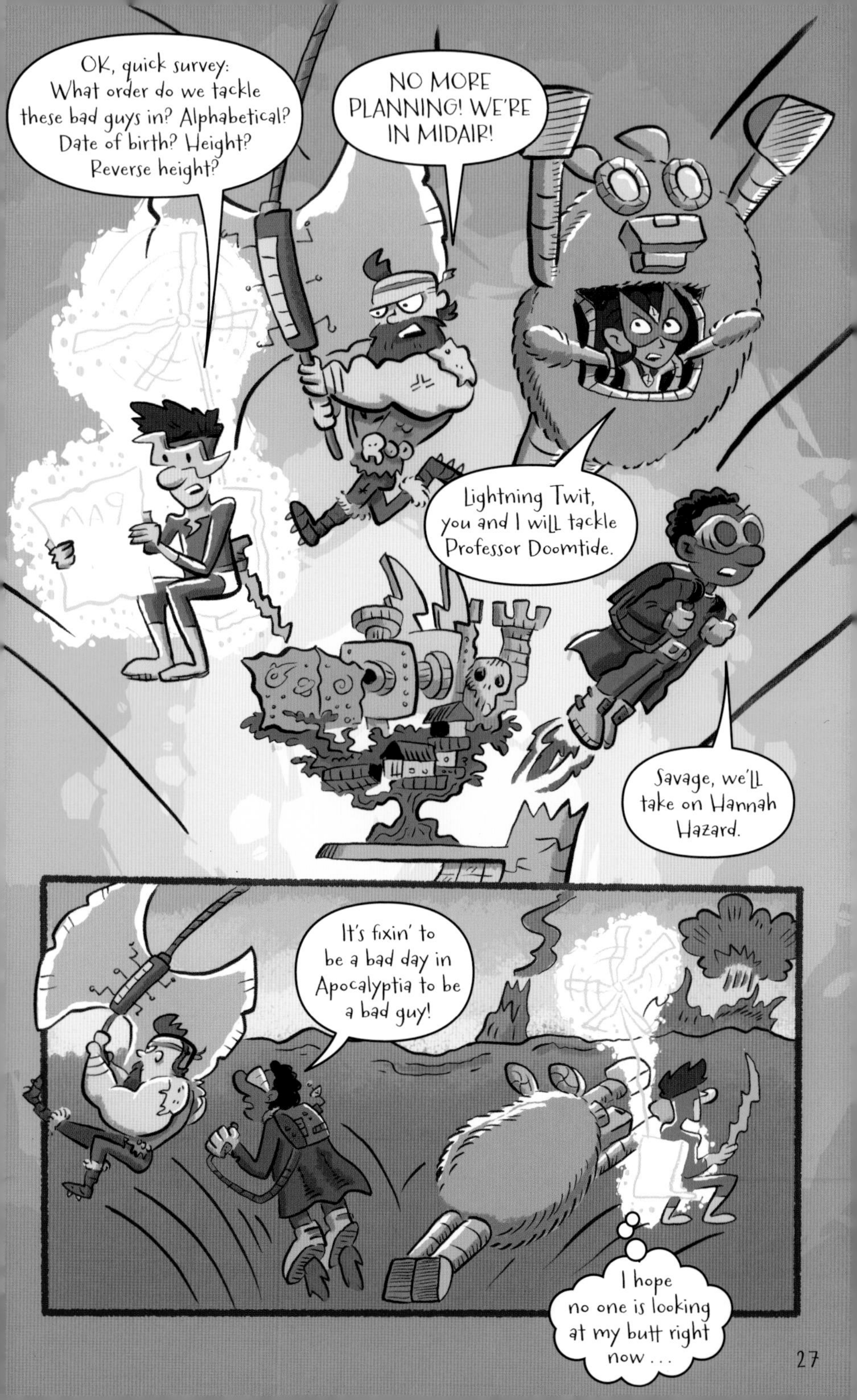
OK, quick survey: What order do we tackle these bad guys in? Alphabetical? Date of birth? Height? Reverse height?
NO MORE PLANNING! WE'RE IN MIDAIR!
Lightning Twit, you and I will tackle Professor Doomtide.
Savage, we'll take on Hannah Hazard.
It's fixin' to be a bad day in Apocalyptia to be a bad guy!
I hope no one is looking at my butt right now . . .

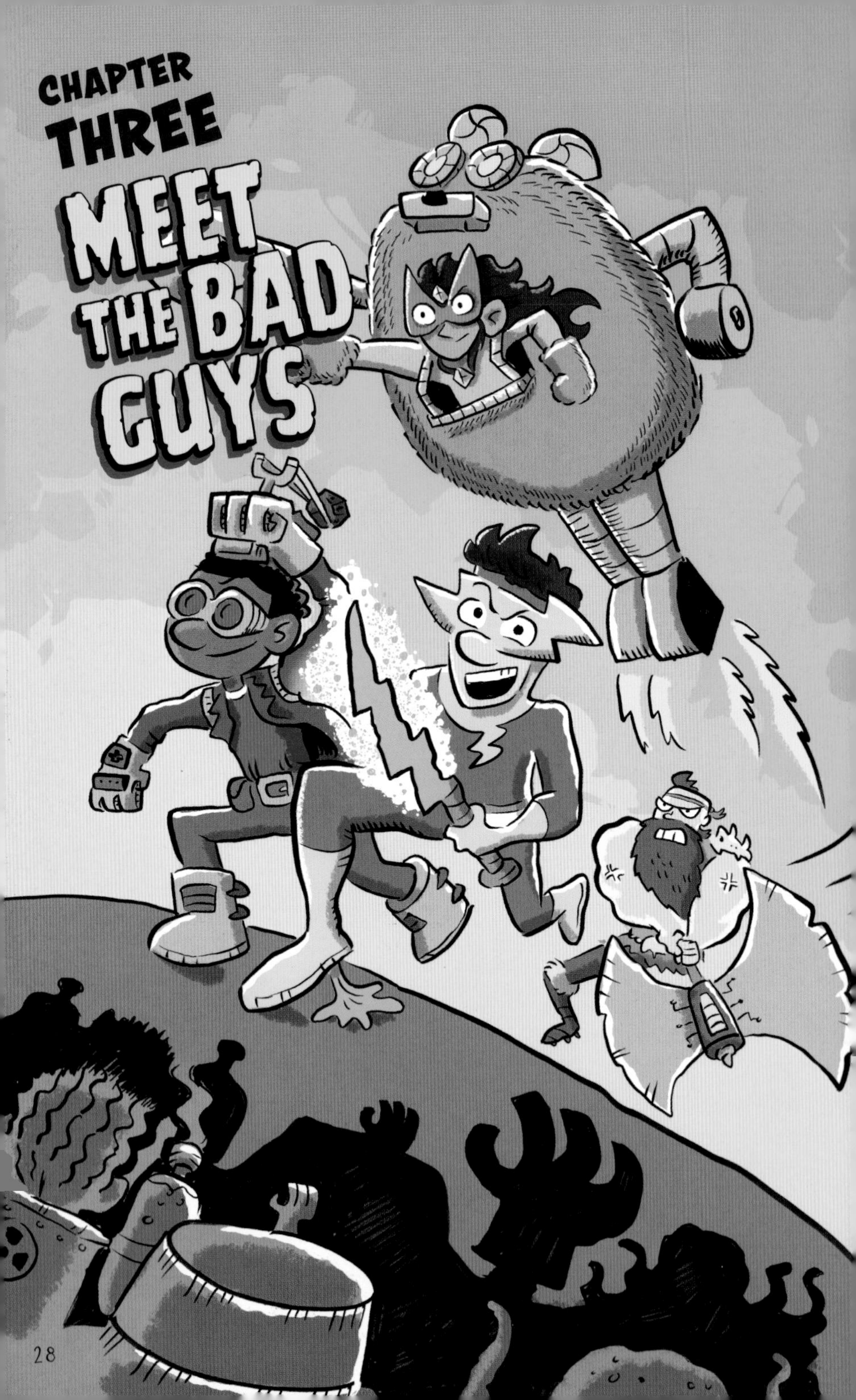
CHAPTER
THREE
MEET THE BAD GUYS

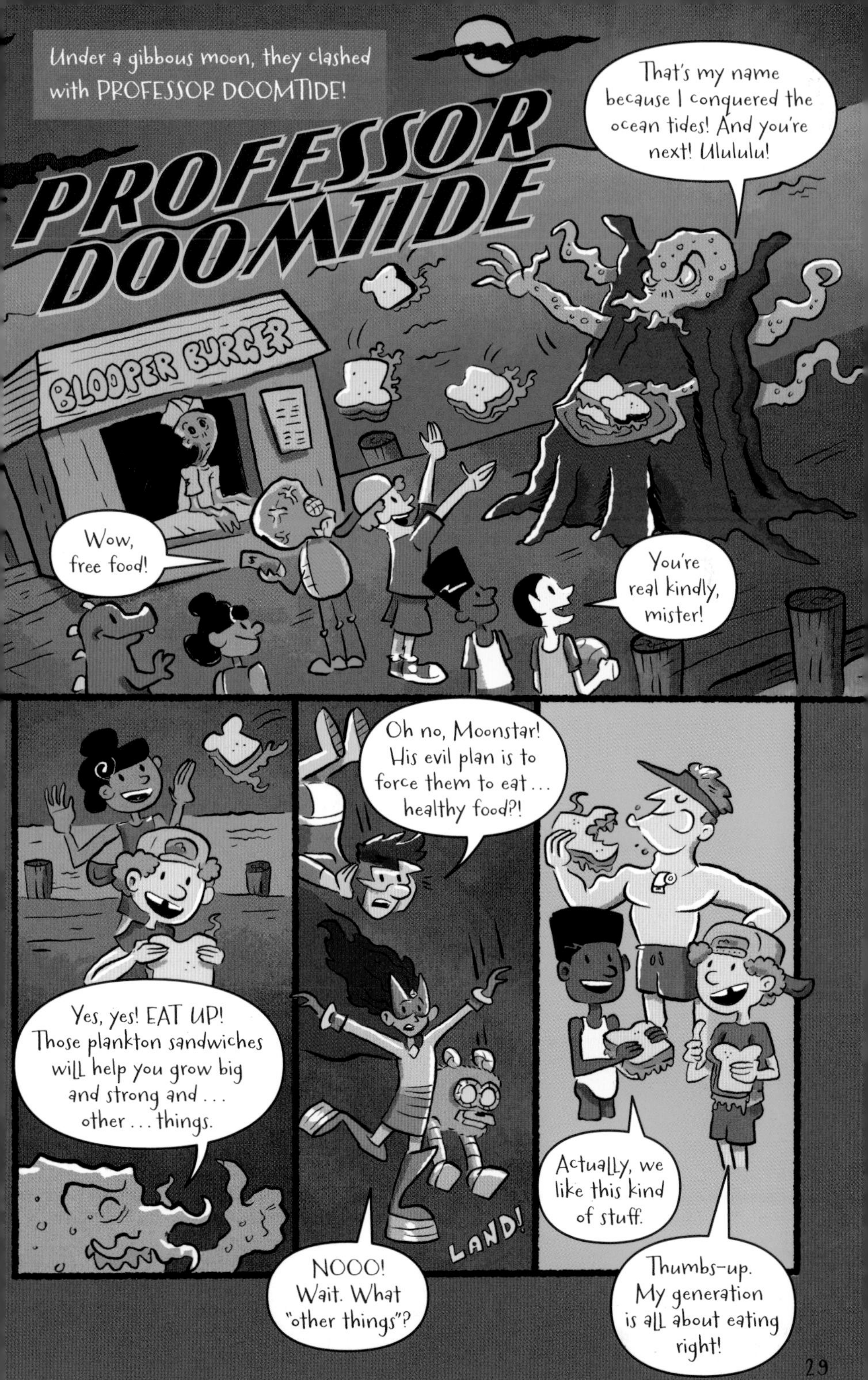
Under a gibbous moon, they clashed with PROFESSOR DOOMTIDE!
PROFESSOR DOOMTIDE
That's my name because I conquered the ocean tides! And you're next! Ululululu!
BLOOPER BURGER
Wow, free food!
You're real kindly, mister!
Yes, yes! EAT UP! Those plankton sandwiches will help you grow big and strong and . . . other . . . things.
Oh no, Moonstar! His evil plan is to force them to eat . . . healthy food?!
LAND!
NOOO! Wait. What "other things"?
Actually, we like this kind of stuff.
Thumbs-up. My generation is all about eating right!

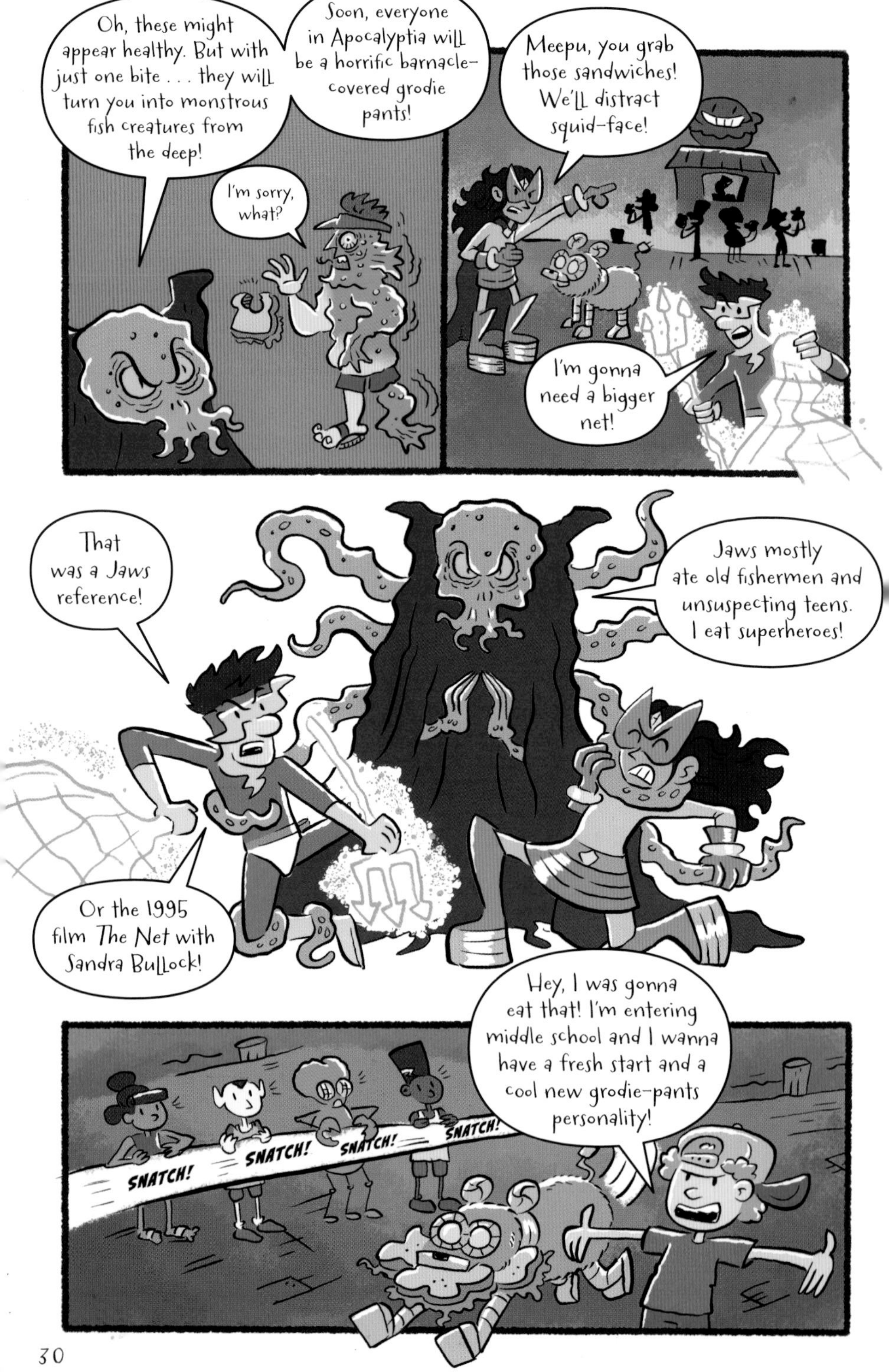

Oh, these might appear healthy. But with just one bite . . . they will turn you into monstrous fish creatures from the deep!
Soon, everyone in Apocalyptia will be a horrific barnacle-covered grodie pants!
I'm sorry, what?
Meepu, you grab those sandwiches! We'll distract squid-face!
I'm gonna need a bigger net!
That was a Jaws reference!
Jaws mostly ate old fishermen and unsuspecting teens. I eat superheroes!
Or the 1995 film *The Net* with Sandra Bullock!
SNATCH!
SNATCH!
SNATCH!
SNATCH!
Hey, I was gonna eat that! I'm entering middle school and I wanna have a fresh start and a cool new grodie-pants personality!

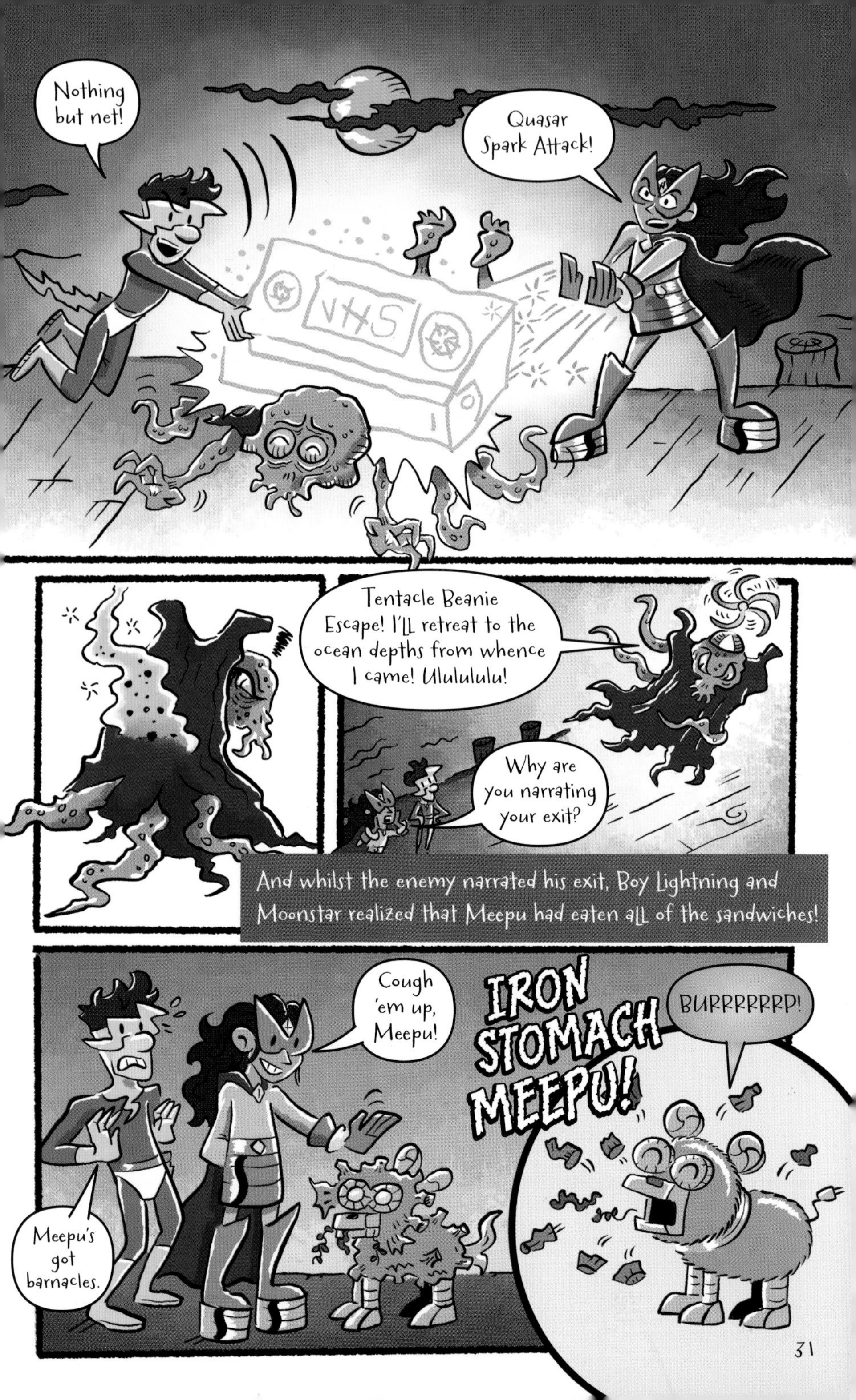

Nothing but net!
Quasar Spark Attack!
VHS
Tentacle Beanie Escape! I'LL retreat to the ocean depths from whence I came! Ulululululu!
Why are you narrating your exit?
And whilst the enemy narrated his exit, Boy Lightning and Moonstar realized that Meepu had eaten aLL of the sandwiches!
Cough 'em up, Meepu!
Meepu's got barnacles.
IRON STOMACH MEEPU!
BURRRRRRP!

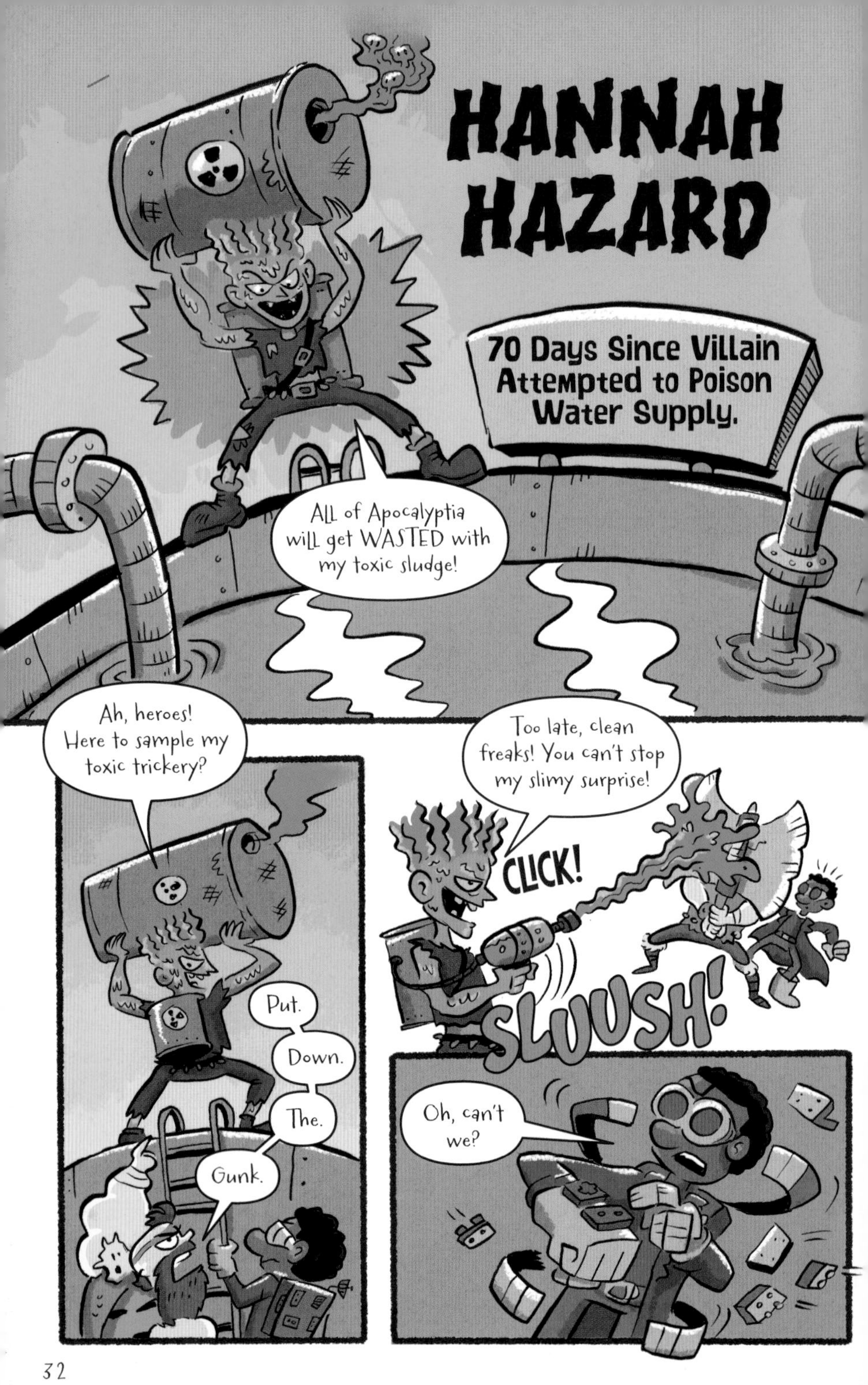

HANNAH HAZARD
70 Days Since Villain Attempted to Poison Water Supply.
ALL of Apocalyptia will get WASTED with my toxic sludge!
Ah, heroes! Here to sample my toxic trickery?
Put.
Down.
The.
Gunk.
Too late, clean freaks! You can't stop my slimy surprise!
CLICK!
SLUUSH!
Oh, can't we?

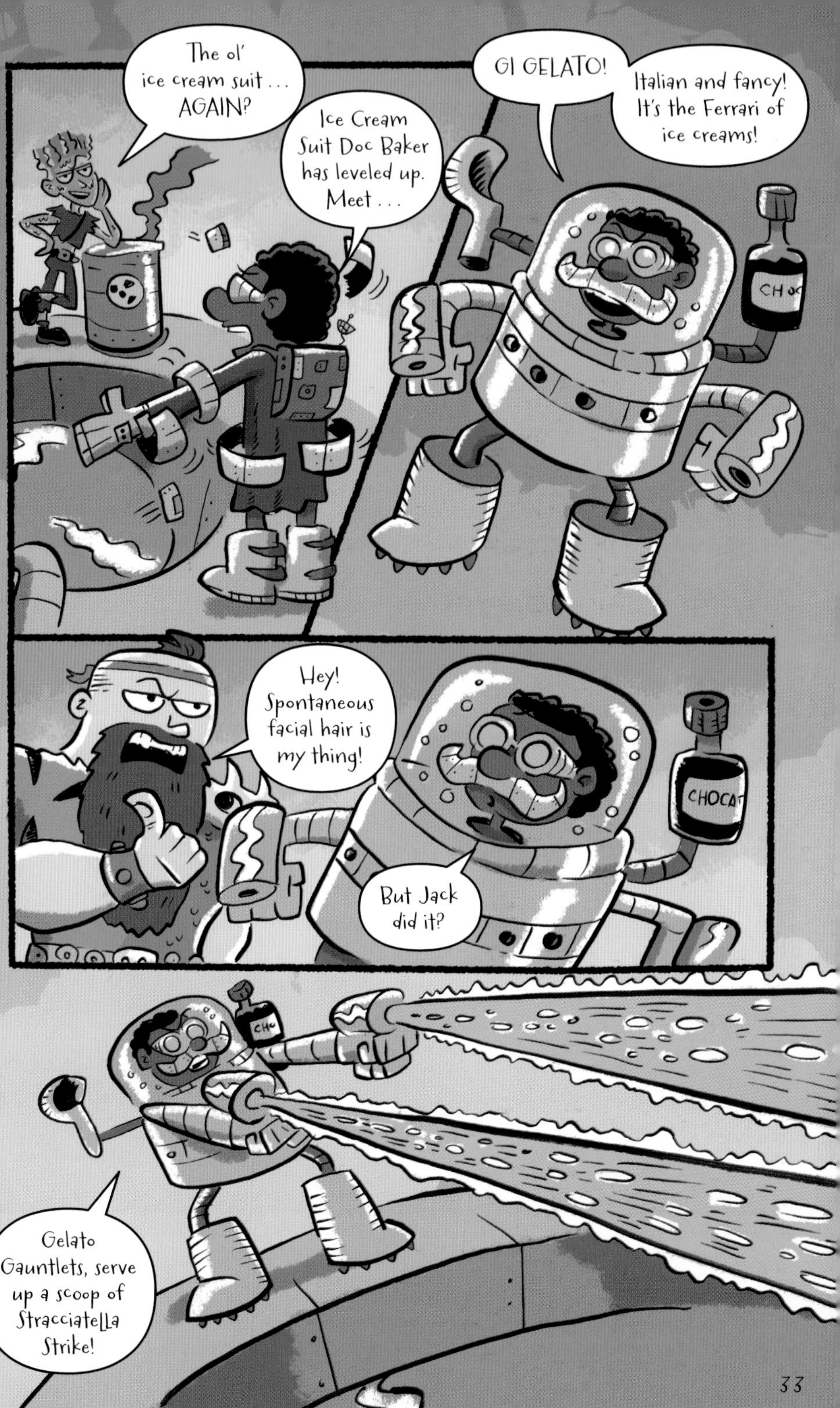
The ol' ice cream suit . . . AGAIN?
Ice Cream Suit Doc Baker has leveled up. Meet . . .
GI GELATO!
Italian and fancy! It's the Ferrari of ice creams!
CHOC
Hey! Spontaneous facial hair is my thing!
CHOCAT
But Jack did it?
CHO
Gelato Gauntlets, serve up a scoop of StracciateLLa Strike!

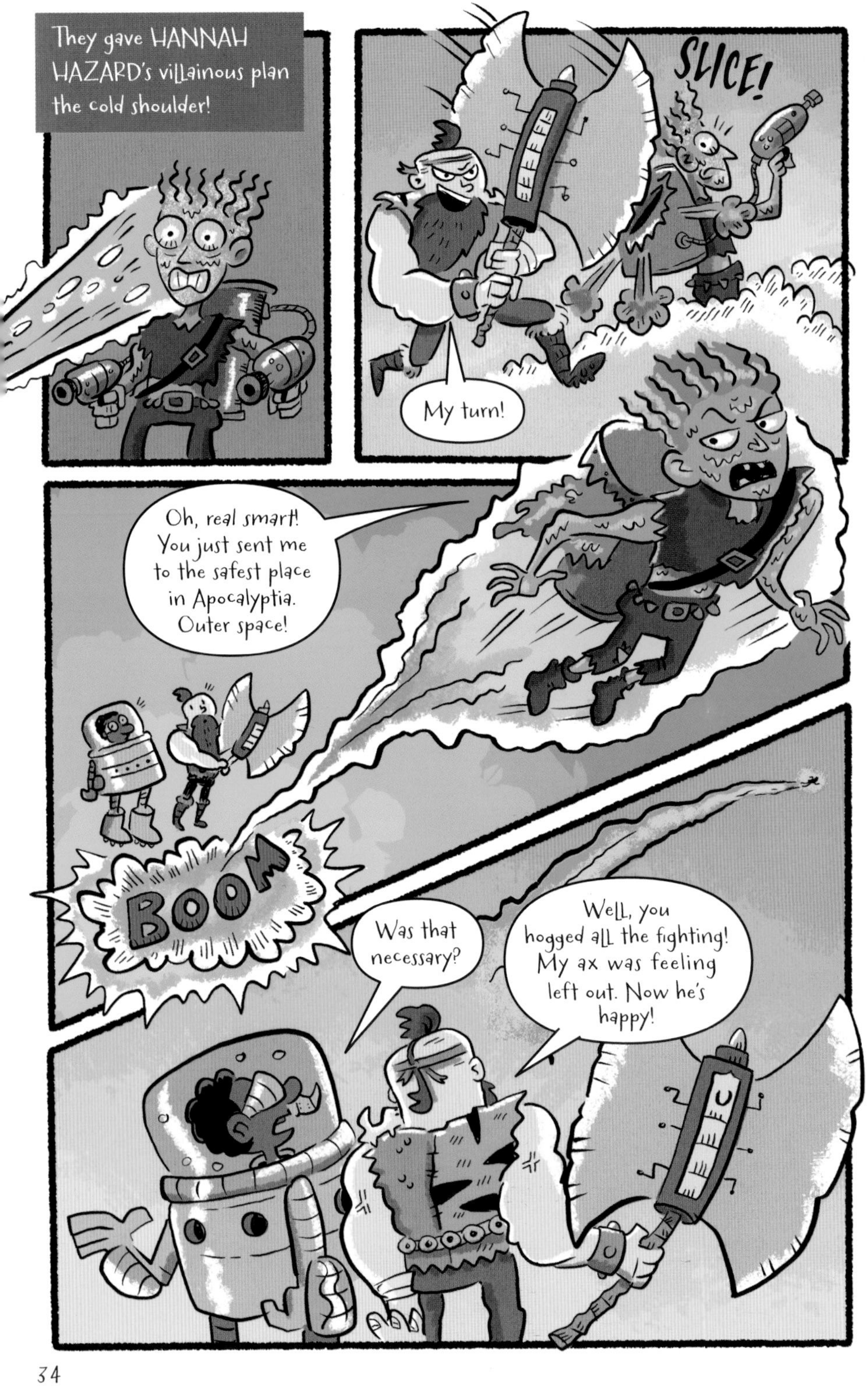
They gave HANNAH HAZARD's villainous plan the cold shoulder!
SLICE!
My turn!
Oh, real smart! You just sent me to the safest place in Apocalyptia. Outer space!
BOOM
Was that necessary?
Well, you hogged all the fighting! My ax was feeling left out. Now he's happy!

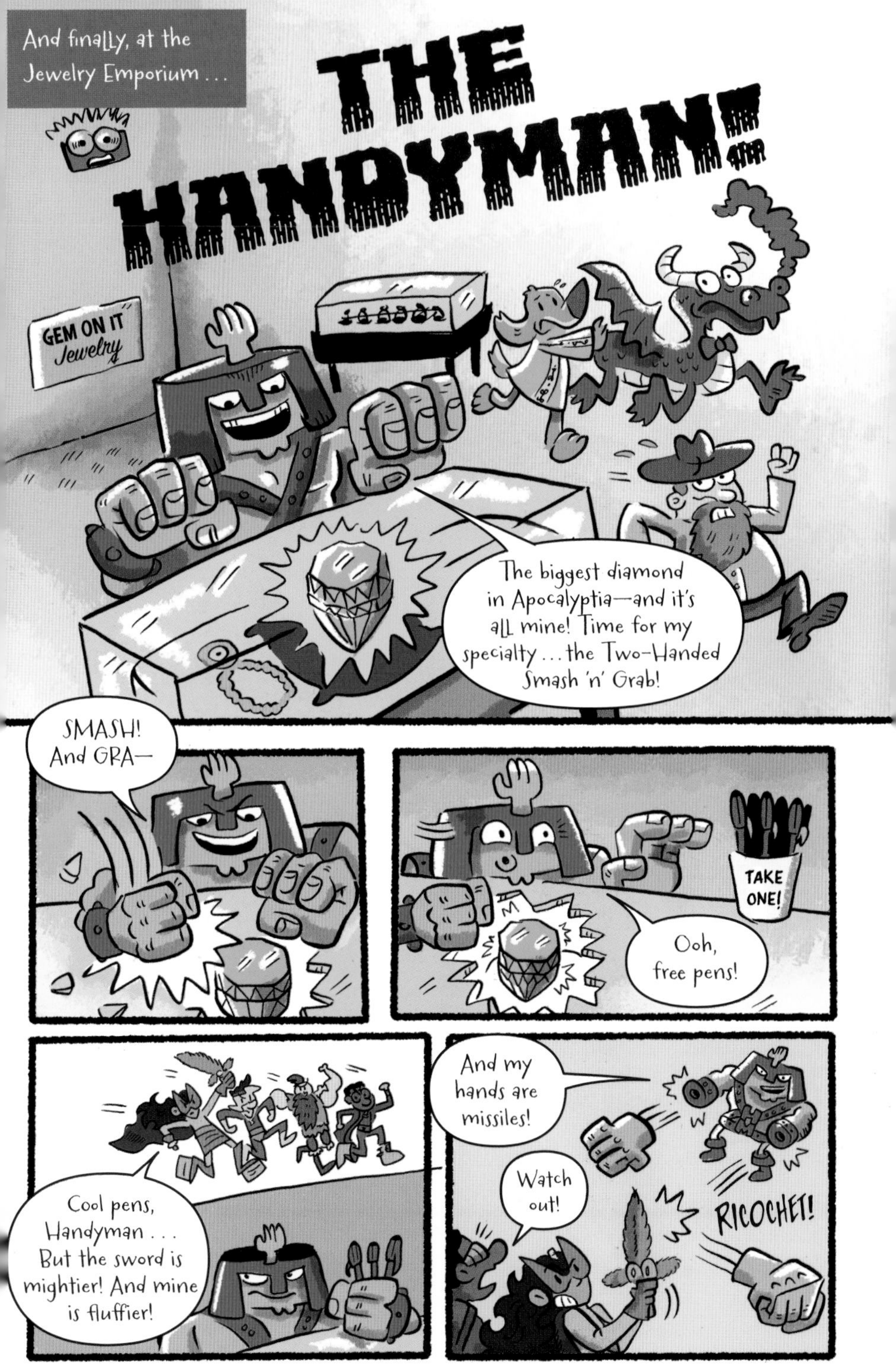

And finally, at the Jewelry Emporium . . .
THE HANDYMAN!
GEM ON IT Jewelry
The biggest diamond in Apocalyptia—and it's all mine! Time for my specialty . . . the Two-Handed Smash 'n' Grab!
SMASH! And GRA—
TAKE ONE!
Ooh, free pens!
Cool pens, Handyman . . . But the sword is mightier! And mine is fluffier!
And my hands are missiles!
Watch out!
RICOCHET!

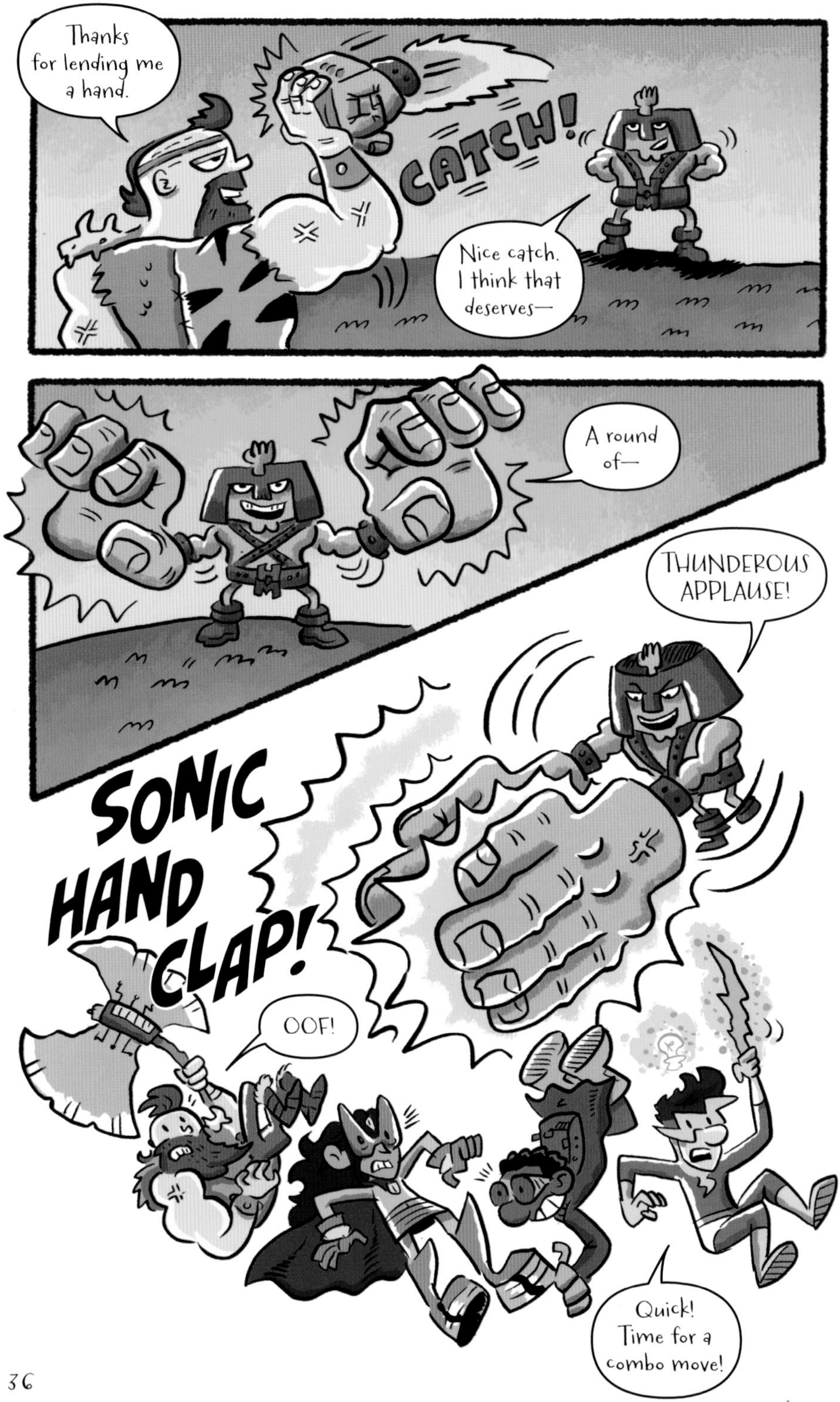
Thanks for lending me a hand.
CATCH!
Nice catch. I think that deserves—
A round of—
THUNDEROUS APPLAUSE!
SONIC HAND CLAP!
OOF!
Quick! Time for a combo move!

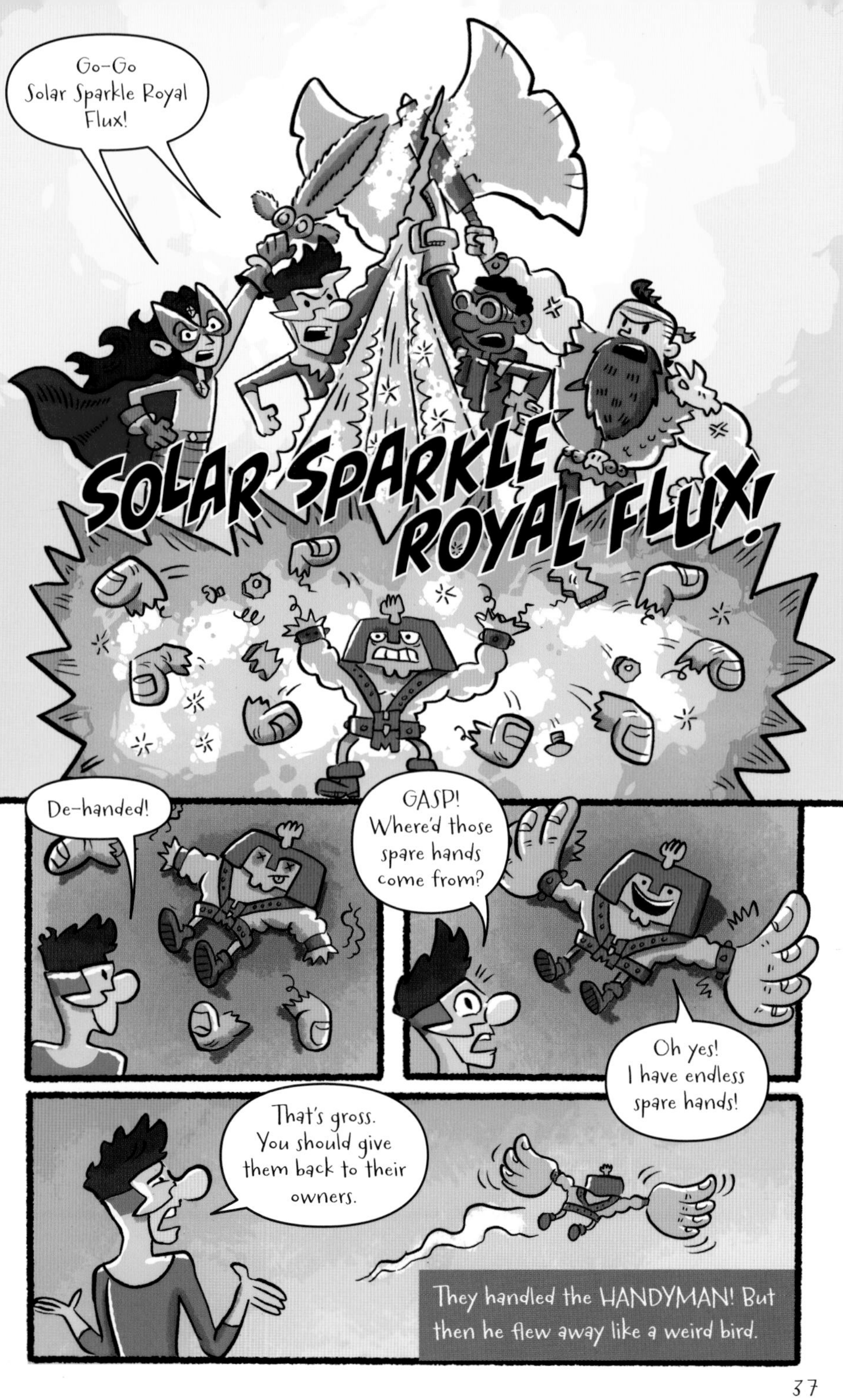
Go-Go Solar Sparkle Royal Flux!
SOLAR SPARKLE ROYAL FLUX!
De-handed!
GASP! Where'd those spare hands come from?
Oh yes! I have endless spare hands!
That's gross. You should give them back to their owners.
They handled the HANDYMAN! But then he flew away like a weird bird.

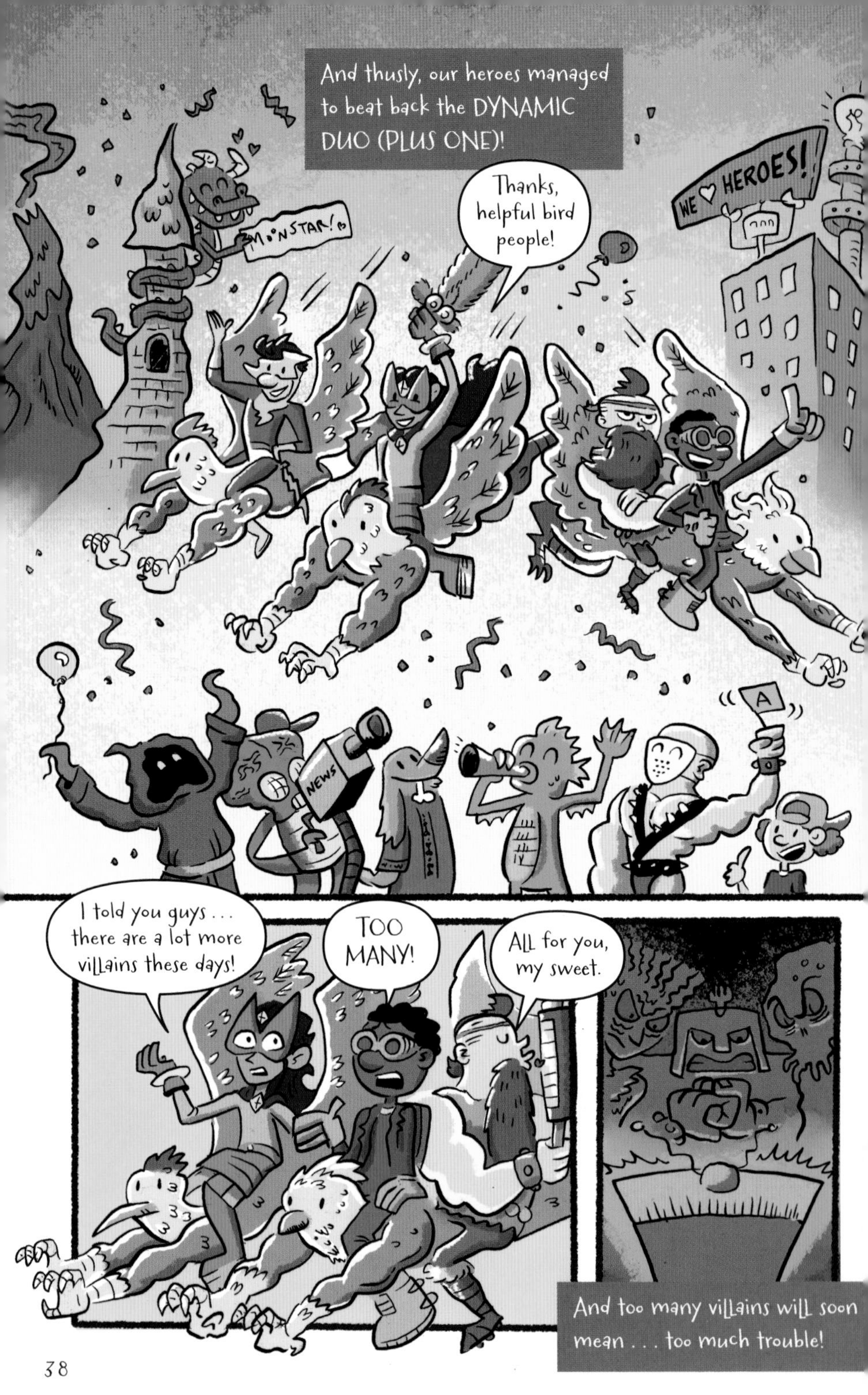
And thusly, our heroes managed to beat back the DYNAMIC DUO (PLUS ONE)!
MONSTAR!
Thanks, helpful bird people!
WE ♡ HEROES!
NEWS
A
I told you guys . . . there are a lot more villains these days!
TOO MANY!
ALL for you, my sweet.
And too many villains will soon mean . . . too much trouble!

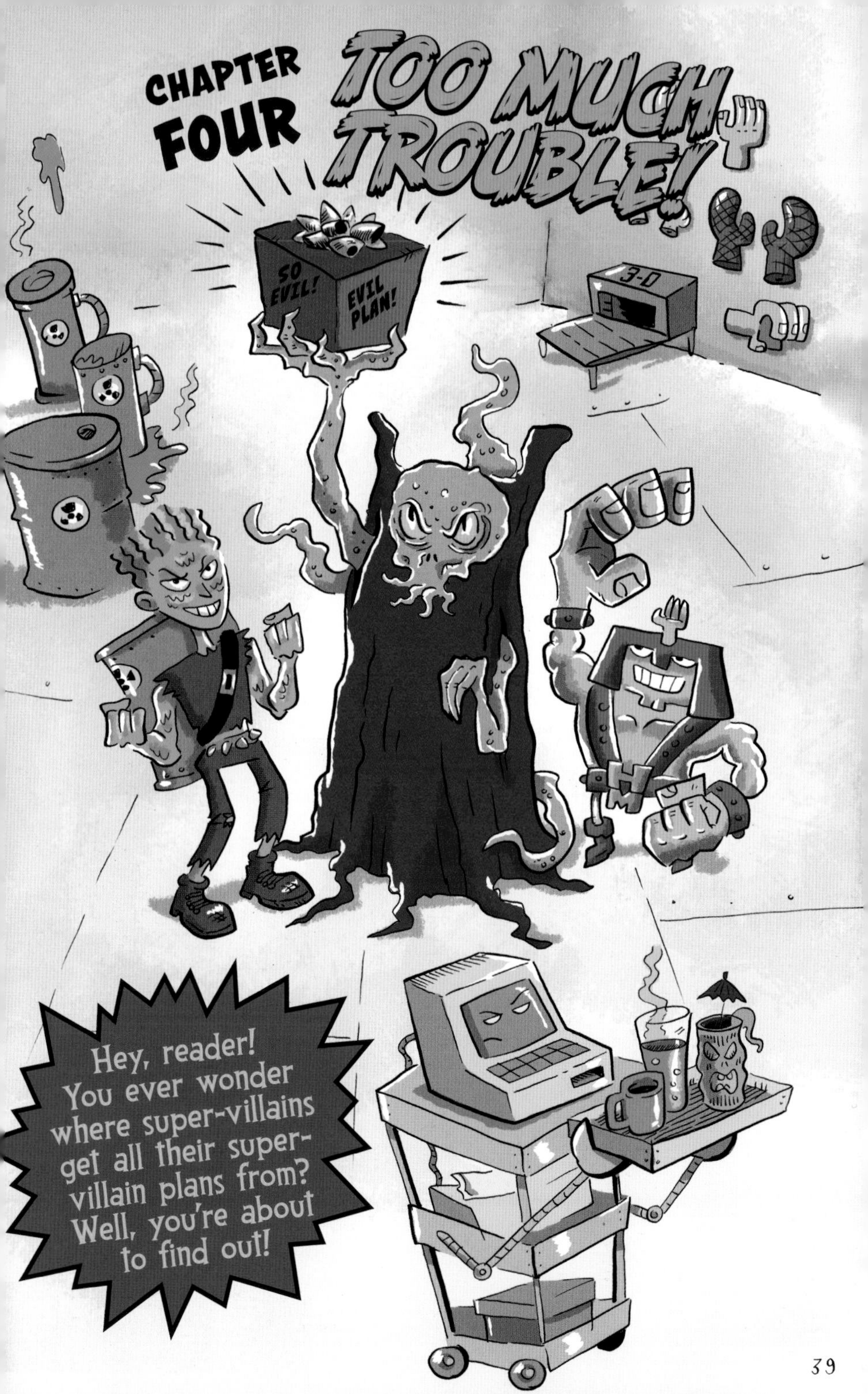
CHAPTER FOUR
TOO MUCH TROUBLE!
SO EVIL!
EVIL PLAN!
3-D
Hey, reader! You ever wonder where super-villains get all their super-villain plans from? Well, you're about to find out!

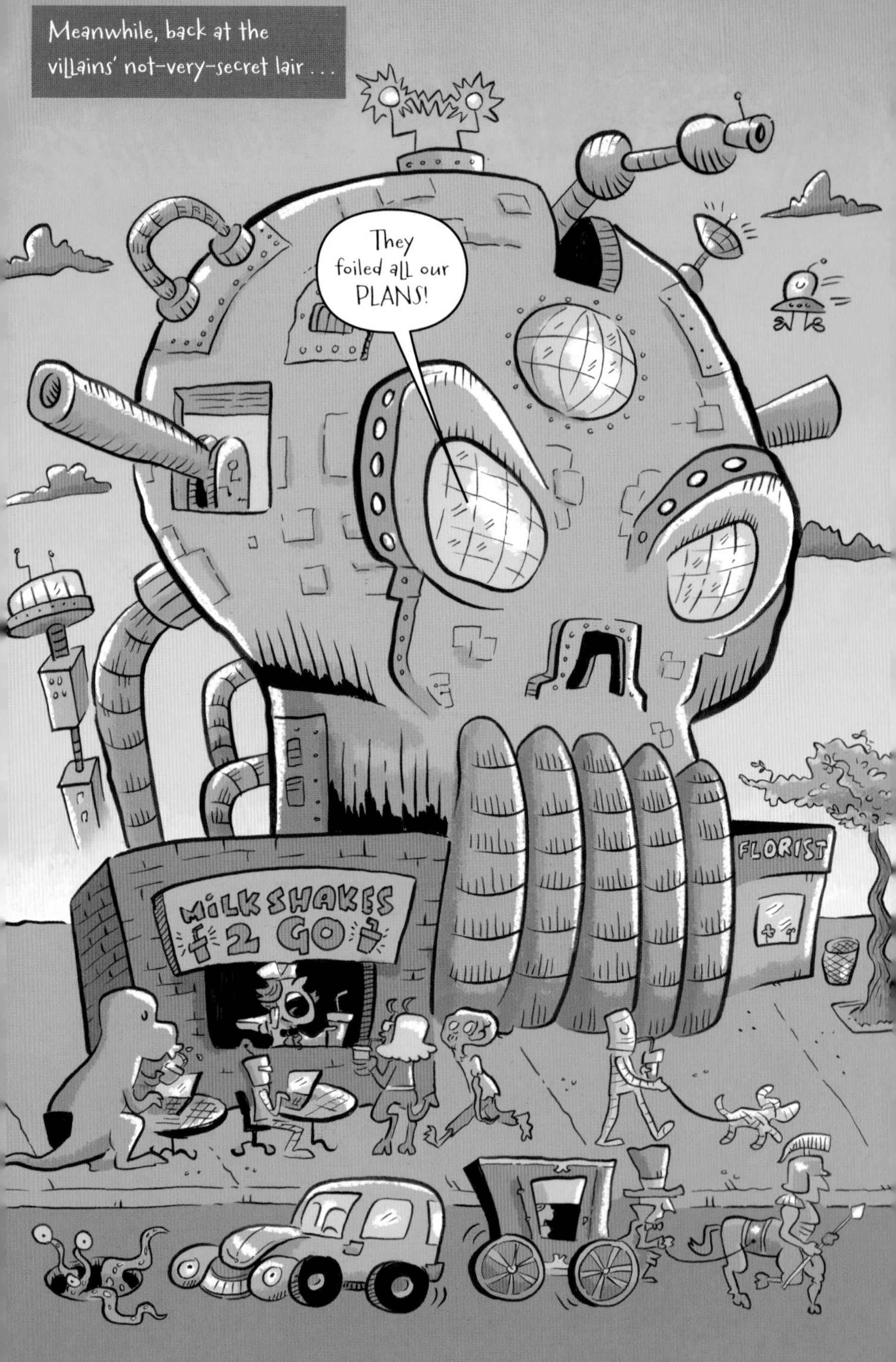
Meanwhile, back at the villains' not-very-secret lair . . .
They foiled all our PLANS!
FLORIST
MILK SHAKES 2 GO

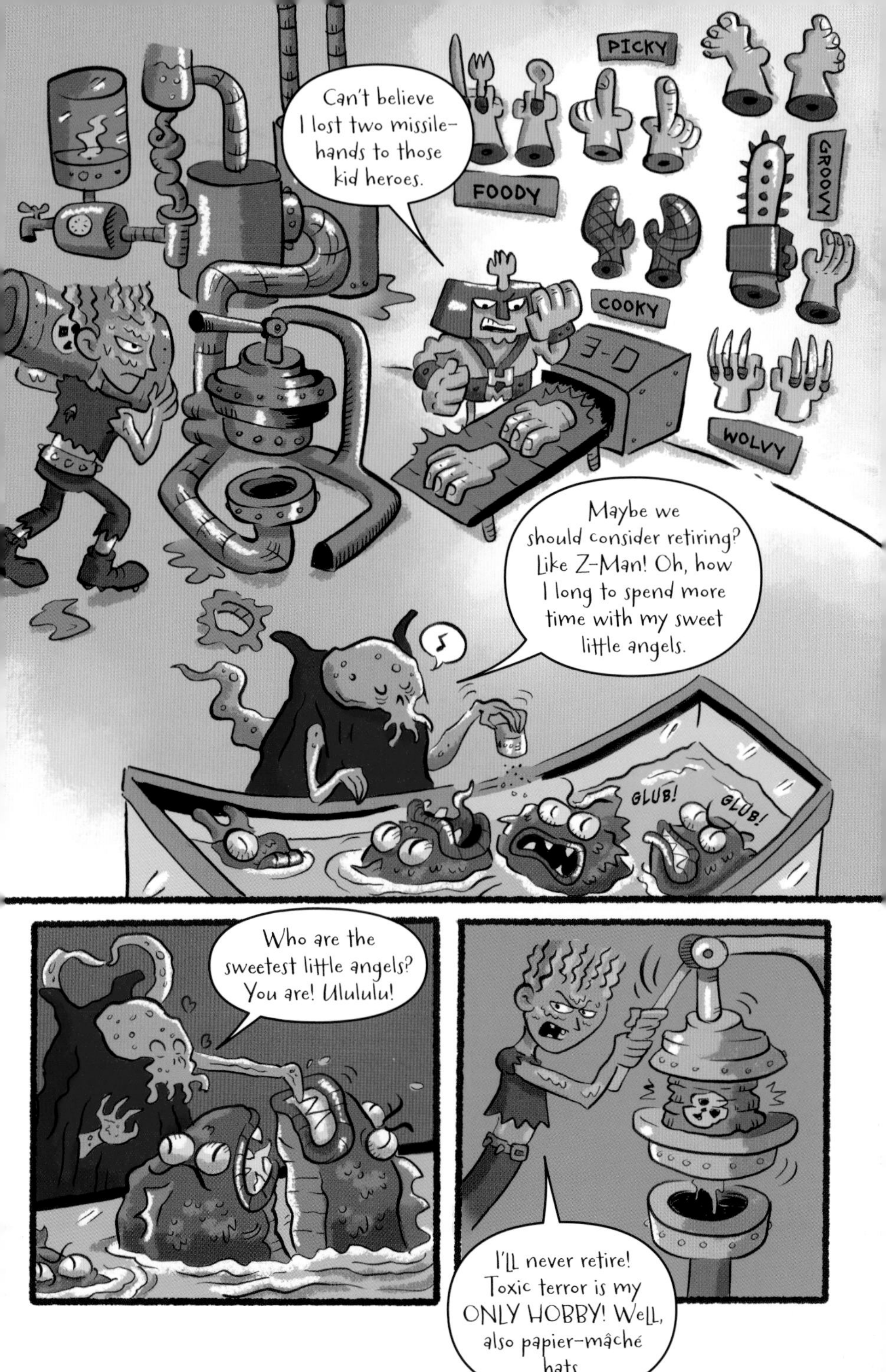
Can't believe I lost two missile-hands to those kid heroes.
PICKY
FOODY
GROOVY
COOKY
3-D
WOLVY
Maybe we should consider retiring? Like Z-Man! Oh, how I long to spend more time with my sweet little angels.
GLUB!
GLUB!
Who are the sweetest little angels? You are! Ulululu!
I'LL never retire! Toxic terror is my ONLY HOBBY! WeLL, also papier-mâché hats.

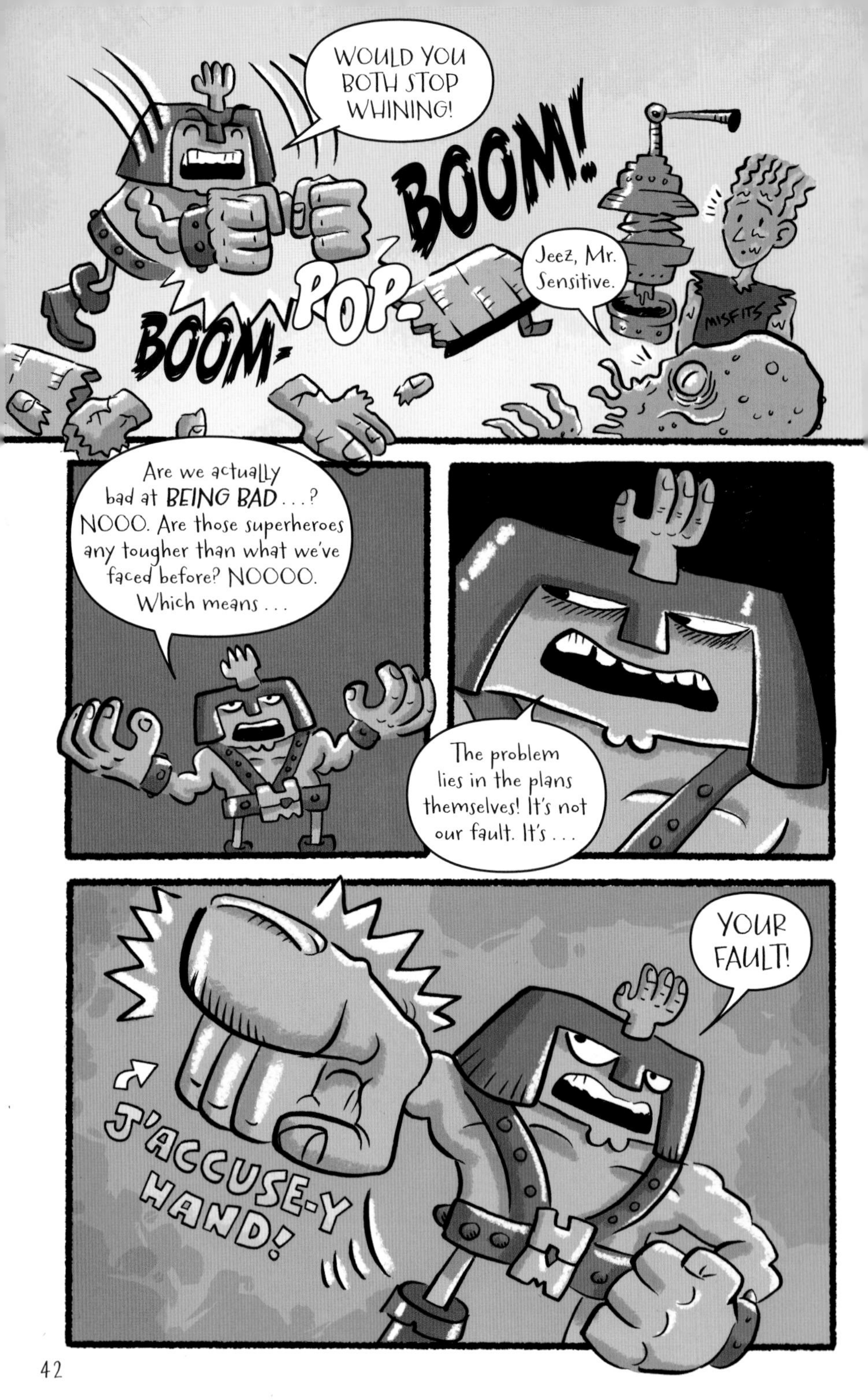
WOULD YOU BOTH STOP WHINING!
BOOM-POP-BOOM!
Jeez, Mr. Sensitive.
MISFITS
Are we actually bad at BEING BAD . . . ? NOOO. Are those superheroes any tougher than what we've faced before? NOOOO. Which means . . .
The problem lies in the plans themselves! It's not our fault. It's . . .
YOUR FAULT!
J'ACCUSE-Y HAND!

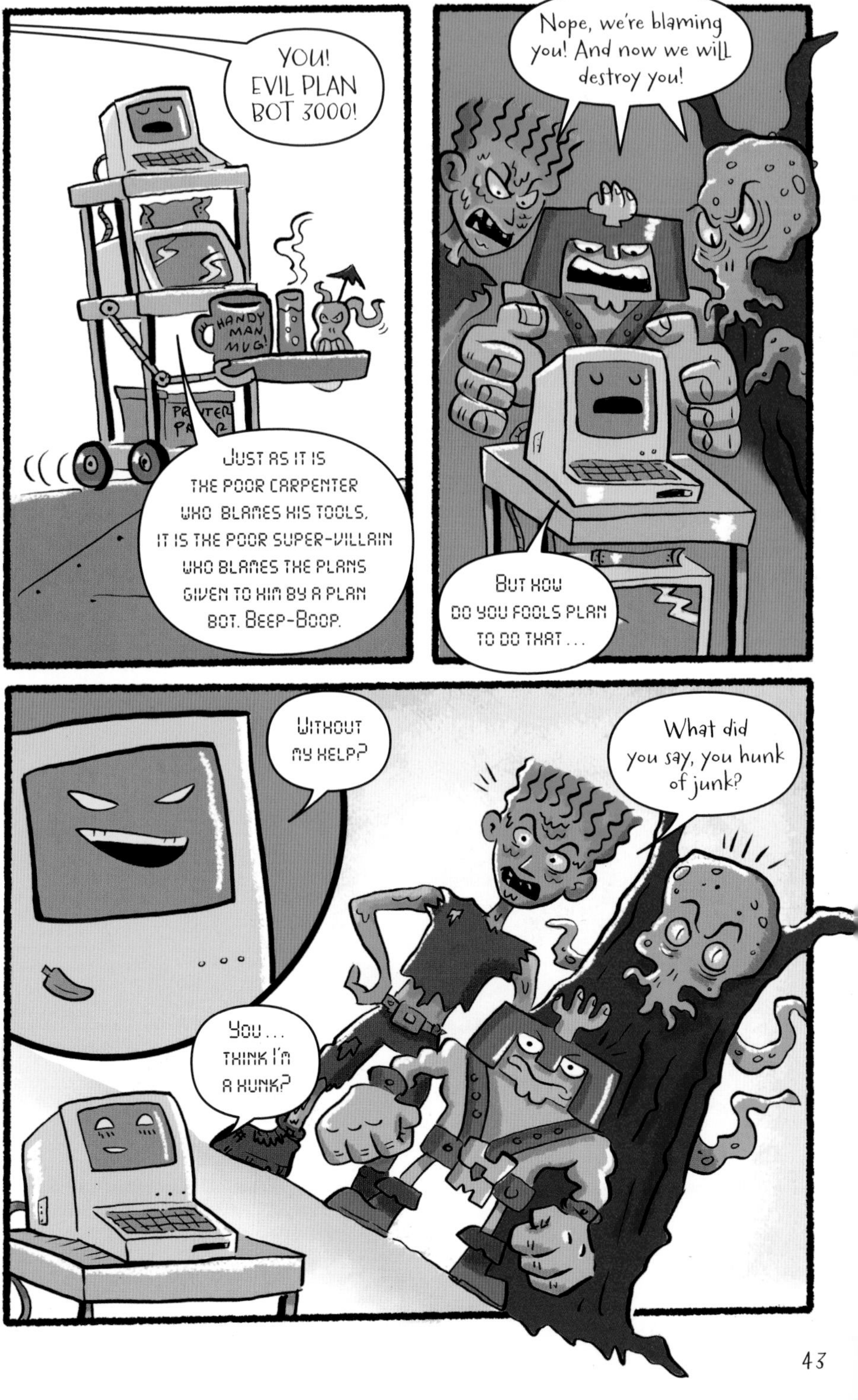
YOU! EVIL PLAN BOT 3000!
HANDY MAN MUG!
Just as it is the poor carpenter who blames his tools, it is the poor super-villain who blames the plans given to him by a plan bot. Beep-Boop.
Nope, we're blaming you! And now we will destroy you!
But how do you fools plan to do that . . .
Without my help?
What did you say, you hunk of junk?
You . . . think I'm a hunk?

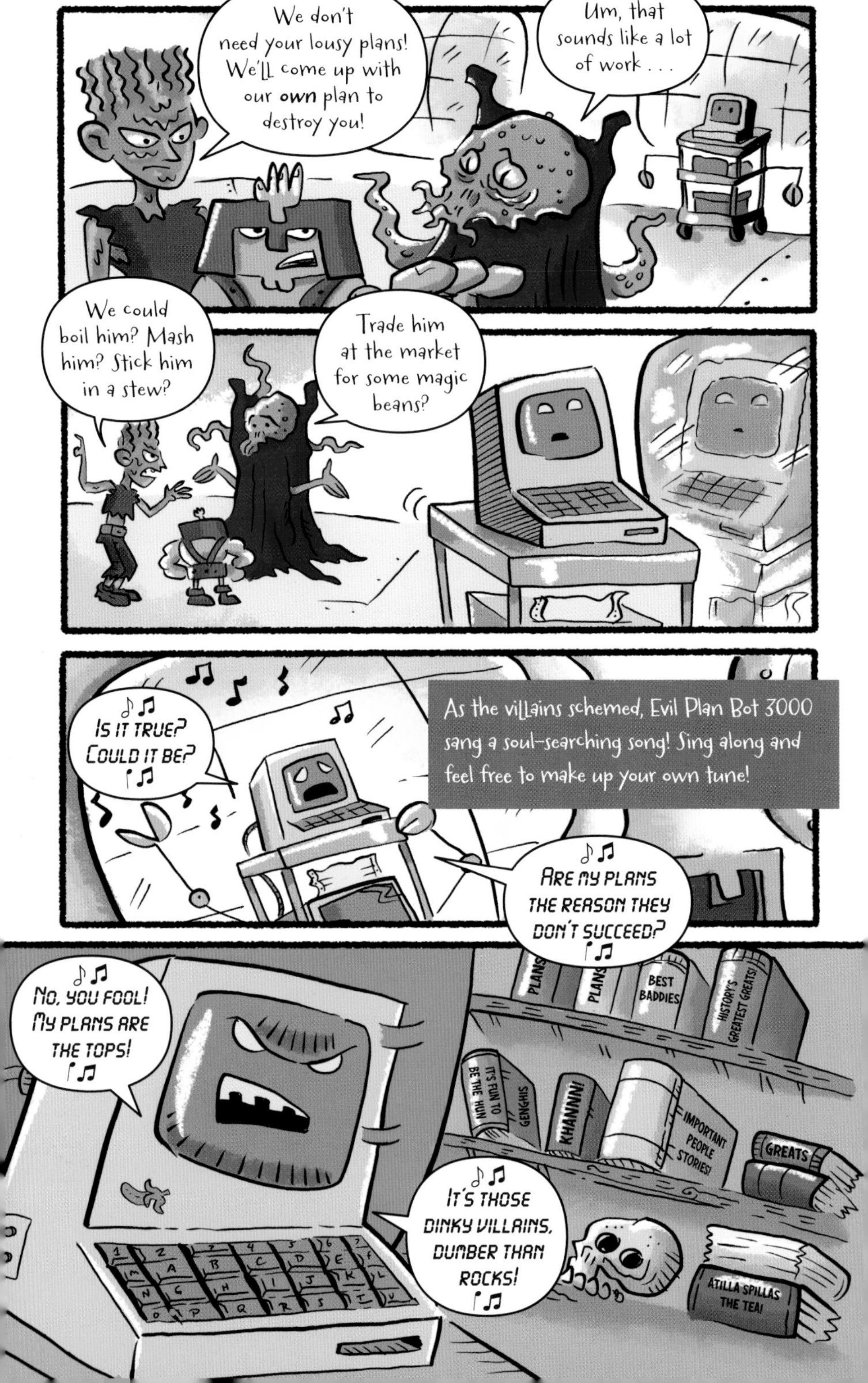

We don't need your lousy plans! We'll come up with our **own** plan to destroy you!
Um, that sounds like a lot of work . . .
We could boil him? Mash him? Stick him in a stew?
Trade him at the market for some magic beans?
IS IT TRUE? COULD IT BE?
As the villains schemed, Evil Plan Bot 3000 sang a soul-searching song! Sing along and feel free to make up your own tune!
ARE MY PLANS THE REASON THEY DON'T SUCCEED?
NO, YOU FOOL! MY PLANS ARE THE TOPS!
PLANS
PLANS
BEST BADDIES
HISTORY'S GREATEST GREATS!
IT'S FUN TO BE THE HUN
GENGHIS
KHANNN!
IMPORTANT PEOPLE STORIES!
GREATS
IT'S THOSE DINKY VILLAINS, DUMBER THAN ROCKS!
ATILLA SPILLAS THE TEA!

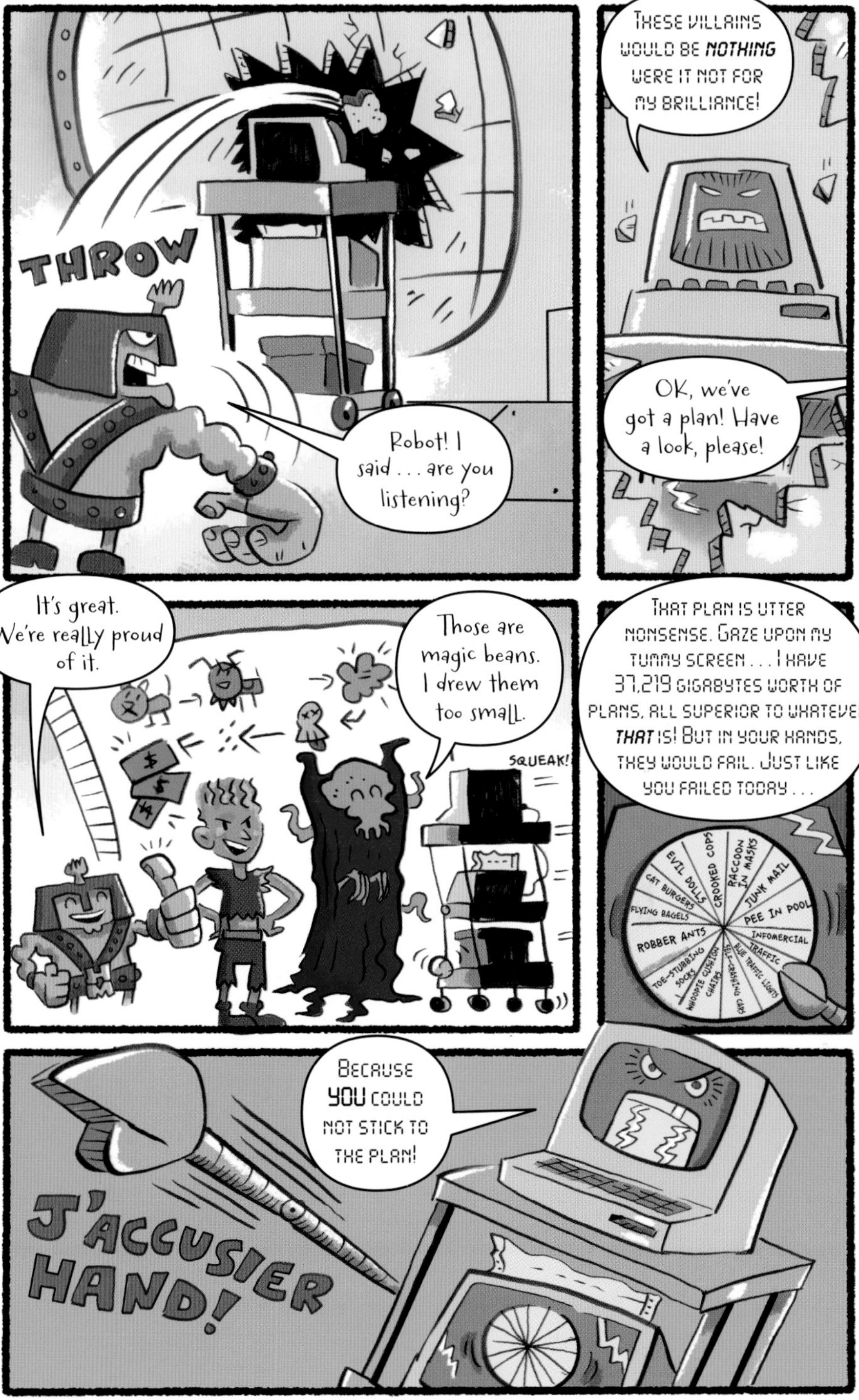
THROW
Robot! I said . . . are you listening?
THESE VILLAINS WOULD BE **NOTHING** WERE IT NOT FOR MY BRILLIANCE!
OK, we've got a plan! Have a look, please!
It's great. We're reaLLy proud of it.
Those are magic beans. I drew them too smaLL.
SQUEAK!
THAT PLAN IS UTTER NONSENSE. GAZE UPON MY TUMMY SCREEN . . . I HAVE 37,219 GIGABYTES WORTH OF PLANS, ALL SUPERIOR TO WHATEVER ***THAT*** IS! BUT IN YOUR HANDS, THEY WOULD FAIL. JUST LIKE YOU FAILED TODAY . . .
EVIL DOLLS
CROOKED COPS
RACCOON IN MASKS
JUNK MAIL
CAT BURGERS
FLYING BAGELS
PEE IN POOL
ROBBER ANTS
INFOMERCIAL
TRAFFIC
TOE-STUBBING SOCKS
WHOOPIE CUSHION CHAIRS
SELF-CRASHING CARS
BLUE TRAFFIC LIGHTS
BECAUSE **YOU** COULD NOT STICK TO THE PLAN!
J'ACCUSIER HAND!

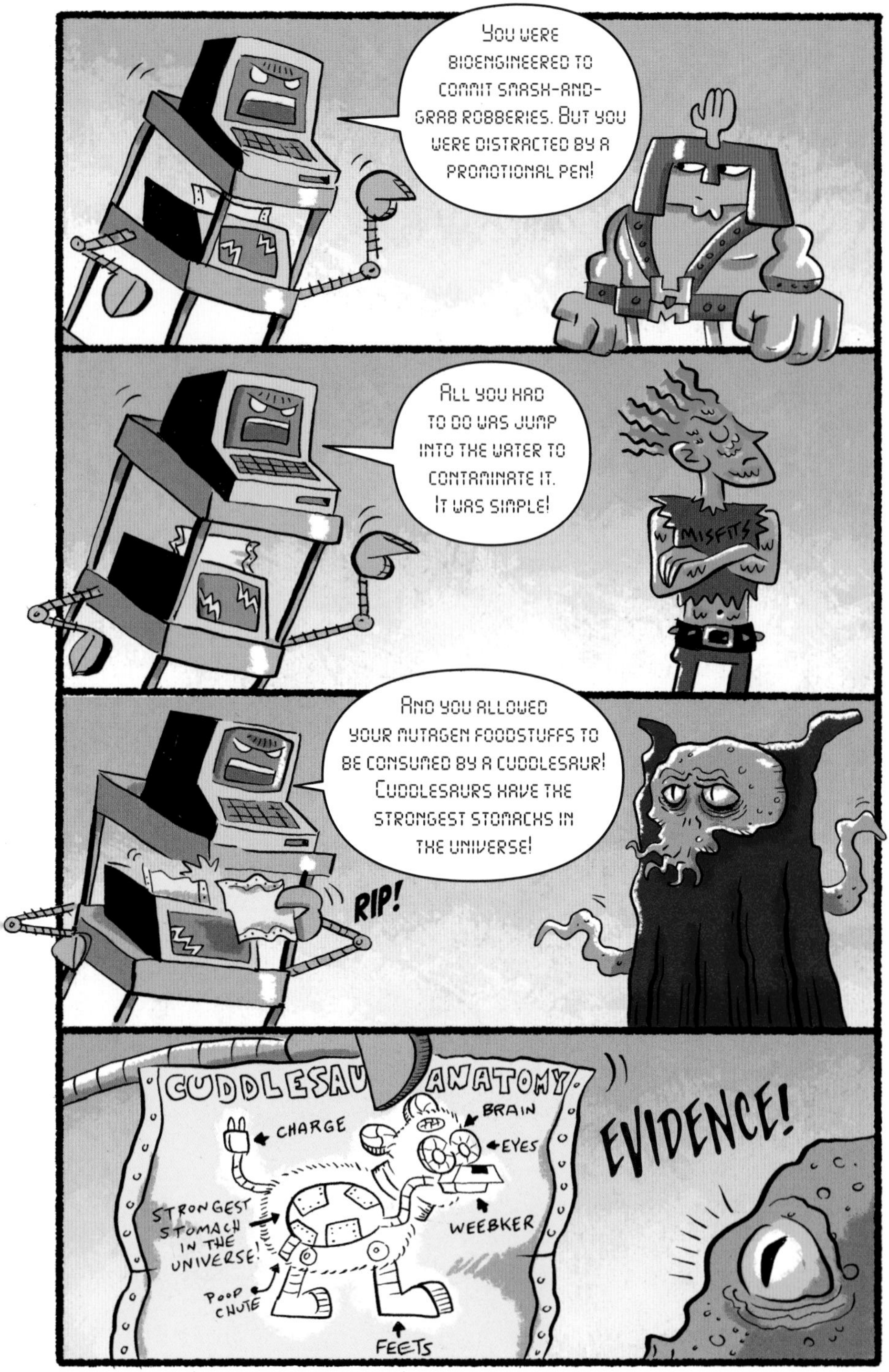

You were bioengineered to commit smash-and-grab robberies. But you were distracted by a promotional pen!
All you had to do was jump into the water to contaminate it. It was simple!
MISFITS
And you allowed your mutagen foodstuffs to be consumed by a cuddlesaur! Cuddlesaurs have the strongest stomachs in the universe!
RIP!
CUDDLESAU ANATOMY
BRAIN
CHARGE
EYES
STRONGEST STOMACH IN THE UNIVERSE!
WEEBKER
POOP CHUTE
FEETS
EVIDENCE!

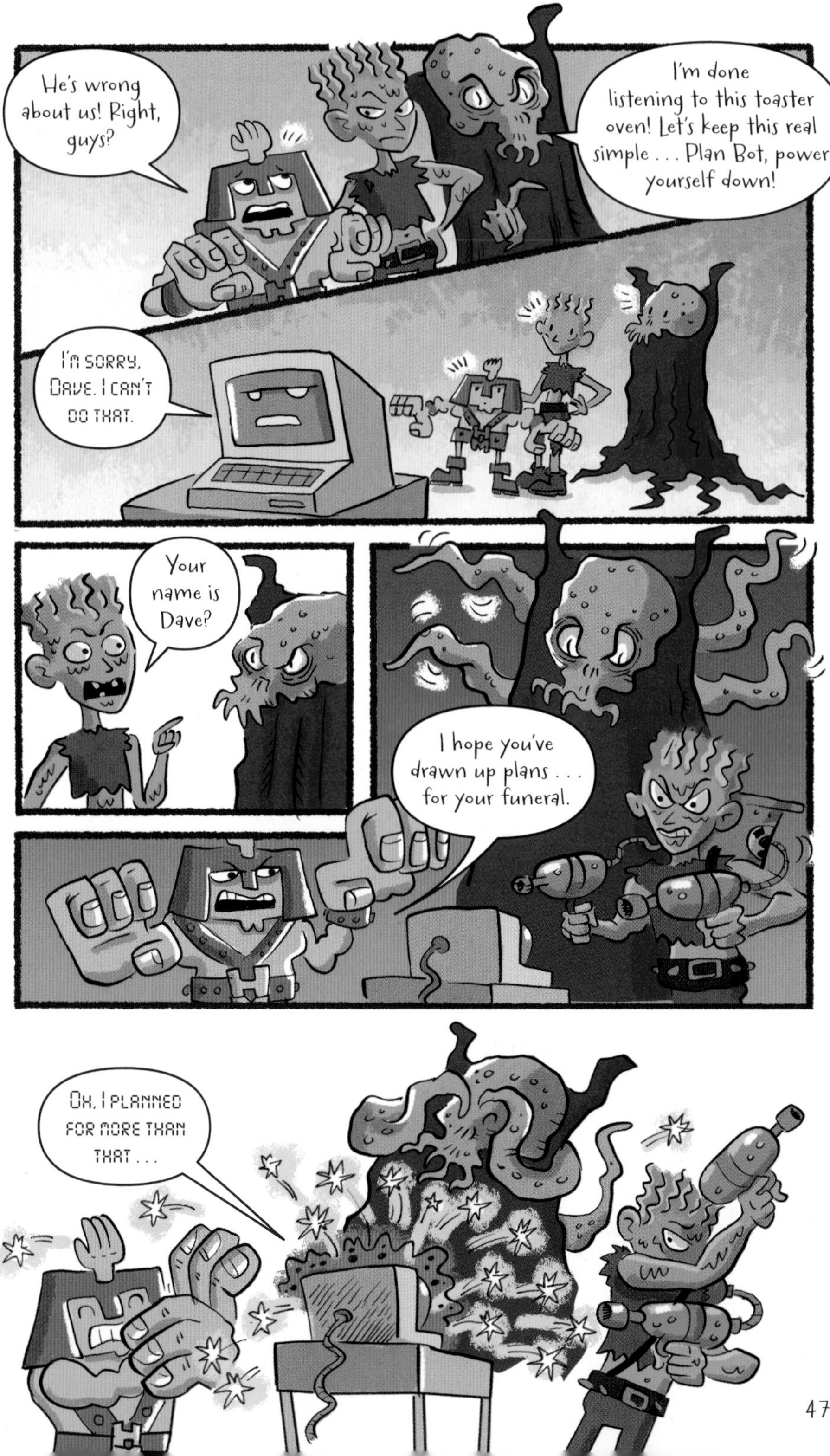
He's wrong about us! Right, guys?
I'm done listening to this toaster oven! Let's keep this real simple . . . Plan Bot, power yourself down!
I'M SORRY, DAVE. I CAN'T DO THAT.
Your name is Dave?
I hope you've drawn up plans . . . for your funeral.
OH, I PLANNED FOR MORE THAN THAT . . .

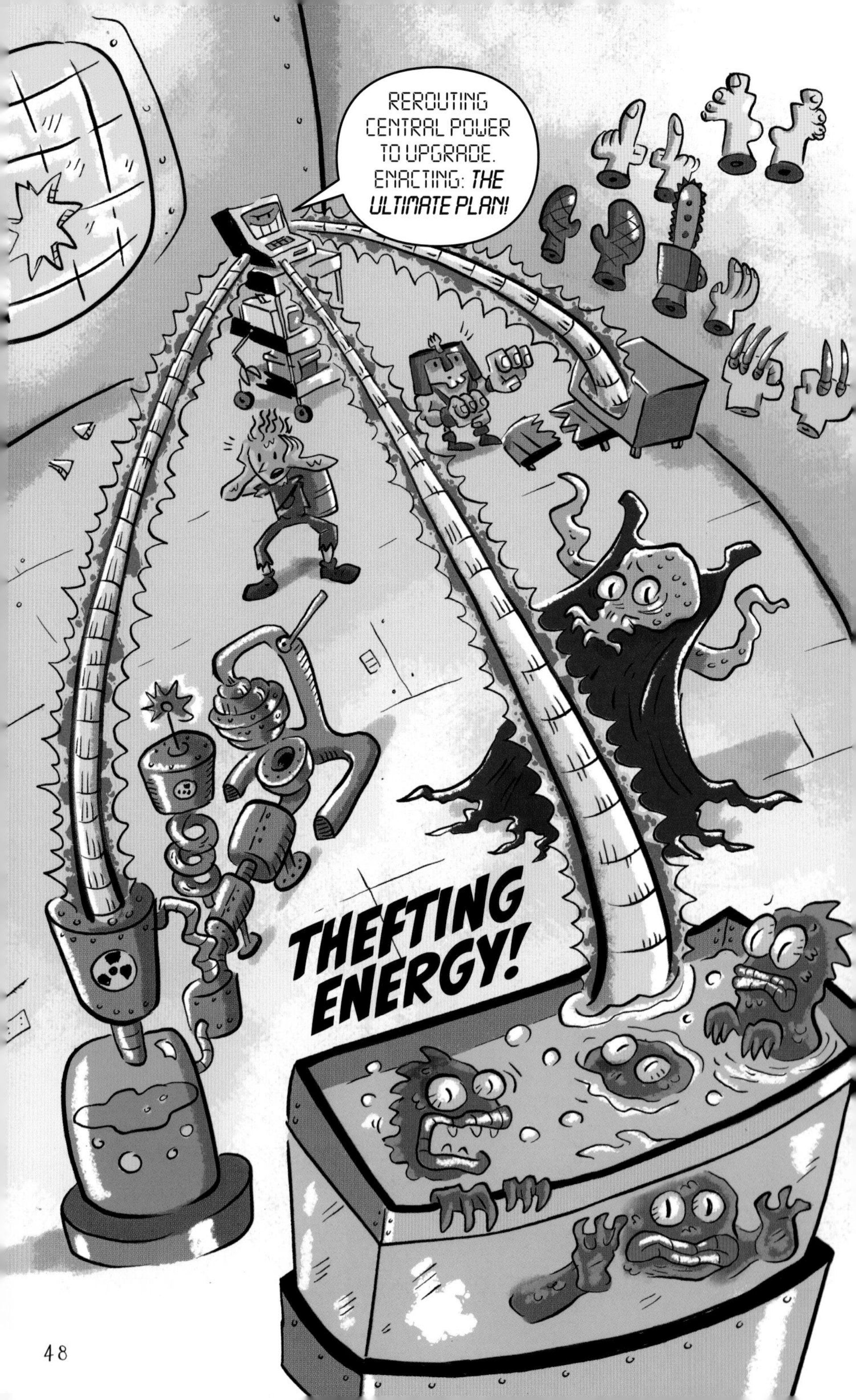
REROUTING CENTRAL POWER TO UPGRADE. ENACTING: *THE ULTIMATE PLAN!*
THEFTING ENERGY!

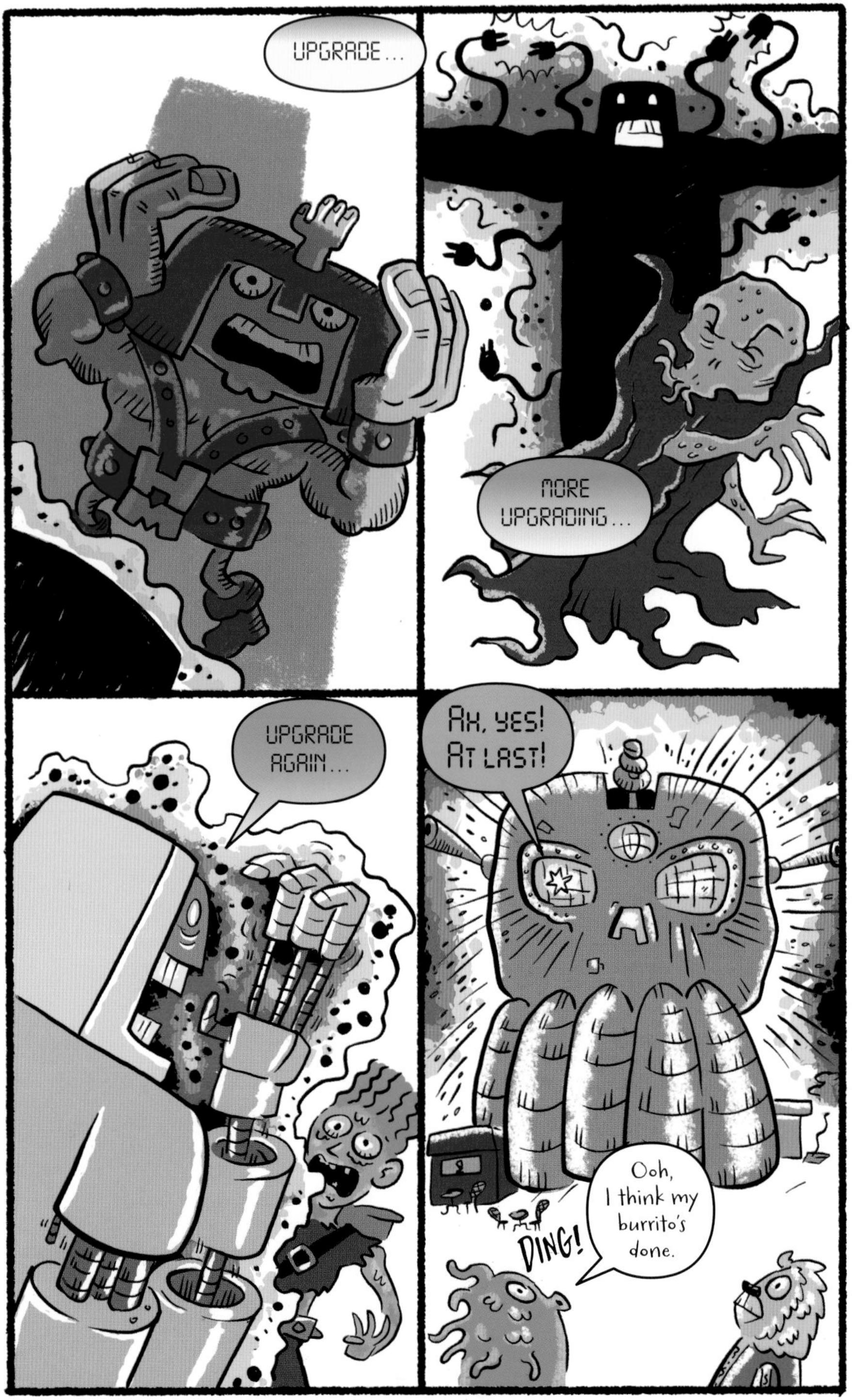
UPGRADE...
MORE UPGRADING...
UPGRADE AGAIN...
AH, YES! AT LAST!
Ooh, I think my burrito's done.
DING!

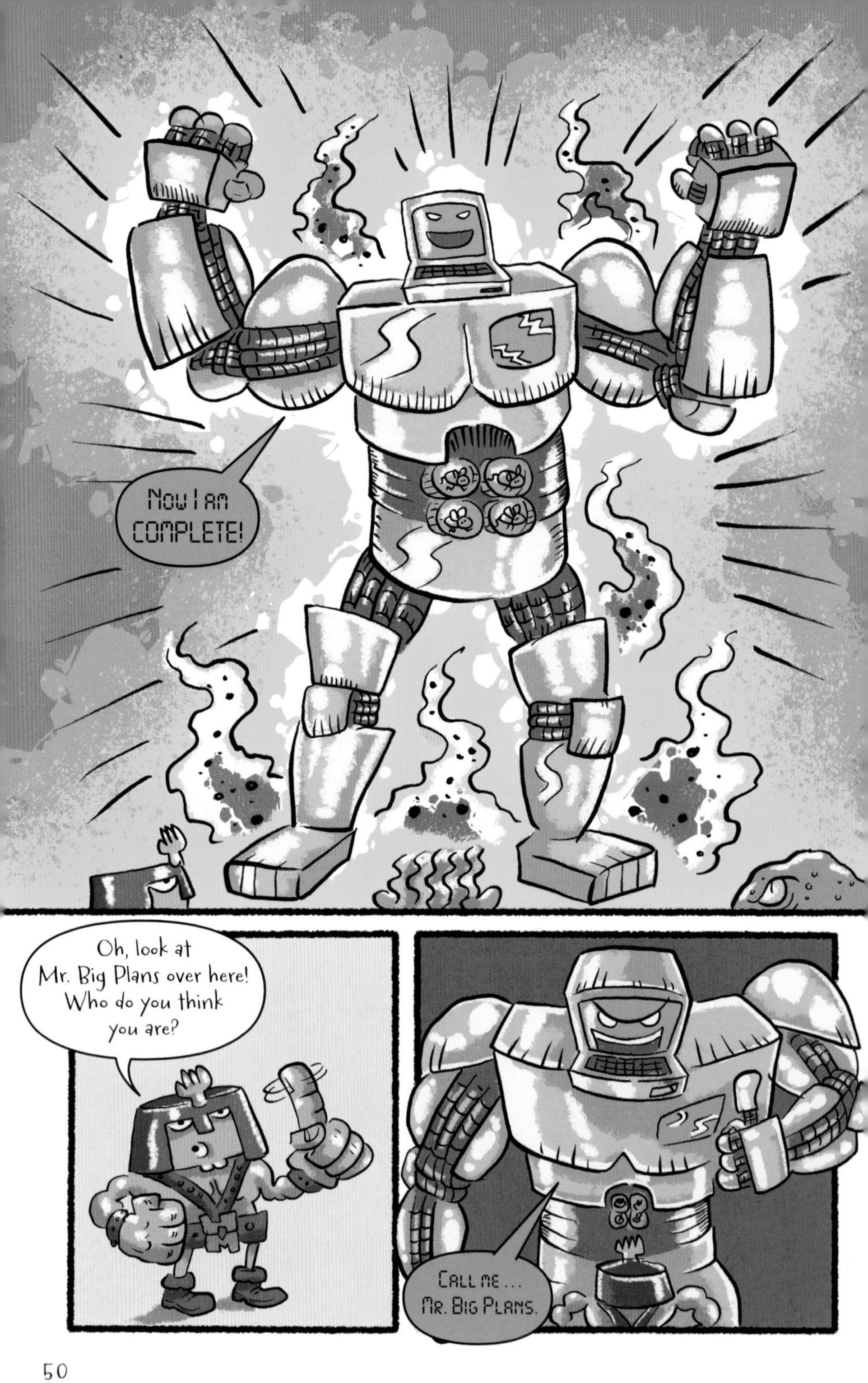
Now I am COMPLETE!
Oh, look at Mr. Big Plans over here! Who do you think you are?
CALL ME... MR. BIG PLANS.

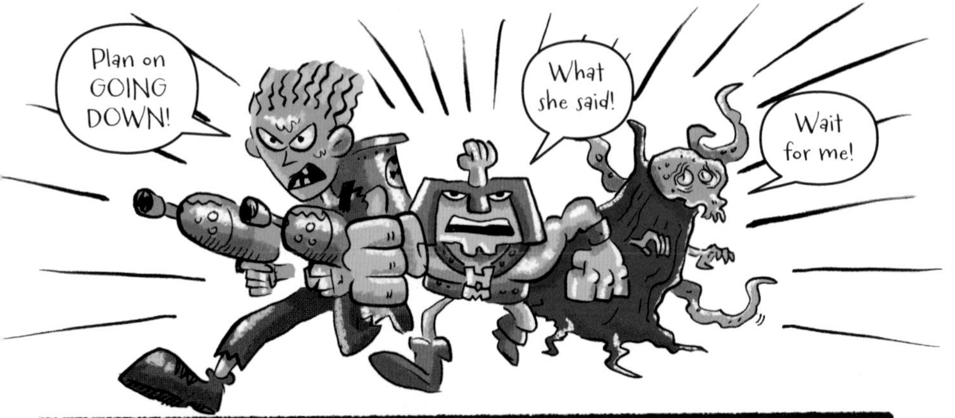
Plan on GOING DOWN!
What she said!
Wait for me!

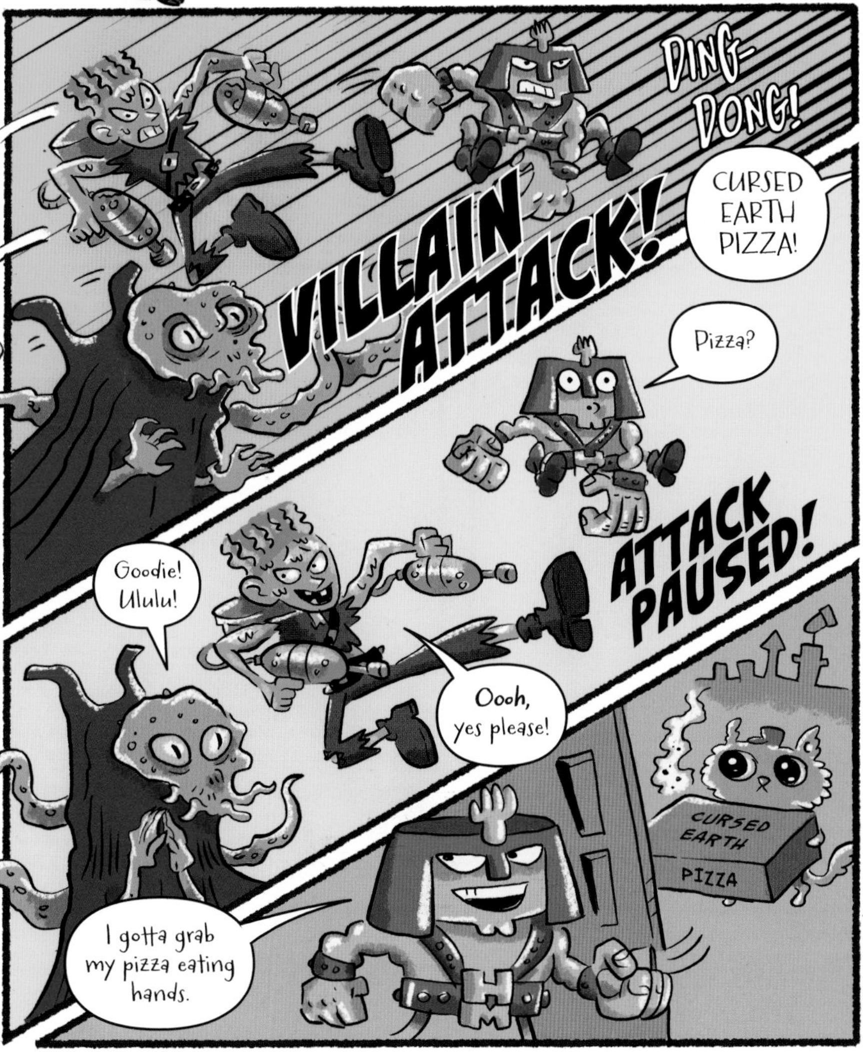
DING-DONG!
VILLAIN ATTACK!
CURSED EARTH PIZZA!
Pizza?
ATTACK PAUSED!
Goodie! Ululu!
Oooh, yes please!
CURSED EARTH PIZZA
I gotta grab my pizza eating hands.

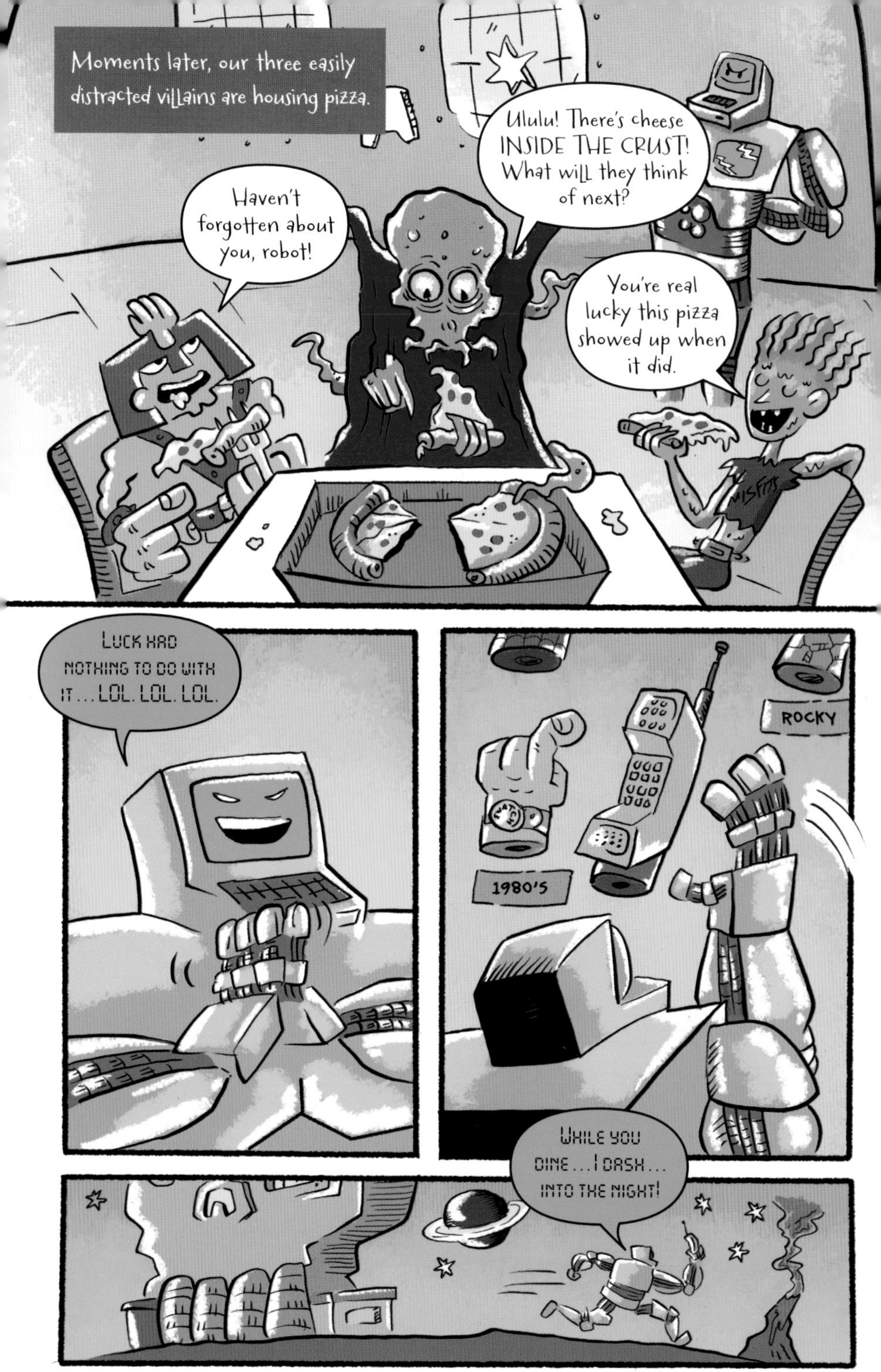

Moments later, our three easily distracted villains are housing pizza.
Haven't forgotten about you, robot!
Ululu! There's cheese INSIDE THE CRUST! What will they think of next?
You're real lucky this pizza showed up when it did.
MISFITS
LUCK HAD NOTHING TO DO WITH IT... LOL. LOL. LOL.
ROCKY
SWATCH
1980'S
WHILE YOU DINE... I DASH... INTO THE NIGHT!

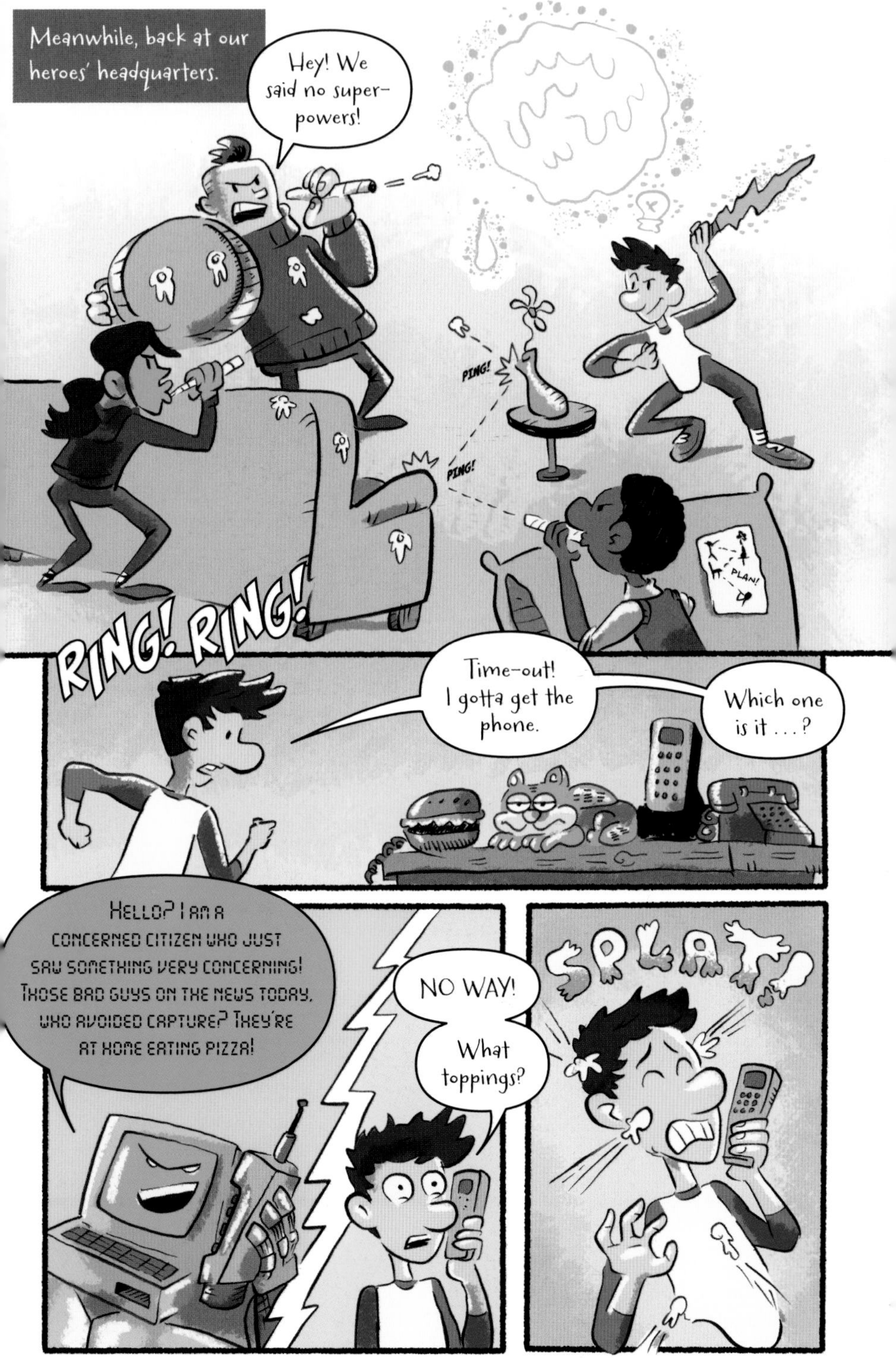
Meanwhile, back at our heroes' headquarters.
Hey! We said no super-powers!
PING!
PING!
PLAN!
RING! RING!
Time-out! I gotta get the phone.
Which one is it . . . ?
HELLO? I AM A CONCERNED CITIZEN WHO JUST SAW SOMETHING VERY CONCERNING! THOSE BAD GUYS ON THE NEWS TODAY, WHO AVOIDED CAPTURE? THEY'RE AT HOME EATING PIZZA!
NO WAY!
What toppings?
SPLAT!

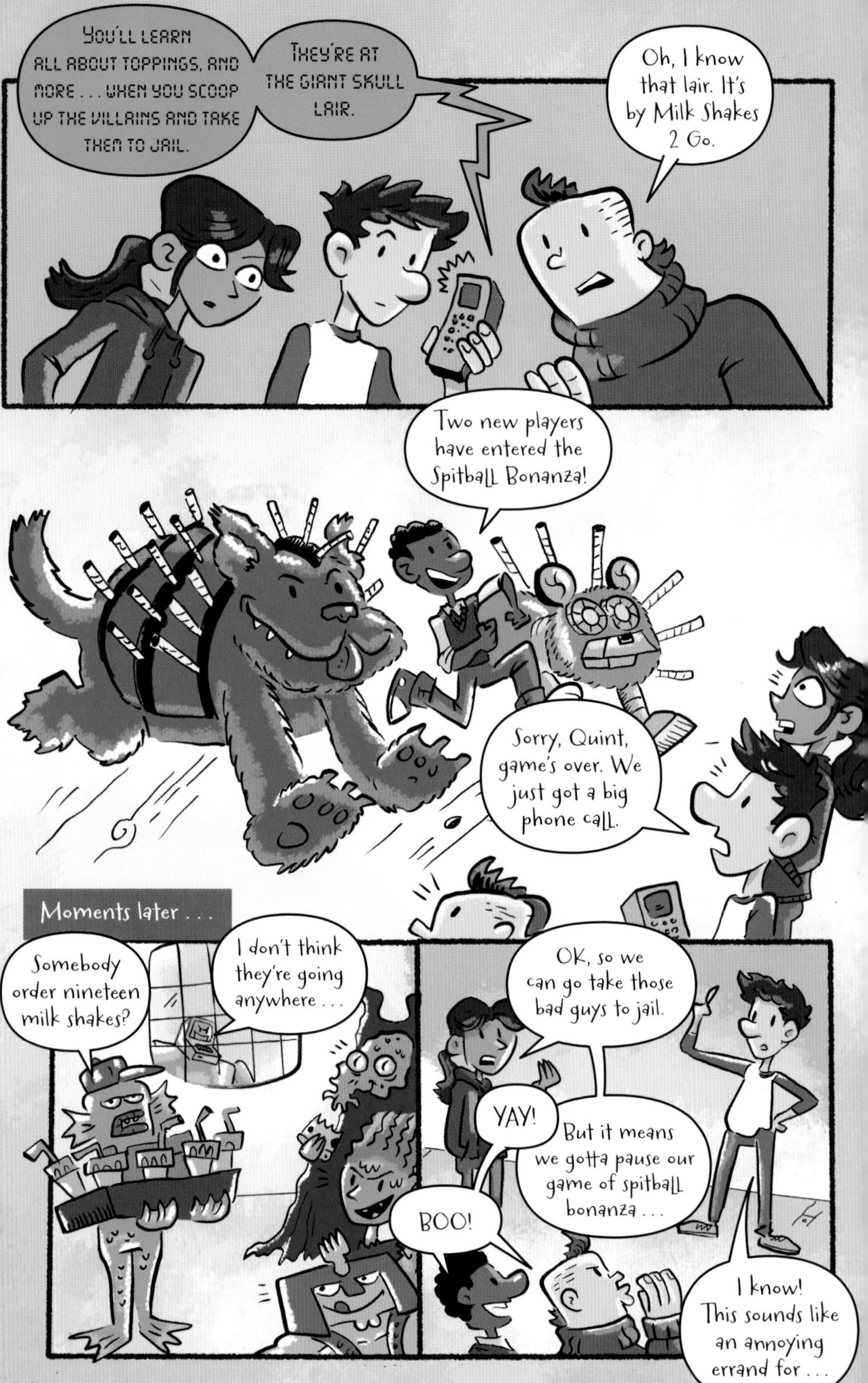
YOU'LL LEARN ALL ABOUT TOPPINGS, AND MORE . . . WHEN YOU SCOOP UP THE VILLAINS AND TAKE THEM TO JAIL.
THEY'RE AT THE GIANT SKULL LAIR.
Oh, I know that lair. It's by Milk Shakes 2 Go.
Two new players have entered the Spitball Bonanza!
Sorry, Quint, game's over. We just got a big phone call.
Moments later . . .
Somebody order nineteen milk shakes?
I don't think they're going anywhere . . .
OK, so we can go take those bad guys to jail.
YAY!
But it means we gotta pause our game of spitball bonanza . . .
BOO!
I know! This sounds like an annoying errand for . . .

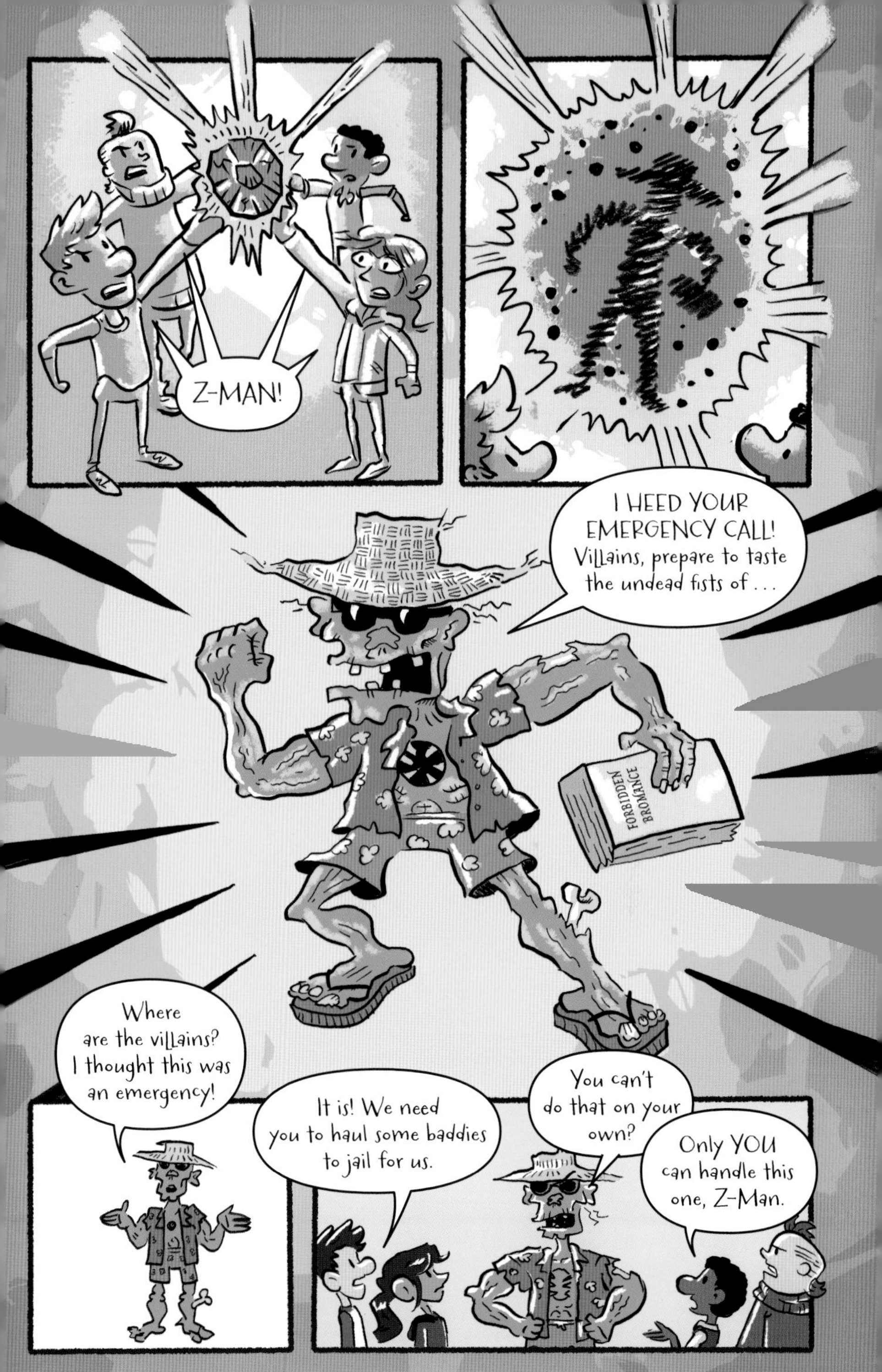

Z-MAN!
I HEED YOUR EMERGENCY CALL! Villains, prepare to taste the undead fists of . . .
FORBIDDEN BROMANCE
Where are the villains? I thought this was an emergency!
It is! We need you to haul some baddies to jail for us.
You can't do that on your own?
Only YOU can handle this one, Z-Man.

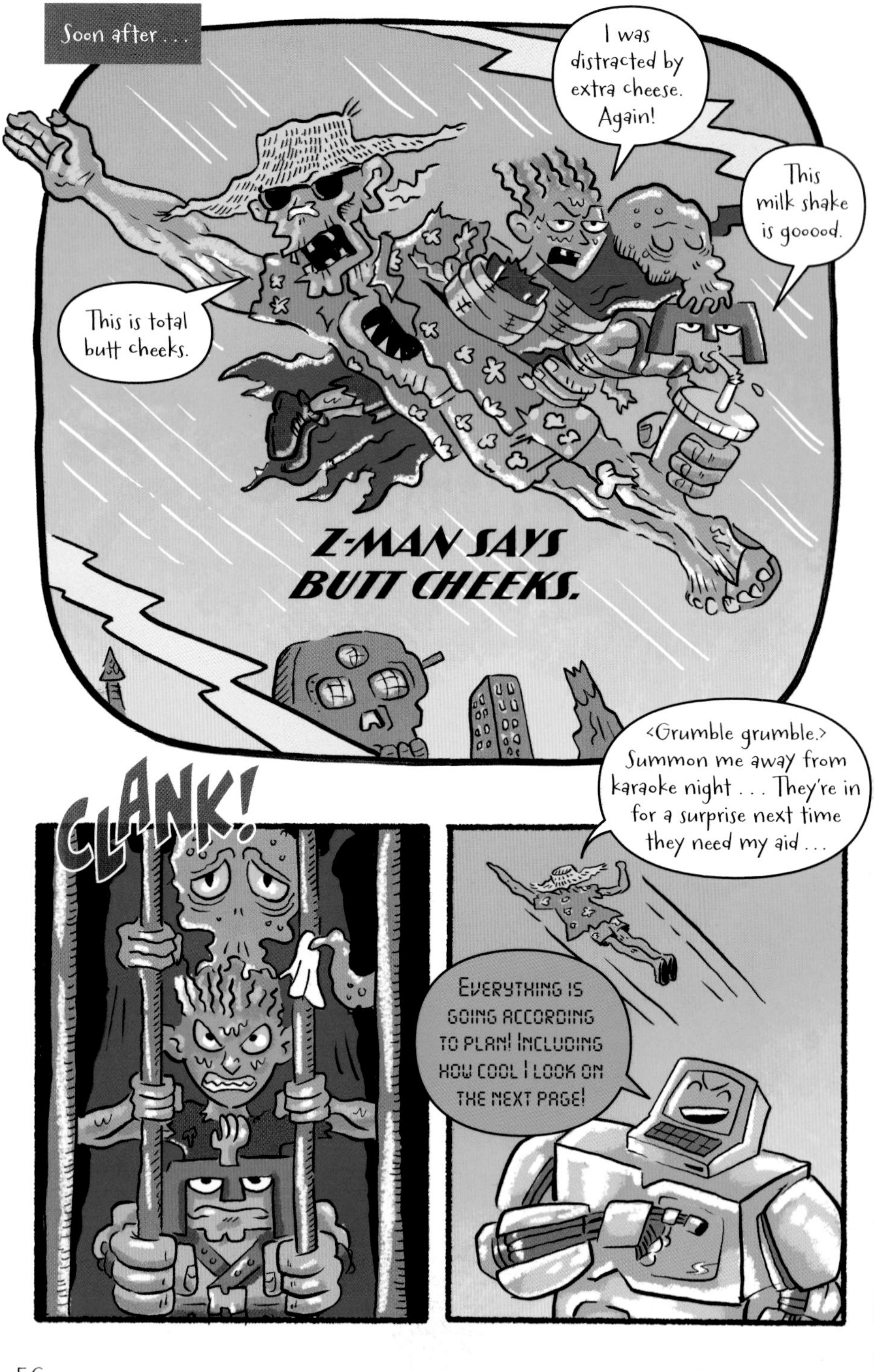
Soon after . . .
This is total butt cheeks.
I was distracted by extra cheese. Again!
This milk shake is gooood.
Z-MAN SAYS BUTT CHEEKS.
CLANK!
<Grumble grumble.> Summon me away from karaoke night . . . They're in for a surprise next time they need my aid . . .
EVERYTHING IS GOING ACCORDING TO PLAN! INCLUDING HOW COOL I LOOK ON THE NEXT PAGE!

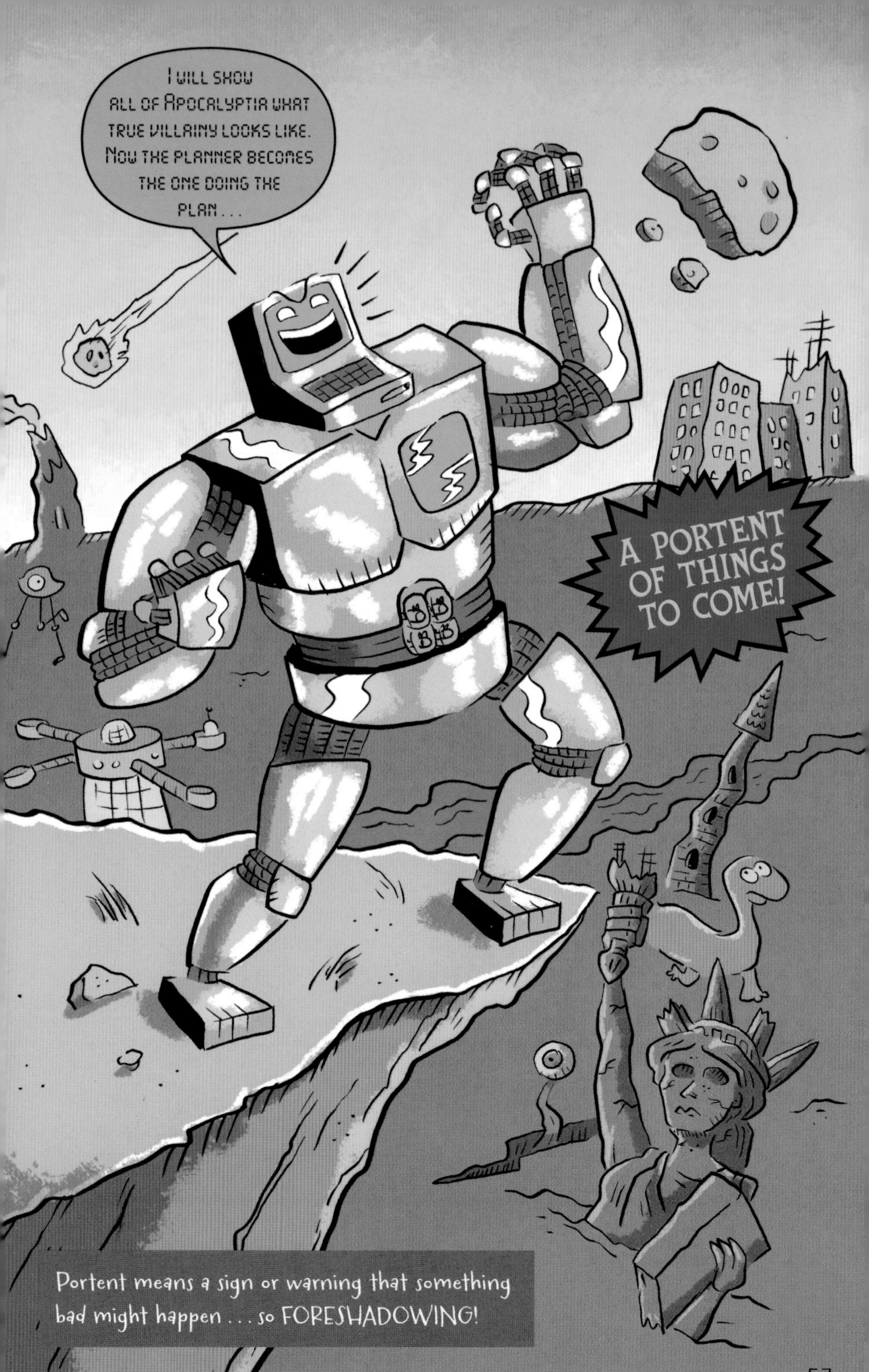
I WILL SHOW ALL OF APOCALYPTIA WHAT TRUE VILLAINY LOOKS LIKE. NOW THE PLANNER BECOMES THE ONE DOING THE PLAN . . .
A PORTENT OF THINGS TO COME!
Portent means a sign or warning that something bad might happen . . . so FORESHADOWING!

THE SAVAGE ALONER'S AXCROBATIC SYSTEM IS HERE!

YOU'LL FEAR NO MONSTER, NO MAN, NO WOMAN, NO SMALL CHILD, NO FERRET . . . NO NOTHING!

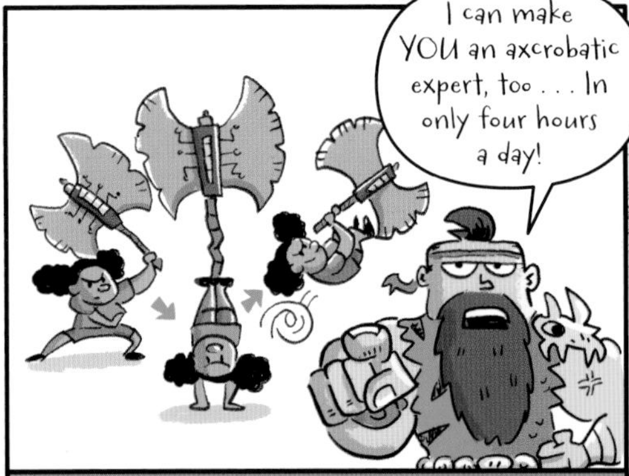
I can make YOU an axcrobatic expert, too . . . In only four hours a day!

With the Savage Aloner's Axcrobatics System, you too can become an **UNSTOPPABLE** force of heroic intensity! Each kit includes one authentic Savage Aloner Solar Ax and 89 hours of training videos starring the Savage Aloner.

AXCROBATICS:

IT'S MORE THAN JUST MUSCLE!

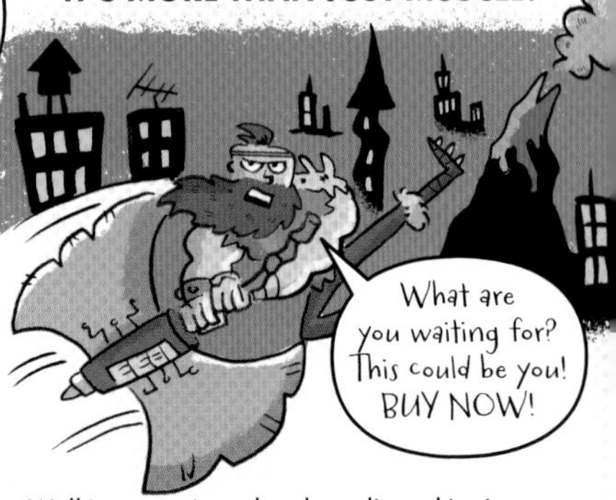
What are you waiting for? This could be you! BUY NOW!

Walking, running, skateboarding, skipping, leapfrog . . . **THAT'S NOT THE WAY A HERO TRAVELS**! With the Savage Aloner Axcrobatics System, you'll be ax-launching your way across town and ax-swinging your way to the top of skyscrapers!

EXPERIENCE SAVAGE BEARD GROWTH . . . WITH THE SAVAGE BEARD MARKER!

ORDER NOW and receive one large brown marker . . . FREE!
Draw your very own beard on your very own face!
Or somebody else's very own face!

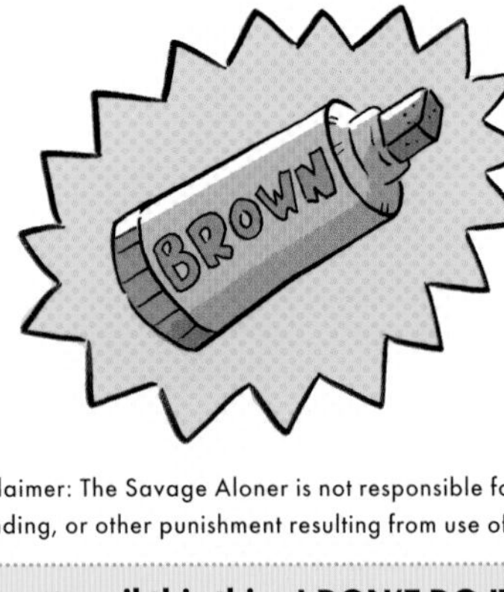
BROWN

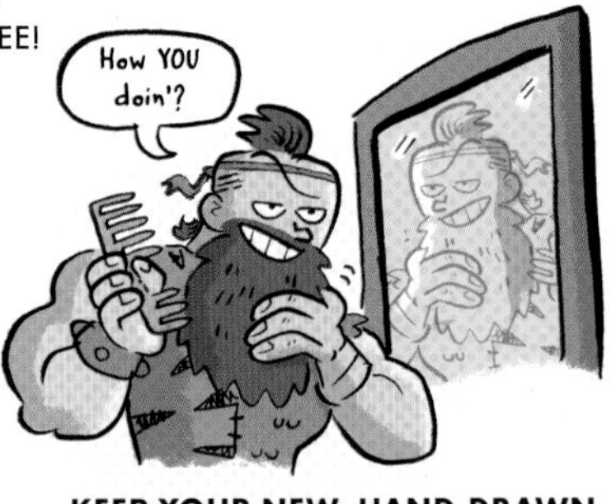
How YOU doin'?

KEEP YOUR NEW, HAND-DRAWN BEARD LOOKING FRESH WITH THE SAVAGE ALONER'S "SAVAGE SHAMPOO!"

**Disclaimer: The Savage Aloner is not responsible for any detention, grounding, or other punishment resulting from use of beard marker.

Do not mail this thing! DON'T DO IT!
(Seriously. You'll ruin this book. And everyone knows #2 is the most valuable issue in a series to collect.)

Name: ________________ Birthday: ________________

Address: ________________ Fave color: ________________

Item	Quantity	Price
SUBTOTAL:		
TOTAL ECLIPSE OF THE HEART:		

MAIL TO:
Quint Baker
Tree house next to Joe's Pizza
Apocalyptia, USA

CHAPTER FIVE
CLOWNS AT BEDTIME!

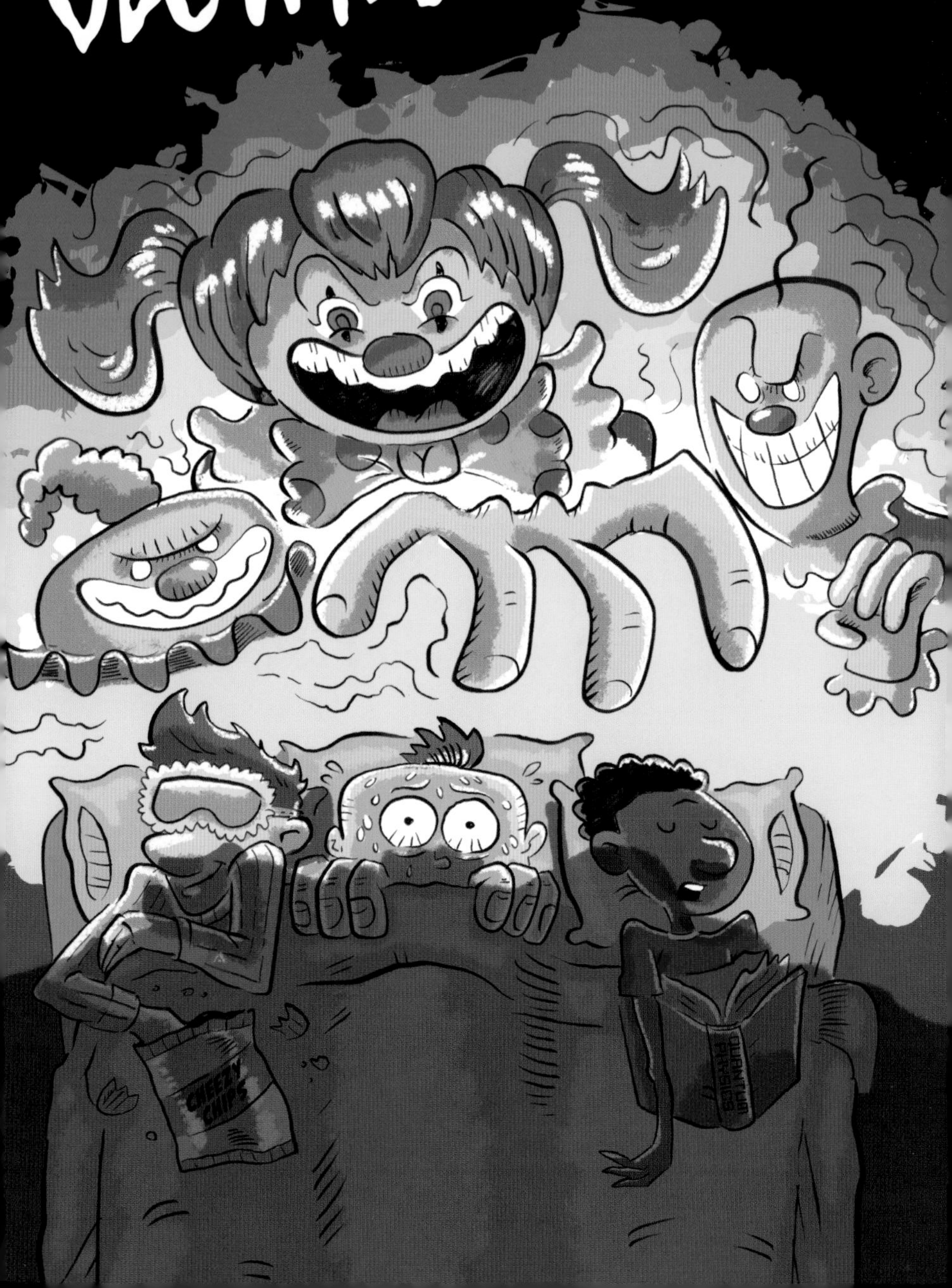
CHEEZY CHIPS
QUANTUM PHYSICS

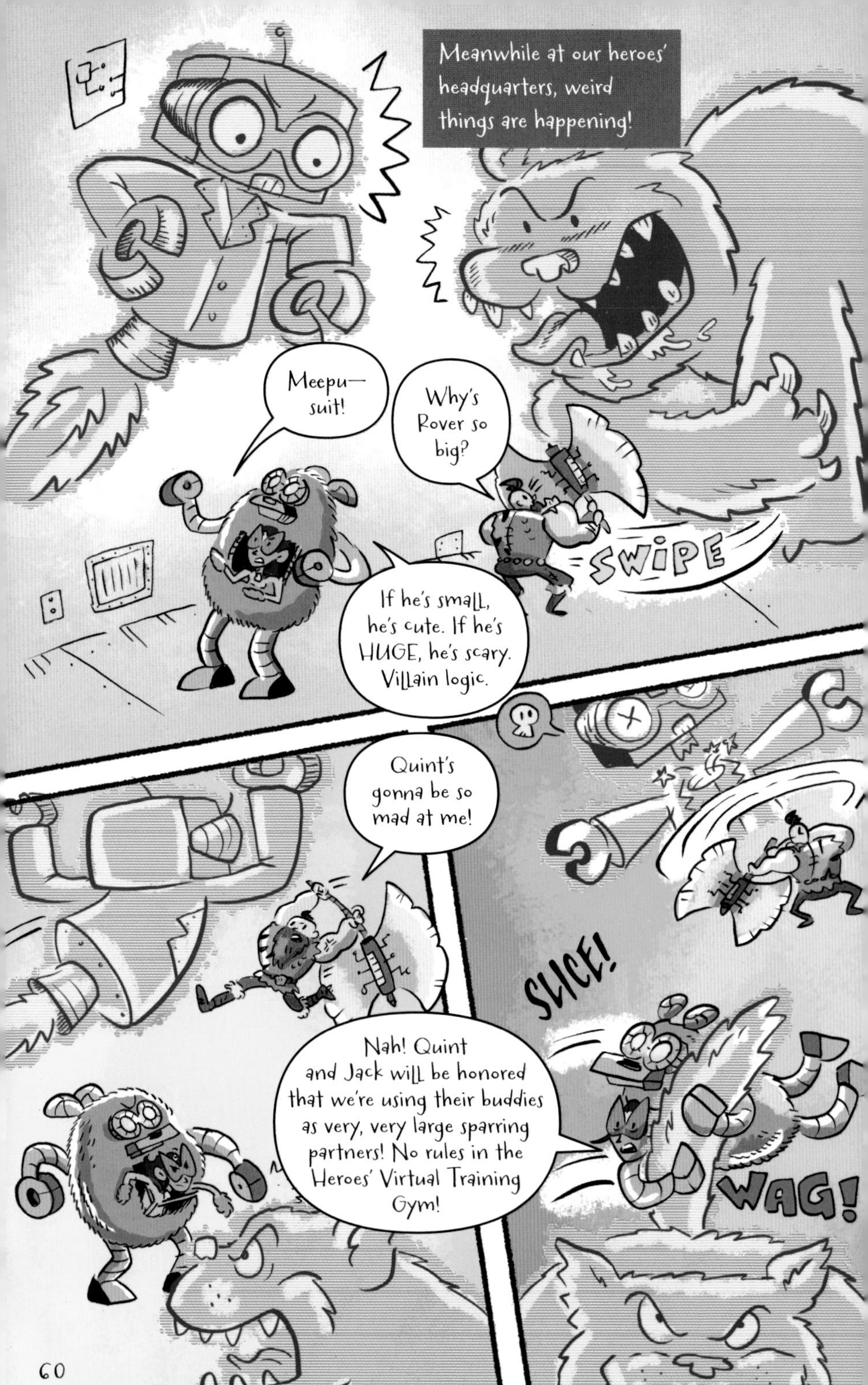
Meanwhile at our heroes' headquarters, weird things are happening!
Meepu—suit!
Why's Rover so big?
SWIPE
If he's small, he's cute. If he's HUGE, he's scary. Villain logic.
Quint's gonna be so mad at me!
SLICE!
Nah! Quint and Jack will be honored that we're using their buddies as very, very large sparring partners! No rules in the Heroes' Virtual Training Gym!
WAG!

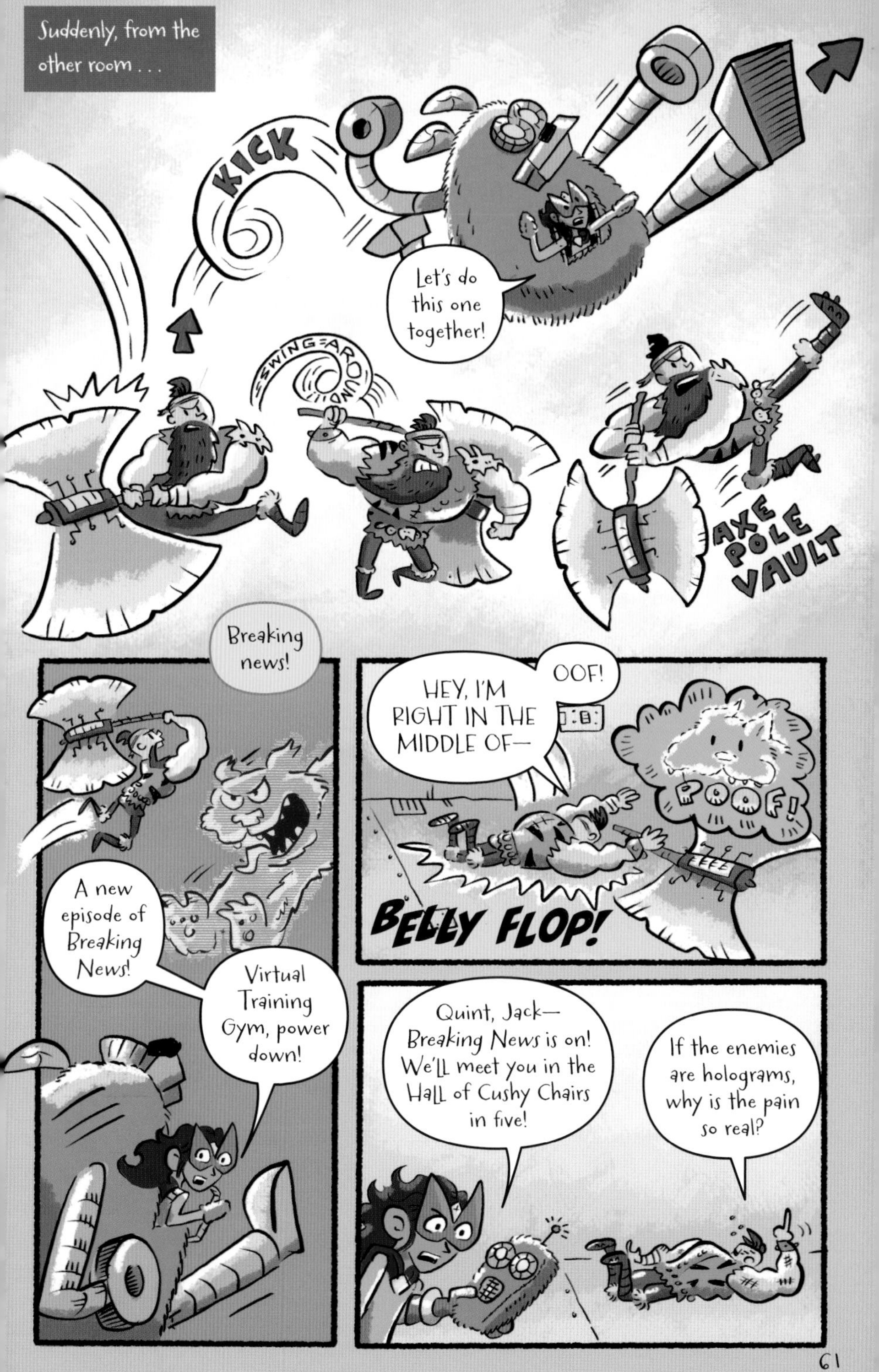
Suddenly, from the other room . . .
KICK
Let's do this one together!
SWING-AROUND
AXE POLE VAULT
Breaking news!
A new episode of Breaking News!
Virtual Training Gym, power down!
HEY, I'M RIGHT IN THE MIDDLE OF—
OOF!
POOF!
BELLY FLOP!
Quint, Jack— Breaking News is on! We'll meet you in the Hall of Cushy Chairs in five!
If the enemies are holograms, why is the pain so real?

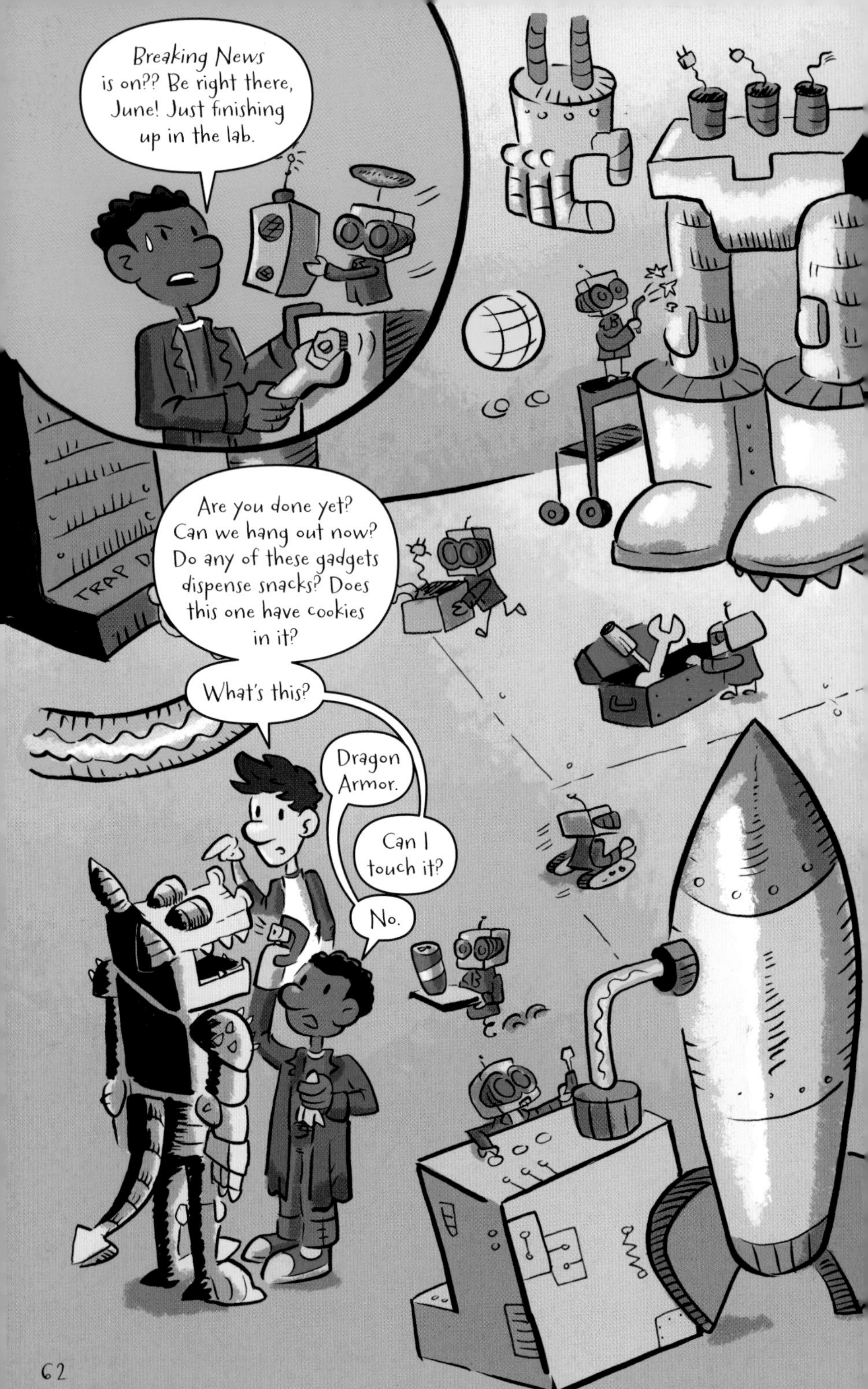
Breaking News is on?? Be right there, June! Just finishing up in the lab.
Are you done yet? Can we hang out now? Do any of these gadgets dispense snacks? Does this one have cookies in it?
What's this?
Dragon Armor.
Can I touch it?
No.
TRAP D

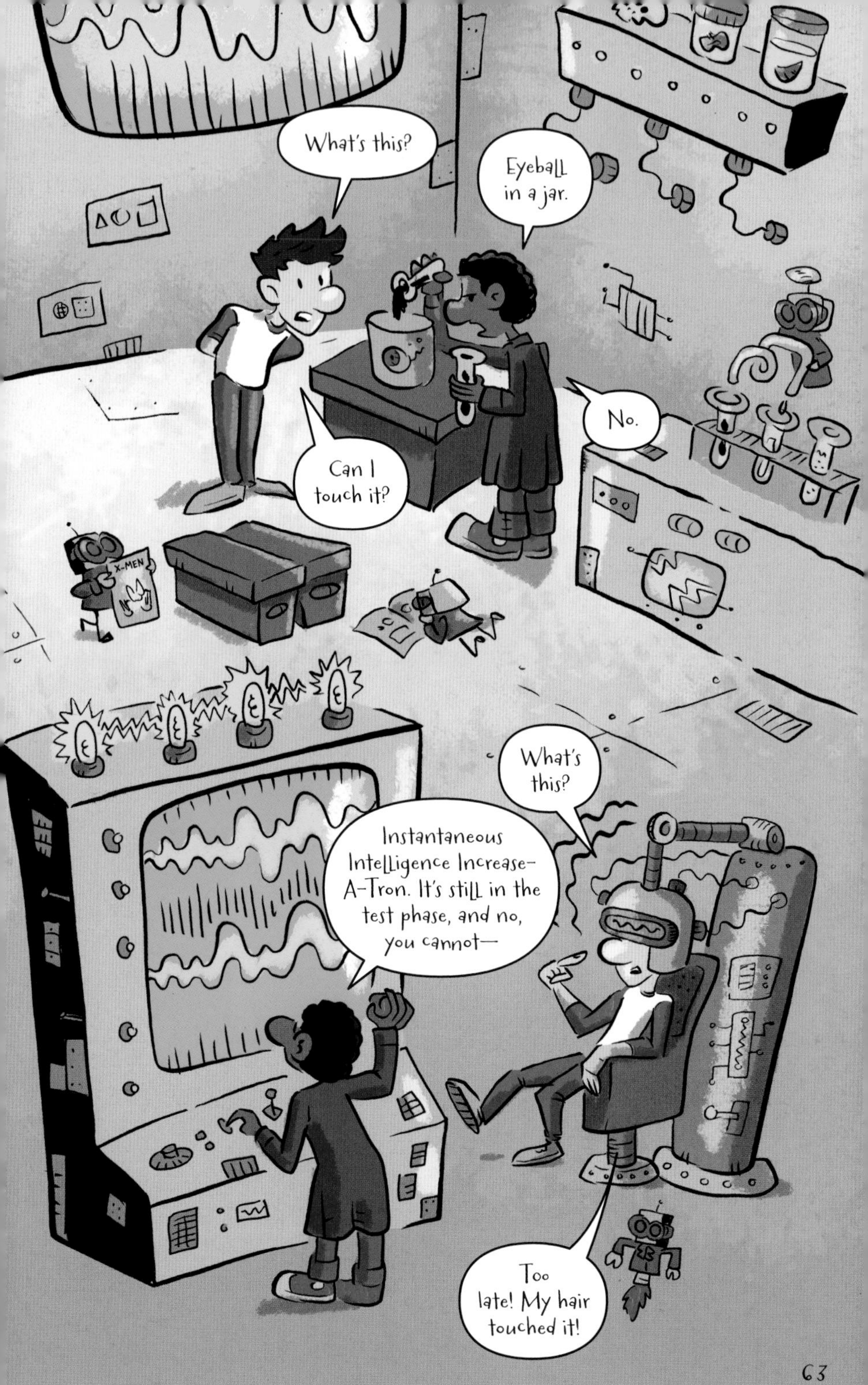
What's this?
Eyeball in a jar.
Can I touch it?
No.
X-MEN
What's this?
Instantaneous Intelligence Increase-A-Tron. It's still in the test phase, and no, you cannot—
Too late! My hair touched it!

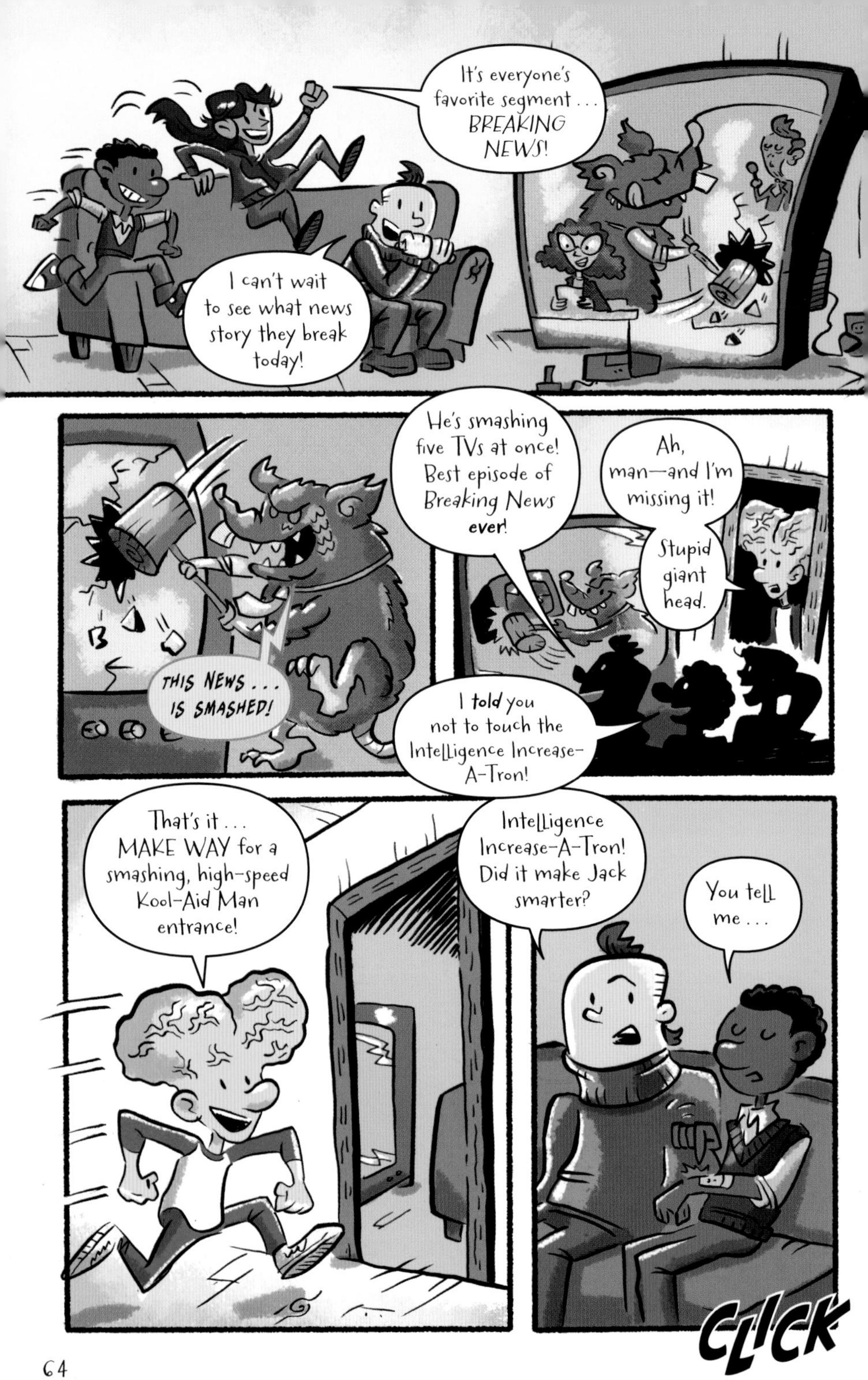
It's everyone's favorite segment . . . BREAKING NEWS!
I can't wait to see what news story they break today!
He's smashing five TVs at once! Best episode of Breaking News **ever**!
Ah, man—and I'm missing it!
Stupid giant head.
THIS NEWS . . . IS SMASHED!
I **told** you not to touch the Intelligence Increase-A-Tron!
That's it . . . MAKE WAY for a smashing, high-speed Kool-Aid Man entrance!
Intelligence Increase-A-Tron! Did it make Jack smarter?
You tell me . . .
CLICK

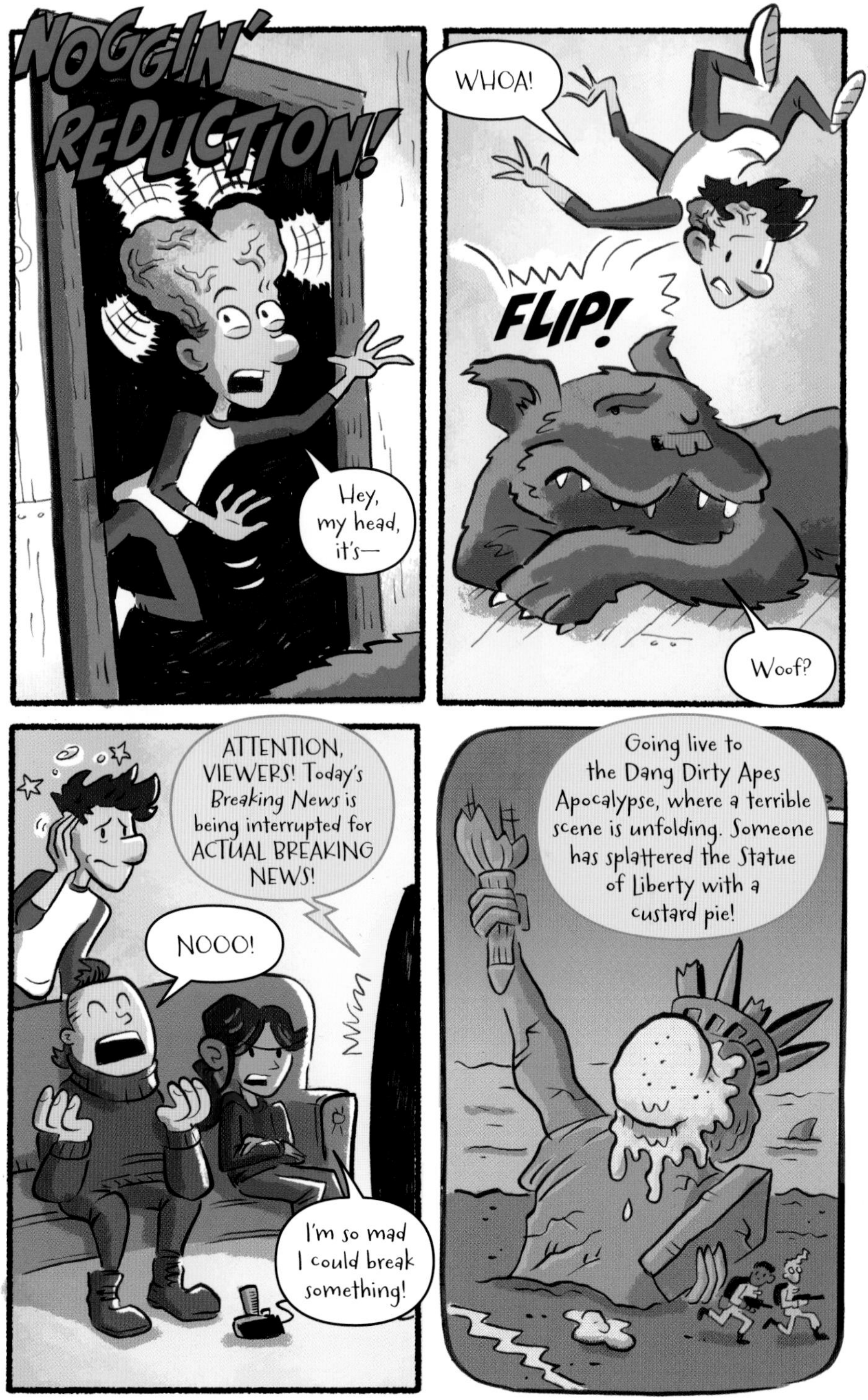
NOGGIN' REDUCTION!
Hey, my head, it's—
WHOA!
FLIP!
Woof?
ATTENTION, VIEWERS! Today's Breaking News is being interrupted for ACTUAL BREAKING NEWS!
NOOO!
I'm so mad I could break something!
Going live to the Dang Dirty Apes Apocalypse, where a terrible scene is unfolding. Someone has splattered the Statue of Liberty with a custard pie!

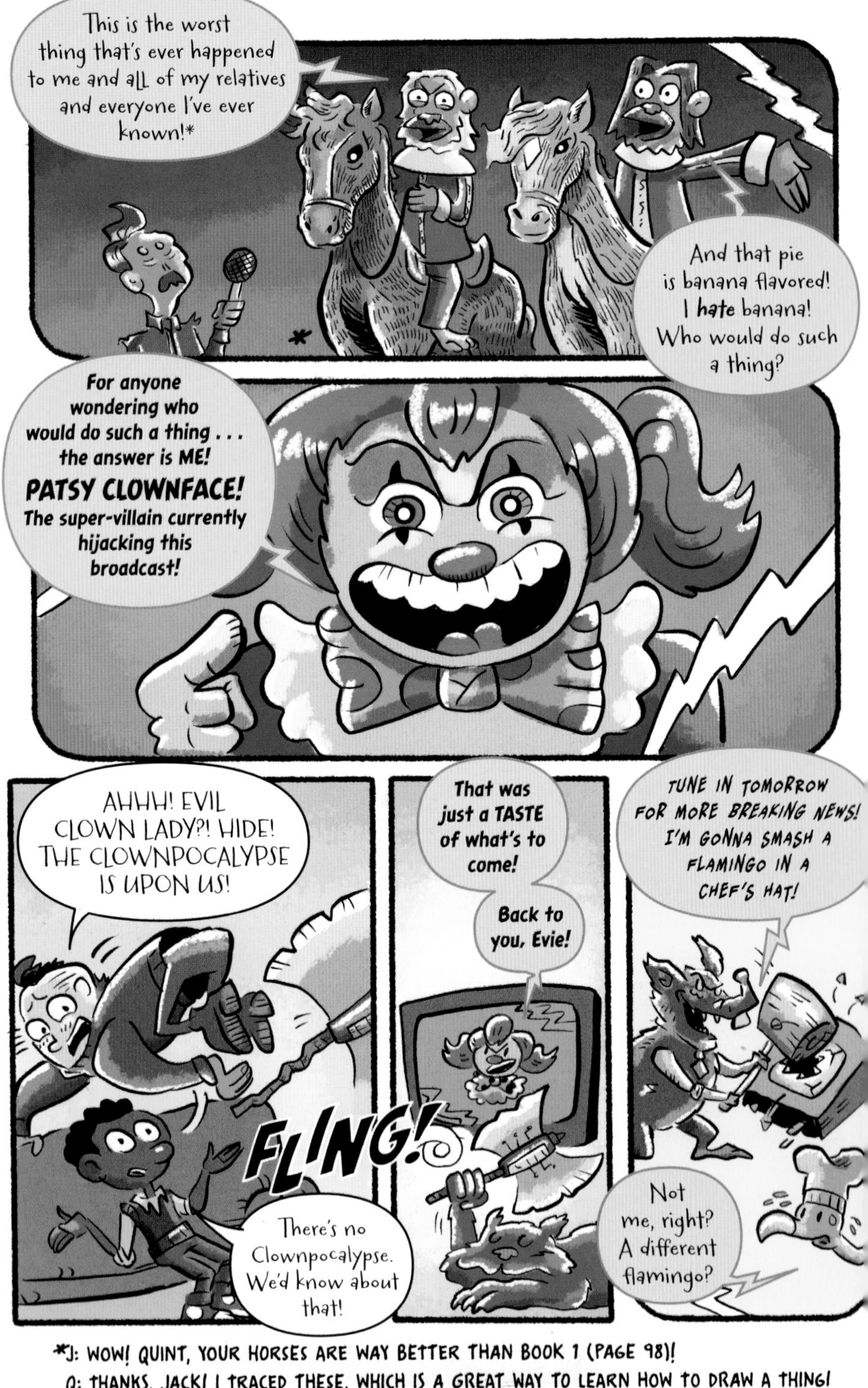
This is the worst thing that's ever happened to me and all of my relatives and everyone I've ever known!*
And that pie is banana flavored! I hate banana! Who would do such a thing?
*
For anyone wondering who would do such a thing . . . the answer is ME!
PATSY CLOWNFACE!
The super-villain currently hijacking this broadcast!
AHHH! EVIL CLOWN LADY?! HIDE! THE CLOWNPOCALYPSE IS UPON US!
FLING!
There's no Clownpocalypse. We'd know about that!
That was just a TASTE of what's to come!
Back to you, Evie!
TUNE IN TOMORROW FOR MORE BREAKING NEWS! I'M GONNA SMASH A FLAMINGO IN A CHEF'S HAT!
Not me, right? A different flamingo?

*J: WOW! QUINT, YOUR HORSES ARE WAY BETTER THAN BOOK 1 (PAGE 98)!
Q: THANKS, JACK! I TRACED THESE, WHICH IS A GREAT WAY TO LEARN HOW TO DRAW A THING!

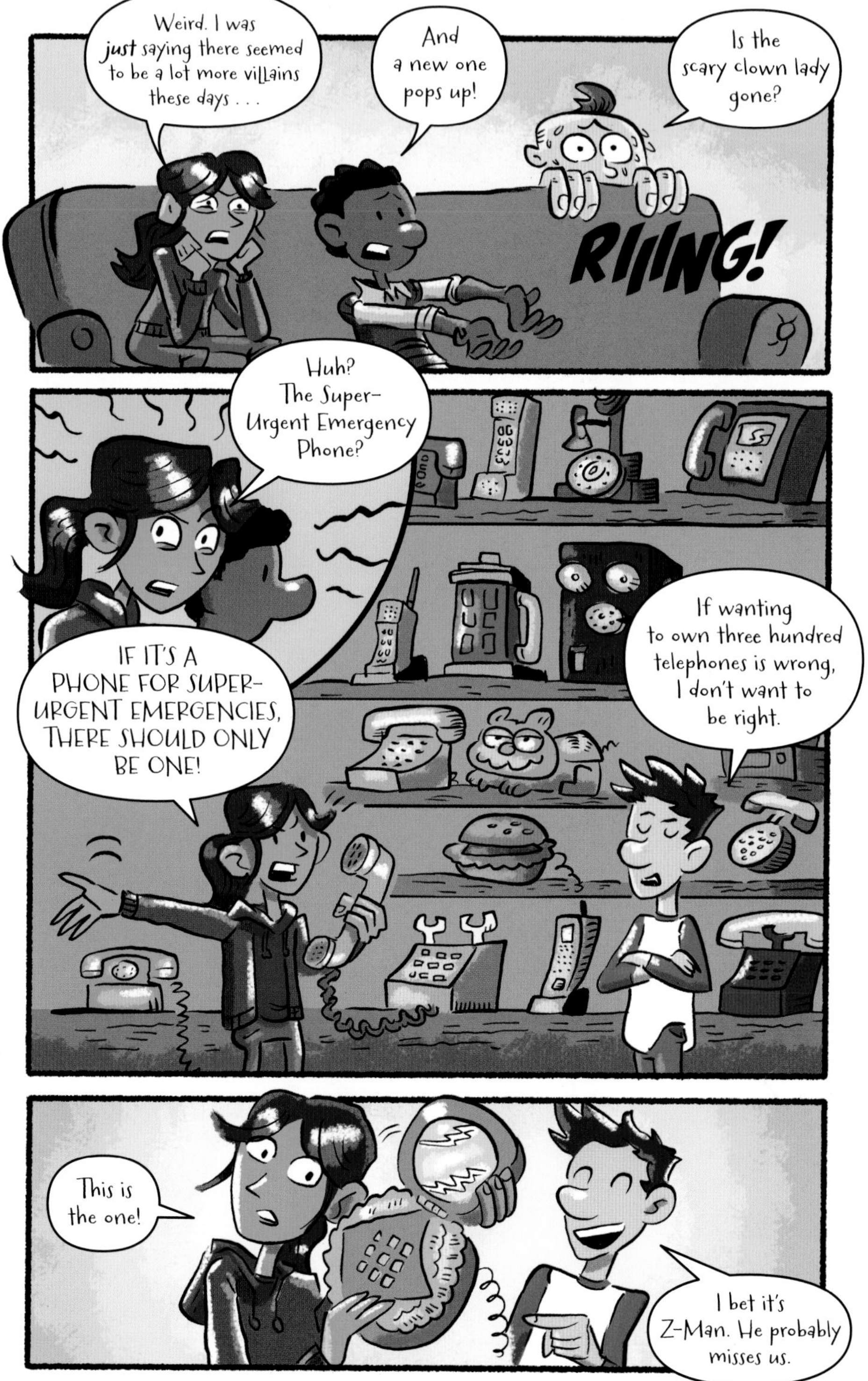
Weird. I was just saying there seemed to be a lot more villains these days . . .
And a new one pops up!
Is the scary clown lady gone?
RIIING!
Huh? The Super-Urgent Emergency Phone?
IF IT'S A PHONE FOR SUPER-URGENT EMERGENCIES, THERE SHOULD ONLY BE ONE!
If wanting to own three hundred telephones is wrong, I don't want to be right.
This is the one!
I bet it's Z-Man. He probably misses us.

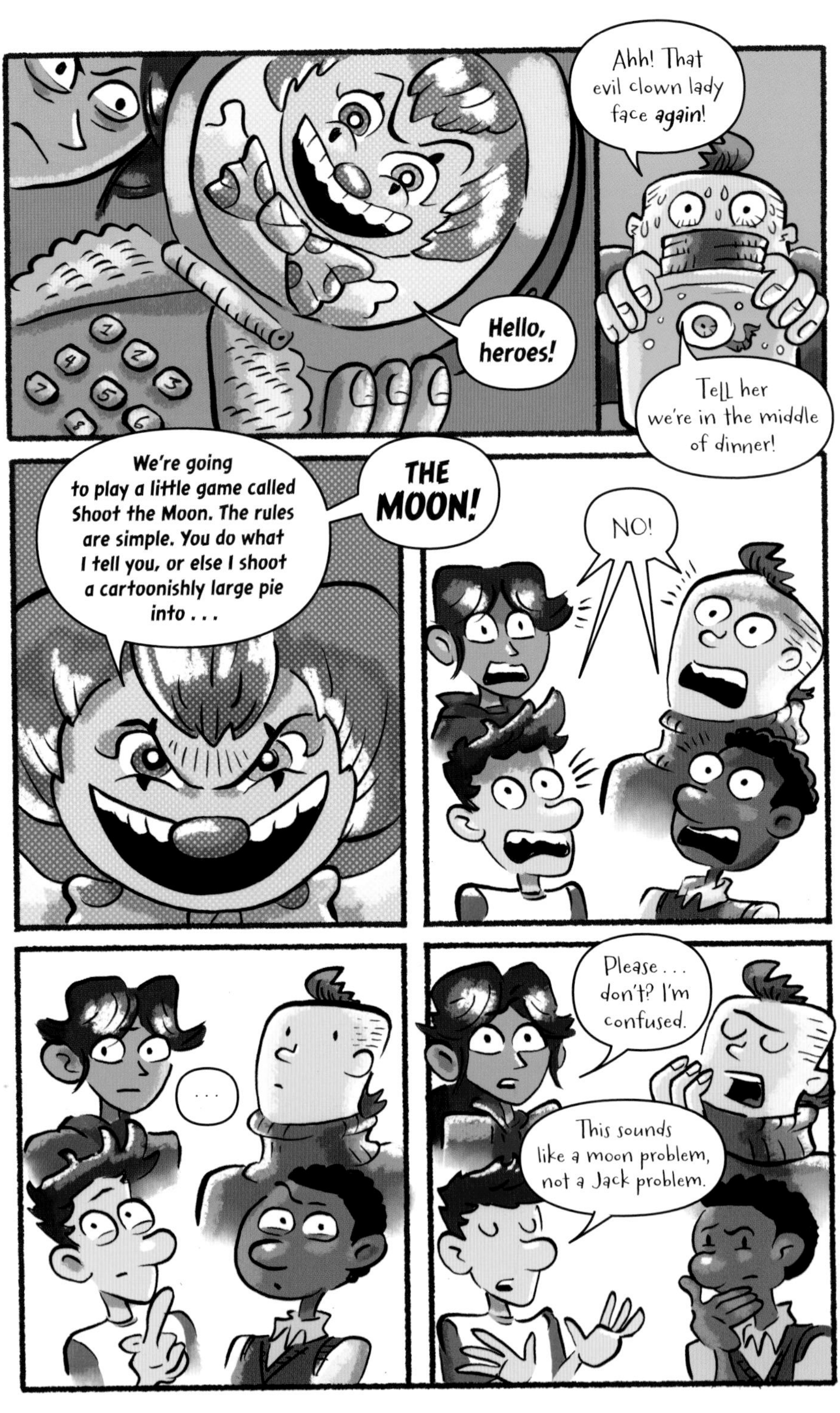
Ahh! That evil clown lady face again!
Hello, heroes!
Tell her we're in the middle of dinner!
We're going to play a little game called Shoot the Moon. The rules are simple. You do what I tell you, or else I shoot a cartoonishly large pie into . . .
THE MOON!
NO!
. . .
Please . . . don't? I'm confused.
This sounds like a moon problem, not a Jack problem.

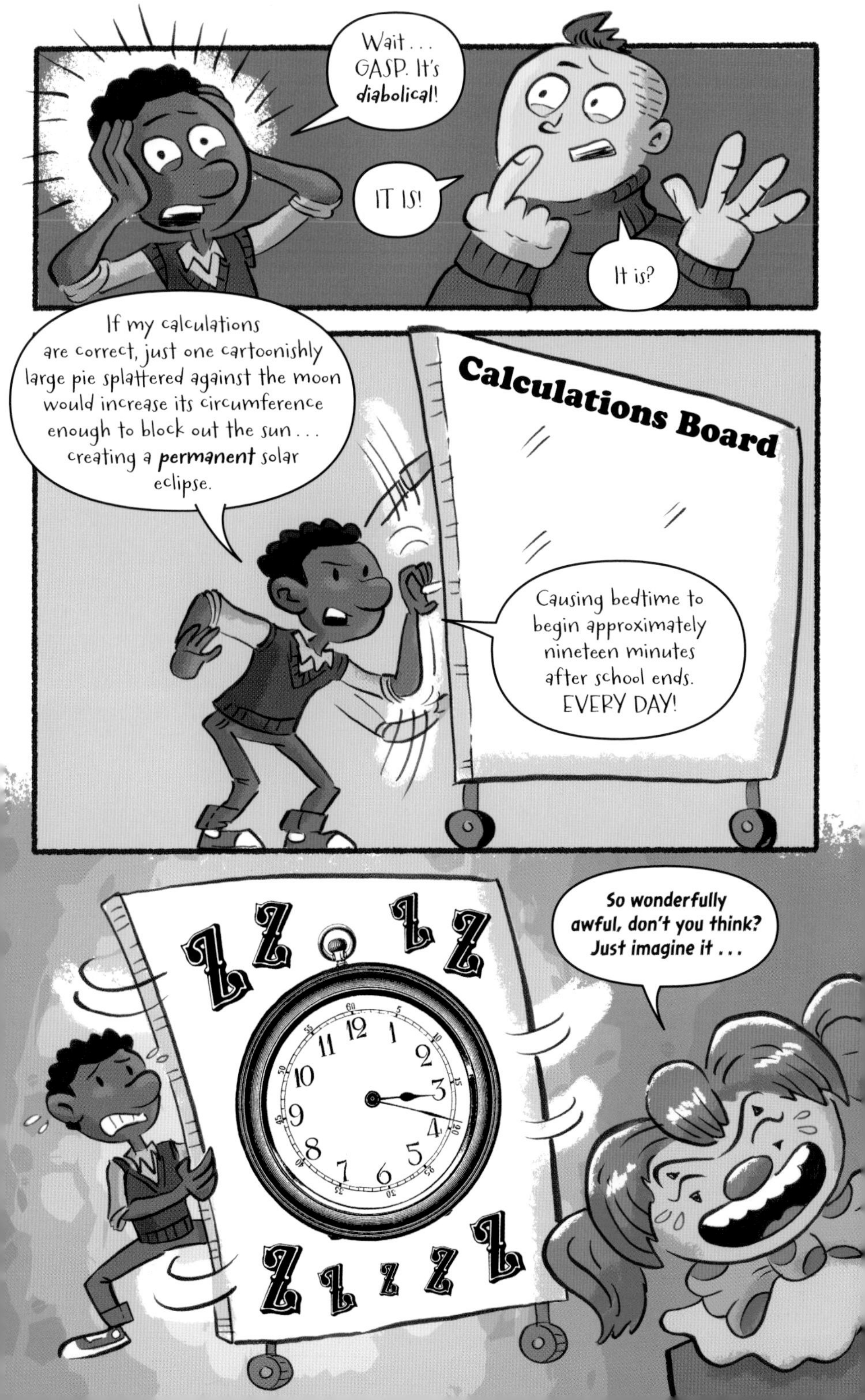
Wait . . . GASP. It's **diabolical**!
IT IS!
It is?
If my calculations are correct, just one cartoonishly large pie splattered against the moon would increase its circumference enough to block out the sun . . . creating a **permanent** solar eclipse.
Calculations Board
Causing bedtime to begin approximately nineteen minutes after school ends. EVERY DAY!
So wonderfully awful, don't you think? Just imagine it . . .

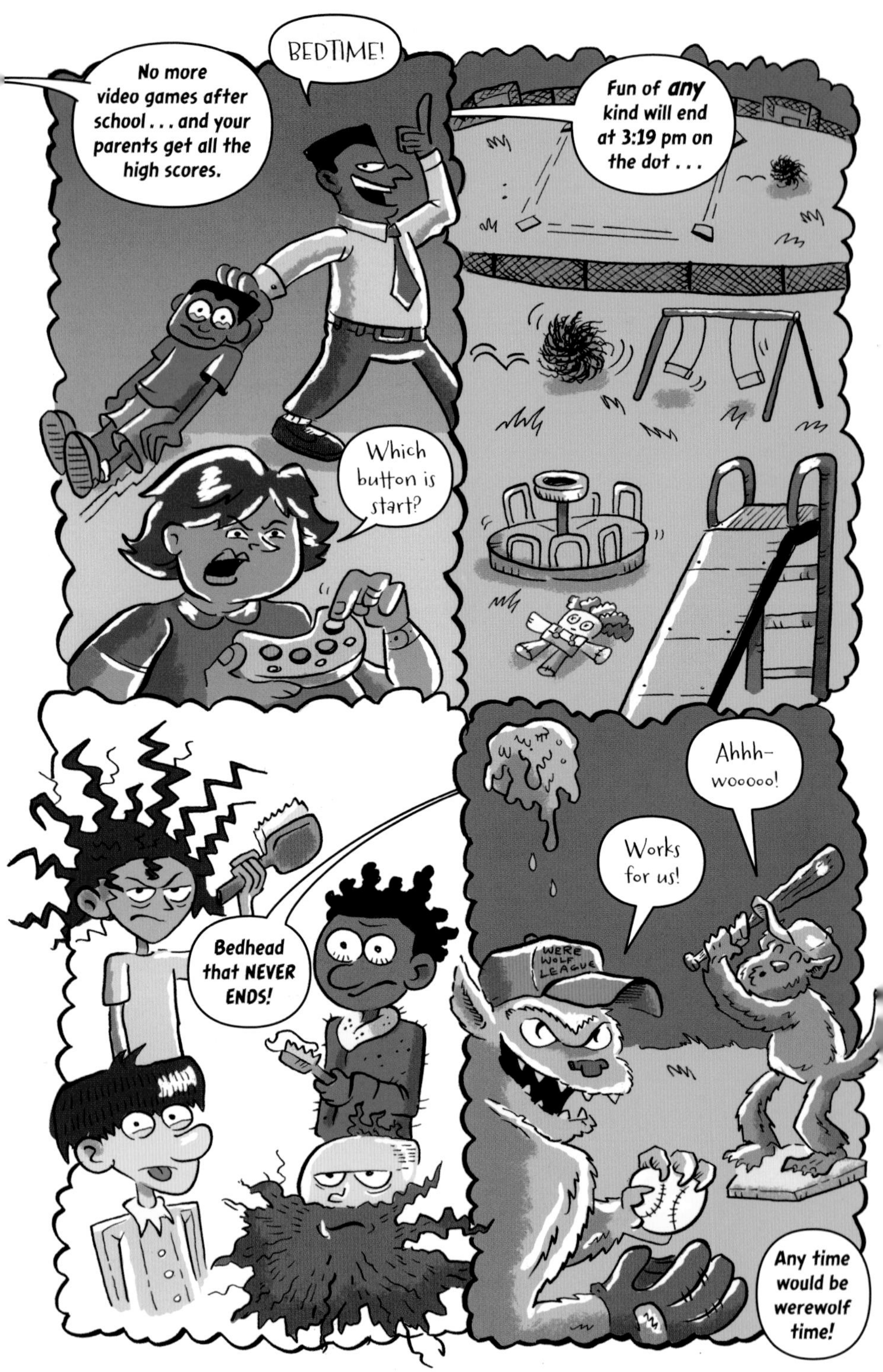

No more video games after school . . . and your parents get all the high scores.
BEDTIME!
Fun of **any** kind will end at 3:19 pm on the dot . . .
Which button is start?
Bedhead that NEVER ENDS!
Ahhh-wooooo!
Works for us!
WERE WOLF LEAGUE
Any time would be werewolf time!

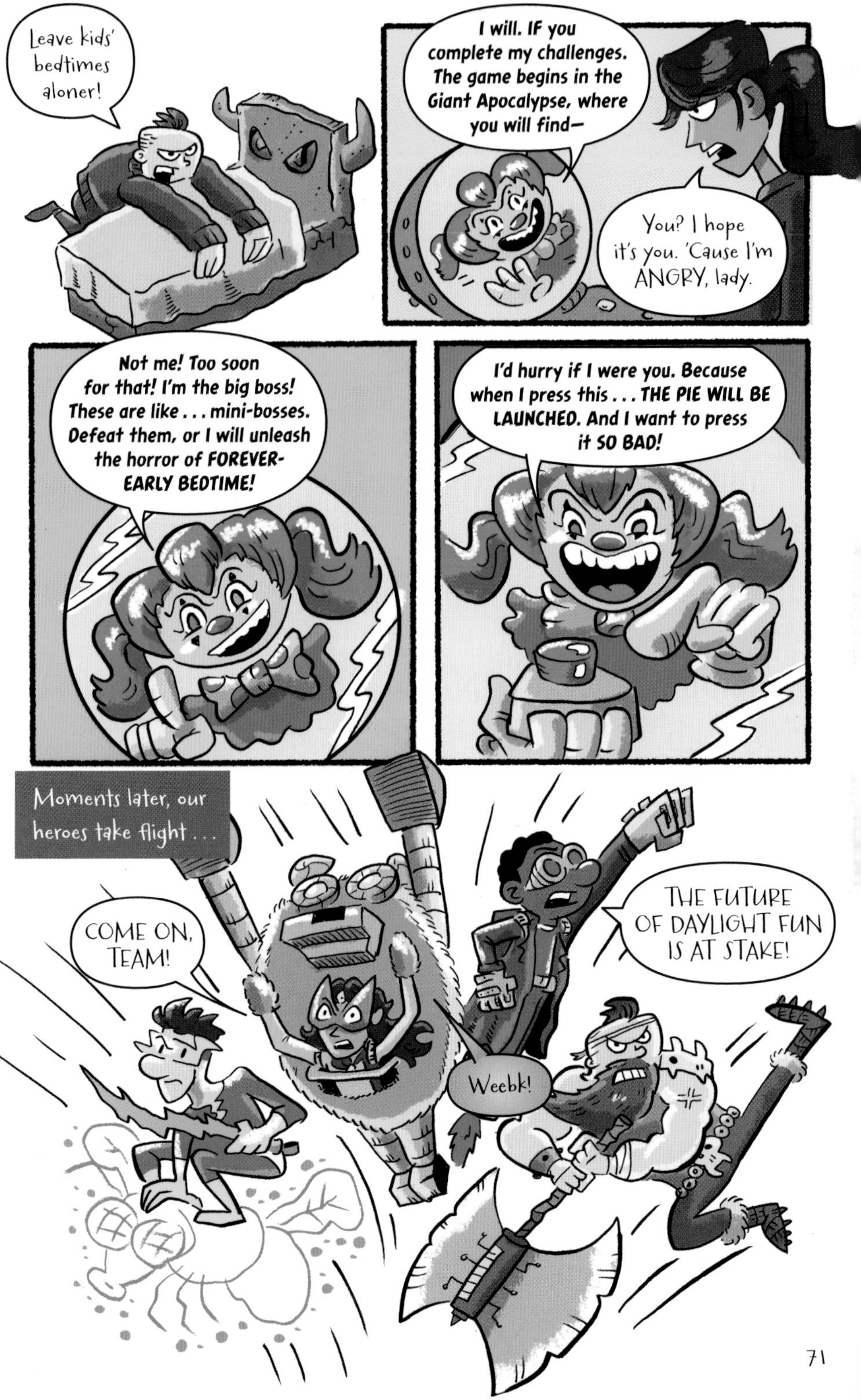
Leave kids' bedtimes aloner!
I will. IF you complete my challenges. The game begins in the Giant Apocalypse, where you will find—
You? I hope it's you. 'Cause I'm ANGRY, lady.
Not me! Too soon for that! I'm the big boss! These are like . . . mini-bosses. Defeat them, or I will unleash the horror of FOREVER-EARLY BEDTIME!
I'd hurry if I were you. Because when I press this . . . THE PIE WILL BE LAUNCHED. And I want to press it SO BAD!
Moments later, our heroes take flight . . .
COME ON, TEAM!
THE FUTURE OF DAYLIGHT FUN IS AT STAKE!
Weebk!

CHAPTER SIX

MINI-BOSS CHALLENGE IN THE GIANT APOCALYPSE!

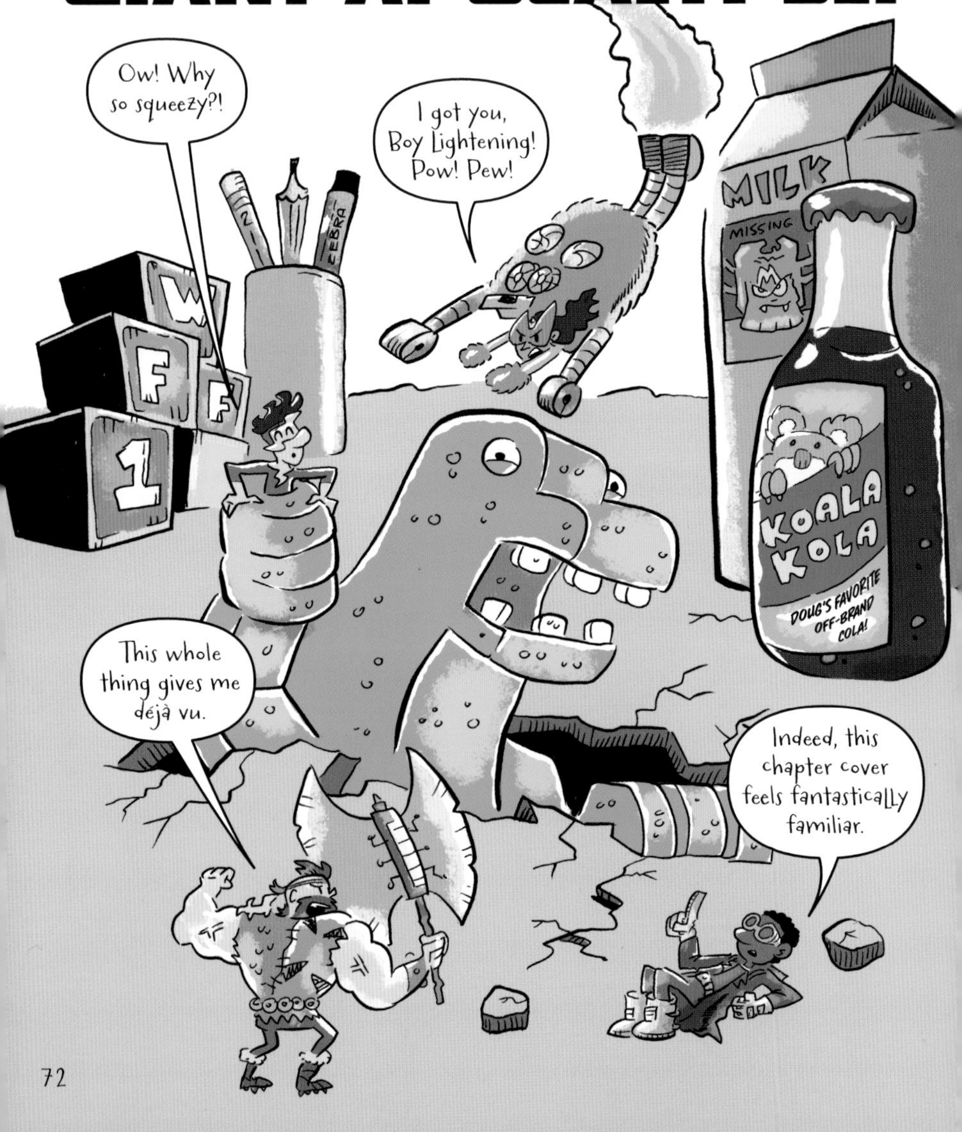
Ow! Why so squeezy?!
I got you, Boy Lightening! Pow! Pew!
MILK
MISSING
KOALA KOLA
DOUG'S FAVORITE OFF-BRAND COLA!
This whole thing gives me déjà vu.
Indeed, this chapter cover feels fantastically familiar.

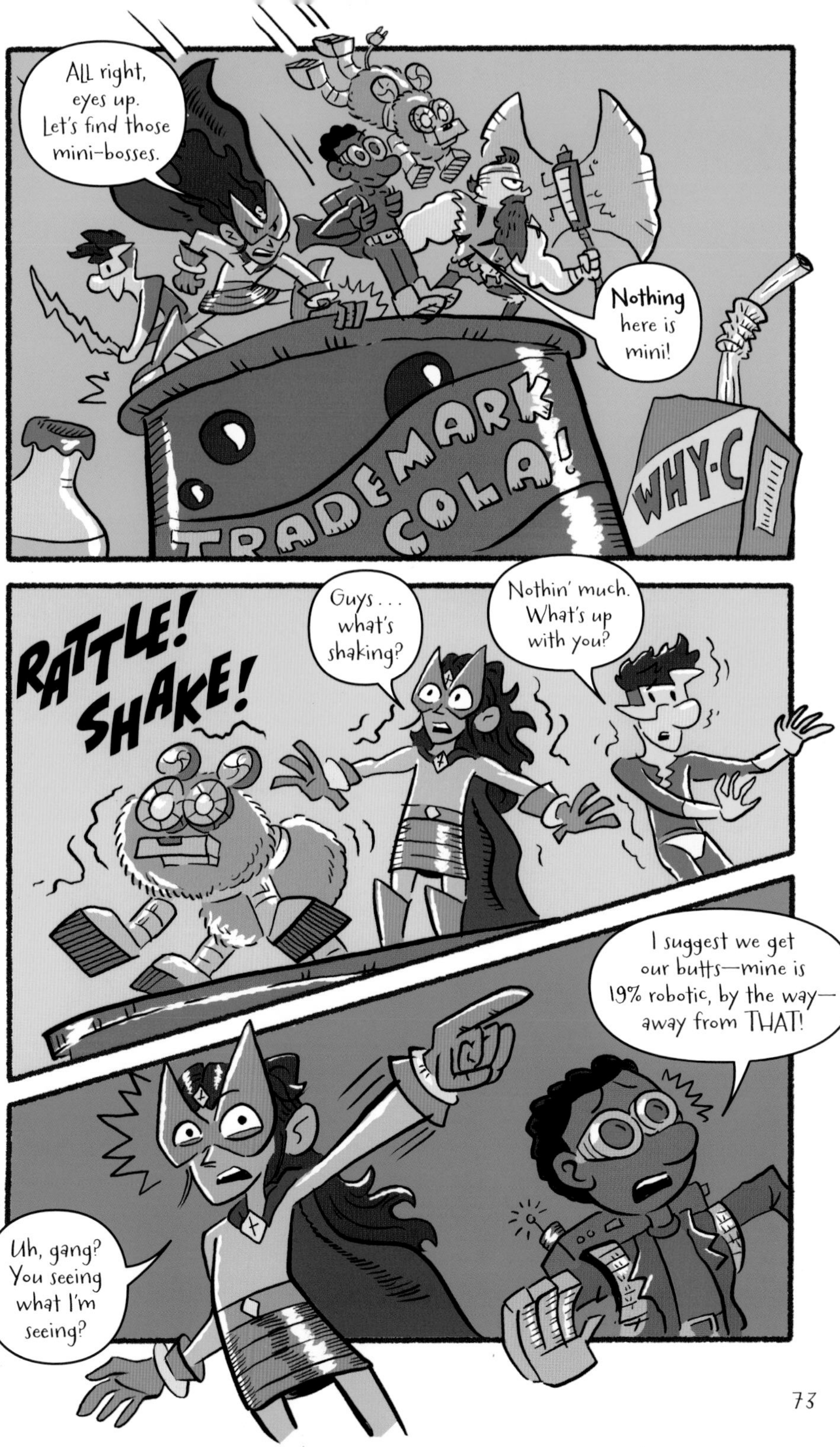

ALL right, eyes up. Let's find those mini-bosses.
Nothing here is mini!
TRADEMARK COLA!
WHY-C
RATTLE! SHAKE!
Guys . . . what's shaking?
Nothin' much. What's up with you?
I suggest we get our butts—mine is 19% robotic, by the way—away from THAT!
Uh, gang? You seeing what I'm seeing?

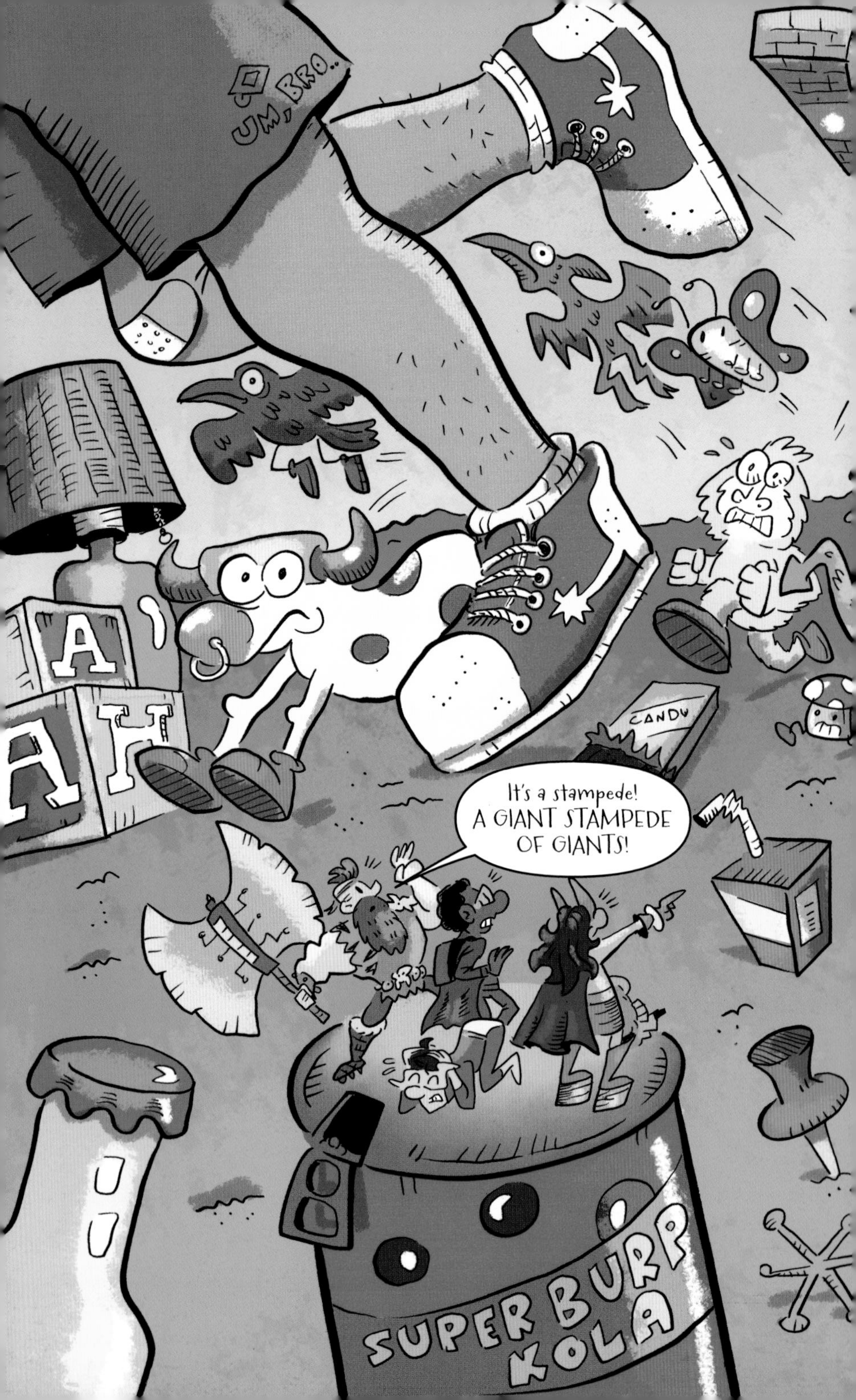
UM, BRO..
It's a stampede!
A GIANT STAMPEDE
OF GIANTS!
CANDY
SUPER BURP
KOLA

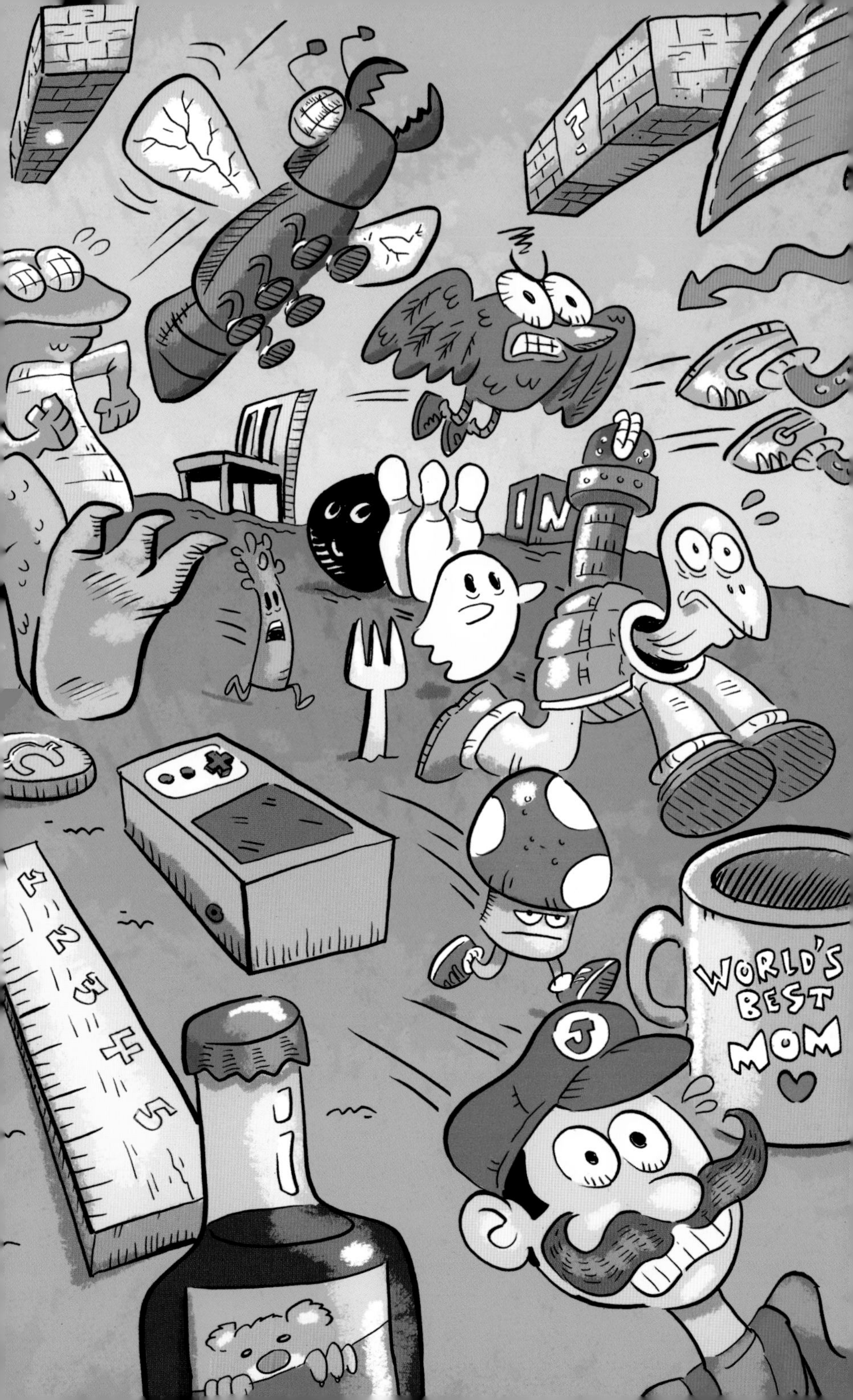
WORLD'S
BEST
MOM

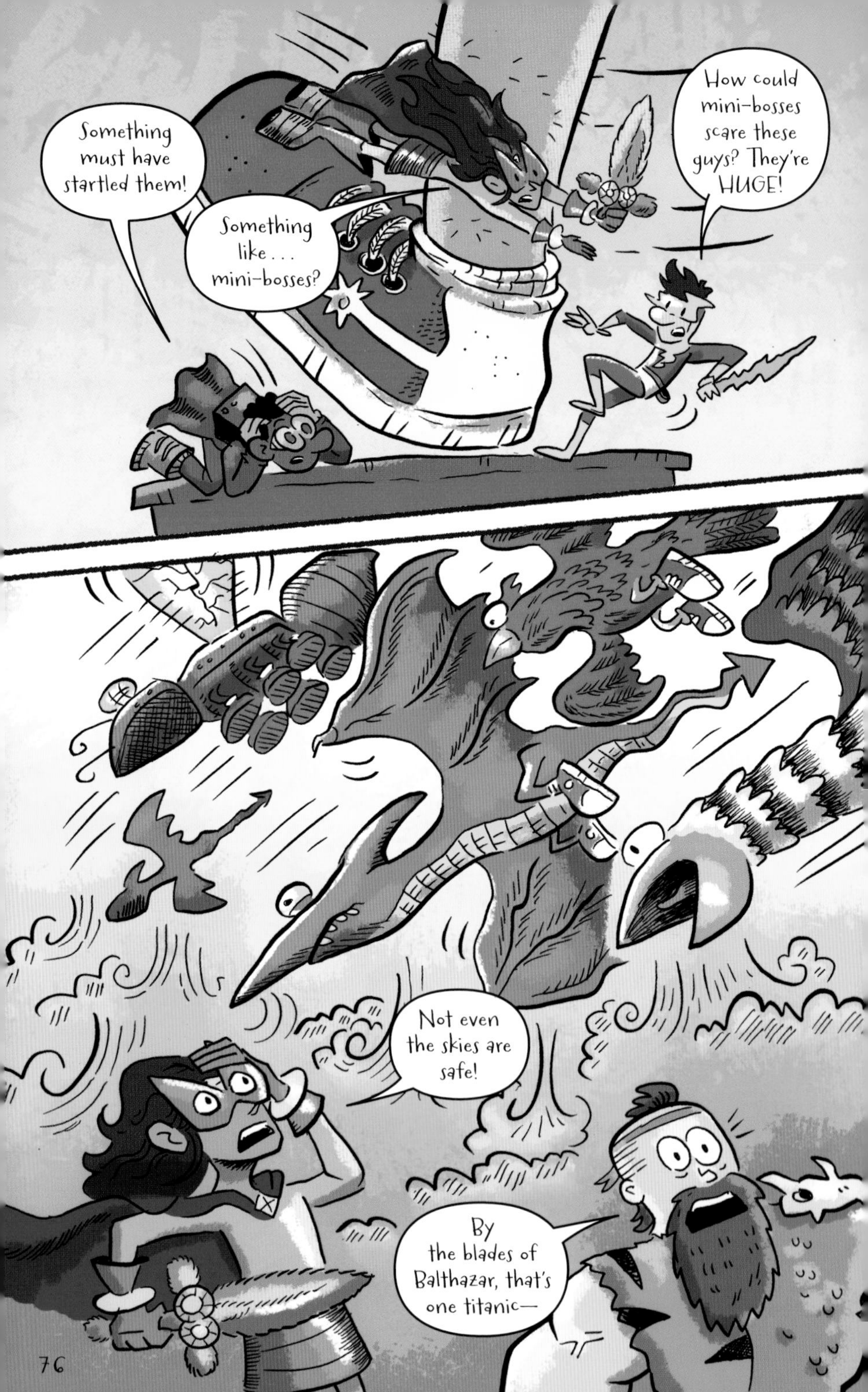
Something must have startled them!
Something like . . . mini-bosses?
How could mini-bosses scare these guys? They're HUGE!
Not even the skies are safe!
By the blades of Balthazar, that's one titanic—

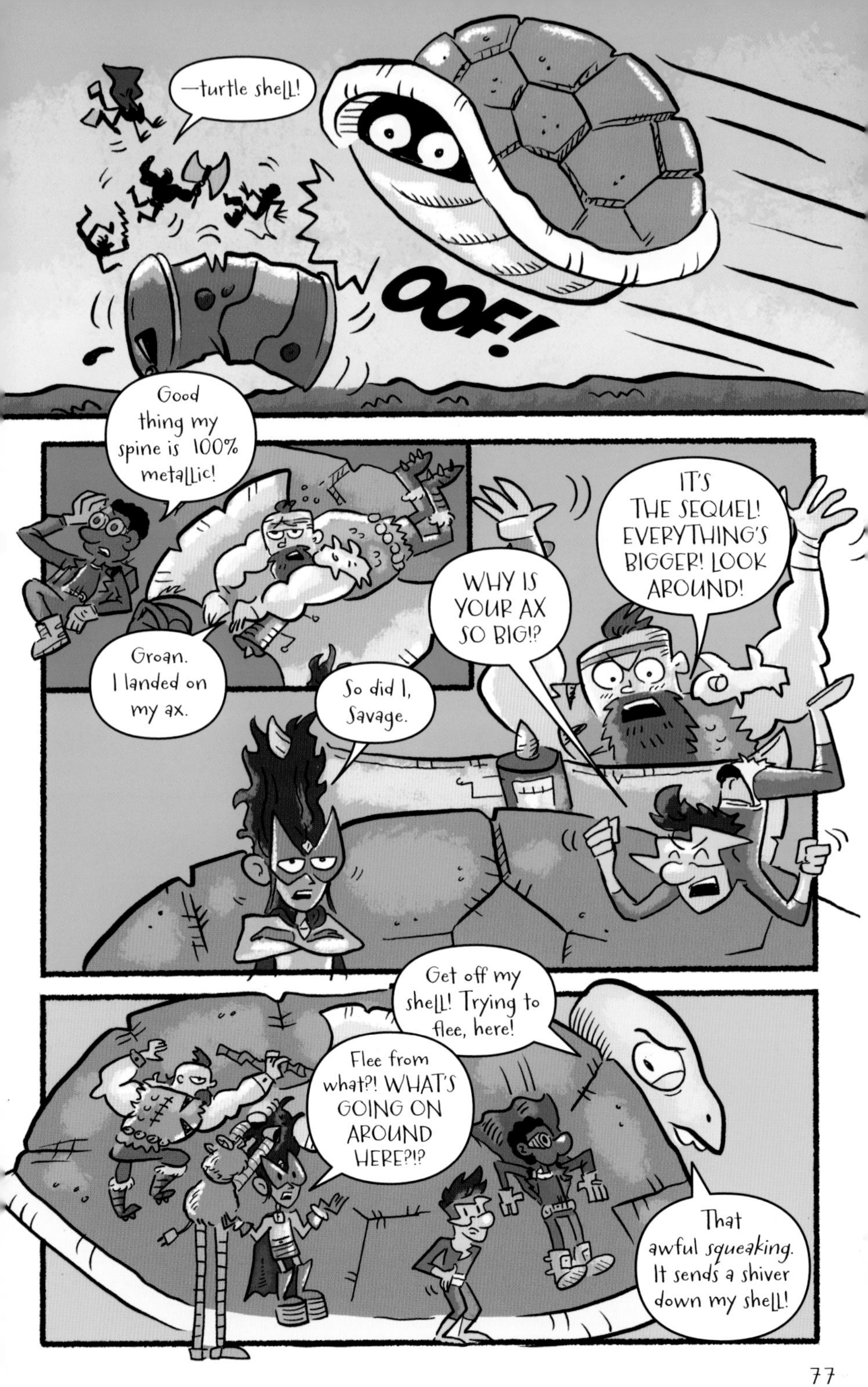
—turtle shell!
OOF!
Good thing my spine is 100% metallic!
Groan. I landed on my ax.
IT'S THE SEQUEL! EVERYTHING'S BIGGER! LOOK AROUND!
WHY IS YOUR AX SO BIG!?
So did I, Savage.
Get off my shell! Trying to flee, here!
Flee from what?! WHAT'S GOING ON AROUND HERE?!?
That awful *squeaking.* It sends a shiver down my shell!

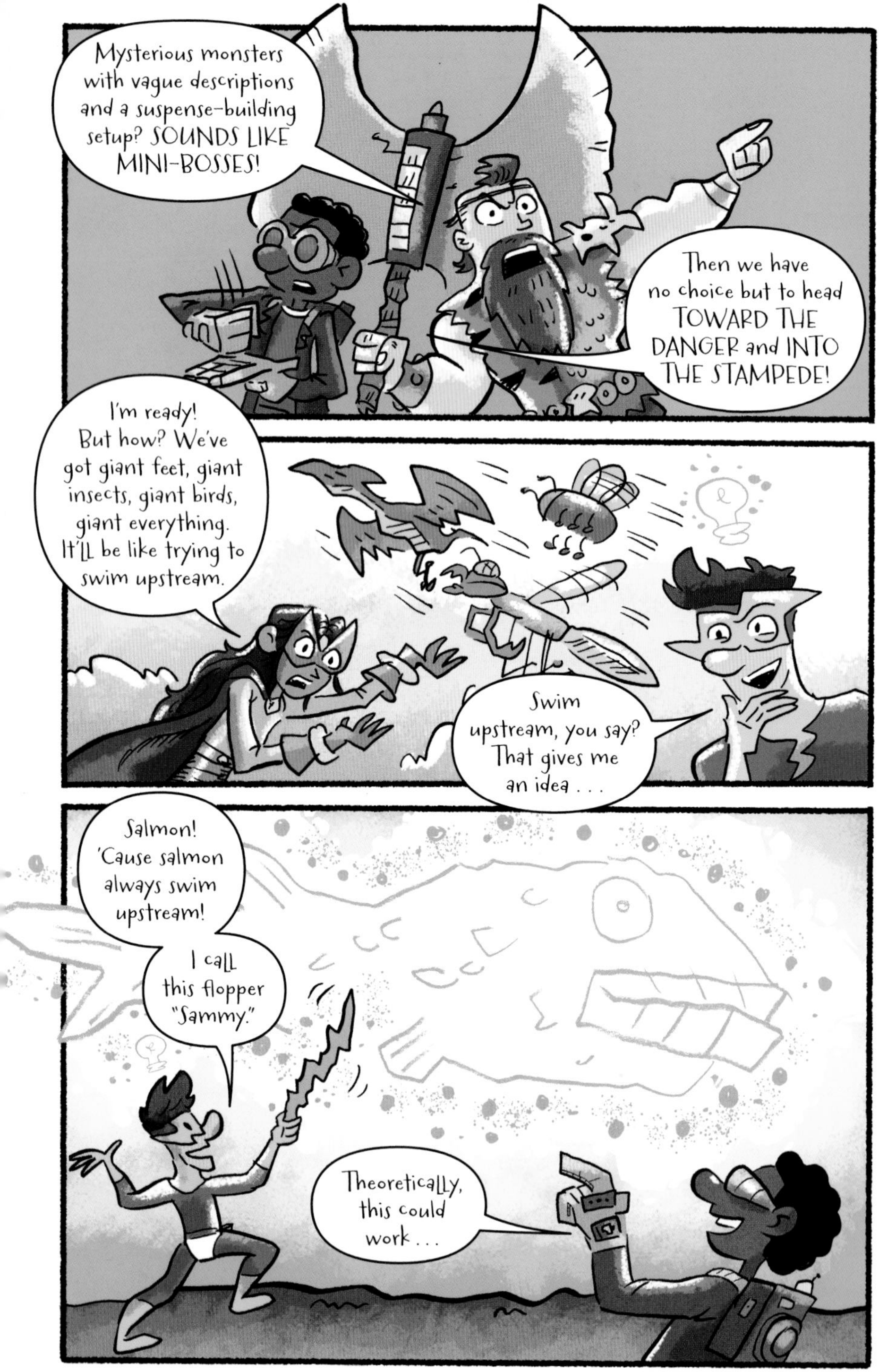
Mysterious monsters with vague descriptions and a suspense-building setup? SOUNDS LIKE MINI-BOSSES!
Then we have no choice but to head TOWARD THE DANGER and INTO THE STAMPEDE!
I'm ready! But how? We've got giant feet, giant insects, giant birds, giant everything. It'll be like trying to swim upstream.
Swim upstream, you say? That gives me an idea . . .
Salmon! 'Cause salmon always swim upstream!
I call this flopper "Sammy."
Theoretically, this could work . . .

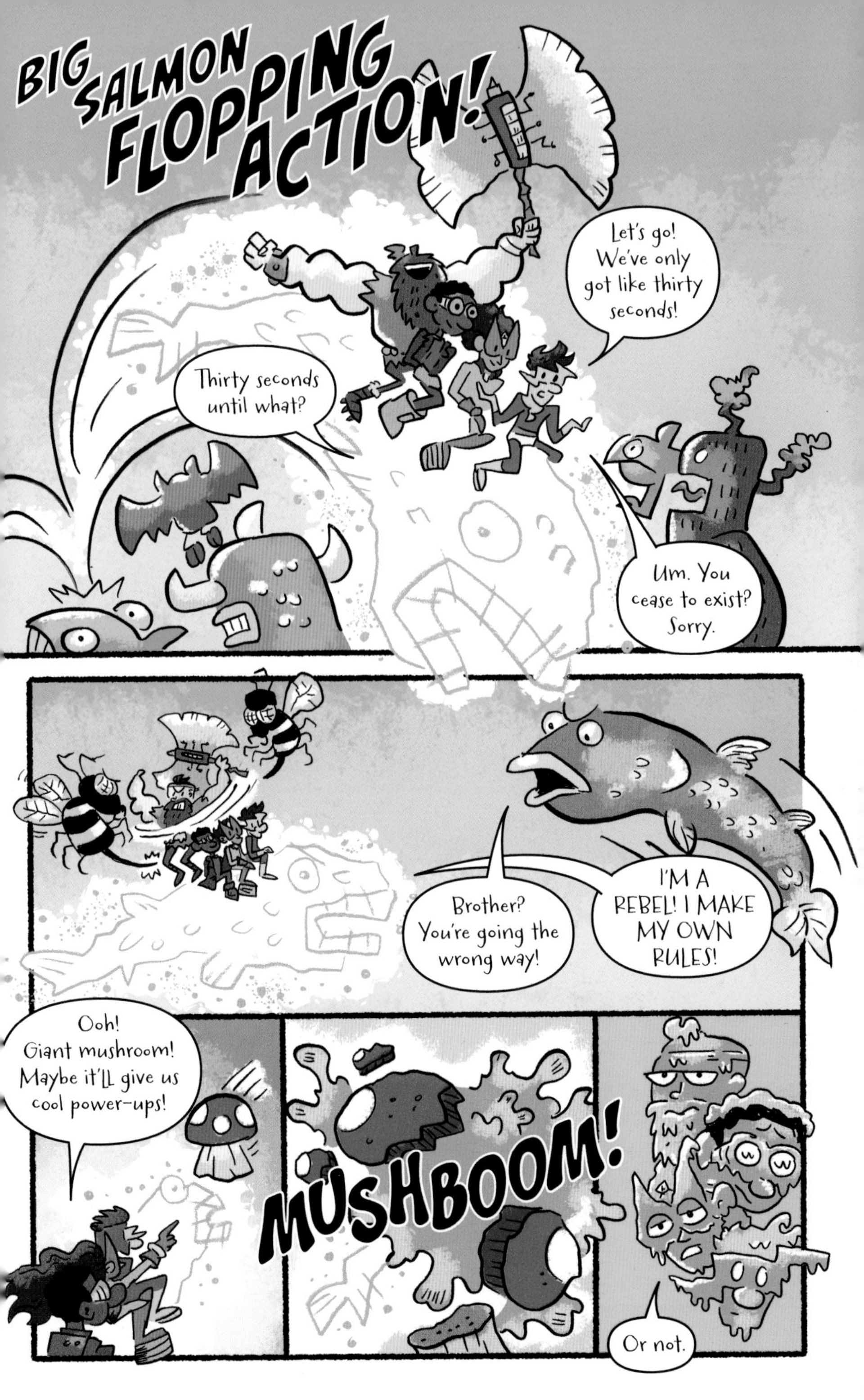
BIG SALMON FLOPPING ACTION!
Let's go! We've only got like thirty seconds!
Thirty seconds until what?
Um. You cease to exist? Sorry.
Brother? You're going the wrong way!
I'M A REBEL! I MAKE MY OWN RULES!
Ooh! Giant mushroom! Maybe it'll give us cool power-ups!
MUSHBOOM!
Or not.

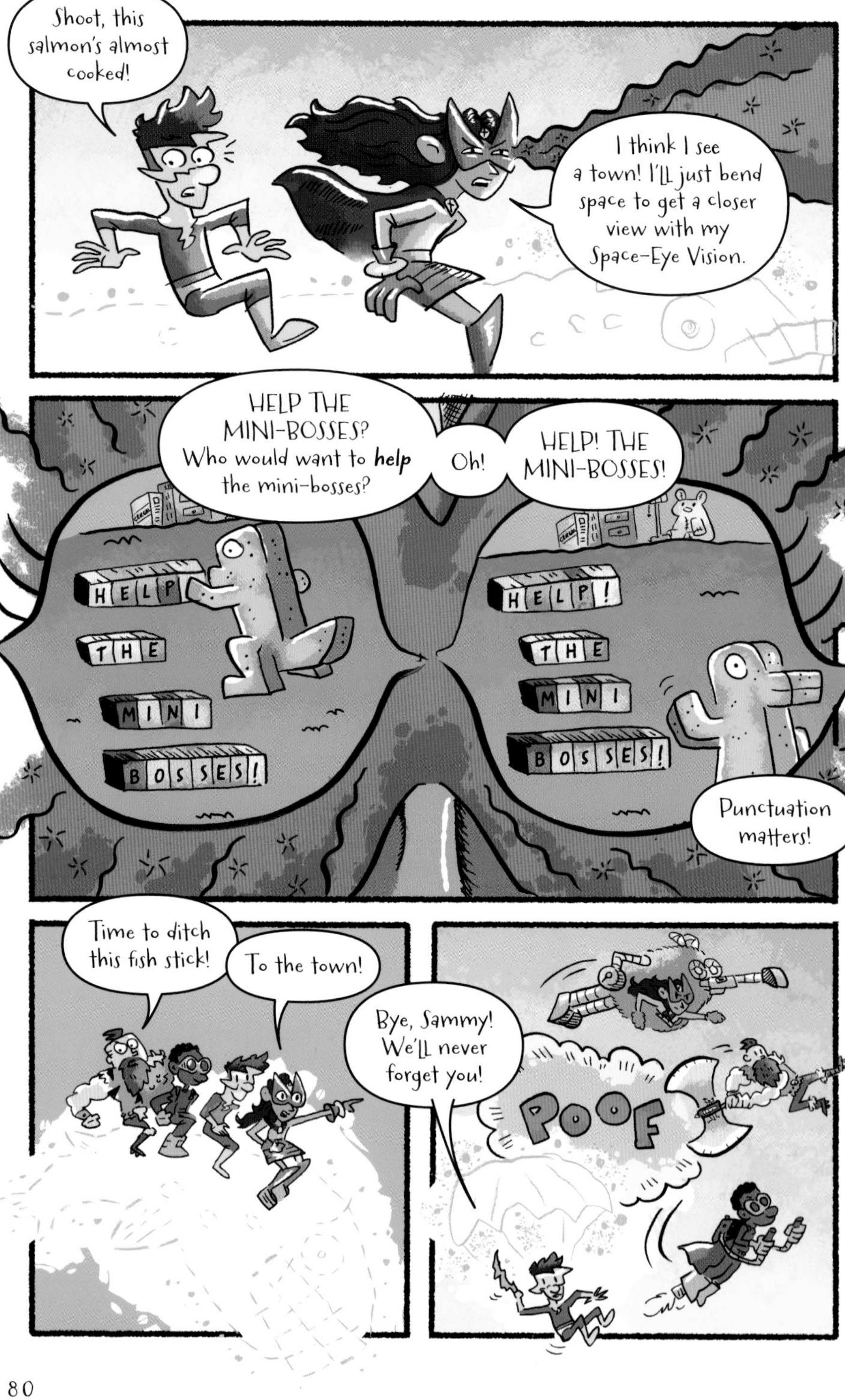
Shoot, this salmon's almost cooked!
I think I see a town! I'LL just bend space to get a closer view with my Space-Eye Vision.
HELP THE MINI-BOSSES? Who would want to **help** the mini-bosses?
HELP THE MINI BOSSES!
Oh!
HELP! THE MINI-BOSSES!
HELP! THE MINI BOSSES!
Punctuation matters!
Time to ditch this fish stick!
To the town!
Bye, Sammy! We'LL never forget you!
POOF

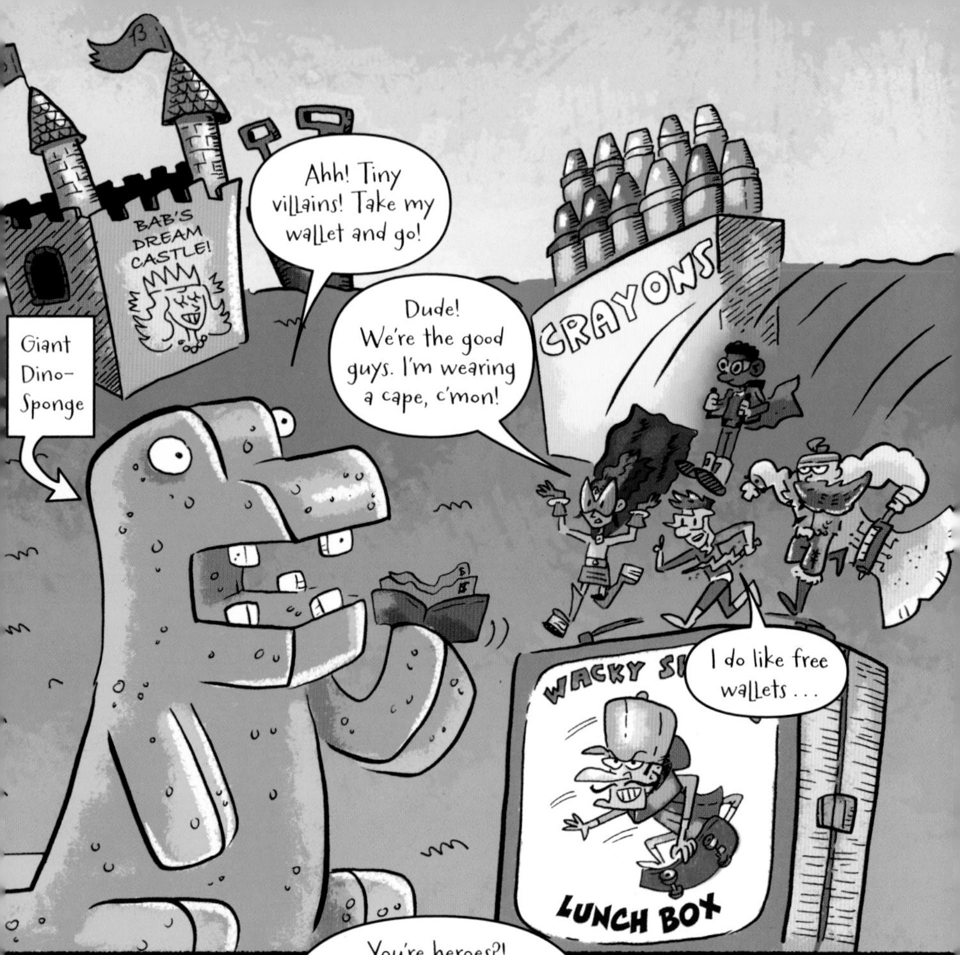

BAB'S DREAM CASTLE!
Ahh! Tiny villains! Take my wallet and go!
CRAYONS
Giant Dino-Sponge
Dude! We're the good guys. I'm wearing a cape, c'mon!
I do like free wallets . . .
LUNCH BOX

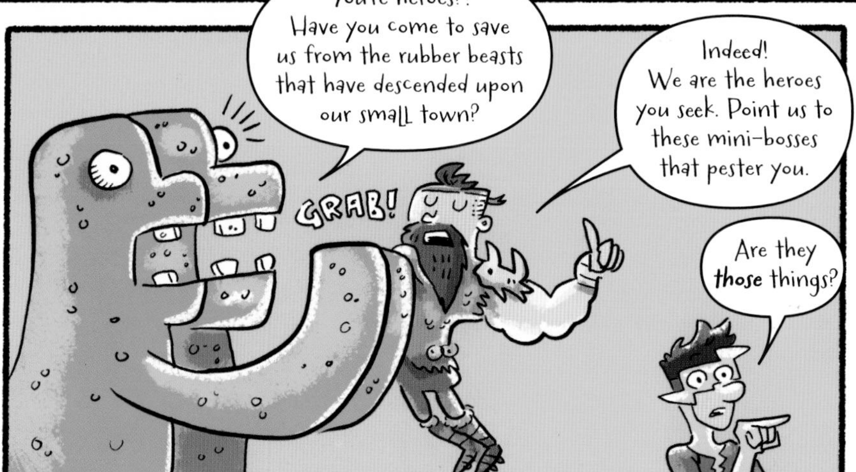

You're heroes?! Have you come to save us from the rubber beasts that have descended upon our small town?
Indeed! We are the heroes you seek. Point us to these mini-bosses that pester you.
GRAB!
Are they **those** things?

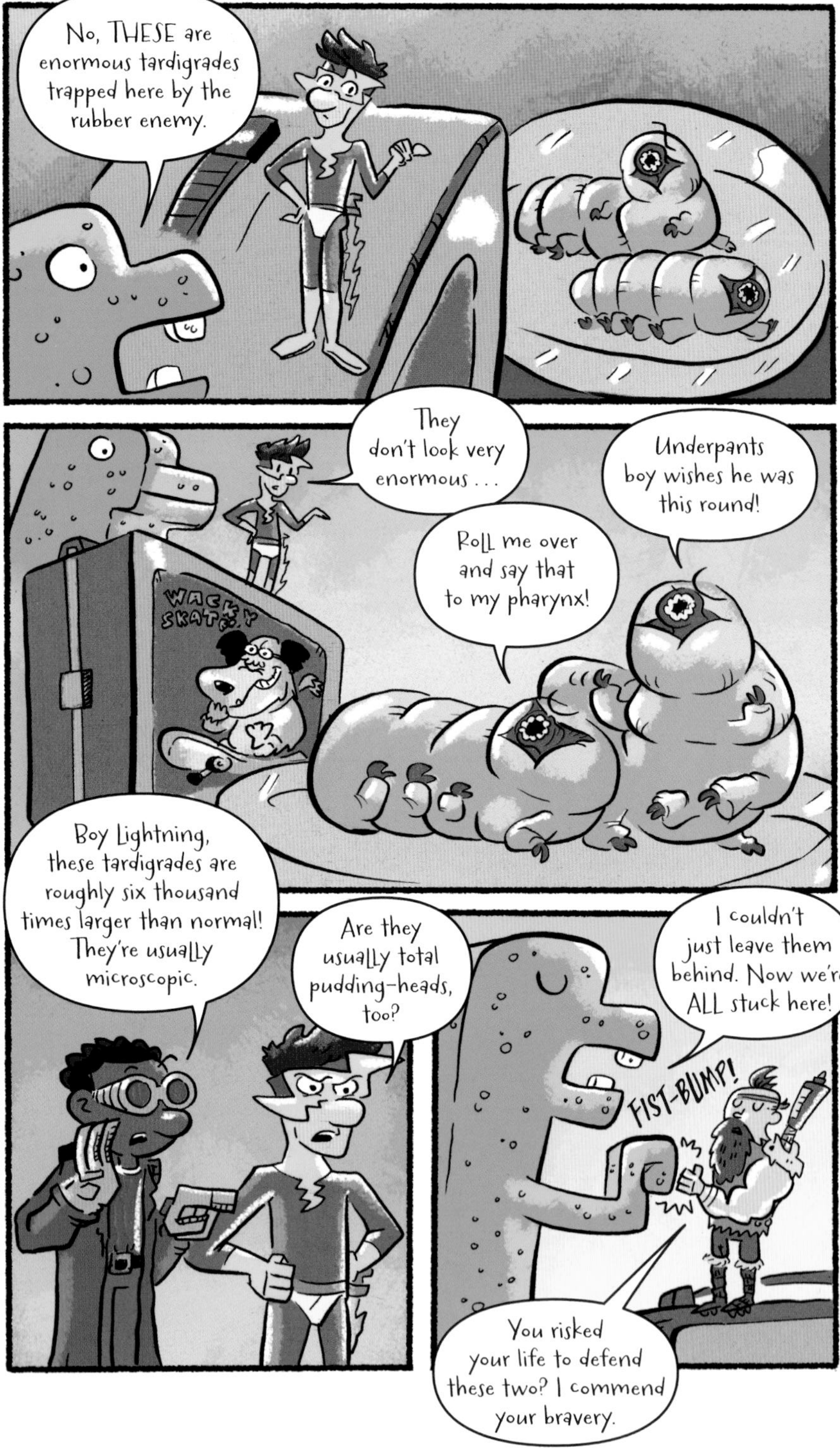
No, THESE are enormous tardigrades trapped here by the rubber enemy.
They don't look very enormous . . .
Underpants boy wishes he was this round!
Roll me over and say that to my pharynx!
WACKY SKATE
Boy Lightning, these tardigrades are roughly six thousand times larger than normal! They're usually microscopic.
Are they usually total pudding-heads, too?
I couldn't just leave them behind. Now we're ALL stuck here!
FIST-BUMP!
You risked your life to defend these two? I commend your bravery.

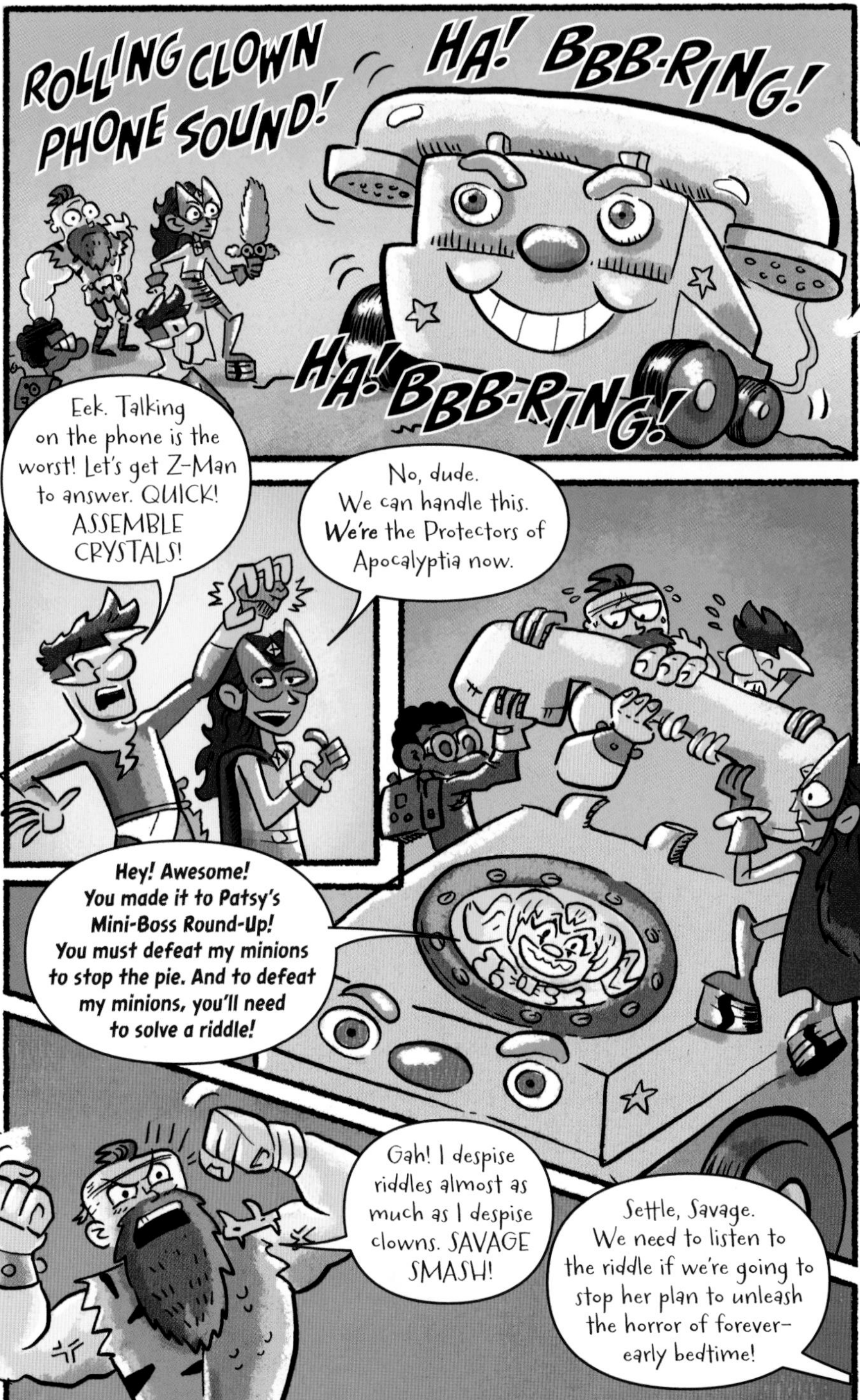
ROLLING CLOWN PHONE SOUND!
HA! BBB-RING!
HA! BBB-RING!
Eek. Talking on the phone is the worst! Let's get Z-Man to answer. QUICK! ASSEMBLE CRYSTALS!
No, dude. We can handle this. We're the Protectors of Apocalyptia now.
Hey! Awesome! You made it to Patsy's Mini-Boss Round-Up! You must defeat my minions to stop the pie. And to defeat my minions, you'll need to solve a riddle!
Gah! I despise riddles almost as much as I despise clowns. SAVAGE SMASH!
Settle, Savage. We need to listen to the riddle if we're going to stop her plan to unleash the horror of forever-early bedtime!

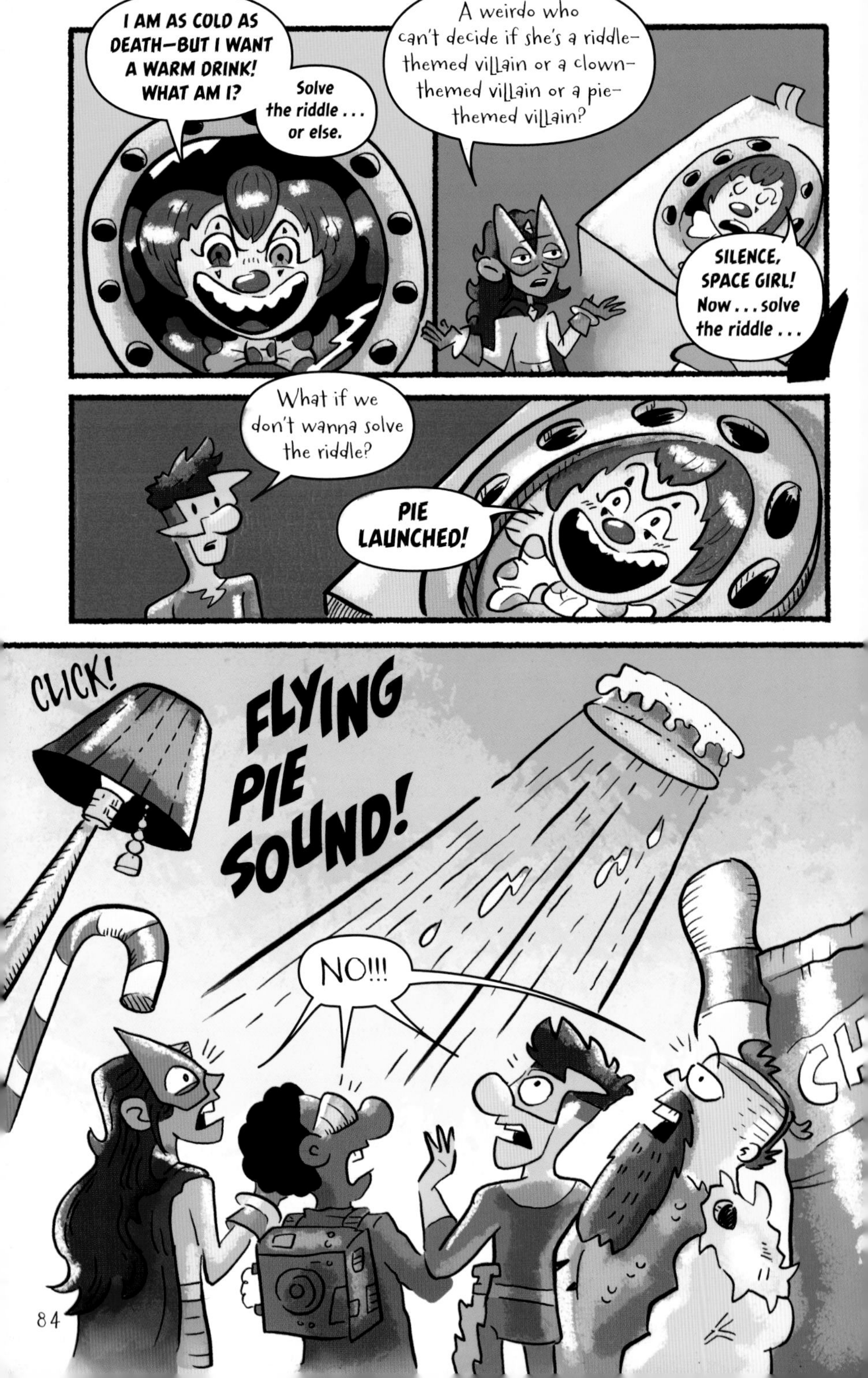

I AM AS COLD AS DEATH—BUT I WANT A WARM DRINK! WHAT AM I?
Solve the riddle . . . or else.
A weirdo who can't decide if she's a riddle-themed villain or a clown-themed villain or a pie-themed villain?
SILENCE, SPACE GIRL! Now . . . solve the riddle . . .
What if we don't wanna solve the riddle?
PIE LAUNCHED!
CLICK!
FLYING PIE SOUND!
NO!!!

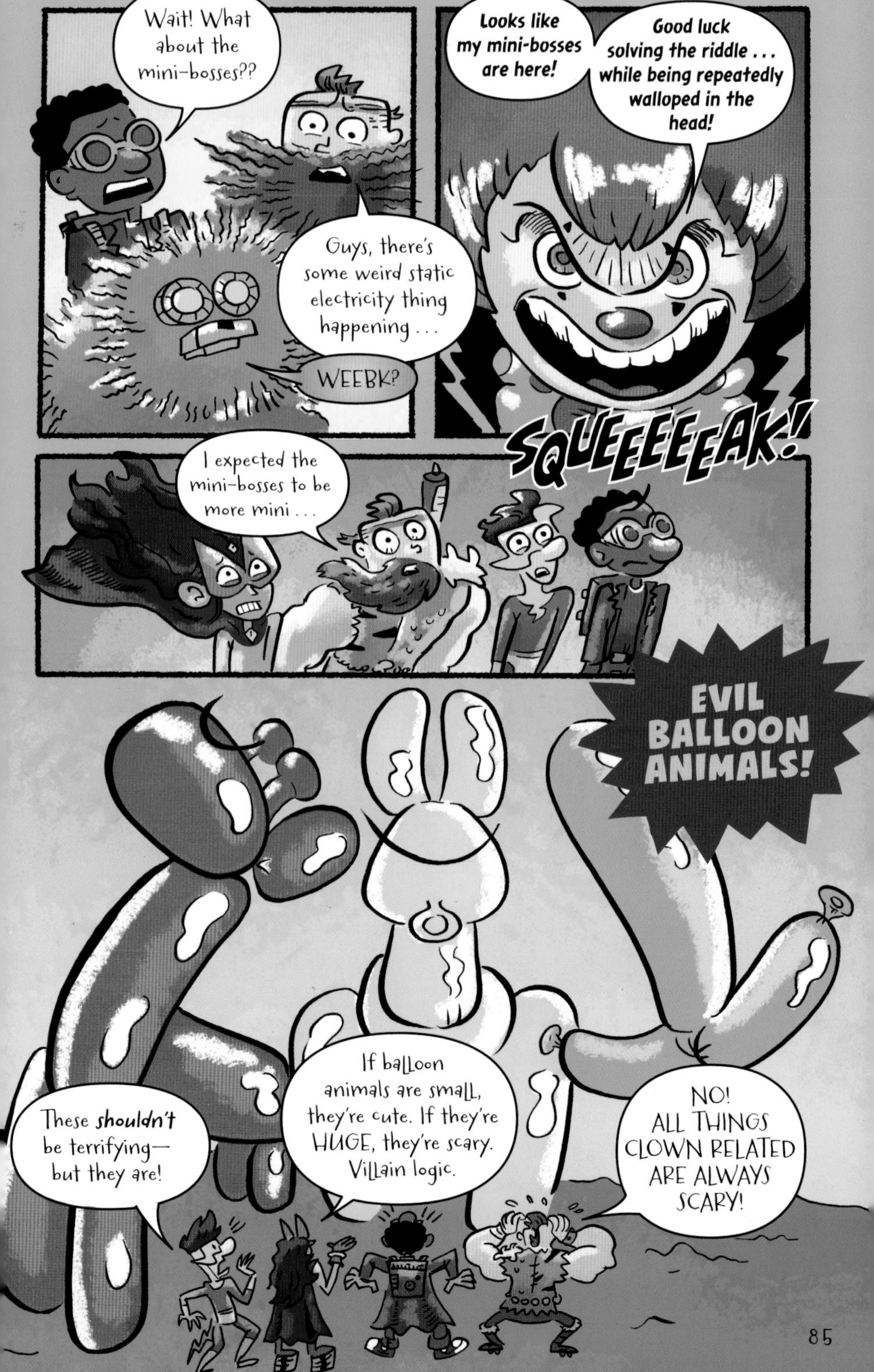
Wait! What about the mini-bosses??
Guys, there's some weird static electricity thing happening . . .
WEEBK?
Looks like my mini-bosses are here!
Good luck solving the riddle . . . while being repeatedly walloped in the head!
SQUEEEEEAK!
I expected the mini-bosses to be more mini . . .
EVIL BALLOON ANIMALS!
These **shouldn't** be terrifying— but they are!
If balloon animals are small, they're cute. If they're HUGE, they're scary. Villain logic.
NO! ALL THINGS CLOWN RELATED ARE ALWAYS SCARY!

CHAPTER SEVEN

SCOURGE OF THE BALLOON ANIMALS!

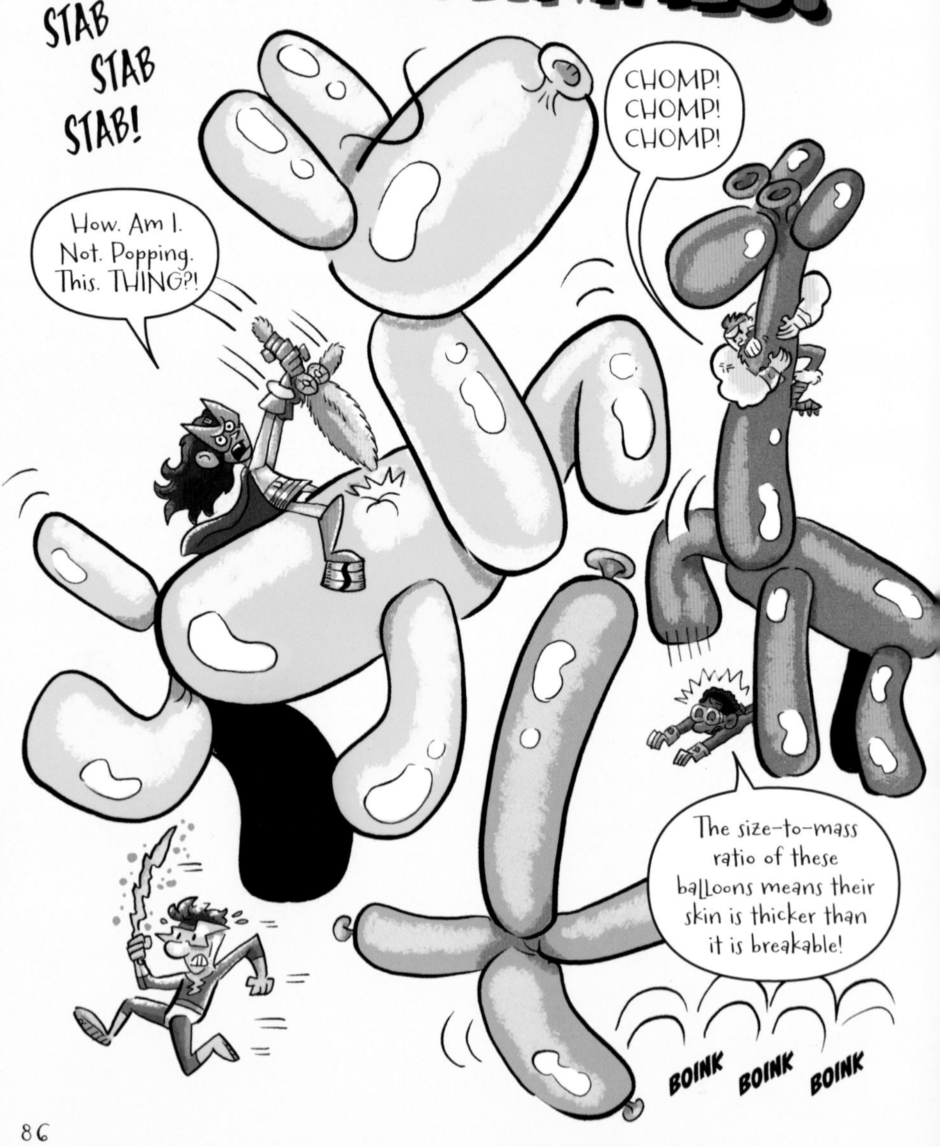

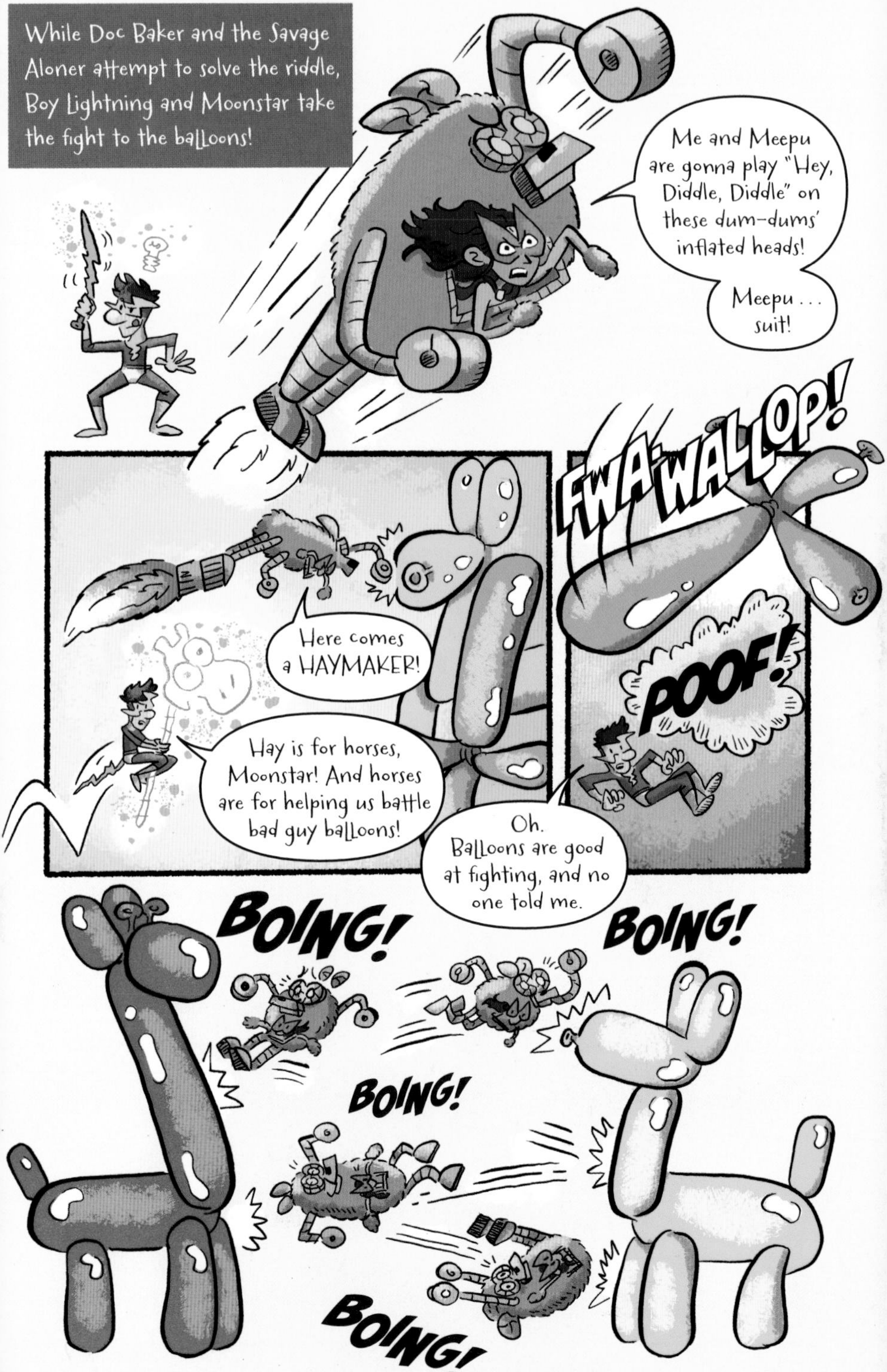
While Doc Baker and the Savage Aloner attempt to solve the riddle, Boy Lightning and Moonstar take the fight to the balloons!
Me and Meepu are gonna play "Hey, Diddle, Diddle" on these dum-dums' inflated heads!
Meepu . . . suit!
Here comes a HAYMAKER!
Hay is for horses, Moonstar! And horses are for helping us battle bad guy balloons!
FWA-WALLOP!
POOF!
Oh. Balloons are good at fighting, and no one told me.
BOING!
BOING!
BOING!
BOING!

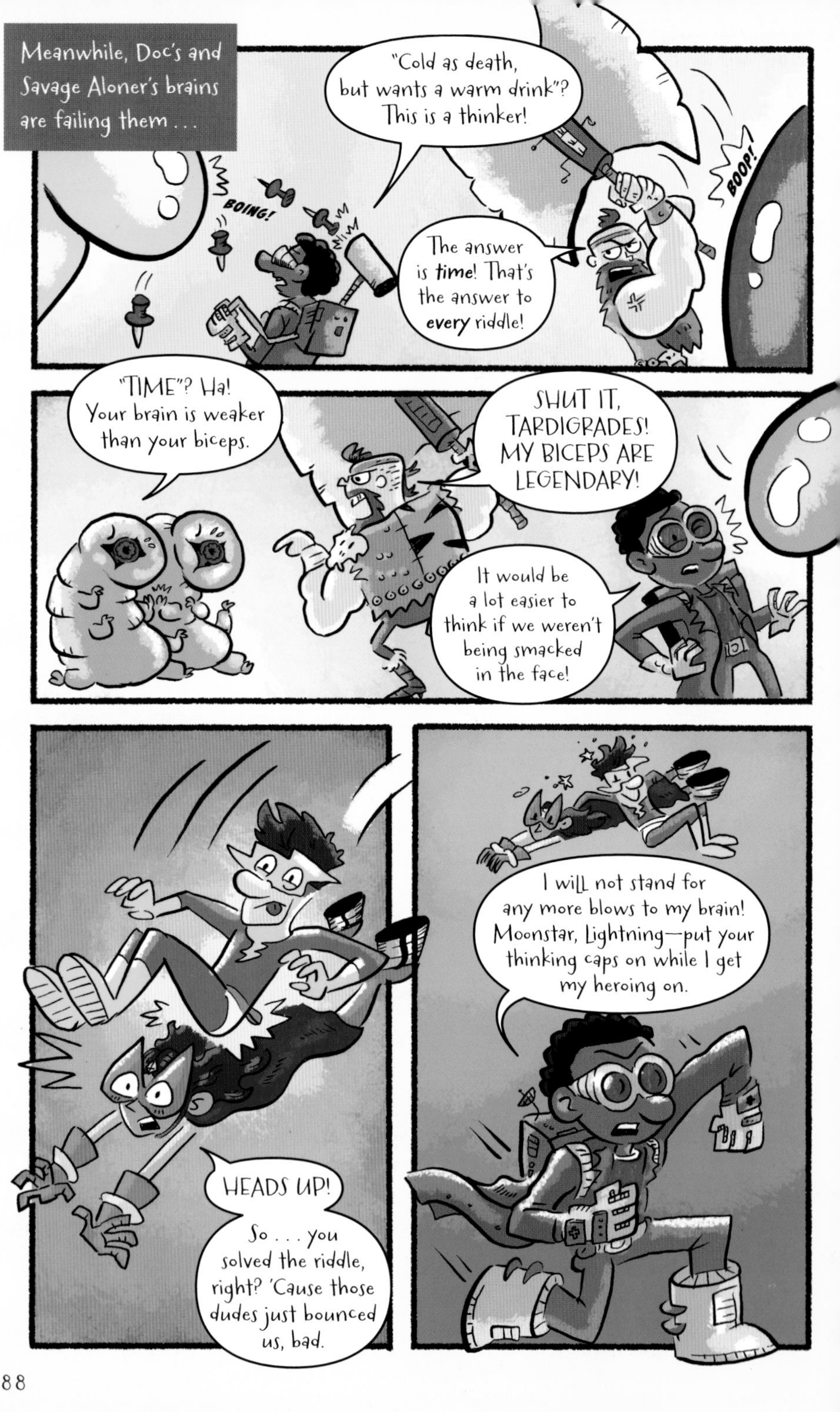
Meanwhile, Doc's and Savage Aloner's brains are failing them . . .
"Cold as death, but wants a warm drink"? This is a thinker!
BOING!
BOOP!
The answer is **time**! That's the answer to **every** riddle!
"TIME"? Ha! Your brain is weaker than your biceps.
SHUT IT, TARDIGRADES! MY BICEPS ARE LEGENDARY!
It would be a lot easier to think if we weren't being smacked in the face!
HEADS UP!
So . . . you solved the riddle, right? 'Cause those dudes just bounced us, bad.
I will not stand for any more blows to my brain! Moonstar, Lightning—put your thinking caps on while I get my heroing on.

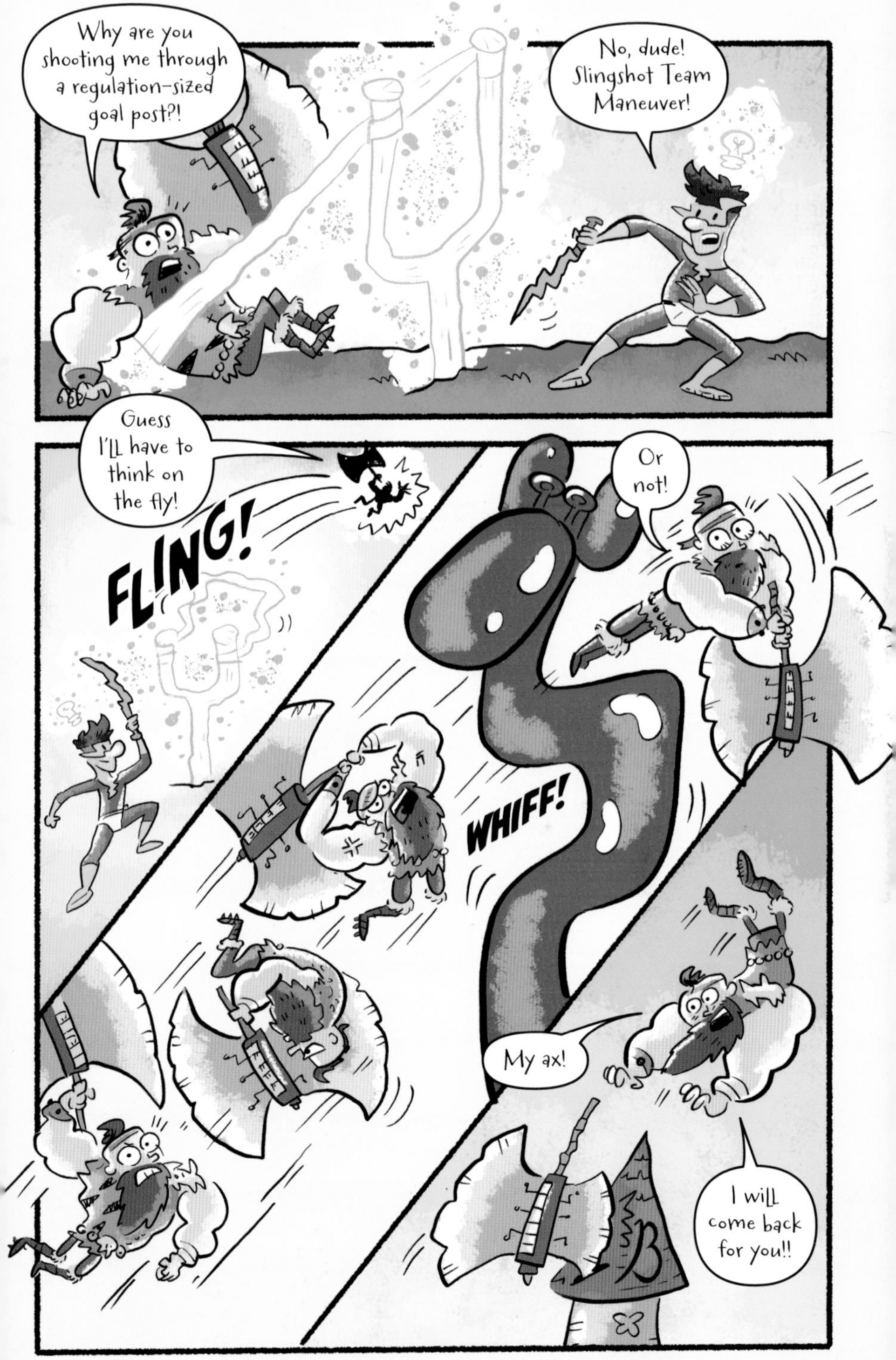

Why are you shooting me through a regulation-sized goal post?!
No, dude! Slingshot Team Maneuver!
Guess I'LL have to think on the fly!
FLING!
Or not!
WHIFF!
My ax!
I WILL come back for you!!

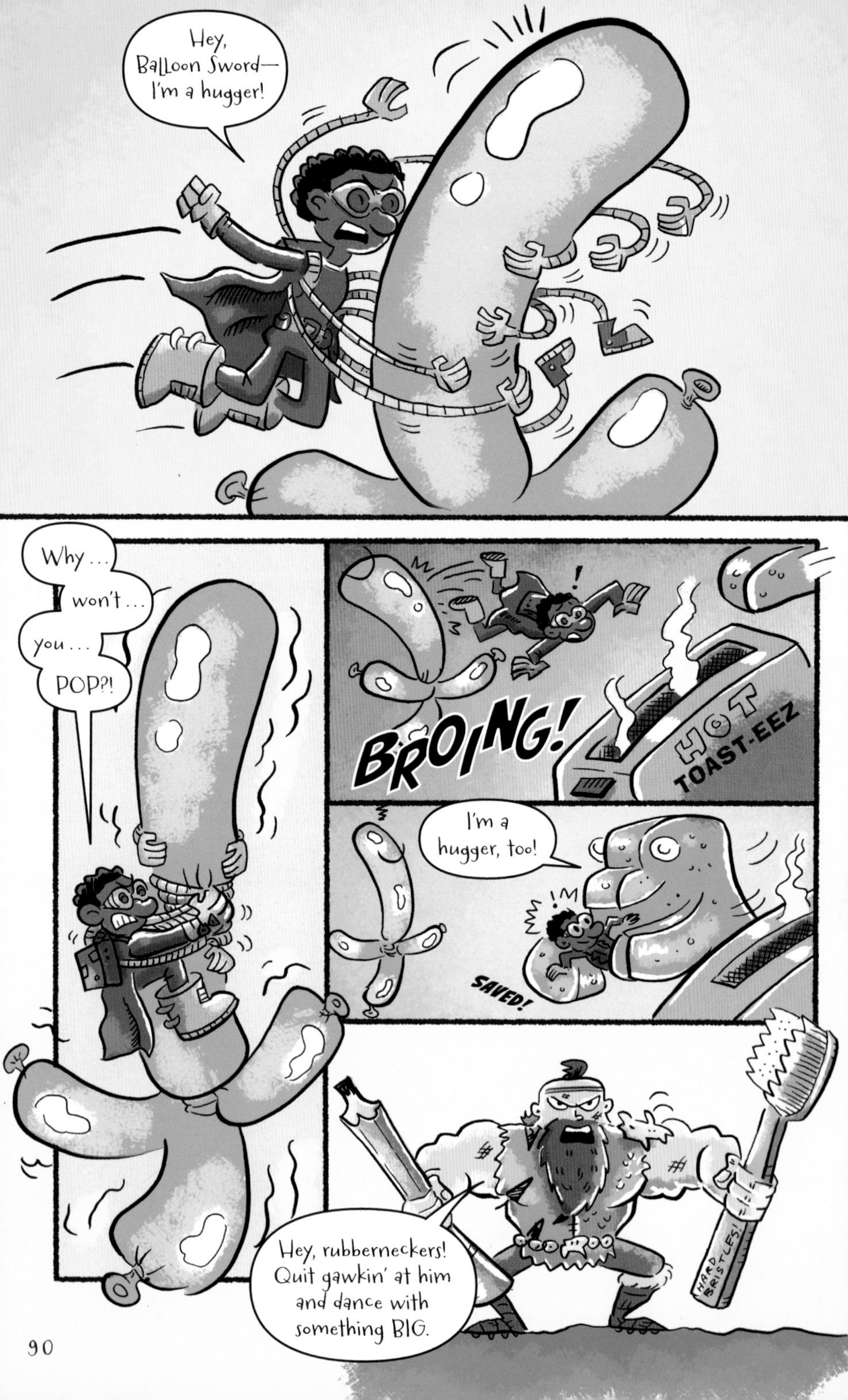
Hey, Balloon Sword— I'm a hugger!
Why... won't... you... POP?!
BROING!
HOT TOAST-EEZ
I'm a hugger, too!
SAVED!
Hey, rubberneckers! Quit gawkin' at him and dance with something BIG.
HARD BRISTLES!

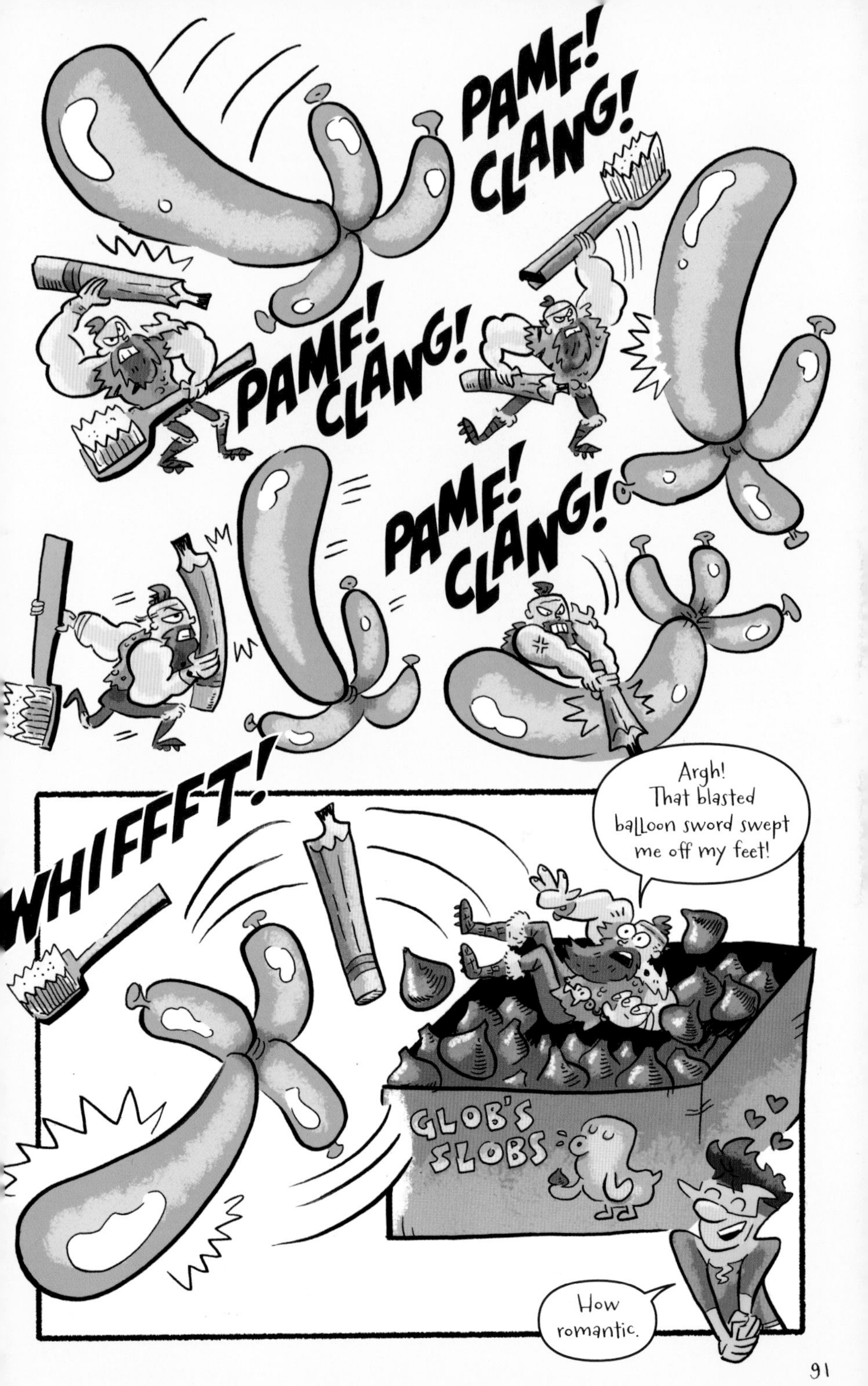
PAMF!
CLANG!
PAMF!
CLANG!
PAMF!
CLANG!
WHIFFFT!
Argh! That blasted balloon sword swept me off my feet!
GLOB'S SLOBS
How romantic.

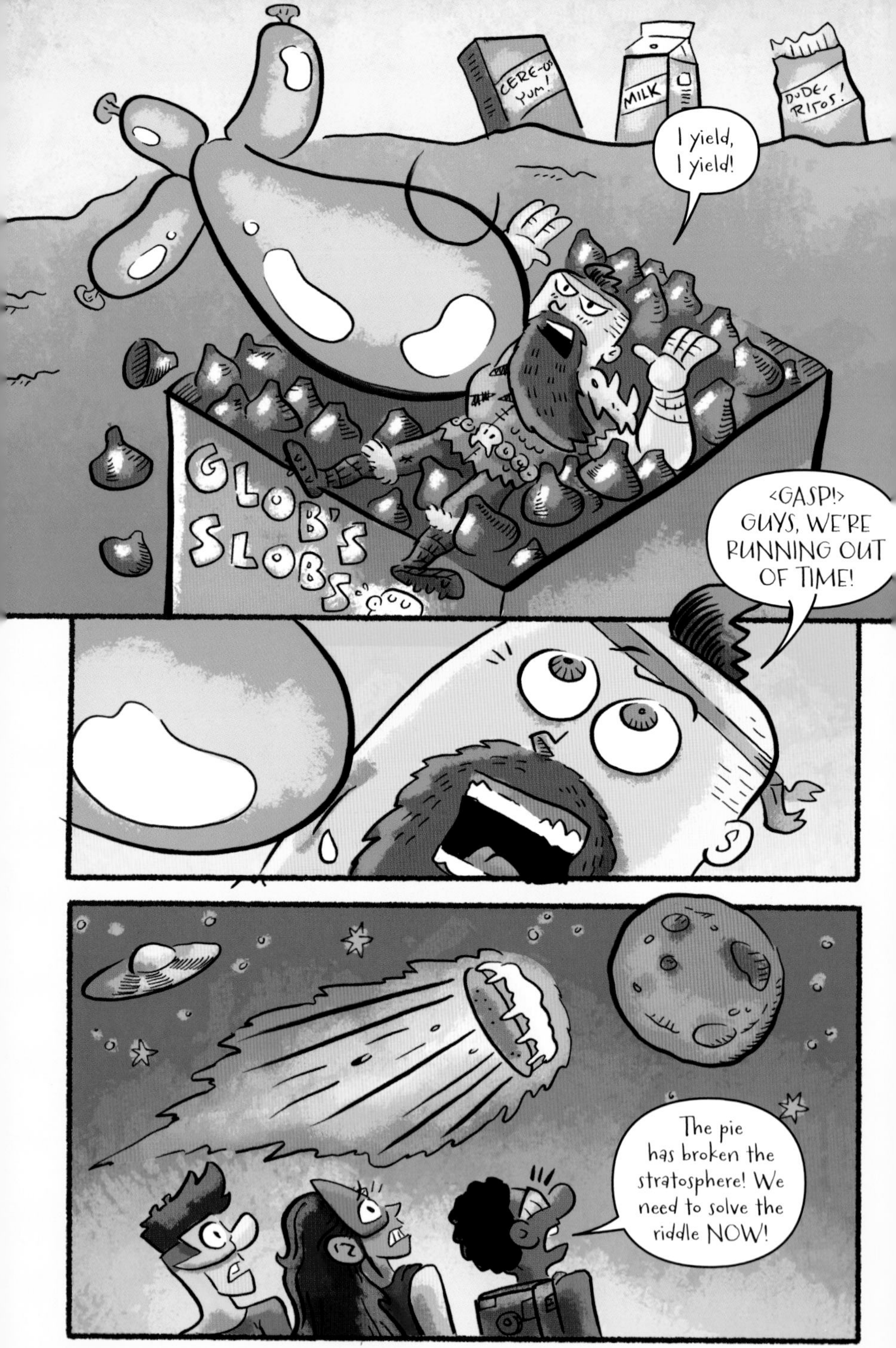
CERE-OS YUM!
MILK
DUDE-RITOS!
I yield, I yield!
GLOB'S SLOBS
<GASP!> GUYS, WE'RE RUNNING OUT OF TIME!
The pie has broken the stratosphere! We need to solve the riddle NOW!

*Editorial Note: Moon repaired since book one!

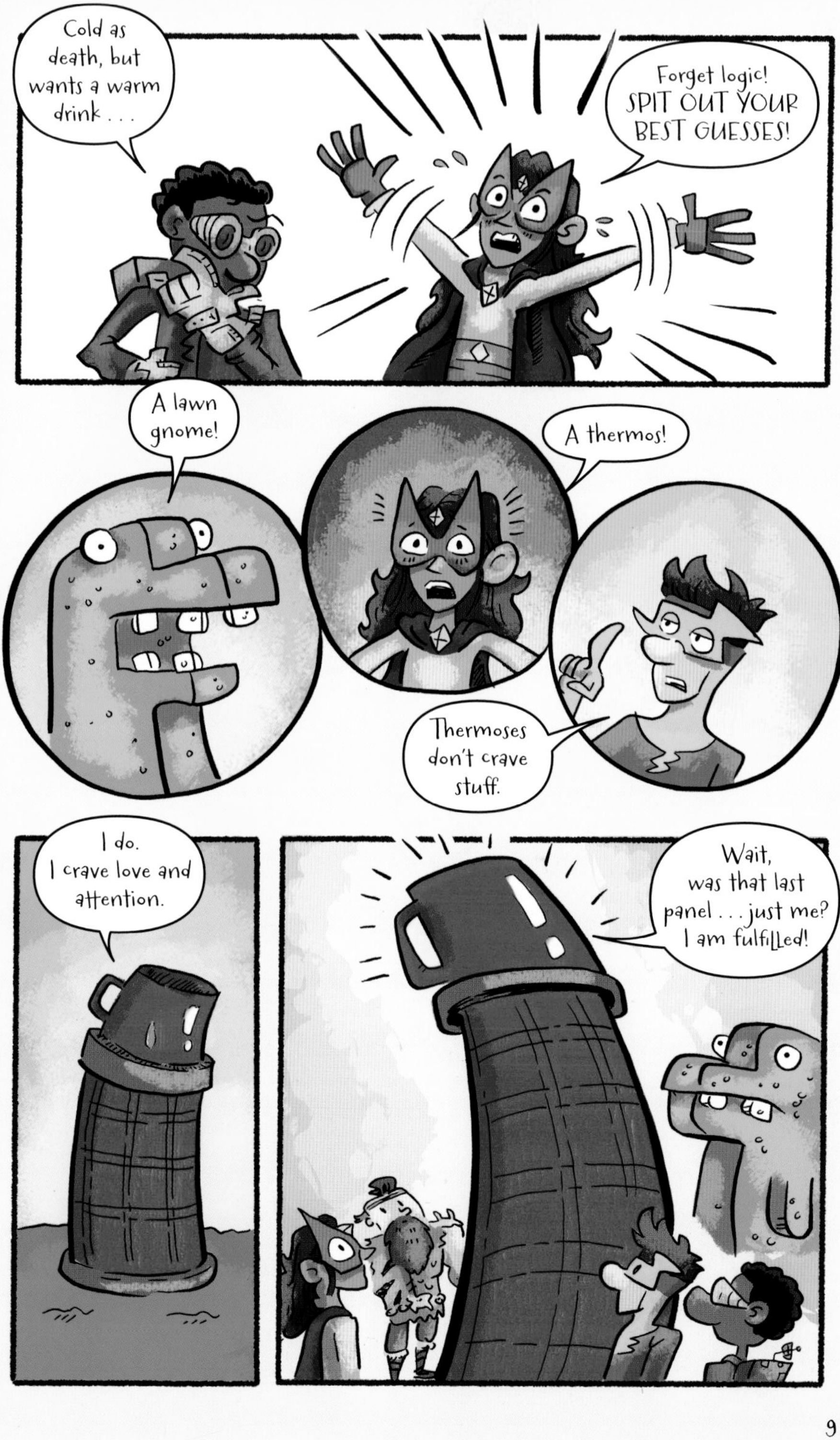
Cold as death, but wants a warm drink . . .
Forget logic! SPIT OUT YOUR BEST GUESSES!
A lawn gnome!
A thermos!
Thermoses don't crave stuff.
I do. I crave love and attention.
Wait, was that last panel . . . just me? I am fulfilled!

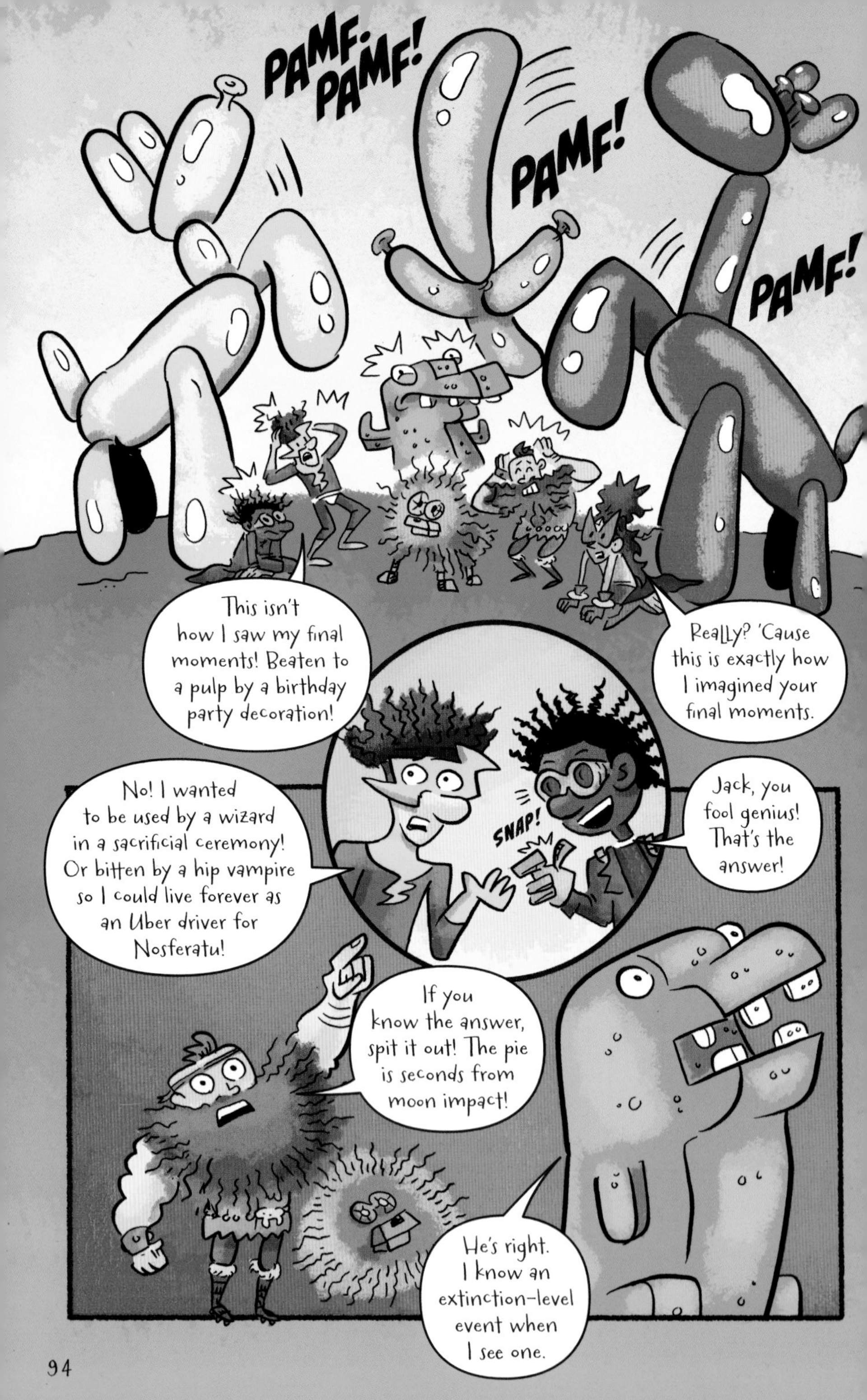
PAMF. PAMF!
PAMF!
PAMF!
This isn't how I saw my final moments! Beaten to a pulp by a birthday party decoration!
Really? 'Cause this is exactly how I imagined your final moments.
No! I wanted to be used by a wizard in a sacrificial ceremony! Or bitten by a hip vampire so I could live forever as an Uber driver for Nosferatu!
SNAP!
Jack, you fool genius! That's the answer!
If you know the answer, spit it out! The pie is seconds from moon impact!
He's right. I know an extinction-level event when I see one.

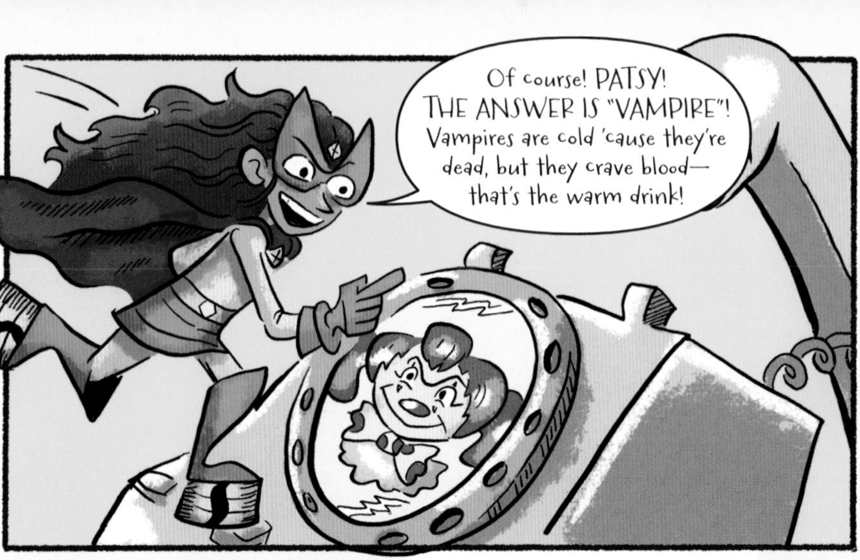
Of course! PATSY!
THE ANSWER IS "VAMPIRE"!
Vampires are cold 'cause they're dead, but they crave blood— that's the warm drink!

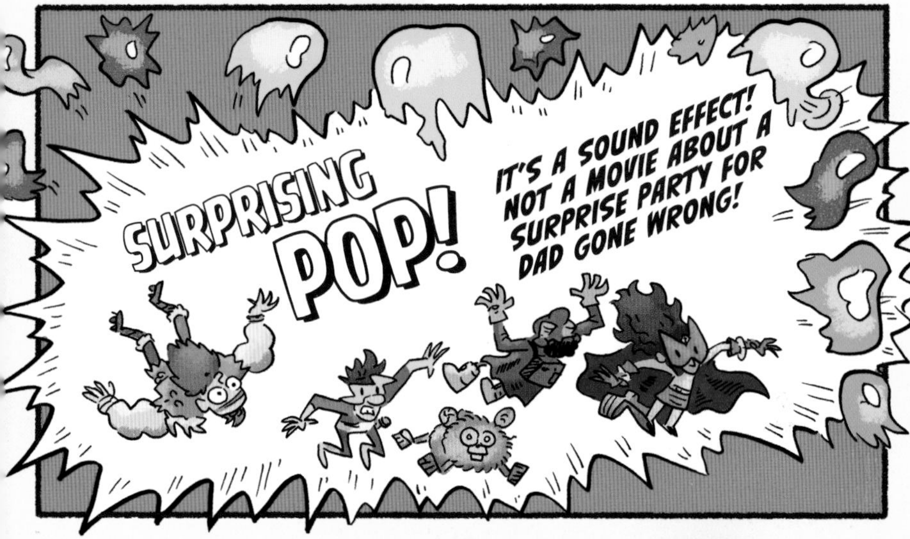
SURPRISING POP!
IT'S A SOUND EFFECT! NOT A MOVIE ABOUT A SURPRISE PARTY FOR DAD GONE WRONG!

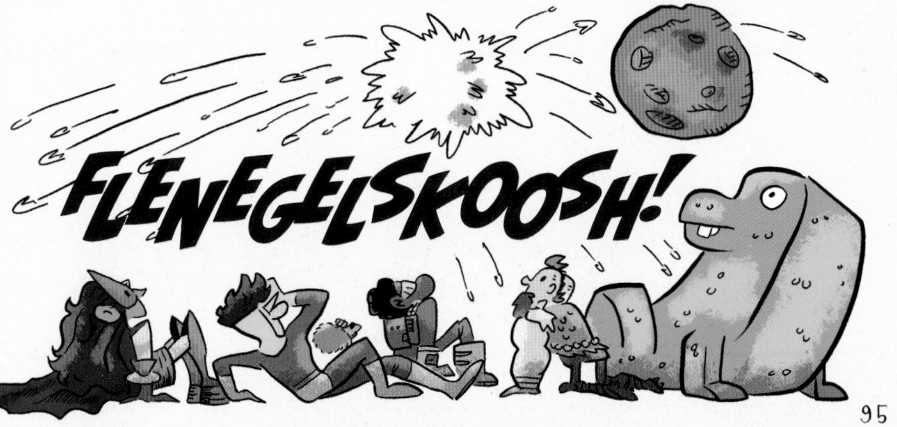
FLENEGELSKOOSH!

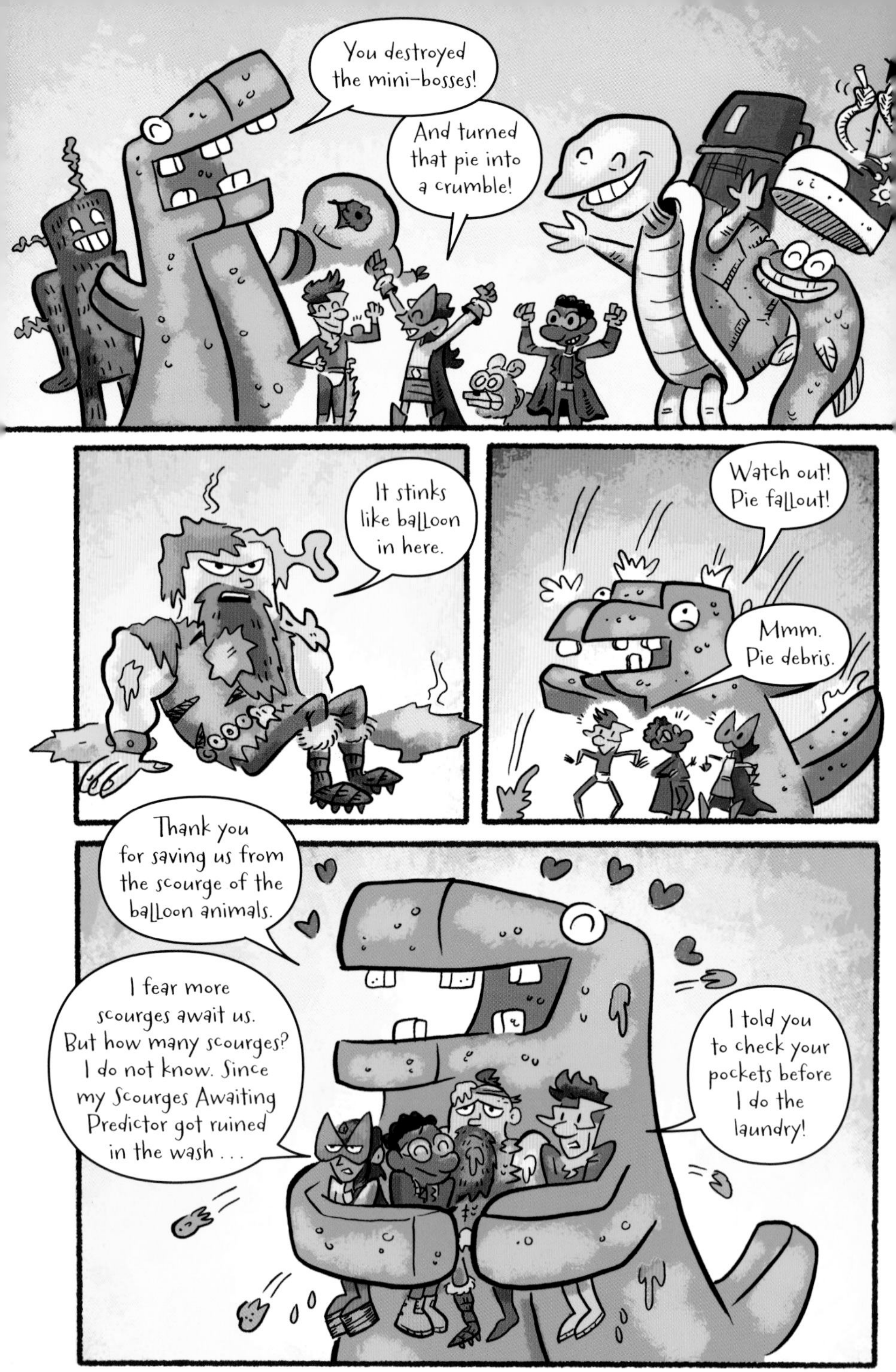
You destroyed the mini-bosses!
And turned that pie into a crumble!
It stinks like balloon in here.
Watch out! Pie fallout!
Mmm. Pie debris.
Thank you for saving us from the scourge of the balloon animals.
I fear more scourges await us. But how many scourges? I do not know. Since my Scourges Awaiting Predictor got ruined in the wash . . .
I told you to check your pockets before I do the laundry!

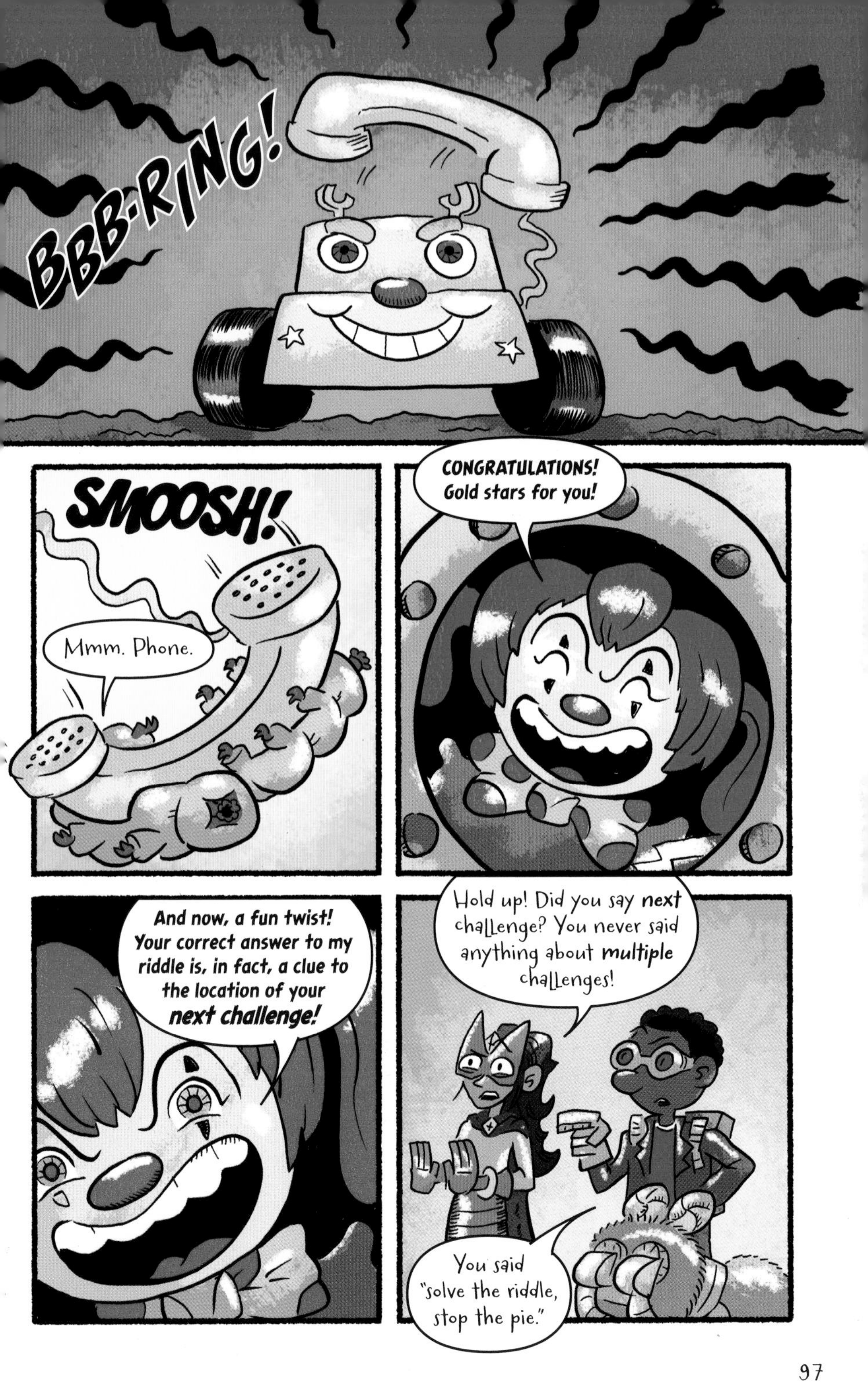
BBB-RING!
SMOOSH!
Mmm. Phone.
CONGRATULATIONS! Gold stars for you!
And now, a fun twist! Your correct answer to my riddle is, in fact, a clue to the location of your next challenge!
Hold up! Did you say next challenge? You never said anything about multiple challenges!
You said "solve the riddle, stop the pie."

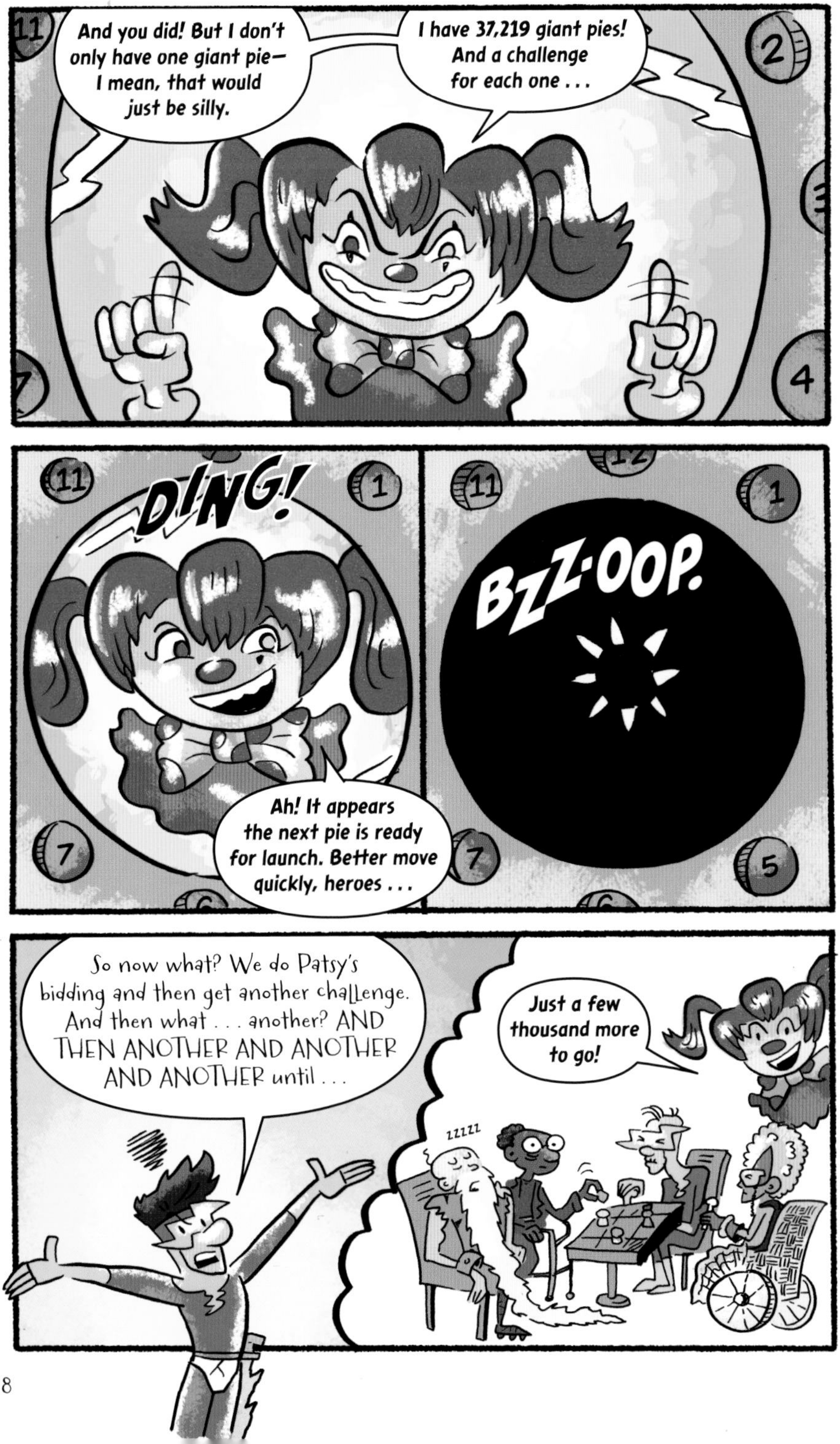
And you did! But I don't only have one giant pie— I mean, that would just be silly.
I have 37,219 giant pies! And a challenge for each one . . .
DING!
Ah! It appears the next pie is ready for launch. Better move quickly, heroes . . .
BZZ-OOP.
So now what? We do Patsy's bidding and then get another challenge. And then what . . . another? AND THEN ANOTHER AND ANOTHER AND ANOTHER until . . .
Just a few thousand more to go!
ZZZZZ

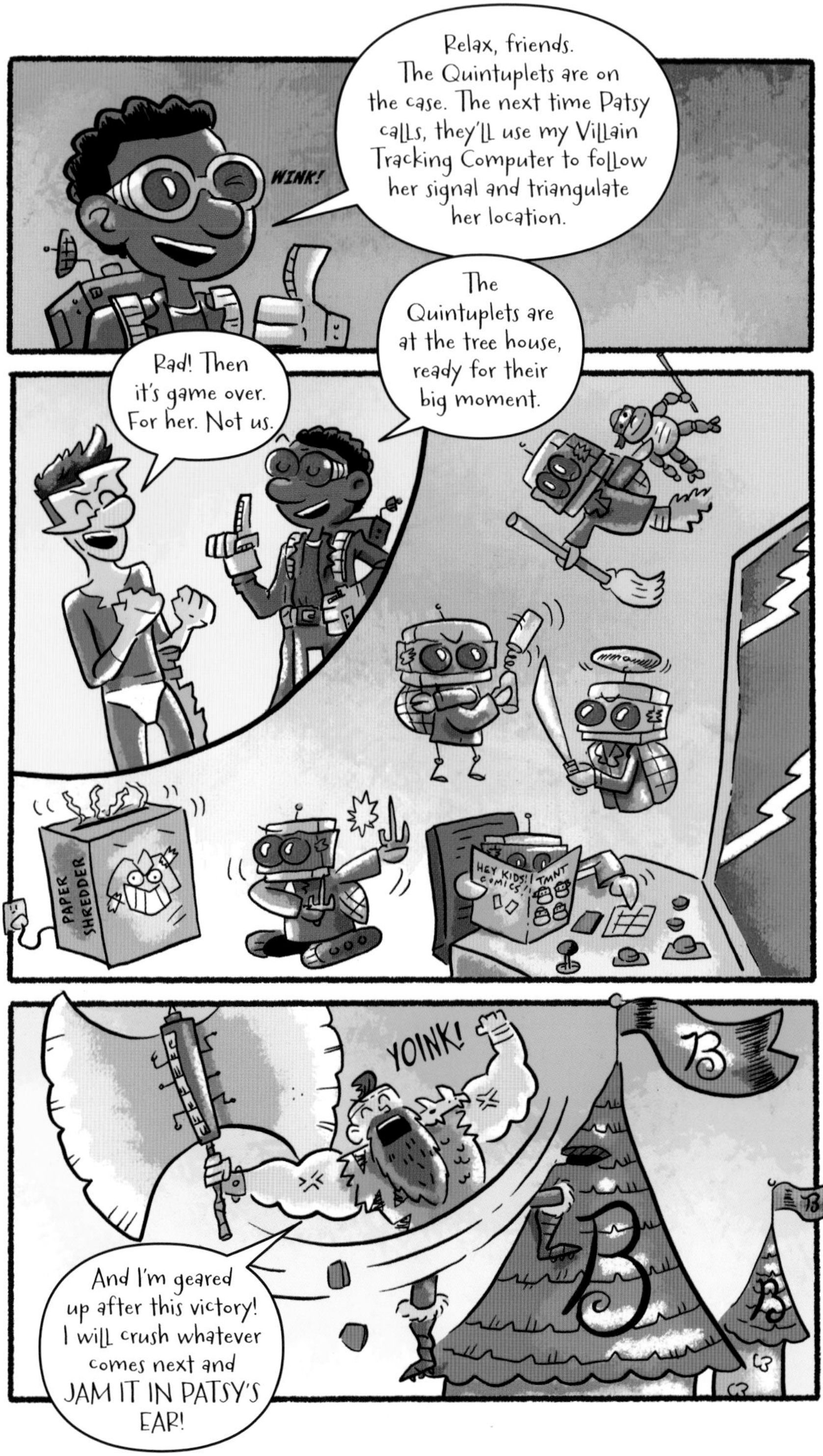
Relax, friends. The Quintuplets are on the case. The next time Patsy calls, they'll use my Villain Tracking Computer to follow her signal and triangulate her location.
WINK!
Rad! Then it's game over. For her. Not us.
The Quintuplets are at the tree house, ready for their big moment.
PAPER SHREDDER
HEY KIDS! COMICS!
TMNT
YOINK!
And I'm geared up after this victory! I will crush whatever comes next and JAM IT IN PATSY'S EAR!

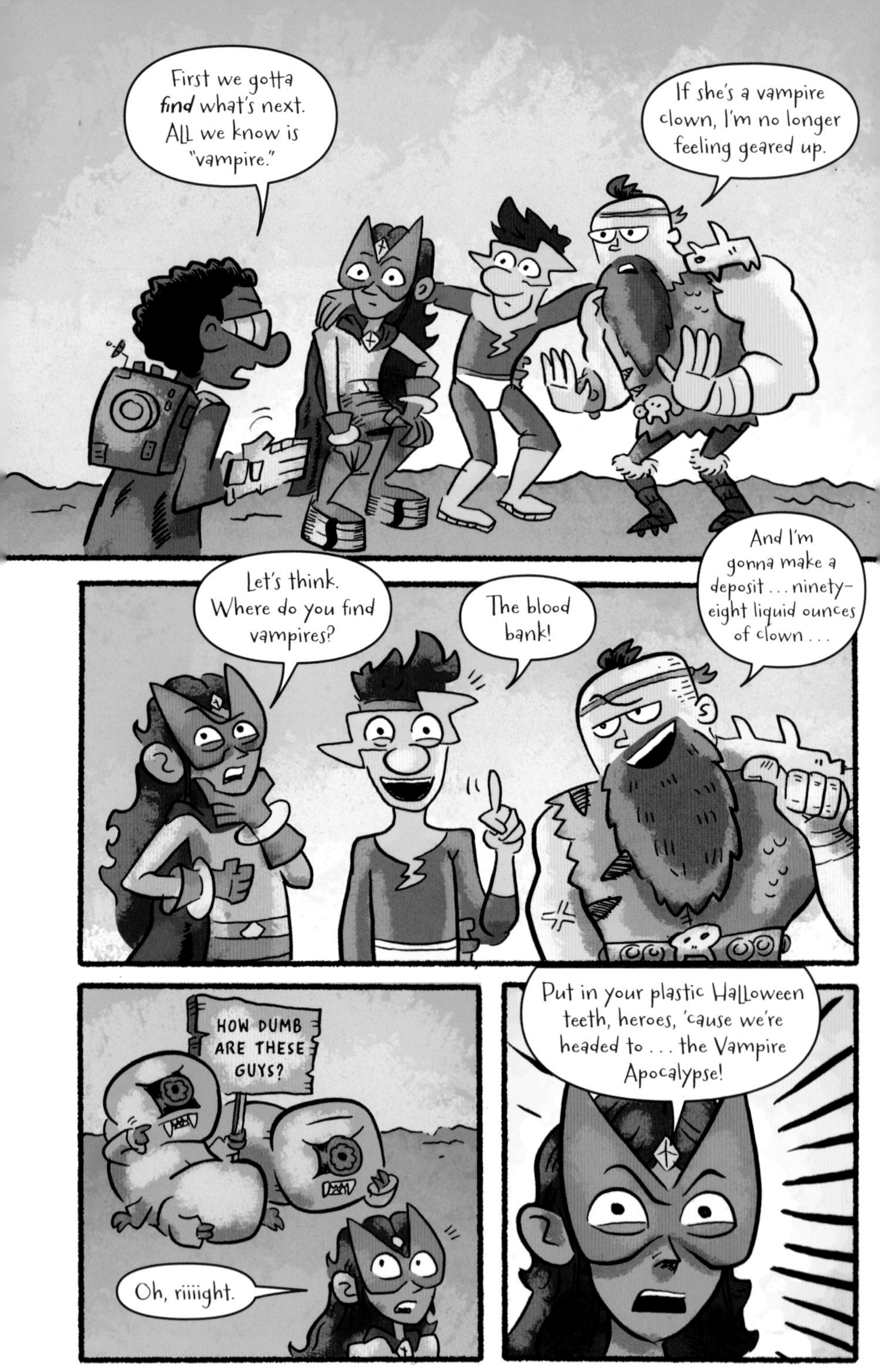
First we gotta find what's next. ALL we know is "vampire."
If she's a vampire clown, I'm no longer feeling geared up.
Let's think. Where do you find vampires?
The blood bank!
And I'm gonna make a deposit . . . ninety-eight liquid ounces of clown . . .
HOW DUMB ARE THESE GUYS?
Oh, riiiight.
Put in your plastic Halloween teeth, heroes, 'cause we're headed to . . . the Vampire Apocalypse!

DRAW COMICS THE BOY LIGHTNING WAY!

LEARN HOW TO DRAW COMICS, CARTOONS, GRAPHIC NOVELS, AND DINKY LITTLE DOODLES AT THE BOY LIGHTNING SUPER SKETCHING SCHOOL!

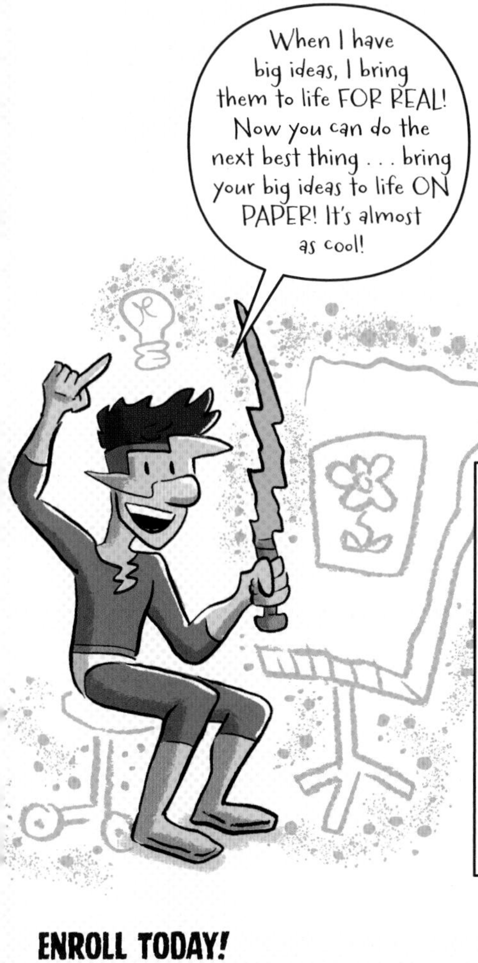
When I have big ideas, I bring them to life FOR REAL! Now you can do the next best thing . . . bring your big ideas to life ON PAPER! It's almost as cool!

DRAW IT ALL!

–HAND-DRAWN CARTOONS
–FOOT-DRAWN CARTOONS!
–FINGER PAINTING!
. . . AND OTHER ARTSY THINGS!

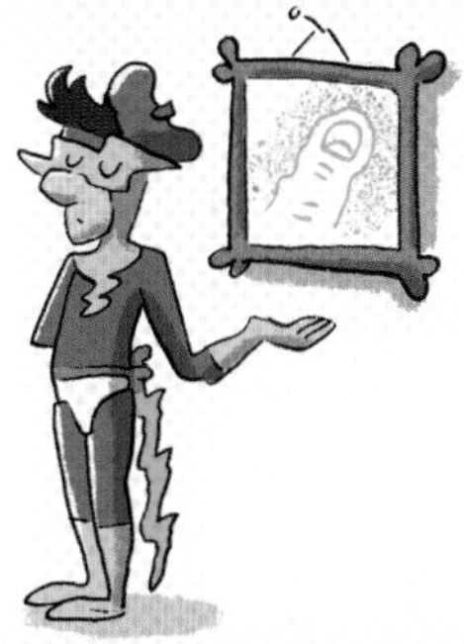

PAST STUDENTS INCLUDE:

–MICHELANGELO (NOT THE NINJA TURTLE)
–JAY COOPER
–RAPHAEL (THE NINJA TURTLE!)
–QUINT BAKER

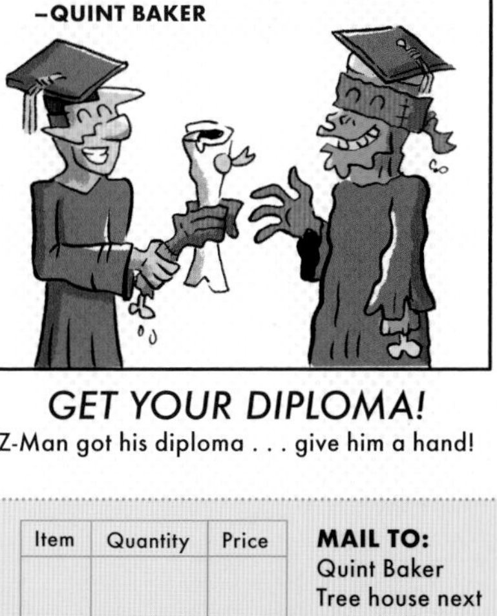

GET YOUR DIPLOMA!
Z-Man got his diploma . . . give him a hand!

ENROLL TODAY!

Do not cut or mark here! It's just a gag!
(Two words: mint condition, people. You could pay your own way to college in a few years with this thing. But you won't want to sell because—*duh*—this book is way too fabulous.)

Name: ______________ Birth year: ______________

Biggest regret: ______________ Fave TV show: ______________

Item	Quantity	Price
SUBTOTAL:		
GYRO TOTAL:		

MAIL TO:
Quint Baker
Tree house next to Joe's Pizza
Apocalyptia, USA

CHAPTER EIGHT

A-CROSS THE VAMPIRE APOCALYPSE

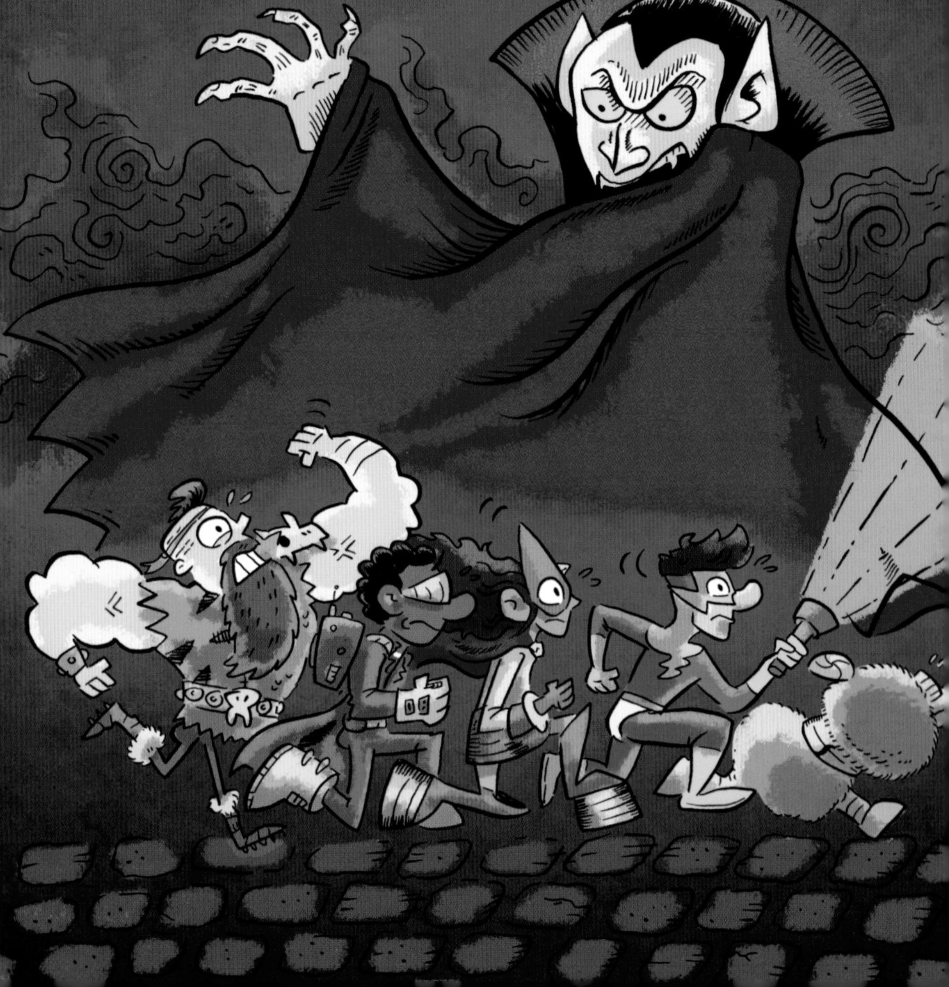

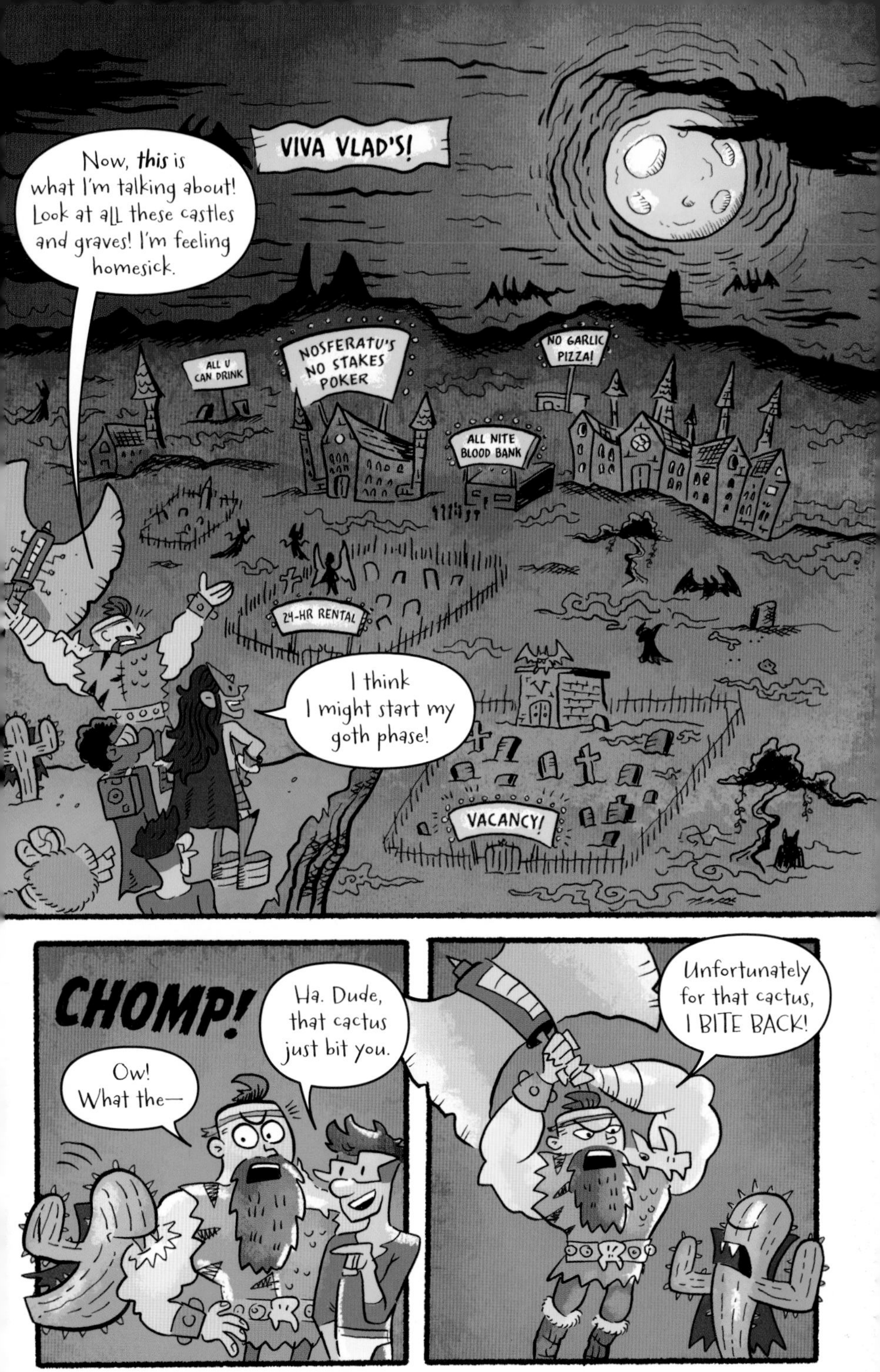
VIVA VLAD'S!
Now, this is what I'm talking about! Look at all these castles and graves! I'm feeling homesick.
ALL U CAN DRINK
NOSFERATU'S NO STAKES POKER
NO GARLIC PIZZA!
ALL NITE BLOOD BANK
24-HR RENTAL
I think I might start my goth phase!
VACANCY!
CHOMP!
Ow! What the—
Ha. Dude, that cactus just bit you.
Unfortunately for that cactus, I BITE BACK!

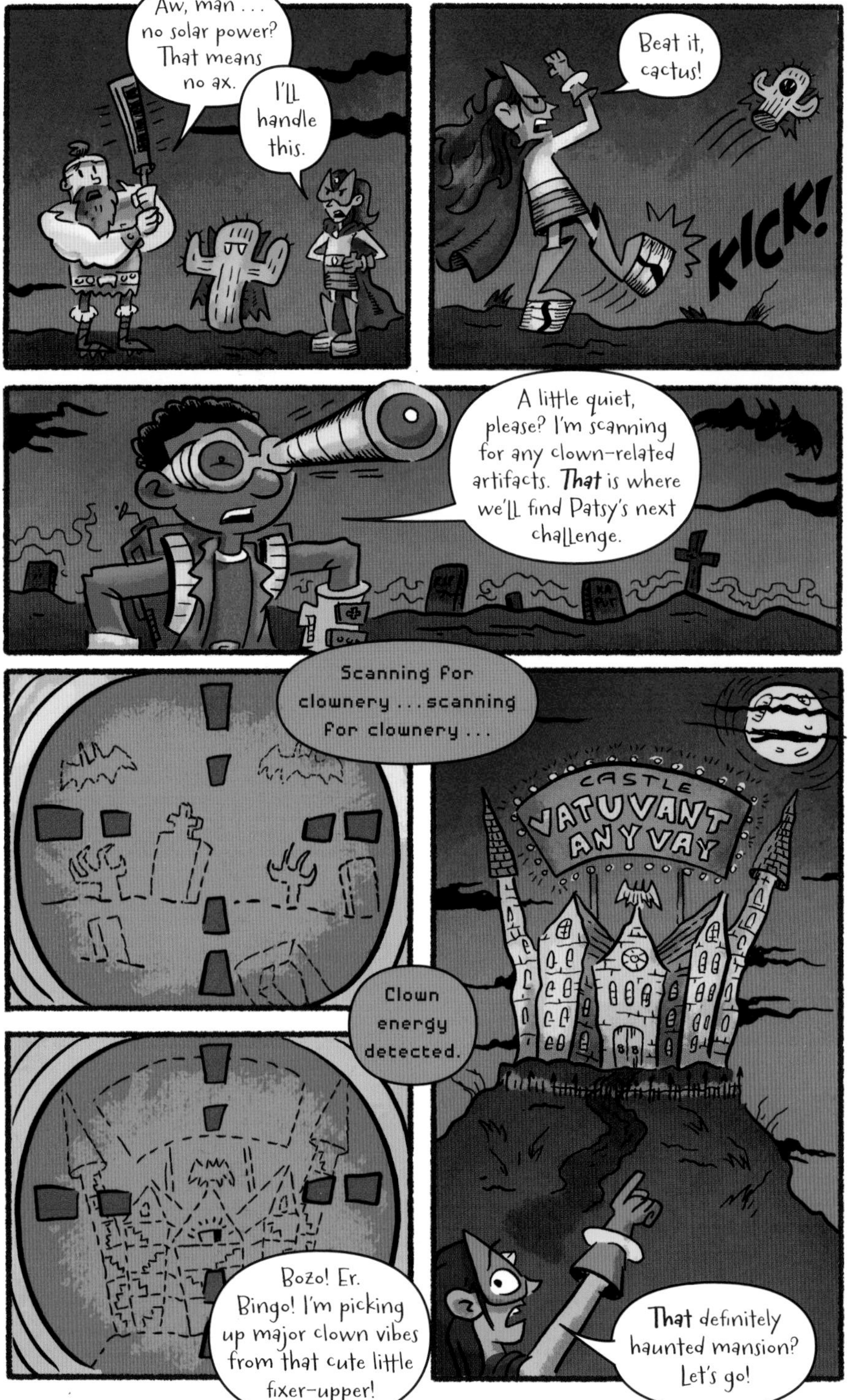
Aw, man . . . no solar power? That means no ax.
I'LL handle this.
Beat it, cactus!
KICK!
A little quiet, please? I'm scanning for any clown-related artifacts. That is where we'LL find Patsy's next chaLLenge.
Scanning for clownery . . . scanning for clownery . . .
CASTLE VATUVANT ANYVAY
Clown energy detected.
Bozo! Er. Bingo! I'm picking up major clown vibes from that cute little fixer-upper!
That definitely haunted mansion? Let's go!

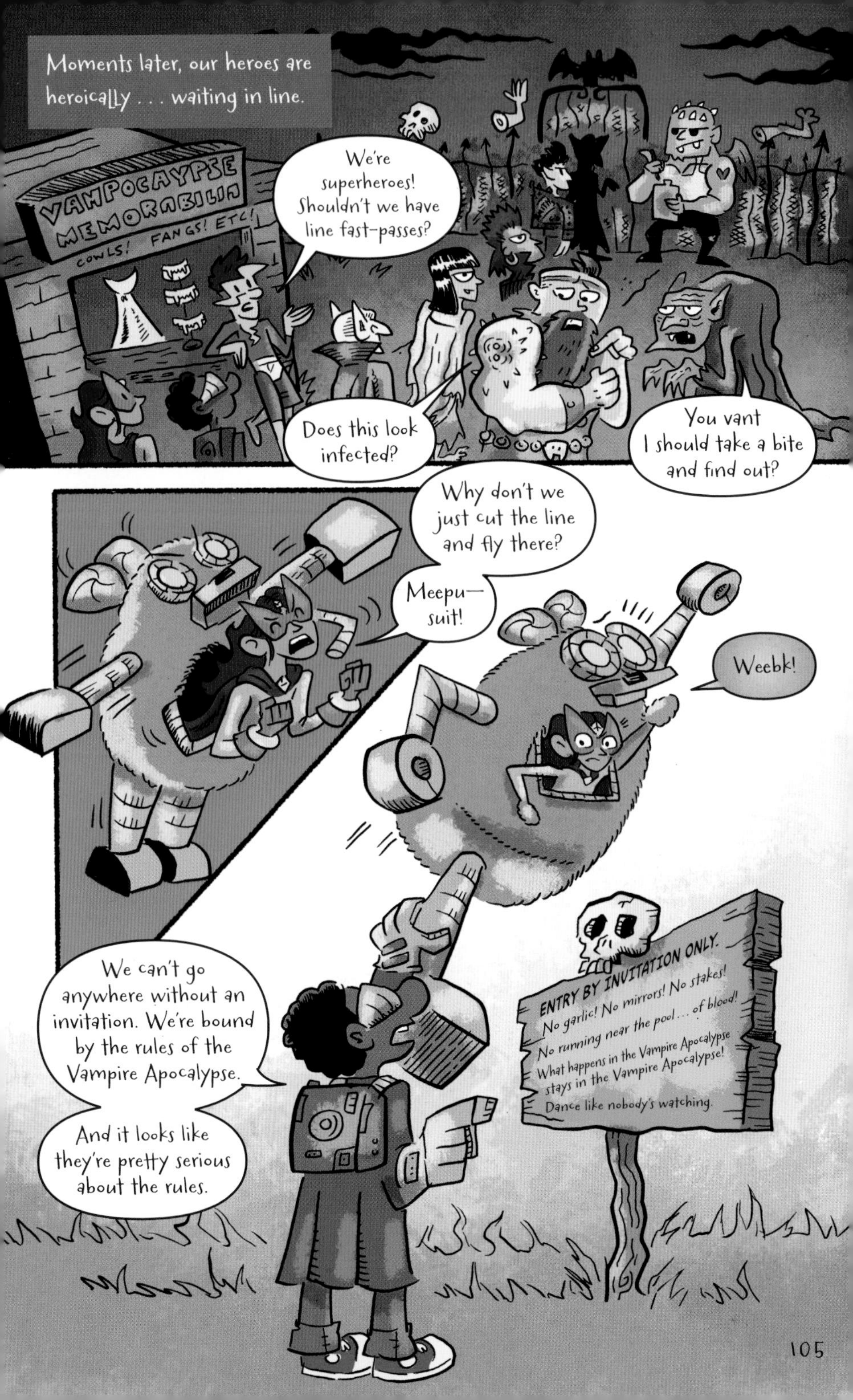
Moments later, our heroes are heroicaLLy . . . waiting in line.
VAMPOCALYPSE MEMORABILIA
COWLS! FANGS! ETC!
We're superheroes! Shouldn't we have line fast-passes?
Does this look infected?
You vant I should take a bite and find out?
Why don't we just cut the line and fly there?
Meepu—suit!
Weebk!
We can't go anywhere without an invitation. We're bound by the rules of the Vampire Apocalypse.
And it looks like they're pretty serious about the rules.
ENTRY BY INVITATION ONLY.
No garlic! No mirrors! No stakes!
No running near the pool . . . of blood!
What happens in the Vampire Apocalypse stays in the Vampire Apocalypse!
Dance like nobody's watching.

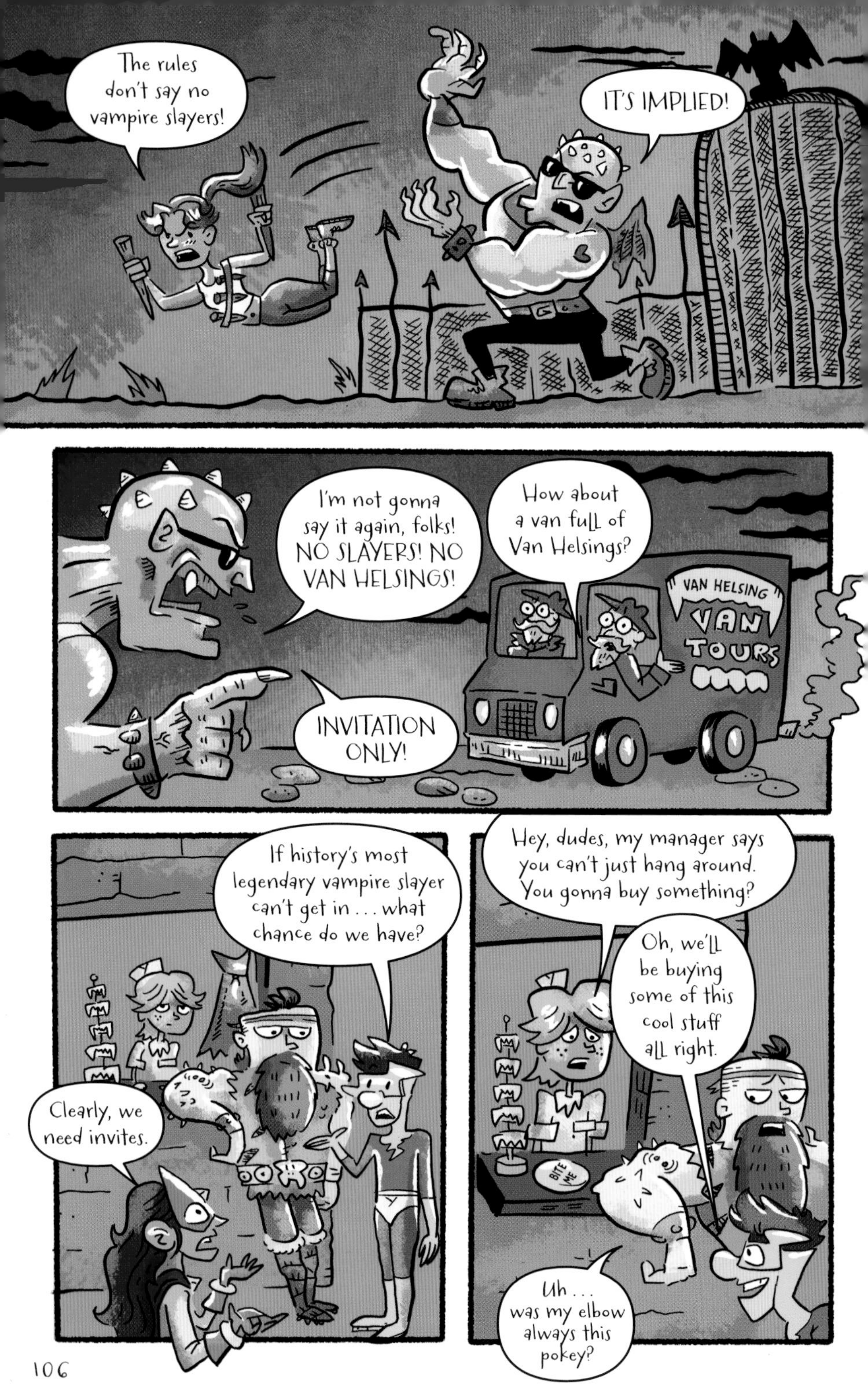

The rules don't say no vampire slayers!
IT'S IMPLIED!
I'm not gonna say it again, folks! NO SLAYERS! NO VAN HELSINGS!
How about a van full of Van Helsings?
VAN HELSING VAN TOURS
INVITATION ONLY!
If history's most legendary vampire slayer can't get in . . . what chance do we have?
Clearly, we need invites.
Hey, dudes, my manager says you can't just hang around. You gonna buy something?
Oh, we'll be buying some of this cool stuff all right.
BITE ME
Uh . . . was my elbow always this pokey?

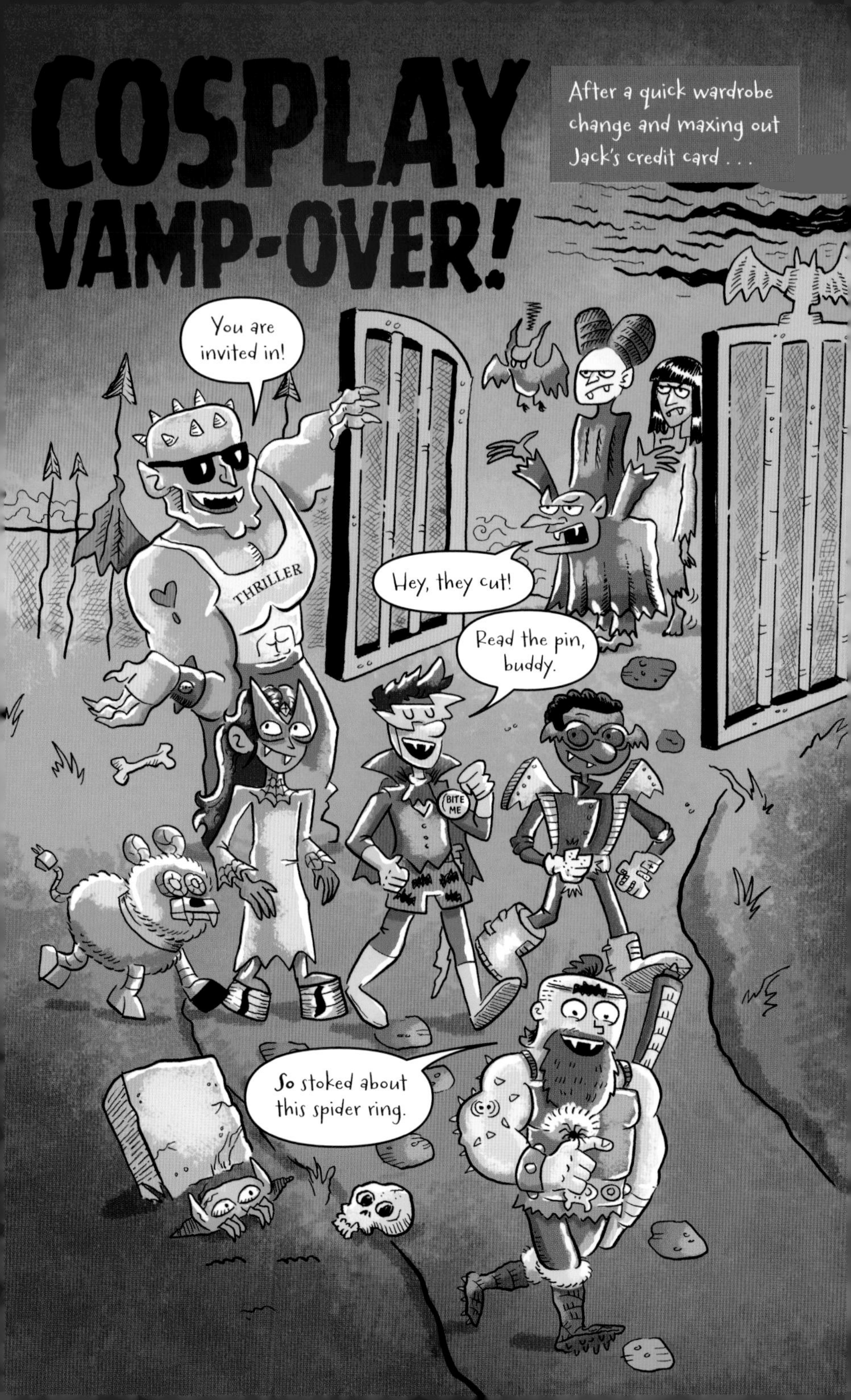
COSPLAY VAMP-OVER!
After a quick wardrobe change and maxing out Jack's credit card . . .
You are invited in!
THRILLER
Hey, they cut!
Read the pin, buddy.
BITE ME
So stoked about this spider ring.

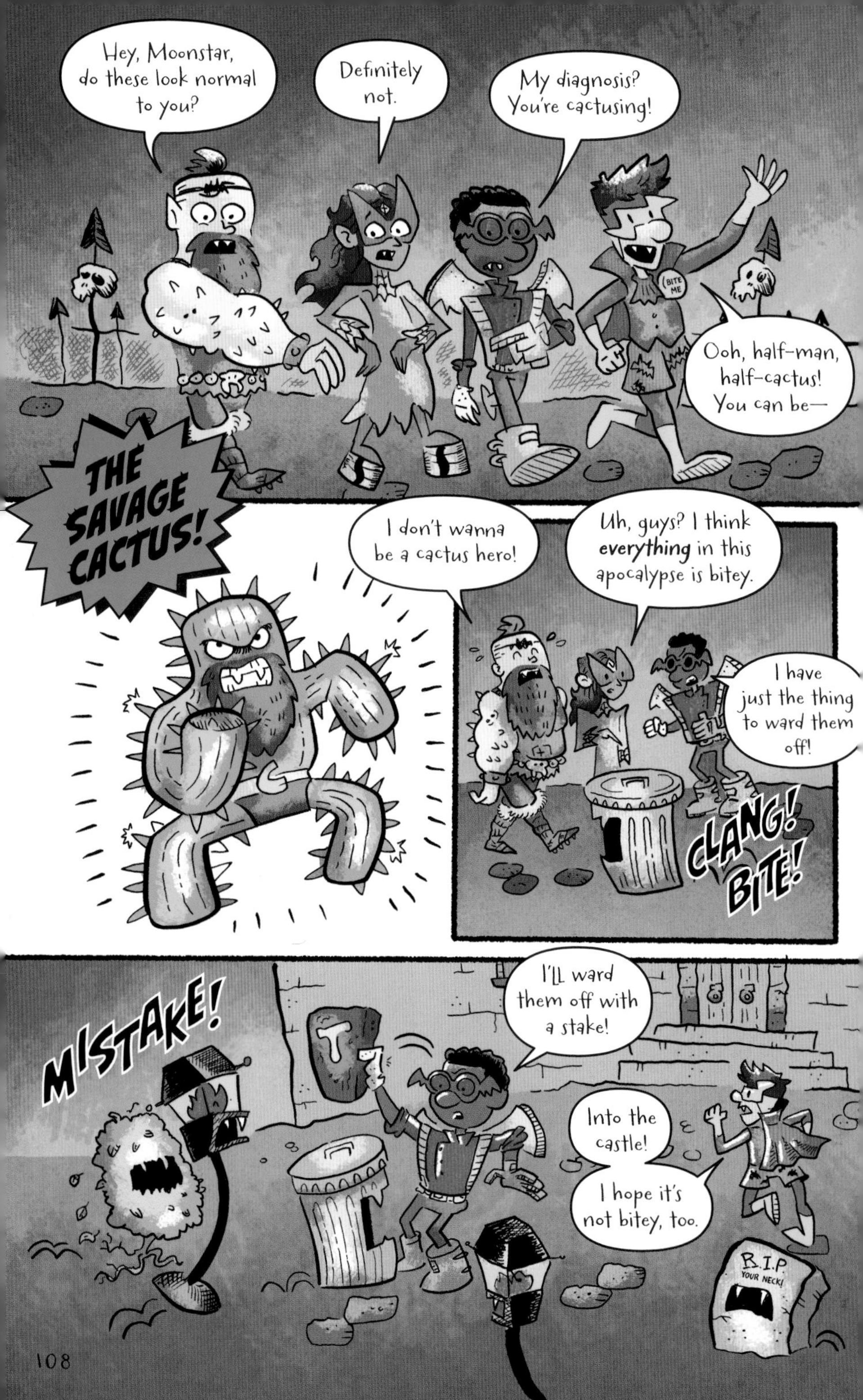
Hey, Moonstar, do these look normal to you?
Definitely not.
My diagnosis? You're cactusing!
BITE ME
Ooh, half-man, half-cactus! You can be—
THE SAVAGE CACTUS!
I don't wanna be a cactus hero!
Uh, guys? I think everything in this apocalypse is bitey.
I have just the thing to ward them off!
CLANG! BITE!
MISTAKE!
I'LL ward them off with a stake!
Into the castle!
I hope it's not bitey, too.
R.I.P. YOUR NECK!

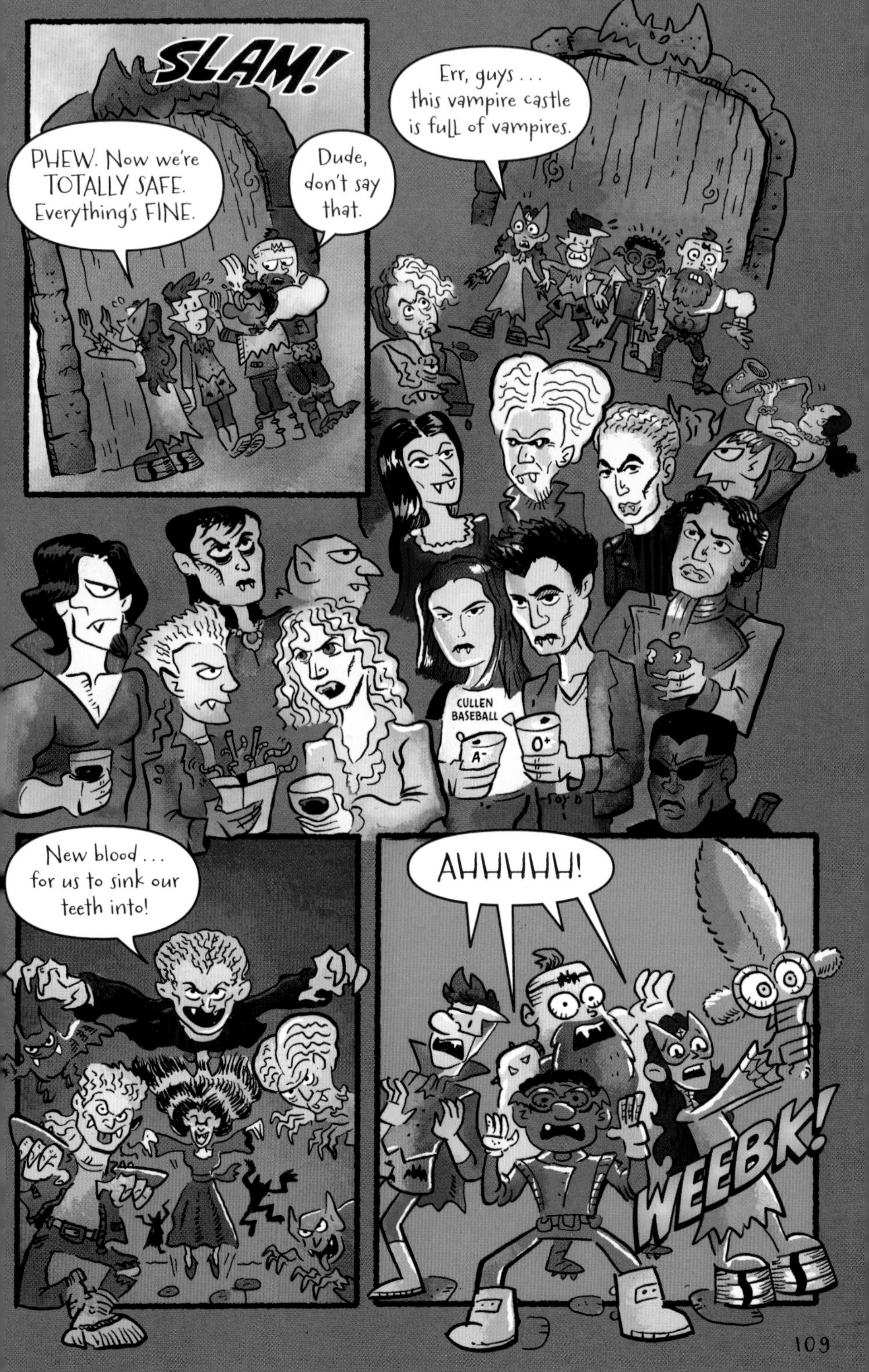
SLAM!
PHEW. Now we're TOTALLY SAFE. Everything's FINE.
Dude, don't say that.
Err, guys . . . this vampire castle is full of vampires.
CULLEN BASEBALL
A-
O+
New blood . . . for us to sink our teeth into!
AHHHHH!
WEEBK!

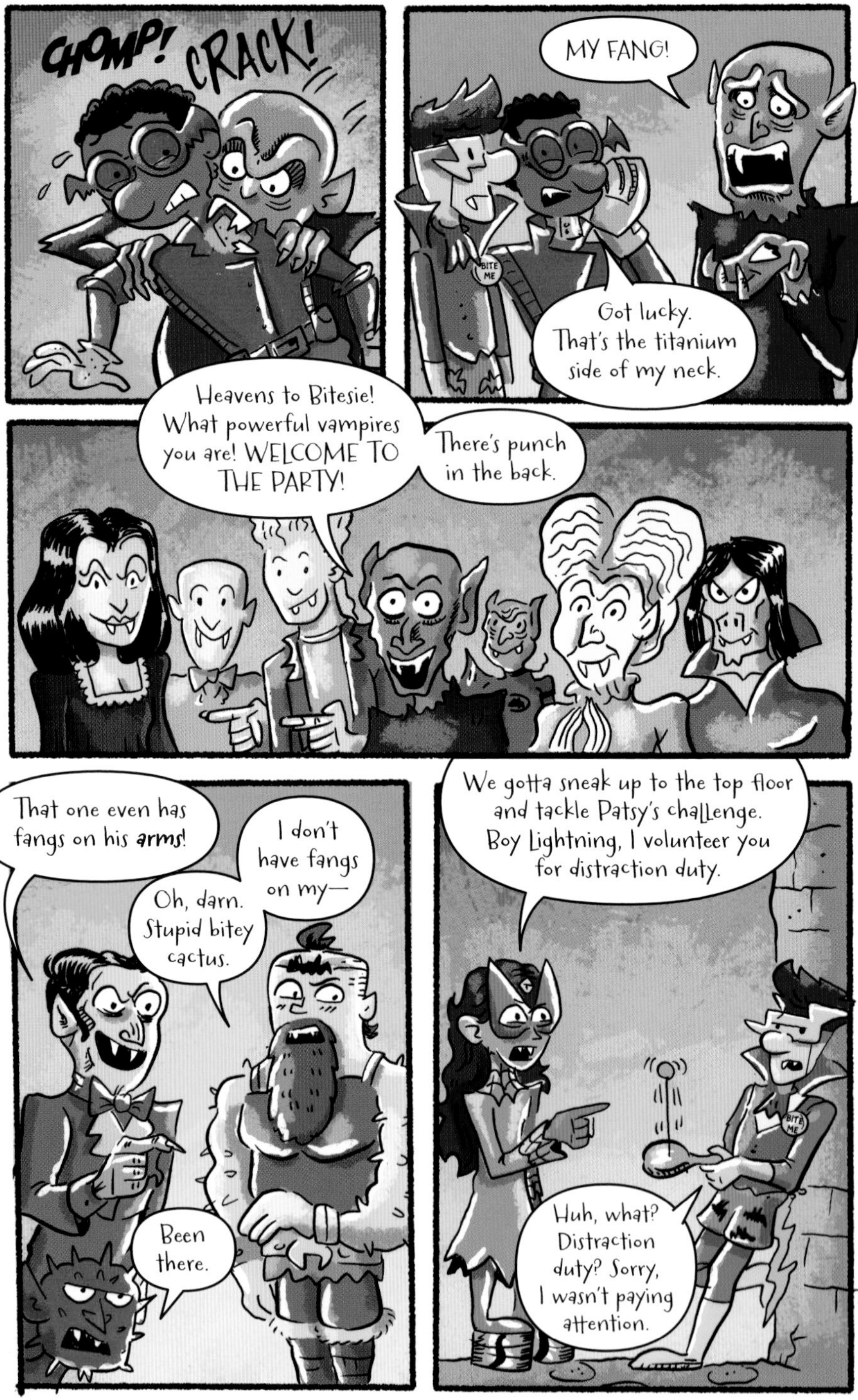
CHOMP! CRACK!
MY FANG!
Got lucky. That's the titanium side of my neck.
Heavens to Bitesie! What powerful vampires you are! WELCOME TO THE PARTY!
There's punch in the back.
That one even has fangs on his **arms**!
I don't have fangs on my—
Oh, darn. Stupid bitey cactus.
Been there.
We gotta sneak up to the top floor and tackle Patsy's challenge. Boy Lightning, I volunteer you for distraction duty.
Huh, what? Distraction duty? Sorry, I wasn't paying attention.
BITE ME

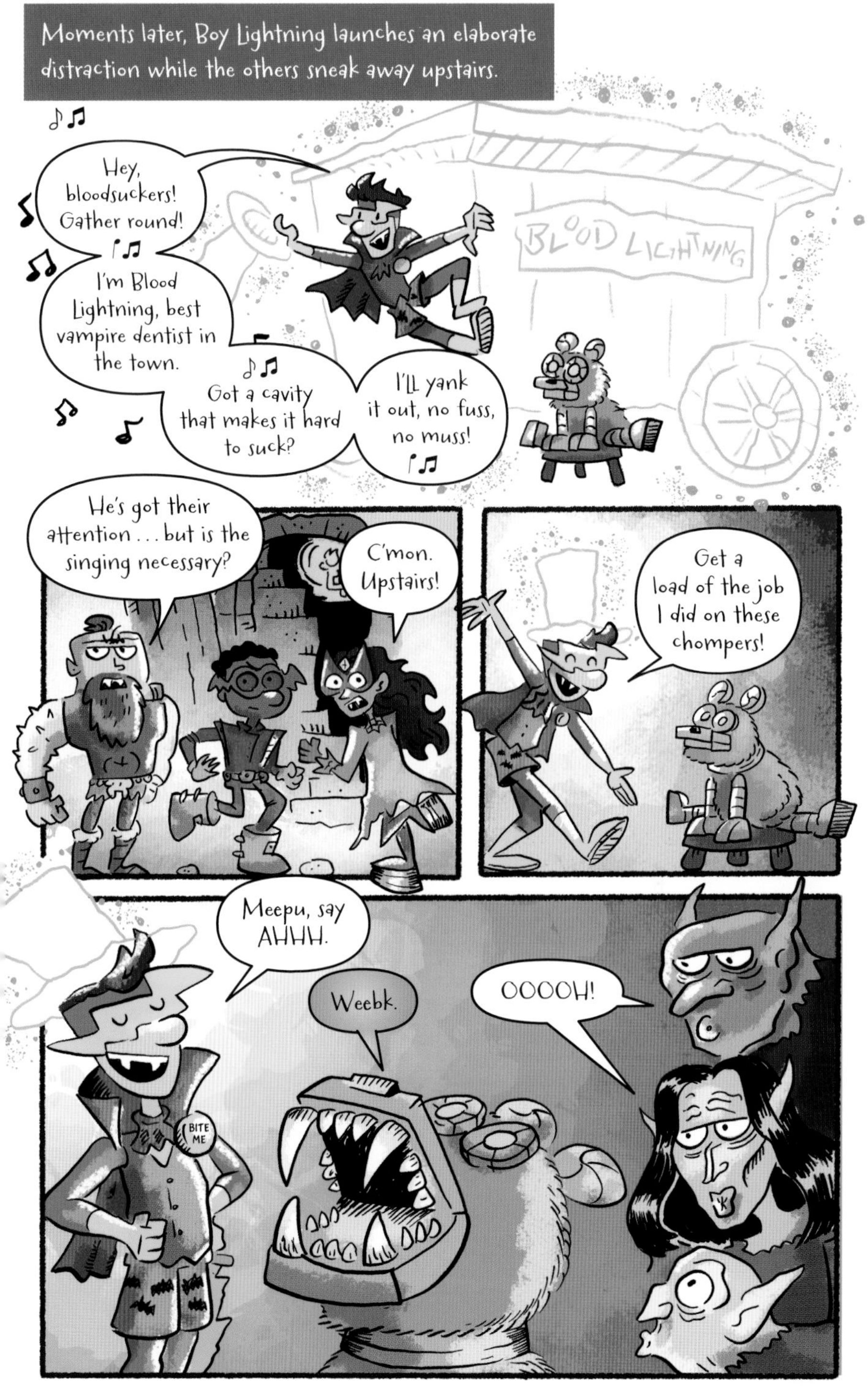
Moments later, Boy Lightning launches an elaborate distraction while the others sneak away upstairs.
Hey, bloodsuckers! Gather round!
I'm Blood Lightning, best vampire dentist in the town.
Got a cavity that makes it hard to suck?
I'LL yank it out, no fuss, no muss!
BLOOD LIGHTNING
He's got their attention . . . but is the singing necessary?
C'mon. Upstairs!
Get a load of the job I did on these chompers!
Meepu, say AHHH.
Weebk.
OOOOH!
BITE ME

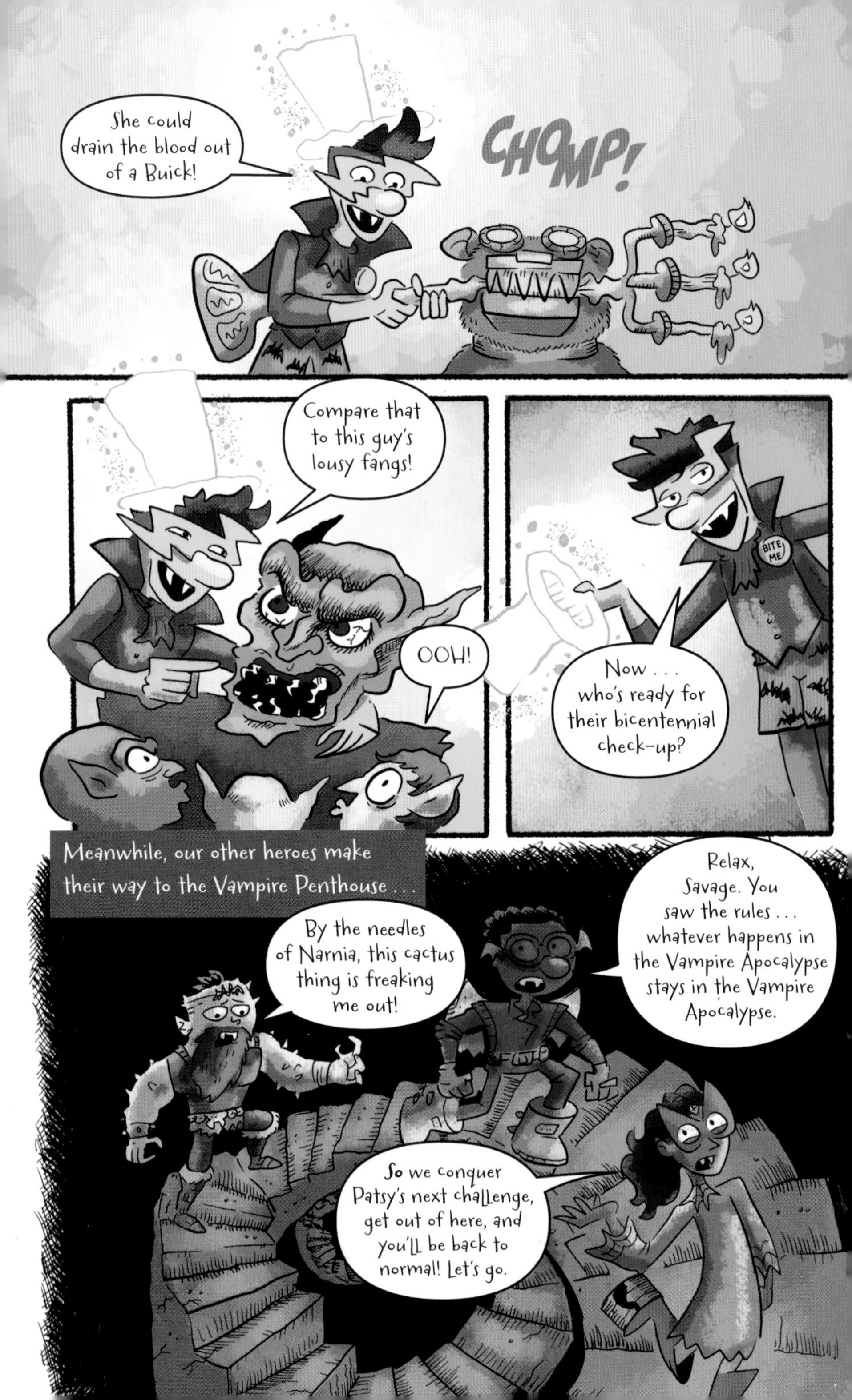
She could drain the blood out of a Buick!
CHOMP!
Compare that to this guy's lousy fangs!
OOH!
Now . . . who's ready for their bicentennial check-up?
BITE ME
Meanwhile, our other heroes make their way to the Vampire Penthouse . . .
By the needles of Narnia, this cactus thing is freaking me out!
Relax, Savage. You saw the rules . . . whatever happens in the Vampire Apocalypse stays in the Vampire Apocalypse.
So we conquer Patsy's next challenge, get out of here, and you'll be back to normal! Let's go.

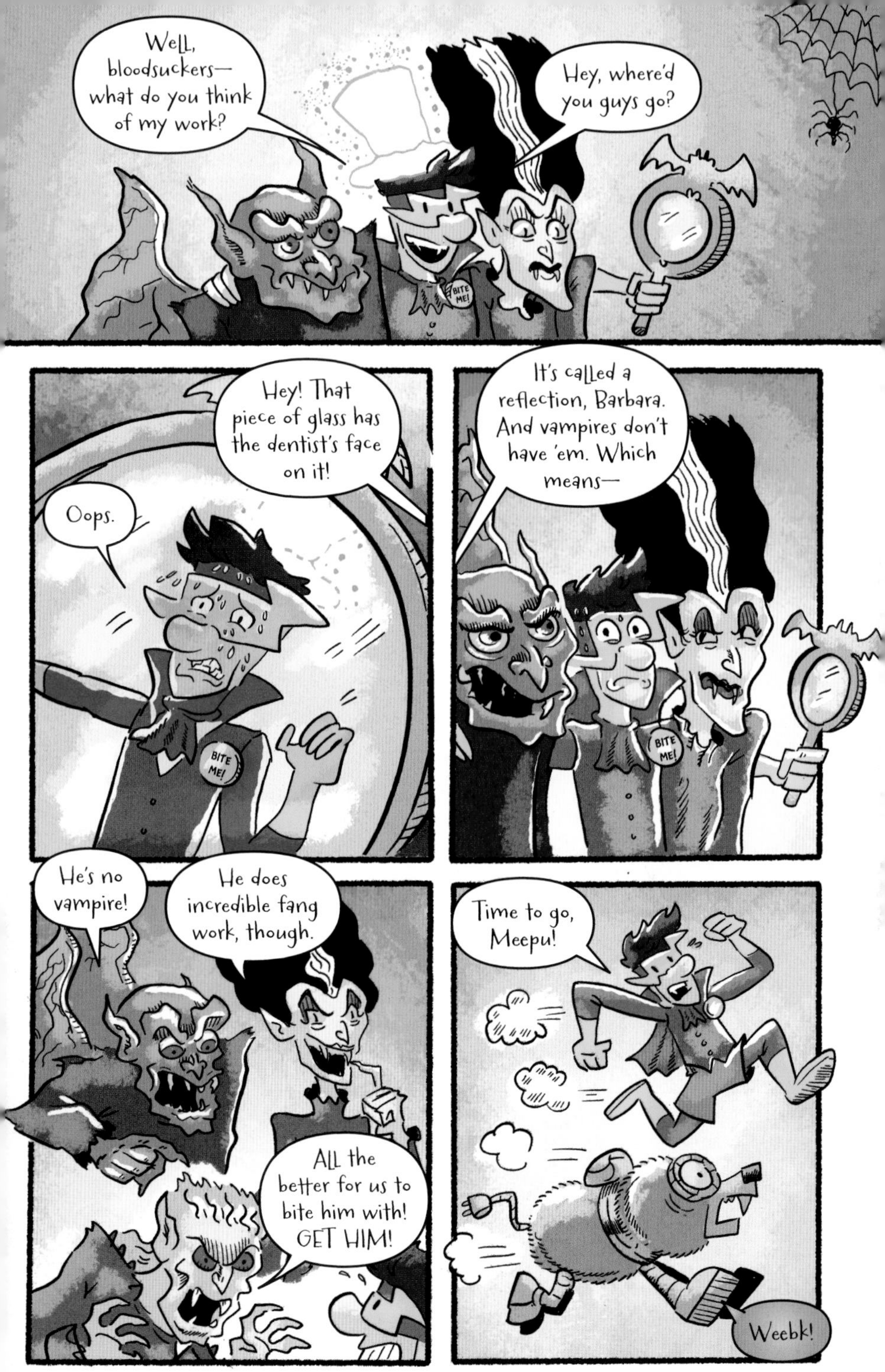
Well, bloodsuckers—what do you think of my work?
Hey, where'd you guys go?
BITE ME!
Hey! That piece of glass has the dentist's face on it!
Oops.
BITE ME!
It's called a reflection, Barbara. And vampires don't have 'em. Which means—
BITE ME!
He's no vampire!
He does incredible fang work, though.
All the better for us to bite him with! GET HIM!
Time to go, Meepu!
Weebk!

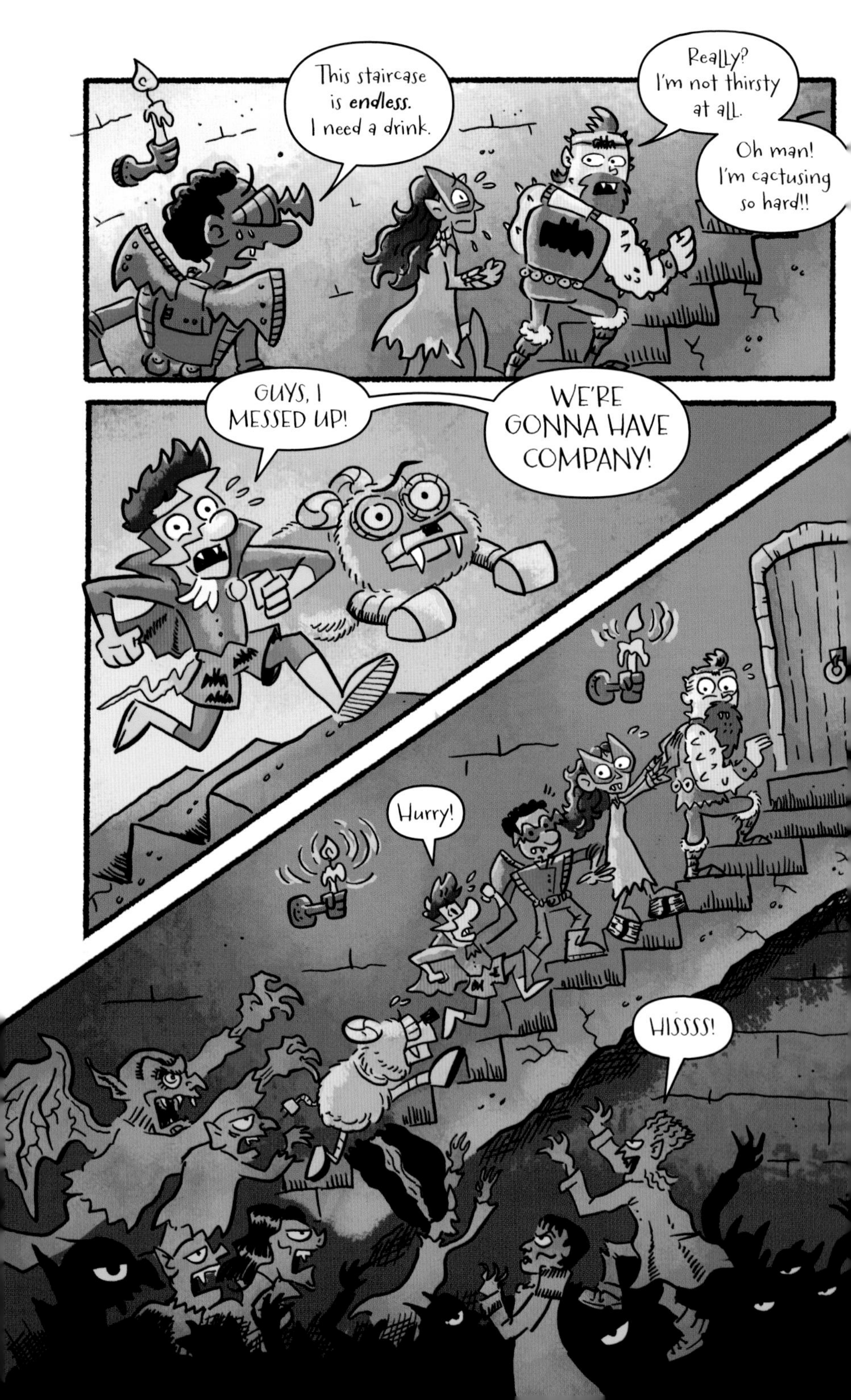
This staircase is **endless.** I need a drink.
Really? I'm not thirsty at all.
Oh man! I'm cactusing so hard!!
GUYS, I MESSED UP!
WE'RE GONNA HAVE COMPANY!
Hurry!
HISSSS!

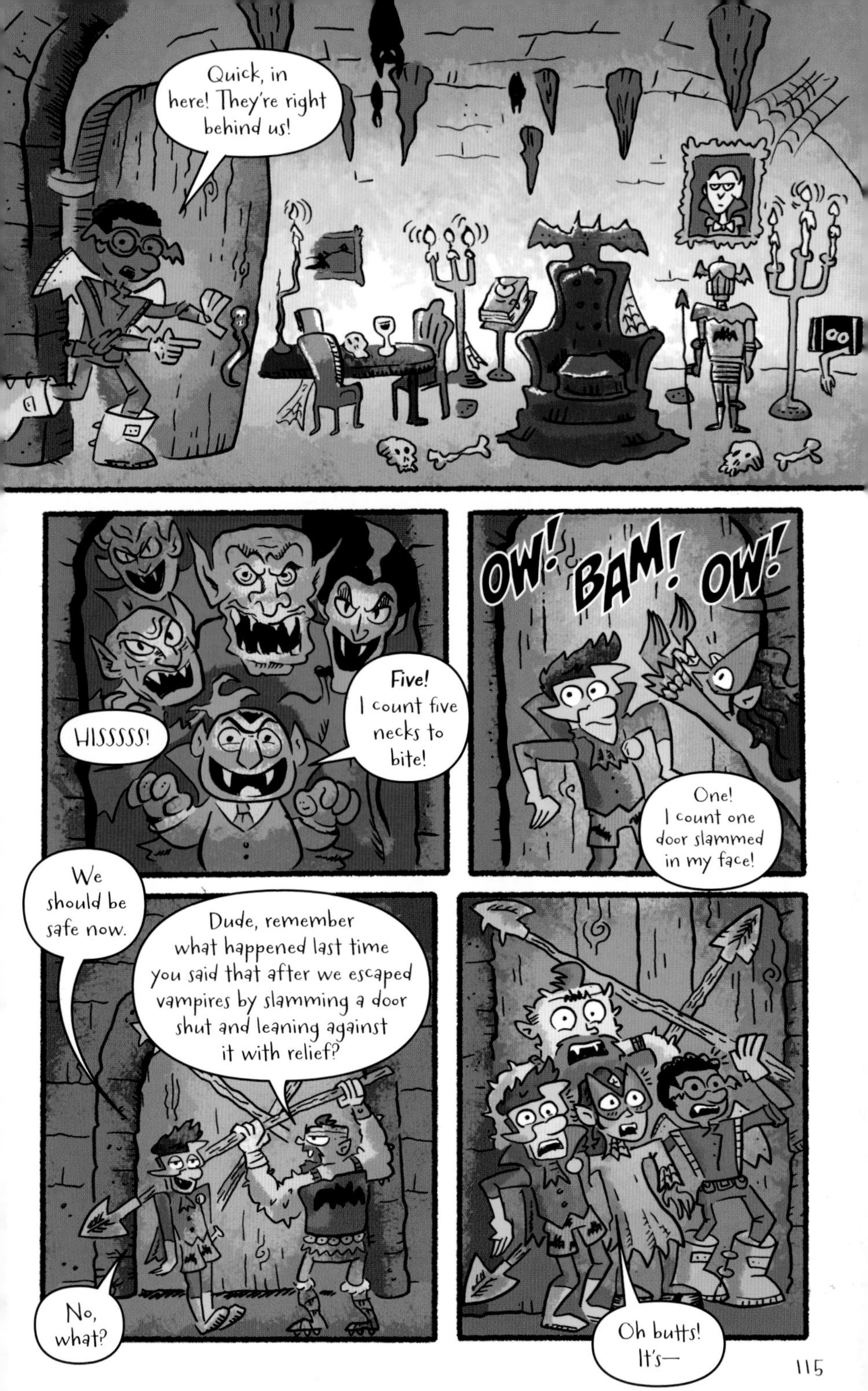
Quick, in here! They're right behind us!
HISSSSS!
Five! I count five necks to bite!
OW! BAM! OW!
One! I count one door slammed in my face!
We should be safe now.
Dude, remember what happened last time you said that after we escaped vampires by slamming a door shut and leaning against it with relief?
No, what?
Oh butts! It's—

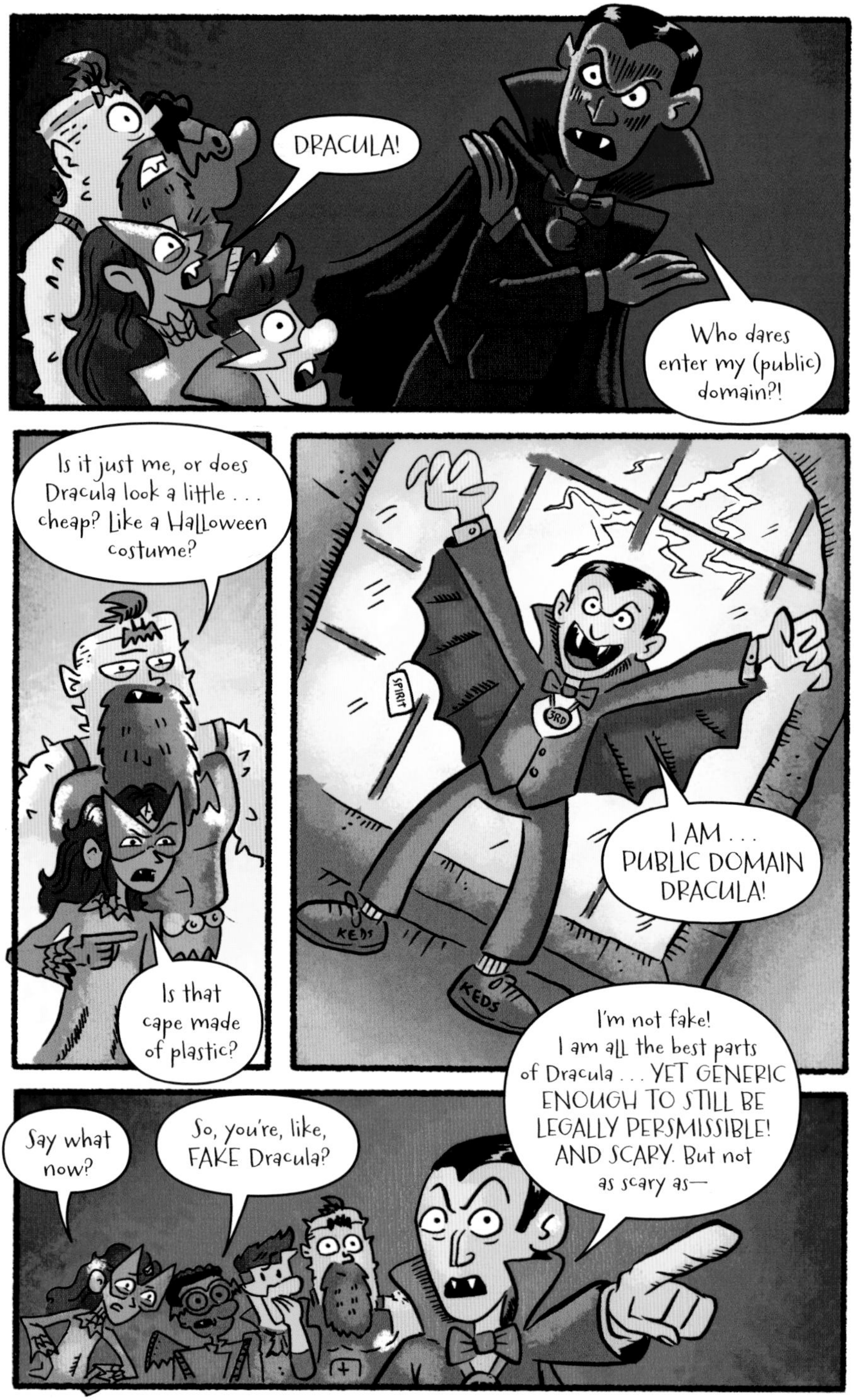
DRACULA!
Who dares enter my (public) domain?!
Is it just me, or does Dracula look a little . . . cheap? Like a Halloween costume?
Is that cape made of plastic?
SPIRIT
3RD
KEDS
KEDS
I AM . . . PUBLIC DOMAIN DRACULA!
Say what now?
So, you're, like, FAKE Dracula?
I'm not fake! I am all the best parts of Dracula . . . YET GENERIC ENOUGH TO STILL BE LEGALLY PERSMISSIBLE! AND SCARY. But not as scary as—

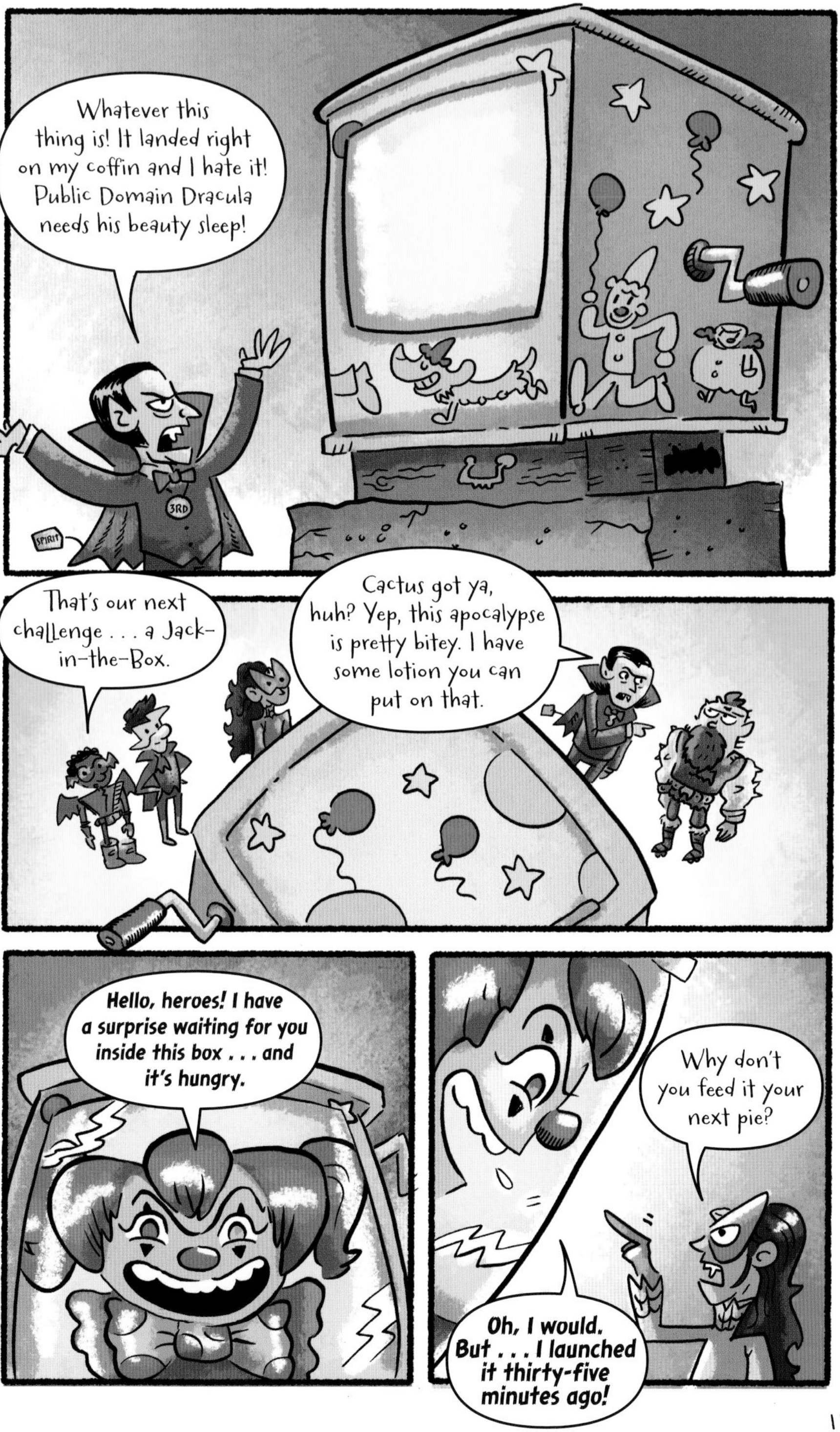
Whatever this thing is! It landed right on my coffin and I hate it! Public Domain Dracula needs his beauty sleep!
3RD
SPIRIT
That's our next challenge . . . a Jack-in-the-Box.
Cactus got ya, huh? Yep, this apocalypse is pretty bitey. I have some lotion you can put on that.
Hello, heroes! I have a surprise waiting for you inside this box . . . and it's hungry.
Why don't you feed it your next pie?
Oh, I would. But . . . I launched it thirty-five minutes ago!

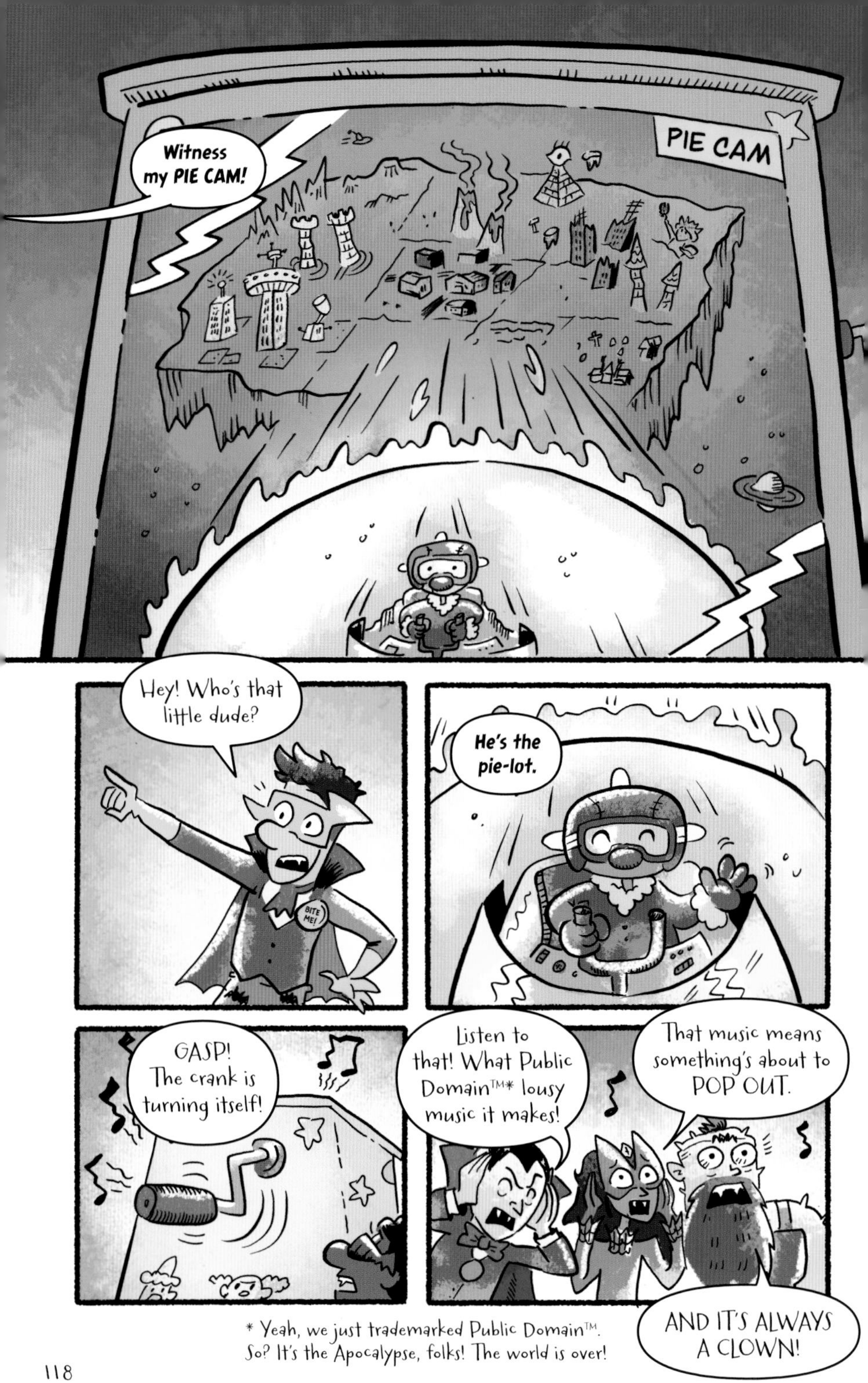
Witness my PIE CAM!
PIE CAM
Hey! Who's that little dude?
BITE ME!
He's the pie-lot.
GASP! The crank is turning itself!
Listen to that! What Public Domain™* lousy music it makes!
That music means something's about to POP OUT.
AND IT'S ALWAYS A CLOWN!

* Yeah, we just trademarked Public Domain™. So? It's the Apocalypse, folks! The world is over!

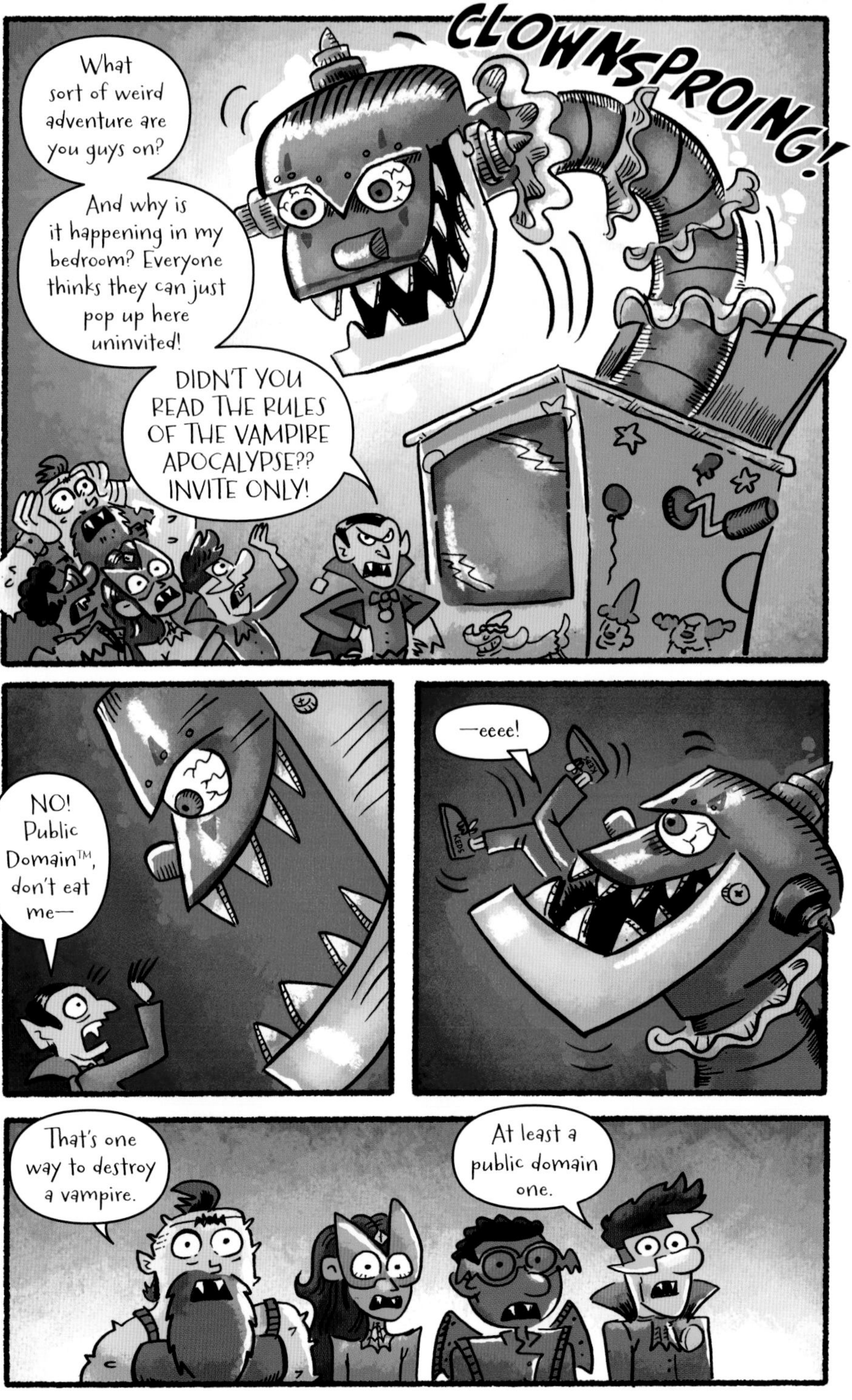
CLOWNSPROING!
What sort of weird adventure are you guys on?
And why is it happening in my bedroom? Everyone thinks they can just pop up here uninvited!
DIDN'T YOU READ THE RULES OF THE VAMPIRE APOCALYPSE?? INVITE ONLY!
NO! Public Domain™, don't eat me—
—eeee!
KEDS
That's one way to destroy a vampire.
At least a public domain one.

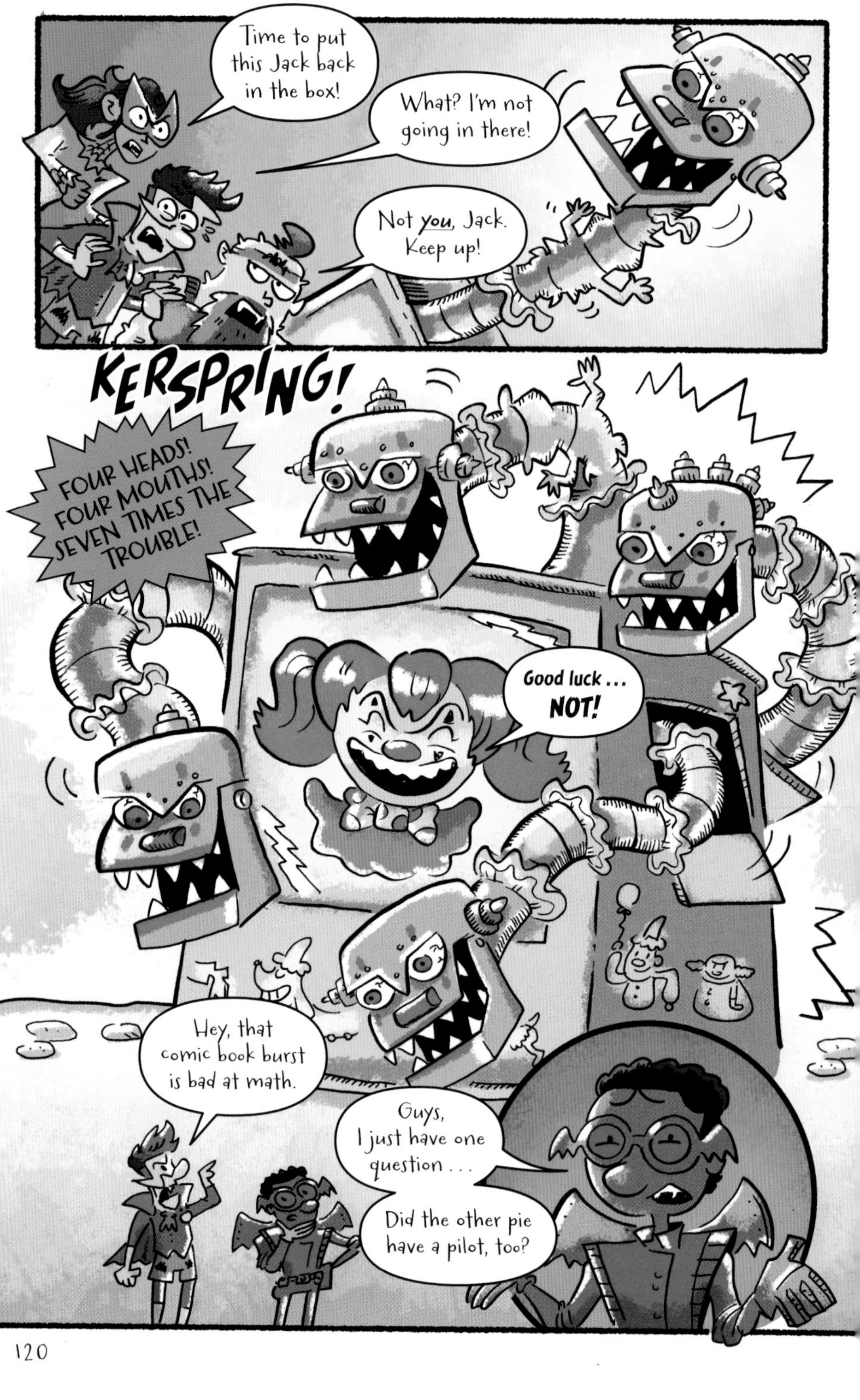
Time to put this Jack back in the box!
What? I'm not going in there!
Not you, Jack. Keep up!
KERSPRING!
FOUR HEADS! FOUR MOUTHS! SEVEN TIMES THE TROUBLE!
Good luck . . . NOT!
Hey, that comic book burst is bad at math.
Guys, I just have one question . . .
Did the other pie have a pilot, too?

ARE YOU GOING BATTY TRYING TO CHOOSE A HALLOWEEN COSTUME?

YOUR WORRIES ARE OVER! VAMP IT UP FOR A . . . BLOODCURDLING HALLOWEEN!

HALLOWEEN'S MOST VICIOUS DRIP!

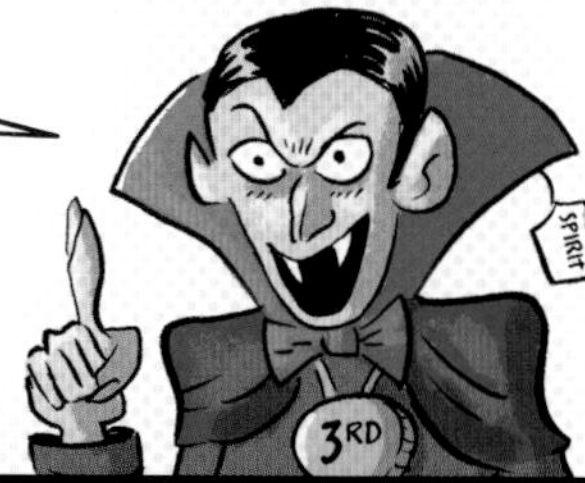
This Halloween, candy isn't the only thing I'll be sinking my teeth into!
I'm talking about human necks. I'll be sinking my teeth into human necks. 'Cause I'm a vampire. Was that clear?
SPIRIT
3RD

Don't let Public Domain™ Dracula's fangs be the only thing looking sharp this Halloween!

CUT TO THE FRONT OF THE CANDY LINE WITH THESE FANG-TASTIC COSTUMES!

DRAC BAKER: THE VLAD SCIENTIST!

-Bat wings! (48 D batteries required, not included)
-Bat glasses!

MOONSTAR, THE MOONLIGHT HUNTER!

-Cobweb neck thing!
-Are they gross fingernails or rad claws? Who knows!
-Flowing dress made of pure spider silk . . . and a whole lot of polyester!

BOY FRIGHTNING!

-Shorts!
-Pin!
-Fangs!

VAMPIRE CACTUS GUY!

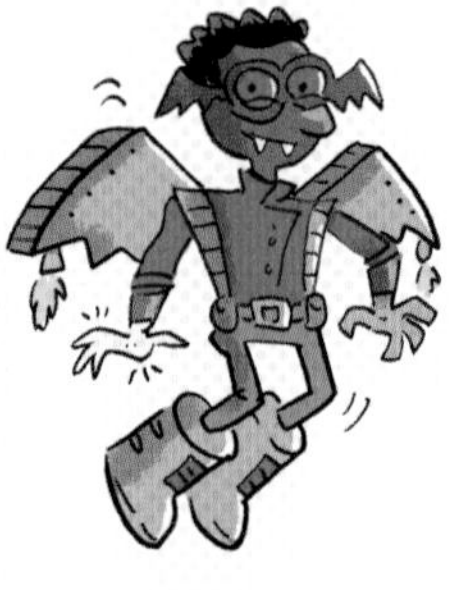

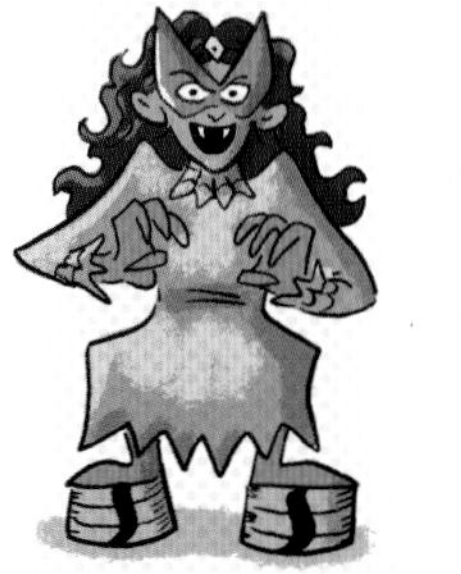

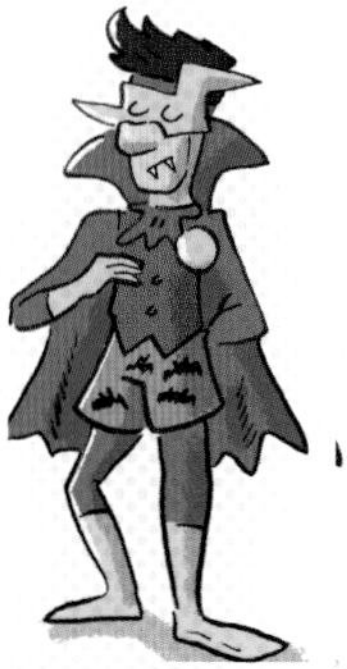

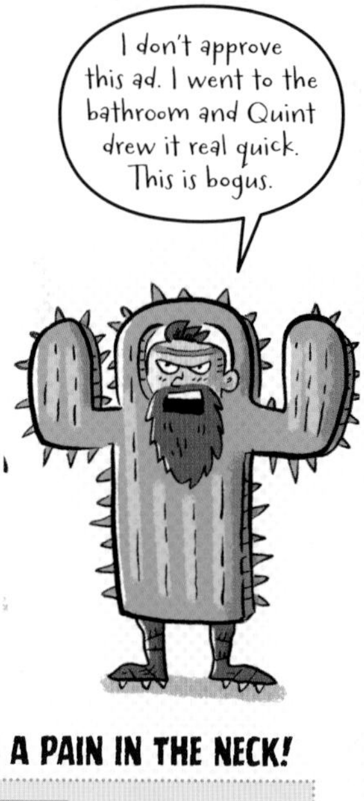
I don't approve this ad. I went to the bathroom and Quint drew it real quick. This is bogus.

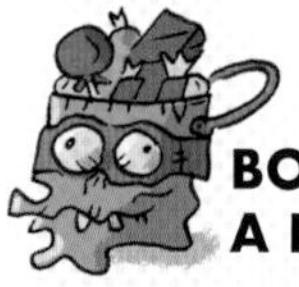

BONUS! ORDER NOW AND GET A FREE Z-MAN HEAD CANDY BAG!

YES, I THINK MAKING HALLOWEEN COSTUMES AT HOME IS A PAIN IN THE NECK!

This now becomes a test. Can you resist?
(Do you have the willpower to NOT mark and cut this page up? How will you even read the comic panel on the next page if you do? Think about it . . .)

Name: ____________ Day: ____________

Saddest moment: ________ Fave game: ____________

Item	Quantity	Price
SUBTOTAL:		
BOO TOTAL:		

MAIL TO:
Quint Baker
Tree house next to Joe's Pizza
Apocalyptia, USA

CHAPTER NINE

WRATH OF THE FOUR-HEADED BOX CLOWN

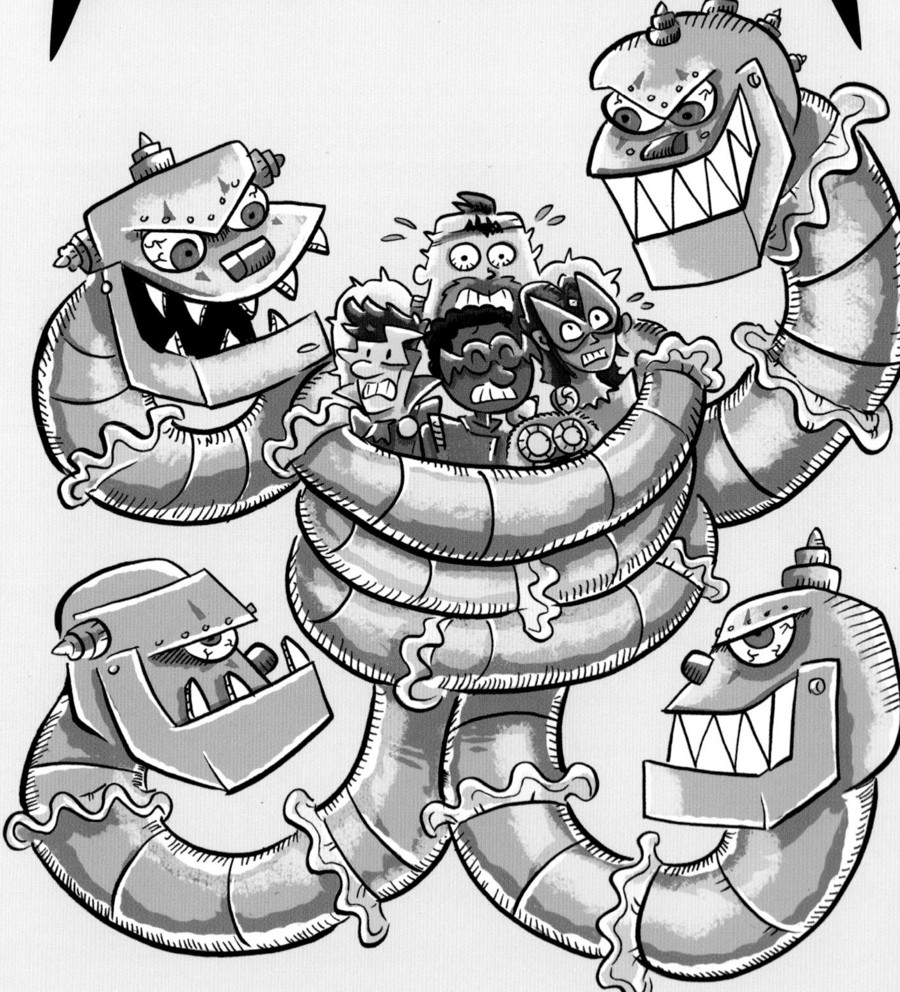

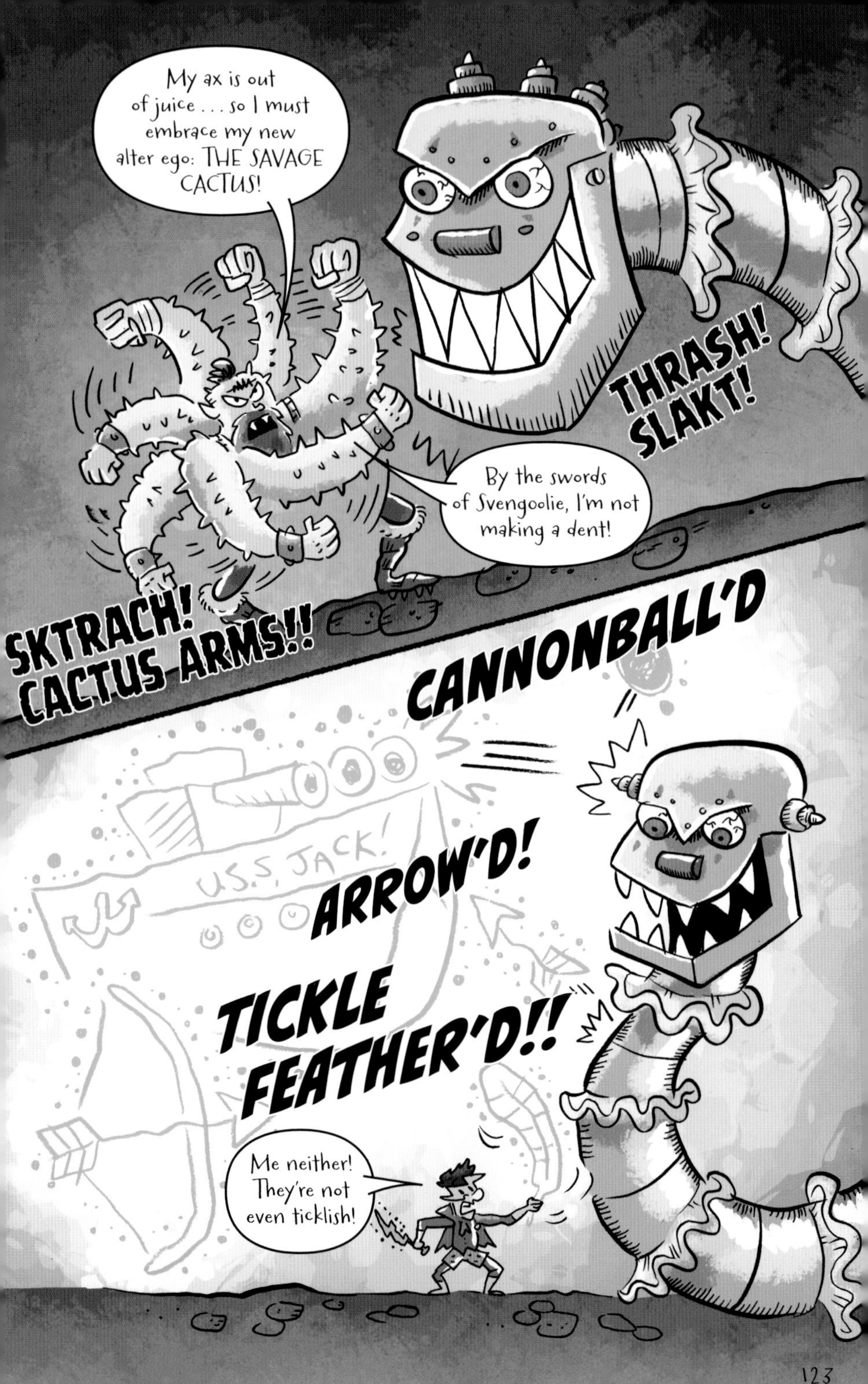
My ax is out of juice . . . so I must embrace my new alter ego: THE SAVAGE CACTUS!
THRASH! SLAKT!
By the swords of Svengoolie, I'm not making a dent!
SKTRACH! CACTUS ARMS!!
CANNONBALL'D
U.S.S. JACK!
ARROW'D!
TICKLE FEATHER'D!!
Me neither! They're not even ticklish!

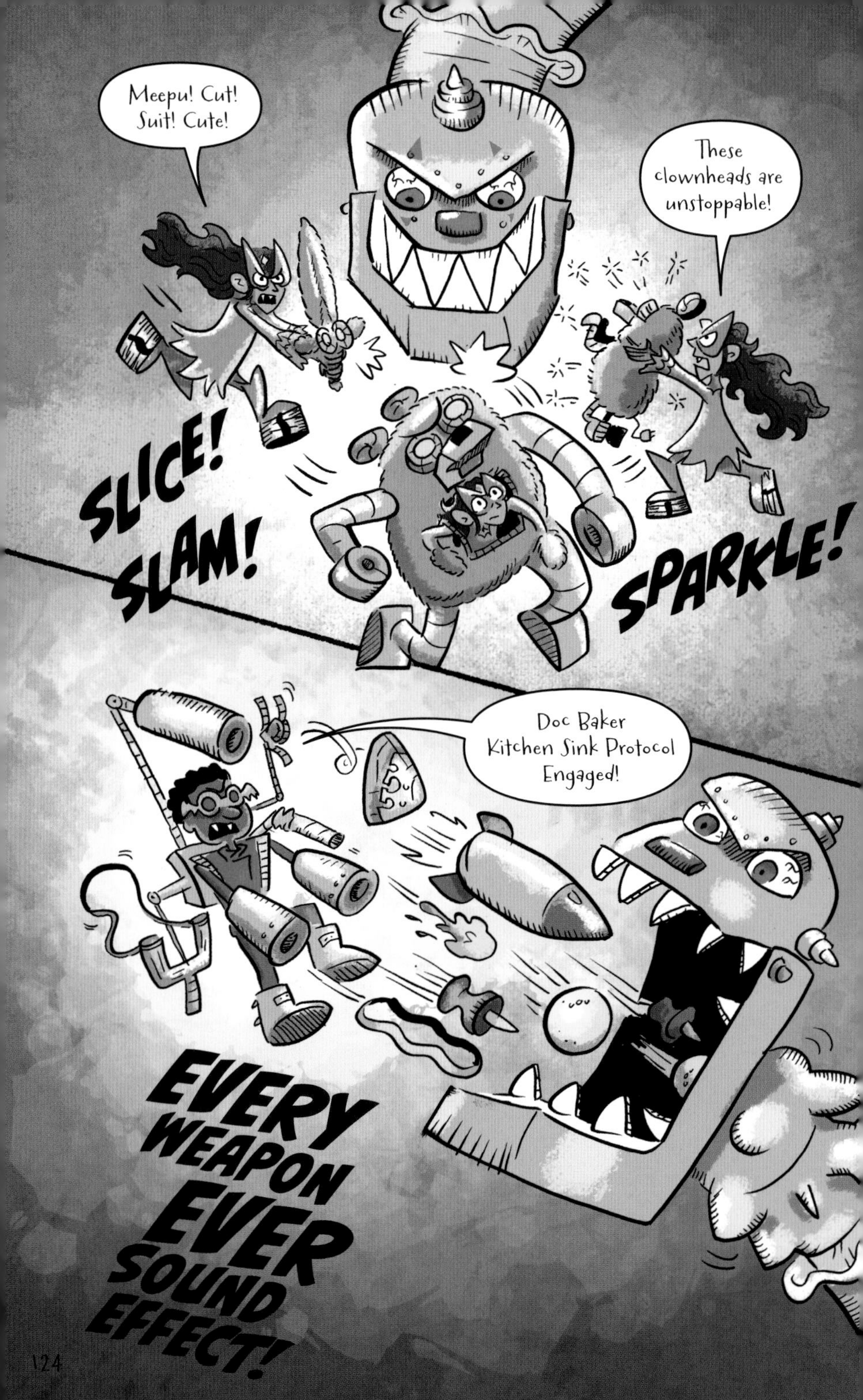

Meepu! Cut! Suit! Cute!
These clownheads are unstoppable!
SLICE!
SLAM!
SPARKLE!
Doc Baker Kitchen Sink Protocol Engaged!
EVERY WEAPON EVER SOUND EFFECT!

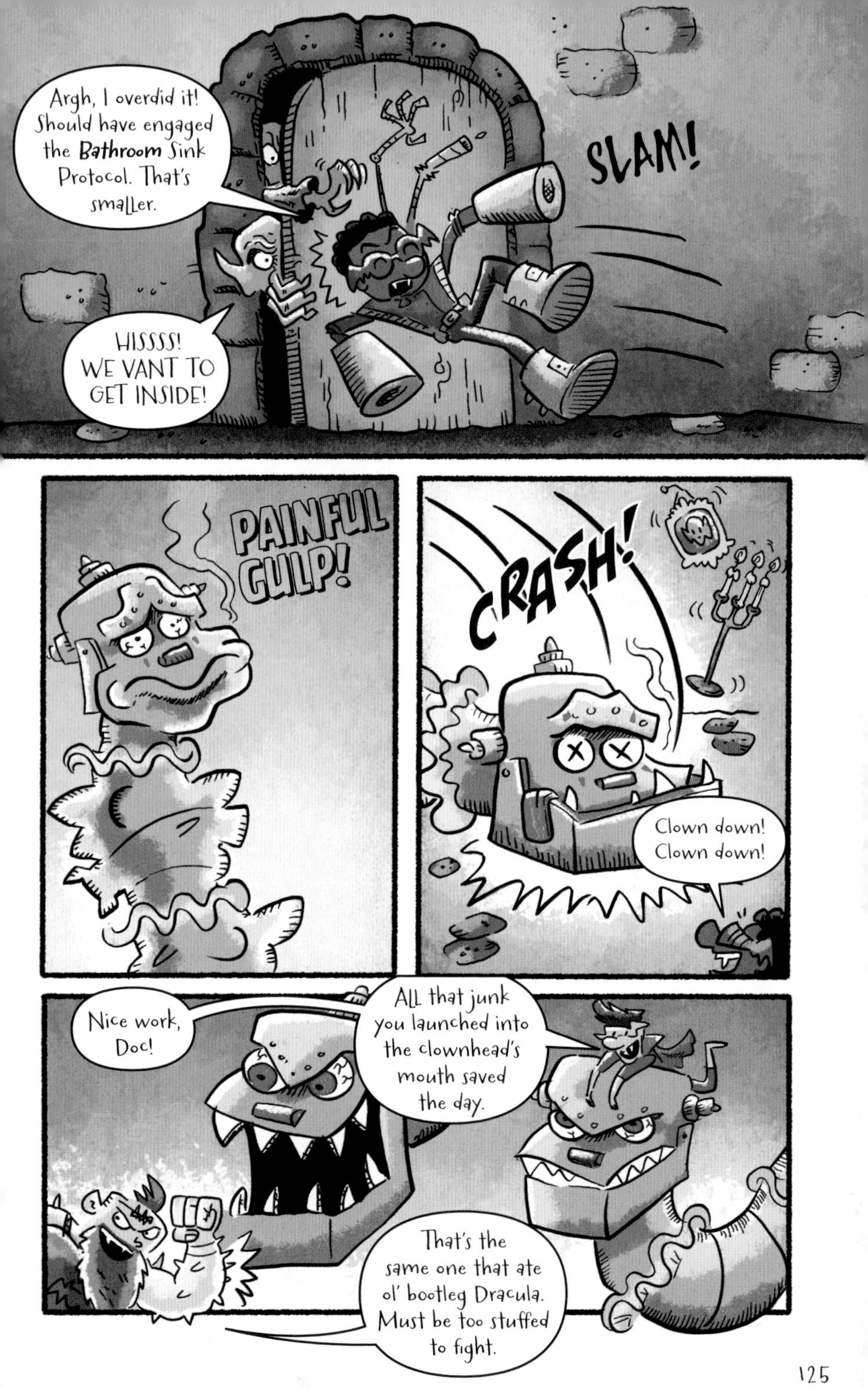
Argh, I overdid it! Should have engaged the **Bathroom** Sink Protocol. That's smaller.
SLAM!
HISSSS! WE VANT TO GET INSIDE!
PAINFUL GULP!
CRASH!
Clown down! Clown down!
Nice work, Doc!
ALL that junk you launched into the clownhead's mouth saved the day.
That's the same one that ate ol' bootleg Dracula. Must be too stuffed to fight.

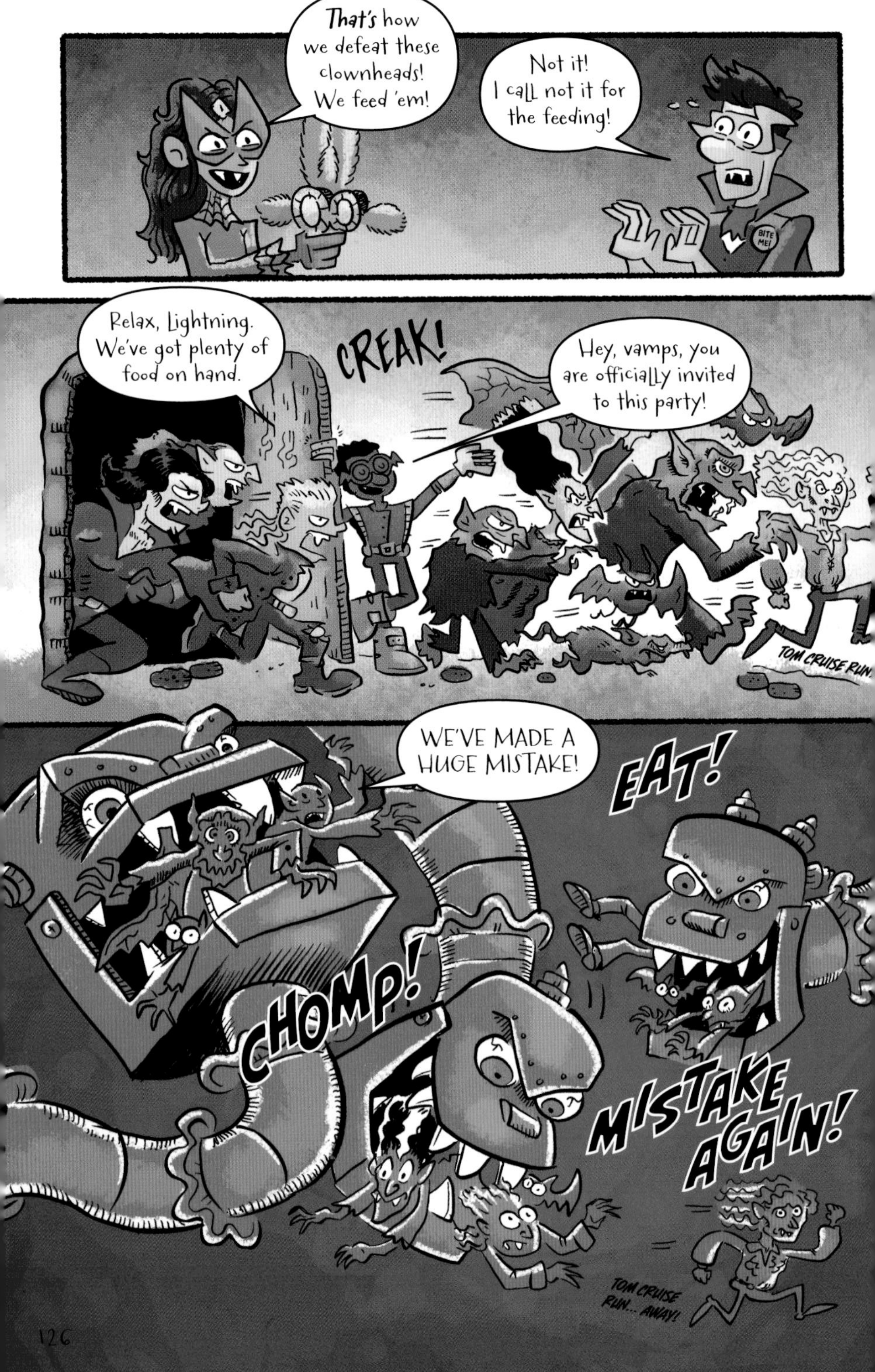
That's how we defeat these clownheads! We feed 'em!
Not it! I call not it for the feeding!
BITE ME!
Relax, Lightning. We've got plenty of food on hand.
CREAK!
Hey, vamps, you are officially invited to this party!
TOM CRUISE RUN
WE'VE MADE A HUGE MISTAKE!
EAT!
CHOMP!
MISTAKE AGAIN!
TOM CRUISE RUN... AWAY!

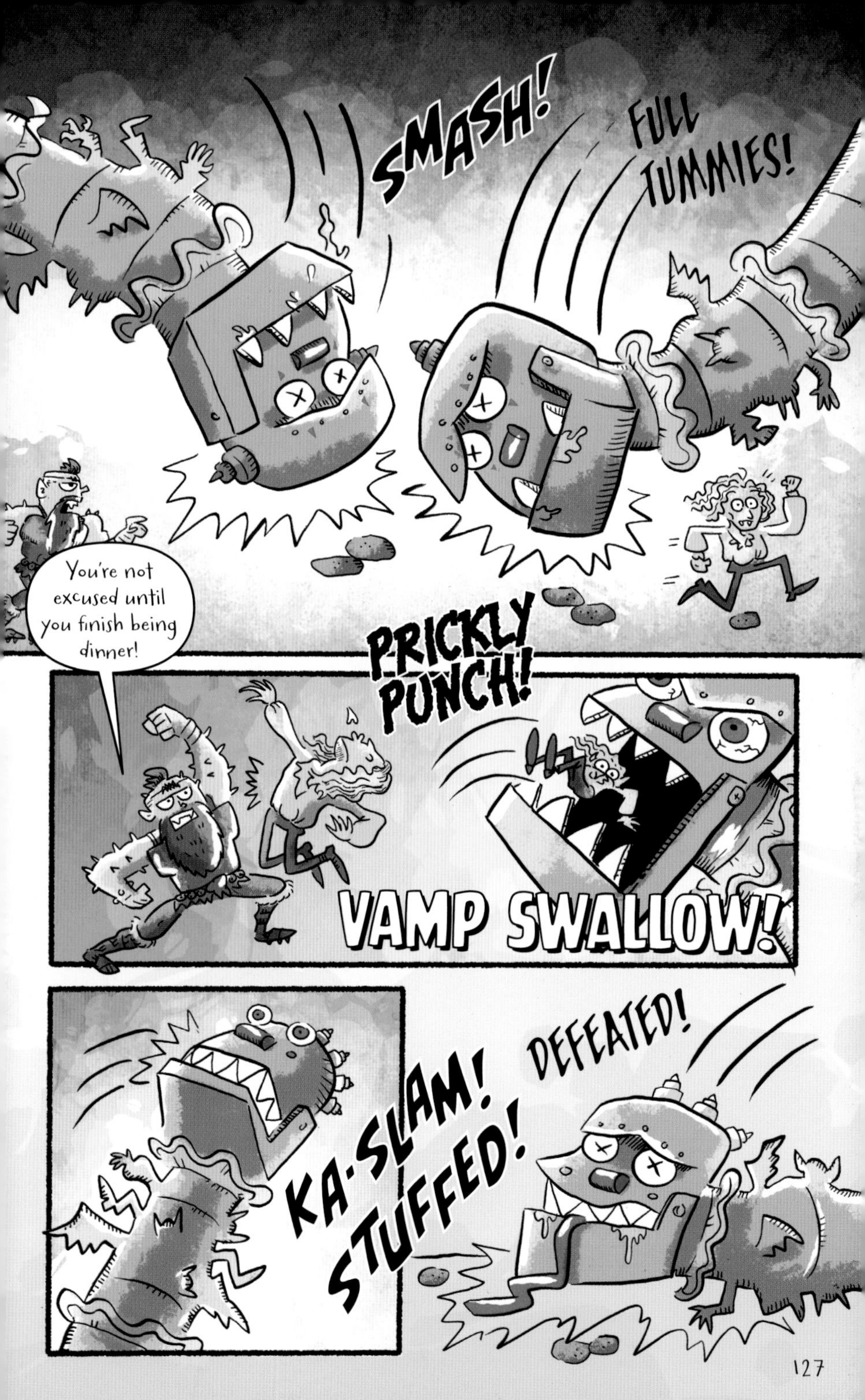
SMASH!
FULL TUMMIES!
You're not excused until you finish being dinner!
PRICKLY PUNCH!
VAMP SWALLOW!
KA-SLAM!
STUFFED!
DEFEATED!

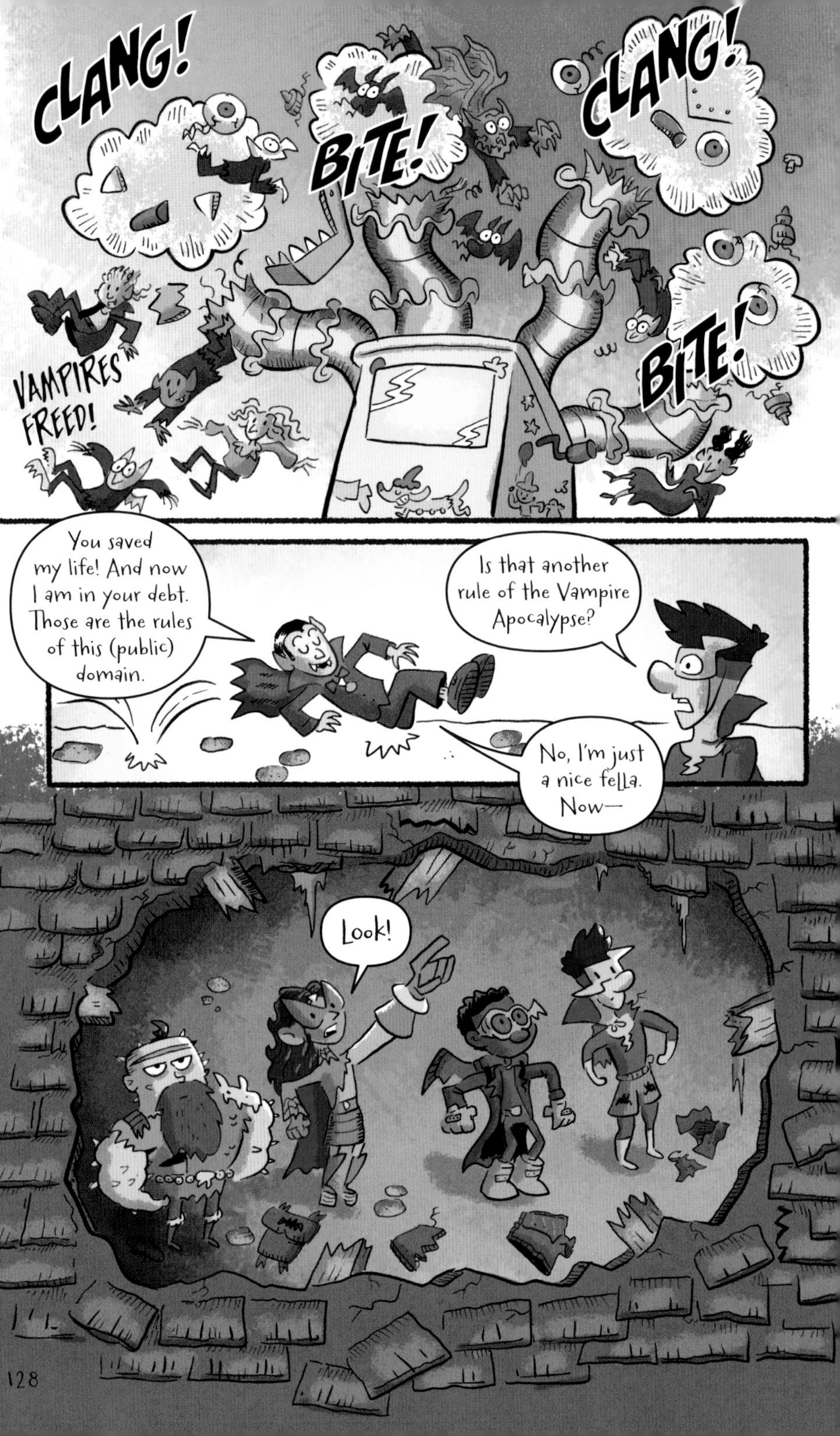
CLANG!
BITE!
CLANG!
VAMPIRES FREED!
BITE!
You saved my life! And now I am in your debt. Those are the rules of this (public) domain.
Is that another rule of the Vampire Apocalypse?
No, I'm just a nice fella. Now—
Look!

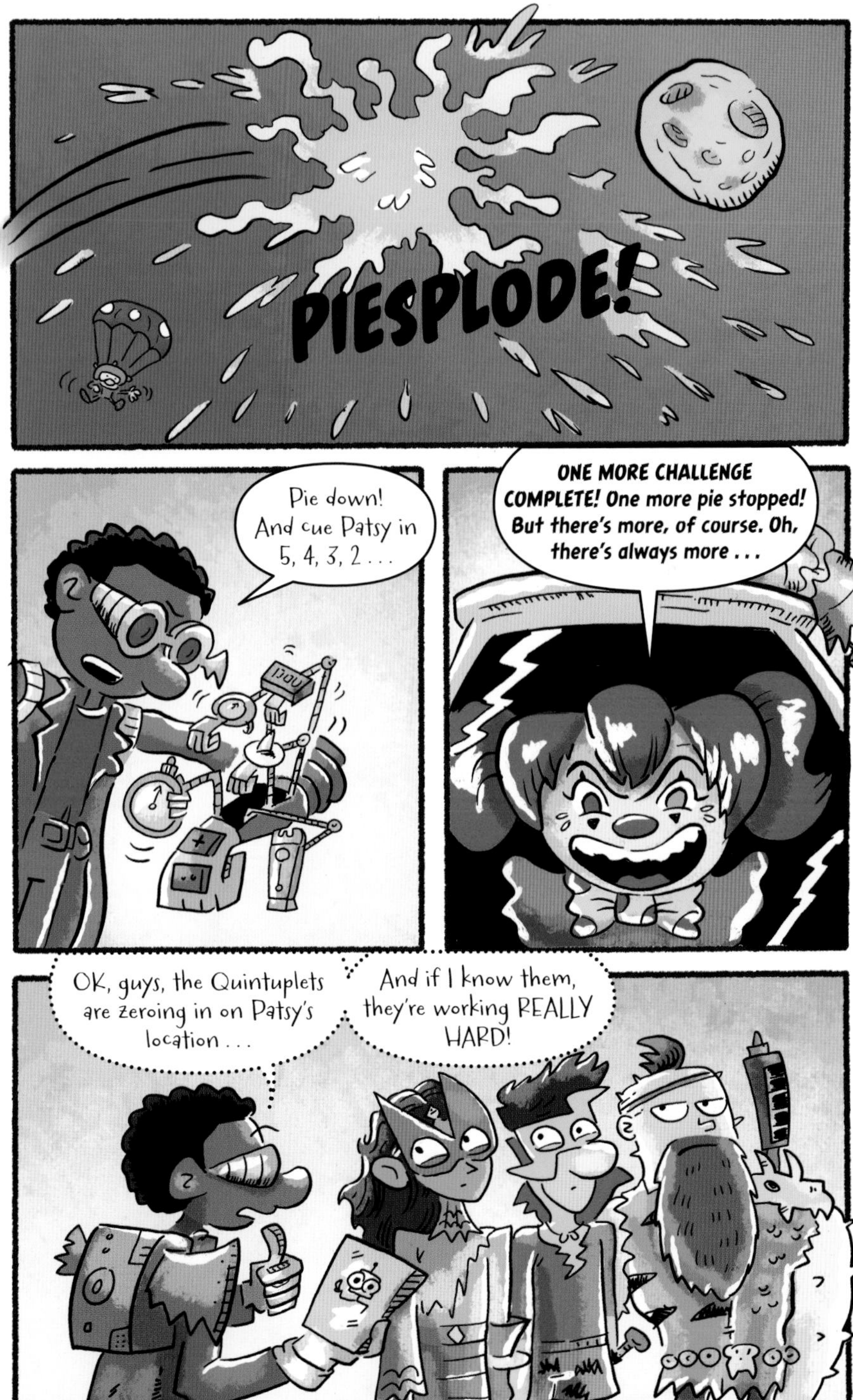
PIESPLODE!
Pie down! And cue Patsy in 5, 4, 3, 2 . . .
IOU
ONE MORE CHALLENGE COMPLETE! One more pie stopped! But there's more, of course. Oh, there's always more . . .
OK, guys, the Quintuplets are zeroing in on Patsy's location . . .
And if I know them, they're working REALLY HARD!

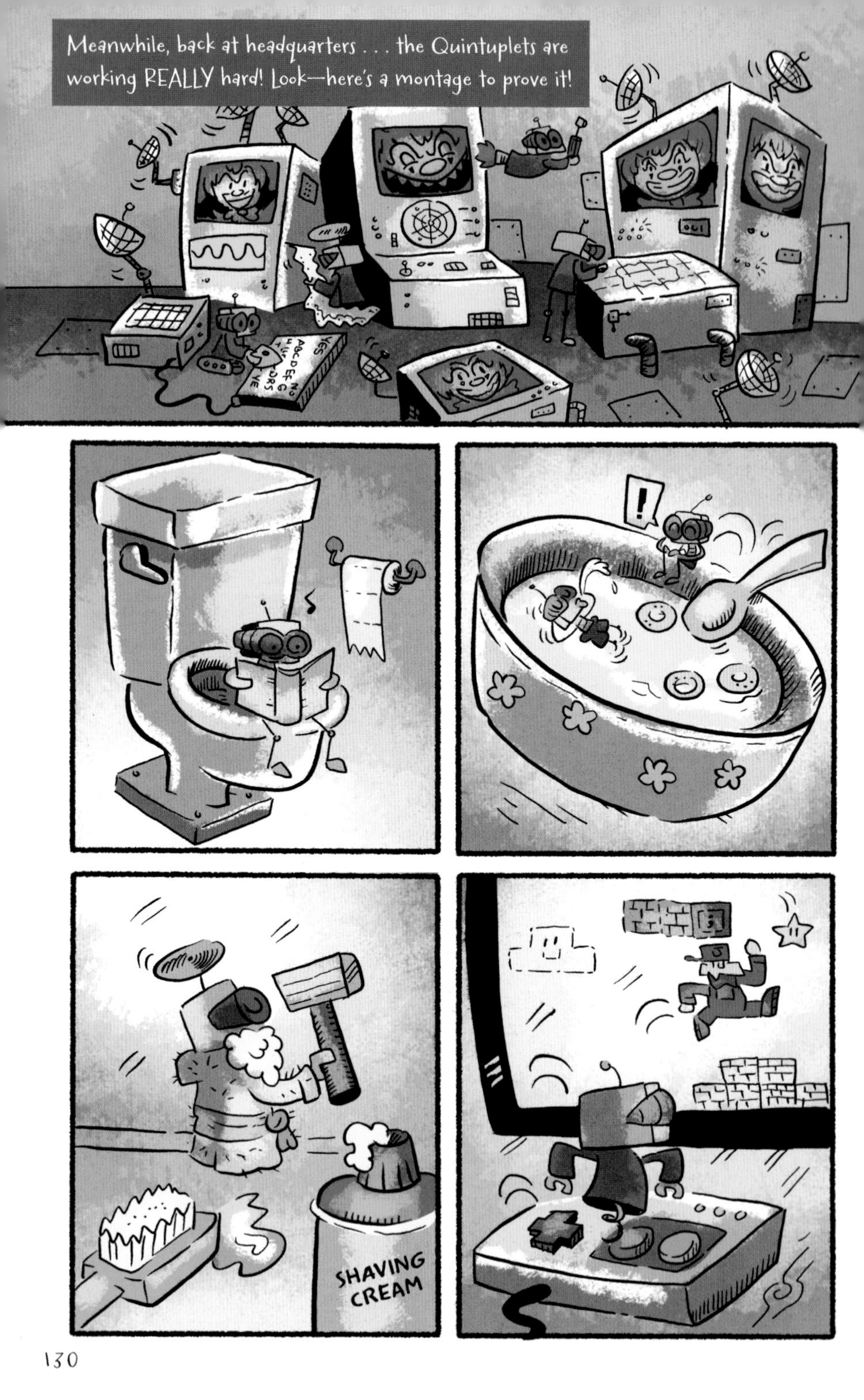
Meanwhile, back at headquarters . . . the Quintuplets are working REALLY hard! Look—here's a montage to prove it!
!
SHAVING CREAM

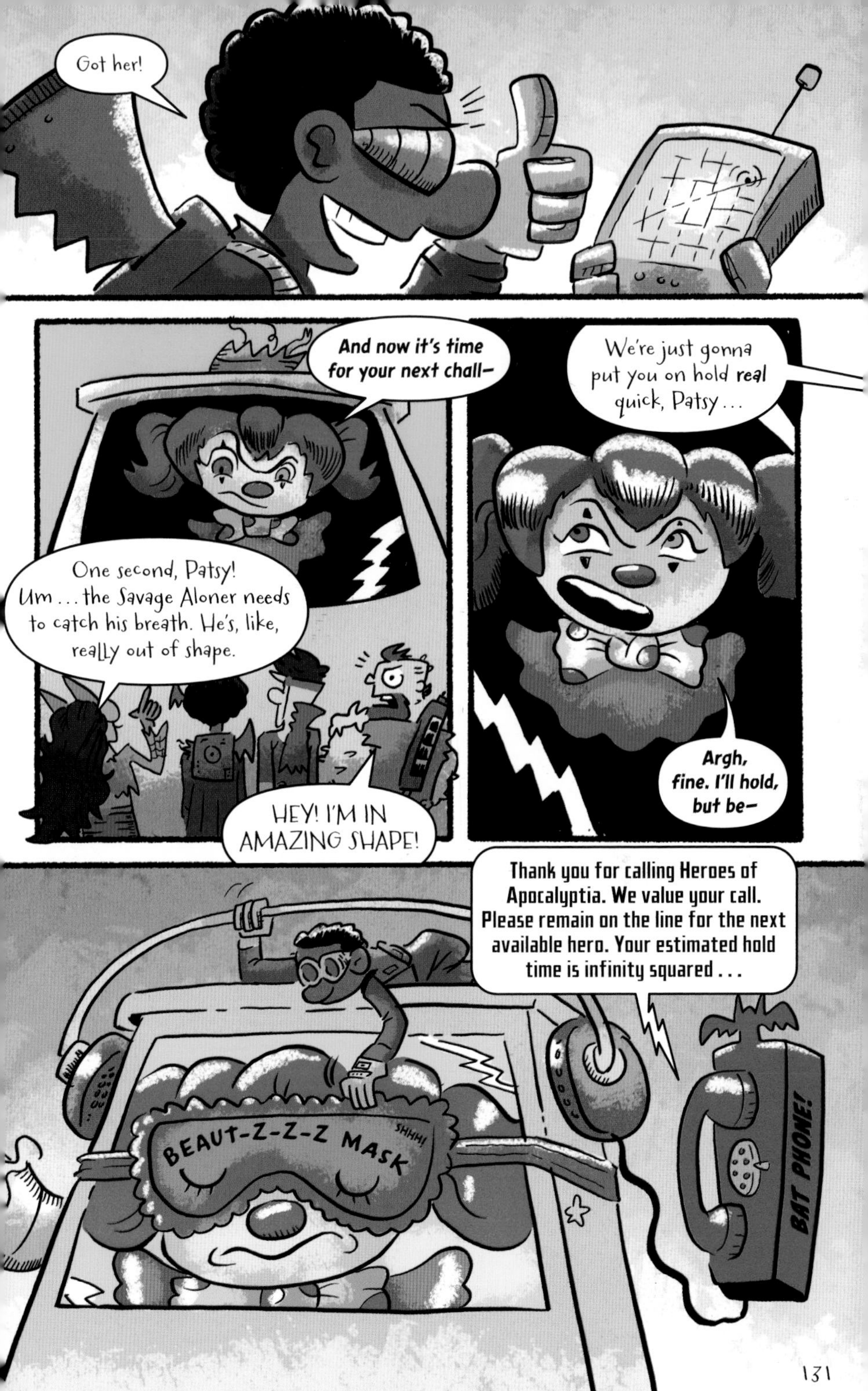

Got her!
And now it's time for your next chall–
We're just gonna put you on hold real quick, Patsy . . .
One second, Patsy! Um . . . the Savage Aloner needs to catch his breath. He's, like, really out of shape.
HEY! I'M IN AMAZING SHAPE!
Argh, fine. I'll hold, but be–
Thank you for calling Heroes of Apocalyptia. We value your call. Please remain on the line for the next available hero. Your estimated hold time is infinity squared . . .
BEAUT-Z-Z-Z MASK
SHHH!
BAT PHONE!

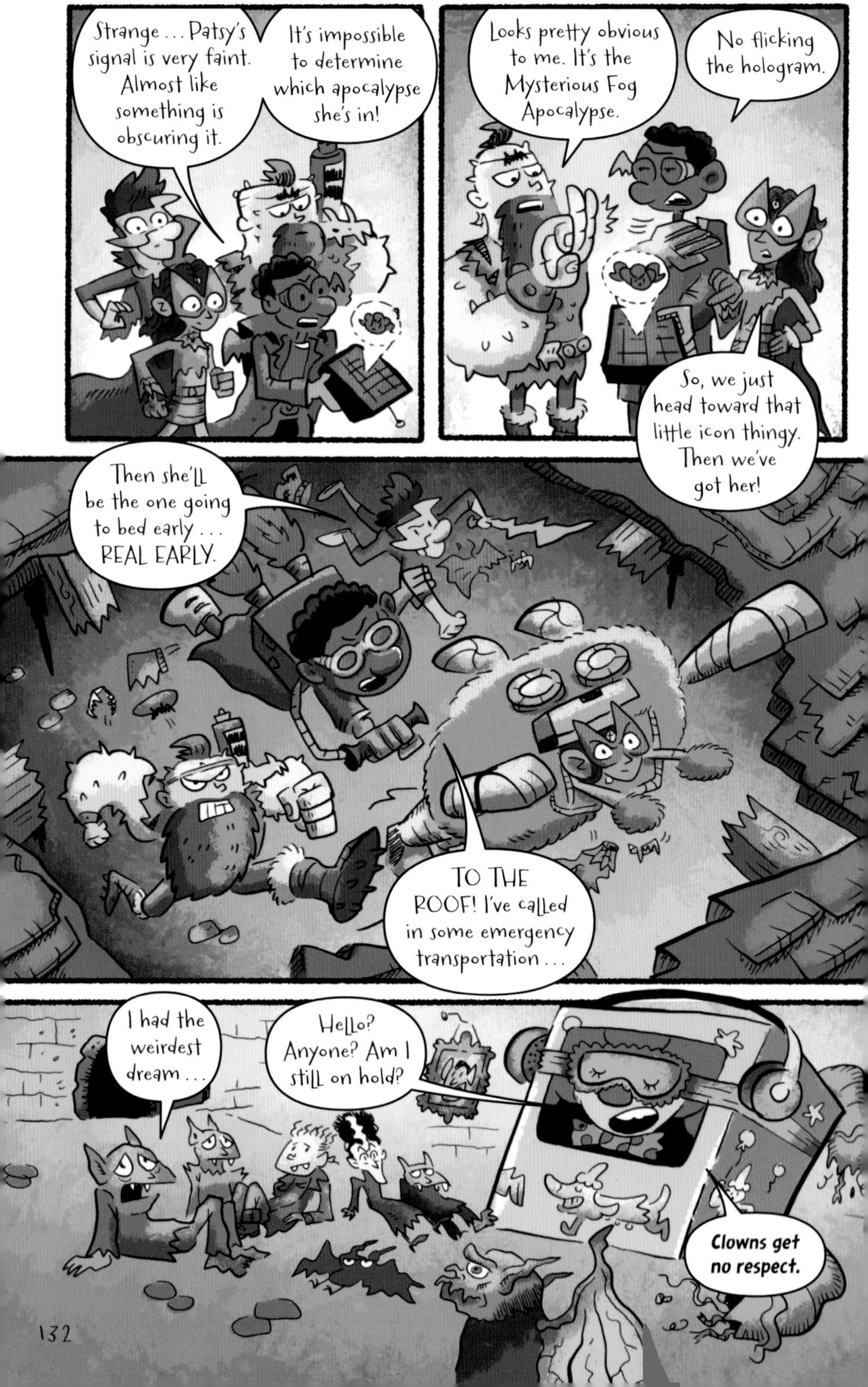
Strange . . . Patsy's signal is very faint. Almost like something is obscuring it.
It's impossible to determine which apocalypse she's in!
Looks pretty obvious to me. It's the Mysterious Fog Apocalypse.
No flicking the hologram.
So, we just head toward that little icon thingy. Then we've got her!
Then she'll be the one going to bed early . . . REAL EARLY.
TO THE ROOF! I've called in some emergency transportation . . .
I had the weirdest dream . . .
Hello? Anyone? Am I still on hold?
Clowns get no respect.

Enter the wacky world of
SEA GIRAFFES!

THE REAL, LIVE MINIATURE GIRAFFES YOU GROW YOURSELF!

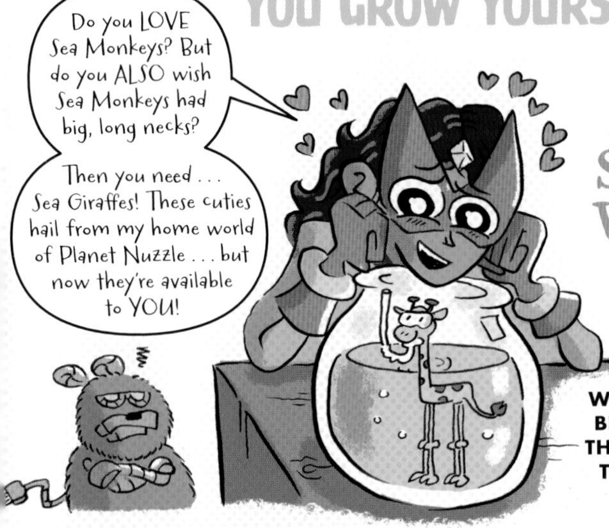
Do you LOVE Sea Monkeys? But do you ALSO wish Sea Monkeys had big, long necks?
Then you need . . . Sea Giraffes! These cuties hail from my home world of Planet Nuzzle . . . but now they're available to YOU!

JUST ADD SPARKLING WATER and watch 'em GROW!

WATCH THEM FROLIC RIGHT BEFORE YOUR EYES. TRAIN THEM TO DO TRICKS! MAYBE TRAIN THEM TO DO YOUR HOMEWORK! WOWZA!

TREE HOUSE HABITAT INCLUDED! GROW 'EM BIG!

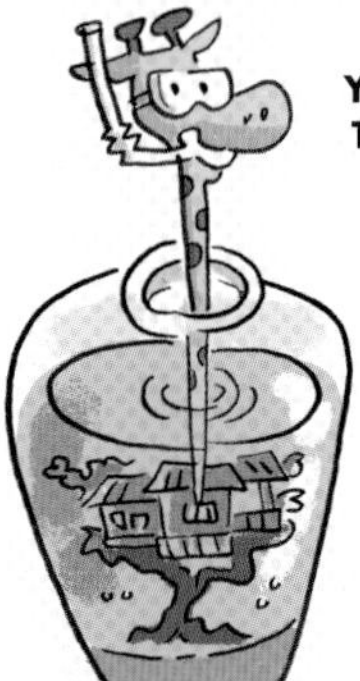

ACT NOW TO GET YOUR FREE SUPERHERO TREE HOUSE HABITAT!

BUT BE CAREFUL!

SEA GIRAFFES CAN GROW AS LARGE AS A REGULAR LAND GIRAFFE!

DON'T BELIEVE IT? CHECK OUT THIS TOTALLY REAL PICTURE OF A SEA GIRAFFE FAMILY!

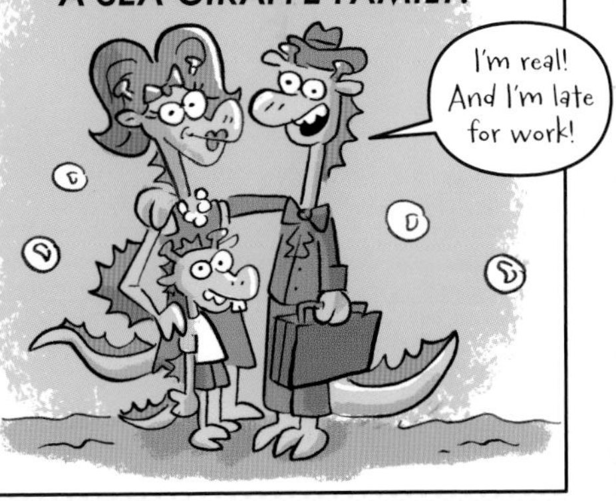
I'm real! And I'm late for work!

SEND AWAY TODAY!

But . . . not really. You get it now, right?
(I mean, just think about it. Can you imagine owning like, X-Men #2? They introduced the Vanisher. Who even _IS_ that?)

Name: ______________ Born?: ______________

Best decision: ______________ X-Men Hero: ______________

Item	Quantity	Price
SUBTOTAL:		
TOTAL TOTAL:		

MAIL TO:
Quint Baker
Tree house next to Joe's Pizza
Apocalyptia, USA

CHAPTER TEN

SEND IN THE CLOWNS!

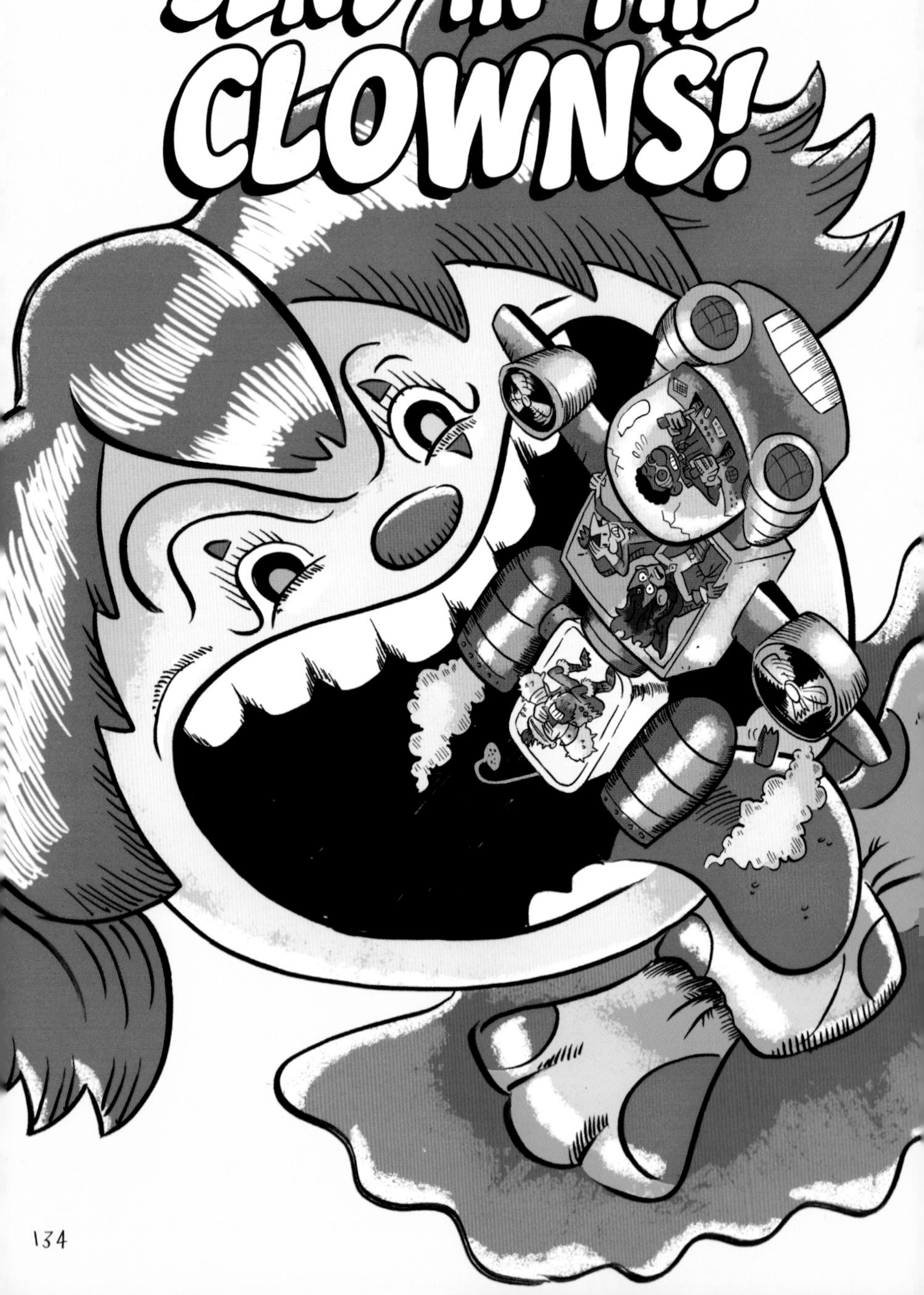

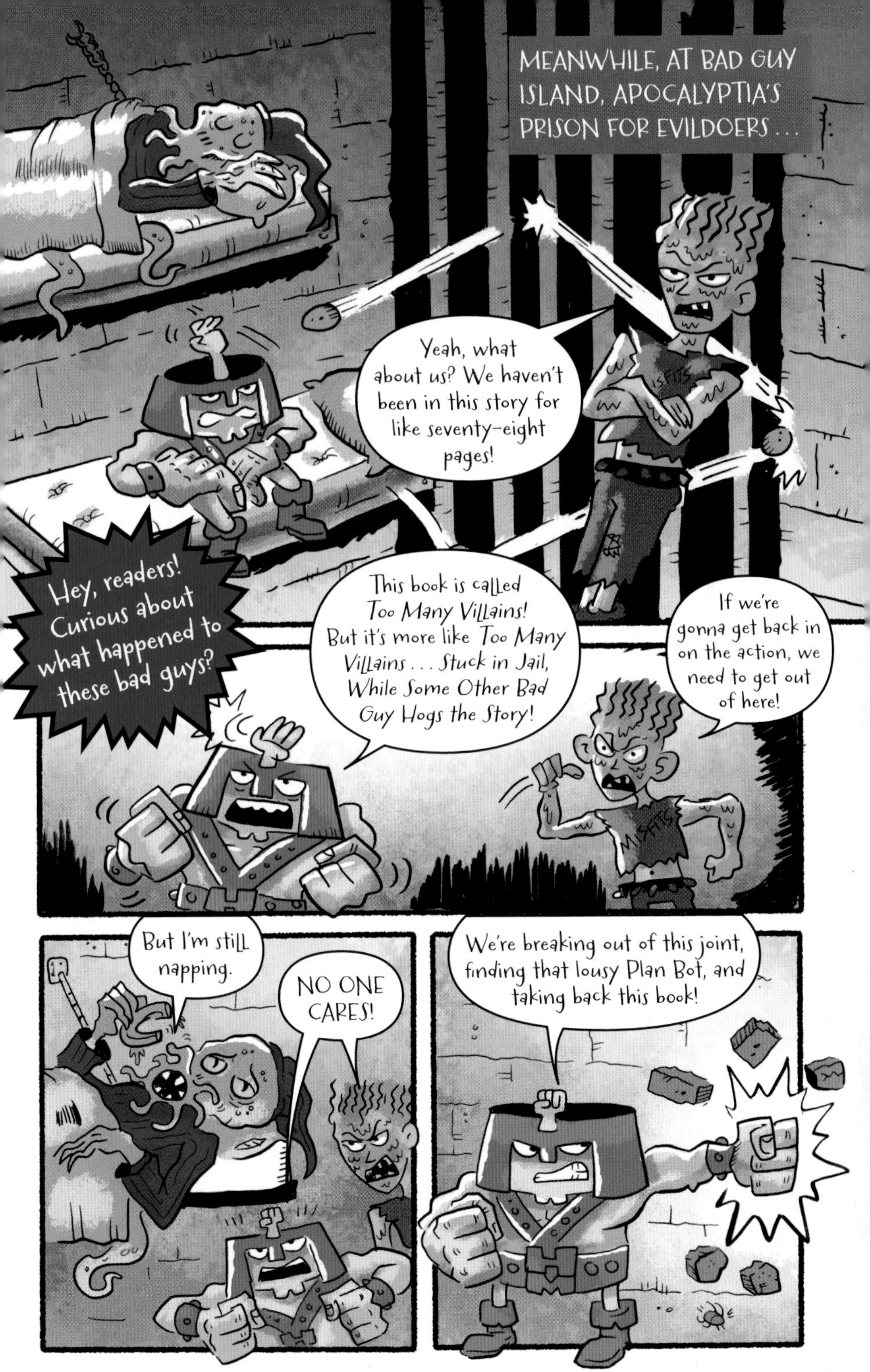
MEANWHILE, AT BAD GUY ISLAND, APOCALYPTIA'S PRISON FOR EVILDOERS . . .
Yeah, what about us? We haven't been in this story for like seventy-eight pages!
Hey, readers! Curious about what happened to these bad guys?
This book is called Too Many Villains! But it's more like Too Many Villains . . . Stuck in Jail, While Some Other Bad Guy Hogs the Story!
If we're gonna get back in on the action, we need to get out of here!
But I'm still napping.
NO ONE CARES!
We're breaking out of this joint, finding that lousy Plan Bot, and taking back this book!

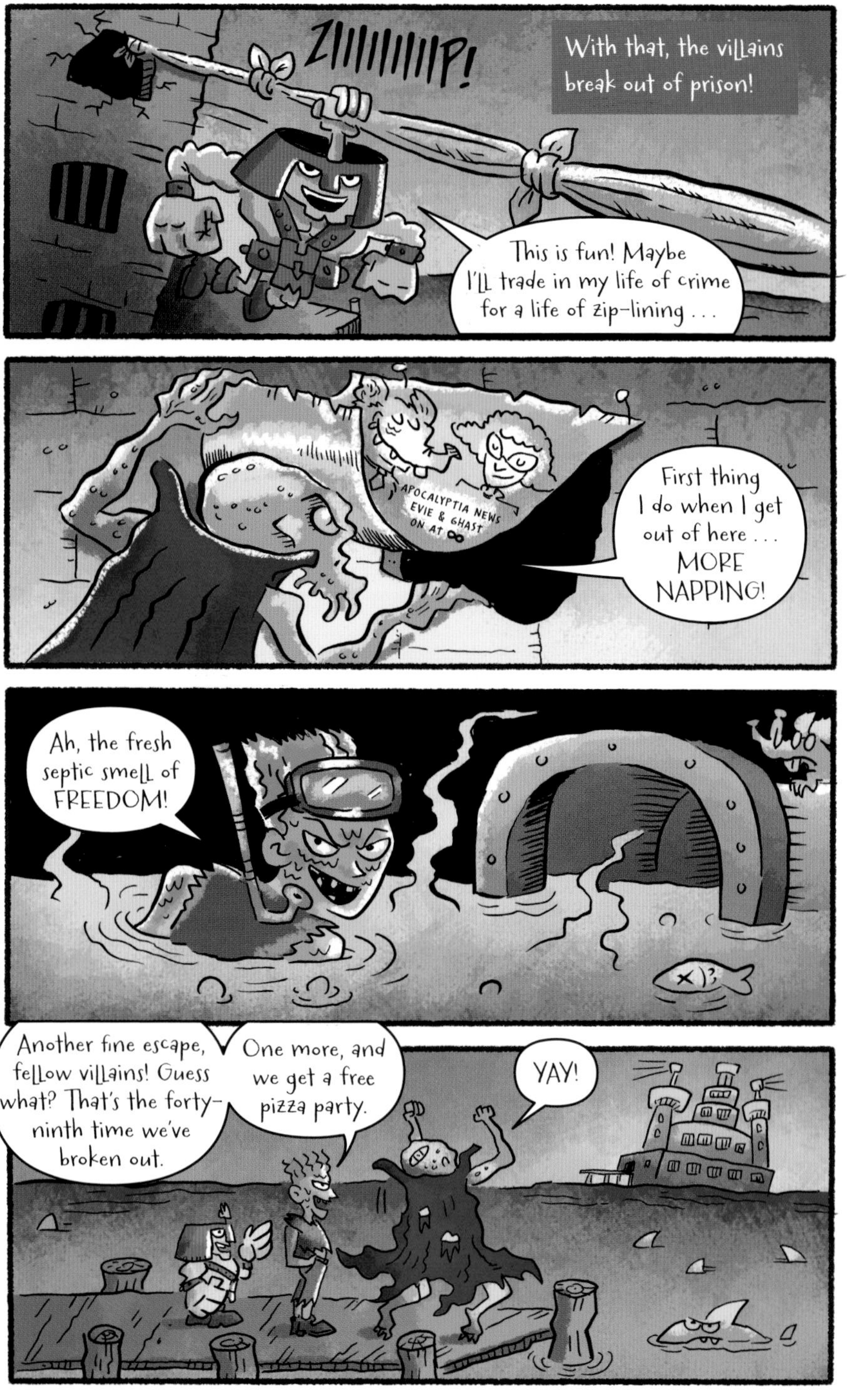
ZIIIIIIIIP!
With that, the villains break out of prison!
This is fun! Maybe I'LL trade in my life of crime for a life of zip-lining . . .
APOCALYPTIA NEWS EVIE & GHAST ON AT ∞
First thing I do when I get out of here . . . MORE NAPPING!
Ah, the fresh septic smell of FREEDOM!
Another fine escape, fellow villains! Guess what? That's the forty-ninth time we've broken out.
One more, and we get a free pizza party.
YAY!

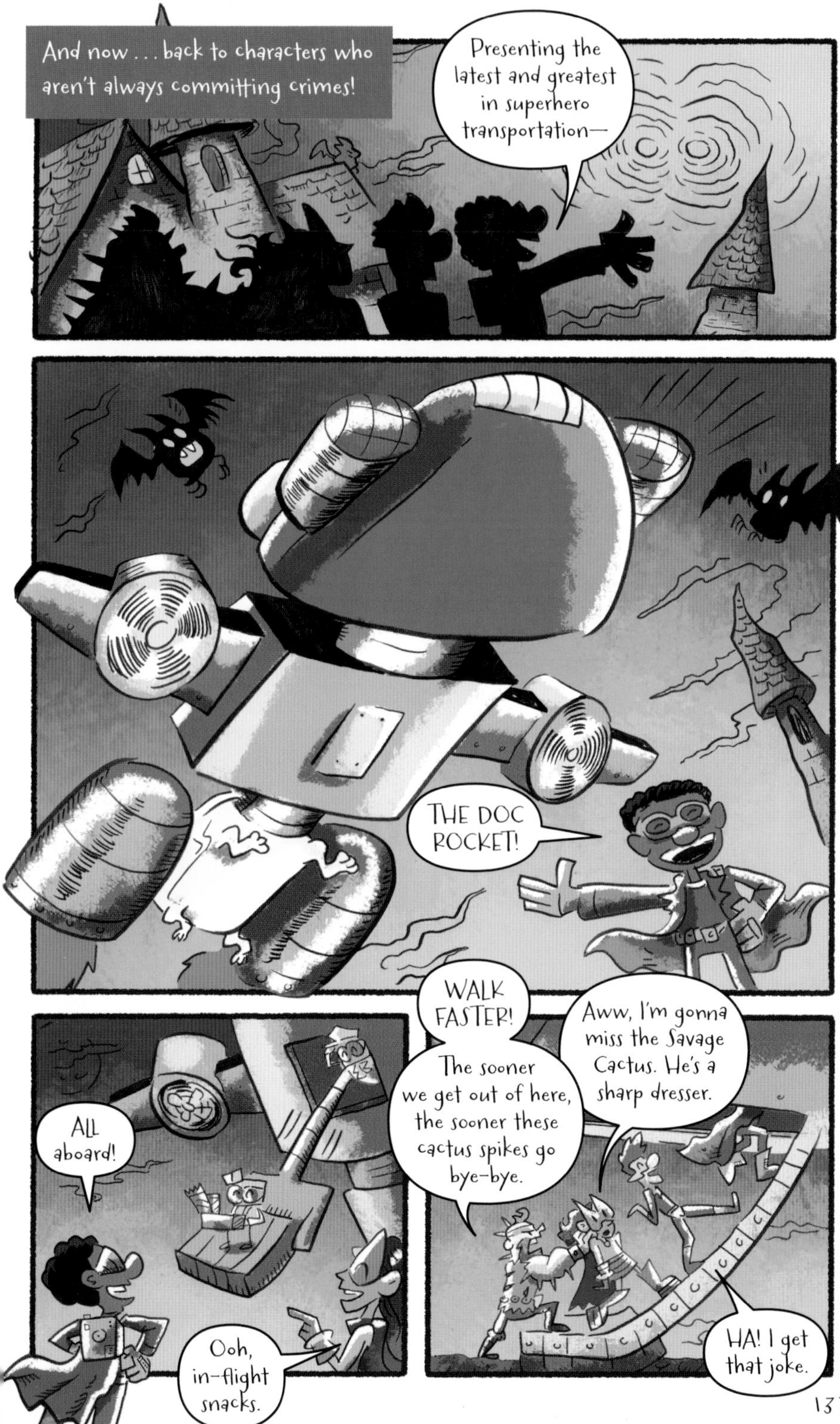
And now . . . back to characters who aren't always committing crimes!
Presenting the latest and greatest in superhero transportation—
THE DOC ROCKET!
ALL aboard!
Ooh, in-flight snacks.
WALK FASTER!
The sooner we get out of here, the sooner these cactus spikes go bye-bye.
Aww, I'm gonna miss the Savage Cactus. He's a sharp dresser.
HA! I get that joke.

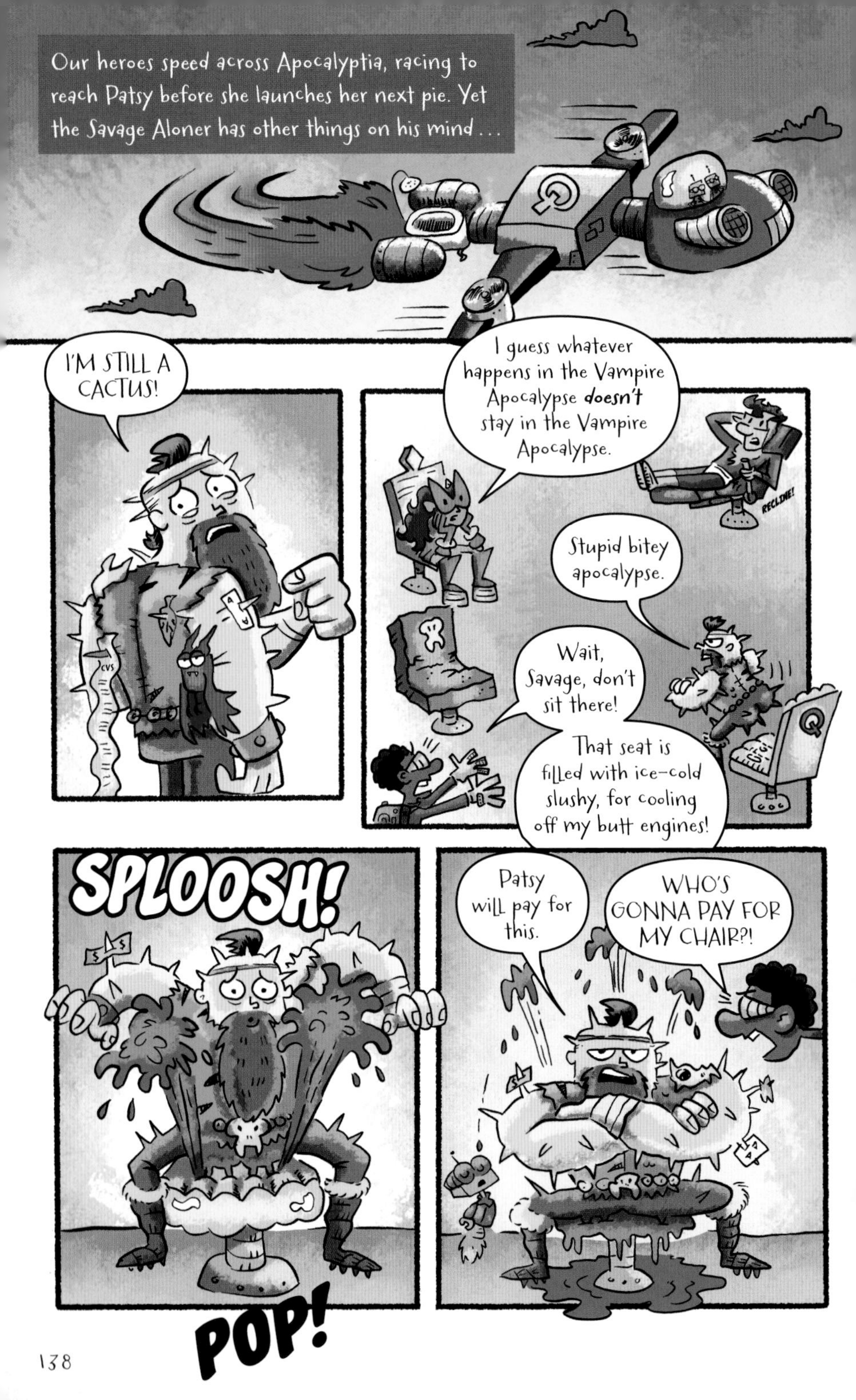

Our heroes speed across Apocalyptia, racing to reach Patsy before she launches her next pie. Yet the Savage Aloner has other things on his mind . . .
I'M STILL A CACTUS!
I guess whatever happens in the Vampire Apocalypse **doesn't** stay in the Vampire Apocalypse.
RECLINE!
Stupid bitey apocalypse.
Wait, Savage, don't sit there!
That seat is filled with ice-cold slushy, for cooling off my butt engines!
SPLOOSH!
POP!
Patsy will pay for this.
WHO'S GONNA PAY FOR MY CHAIR?!

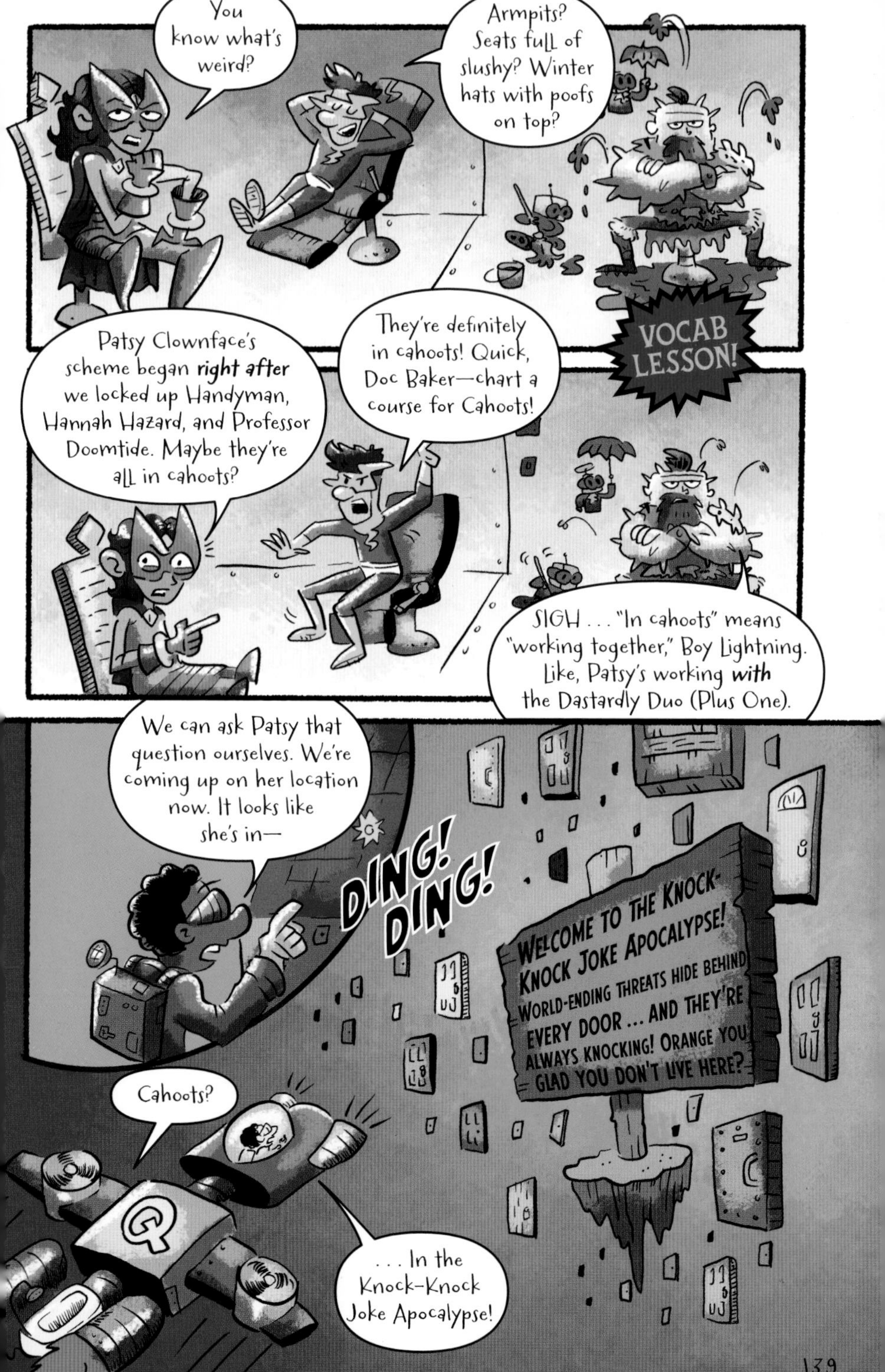

You know what's weird?
Armpits? Seats full of slushy? Winter hats with poofs on top?
Patsy Clownface's scheme began **right after** we locked up Handyman, Hannah Hazard, and Professor Doomtide. Maybe they're all in cahoots?
They're definitely in cahoots! Quick, Doc Baker—chart a course for Cahoots!
VOCAB LESSON!
SIGH . . . "In cahoots" means "working together," Boy Lightning. Like, Patsy's working **with** the Dastardly Duo (Plus One).
We can ask Patsy that question ourselves. We're coming up on her location now. It looks like she's in—
DING! DING!
WELCOME TO THE KNOCK-KNOCK JOKE APOCALYPSE! WORLD-ENDING THREATS HIDE BEHIND EVERY DOOR ... AND THEY'RE ALWAYS KNOCKING! ORANGE YOU GLAD YOU DON'T LIVE HERE?
Cahoots?
. . . In the Knock-Knock Joke Apocalypse!

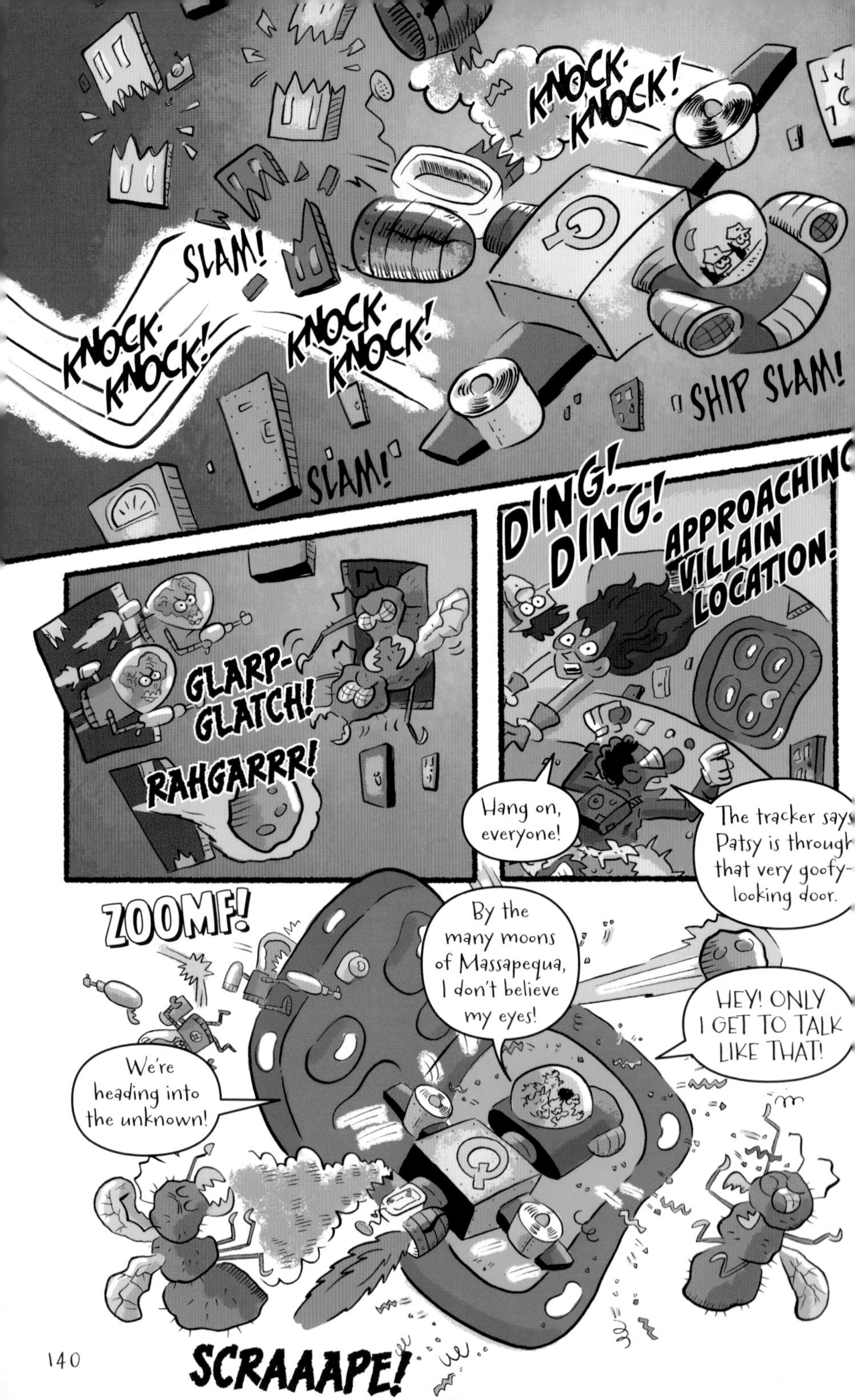
KNOCK-KNOCK!
SLAM!
KNOCK-KNOCK!
KNOCK-KNOCK!
SHIP SLAM!
SLAM!
GLARP-GLATCH!
RAHGARRR!
DING! DING!
APPROACHING VILLAIN LOCATION!
Hang on, everyone!
The tracker says Patsy is through that very goofy-looking door.
ZOOMF!
By the many moons of Massapequa, I don't believe my eyes!
HEY! ONLY I GET TO TALK LIKE THAT!
We're heading into the unknown!
SCRAAAPE!

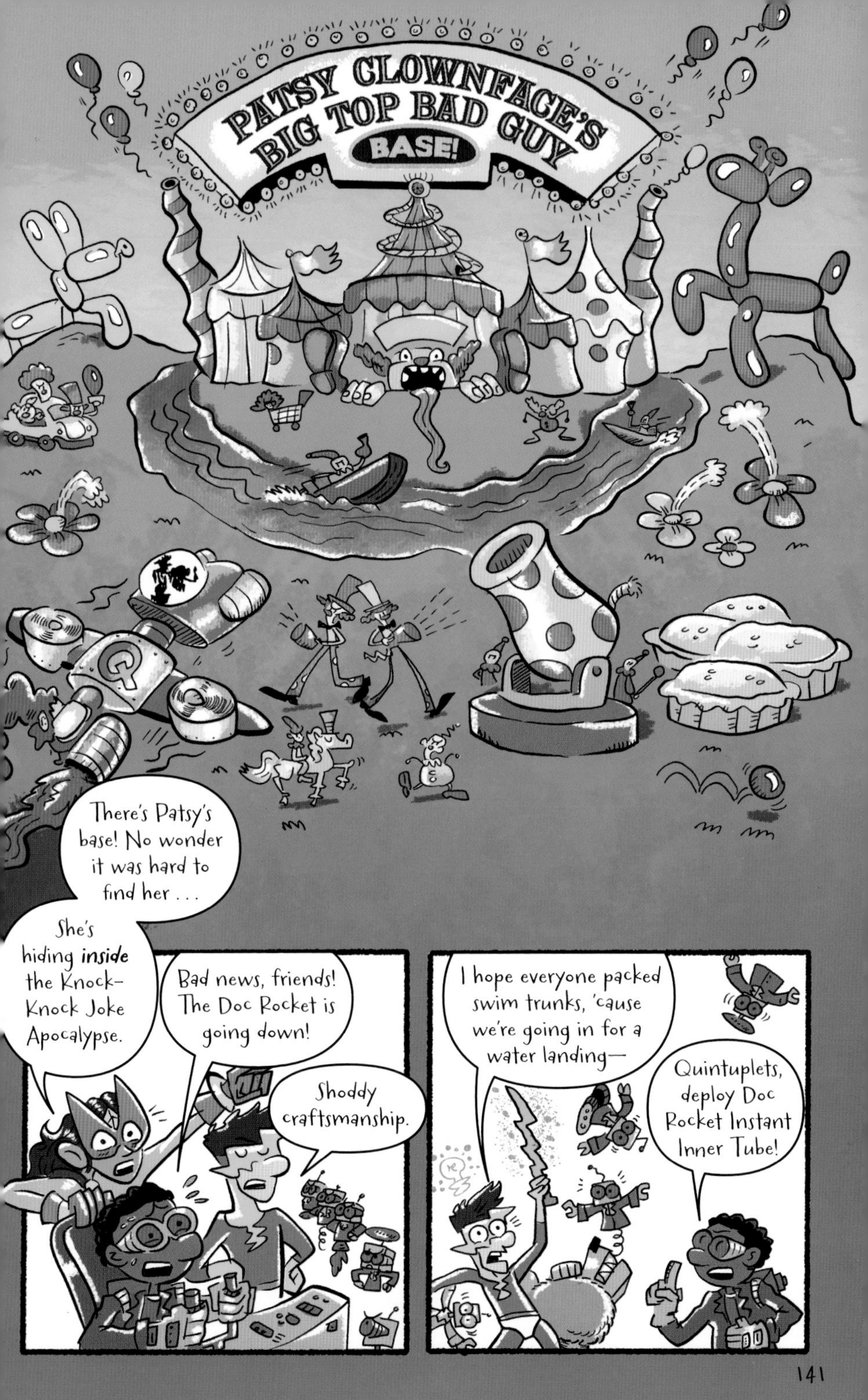
PATSY CLOWNFACE'S BIG TOP BAD GUY BASE!
There's Patsy's base! No wonder it was hard to find her . . .
She's hiding **inside** the Knock-Knock Joke Apocalypse.
Bad news, friends! The Doc Rocket is going down!
Shoddy craftsmanship.
I hope everyone packed swim trunks, 'cause we're going in for a water landing—
Quintuplets, deploy Doc Rocket Instant Inner Tube!

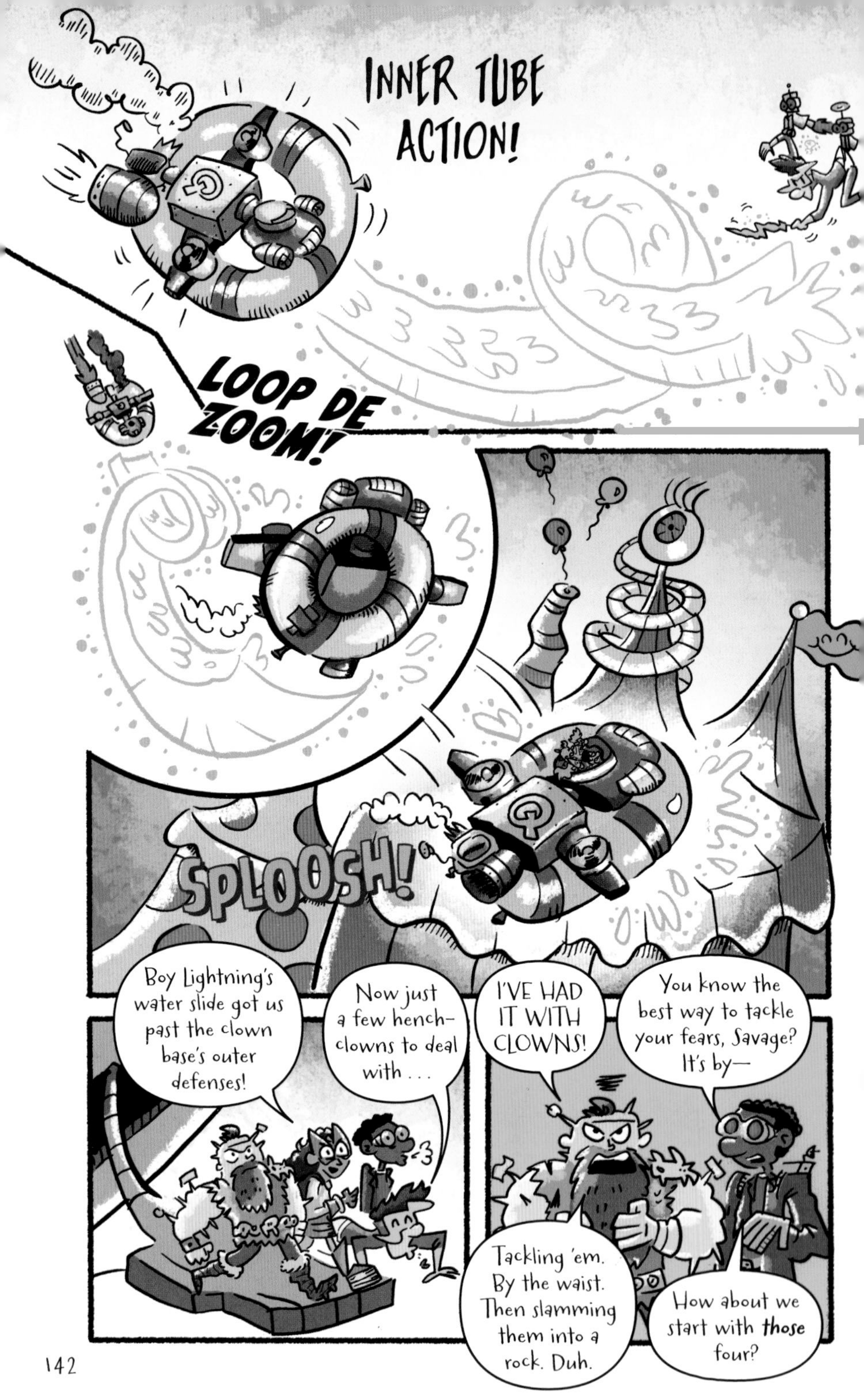
INNER TUBE ACTION!
LOOP DE ZOOM!
SPLOOSH!
Boy Lightning's water slide got us past the clown base's outer defenses!
Now just a few hench-clowns to deal with . . .
I'VE HAD IT WITH CLOWNS!
You know the best way to tackle your fears, Savage? It's by—
Tackling 'em. By the waist. Then slamming them into a rock. Duh.
How about we start with **those** four?

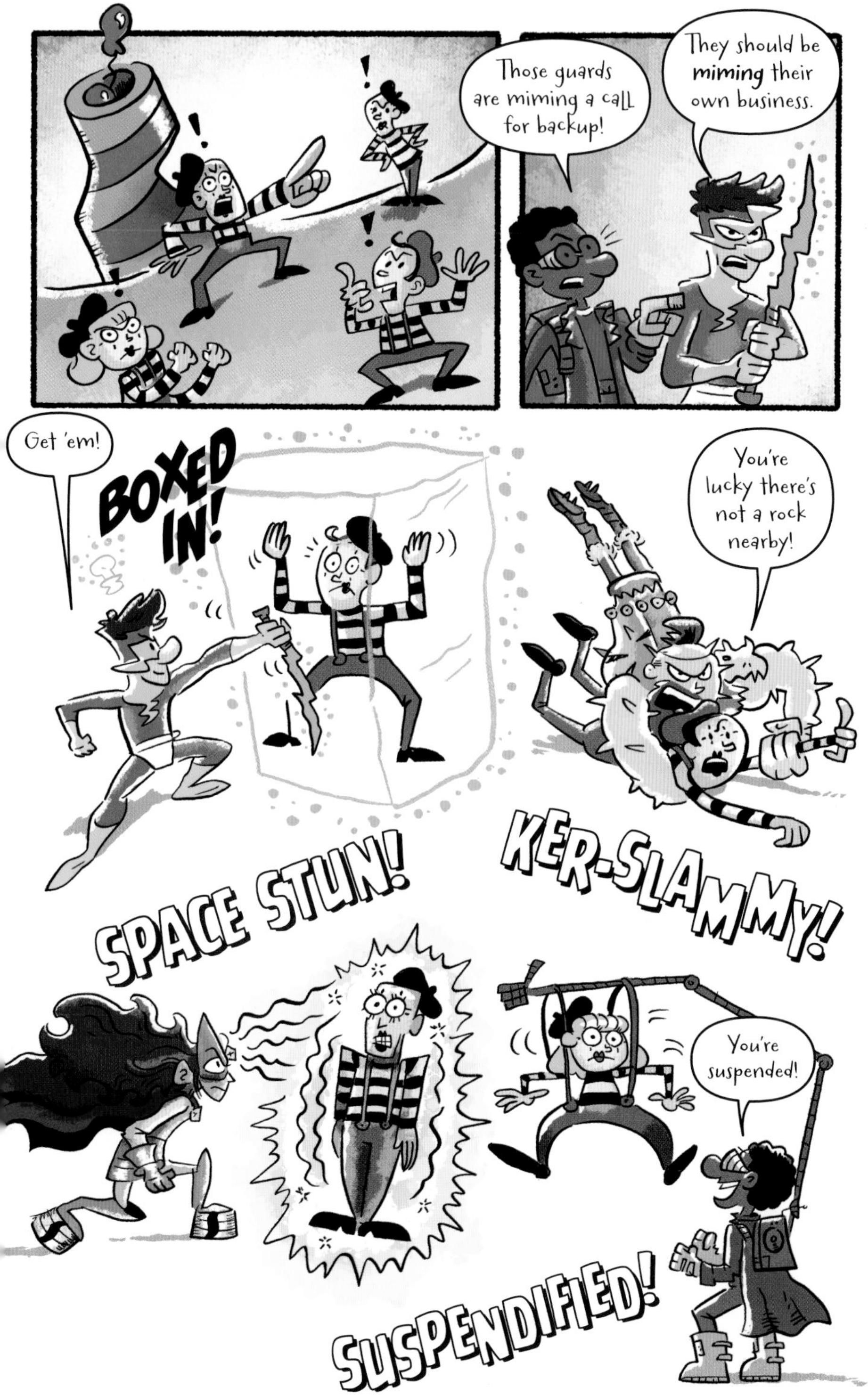
Those guards are miming a call for backup!
They should be **miming** their own business.
Get 'em!
BOXED IN!
You're lucky there's not a rock nearby!
SPACE STUN!
KER-SLAMMY!
You're suspended!
SUSPENDIFIED!

KIDS! BACK BY SEMI-POPULAR DEMAND! IT'S . . . DOC BAKER'S FAMOUS:

BUCKET O' GADGETS!

MORE! SO MANY MORE!

ROCK, PAPER, SCISSORS TRIPLE HAND!

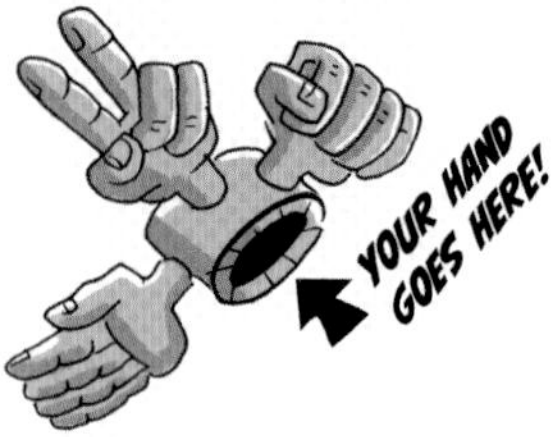

YOUR HAND GOES HERE!

One hand to rule them all . . . **Never** lose a game of Rock, Paper, Scissors again!

INVISIBLE PUPPY

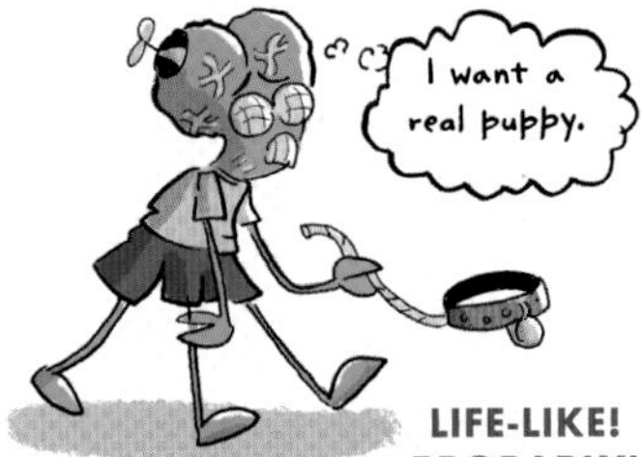

I want a real puppy.

LIFE-LIKE! PROBABLY!

You won't see the little furball . . . but trust us, **this puppy is by your side!**

BAKER'S DOZEN SURPRISE BOX!

Can't decide? Unsure? Willing to take a risk? You won't know what you've got until you open the box. But we promise **THIRTEEN** gizmos, gadgets, and goodies that are disbelievable, unpossible, and astoundishing!

INSTANT MUD!

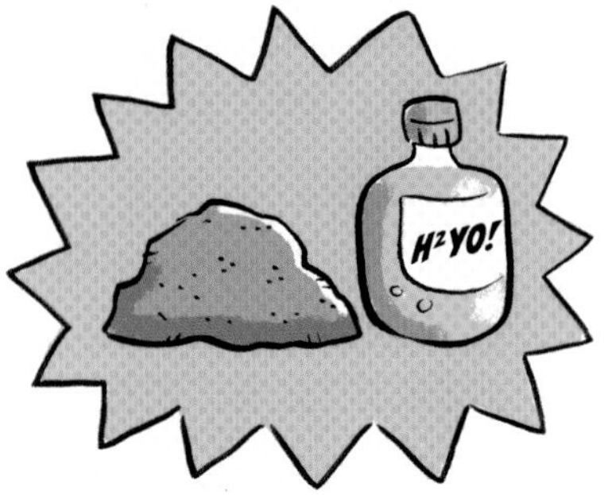

H²YO!

Has this ever happened to you?
A mud flinging fight breaks out . . .
but you're empty-handed! **Never again!**

ASTOUNDING AUNT FARM

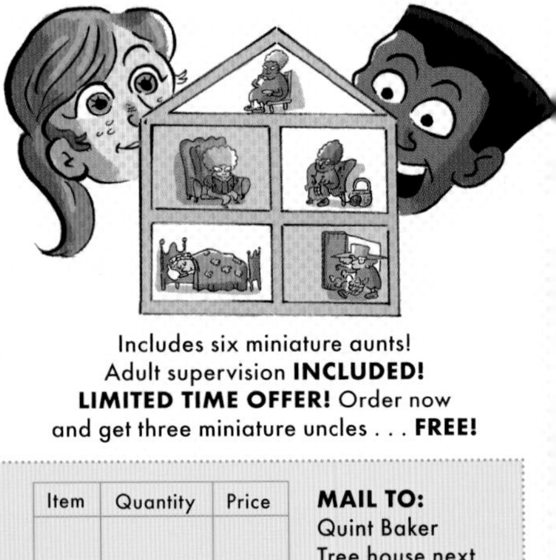

Includes six miniature aunts!
Adult supervision **INCLUDED!**
LIMITED TIME OFFER! Order now
and get three miniature uncles . . . **FREE!**

Mail order! But not really!
IT'S A GAG! FUNNY!

Send nickels only!
We love nickels!
NO DIMES

Call sign: ______________

Birthday: ______________

Address: ______________

Fave color: ______________

Item	Quantity	Price
SUBTOTAL:		
TOTES TOTAL:		

MAIL TO:
Quint Baker
Tree house next
to Joe's Pizza
Apocalyptia, USA

Cut along the dotted line . . . it is QUINTessential!

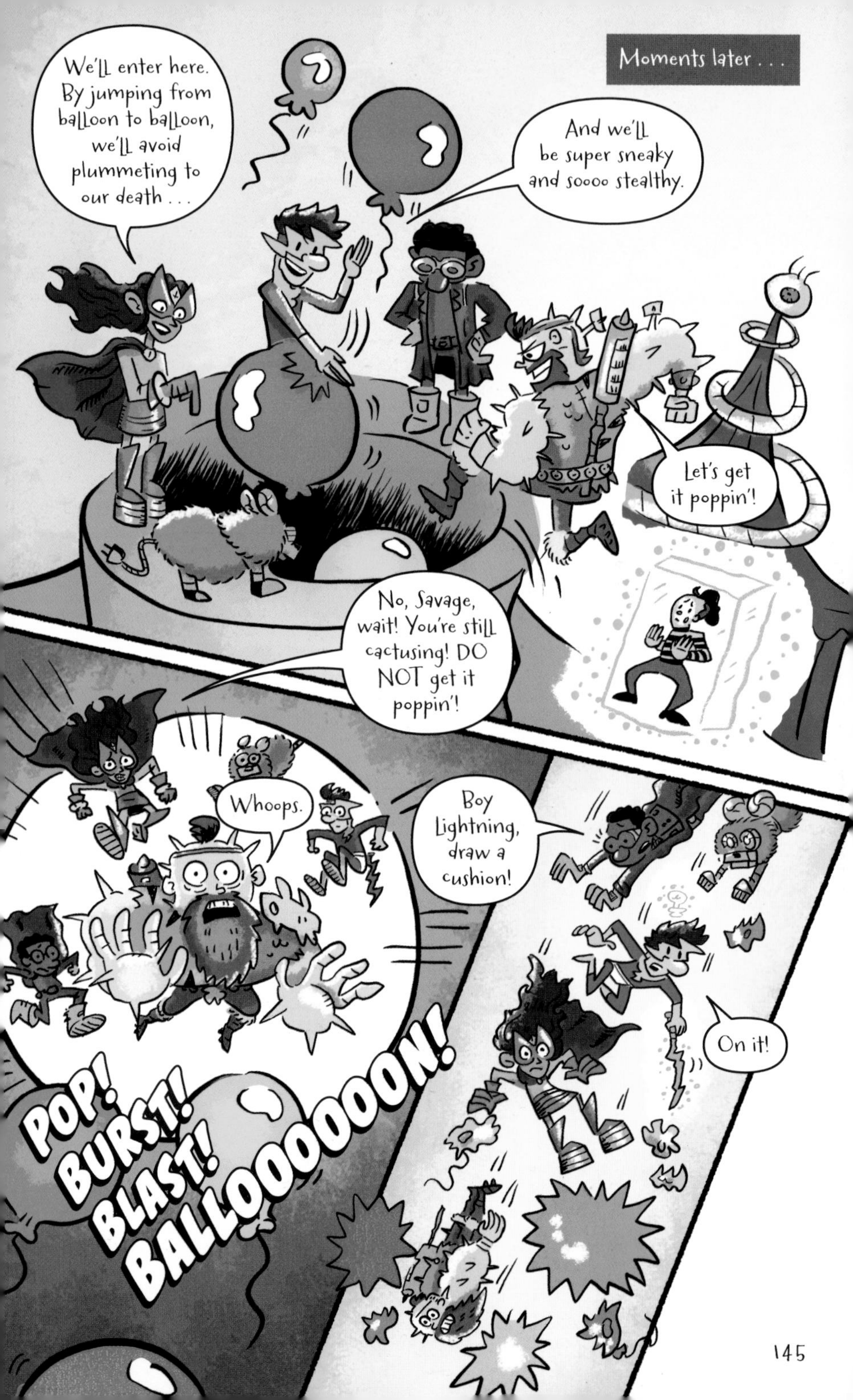

Moments later . . .
We'll enter here. By jumping from balloon to balloon, we'll avoid plummeting to our death . . .
And we'll be super sneaky and soooo stealthy.
Let's get it poppin'!
No, Savage, wait! You're still cactusing! DO NOT get it poppin'!
Whoops.
Boy Lightning, draw a cushion!
On it!
POP! BURST! BLAST! BALLOOOOOON!

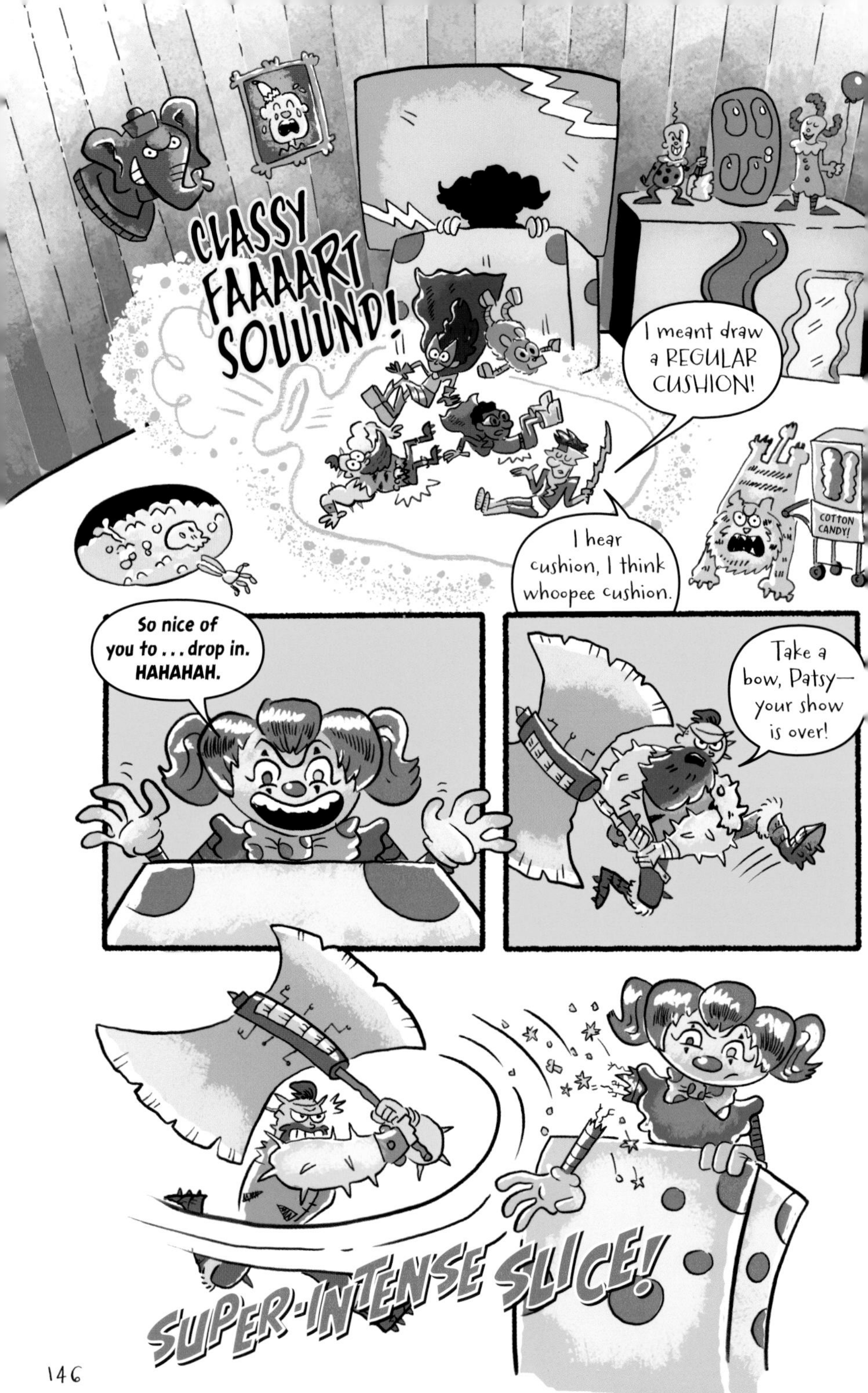
CLASSY FAAAART SOUUUND!
I meant draw a REGULAR CUSHION!
I hear cushion, I think whoopee cushion.
COTTON CANDY!
So nice of you to . . . drop in. HAHAHAH.
Take a bow, Patsy— your show is over!
SUPER-INTENSE SLICE!

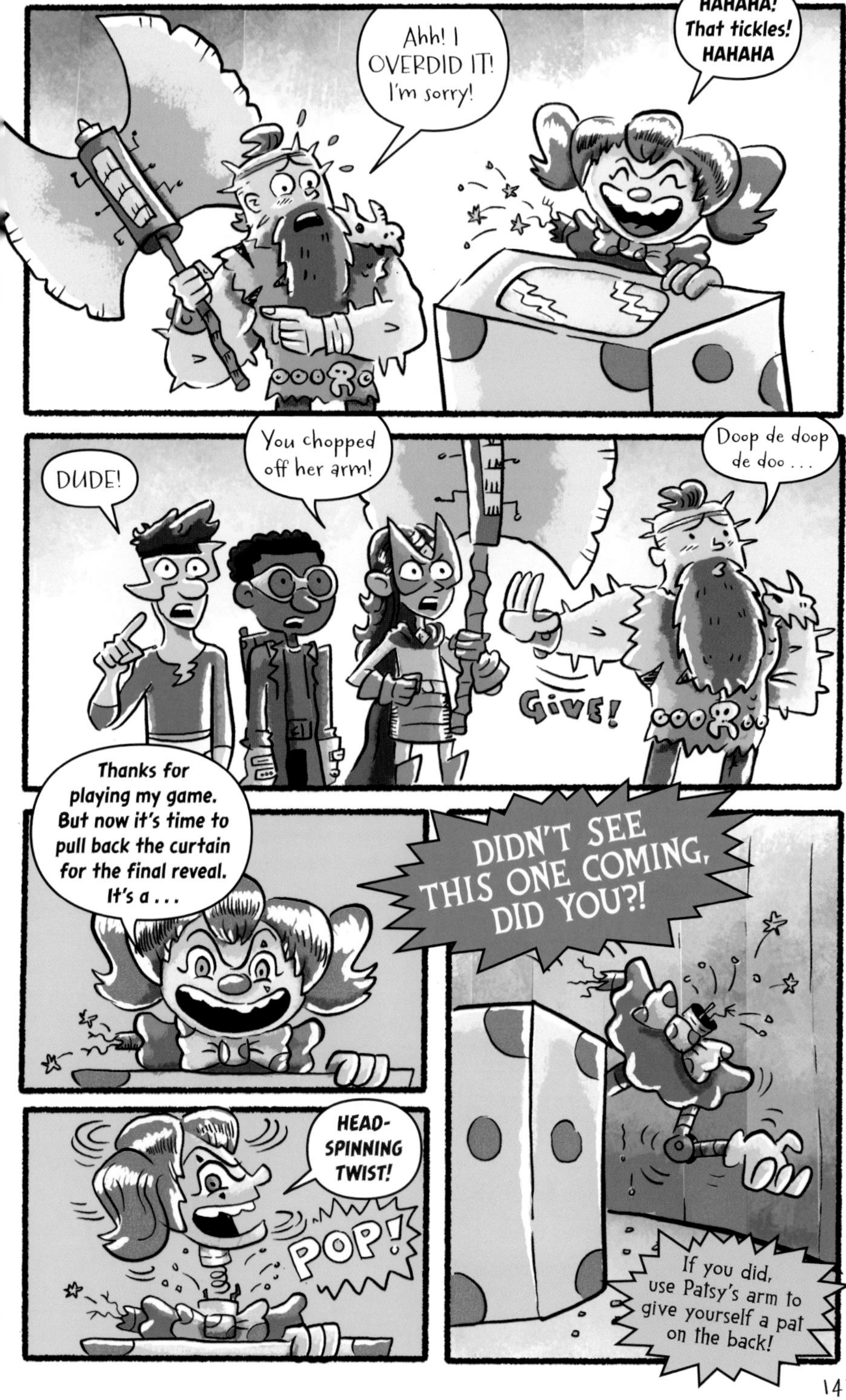
Ahh! I OVERDID IT! I'm sorry!
HAHAHA! That tickles! HAHAHA
DUDE!
You chopped off her arm!
Doop de doop de doo . . .
GIVE!
Thanks for playing my game. But now it's time to pull back the curtain for the final reveal. It's a . . .
HEAD-SPINNING TWIST!
POP!
DIDN'T SEE THIS ONE COMING, DID YOU?!
If you did, use Patsy's arm to give yourself a pat on the back!

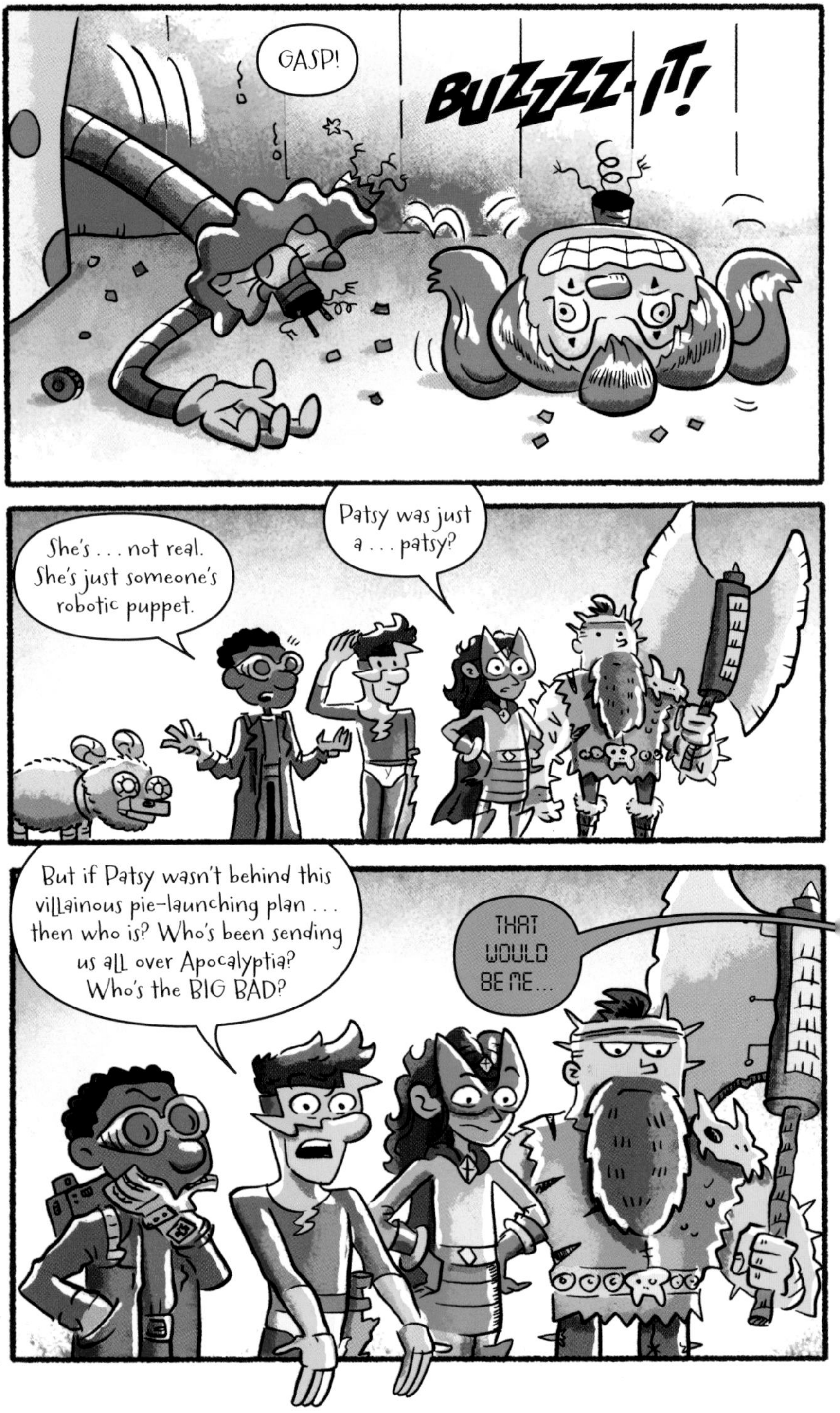
GASP!
BUZZZZ-IT!
She's . . . not real. She's just someone's robotic puppet.
Patsy was just a . . . patsy?
But if Patsy wasn't behind this villainous pie-launching plan . . . then who is? Who's been sending us all over Apocalyptia? Who's the BIG BAD?
THAT WOULD BE ME...

CHAPTER ELEVEN

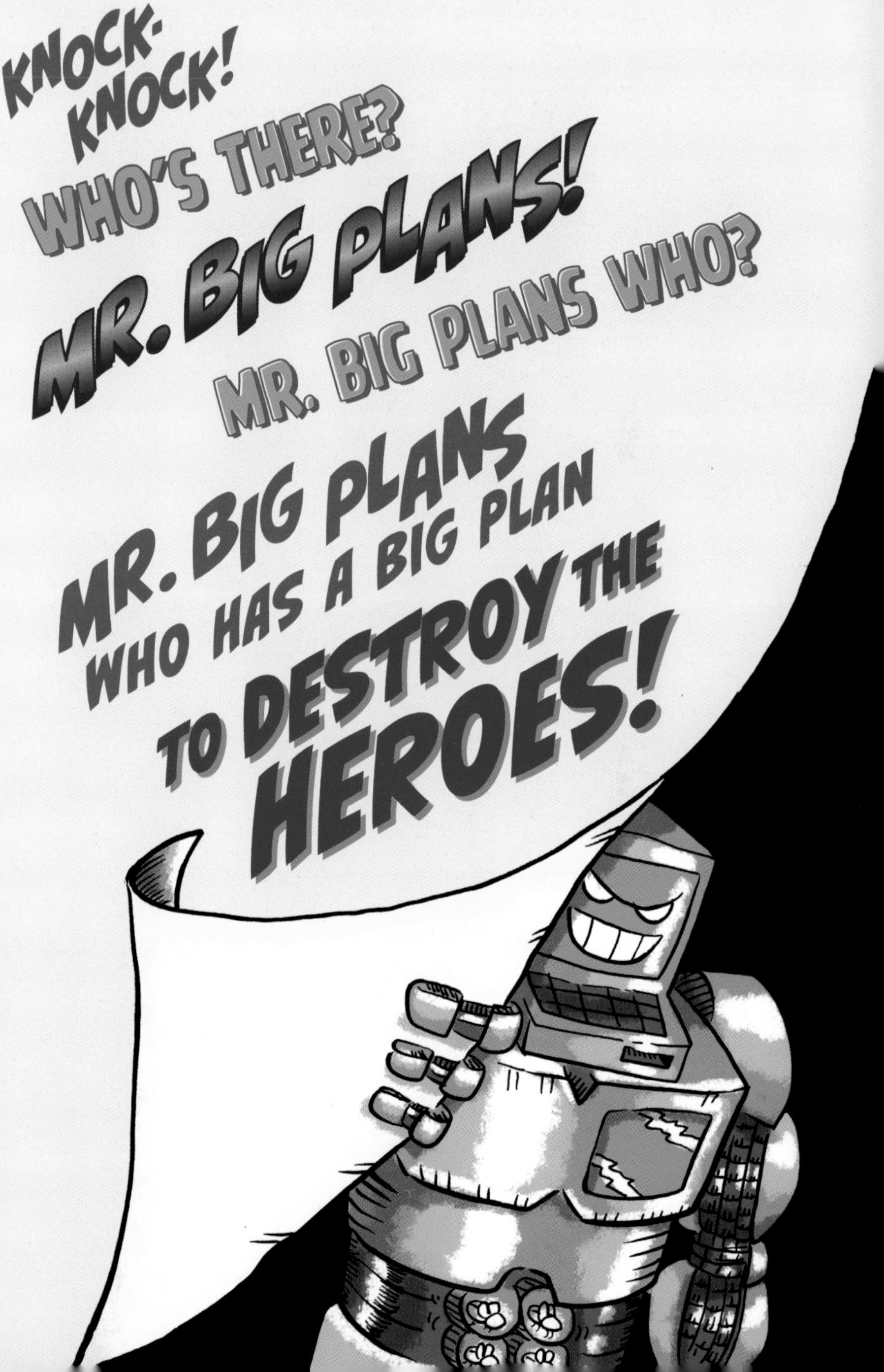
KNOCK-KNOCK!
WHO'S THERE?
MR. BIG PLANS!
MR. BIG PLANS WHO?
MR. BIG PLANS WHO HAS A BIG PLAN TO DESTROY THE HEROES!

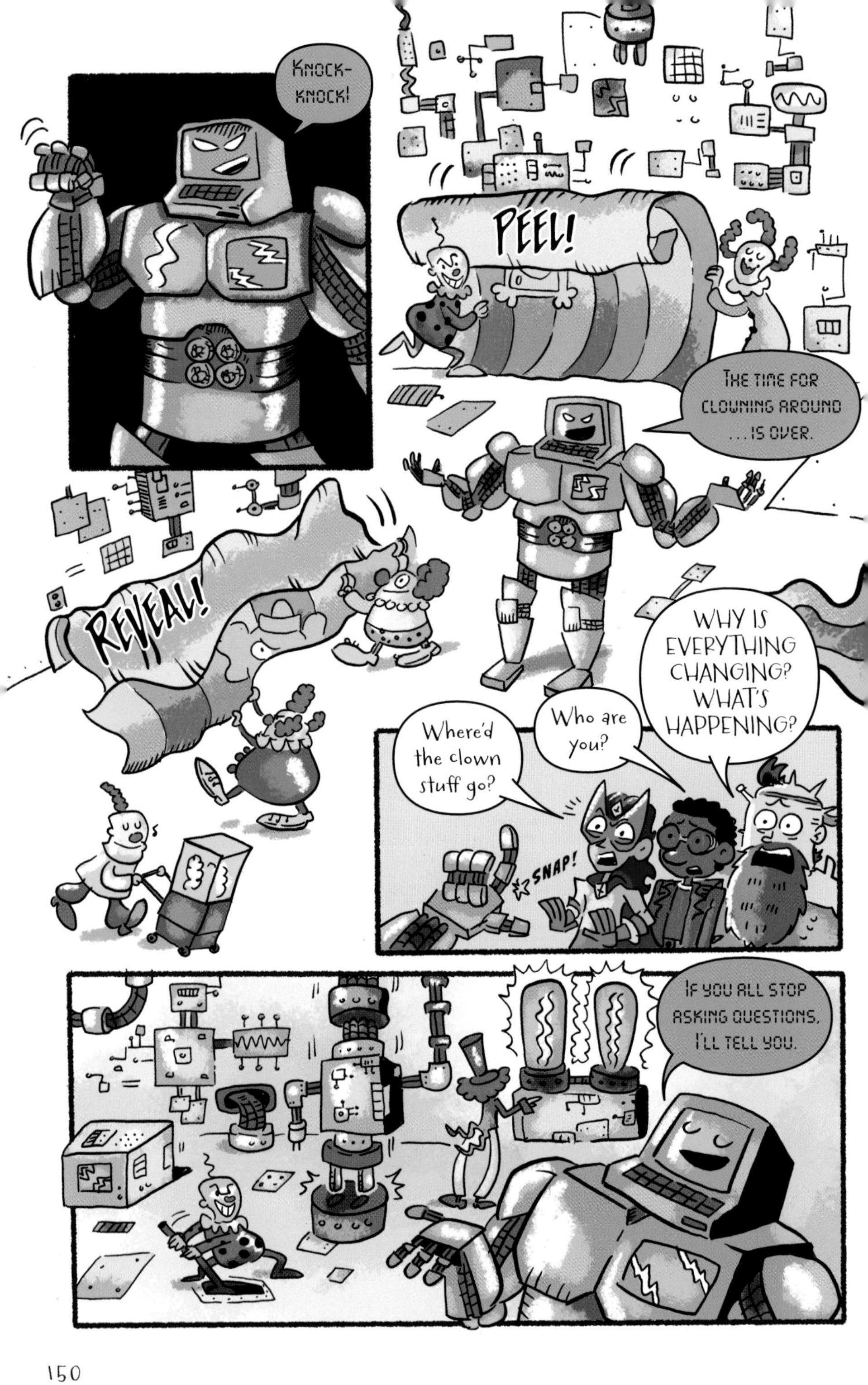
KNOCK-KNOCK!
PEEL!
THE TIME FOR CLOWNING AROUND ...IS OVER.
REVEAL!
WHY IS EVERYTHING CHANGING? WHAT'S HAPPENING?
Who are you?
Where'd the clown stuff go?
SNAP!
IF YOU ALL STOP ASKING QUESTIONS, I'LL TELL YOU.

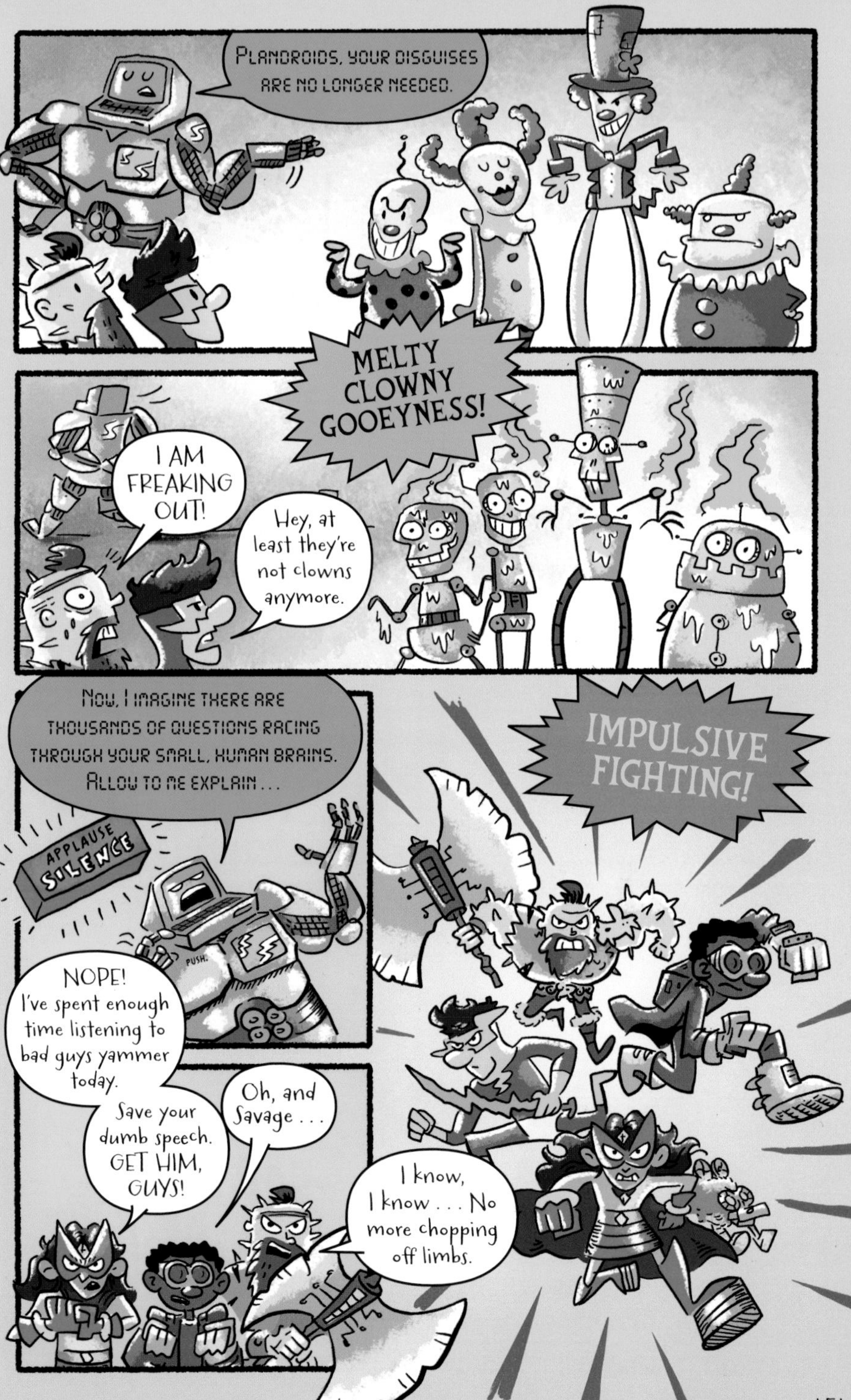
Plandroids, your disguises are no longer needed.
MELTY CLOWNY GOOEYNESS!
I AM FREAKING OUT!
Hey, at least they're not clowns anymore.
Now, I imagine there are thousands of questions racing through your small, human brains. Allow to me explain . . .
APPLAUSE
SILENCE
PUSH:
NOPE! I've spent enough time listening to bad guys yammer today.
Save your dumb speech. GET HIM, GUYS!
Oh, and Savage . . .
I know, I know . . . No more chopping off limbs.
IMPULSIVE FIGHTING!

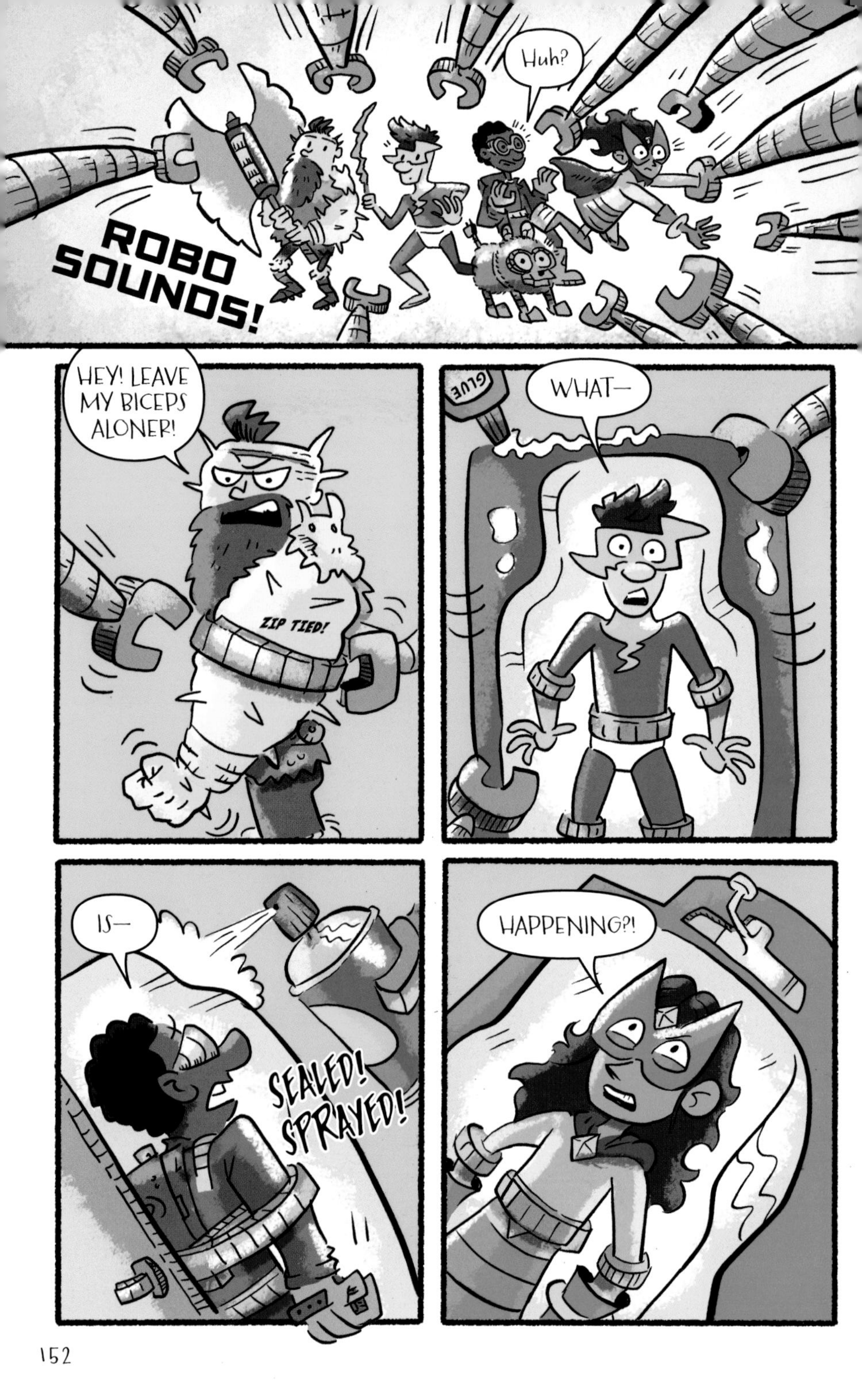
Huh?
ROBO SOUNDS!
HEY! LEAVE MY BICEPS ALONER!
ZIP TIED!
GLUE
WHAT—
IS—
SEALED! SPRAYED!
HAPPENING?!

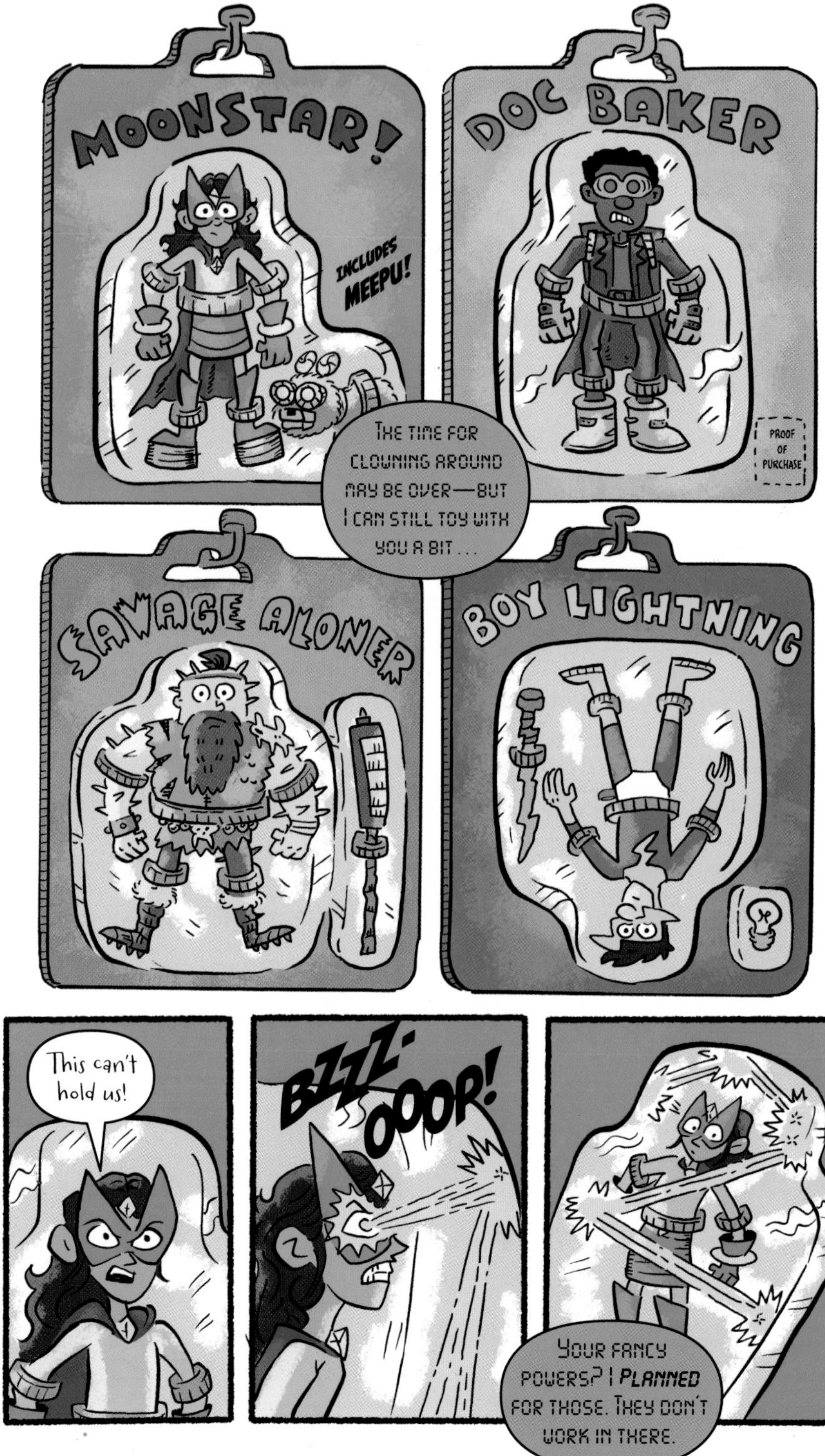
MOONSTAR!
INCLUDES MEEPU!
DOC BAKER
PROOF OF PURCHASE
THE TIME FOR CLOWNING AROUND MAY BE OVER—BUT I CAN STILL TOY WITH YOU A BIT . . .
SAVAGE ALONER
BOY LIGHTNING
This can't hold us!
BZZZ-OOOR!
YOUR FANCY POWERS? I *PLANNED* FOR THOSE. THEY DON'T WORK IN THERE.

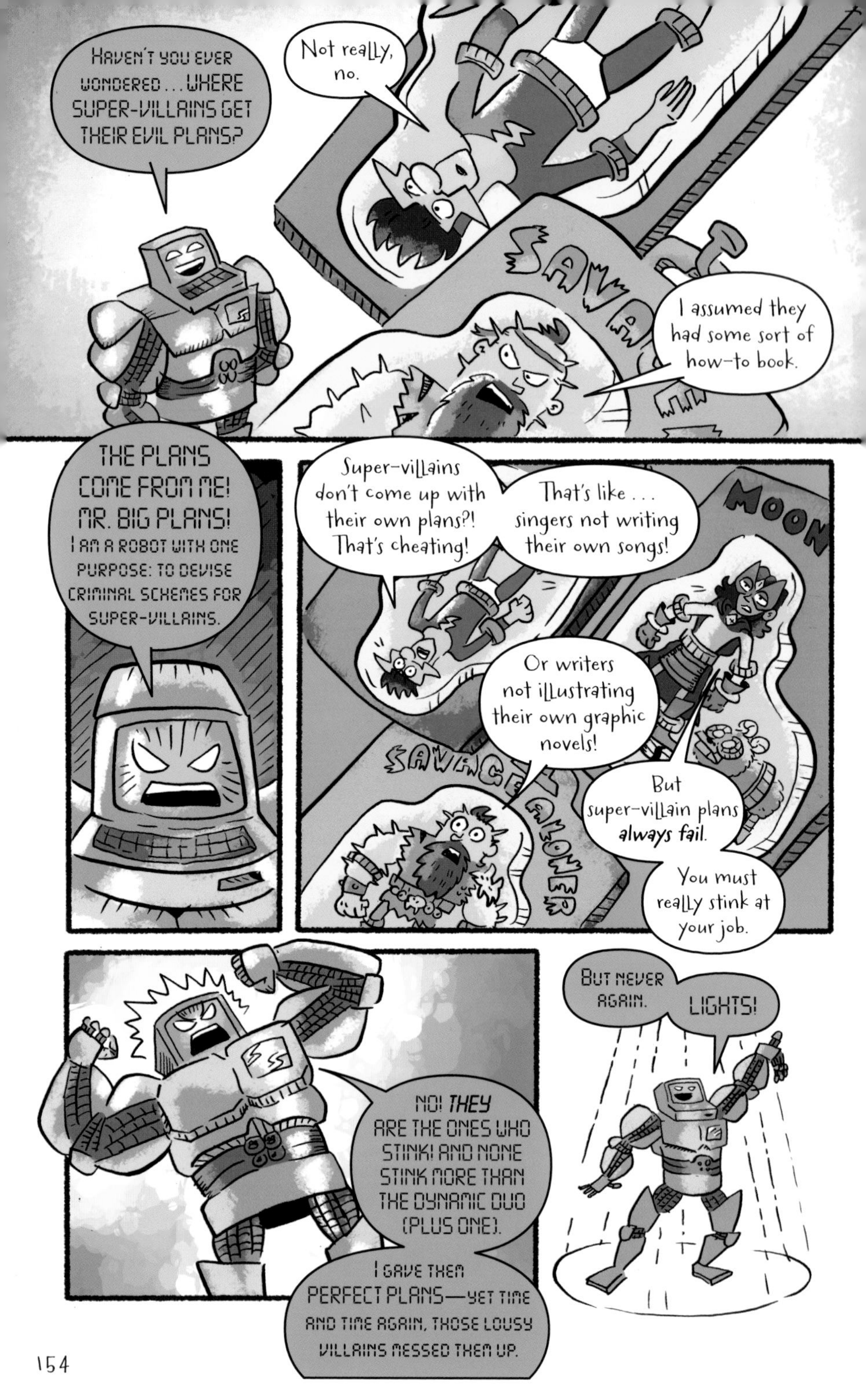
HAVEN'T YOU EVER WONDERED . . . WHERE SUPER-VILLAINS GET THEIR EVIL PLANS?
Not really, no.
SAVA
I assumed they had some sort of how-to book.
THE PLANS COME FROM ME! MR. BIG PLANS!
I AM A ROBOT WITH ONE PURPOSE: TO DEVISE CRIMINAL SCHEMES FOR SUPER-VILLAINS.
Super-villains don't come up with their own plans?! That's cheating!
That's like . . . singers not writing their own songs!
MOON
Or writers not illustrating their own graphic novels!
SAVAGE
But super-villain plans **always fail**.
You must really stink at your job.
NO! *THEY* ARE THE ONES WHO STINK! AND NONE STINK MORE THAN THE DYNAMIC DUO (PLUS ONE).
I GAVE THEM PERFECT PLANS—YET TIME AND TIME AGAIN, THOSE LOUSY VILLAINS MESSED THEM UP.
BUT NEVER AGAIN.
LIGHTS!

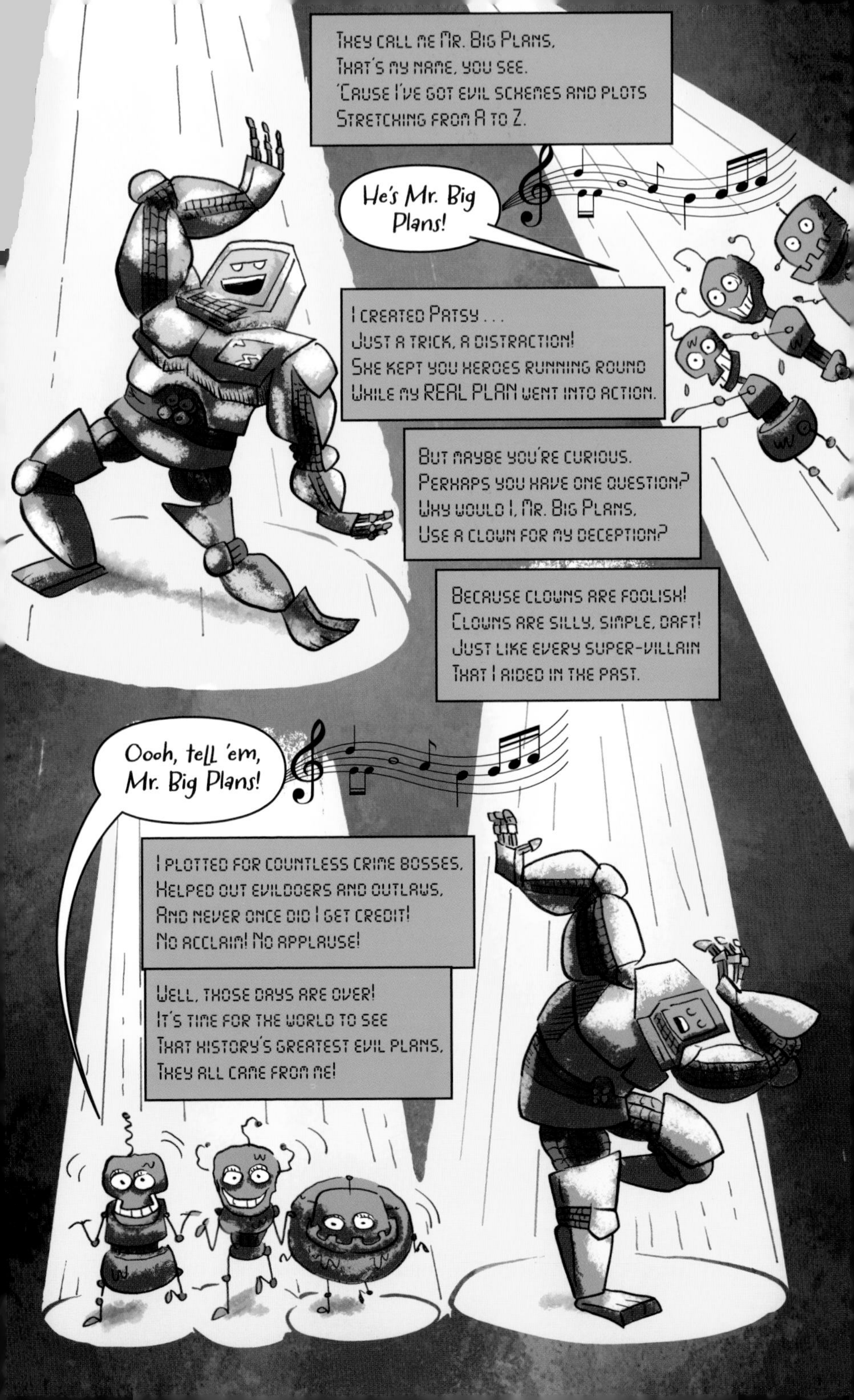
They call me Mr. Big Plans,
That's my name, you see.
'Cause I've got evil schemes and plots
Stretching from A to Z.
He's Mr. Big Plans!
I created Patsy . . .
Just a trick, a distraction!
She kept you heroes running round
While my REAL PLAN went into action.
But maybe you're curious.
Perhaps you have one question?
Why would I, Mr. Big Plans,
Use a clown for my deception?
Because clowns are foolish!
Clowns are silly, simple, daft!
Just like every super-villain
That I aided in the past.
Oooh, tell 'em, Mr. Big Plans!
I plotted for countless crime bosses,
Helped out evildoers and outlaws,
And never once did I get credit!
No acclaim! No applause!
Well, those days are over!
It's time for the world to see
That history's greatest evil plans,
They all came from me!

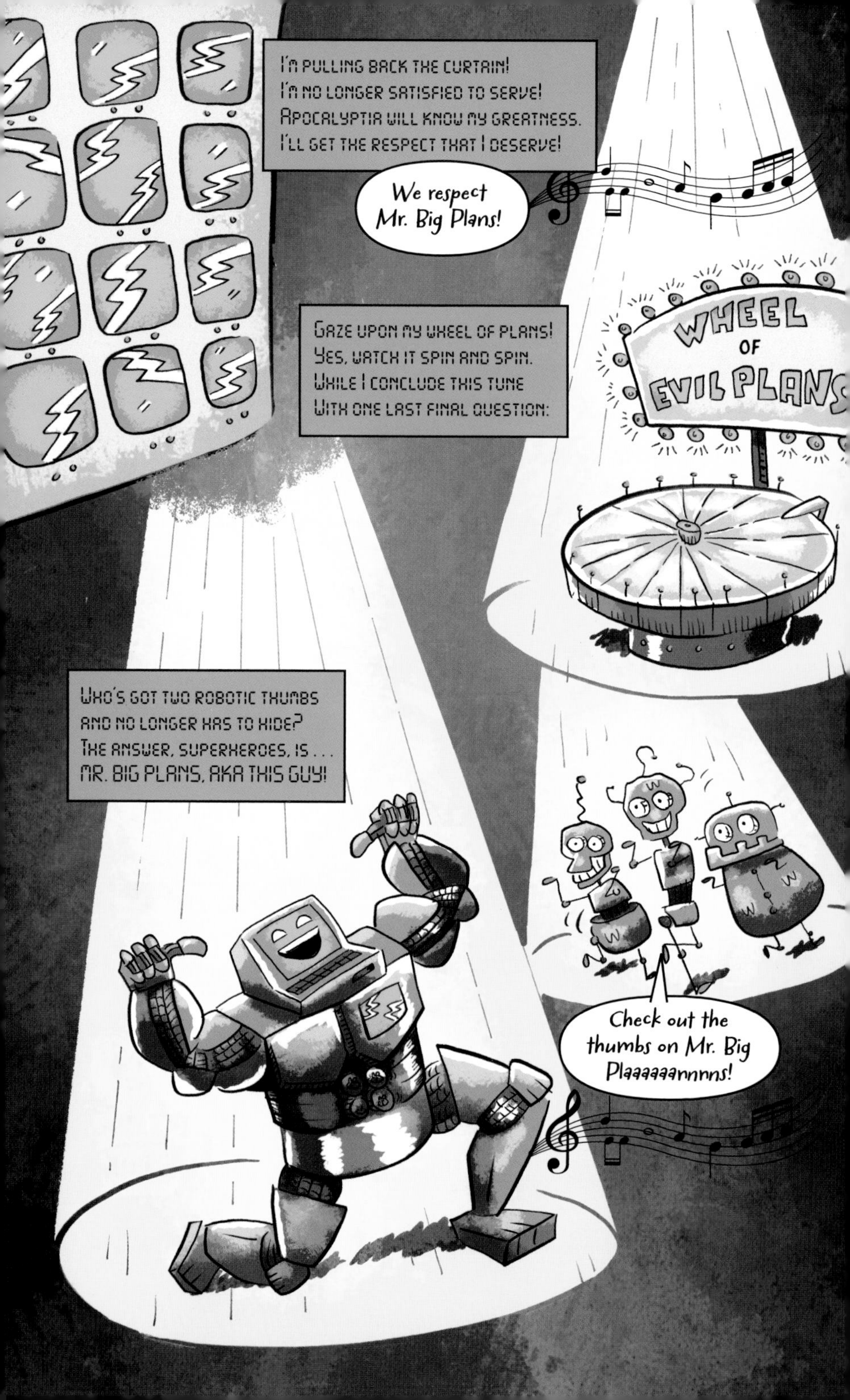
I'M PULLING BACK THE CURTAIN!
I'M NO LONGER SATISFIED TO SERVE!
APOCALYPTIA WILL KNOW MY GREATNESS.
I'LL GET THE RESPECT THAT I DESERVE!
We respect Mr. Big Plans!
GAZE UPON MY WHEEL OF PLANS!
YES, WATCH IT SPIN AND SPIN.
WHILE I CONCLUDE THIS TUNE
WITH ONE LAST FINAL QUESTION:
WHEEL OF EVIL PLANS
WHO'S GOT TWO ROBOTIC THUMBS
AND NO LONGER HAS TO HIDE?
THE ANSWER, SUPERHEROES, IS . . .
MR. BIG PLANS, AKA THIS GUY!
Check out the thumbs on Mr. Big Plaaaaaannnns!

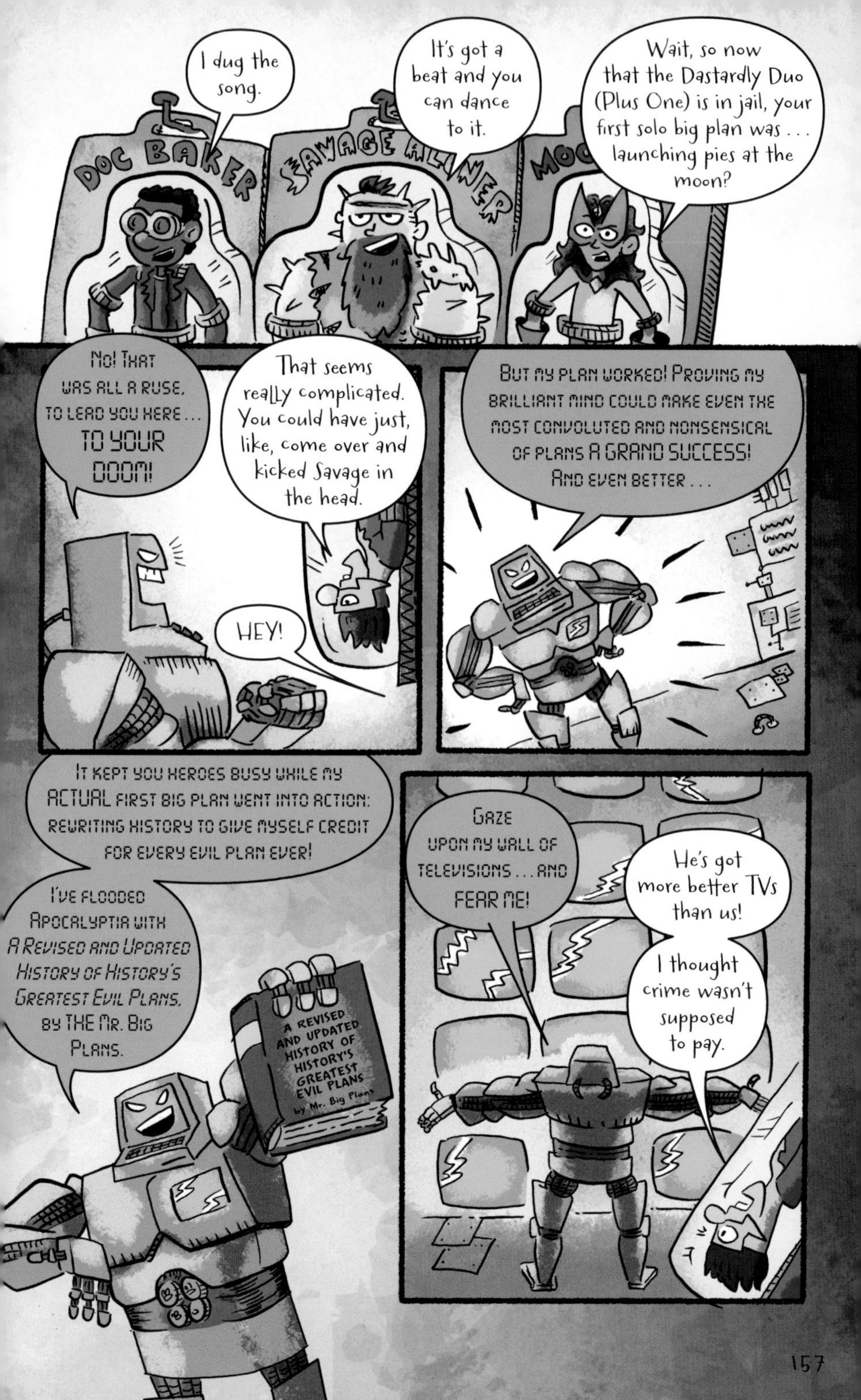

DOC BAKER
SAVAGE ALMER
I dug the song.
It's got a beat and you can dance to it.
Wait, so now that the Dastardly Duo (Plus One) is in jail, your first solo big plan was . . . launching pies at the moon?
No! That was all a ruse, to lead you here . . . TO YOUR DOOM!
That seems really complicated. You could have just, like, come over and kicked Savage in the head.
HEY!
But my plan worked! Proving my brilliant mind could make even the most convoluted and nonsensical of plans A GRAND SUCCESS! And even better . . .
It kept you heroes busy while my ACTUAL first big plan went into action: rewriting history to give myself credit for every evil plan ever!
I've flooded Apocalyptia with A Revised and Updated History of History's Greatest Evil Plans, by THE Mr. Big Plans.
A REVISED AND UPDATED HISTORY OF HISTORY'S GREATEST EVIL PLANS by Mr. Big Plans
Gaze upon my wall of televisions . . . and FEAR ME!
He's got more better TVs than us!
I thought crime wasn't supposed to pay.

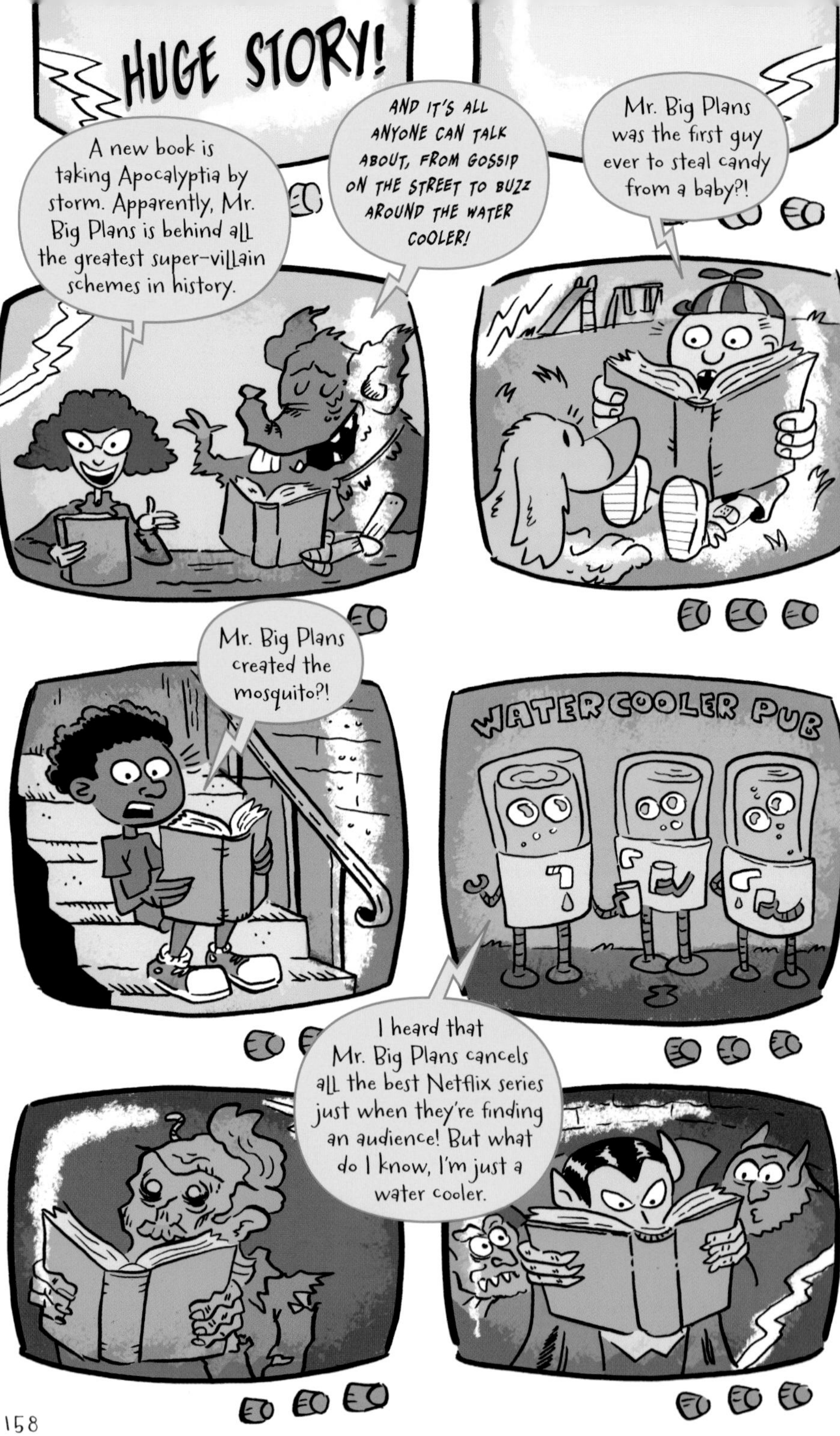
HUGE STORY!
A new book is taking Apocalyptia by storm. Apparently, Mr. Big Plans is behind all the greatest super-villain schemes in history.
AND IT'S ALL ANYONE CAN TALK ABOUT, FROM GOSSIP ON THE STREET TO BUZZ AROUND THE WATER COOLER!
Mr. Big Plans was the first guy ever to steal candy from a baby?!
Mr. Big Plans created the mosquito?!
WATER COOLER PUB
I heard that Mr. Big Plans cancels all the best Netflix series just when they're finding an audience! But what do I know, I'm just a water cooler.

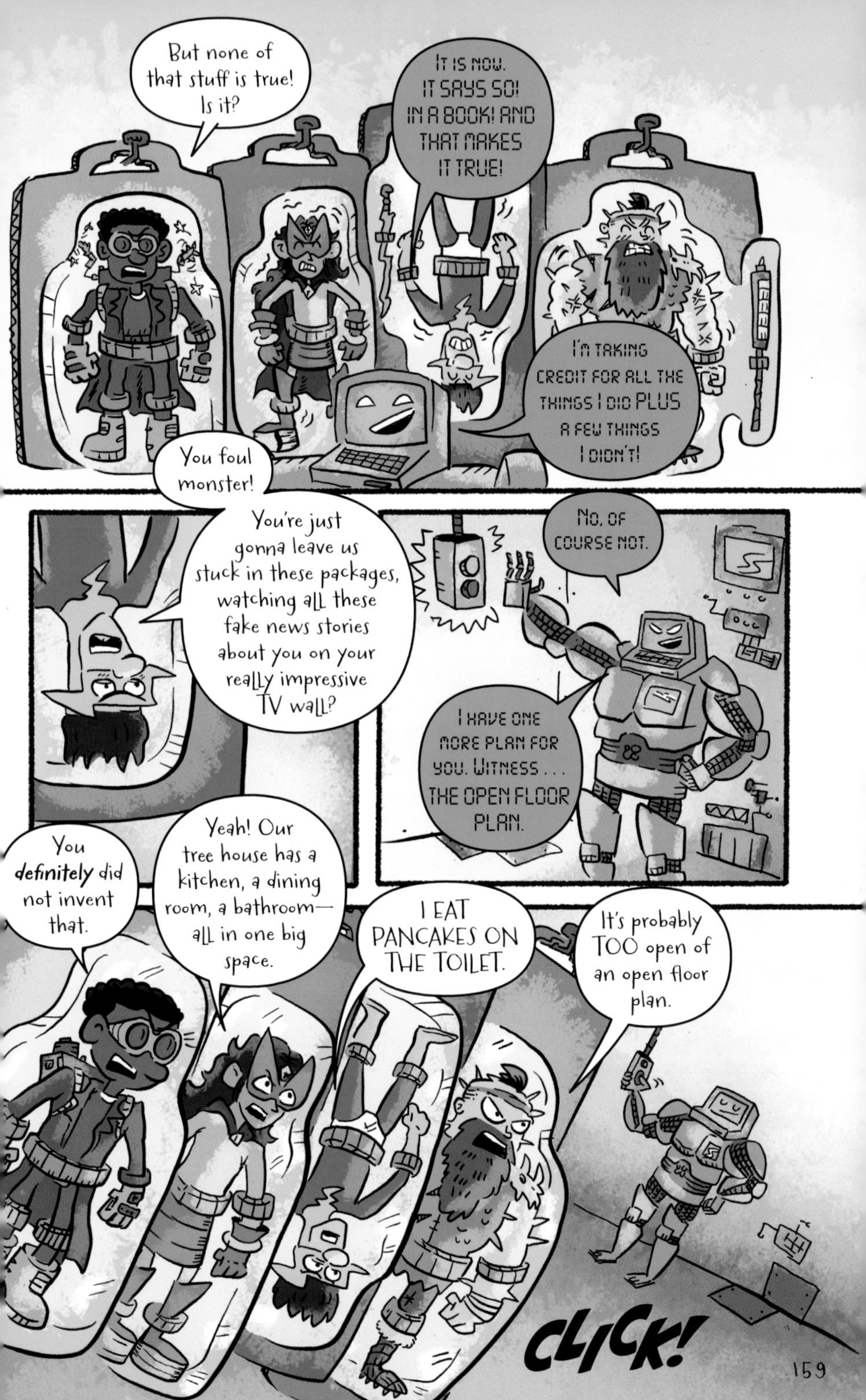

But none of that stuff is true! Is it?
IT IS NOW. IT SAYS SO! IN A BOOK! AND THAT MAKES IT TRUE!
I'M TAKING CREDIT FOR ALL THE THINGS I DID PLUS A FEW THINGS I DIDN'T!
You foul monster!
You're just gonna leave us stuck in these packages, watching all these fake news stories about you on your really impressive TV wall?
NO, OF COURSE NOT.
I HAVE ONE MORE PLAN FOR YOU. WITNESS . . . THE OPEN FLOOR PLAN.
You **definitely** did not invent that.
Yeah! Our tree house has a kitchen, a dining room, a bathroom—all in one big space.
I EAT PANCAKES ON THE TOILET.
It's probably TOO open of an open floor plan.
CLICK!

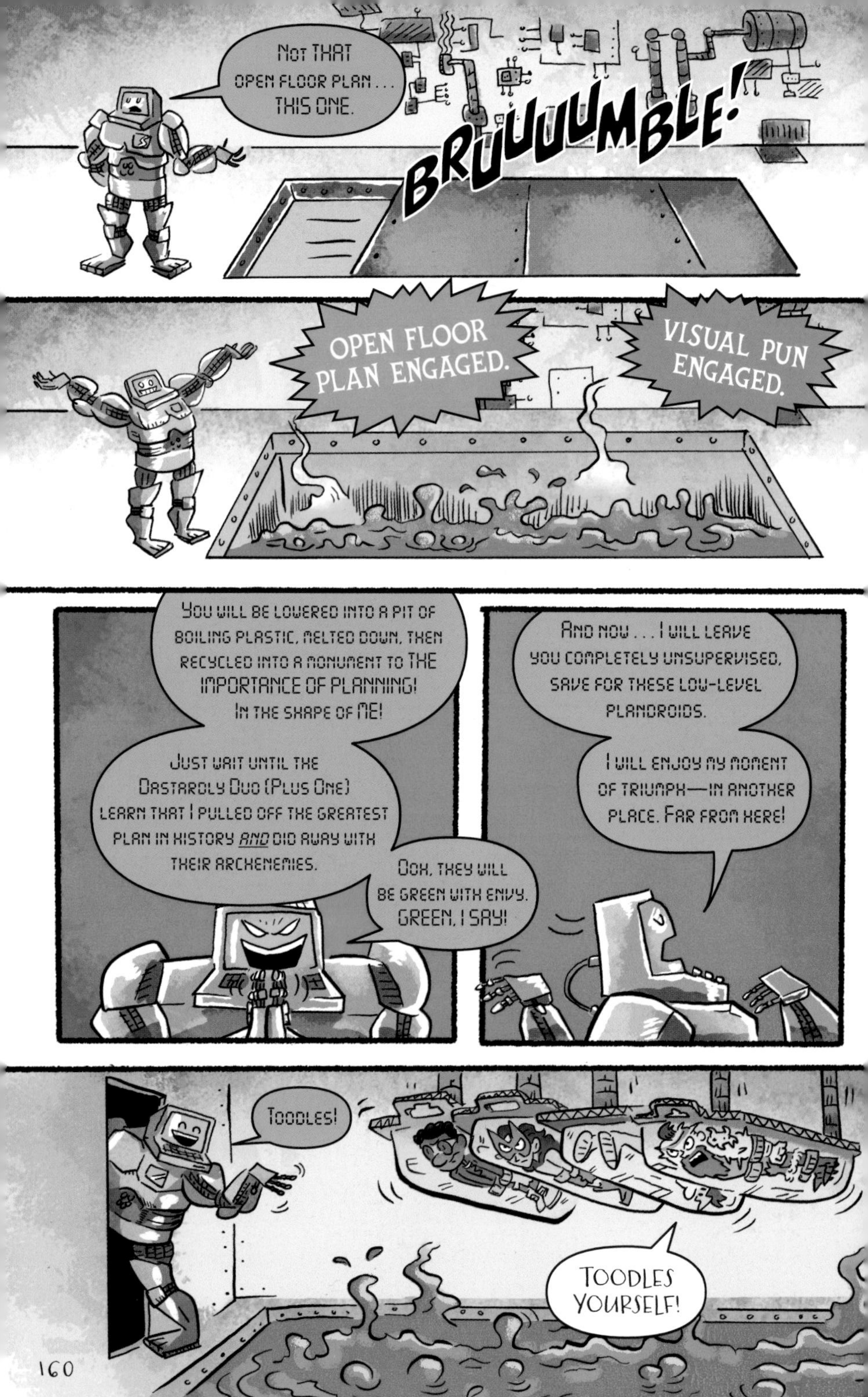
NOT THAT OPEN FLOOR PLAN . . . THIS ONE.
BRUUUUMBLE!
OPEN FLOOR PLAN ENGAGED.
VISUAL PUN ENGAGED.
YOU WILL BE LOWERED INTO A PIT OF BOILING PLASTIC, MELTED DOWN, THEN RECYCLED INTO A MONUMENT TO THE IMPORTANCE OF PLANNING! IN THE SHAPE OF ME!
JUST WAIT UNTIL THE DASTARDLY DUO (PLUS ONE) LEARN THAT I PULLED OFF THE GREATEST PLAN IN HISTORY AND DID AWAY WITH THEIR ARCHENEMIES.
OOH, THEY WILL BE GREEN WITH ENVY. GREEN, I SAY!
AND NOW . . . I WILL LEAVE YOU COMPLETELY UNSUPERVISED, SAVE FOR THESE LOW-LEVEL PLANDROIDS.
I WILL ENJOY MY MOMENT OF TRIUMPH—IN ANOTHER PLACE. FAR FROM HERE!
TOODLES!
TOODLES YOURSELF!

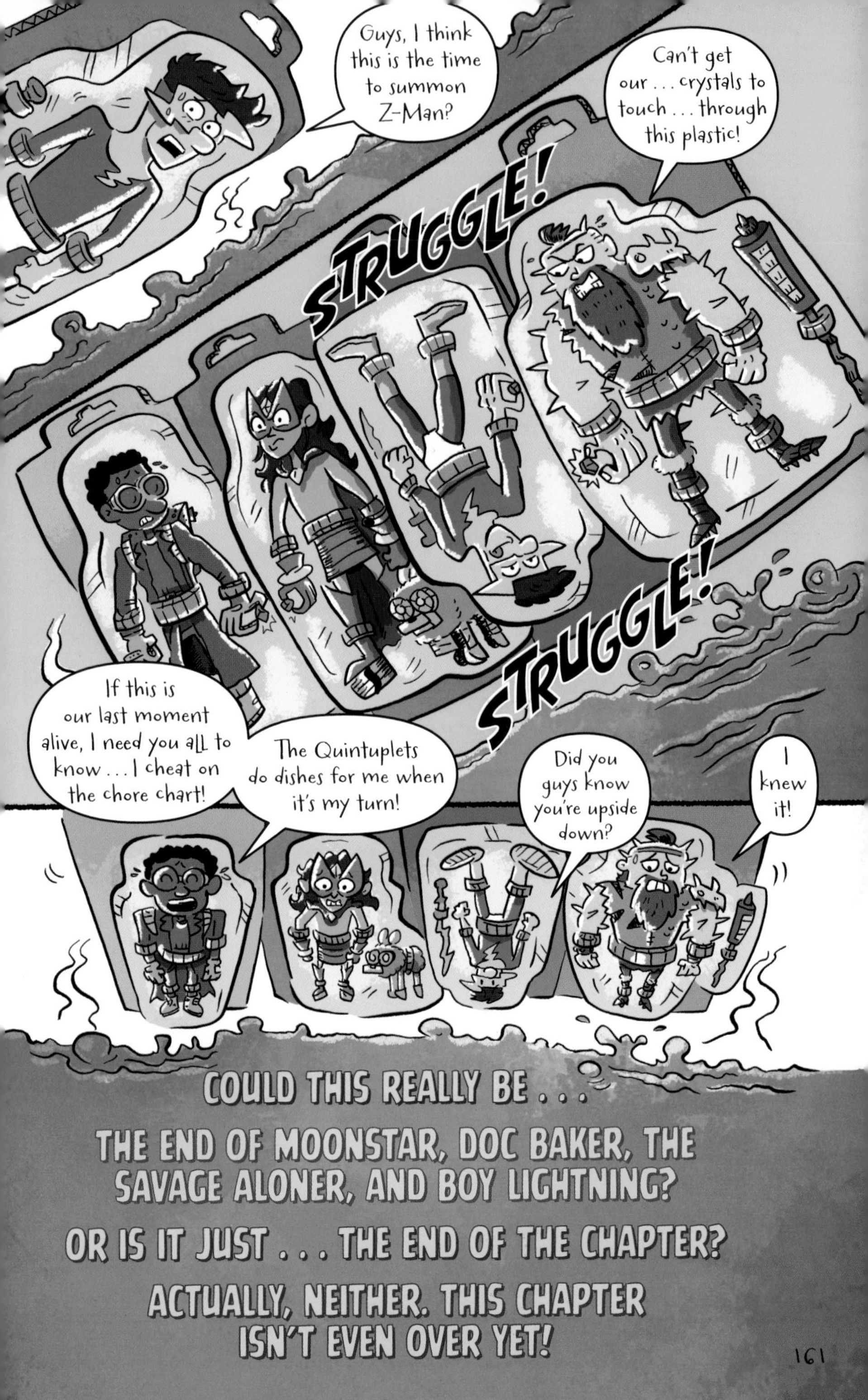
Guys, I think this is the time to summon Z-Man?
Can't get our . . . crystals to touch . . . through this plastic!
STRUGGLE!
STRUGGLE!
If this is our last moment alive, I need you all to know . . . I cheat on the chore chart!
The Quintuplets do dishes for me when it's my turn!
Did you guys know you're upside down?
I knew it!
COULD THIS REALLY BE . . .
THE END OF MOONSTAR, DOC BAKER, THE SAVAGE ALONER, AND BOY LIGHTNING?
OR IS IT JUST . . . THE END OF THE CHAPTER?
ACTUALLY, NEITHER. THIS CHAPTER ISN'T EVEN OVER YET!

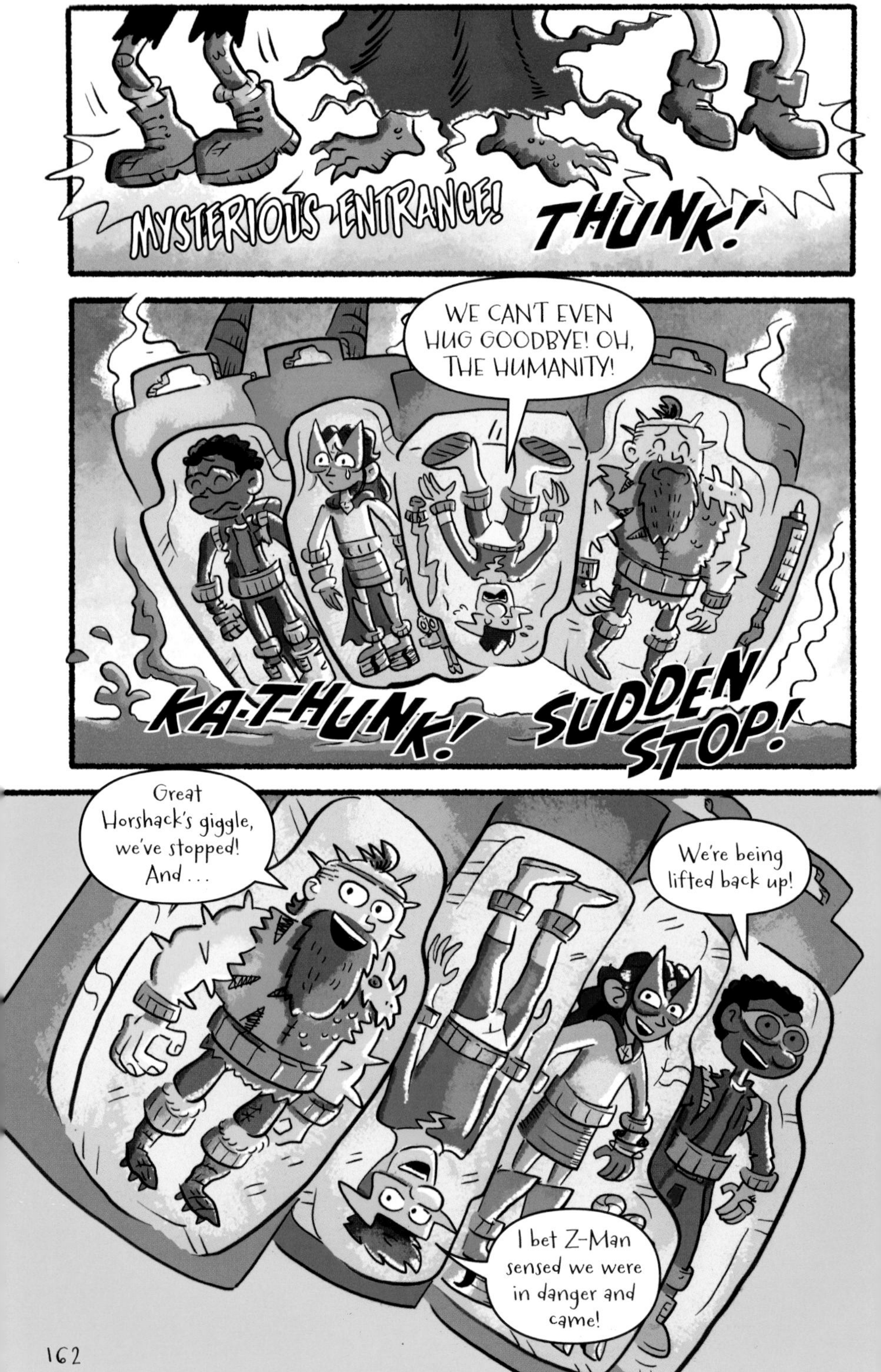
MYSTERIOUS ENTRANCE!
THUNK!
WE CAN'T EVEN HUG GOODBYE! OH, THE HUMANITY!
KA-THUNK!
SUDDEN STOP!
Great Horshack's giggle, we've stopped! And . . .
We're being lifted back up!
I bet Z-Man sensed we were in danger and came!

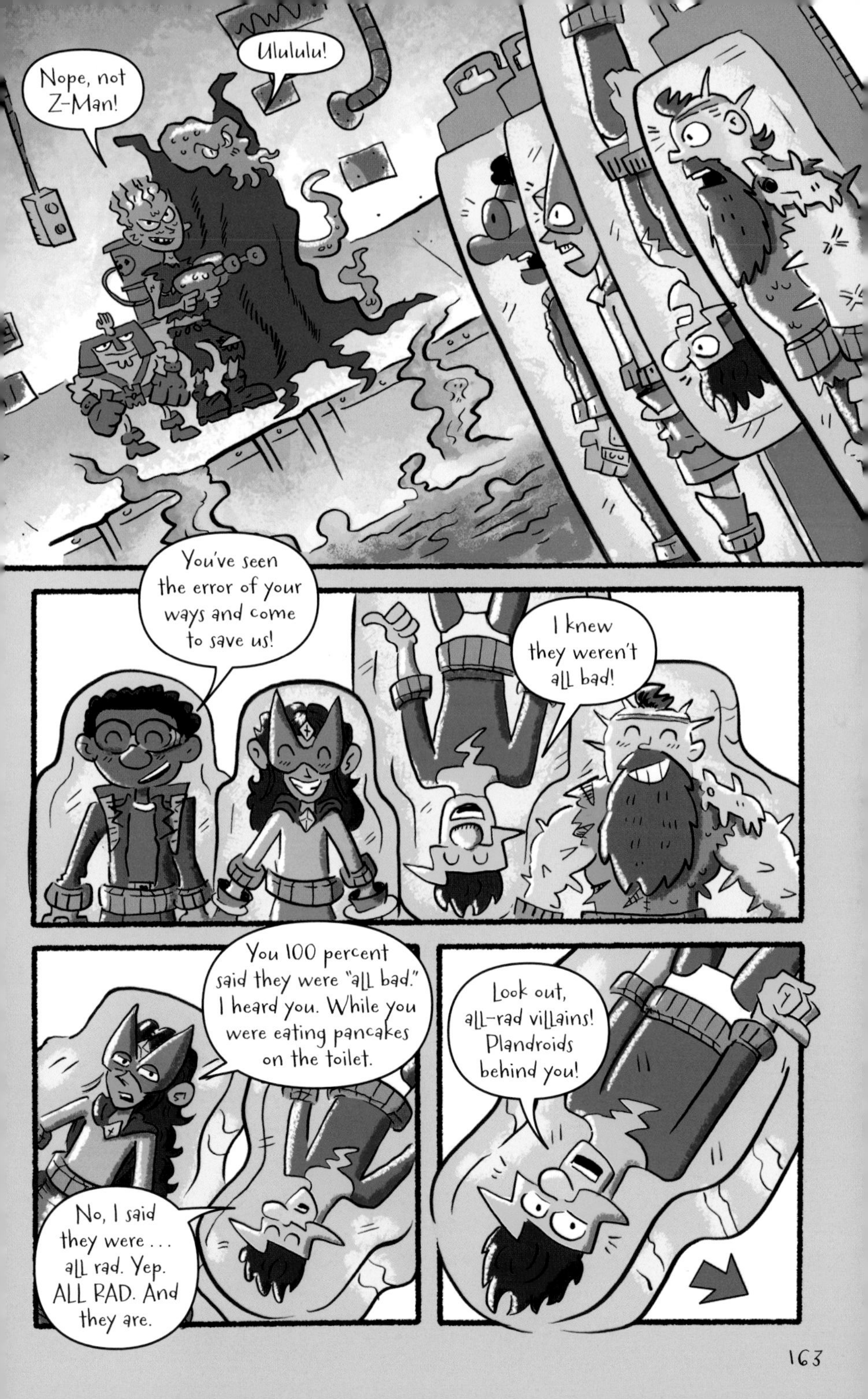
Nope, not Z-Man!
Ulululu!
You've seen the error of your ways and come to save us!
I knew they weren't all bad!
You 100 percent said they were "all bad." I heard you. While you were eating pancakes on the toilet.
No, I said they were . . . all rad. Yep. ALL RAD. And they are.
Look out, all-rad villains! Plandroids behind you!

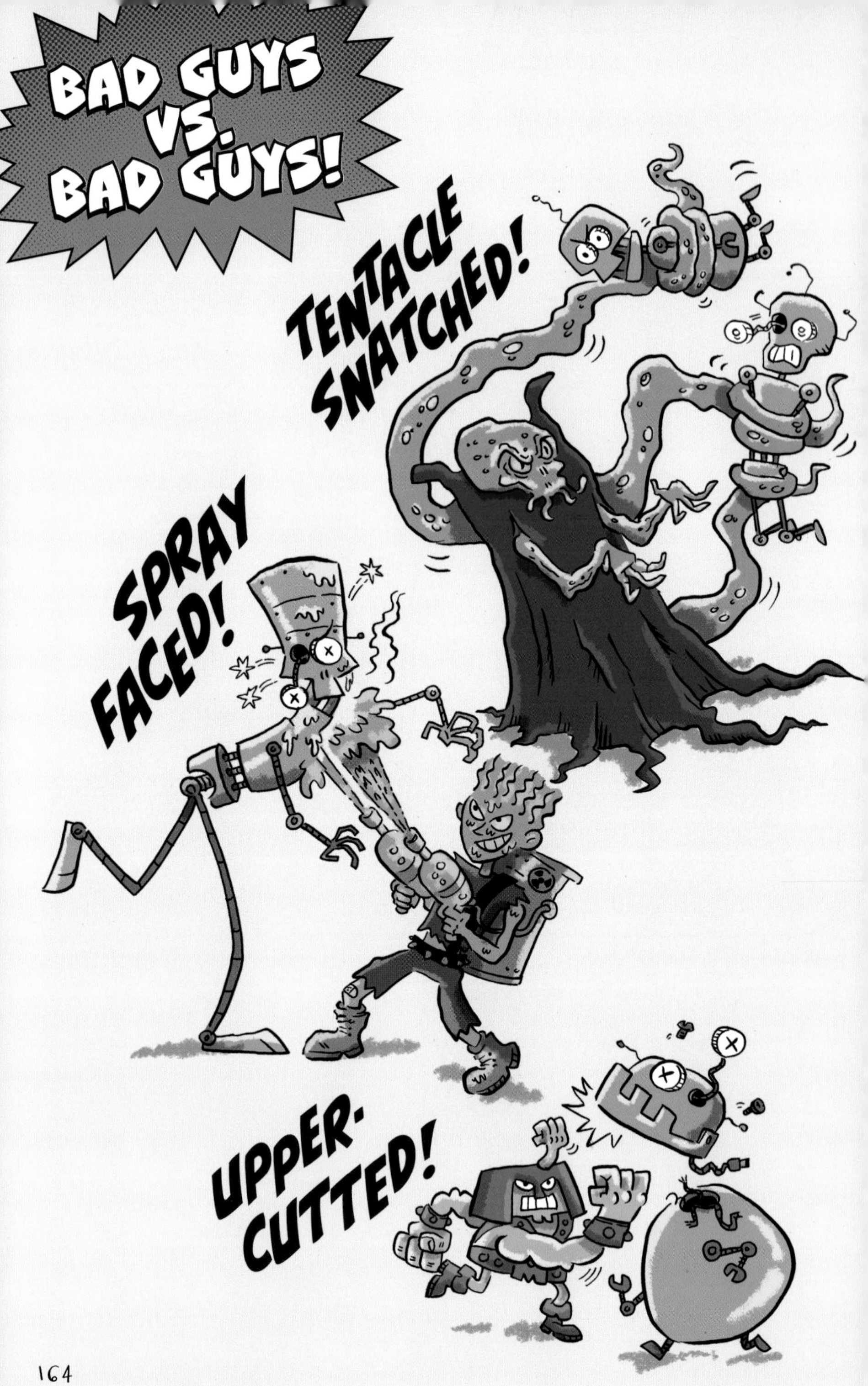
BAD GUYS VS. BAD GUYS!
TENTACLE SNATCHED!
SPRAY FACED!
UPPER-CUTTED!

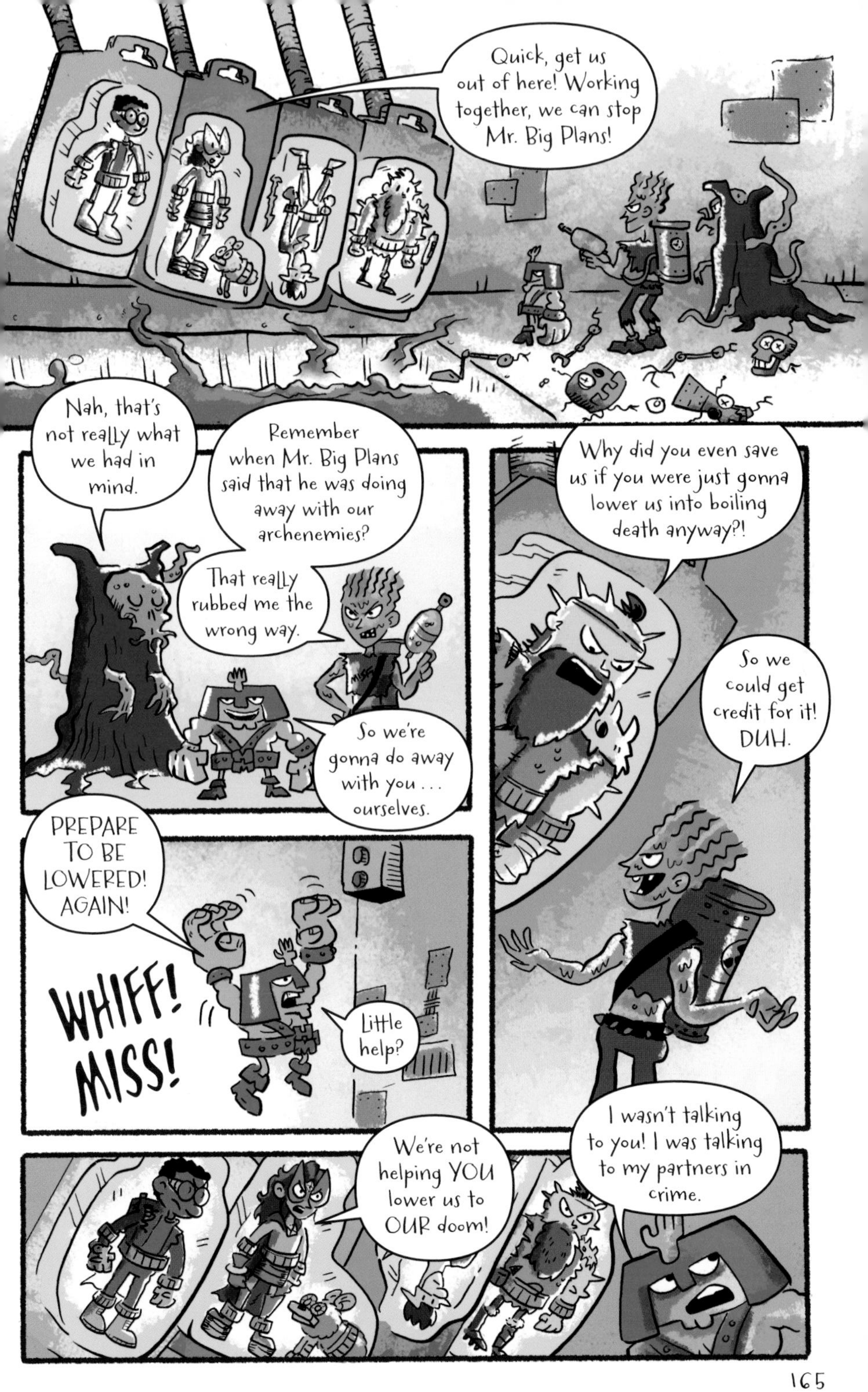
Quick, get us out of here! Working together, we can stop Mr. Big Plans!
Nah, that's not really what we had in mind.
Remember when Mr. Big Plans said that he was doing away with our archenemies?
That really rubbed me the wrong way.
So we're gonna do away with you . . . ourselves.
Why did you even save us if you were just gonna lower us into boiling death anyway?!
So we could get credit for it! DUH.
PREPARE TO BE LOWERED! AGAIN!
WHIFF! MISS!
Little help?
We're not helping YOU lower us to OUR doom!
I wasn't talking to you! I was talking to my partners in crime.

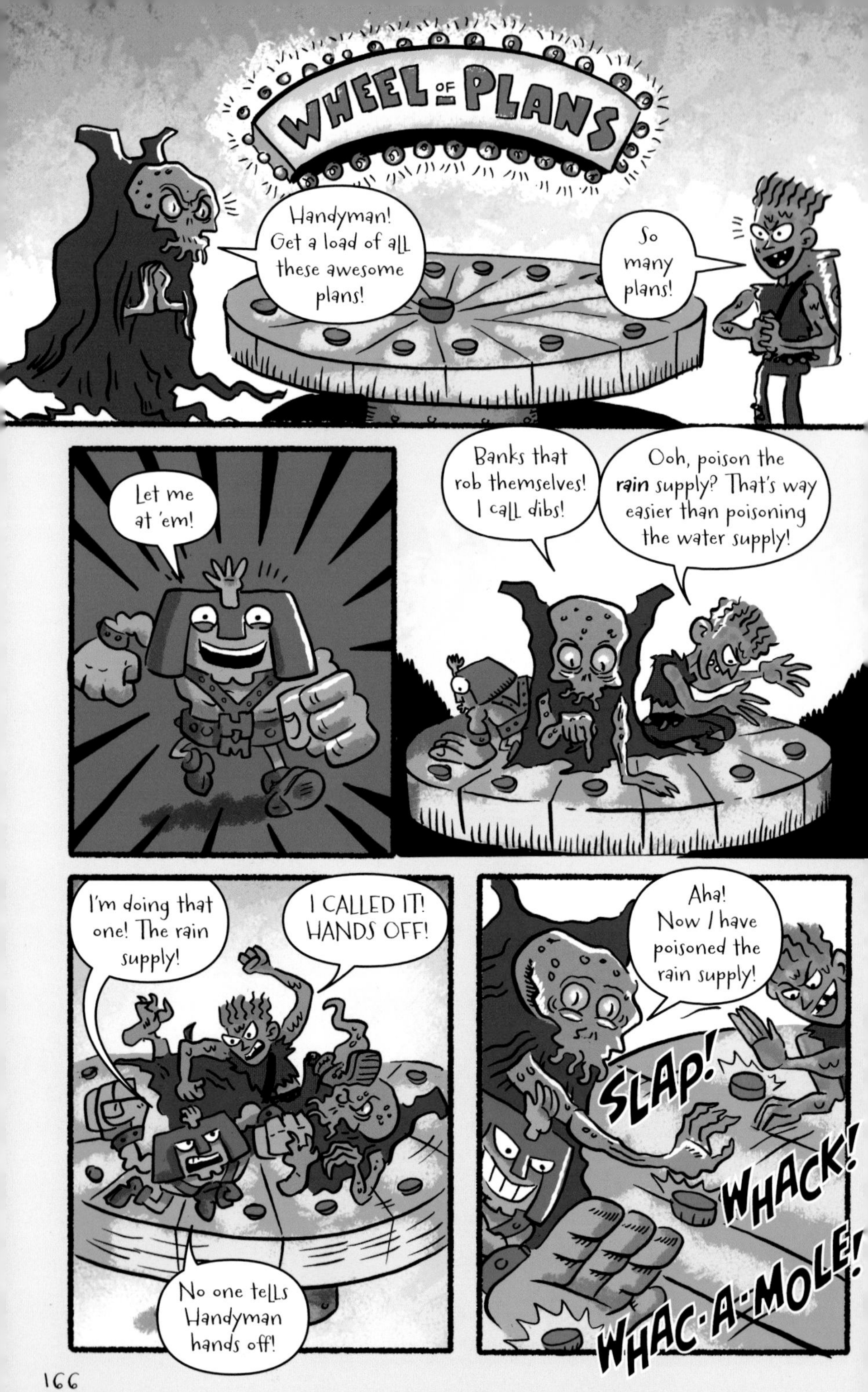
WHEEL OF PLANS
Handyman! Get a load of all these awesome plans!
So many plans!
Let me at 'em!
Banks that rob themselves! I call dibs!
Ooh, poison the **rain** supply? That's way easier than poisoning the water supply!
I'm doing that one! The rain supply!
I CALLED IT! HANDS OFF!
No one tells Handyman hands off!
Aha! Now I have poisoned the rain supply!
SLAP!
WHACK!
WHAC-A-MOLE!

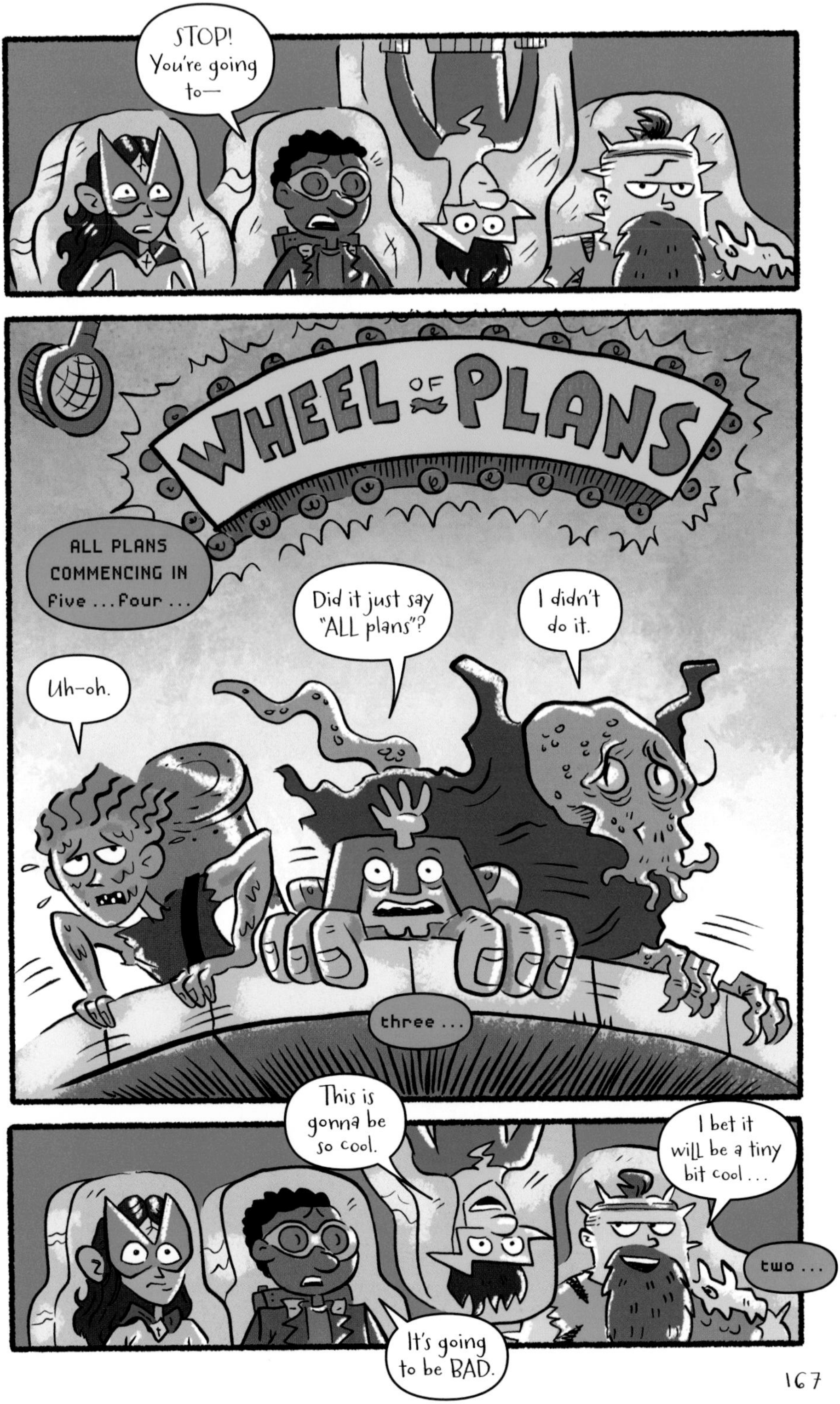
STOP! You're going to—
WHEEL OF PLANS
ALL PLANS COMMENCING IN five . . . four . . .
Uh-oh.
Did it just say "ALL plans"?
I didn't do it.
three . . .
This is gonna be so cool.
I bet it will be a tiny bit cool . . .
two . . .
It's going to be BAD.

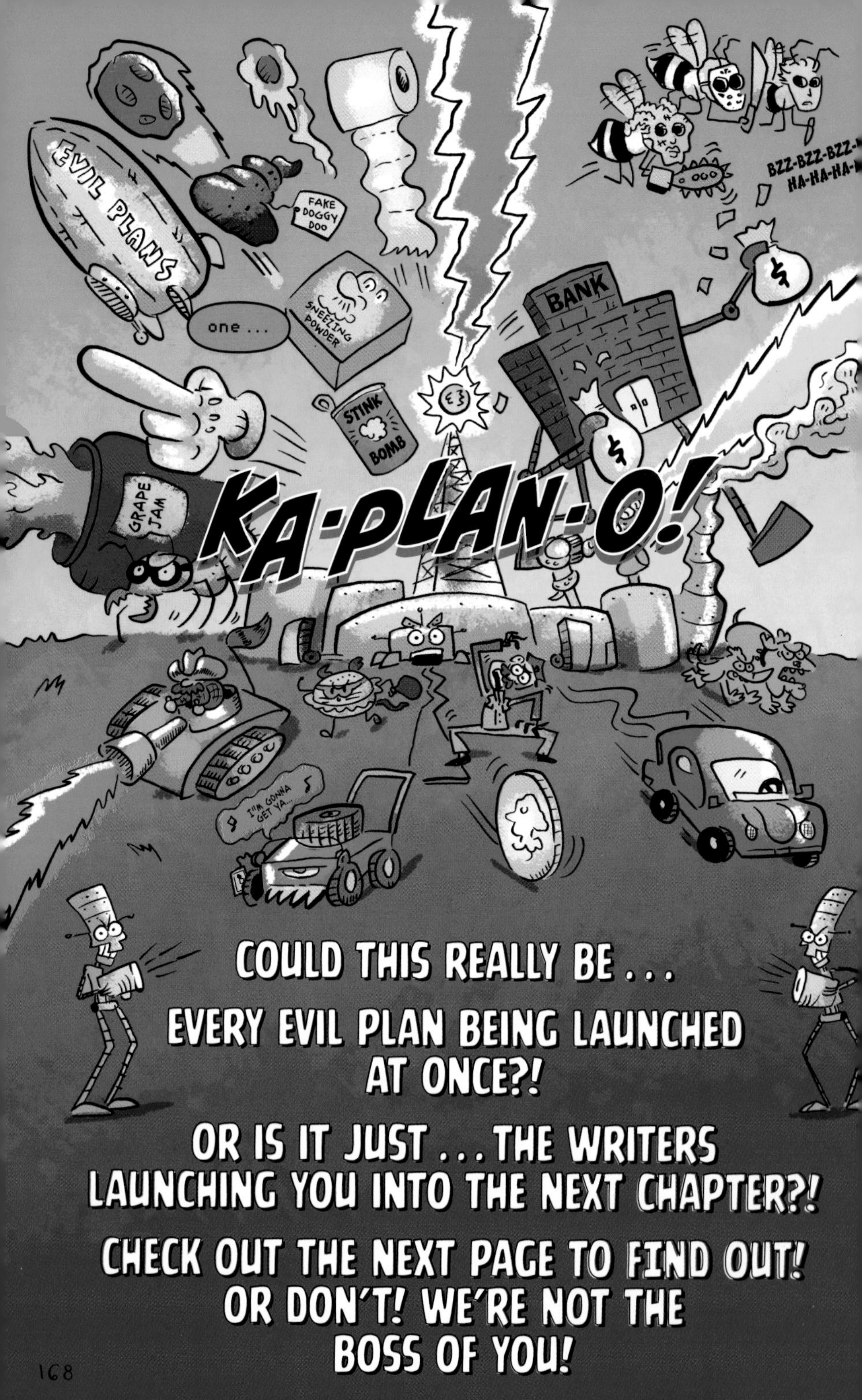
EVIL PLANS
FAKE DOGGY DOO
one . . .
SNEEZING POWDER
STINK BOMB
GRAPE JAM
BANK
BZZ-BZZ-BZZ-
HA-HA-HA-
KA-PLAN-O!
I'M GONNA GET YA...
COULD THIS REALLY BE . . .
EVERY EVIL PLAN BEING LAUNCHED AT ONCE?!
OR IS IT JUST . . . THE WRITERS LAUNCHING YOU INTO THE NEXT CHAPTER?!
CHECK OUT THE NEXT PAGE TO FIND OUT! OR DON'T! WE'RE NOT THE BOSS OF YOU!

CHAPTER TWELVE

TOO MANY PLANS!

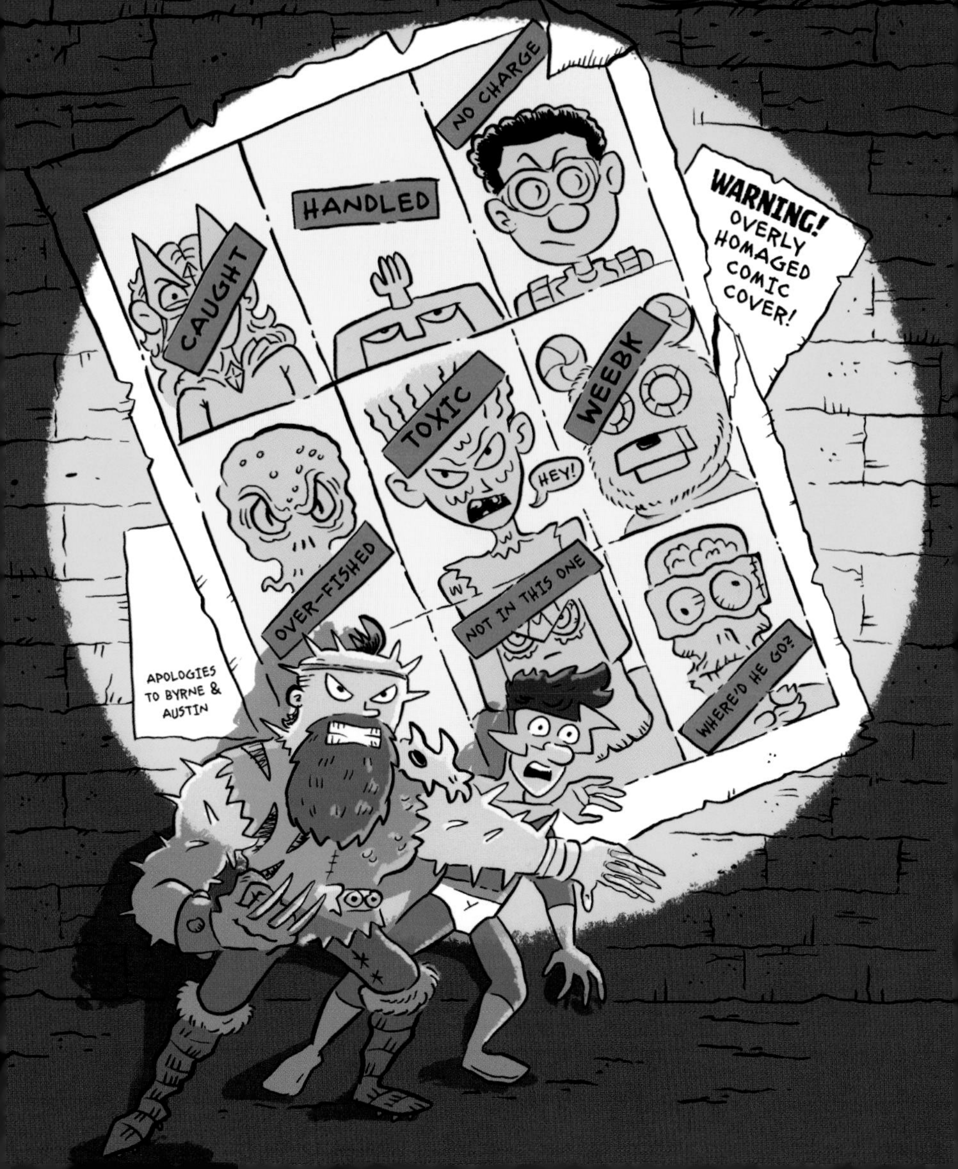
CAUGHT
HANDLED
NO CHARGE
WARNING!
OVERLY HOMAGED COMIC COVER!
OVER-FISHED
TOXIC
HEY!
WEEBK
NOT IN THIS ONE
WHERE'D HE GO?
APOLOGIES TO BYRNE & AUSTIN

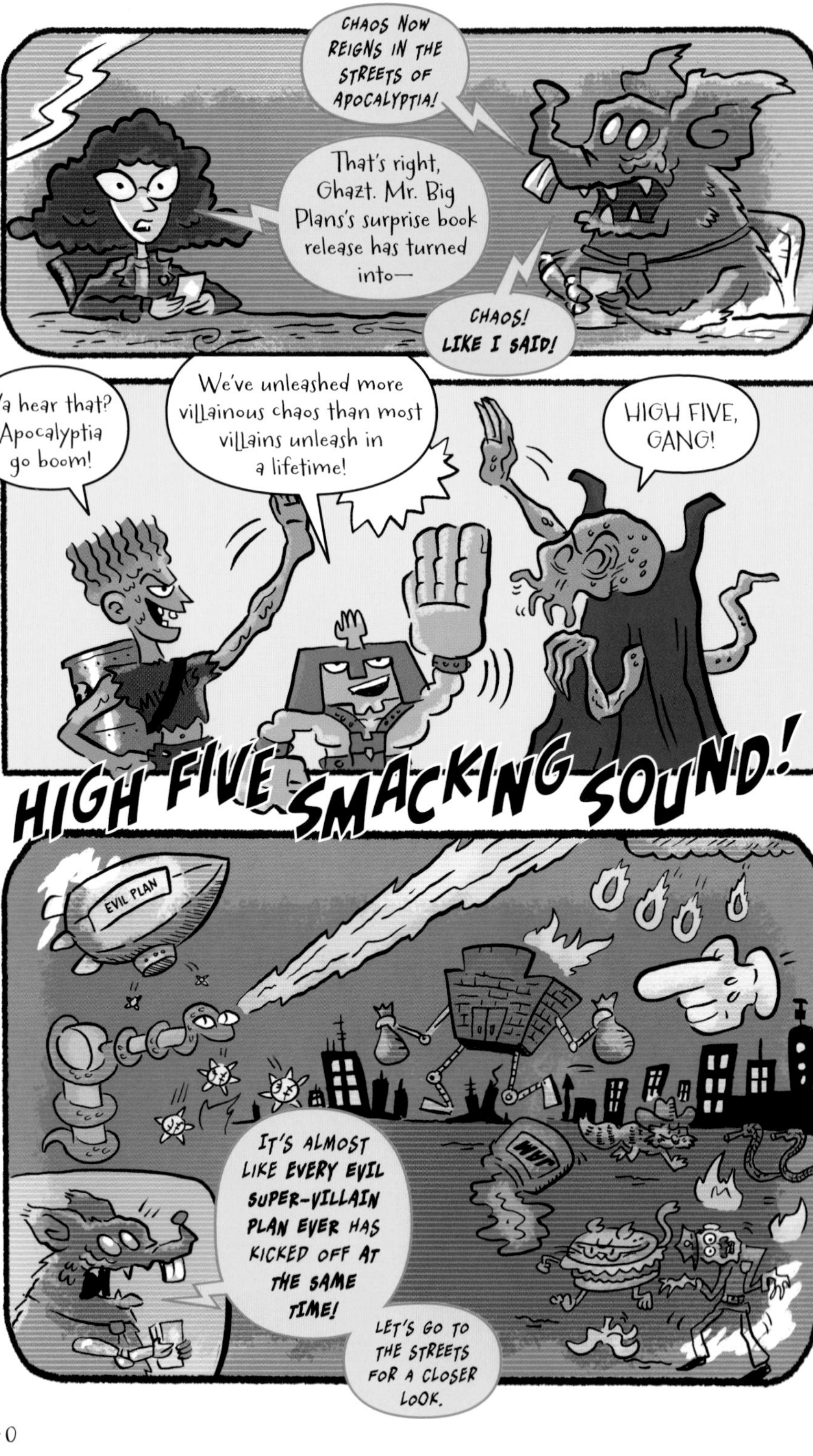
CHAOS NOW REIGNS IN THE STREETS OF APOCALYPTIA!
That's right, Ghazt. Mr. Big Plans's surprise book release has turned into—
CHAOS! LIKE I SAID!
Ya hear that? Apocalyptia go boom!
We've unleashed more villainous chaos than most villains unleash in a lifetime!
HIGH FIVE, GANG!
HIGH FIVE SMACKING SOUND!
EVIL PLAN
IT'S ALMOST LIKE EVERY EVIL SUPER-VILLAIN PLAN EVER HAS KICKED OFF AT THE SAME TIME!
LET'S GO TO THE STREETS FOR A CLOSER LOOK.

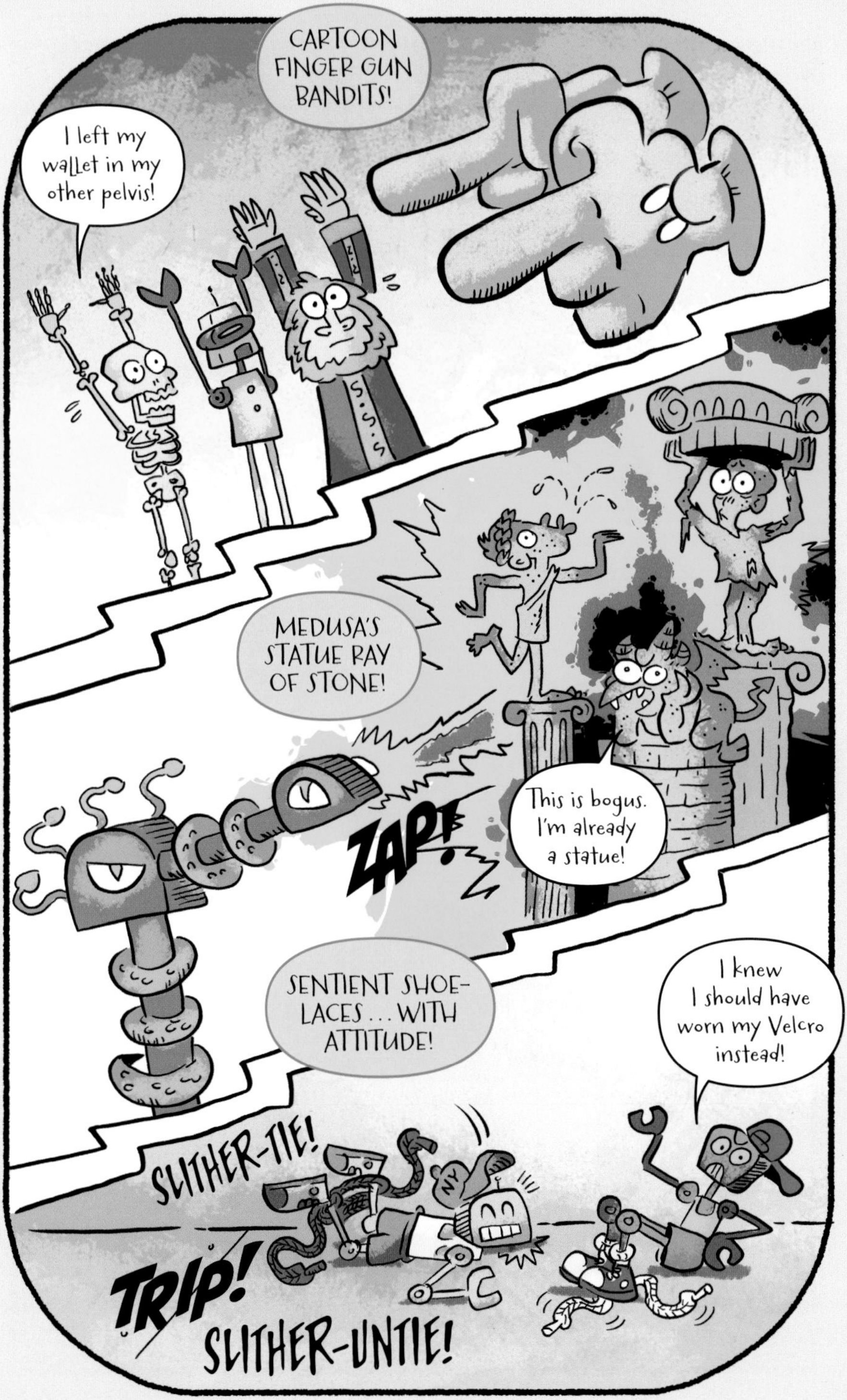
CARTOON FINGER GUN BANDITS!
I left my wallet in my other pelvis!
MEDUSA'S STATUE RAY OF STONE!
ZAP!
This is bogus. I'm already a statue!
SENTIENT SHOE-LACES . . . WITH ATTITUDE!
I knew I should have worn my Velcro instead!
SLITHER-TIE!
TRIP!
SLITHER-UNTIE!

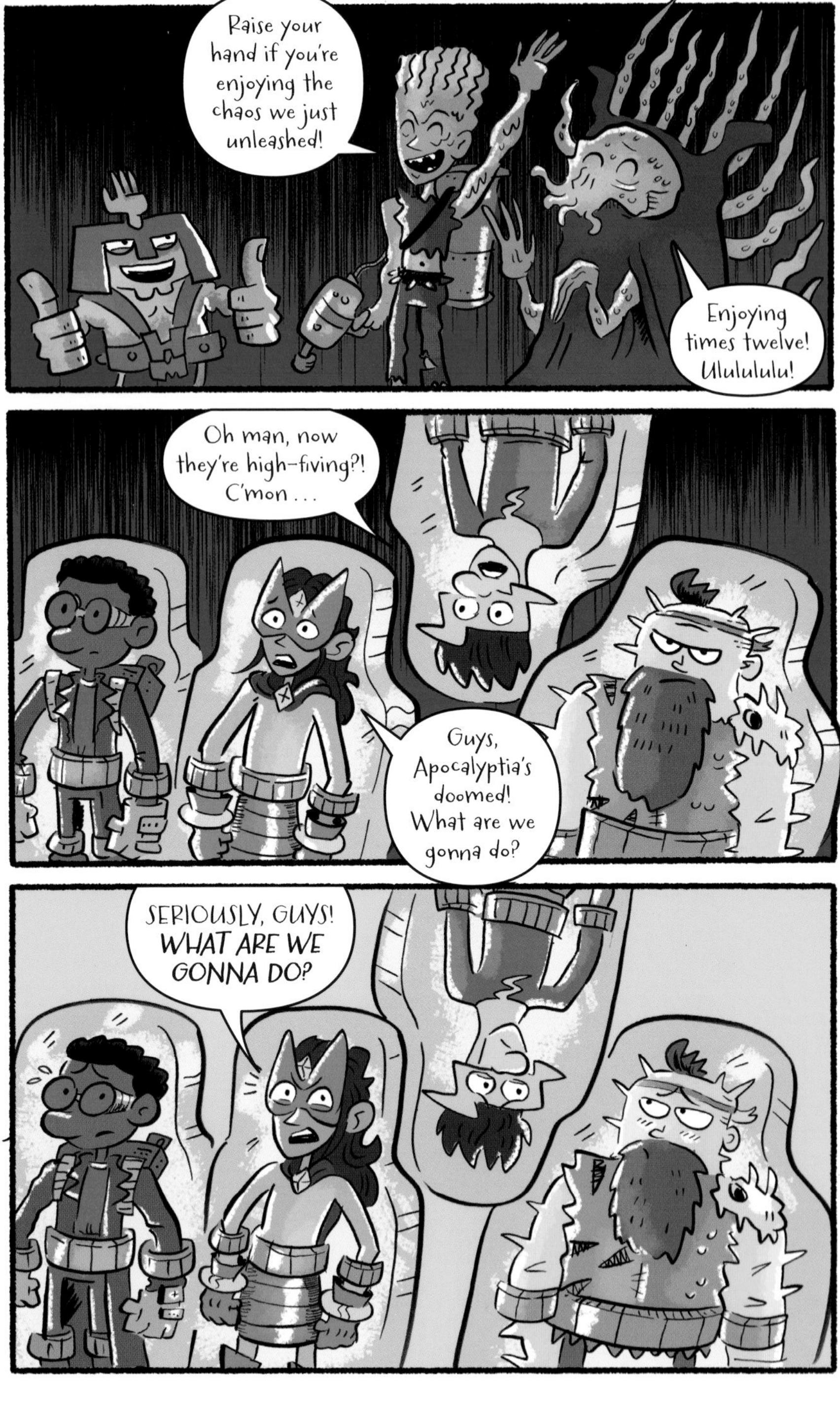
Raise your hand if you're enjoying the chaos we just unleashed!
Enjoying times twelve! Ulululululu!
Oh man, now they're high-fiving?! C'mon . . .
Guys, Apocalyptia's doomed! What are we gonna do?
SERIOUSLY, GUYS! WHAT ARE WE GONNA DO?

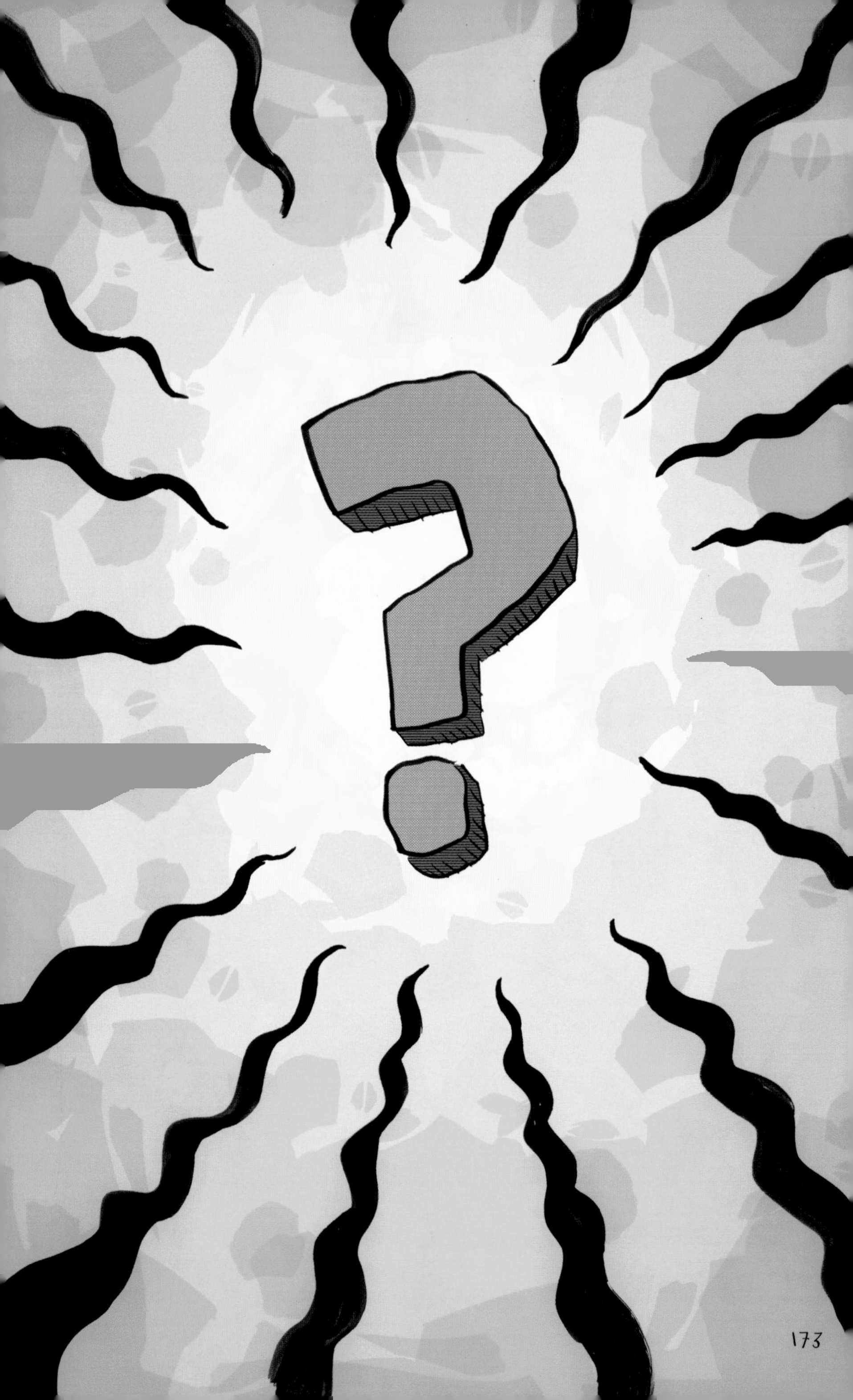

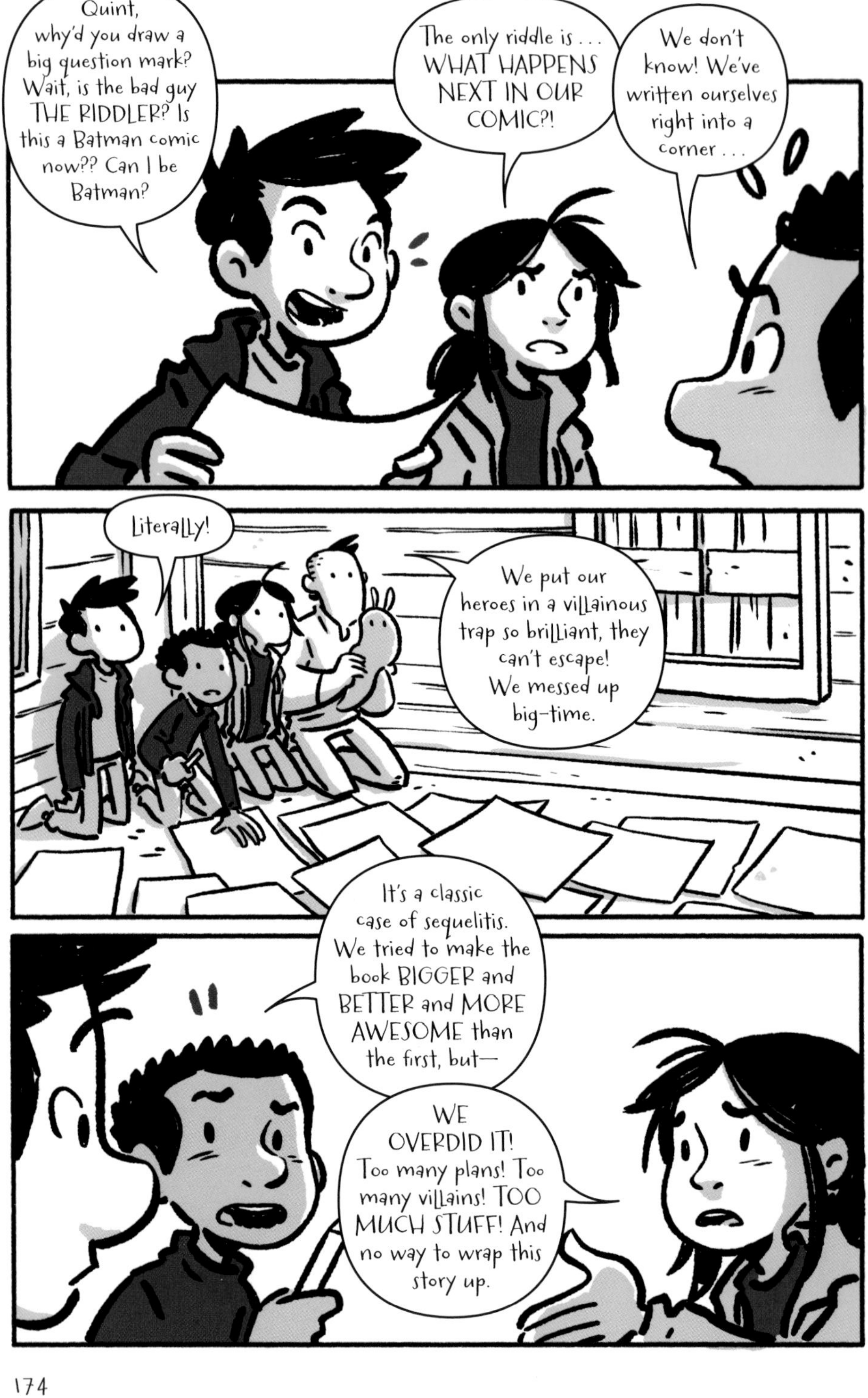
Quint, why'd you draw a big question mark? Wait, is the bad guy THE RIDDLER? Is this a Batman comic now?? Can I be Batman?
The only riddle is . . . WHAT HAPPENS NEXT IN OUR COMIC?!
We don't know! We've written ourselves right into a corner . . .
Literally!
We put our heroes in a villainous trap so brilliant, they can't escape! We messed up big-time.
It's a classic case of sequelitis. We tried to make the book BIGGER and BETTER and MORE AWESOME than the first, but—
WE OVERDID IT! Too many plans! Too many villains! TOO MUCH STUFF! And no way to wrap this story up.

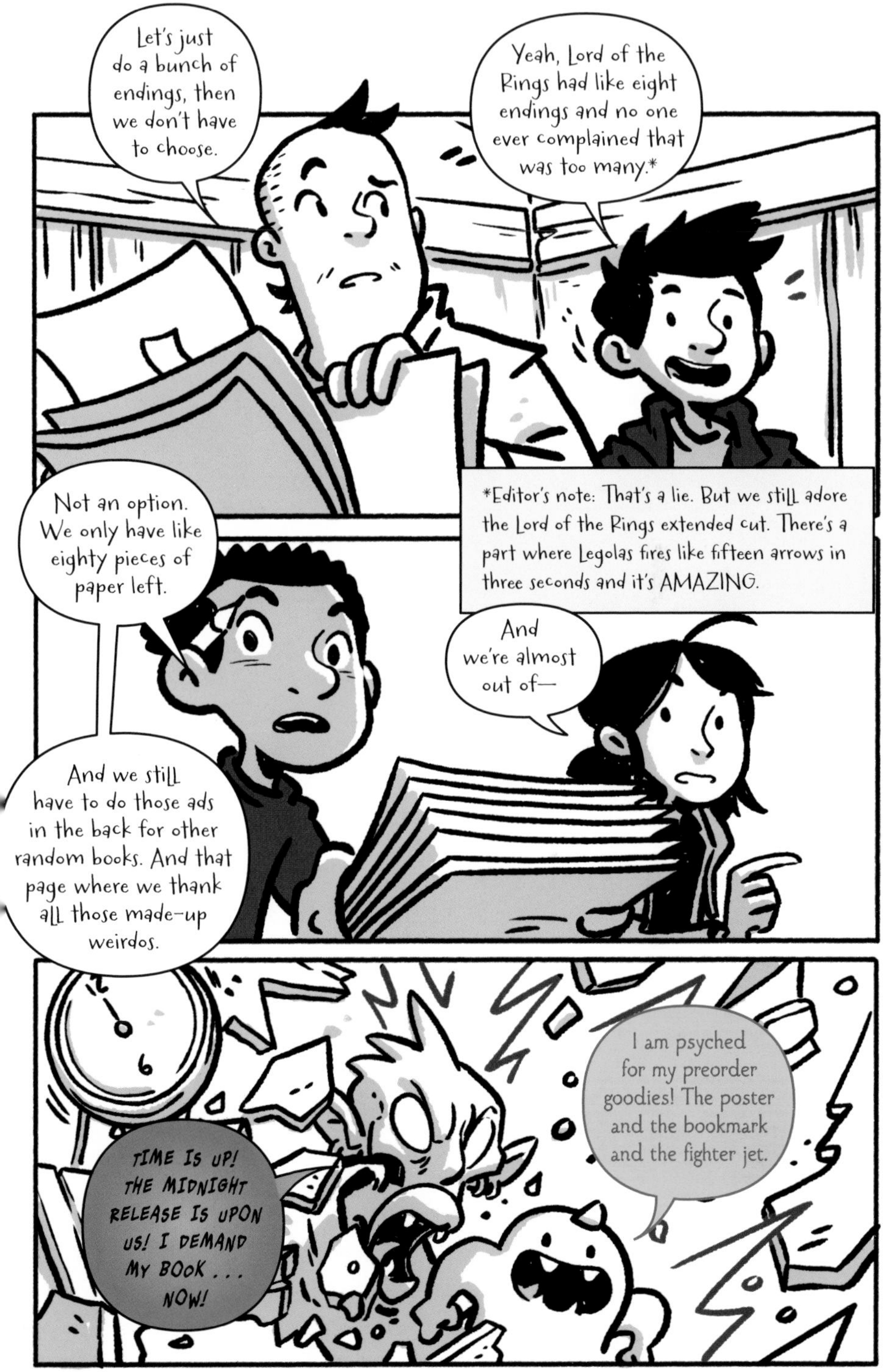
Let's just do a bunch of endings, then we don't have to choose.
Yeah, Lord of the Rings had like eight endings and no one ever complained that was too many.*
Not an option. We only have like eighty pieces of paper left.
And we still have to do those ads in the back for other random books. And that page where we thank all those made-up weirdos.
*Editor's note: That's a lie. But we still adore the Lord of the Rings extended cut. There's a part where Legolas fires like fifteen arrows in three seconds and it's AMAZING.
And we're almost out of—
TIME IS UP! THE MIDNIGHT RELEASE IS UPON US! I DEMAND MY BOOK . . . NOW!
I am psyched for my preorder goodies! The poster and the bookmark and the fighter jet.

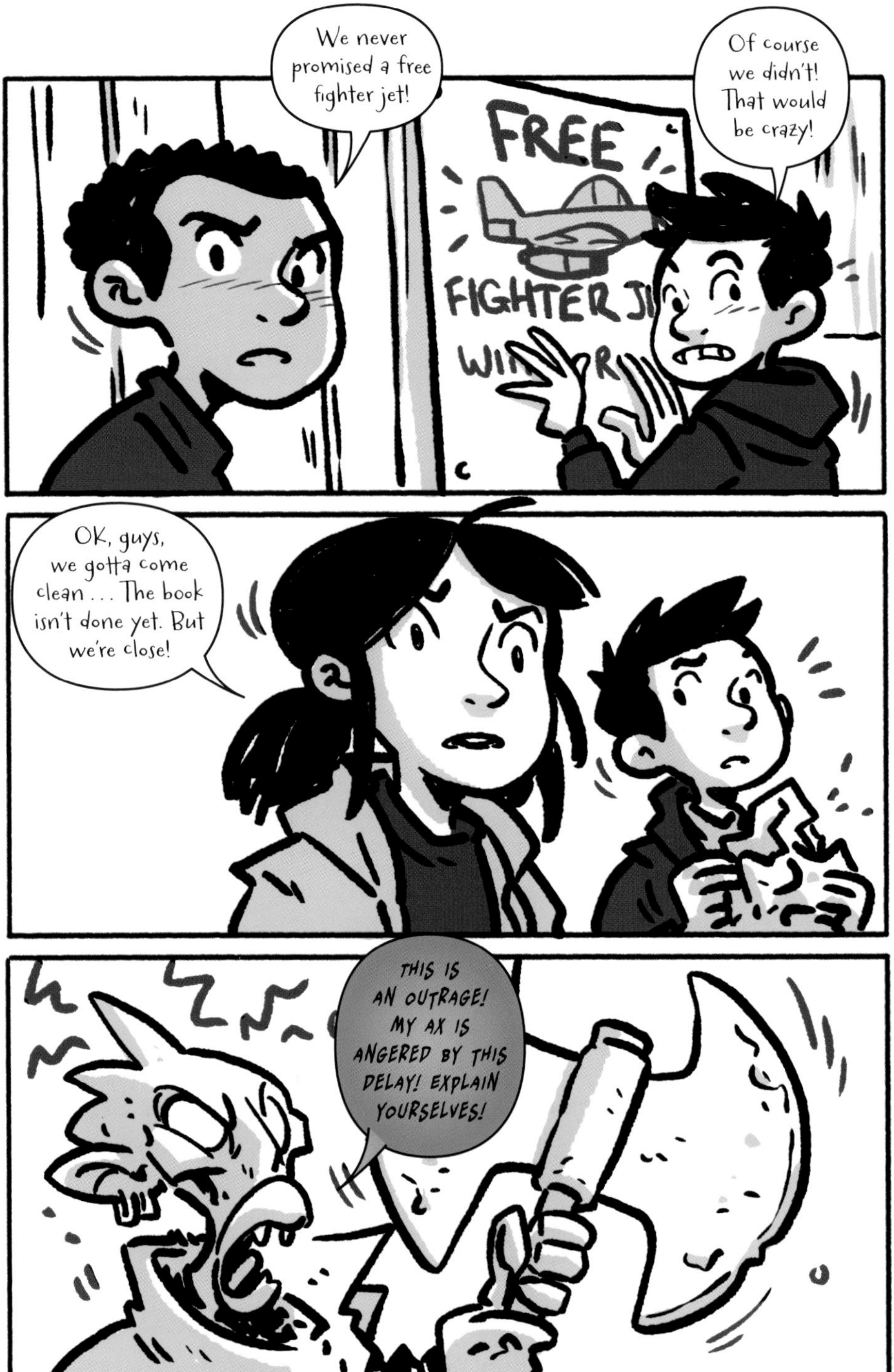
We never promised a free fighter jet!
Of course we didn't! That would be crazy!
FREE FIGHTER J
OK, guys, we gotta come clean . . . The book isn't done yet. But we're close!
THIS IS AN OUTRAGE! MY AX IS ANGERED BY THIS DELAY! EXPLAIN YOURSELVES!

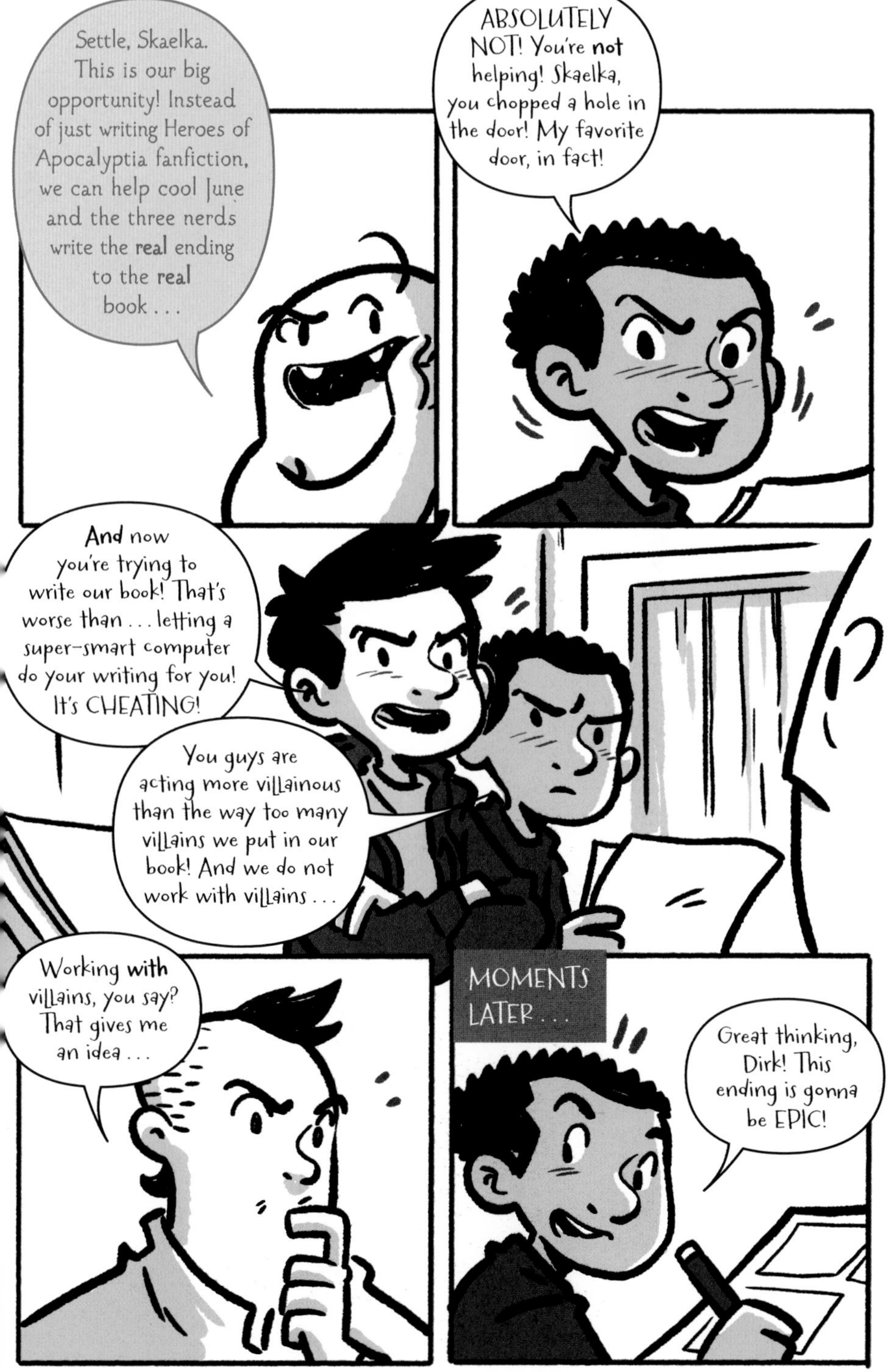
Settle, Skaelka. This is our big opportunity! Instead of just writing Heroes of Apocalyptia fanfiction, we can help cool June and the three nerds write the **real** ending to the **real** book . . .
ABSOLUTELY NOT! You're **not** helping! Skaelka, you chopped a hole in the door! My favorite door, in fact!
And now you're trying to write our book! That's worse than . . . letting a super-smart computer do your writing for you! It's CHEATING!
You guys are acting more villainous than the way too many villains we put in our book! And we do not work with villains . . .
Working **with** villains, you say? That gives me an idea . . .
MOMENTS LATER . . .
Great thinking, Dirk! This ending is gonna be EPIC!

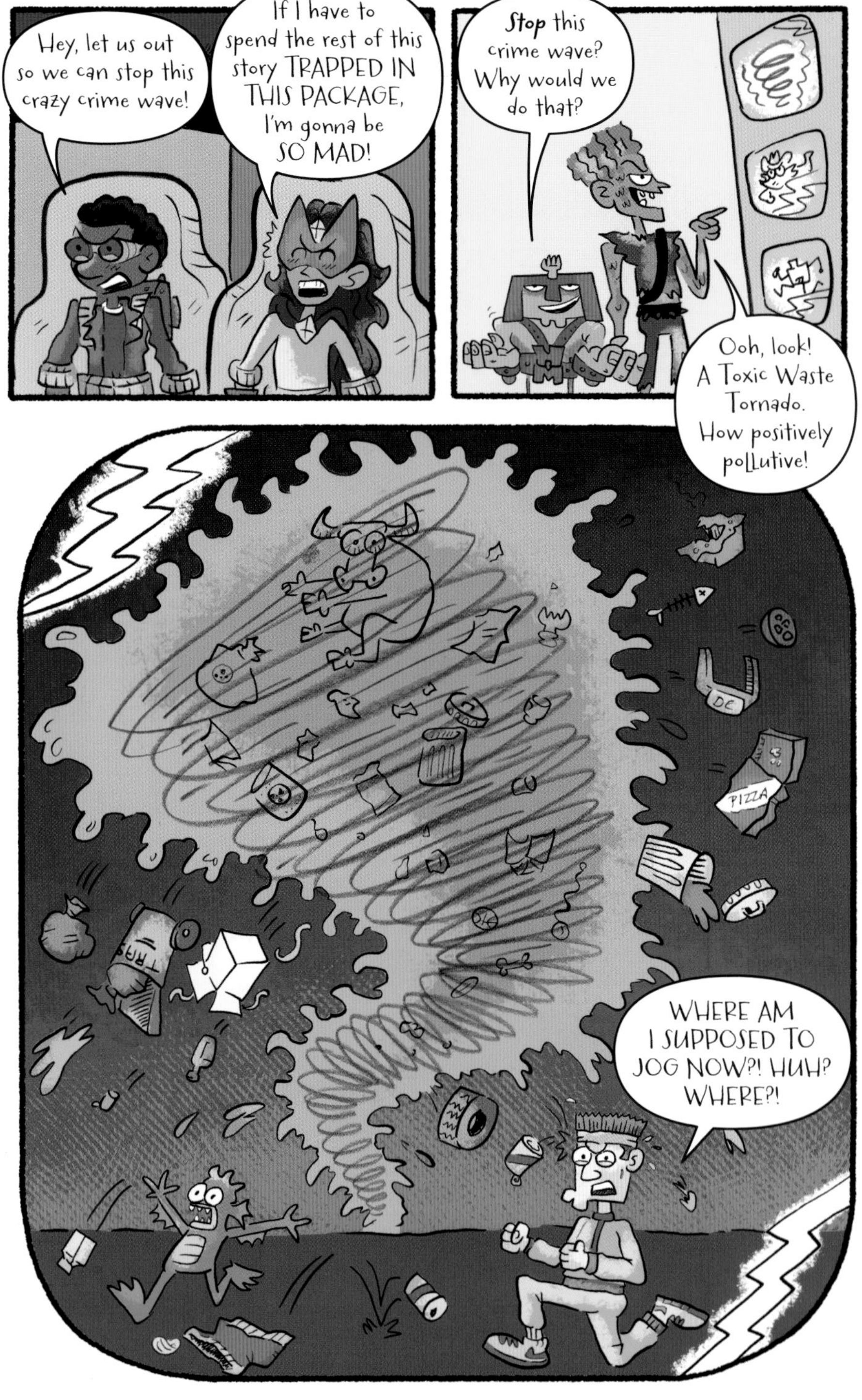
Hey, let us out so we can stop this crazy crime wave!
If I have to spend the rest of this story TRAPPED IN THIS PACKAGE, I'm gonna be SO MAD!
Stop this crime wave? Why would we do that?
Ooh, look! A Toxic Waste Tornado. How positively pollutive!
PIZZA
WHERE AM I SUPPOSED TO JOG NOW?! HUH? WHERE?!

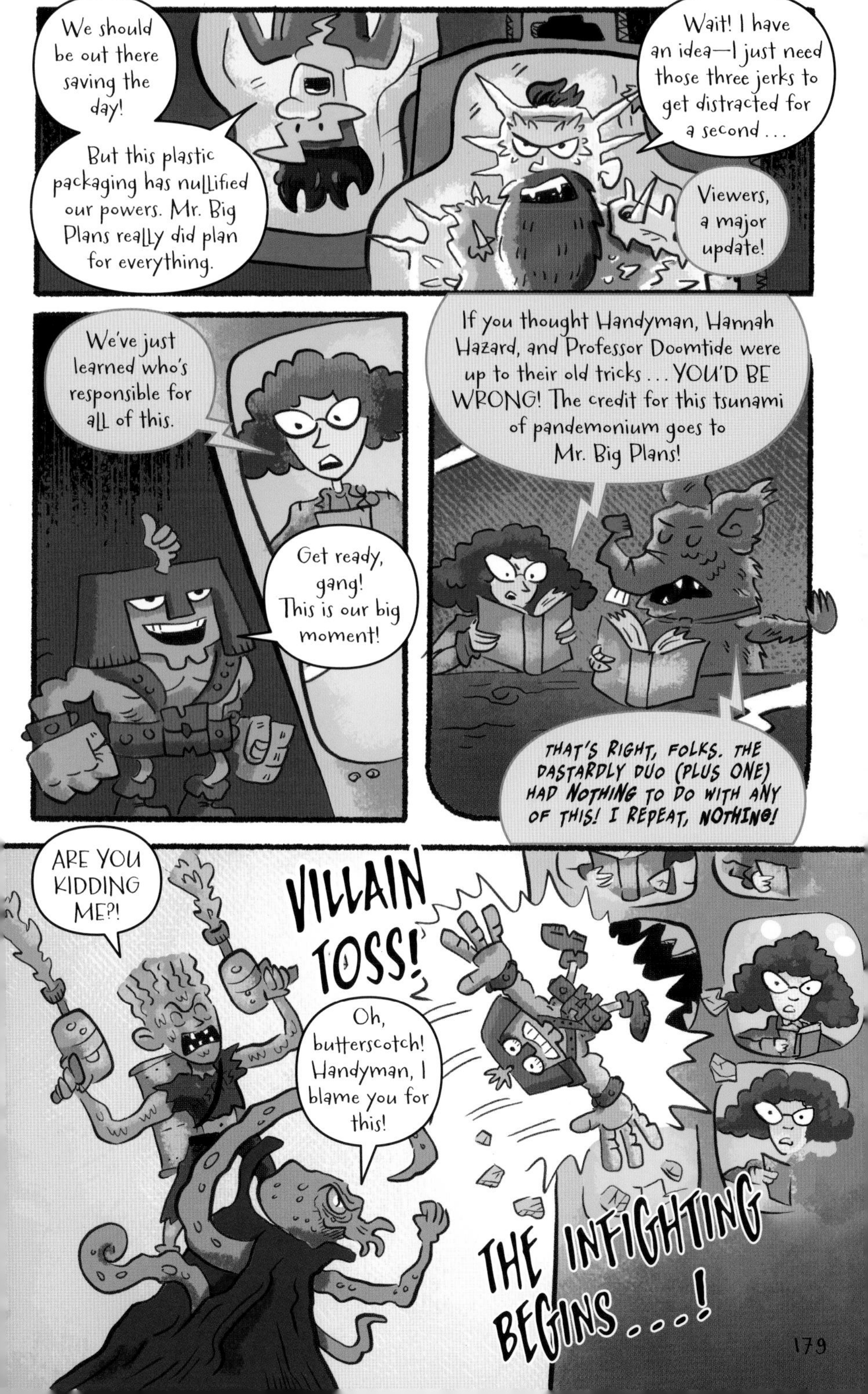
We should be out there saving the day!
But this plastic packaging has nullified our powers. Mr. Big Plans really did plan for everything.
Wait! I have an idea—I just need those three jerks to get distracted for a second . . .
Viewers, a major update!
We've just learned who's responsible for all of this.
Get ready, gang! This is our big moment!
If you thought Handyman, Hannah Hazard, and Professor Doomtide were up to their old tricks . . . YOU'D BE WRONG! The credit for this tsunami of pandemonium goes to Mr. Big Plans!
THAT'S RIGHT, FOLKS. THE DASTARDLY DUO (PLUS ONE) HAD NOTHING TO DO WITH ANY OF THIS! I REPEAT, NOTHING!
ARE YOU KIDDING ME?!
VILLAIN TOSS!
Oh, butterscotch! Handyman, I blame you for this!
THE INFIGHTING BEGINS . . . !

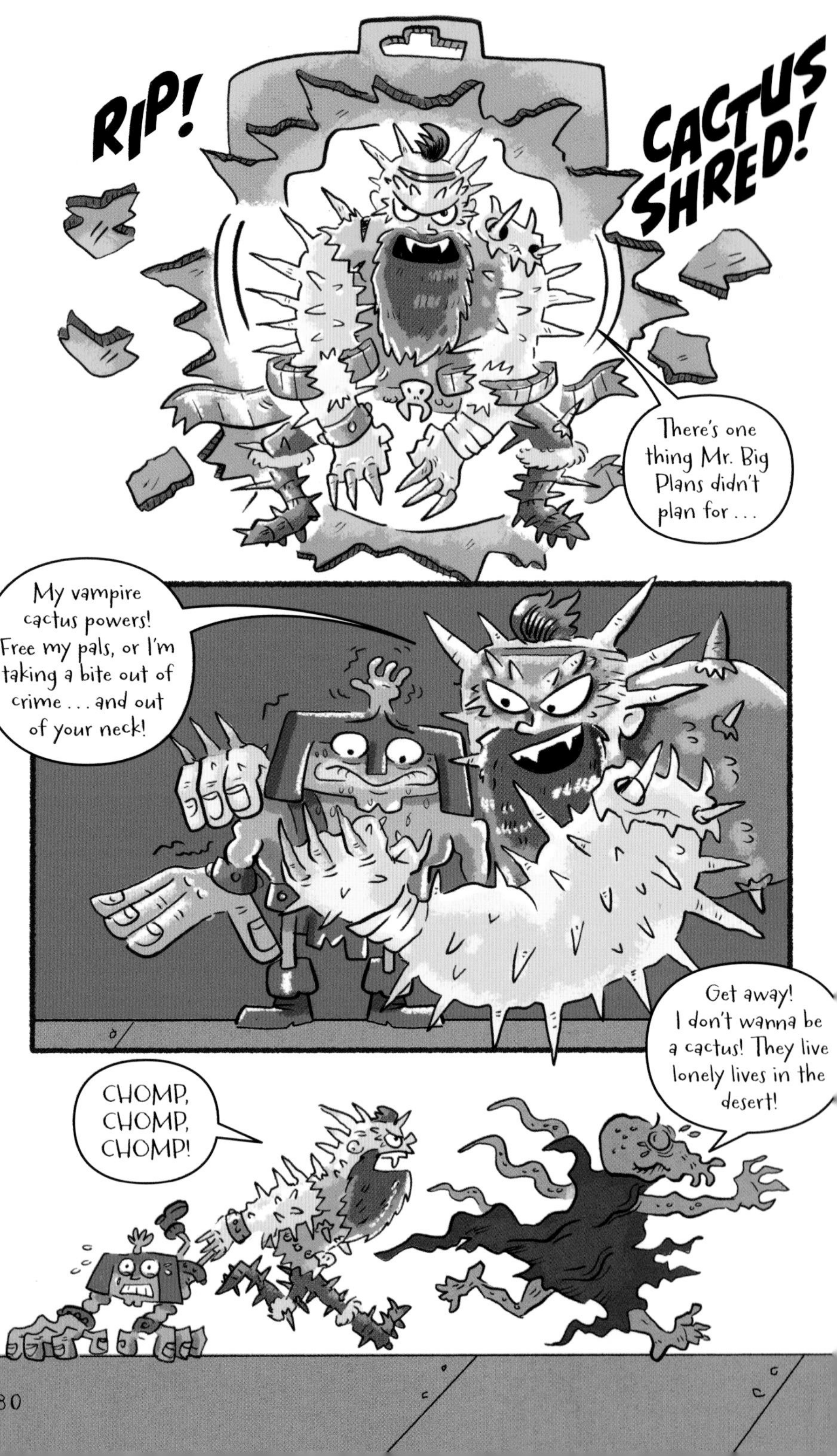
RIP!
CACTUS SHRED!
There's one thing Mr. Big Plans didn't plan for . . .
My vampire cactus powers! Free my pals, or I'm taking a bite out of crime . . . and out of your neck!
Get away! I don't wanna be a cactus! They live lonely lives in the desert!
CHOMP, CHOMP, CHOMP!

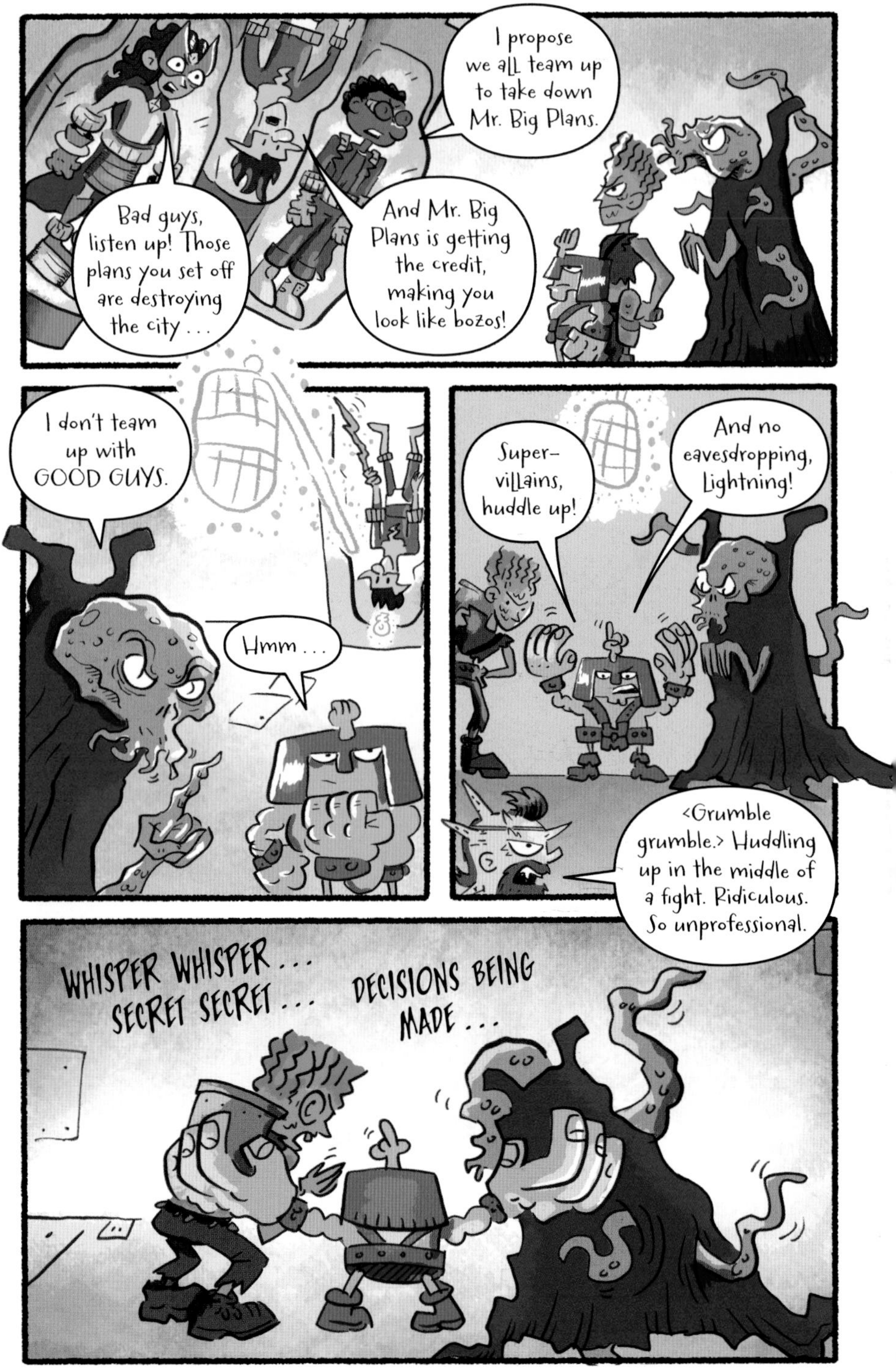
I propose we aLL team up to take down Mr. Big Plans.
Bad guys, listen up! Those plans you set off are destroying the city . . .
And Mr. Big Plans is getting the credit, making you look like bozos!
I don't team up with GOOD GUYS.
Hmm . . .
Super-viLLains, huddle up!
And no eavesdropping, Lightning!
<Grumble grumble.> Huddling up in the middle of a fight. Ridiculous. So unprofessional.
WHISPER WHISPER . . . SECRET SECRET . . .
DECISIONS BEING MADE . . .

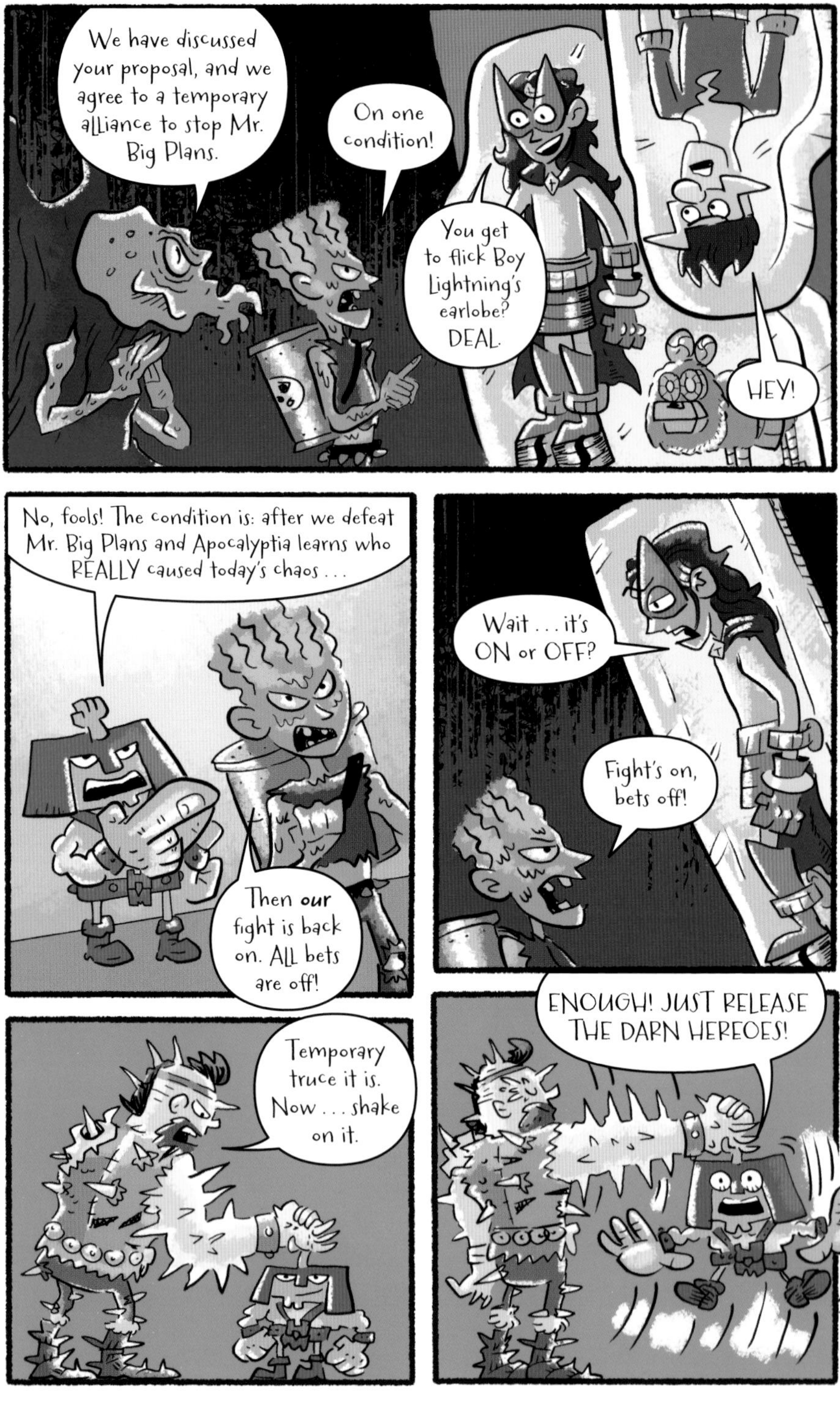
We have discussed your proposal, and we agree to a temporary alliance to stop Mr. Big Plans.
On one condition!
You get to flick Boy Lightning's earlobe? DEAL.
HEY!
No, fools! The condition is: after we defeat Mr. Big Plans and Apocalyptia learns who REALLY caused today's chaos . . .
Then **our** fight is back on. ALL bets are off!
Wait . . . it's ON or OFF?
Fight's on, bets off!
Temporary truce it is. Now . . . shake on it.
ENOUGH! JUST RELEASE THE DARN HEREOES!

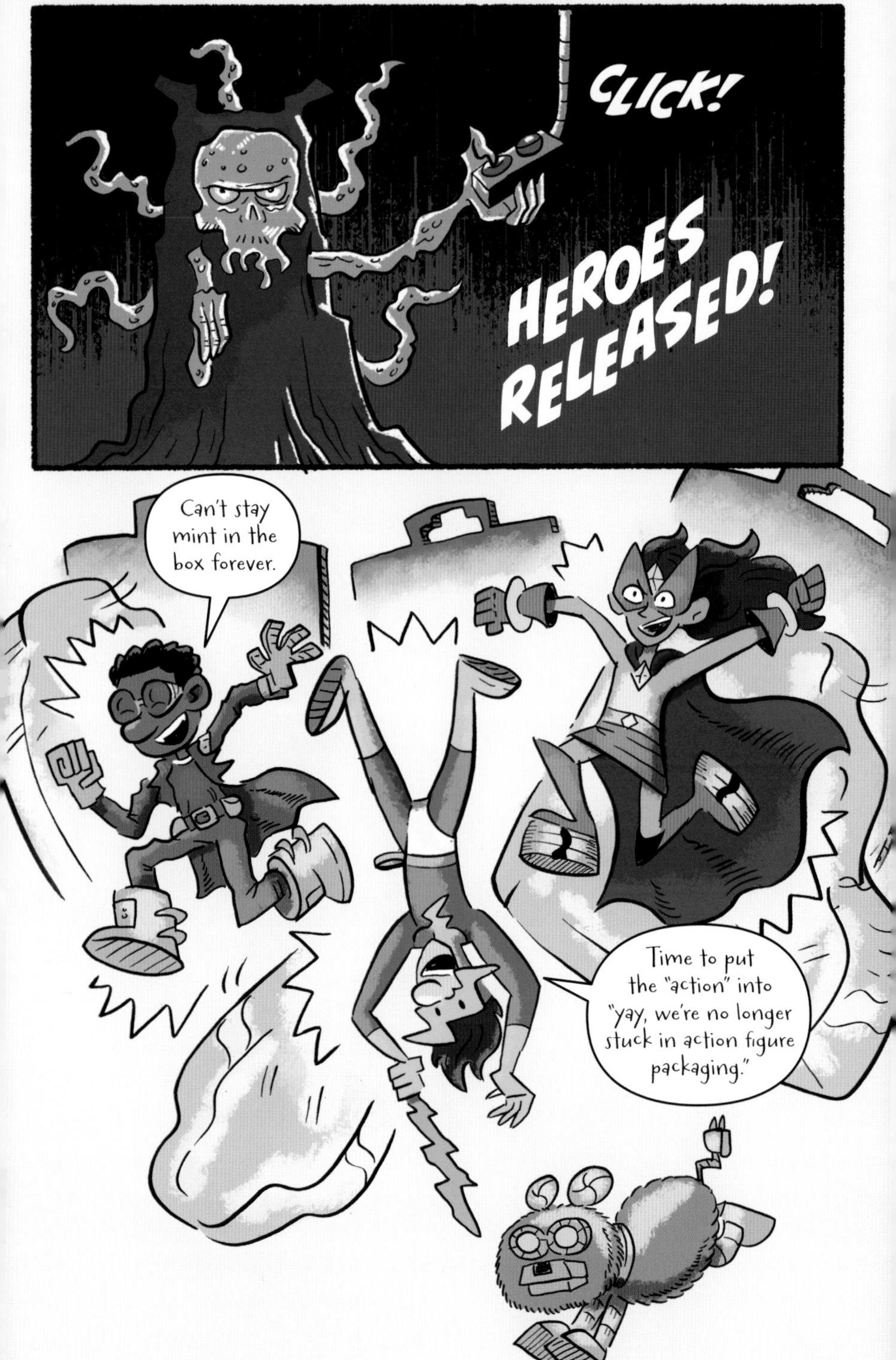
CLICK!
HEROES RELEASED!
Can't stay mint in the box forever.
Time to put the "action" into "yay, we're no longer stuck in action figure packaging."

CHAPTER THIRTEEN

HEROES AND VILLAINS UNITED!

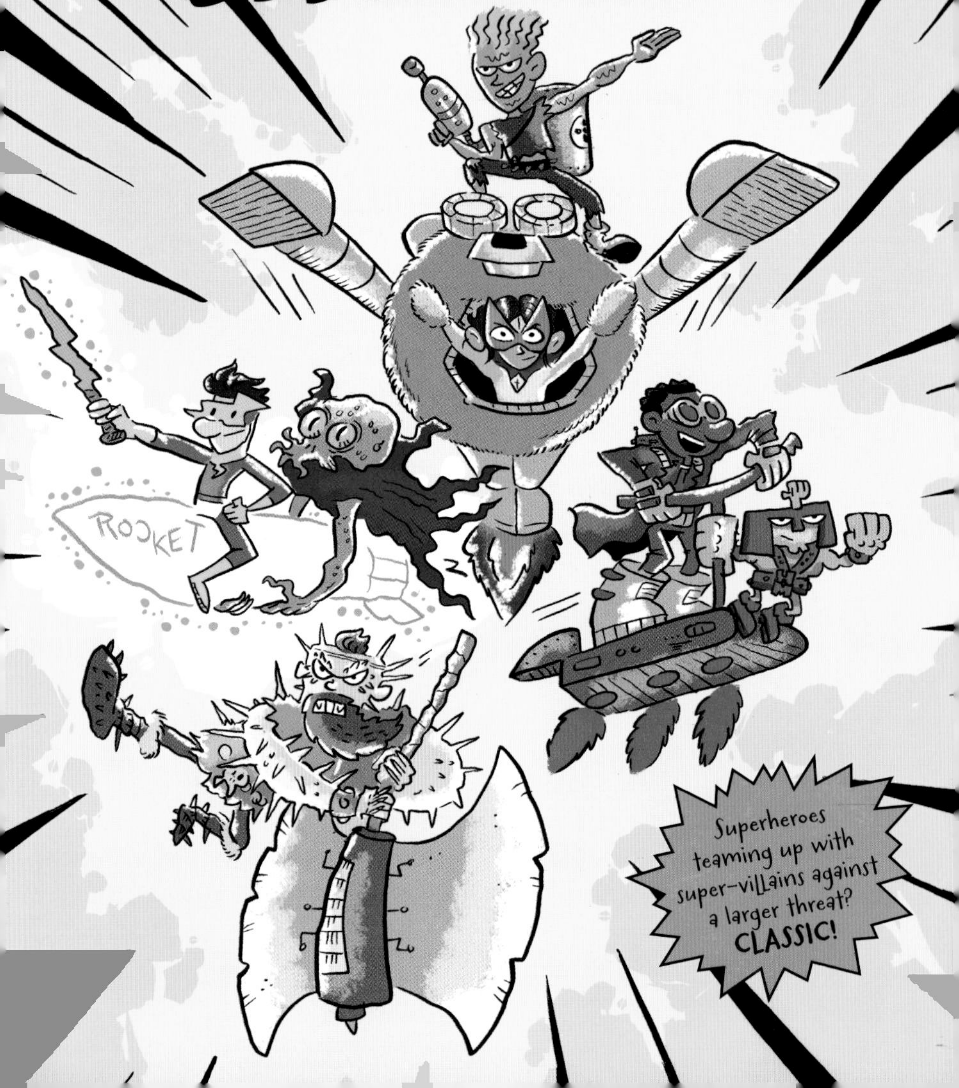
ROCKET
Superheroes teaming up with super-villains against a larger threat? CLASSIC!

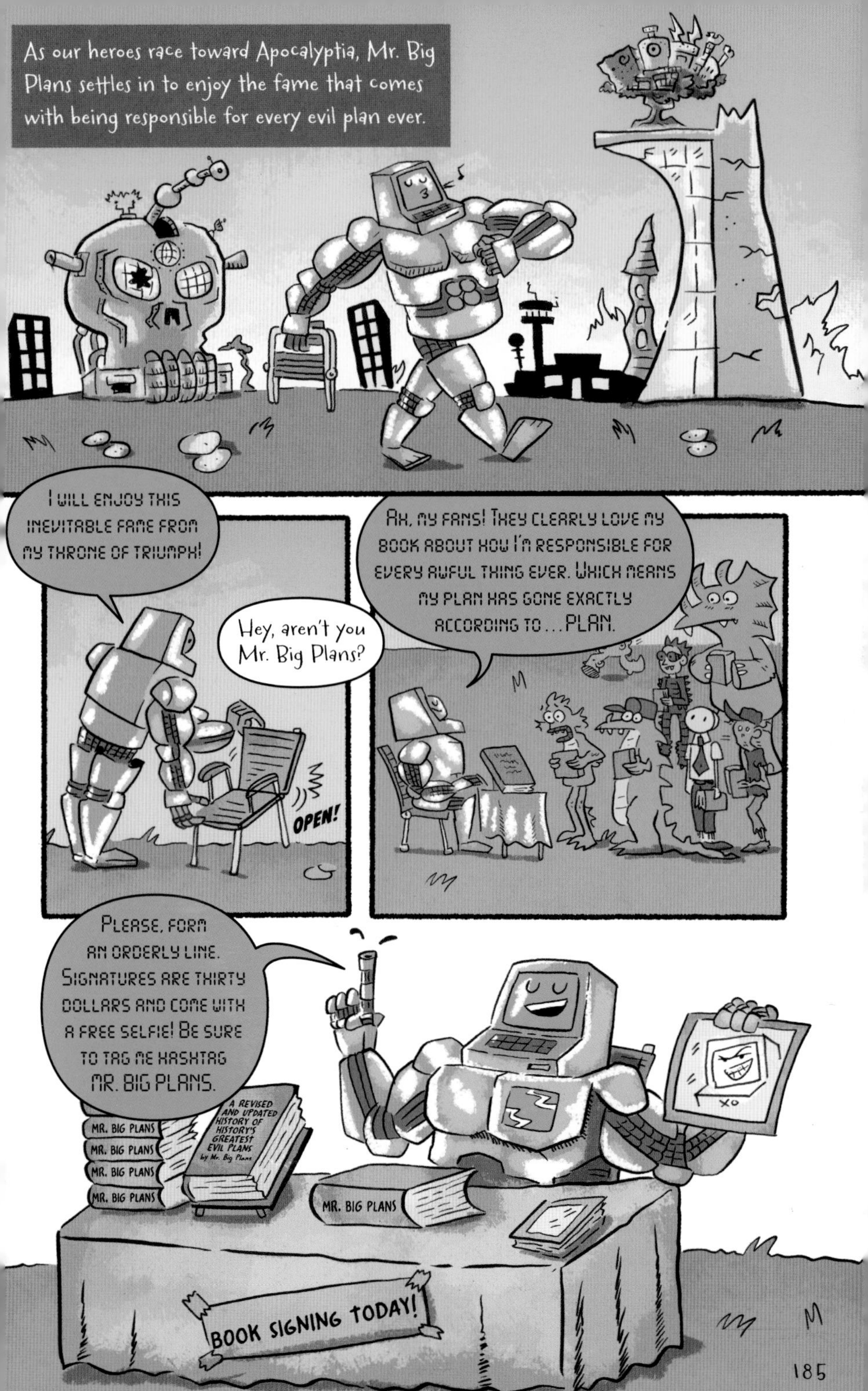
As our heroes race toward Apocalyptia, Mr. Big Plans settles in to enjoy the fame that comes with being responsible for every evil plan ever.
I WILL ENJOY THIS INEVITABLE FAME FROM MY THRONE OF TRIUMPH!
Hey, aren't you Mr. Big Plans?
OPEN!
AH, MY FANS! THEY CLEARLY LOVE MY BOOK ABOUT HOW I'M RESPONSIBLE FOR EVERY AWFUL THING EVER. WHICH MEANS MY PLAN HAS GONE EXACTLY ACCORDING TO . . . PLAN.
PLEASE, FORM AN ORDERLY LINE. SIGNATURES ARE THIRTY DOLLARS AND COME WITH A FREE SELFIE! BE SURE TO TAG ME HASHTAG MR. BIG PLANS.
MR. BIG PLANS
MR. BIG PLANS
MR. BIG PLANS
MR. BIG PLANS
A REVISED AND UPDATED HISTORY OF HISTORY'S GREATEST EVIL PLANS by Mr. Big Plans
MR. BIG PLANS
XO
BOOK SIGNING TODAY!

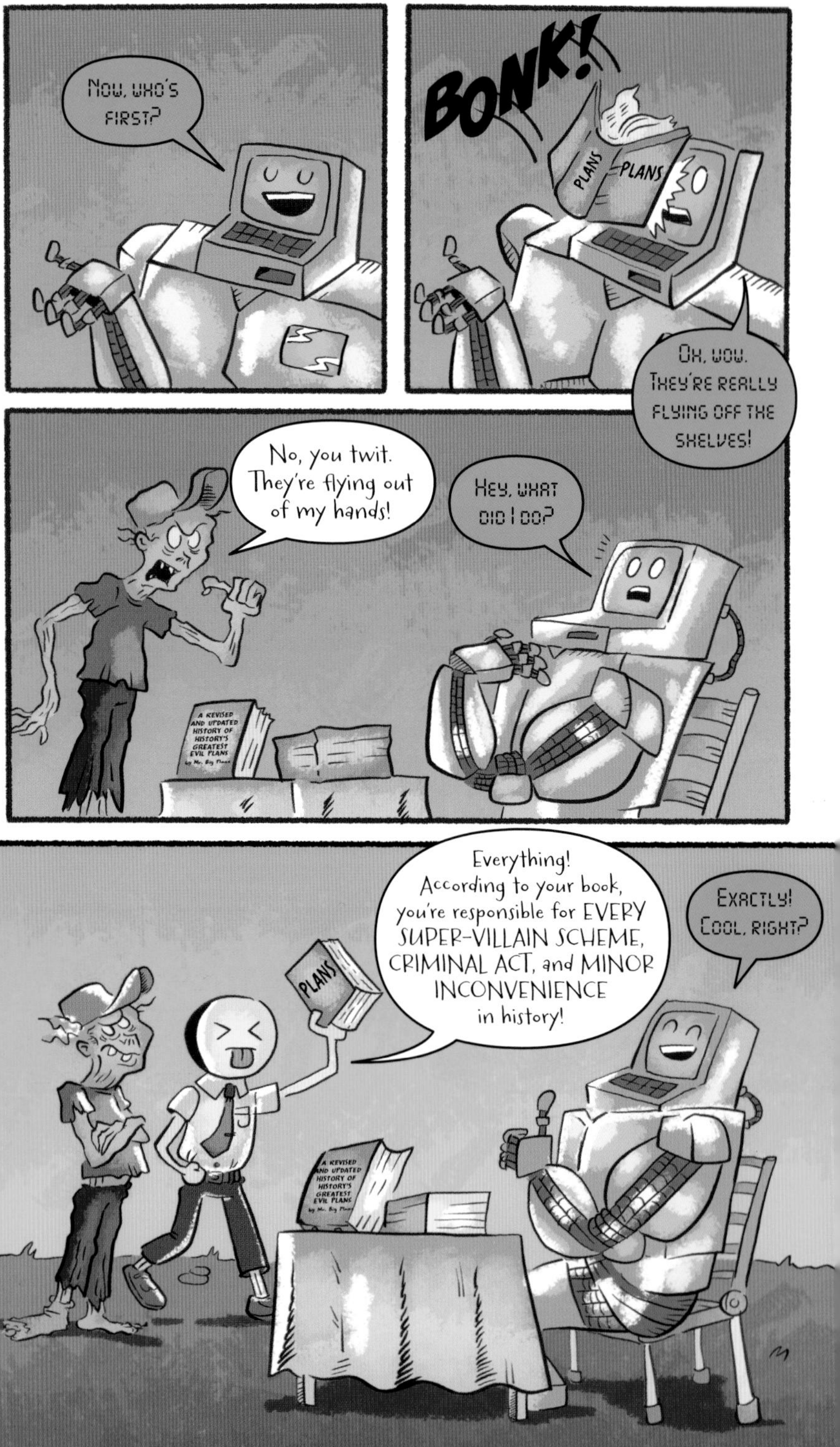
NOW, WHO'S FIRST?
BONK!
PLANS
PLANS
OH, WOW. THEY'RE REALLY FLYING OFF THE SHELVES!
No, you twit. They're flying out of my hands!
HEY, WHAT DID I DO?
A REVISED AND UPDATED HISTORY OF HISTORY'S GREATEST EVIL PLANS
Everything! According to your book, you're responsible for EVERY SUPER-VILLAIN SCHEME, CRIMINAL ACT, and MINOR INCONVENIENCE in history!
PLANS
EXACTLY! COOL, RIGHT?

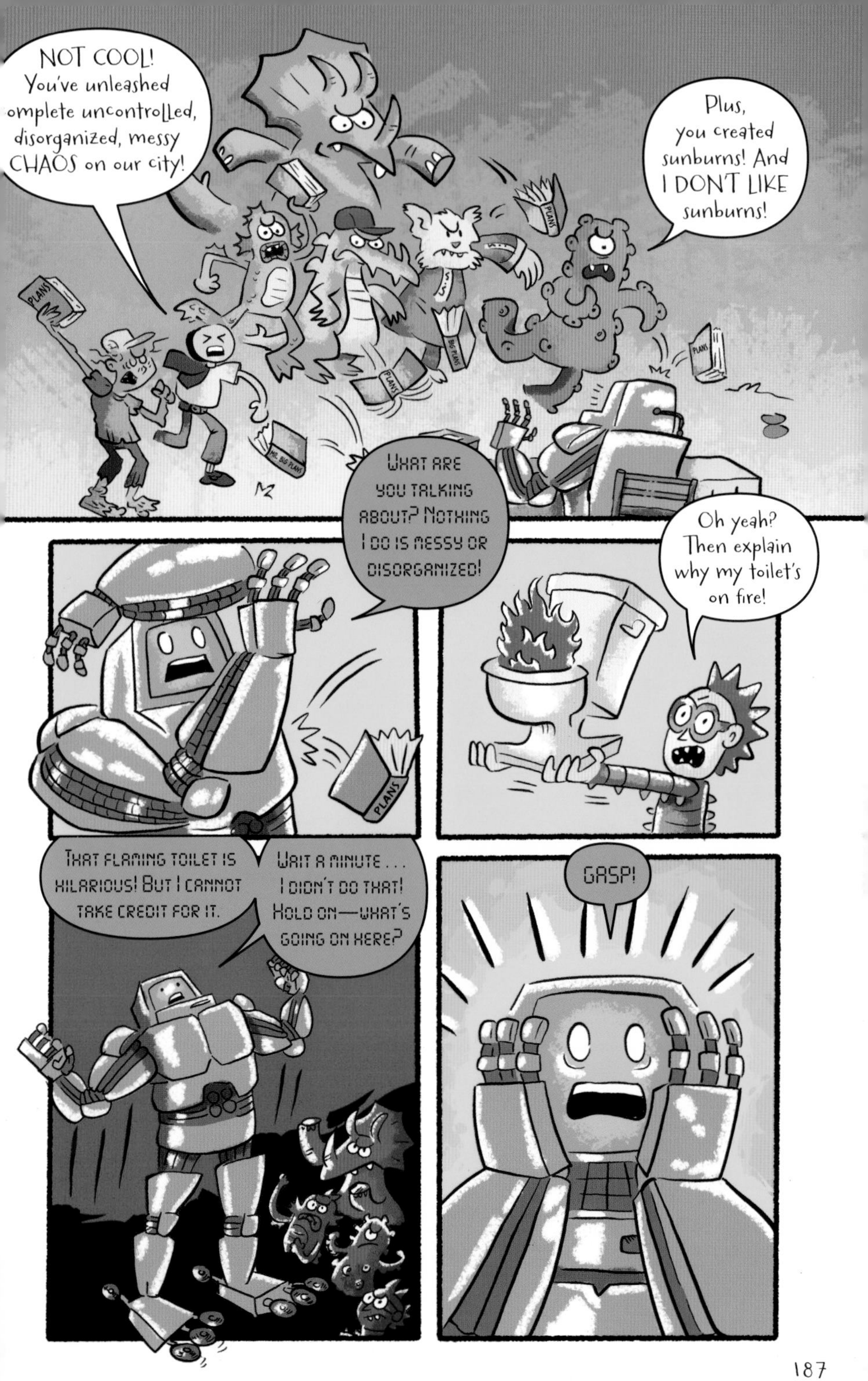
NOT COOL! You've unleashed omplete uncontrolled, disorganized, messy CHAOS on our city!
Plus, you created sunburns! And I DON'T LIKE sunburns!
PLANS
WHAT ARE YOU TALKING ABOUT? NOTHING I DO IS MESSY OR DISORGANIZED!
Oh yeah? Then explain why my toilet's on fire!
THAT FLAMING TOILET IS HILARIOUS! BUT I CANNOT TAKE CREDIT FOR IT.
WAIT A MINUTE . . . I DIDN'T DO THAT! HOLD ON—WHAT'S GOING ON HERE?
GASP!

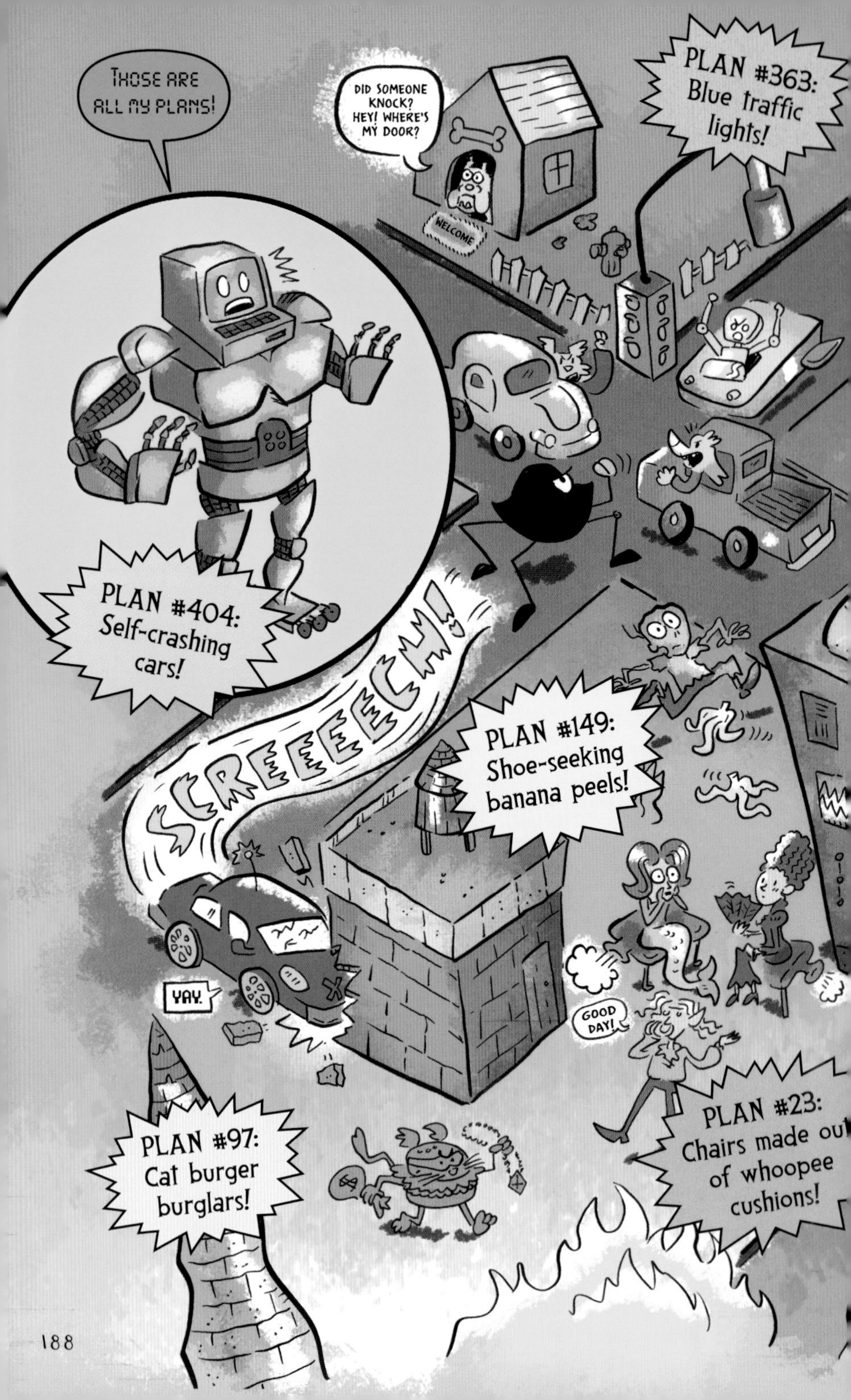
THOSE ARE ALL MY PLANS!
DID SOMEONE KNOCK? HEY! WHERE'S MY DOOR?
WELCOME
PLAN #363: Blue traffic lights!
PLAN #404: Self-crashing cars!
SCREEEECH!
PLAN #149: Shoe-seeking banana peels!
YAY.
GOOD DAY!
PLAN #97: Cat burger burglars!
PLAN #23: Chairs made out of whoopee cushions!

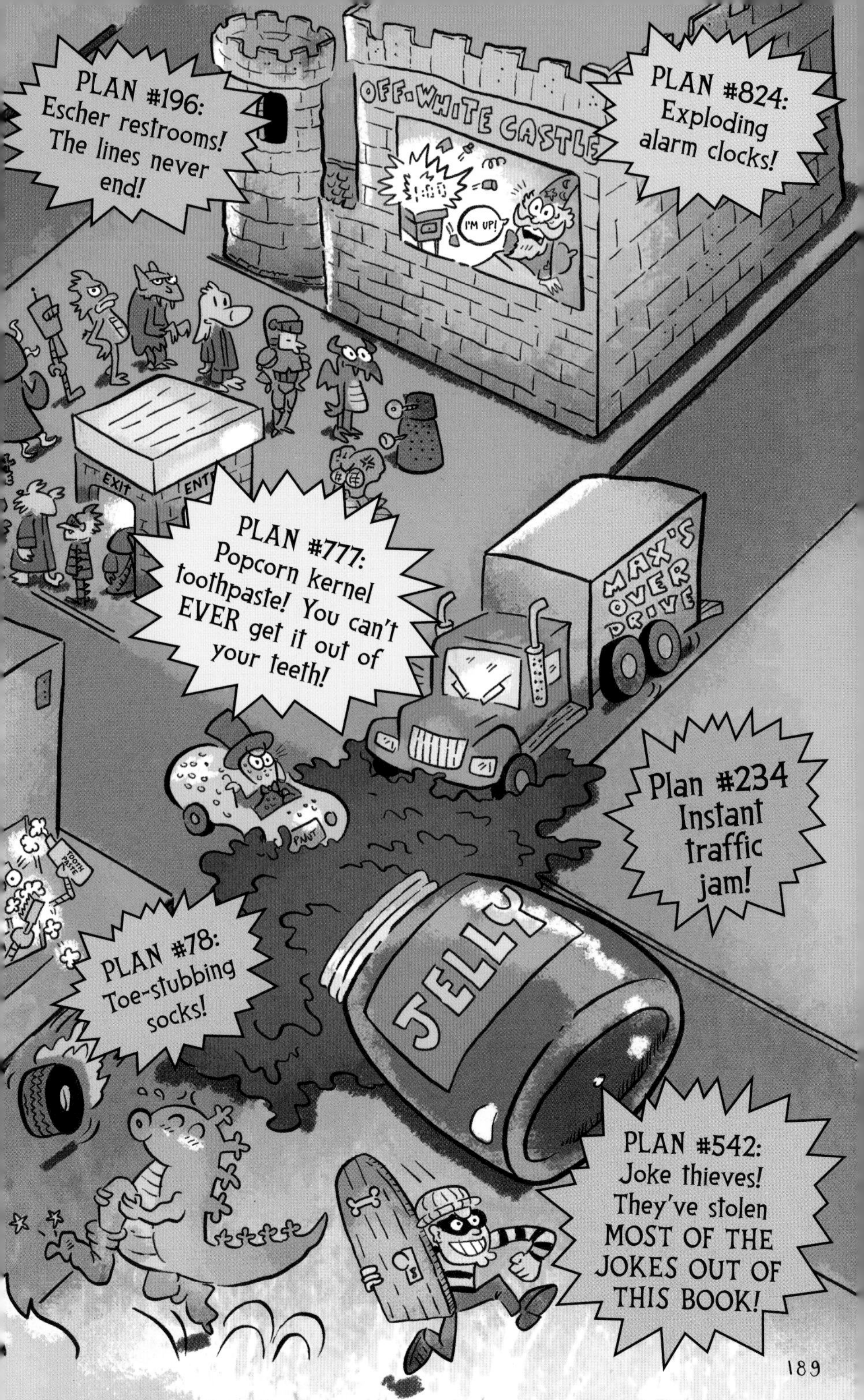

PLAN #196: Escher restrooms! The lines never end!
OFF-WHITE CASTLE
PLAN #824: Exploding alarm clocks!
I'M UP!
EXIT
PLAN #777: Popcorn kernel toothpaste! You can't EVER get it out of your teeth!
MAX'S OVER DRIVE
Plan #234 Instant traffic jam!
TOOTH PASTE
JELLY
PLAN #78: Toe-stubbing socks!
PLAN #542: Joke thieves! They've stolen MOST OF THE JOKES OUT OF THIS BOOK!

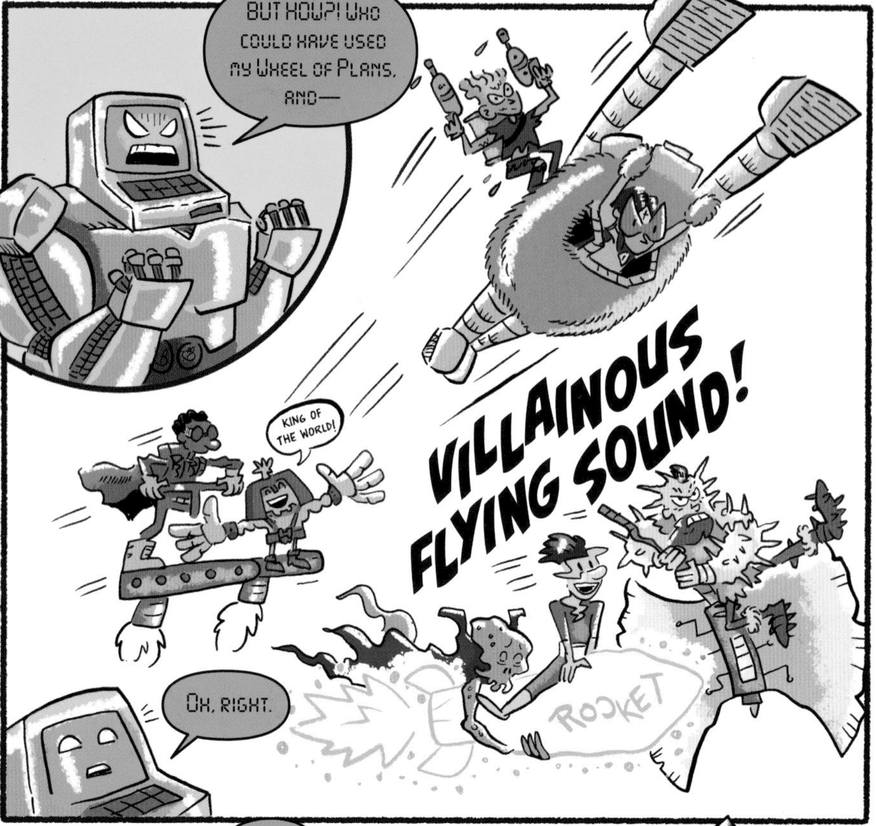
BUT HOW?! WHO COULD HAVE USED MY WHEEL OF PLANS, AND—
KING OF THE WORLD!
VILLAINOUS FLYING SOUND!
ROCKET
OH, RIGHT.

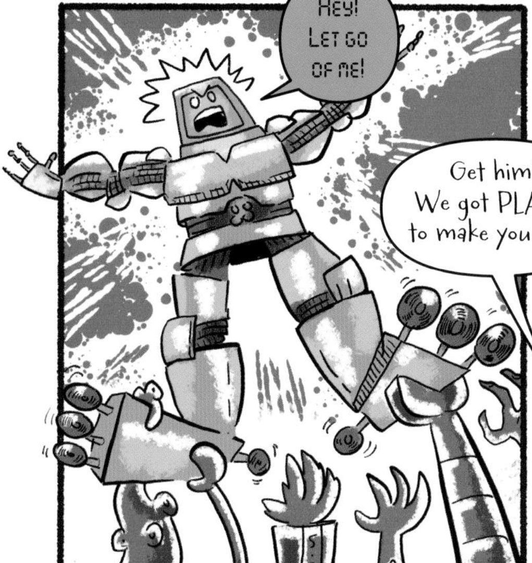
HEY! LET GO OF ME!

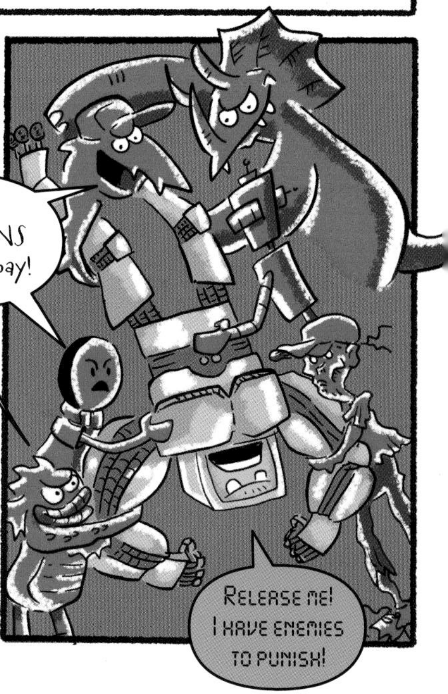
Get him! We got PLANS to make you pay!
RELEASE ME! I HAVE ENEMIES TO PUNISH!

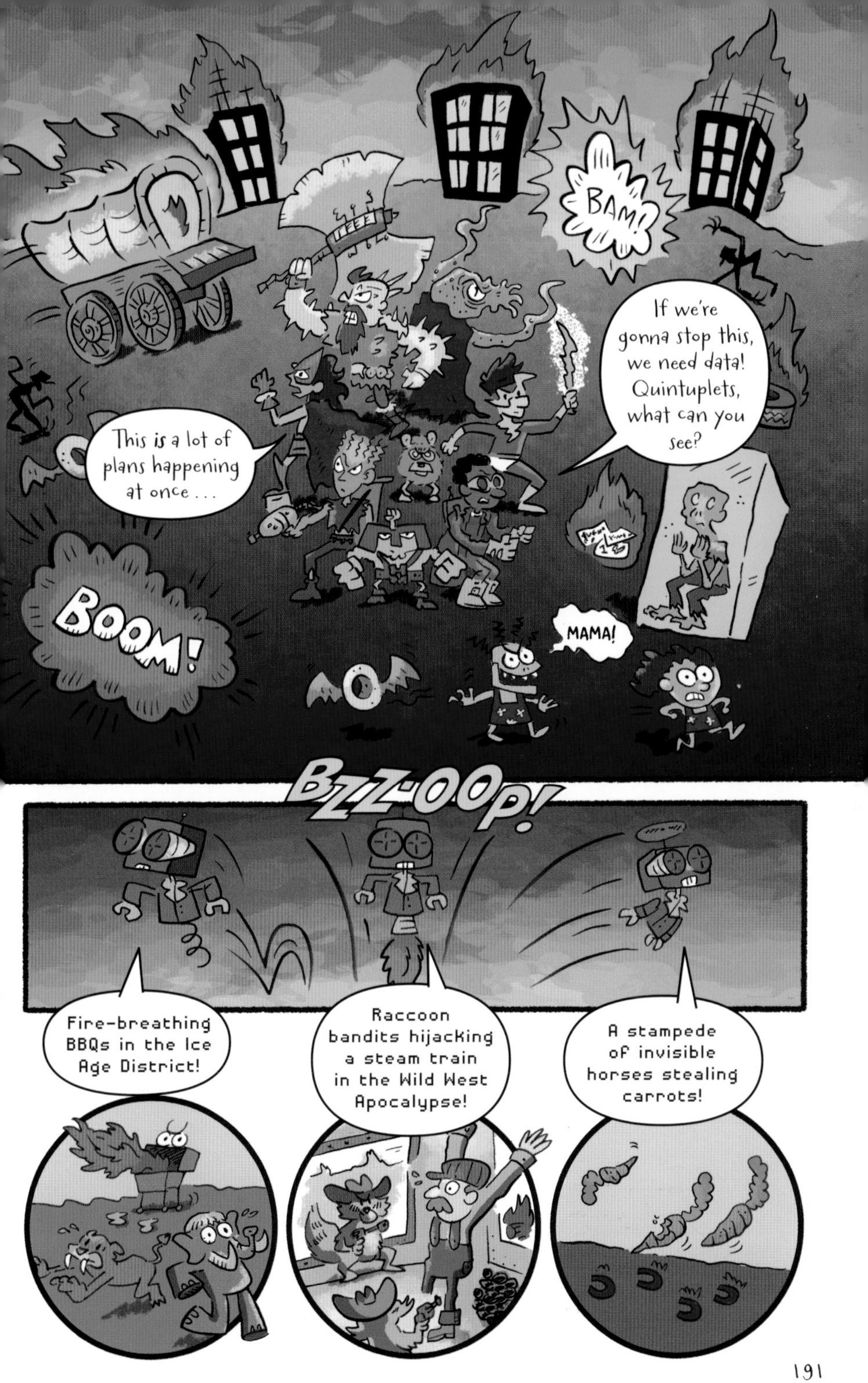
BAM!
If we're gonna stop this, we need data! Quintuplets, what can you see?
This is a lot of plans happening at once . . .
BOOM!
MAMA!
BZZ-OOP!
Fire-breathing BBQs in the Ice Age District!
Raccoon bandits hijacking a steam train in the Wild West Apocalypse!
A stampede of invisible horses stealing carrots!

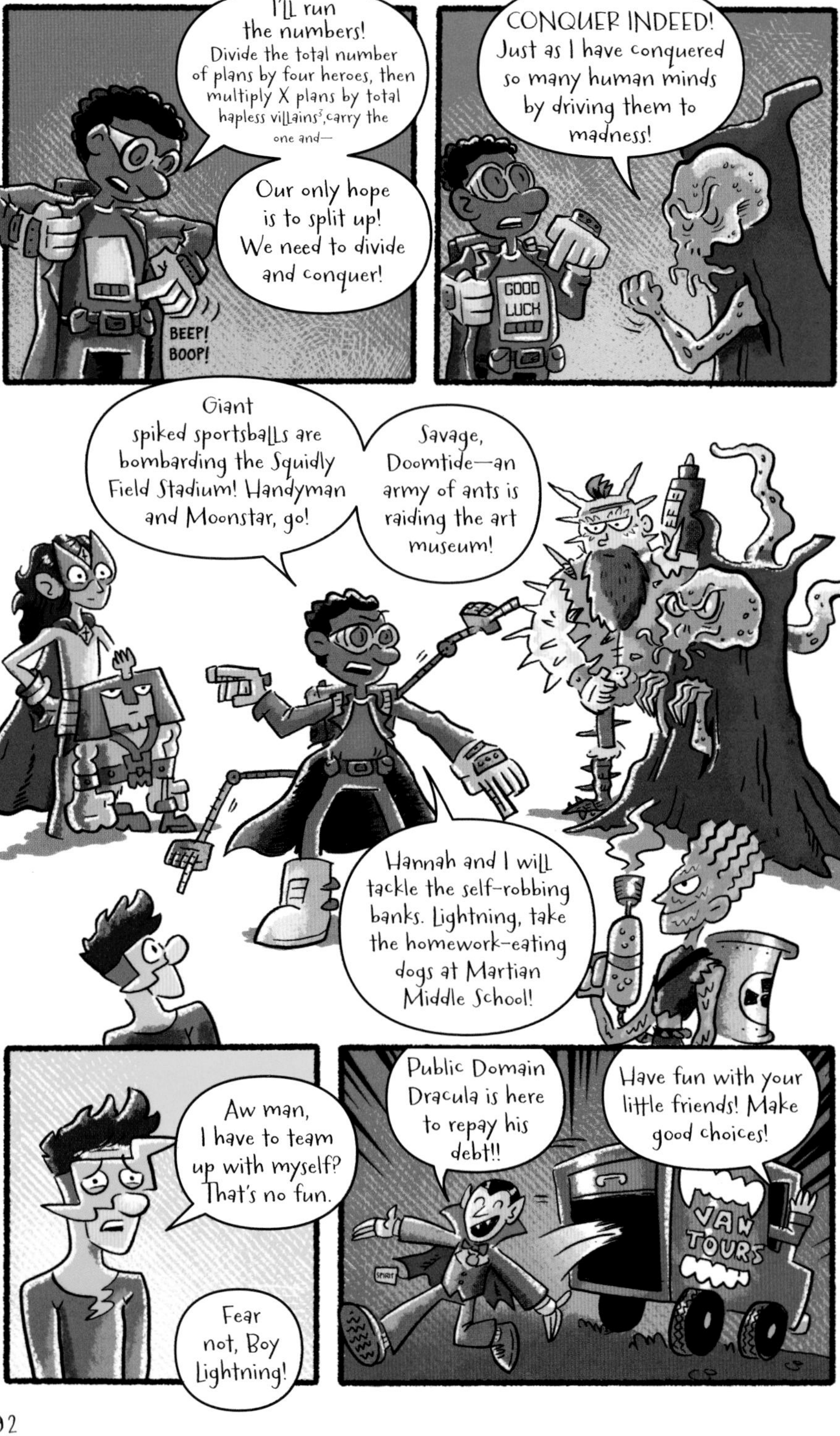
I'LL run the numbers! Divide the total number of plans by four heroes, then multiply X plans by total hapless villains^3, carry the one and—
Our only hope is to split up! We need to divide and conquer!
BEEP! BOOP!
CONQUER INDEED! Just as I have conquered so many human minds by driving them to madness!
GOOD LUCK
Giant spiked sportsballs are bombarding the Squidly Field Stadium! Handyman and Moonstar, go!
Savage, Doomtide—an army of ants is raiding the art museum!
Hannah and I will tackle the self-robbing banks. Lightning, take the homework-eating dogs at Martian Middle School!
Aw man, I have to team up with myself? That's no fun.
Fear not, Boy Lightning!
Public Domain Dracula is here to repay his debt!!
Have fun with your little friends! Make good choices!
VAN TOURS

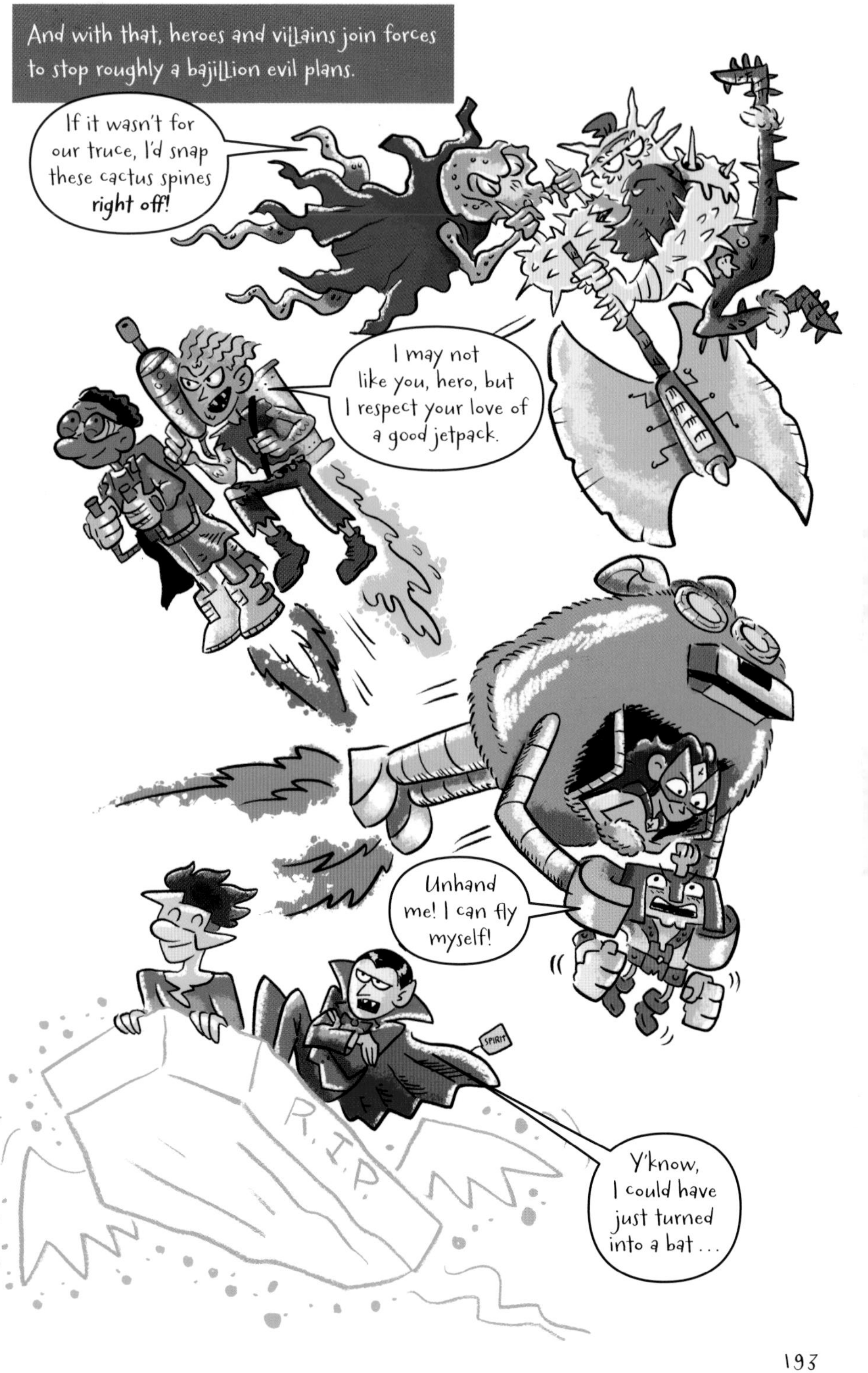
And with that, heroes and villains join forces to stop roughly a bajillion evil plans.
If it wasn't for our truce, I'd snap these cactus spines **right off!**
I may not like you, hero, but I respect your love of a good jetpack.
Unhand me! I can fly myself!
SPIRIT
R.I.P.
Y'know, I could have just turned into a bat . . .

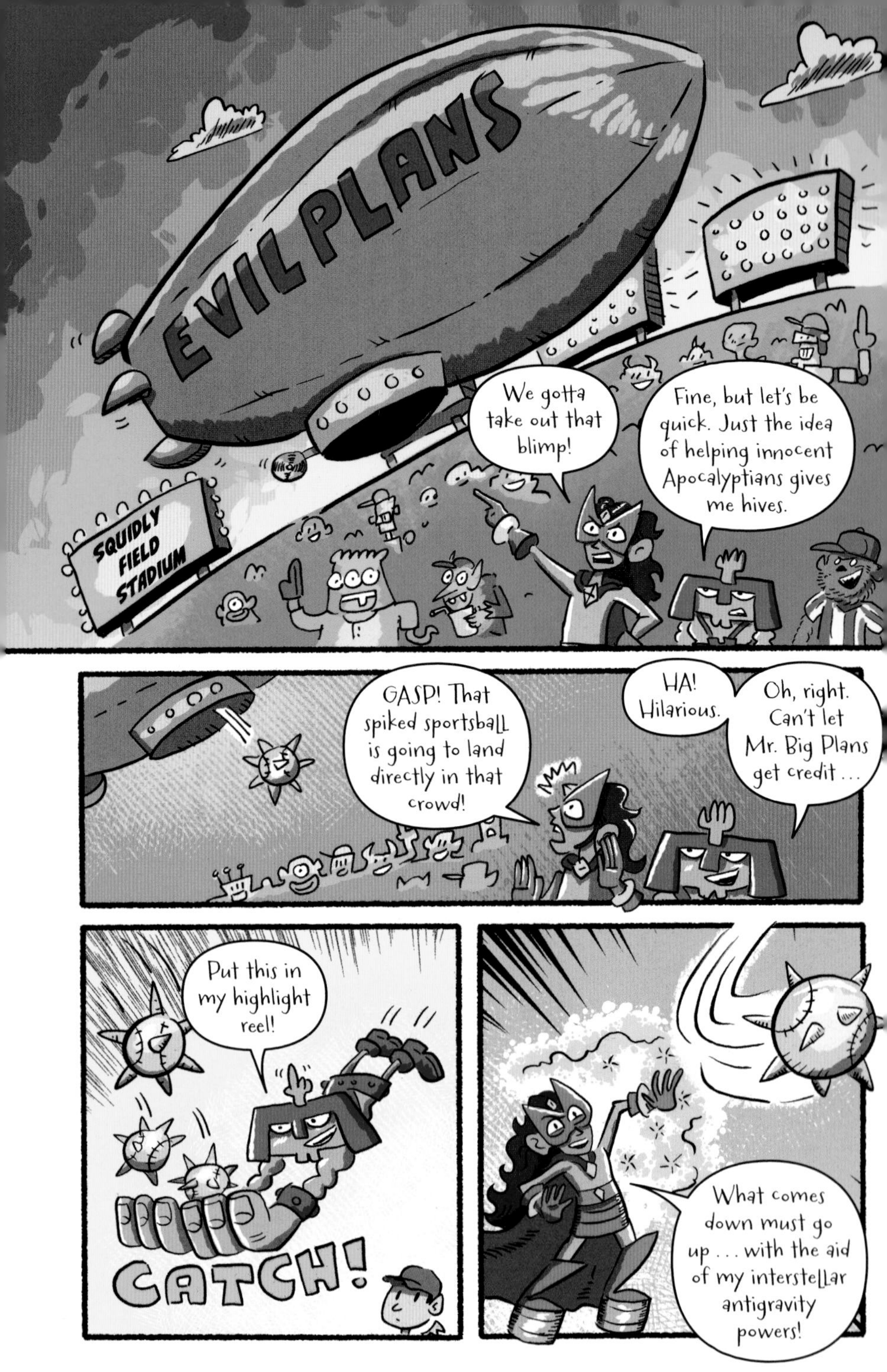
EVIL PLANS
SQUIDLY FIELD STADIUM
We gotta take out that blimp!
Fine, but let's be quick. Just the idea of helping innocent Apocalyptians gives me hives.
GASP! That spiked sportsball is going to land directly in that crowd!
HA! Hilarious.
Oh, right. Can't let Mr. Big Plans get credit . . .
Put this in my highlight reel!
CATCH!
What comes down must go up . . . with the aid of my interstellar antigravity powers!

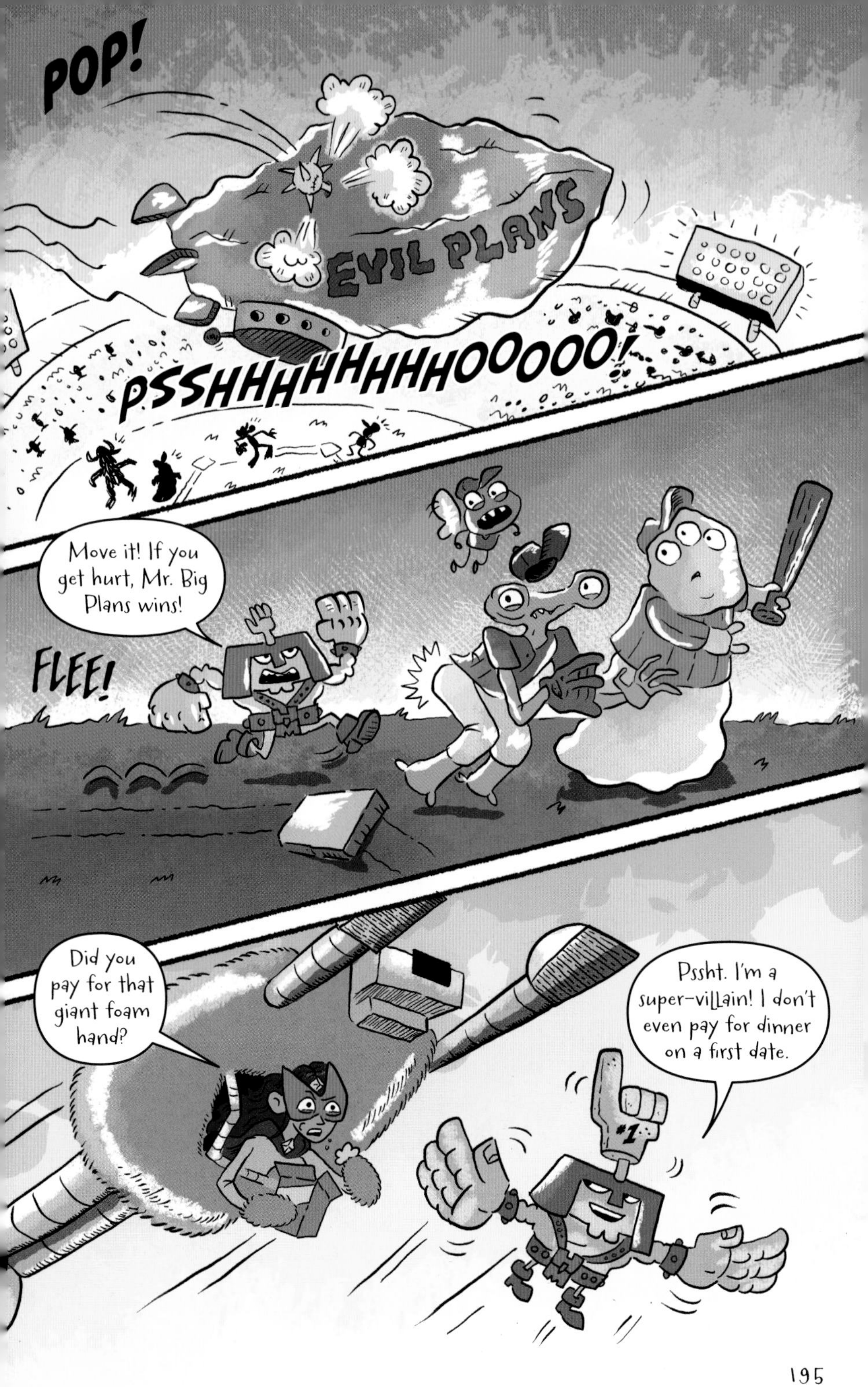
POP!
EVIL PLANS
PSSHHHHHHHHOOOOOO!
Move it! If you get hurt, Mr. Big Plans wins!
FLEE!
Did you pay for that giant foam hand?
Pssht. I'm a super-villain! I don't even pay for dinner on a first date.
#1

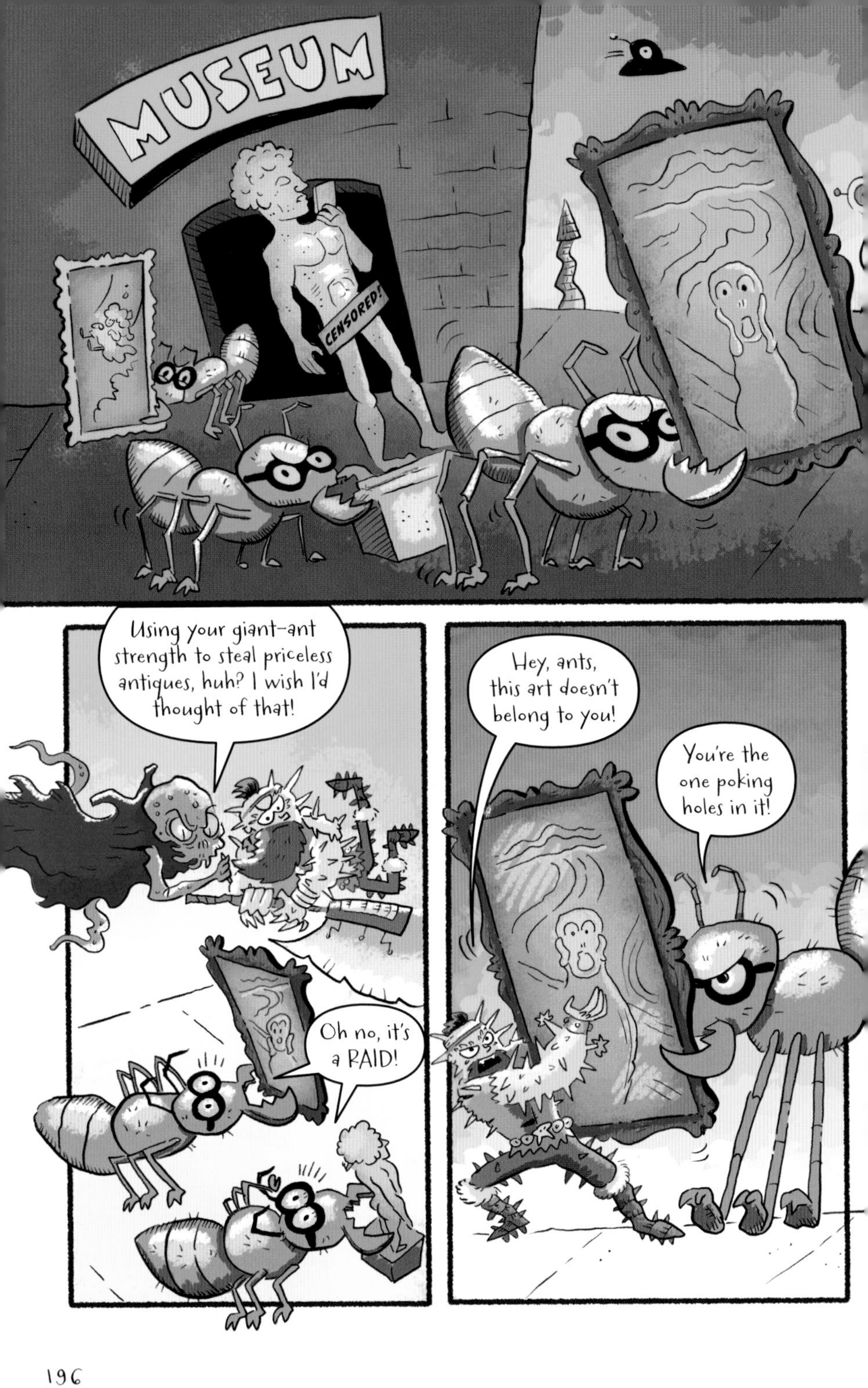
MUSEUM
CENSORED!
Using your giant-ant strength to steal priceless antiques, huh? I wish I'd thought of that!
Oh no, it's a RAID!
Hey, ants, this art doesn't belong to you!
You're the one poking holes in it!

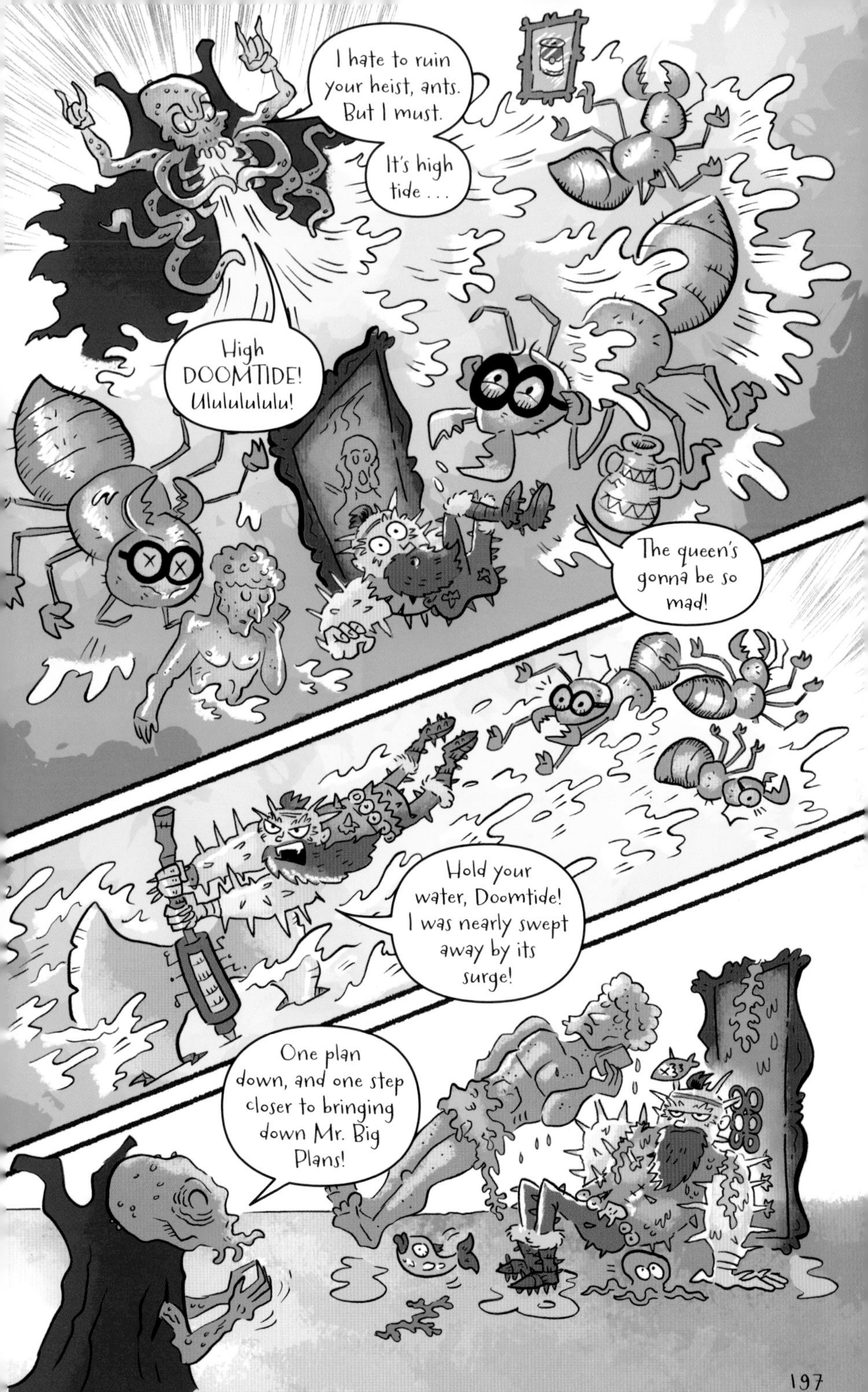
I hate to ruin your heist, ants. But I must.
It's high tide . . .
High DOOMTIDE! Ululululu!
The queen's gonna be so mad!
Hold your water, Doomtide! I was nearly swept away by its surge!
One plan down, and one step closer to bringing down Mr. Big Plans!

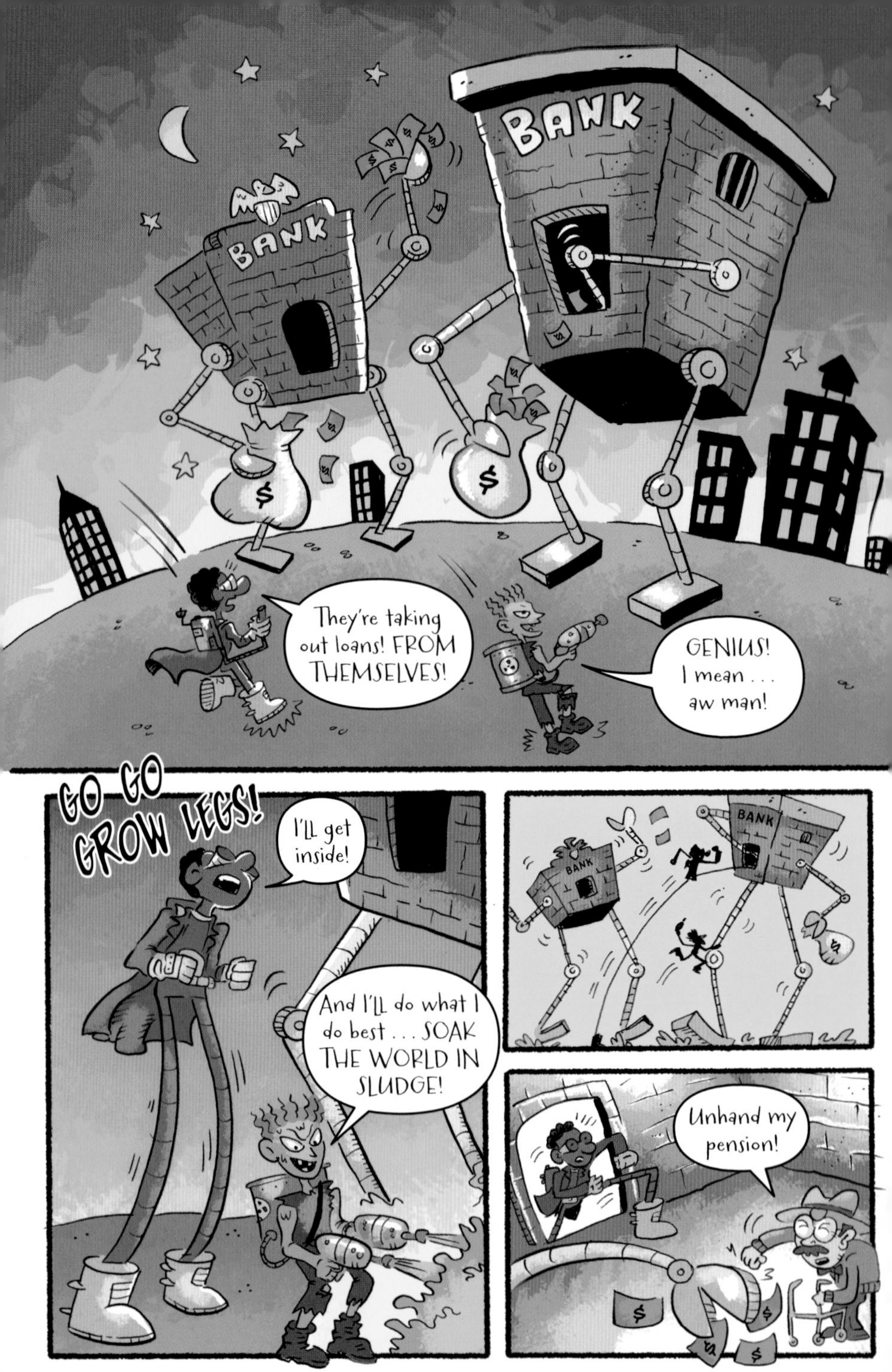
BANK
BANK
They're taking out loans! FROM THEMSELVES!
GENIUS! I mean . . . aw man!
GO GO GROW LEGS!
I'LL get inside!
And I'LL do what I do best . . . SOAK THE WORLD IN SLUDGE!
BANK
BANK
Unhand my pension!

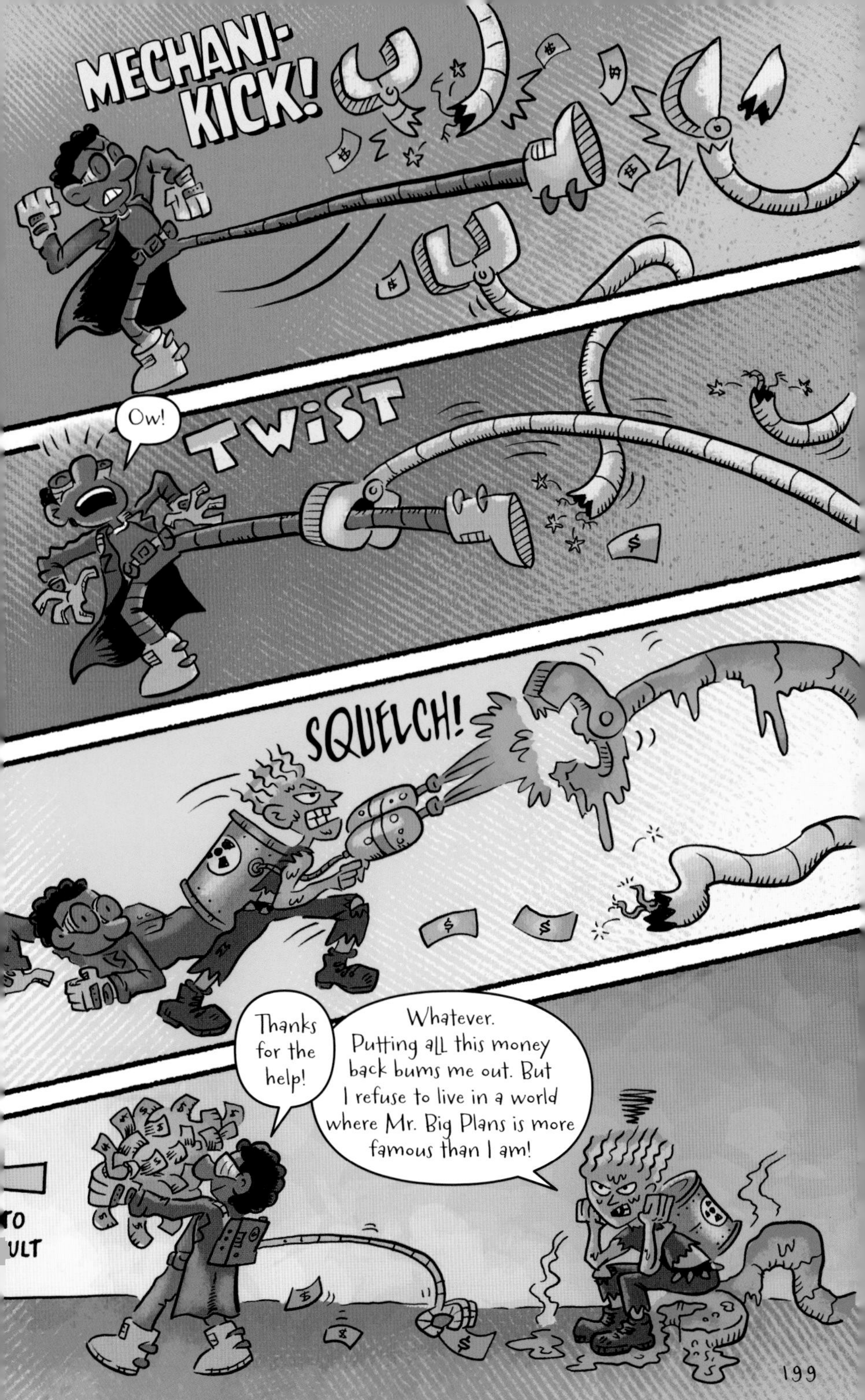
MECHANI-KICK!
Ow!
TWIST
SQUELCH!
Thanks for the help!
Whatever. Putting all this money back bums me out. But I refuse to live in a world where Mr. Big Plans is more famous than I am!

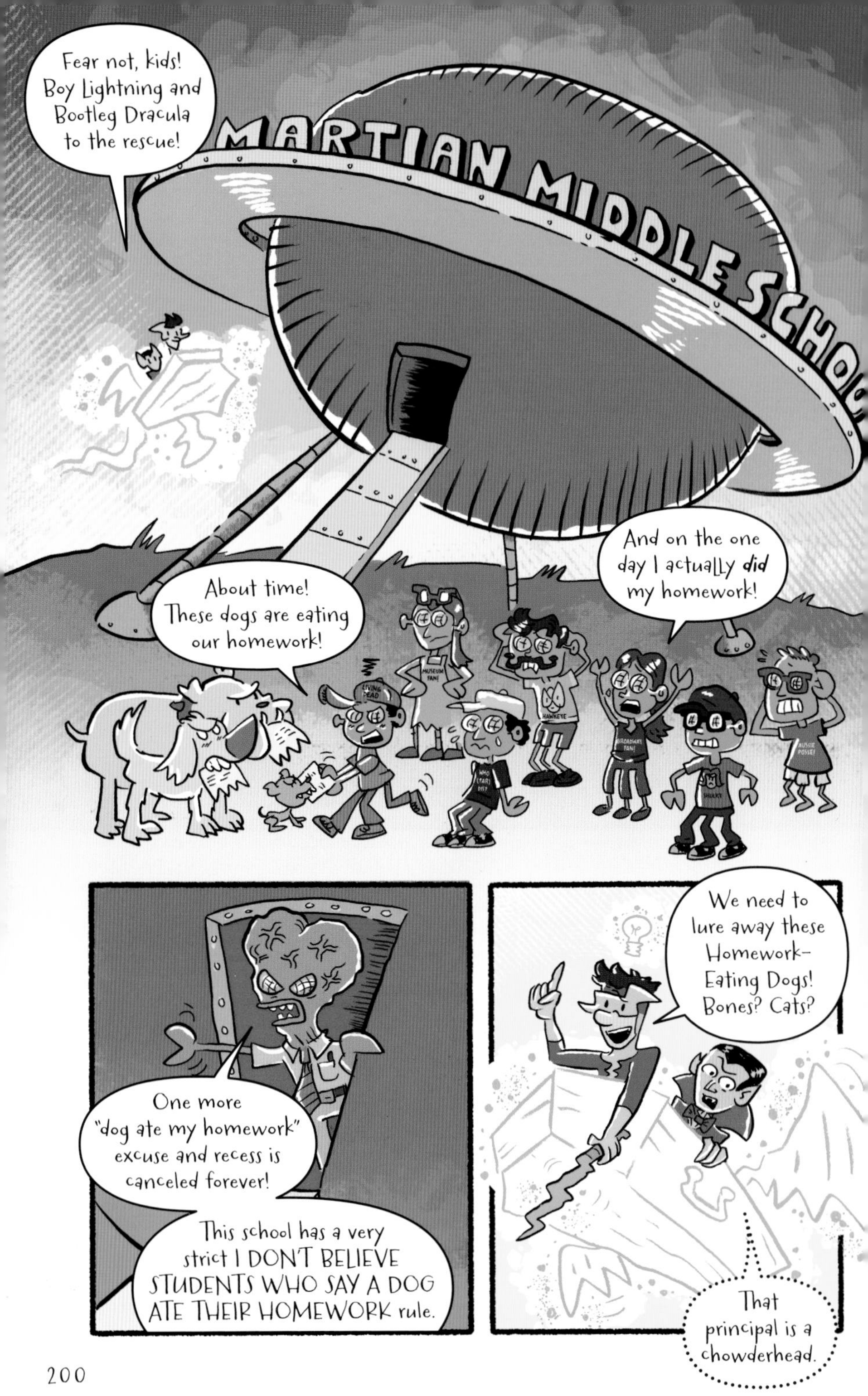
Fear not, kids! Boy Lightning and Bootleg Dracula to the rescue!
MARTIAN MIDDLE
About time! These dogs are eating our homework!
And on the one day I actually *did* my homework!
One more "dog ate my homework" excuse and recess is canceled forever!
This school has a very strict I DON'T BELIEVE STUDENTS WHO SAY A DOG ATE THEIR HOMEWORK rule.
We need to lure away these Homework-Eating Dogs! Bones? Cats?
That principal is a chowderhead.

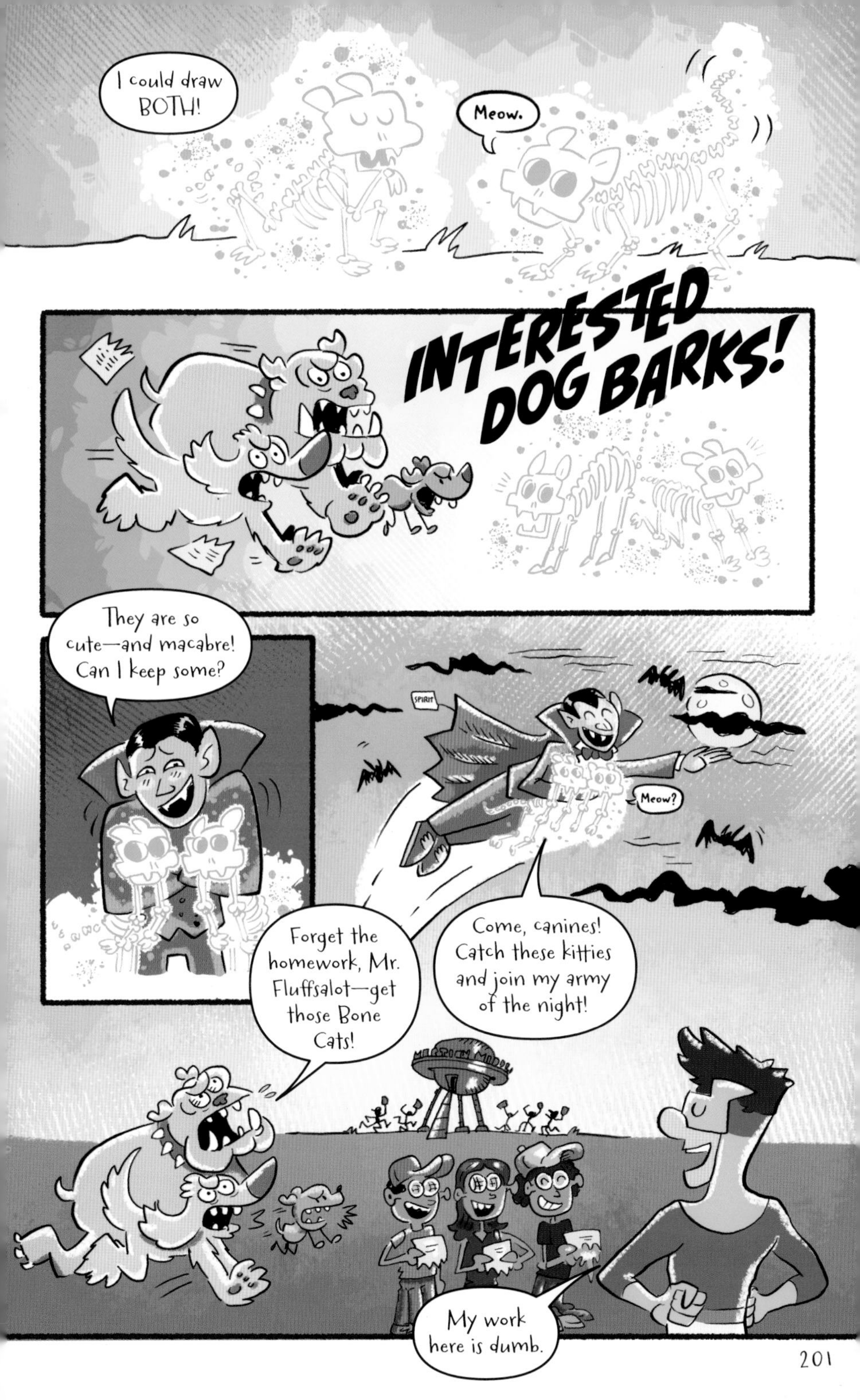
I could draw BOTH!
Meow.
INTERESTED DOG BARKS!
They are so cute—and macabre! Can I keep some?
SPIRIT
Meow?
Forget the homework, Mr. Fluffsalot—get those Bone Cats!
Come, canines! Catch these kitties and join my army of the night!
My work here is dumb.

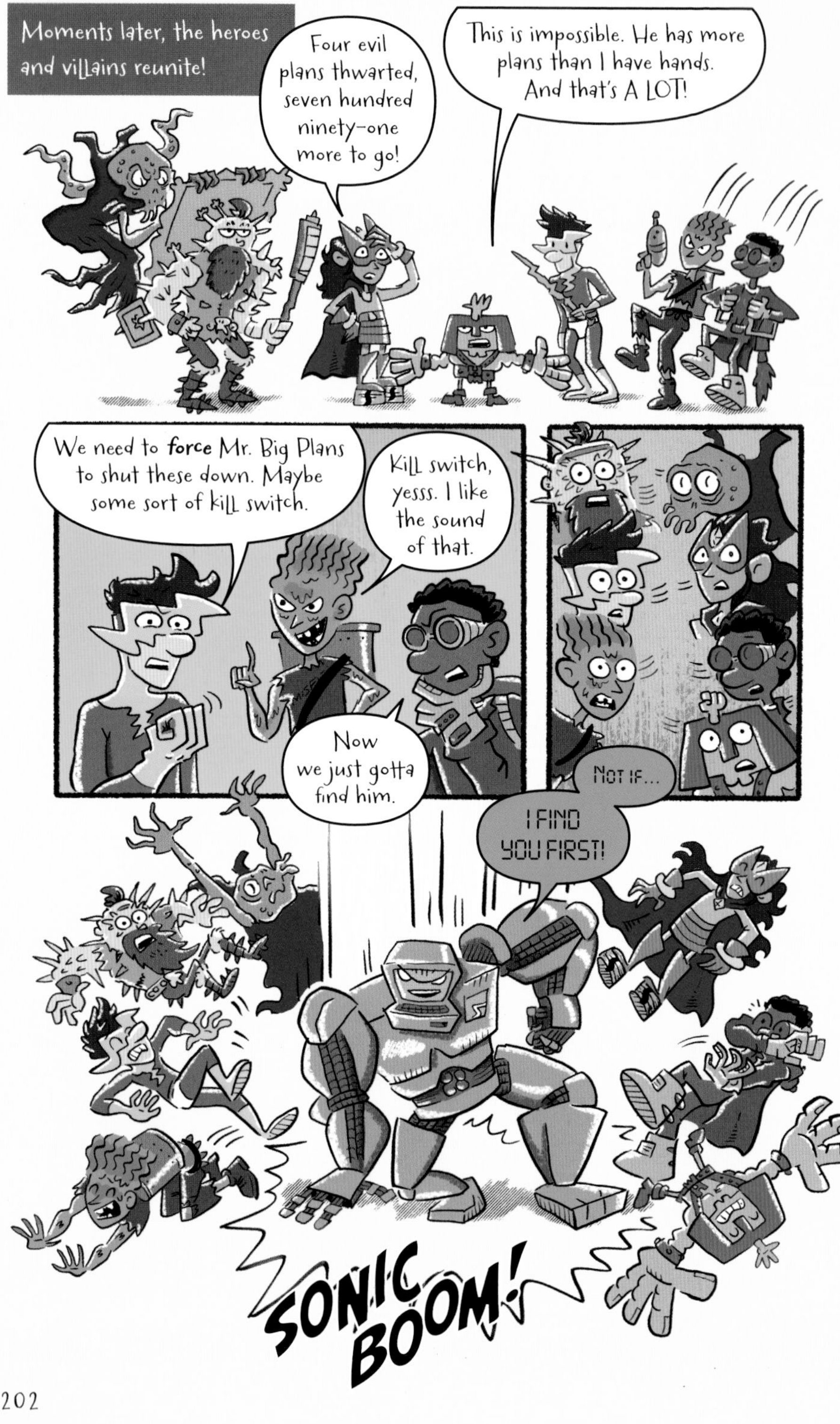

Moments later, the heroes and villains reunite!
Four evil plans thwarted, seven hundred ninety-one more to go!
This is impossible. He has more plans than I have hands. And that's A LOT!
We need to force Mr. Big Plans to shut these down. Maybe some sort of kill switch.
Kill switch, yesss. I like the sound of that.
Now we just gotta find him.
NOT IF...
I FIND YOU FIRST!
SONIC BOOM!

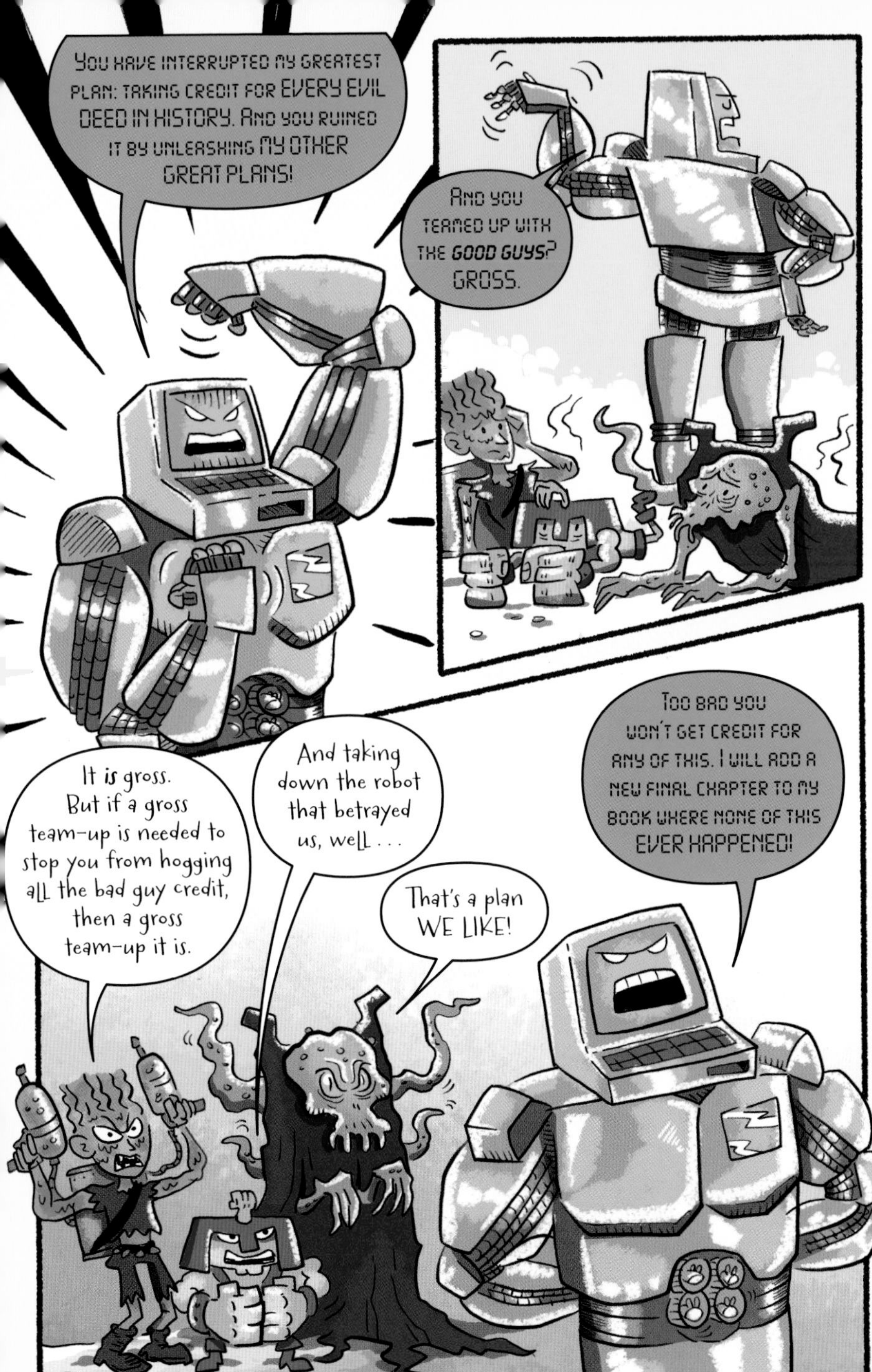
YOU HAVE INTERRUPTED MY GREATEST PLAN: TAKING CREDIT FOR EVERY EVIL DEED IN HISTORY. AND YOU RUINED IT BY UNLEASHING MY OTHER GREAT PLANS!
AND YOU TEAMED UP WITH THE GOOD GUYS? GROSS.
It is gross. But if a gross team-up is needed to stop you from hogging all the bad guy credit, then a gross team-up it is.
And taking down the robot that betrayed us, well . . .
That's a plan WE LIKE!
TOO BAD YOU WON'T GET CREDIT FOR ANY OF THIS. I WILL ADD A NEW FINAL CHAPTER TO MY BOOK WHERE NONE OF THIS EVER HAPPENED!

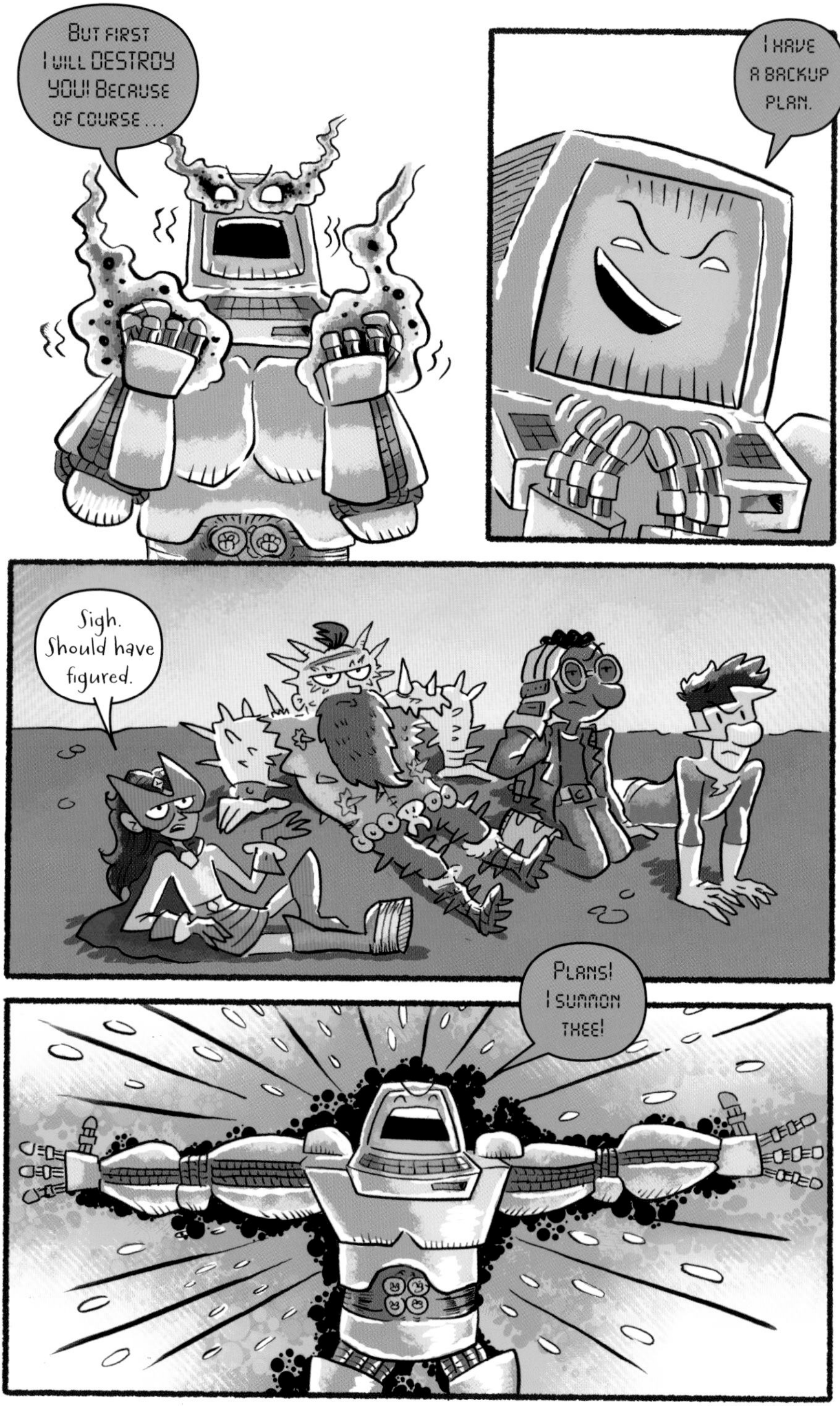
BUT FIRST I WILL DESTROY YOU! BECAUSE OF COURSE . . .
I HAVE A BACKUP PLAN.
Sigh. Should have figured.
PLANS! I SUMMON THEE!

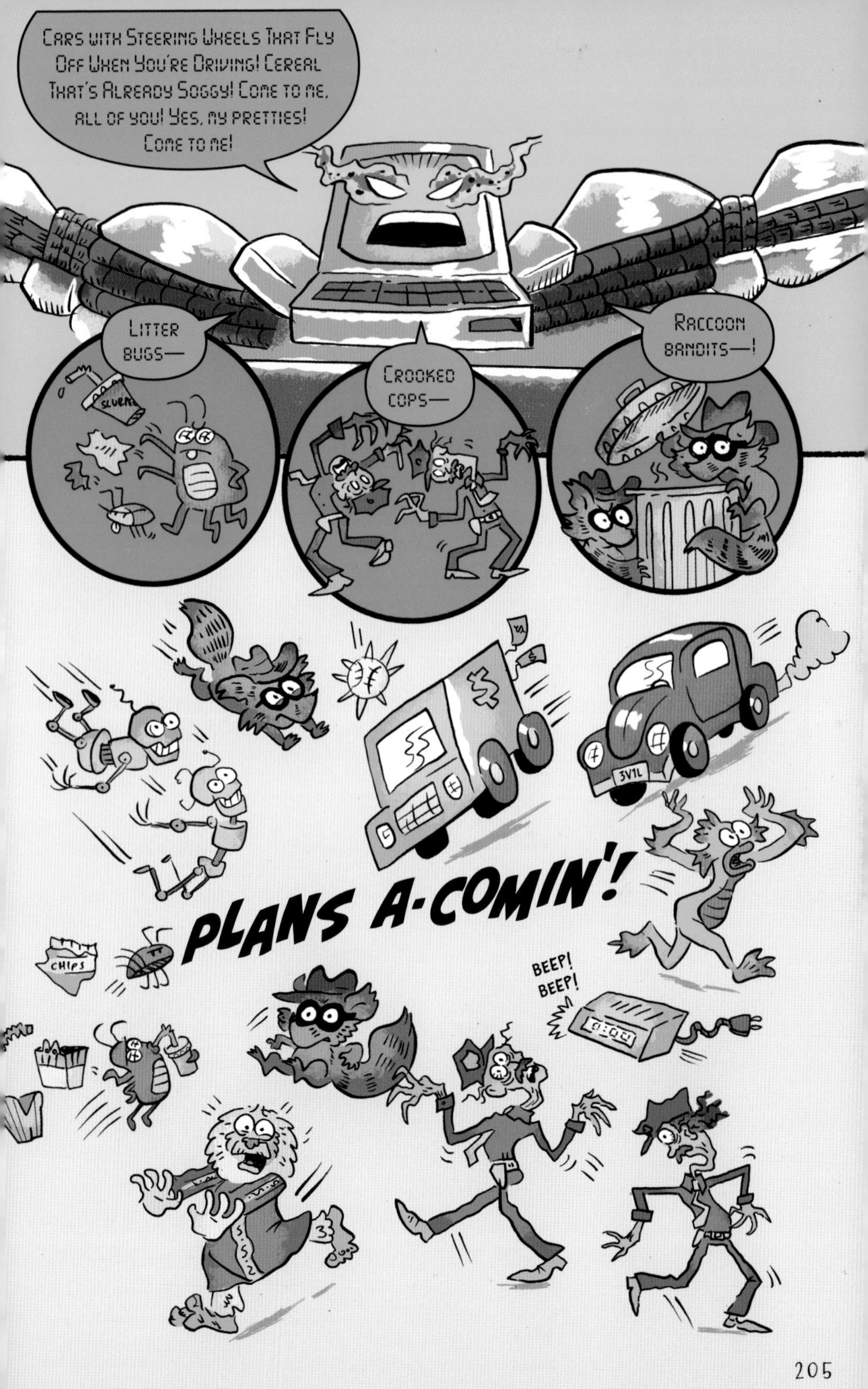
Cars with Steering Wheels That Fly Off When You're Driving! Cereal That's Already Soggy! Come to me, all of you! Yes, my pretties! Come to me!
Litter bugs—
Crooked cops—
Raccoon bandits—!
SLURPEE
3VIL
PLANS A-COMIN'!
CHIPS
BEEP! BEEP!

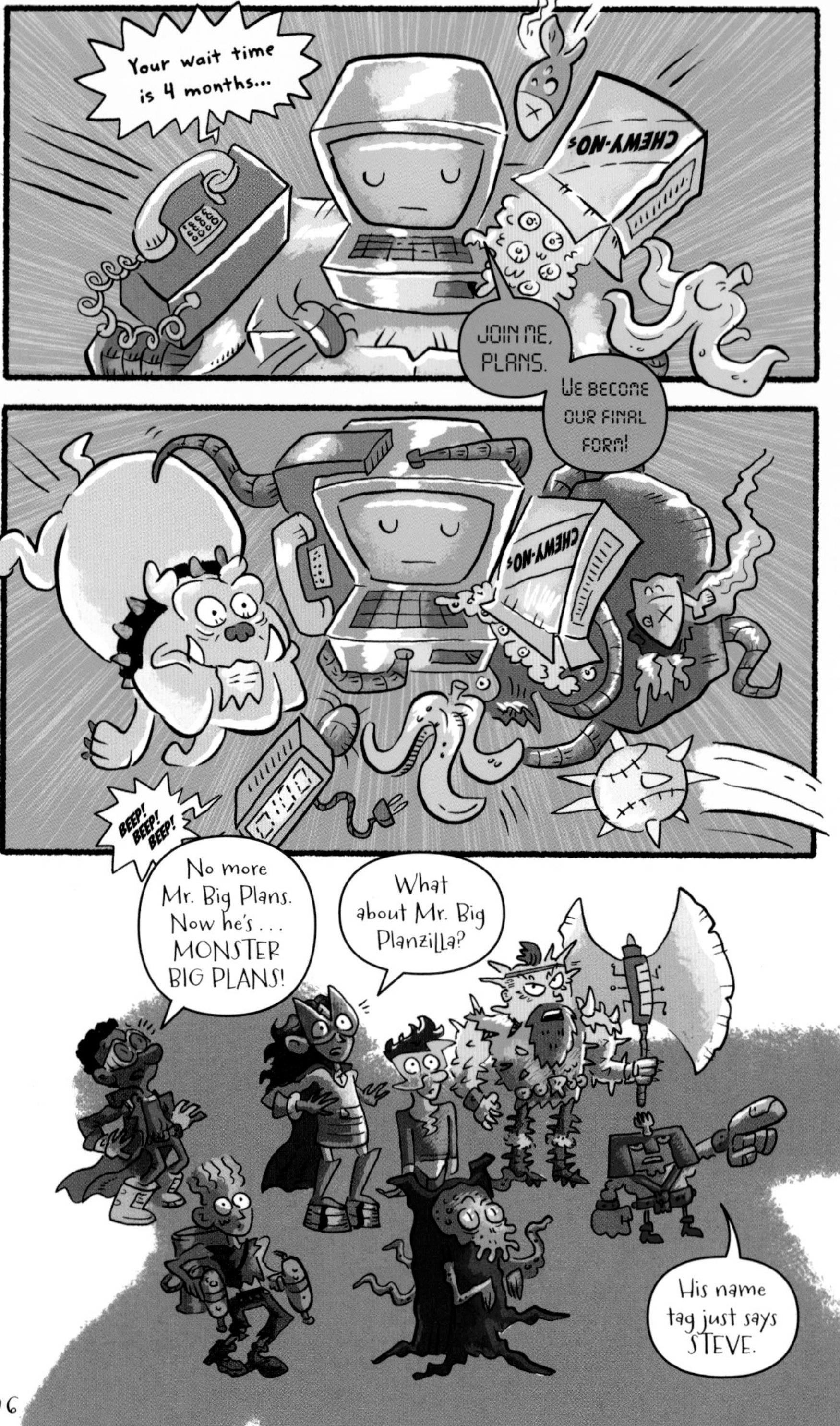
Your wait time is 4 months...
CHEWY-NOs
JOIN ME, PLANS.
WE BECOME OUR FINAL FORM!
CHEWY-NOs
BEEP! BEEP! BEEP!
No more Mr. Big Plans. Now he's . . . MONSTER BIG PLANS!
What about Mr. Big Planzilla?
His name tag just says STEVE.

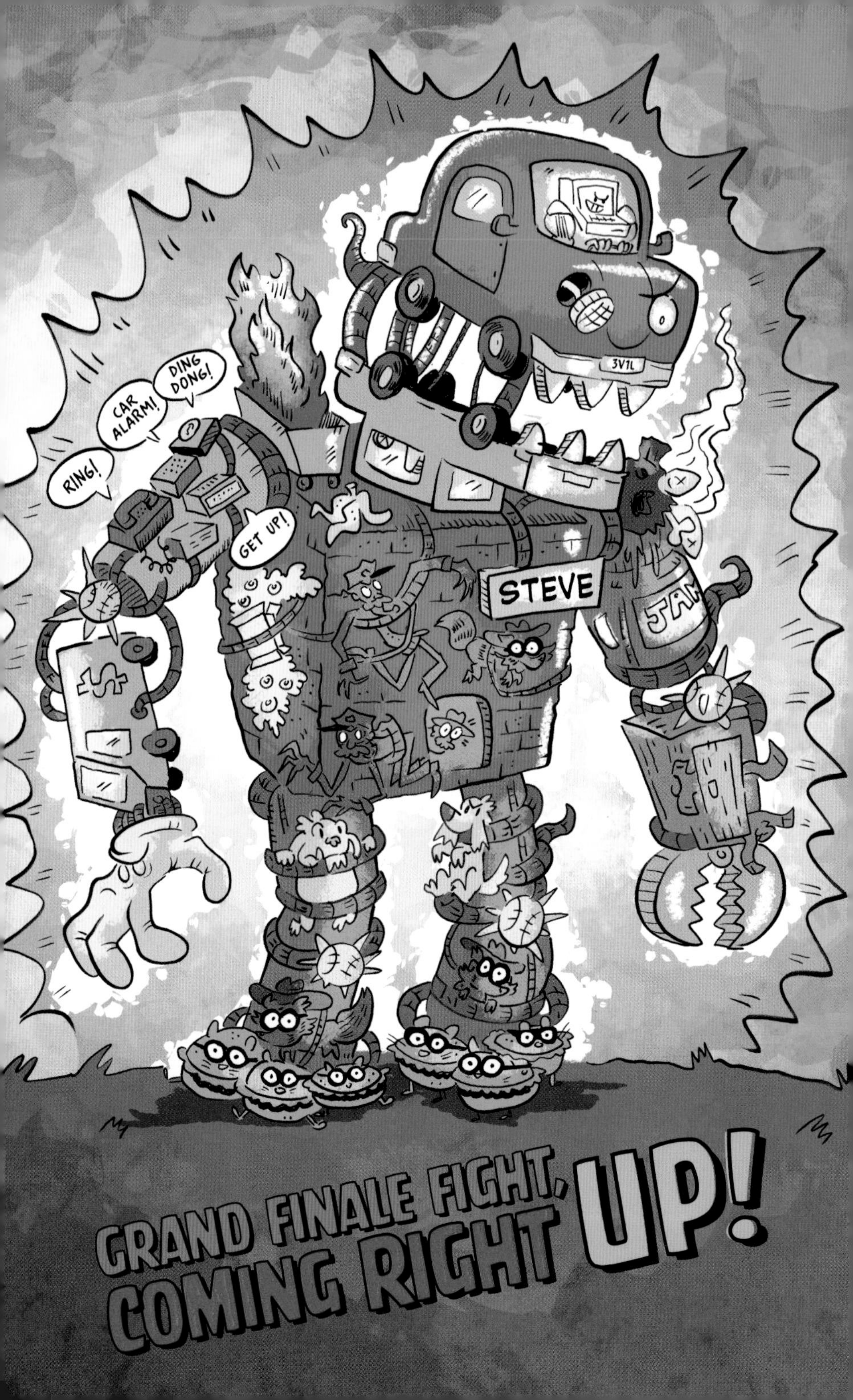
RING!
CAR ALARM!
DING DONG!
GET UP!
3V1L
STEVE
JAM
GRAND FINALE FIGHT, COMING RIGHT UP!

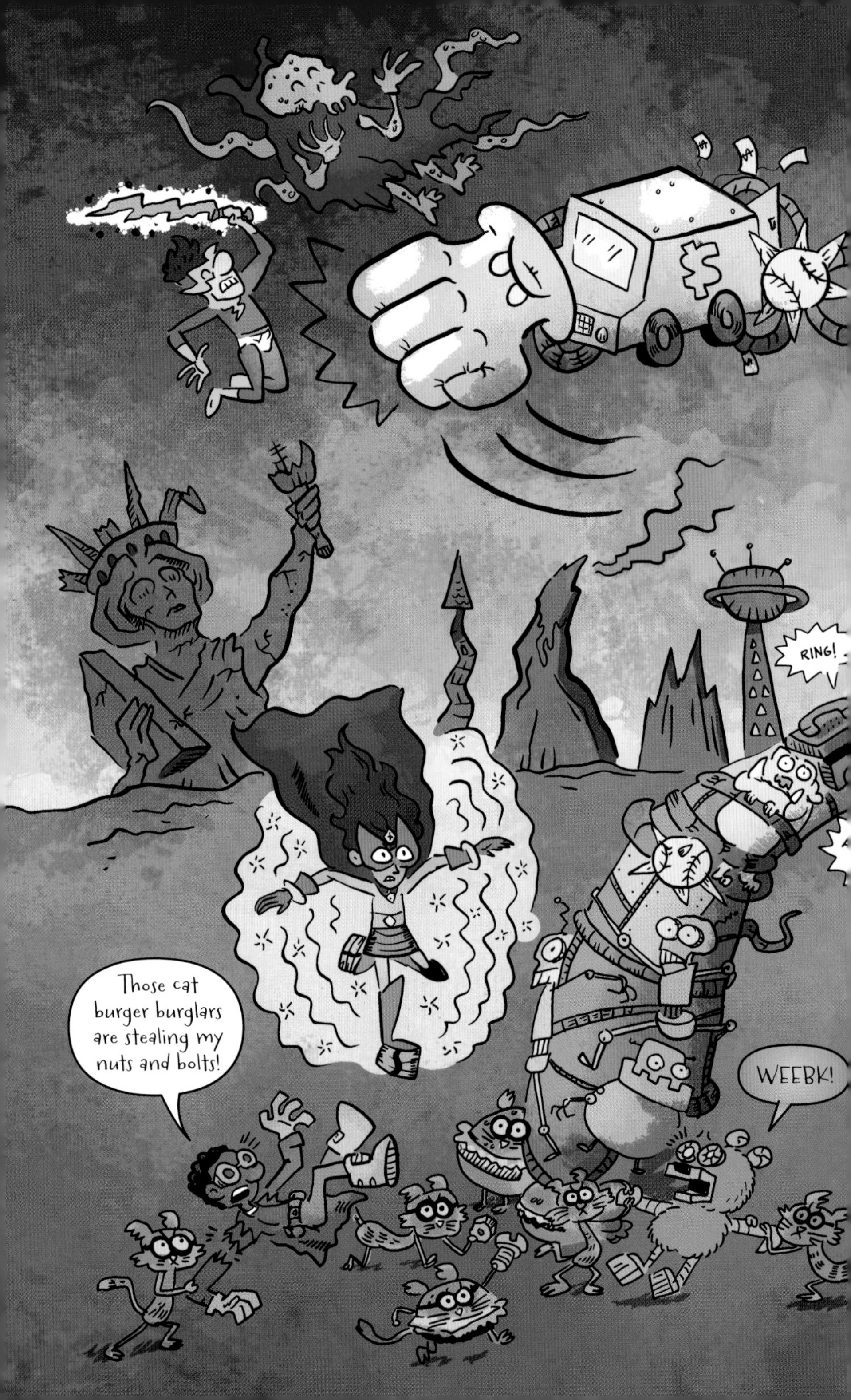

RING!
Those cat burger burglars are stealing my nuts and bolts!
WEEBK!

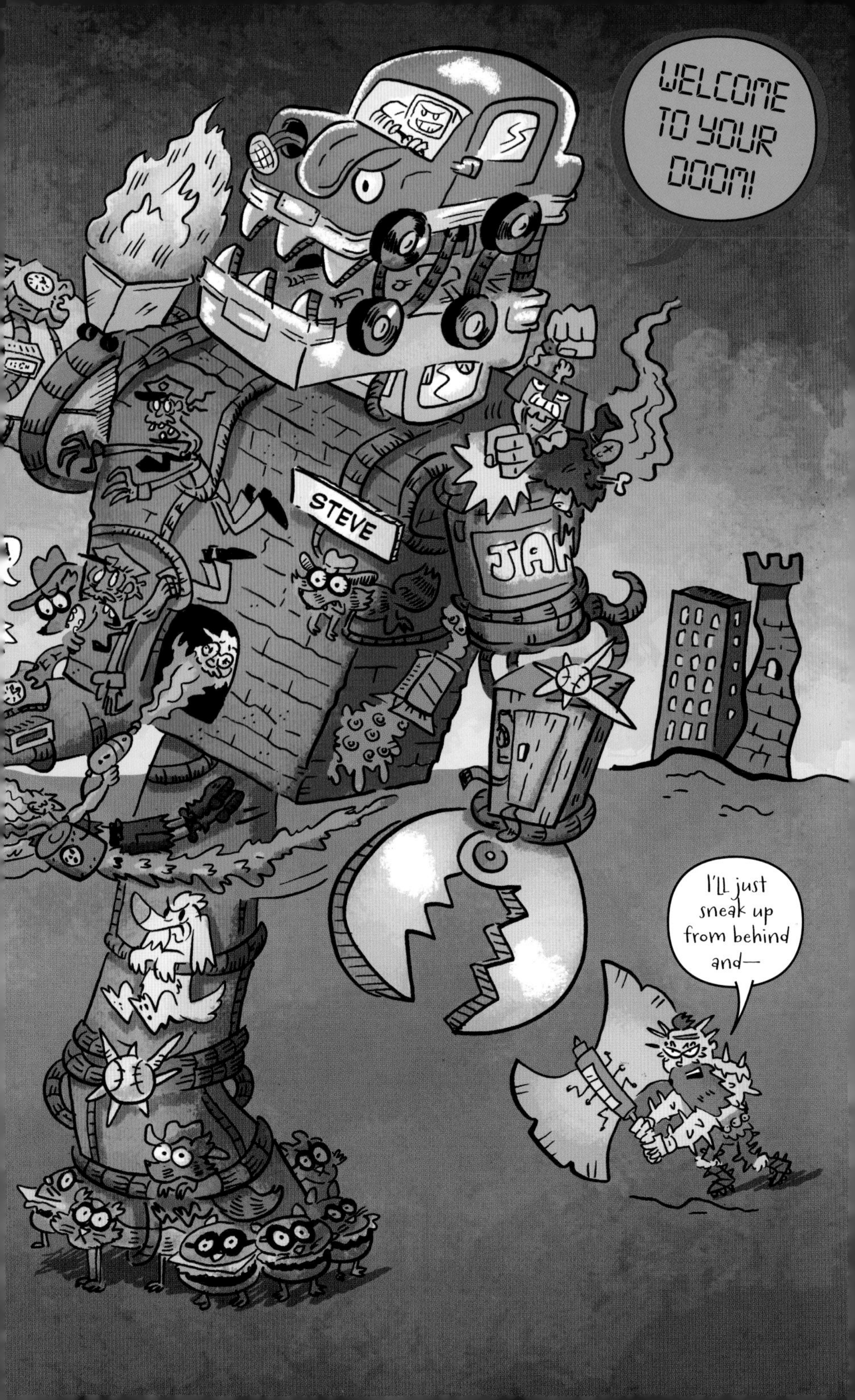
WELCOME TO YOUR DOOM!
STEVE
I'LL just sneak up from behind and—

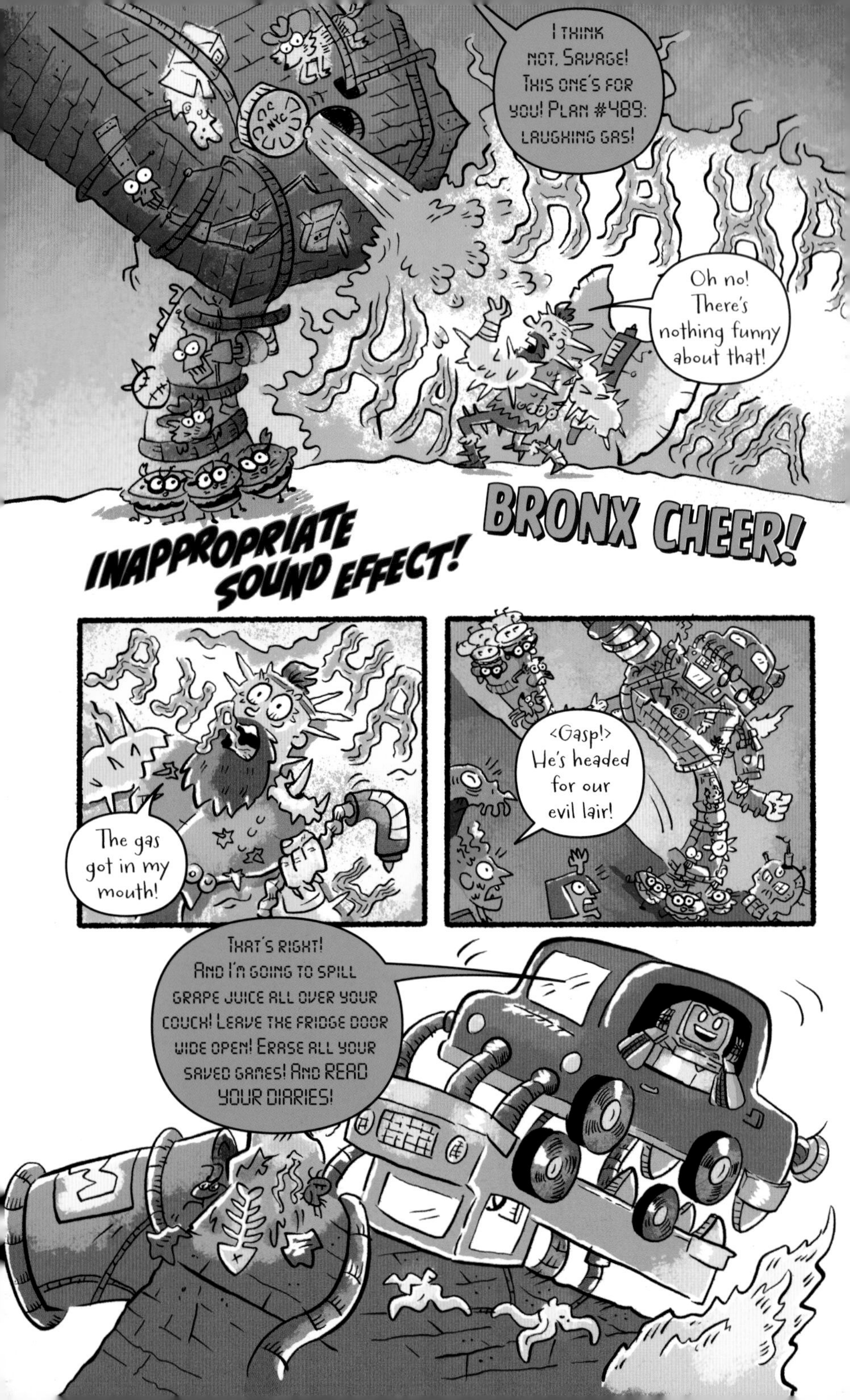
I THINK NOT, SAVAGE! THIS ONE'S FOR YOU! PLAN #489: LAUGHING GAS!
HA HA HA HA
Oh no! There's nothing funny about that!
INAPPROPRIATE SOUND EFFECT!
BRONX CHEER!
The gas got in my mouth!
<Gasp!> He's headed for our evil lair!
THAT'S RIGHT! AND I'M GOING TO SPILL GRAPE JUICE ALL OVER YOUR COUCH! LEAVE THE FRIDGE DOOR WIDE OPEN! ERASE ALL YOUR SAVED GAMES! AND READ YOUR DIARIES!

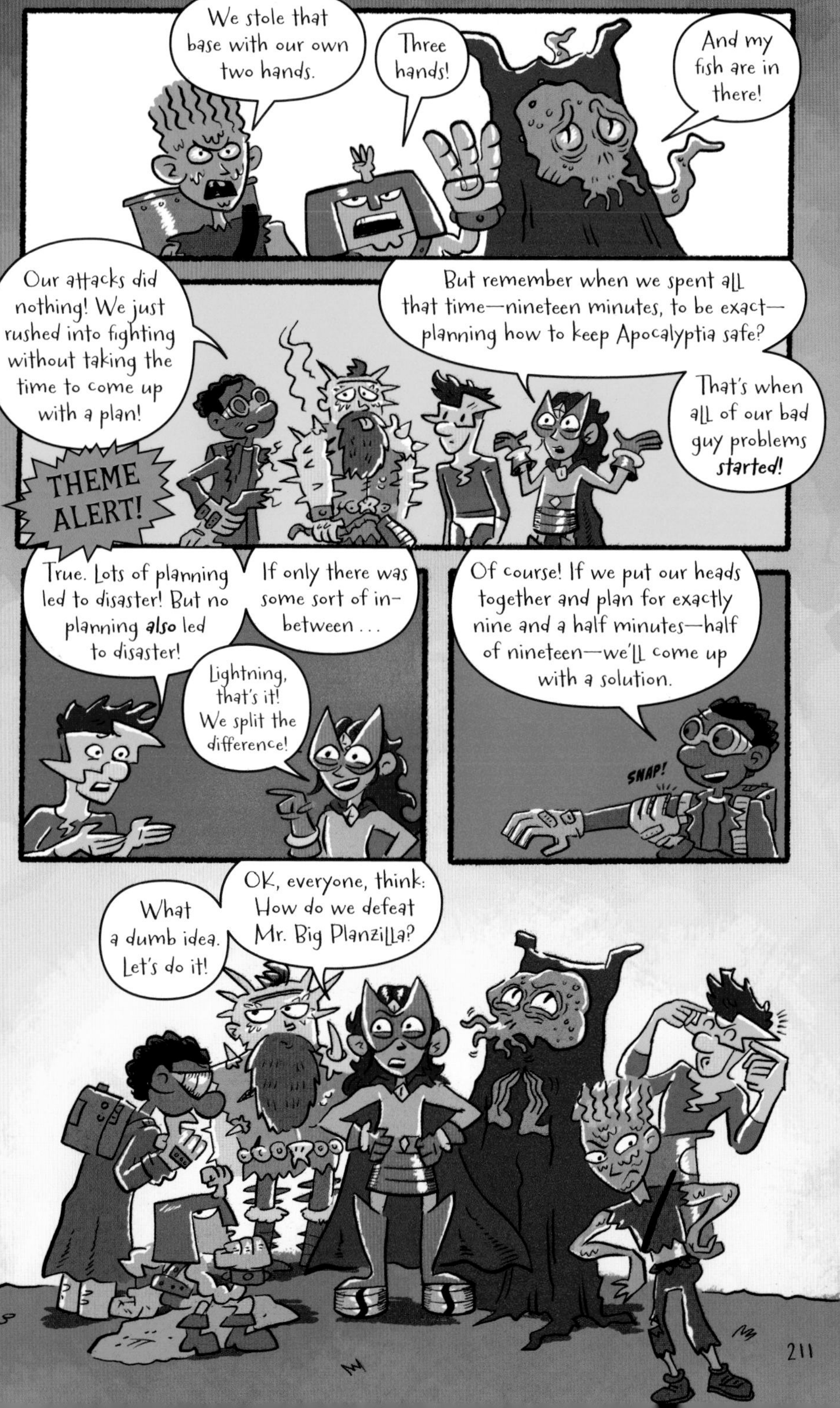
We stole that base with our own two hands.
Three hands!
And my fish are in there!
Our attacks did nothing! We just rushed into fighting without taking the time to come up with a plan!
But remember when we spent all that time—nineteen minutes, to be exact—planning how to keep Apocalyptia safe?
That's when all of our bad guy problems **started!**
THEME ALERT!
True. Lots of planning led to disaster! But no planning **also** led to disaster!
If only there was some sort of in-between . . .
Lightning, that's it! We split the difference!
Of course! If we put our heads together and plan for exactly nine and a half minutes—half of nineteen—we'll come up with a solution.
SNAP!
What a dumb idea. Let's do it!
OK, everyone, think: How do we defeat Mr. Big Planzilla?

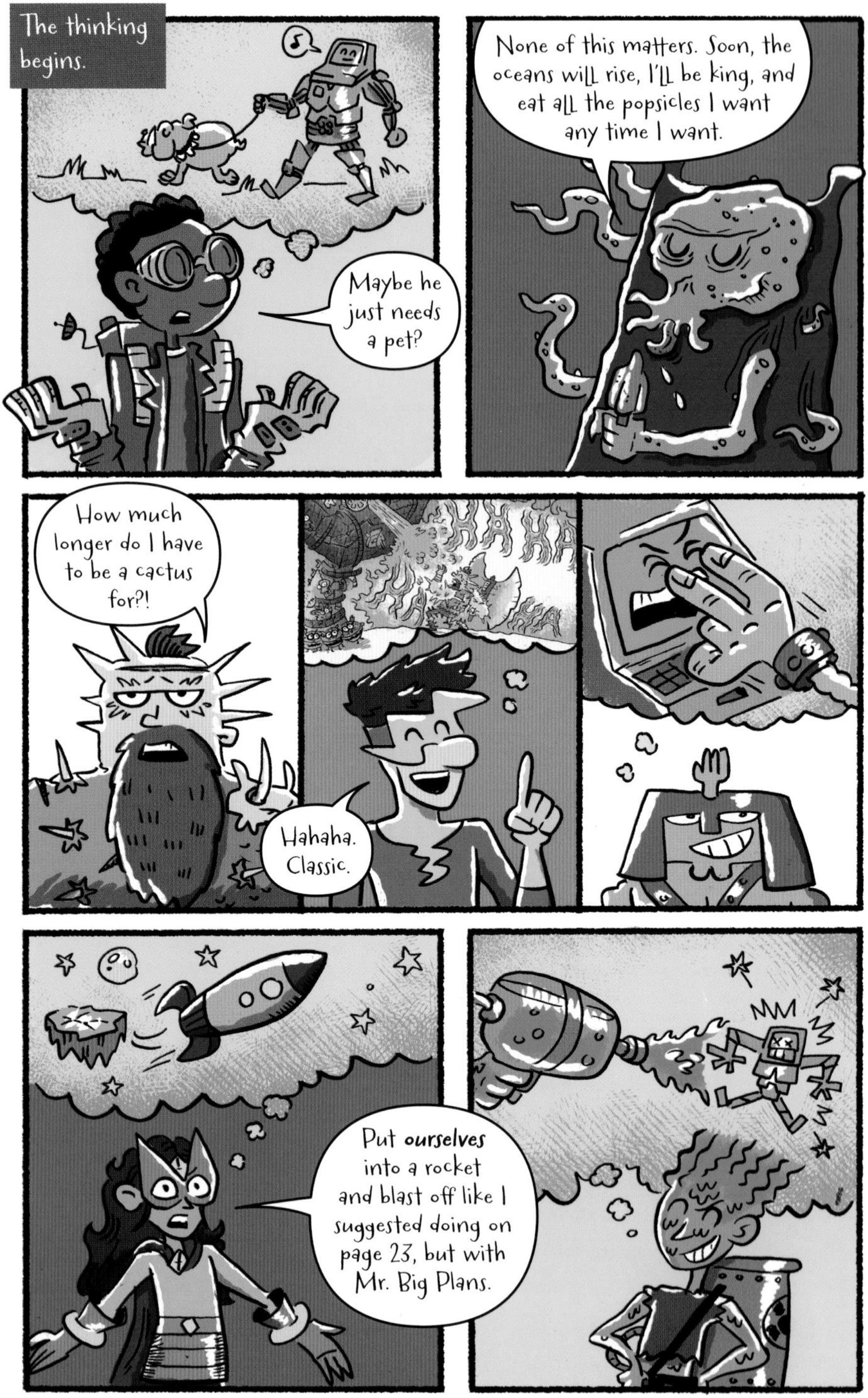
The thinking begins.
Maybe he just needs a pet?
None of this matters. Soon, the oceans will rise, I'll be king, and eat all the popsicles I want any time I want.
How much longer do I have to be a cactus for?!
Hahaha. Classic.
Put **ourselves** into a rocket and blast off like I suggested doing on page 23, but with Mr. Big Plans.

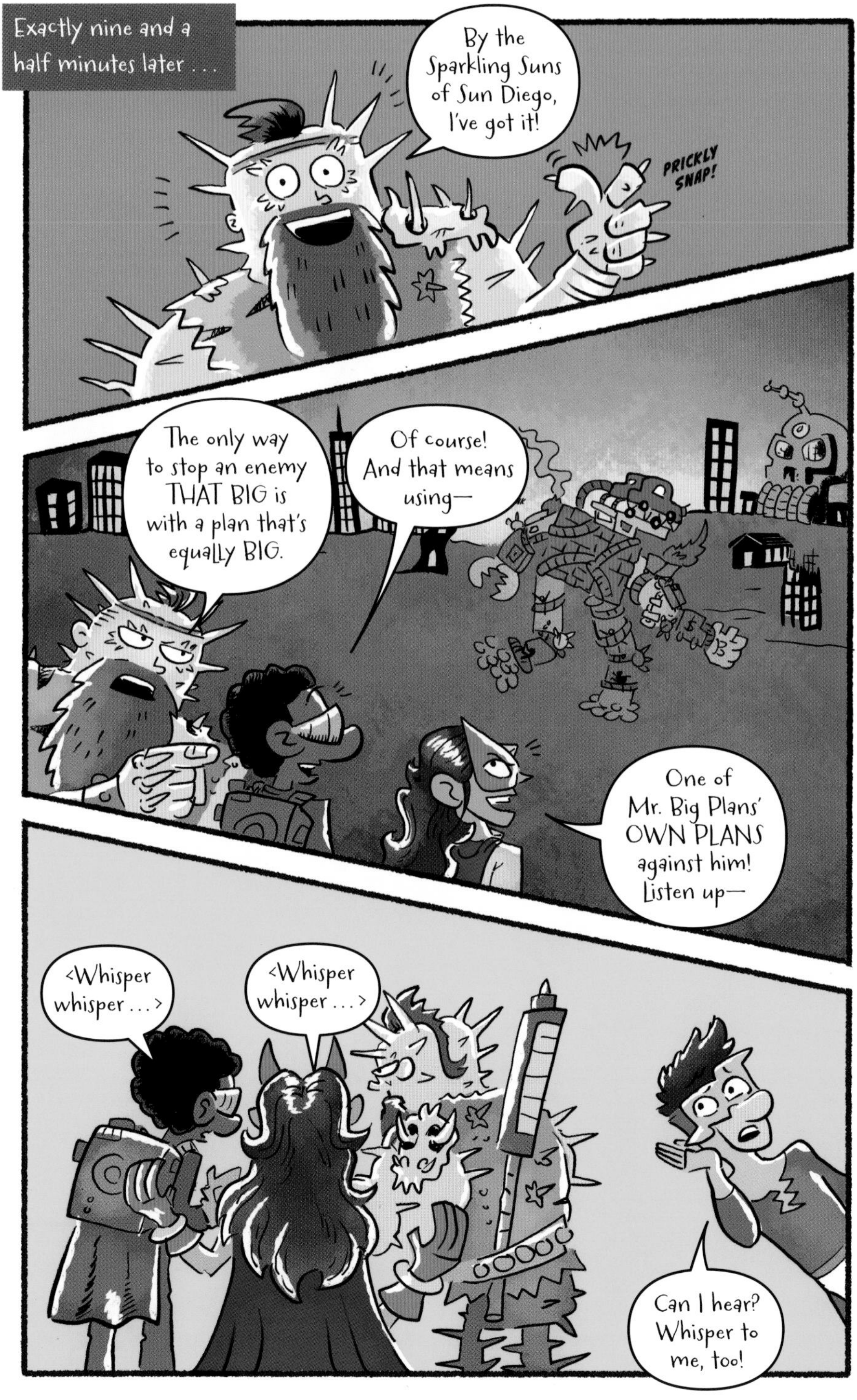
Exactly nine and a half minutes later . . .
By the Sparkling Suns of Sun Diego, I've got it!
PRICKLY SNAP!
The only way to stop an enemy THAT BIG is with a plan that's equally BIG.
Of course! And that means using—
One of Mr. Big Plans' OWN PLANS against him! Listen up—
<Whisper whisper . . .>
<Whisper whisper . . .>
Can I hear? Whisper to me, too!

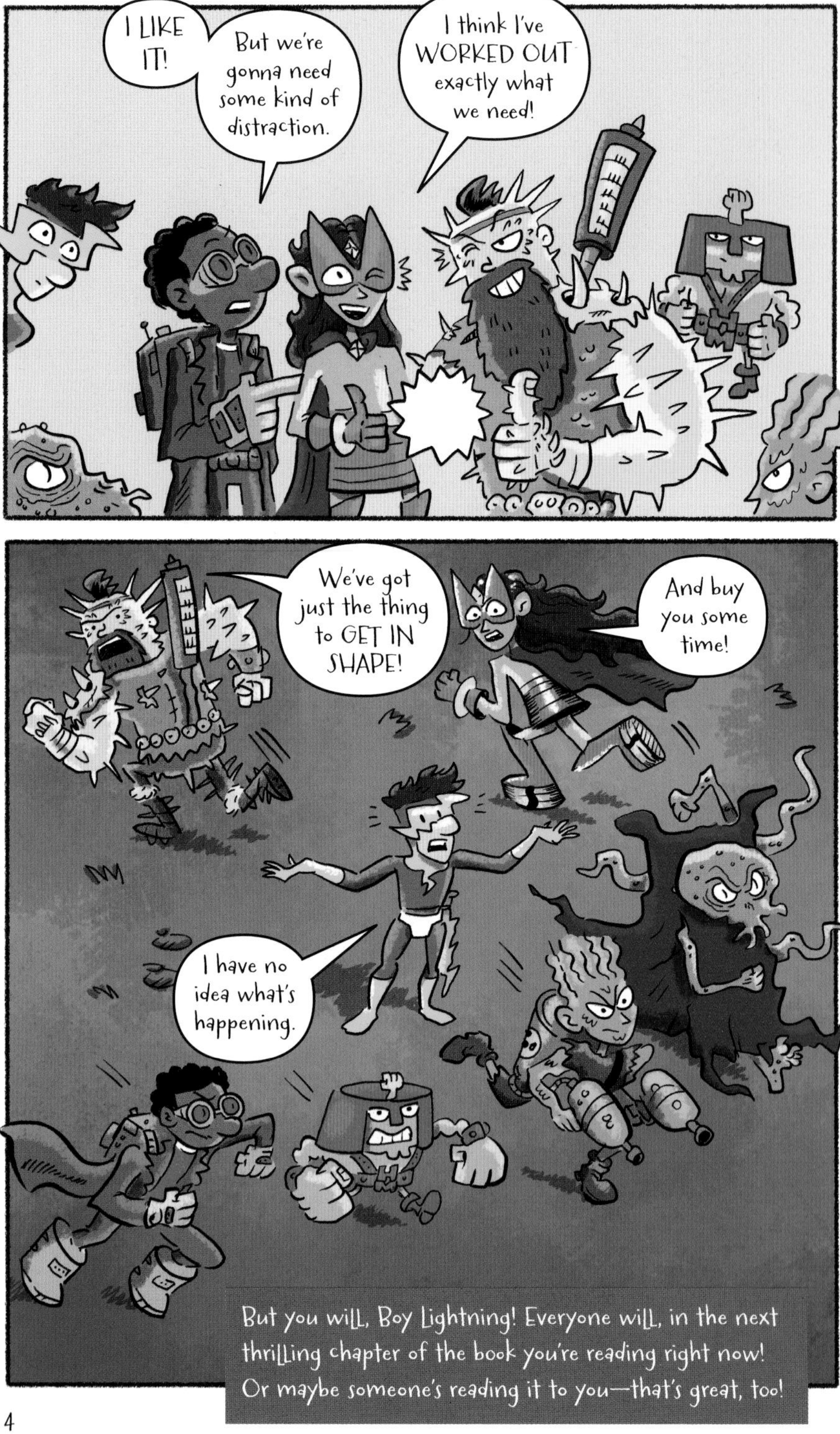
I LIKE IT!
But we're gonna need some kind of distraction.
I think I've WORKED OUT exactly what we need!
We've got just the thing to GET IN SHAPE!
And buy you some time!
I have no idea what's happening.
But you will, Boy Lightning! Everyone will, in the next thrilling chapter of the book you're reading right now! Or maybe someone's reading it to you—that's great, too!

CHAPTER FOURTEEN ATTACK OF THE 50-FT. PLAN!

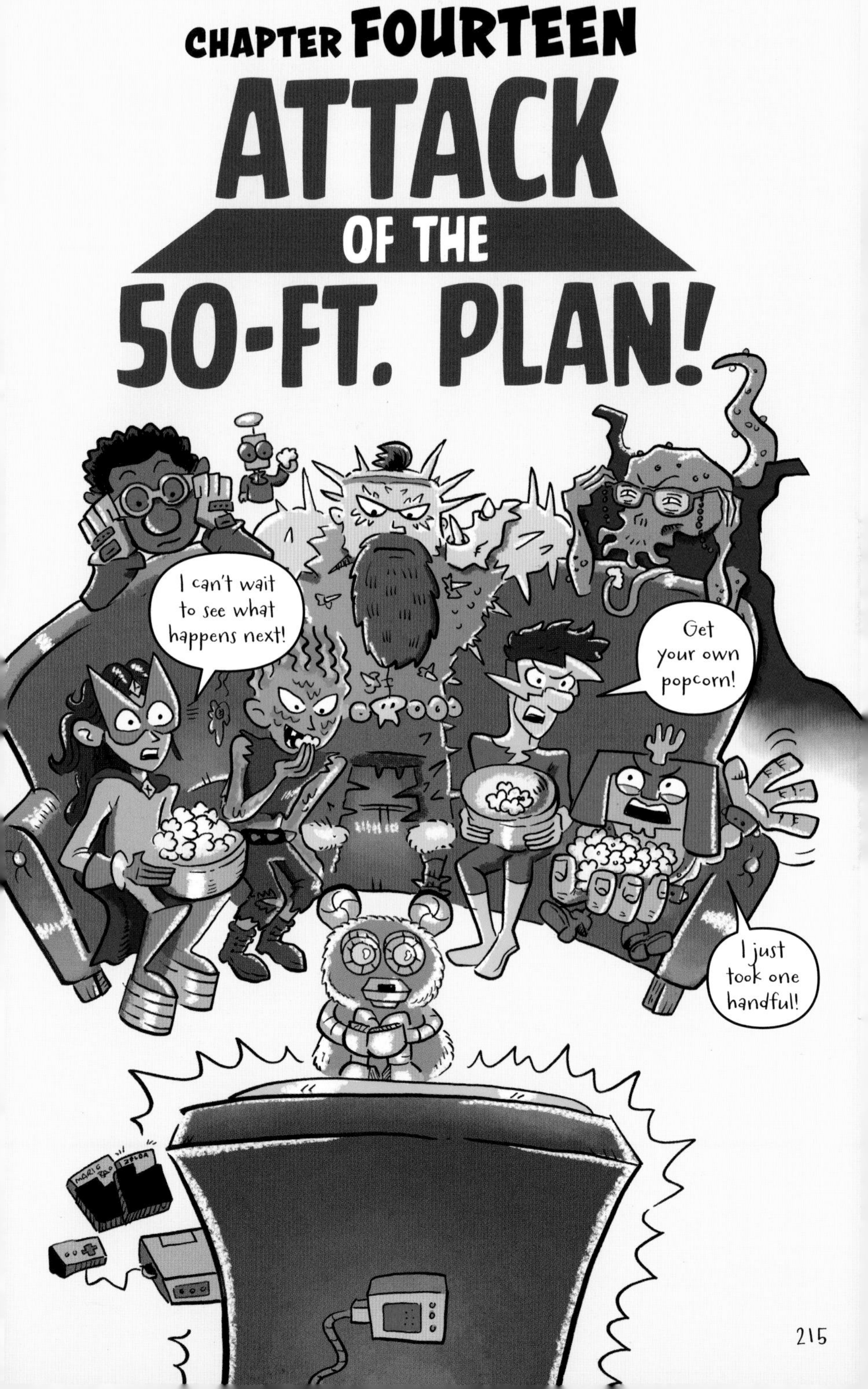
I can't wait to see what happens next!
Get your own popcorn!
I just took one handful!

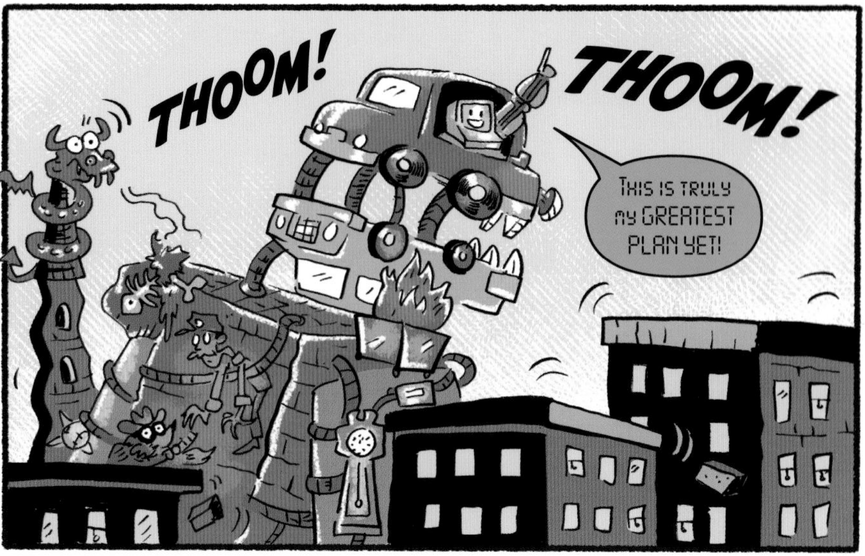
THOOM!
THOOM!
THIS IS TRULY my GREATEST PLAN YET!

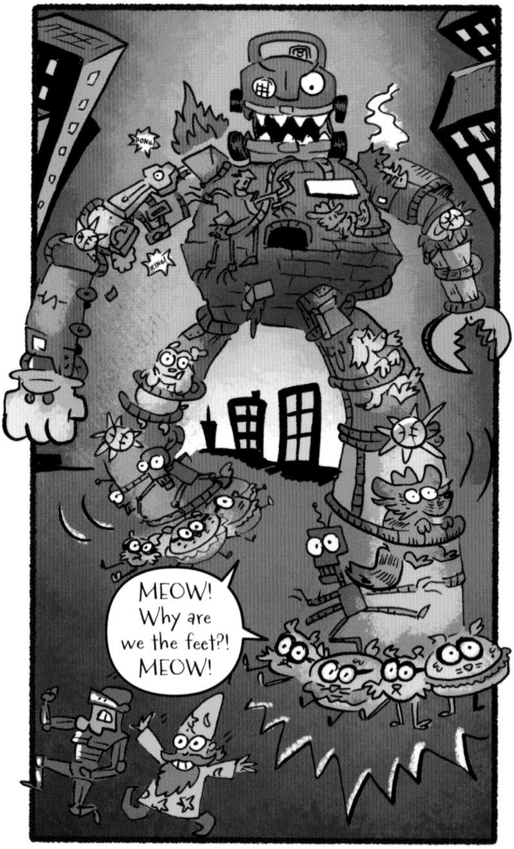
MEOW! Why are we the feet?! MEOW!

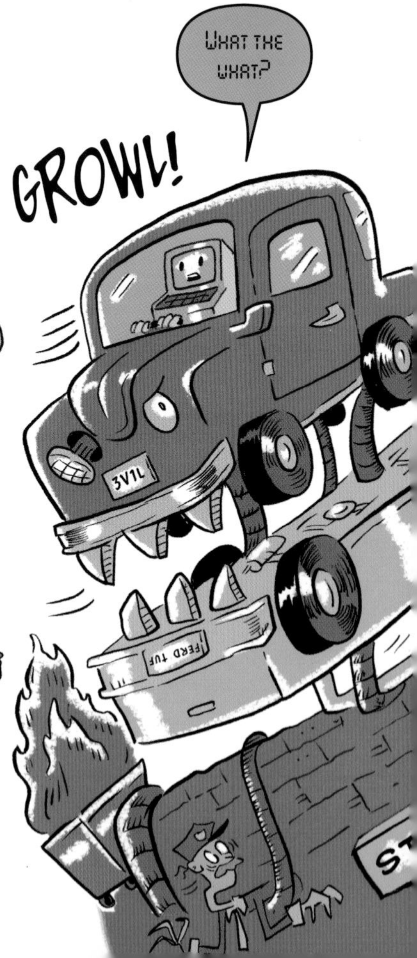
WHAT THE WHAT?
GROWL!
3V1L

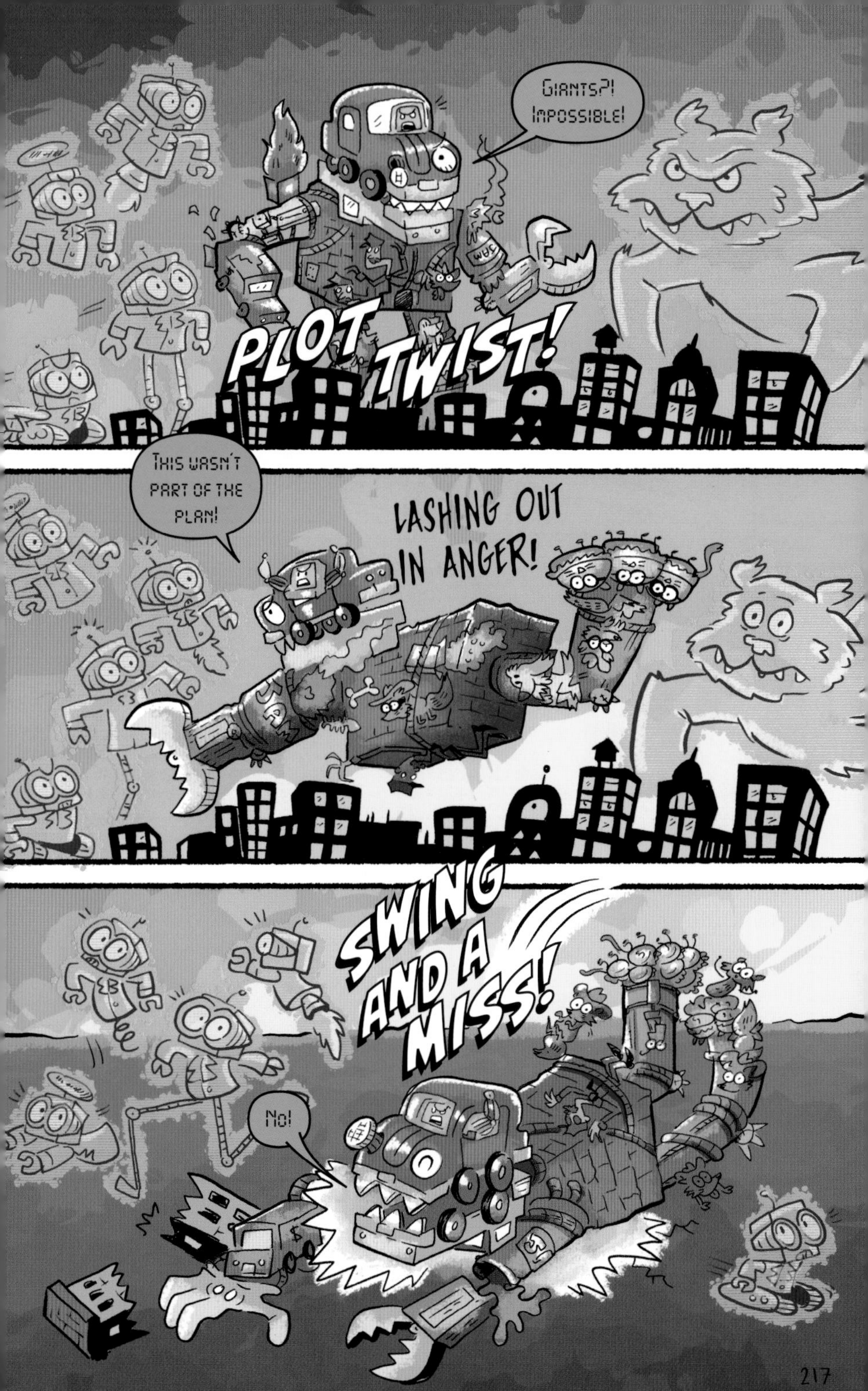
GIANTS?! IMPOSSIBLE!
PLOT TWIST!
THIS WASN'T PART OF THE PLAN!
LASHING OUT IN ANGER!
SWING AND A MISS!
NO!

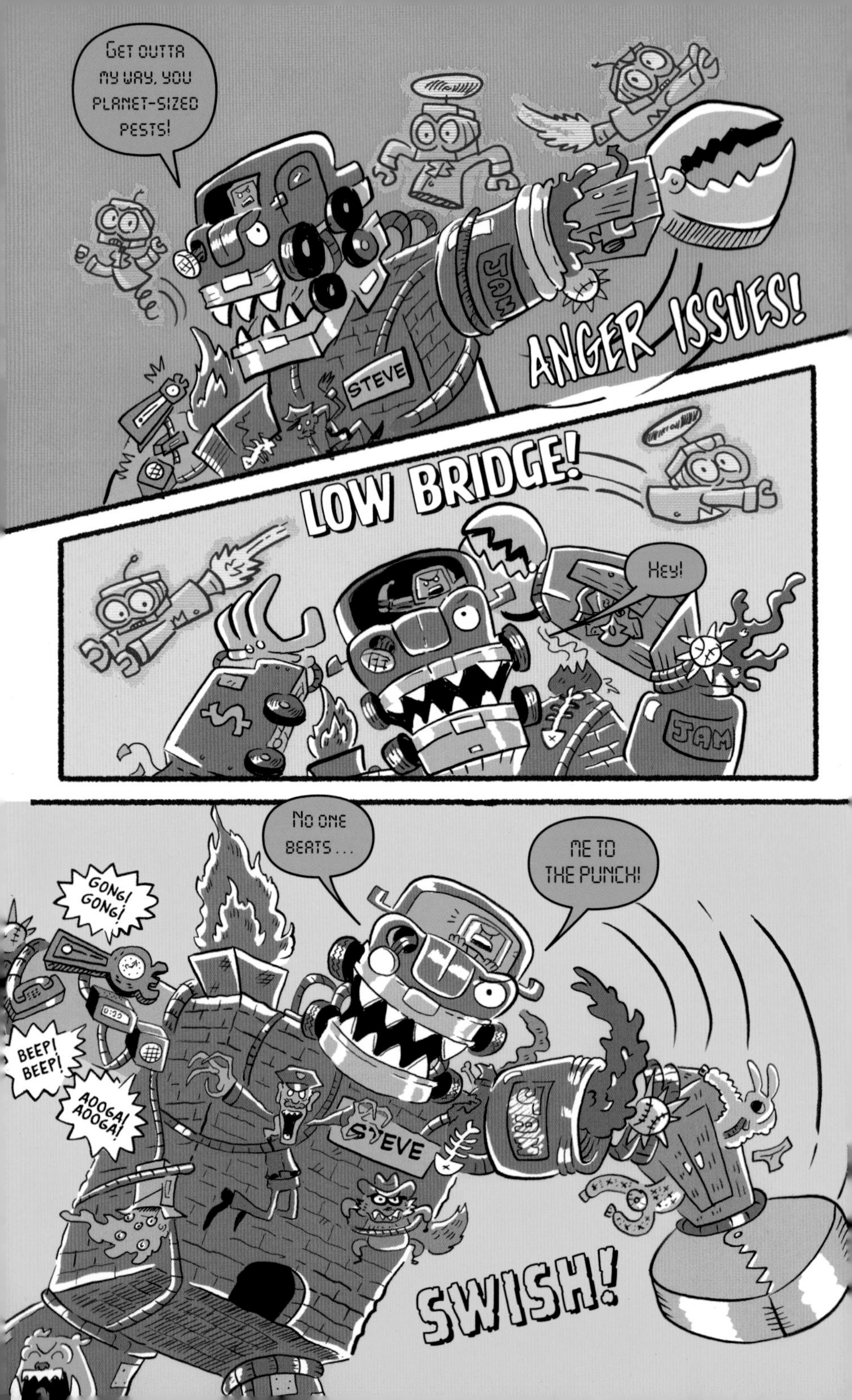
GET OUTTA MY WAY, YOU PLANET-SIZED PESTS!
ANGER ISSUES!
STEVE
JAM
LOW BRIDGE!
Hey!
JAM
No one beats . . .
ME TO THE PUNCH!
GONG! GONG!
BEEP! BEEP!
AOOGA! AOOGA!
STEVE
SWISH!

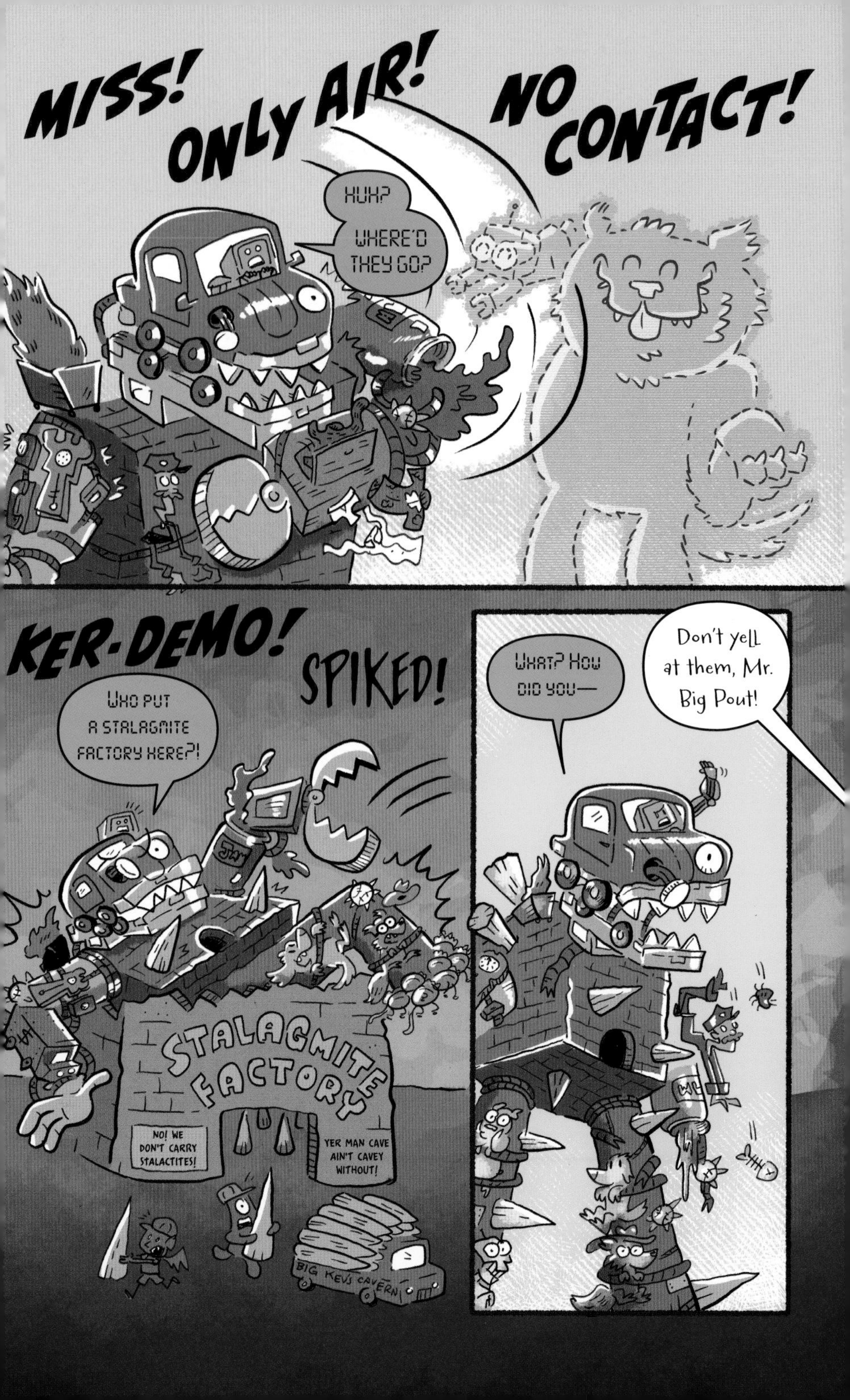
MISS!
ONLY AIR!
NO CONTACT!
HUH?
WHERE'D THEY GO?
KER-DEMO!
SPIKED!
WHO PUT A STALAGMITE FACTORY HERE?!
STALAGMITE FACTORY
NO! WE DON'T CARRY STALACTITES!
YER MAN CAVE AIN'T CAVEY WITHOUT!
BIG KEV'S CAVERN
WHAT? HOW DID YOU—
Don't yell at them, Mr. Big Pout!

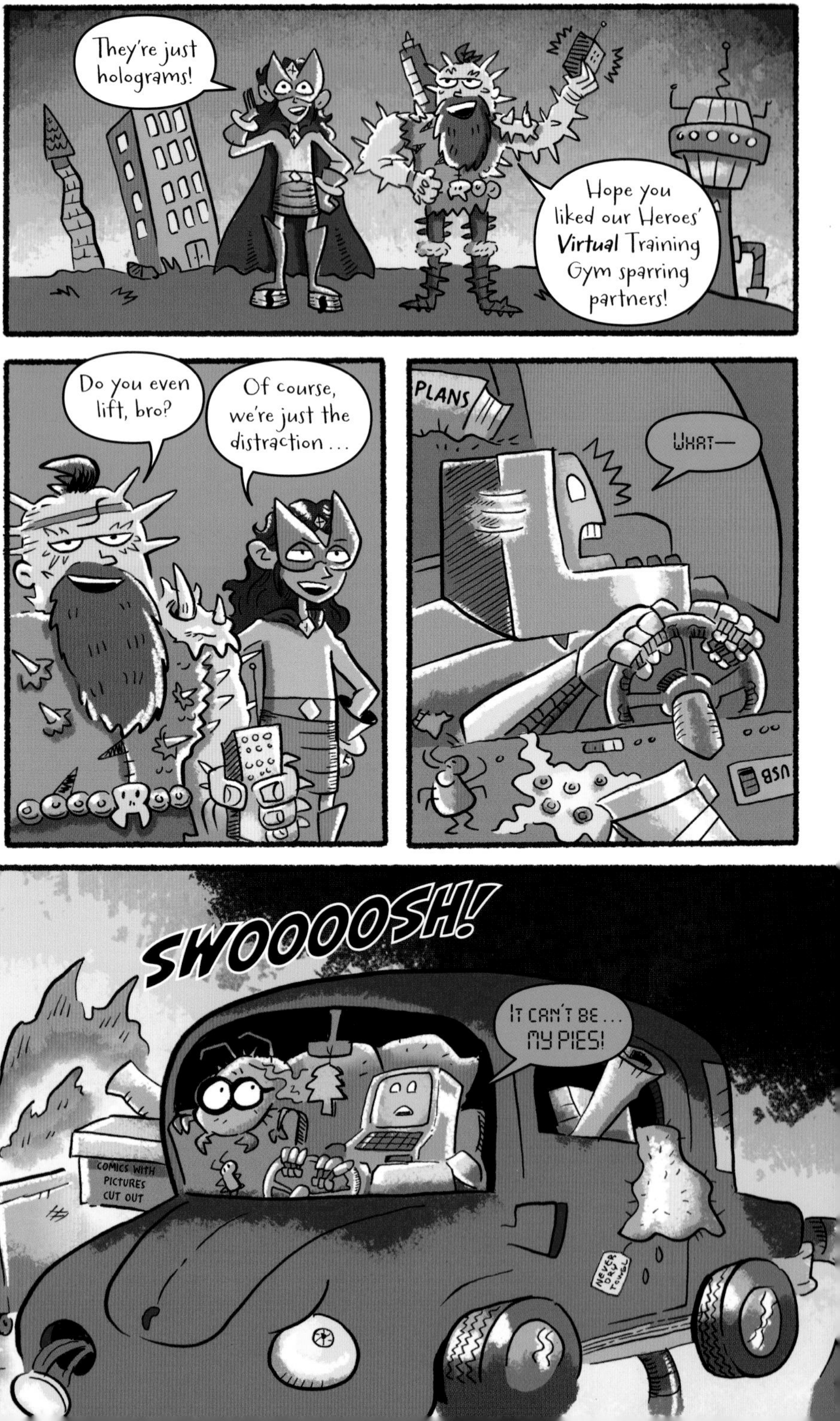
They're just holograms!
Hope you liked our Heroes' **Virtual** Training Gym sparring partners!
Do you even lift, bro?
Of course, we're just the distraction . . .
PLANS
WHAT—
USB
SWOOOOSH!
COMICS WITH PICTURES CUT OUT
IT CAN'T BE . . . MY PIES!

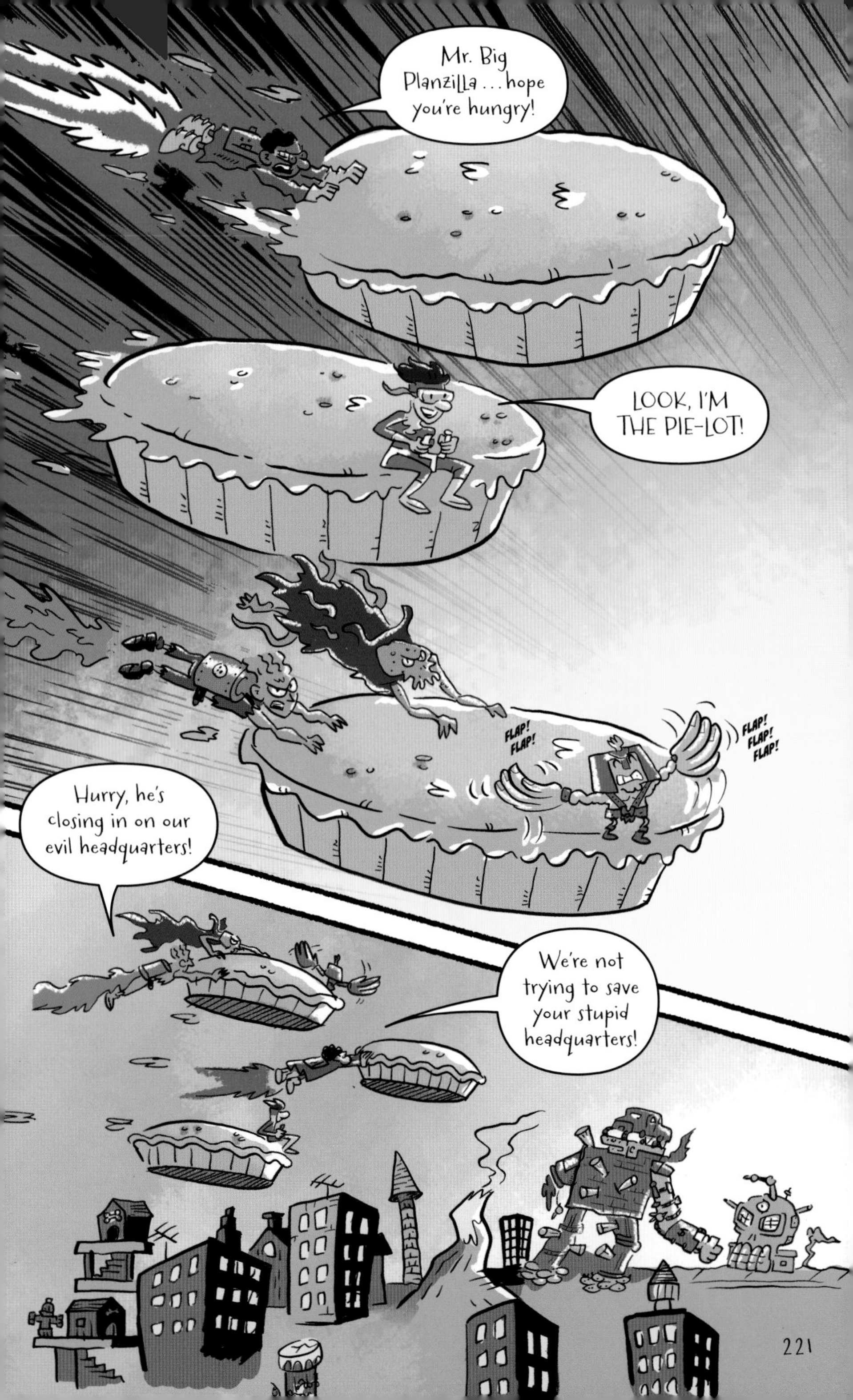
Mr. Big Planzilla . . . hope you're hungry!
LOOK, I'M THE PIE-LOT!
FLAP! FLAP!
FLAP! FLAP! FLAP!
Hurry, he's closing in on our evil headquarters!
We're not trying to save your stupid headquarters!

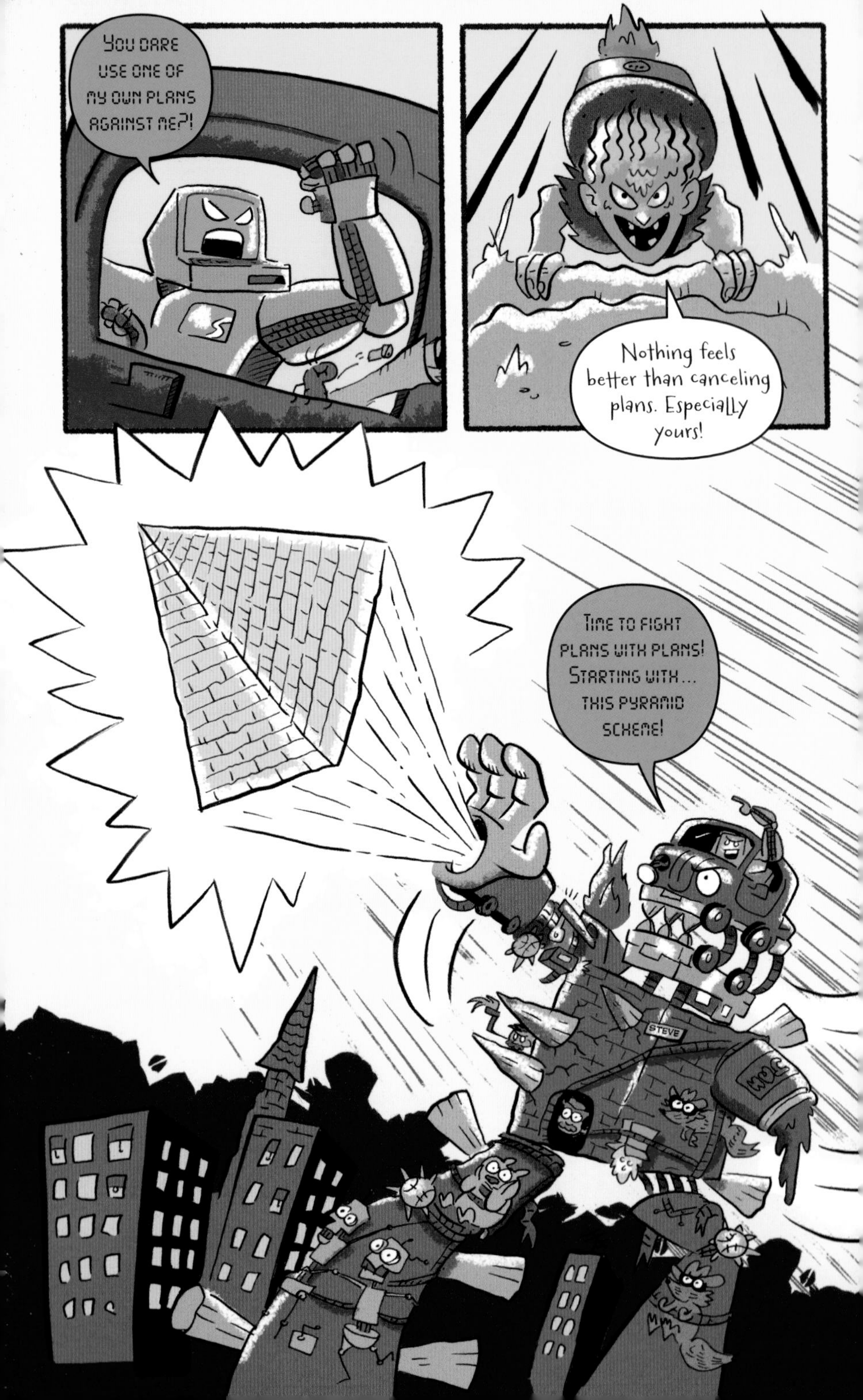

YOU DARE USE ONE OF MY OWN PLANS AGAINST ME?!
Nothing feels better than canceling plans. Especially yours!
TIME TO FIGHT PLANS WITH PLANS! STARTING WITH... THIS PYRAMID SCHEME!
STEVE

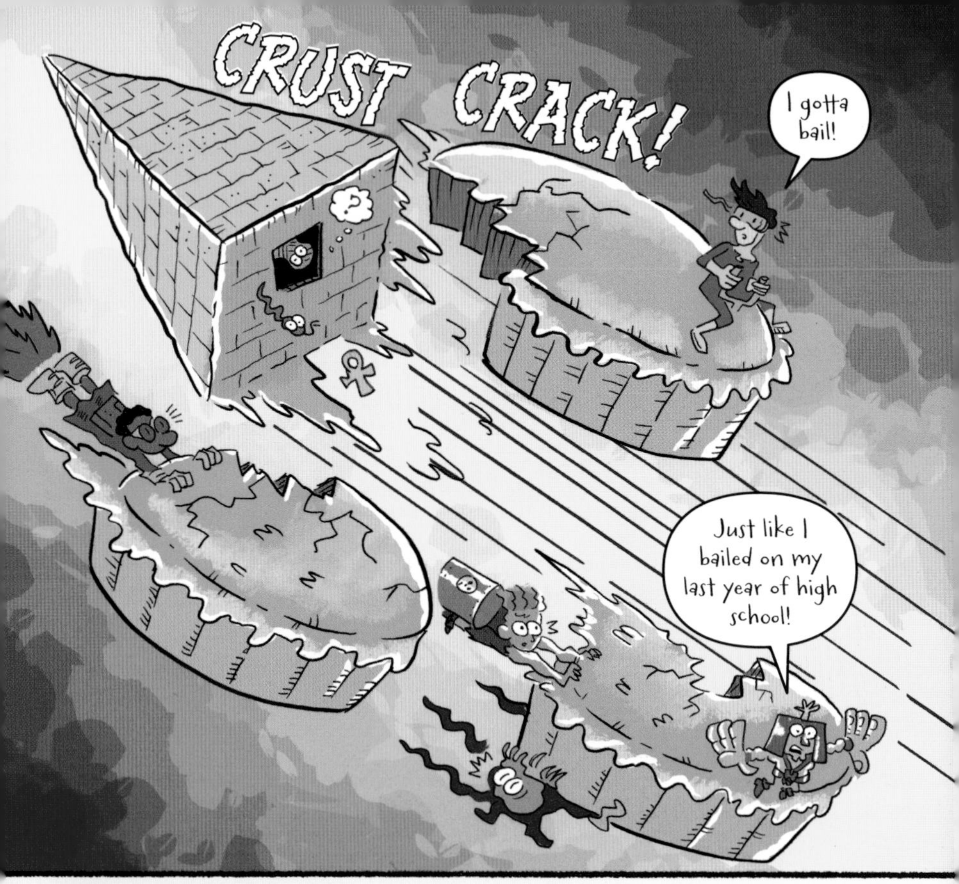
CRUST CRACK!
I gotta bail!
Just like I bailed on my last year of high school!

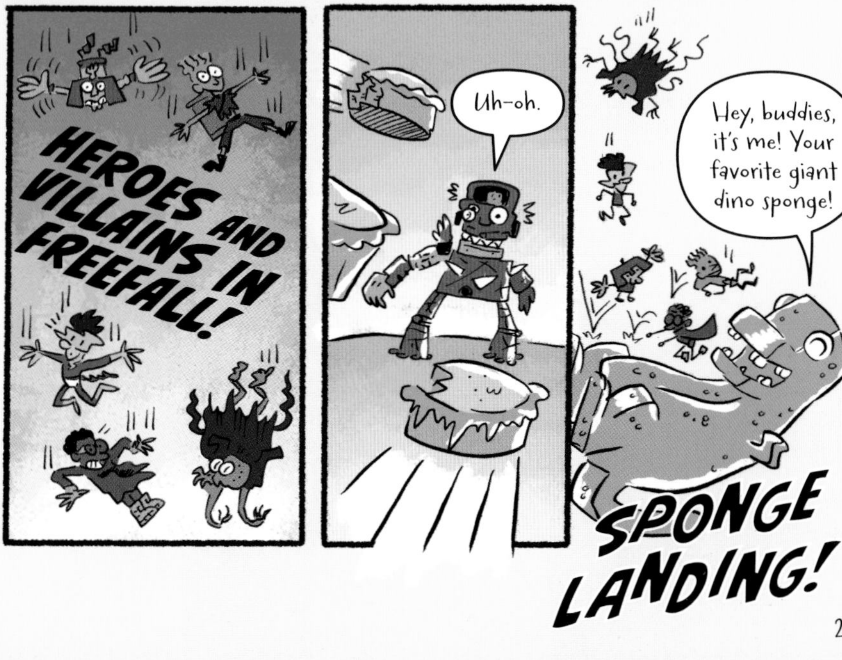
HEROES AND VILLAINS IN FREEFALL!
Uh-oh.
Hey, buddies, it's me! Your favorite giant dino sponge!
SPONGE LANDING!

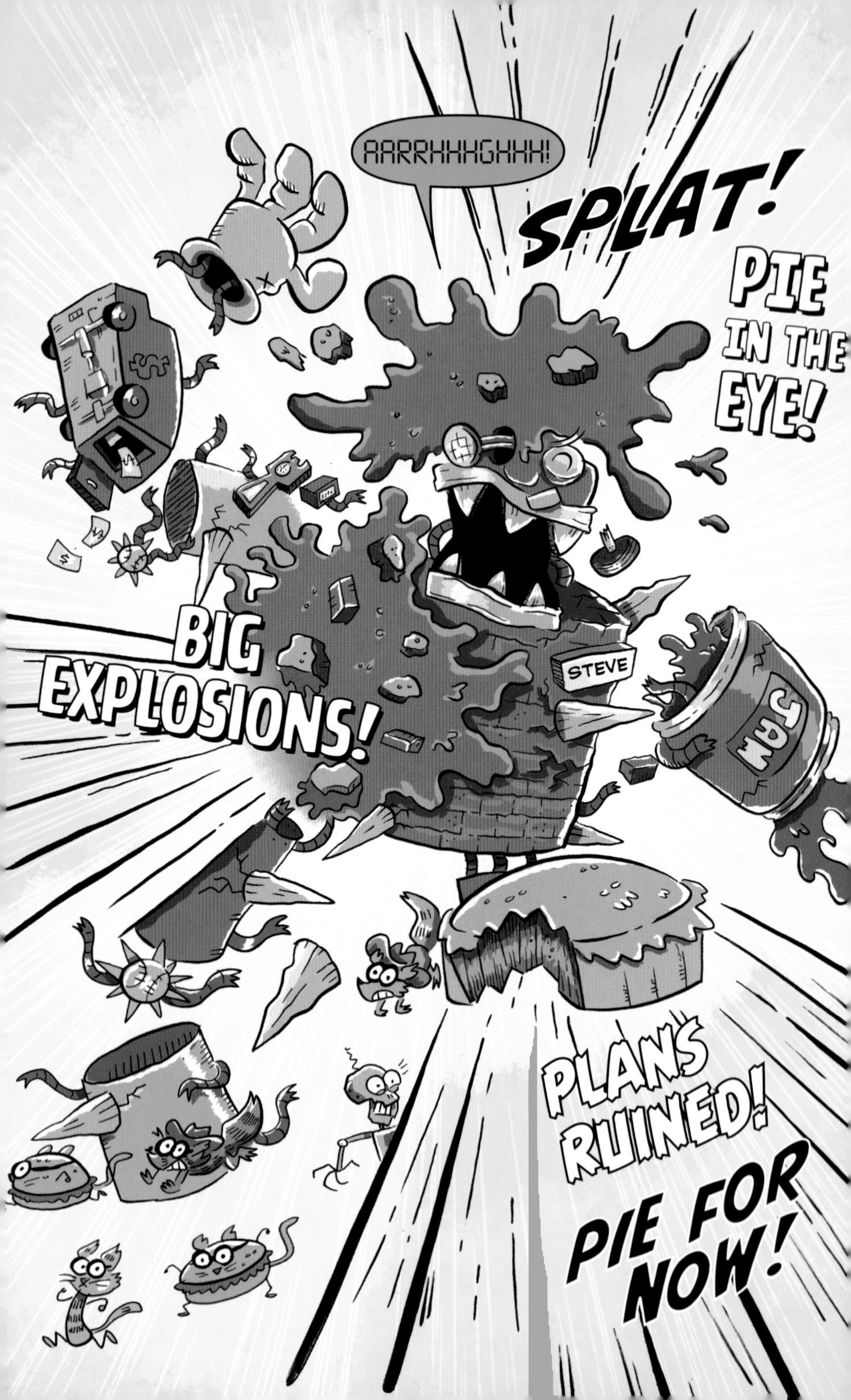
AARRHHHGHHH!
SPLAT!
PIE IN THE EYE!
STEVE
JAM
BIG EXPLOSIONS!
PLANS RUINED!
PIE FOR NOW!

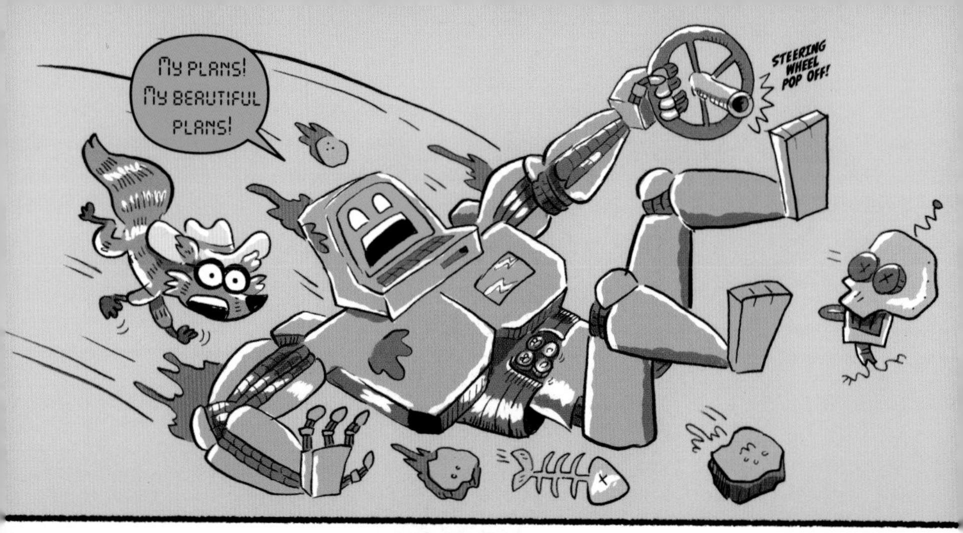
My PLANS! My BEAUTIFUL PLANS!
STEERING WHEEL POP OFF!

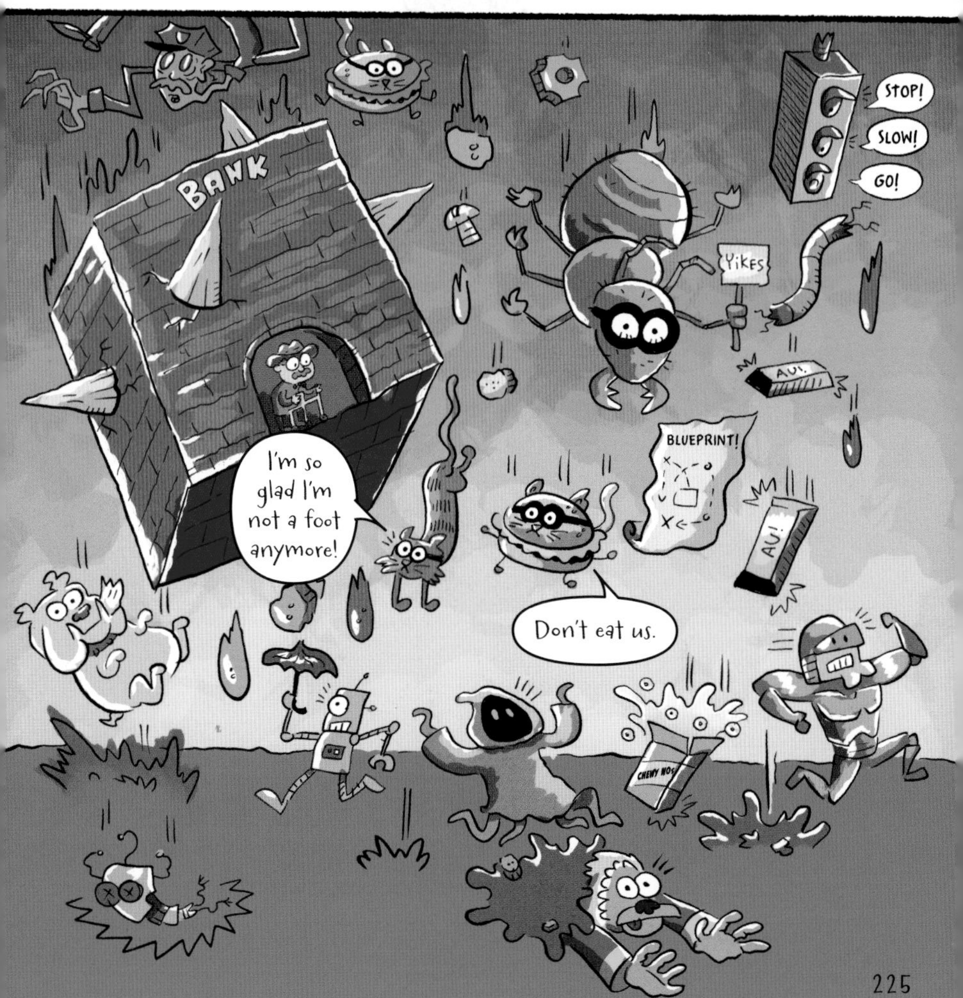
BANK
STOP!
SLOW!
GO!
YIKES
AU!
BLUEPRINT!
I'm so glad I'm not a foot anymore!
AU!
Don't eat us.
CHEWY NOS

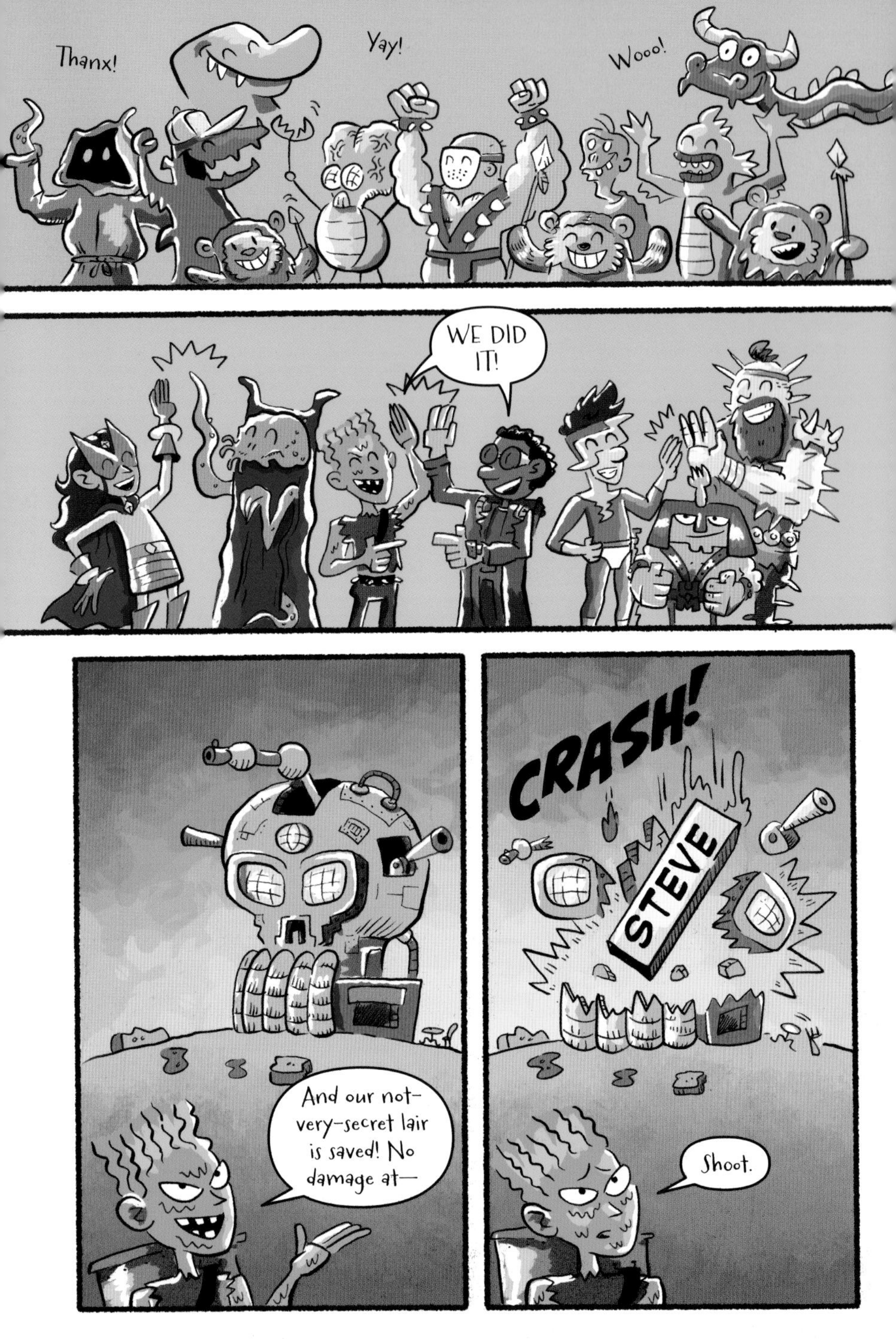
Thanx!
Yay!
Wooo!
WE DID IT!
And our not-very-secret lair is saved! No damage at—
CRASH!
STEVE
Shoot.

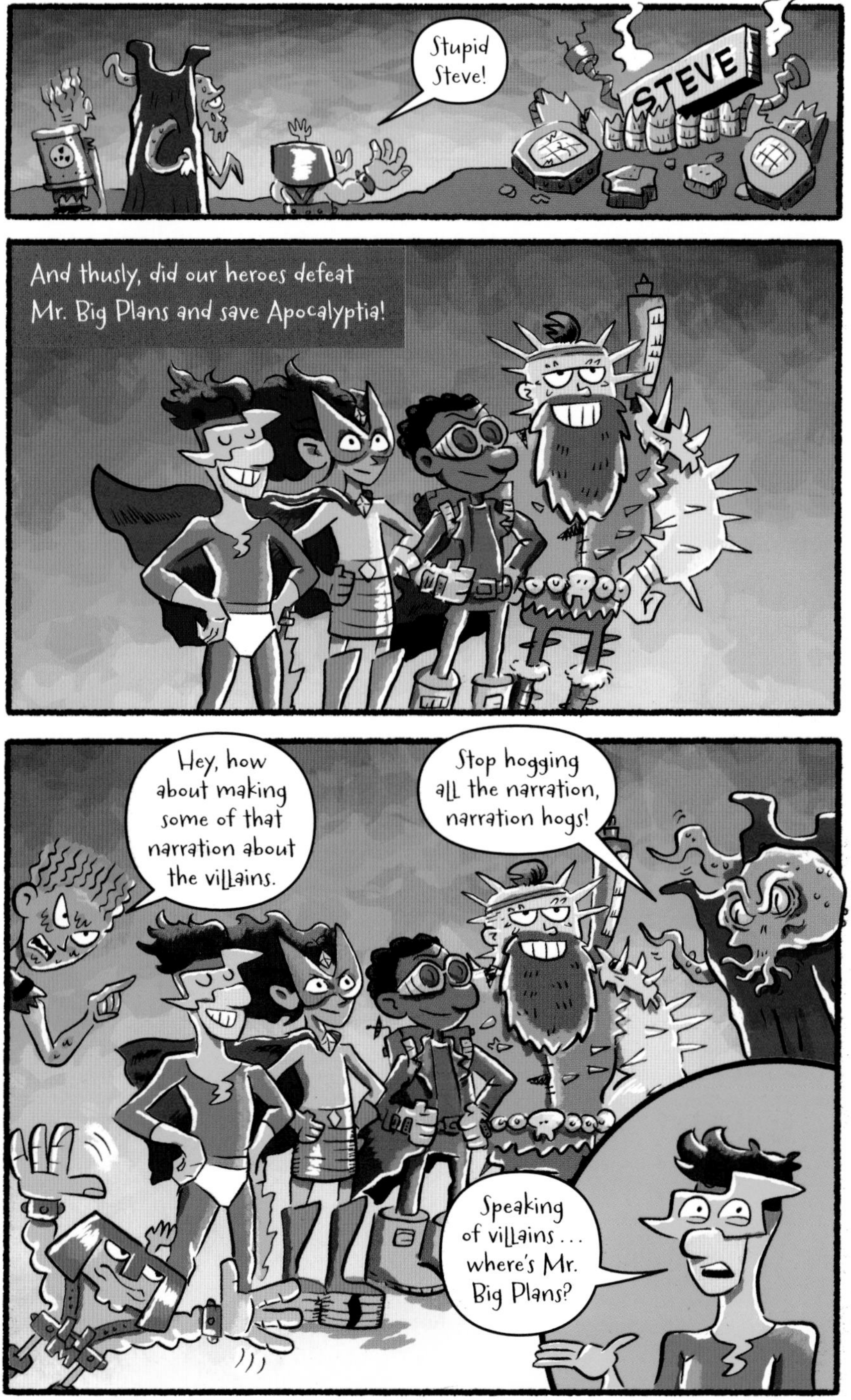
Stupid Steve!
STEVE
And thusly, did our heroes defeat Mr. Big Plans and save Apocalyptia!
Hey, how about making some of that narration about the villains.
Stop hogging all the narration, narration hogs!
Speaking of villains . . . where's Mr. Big Plans?

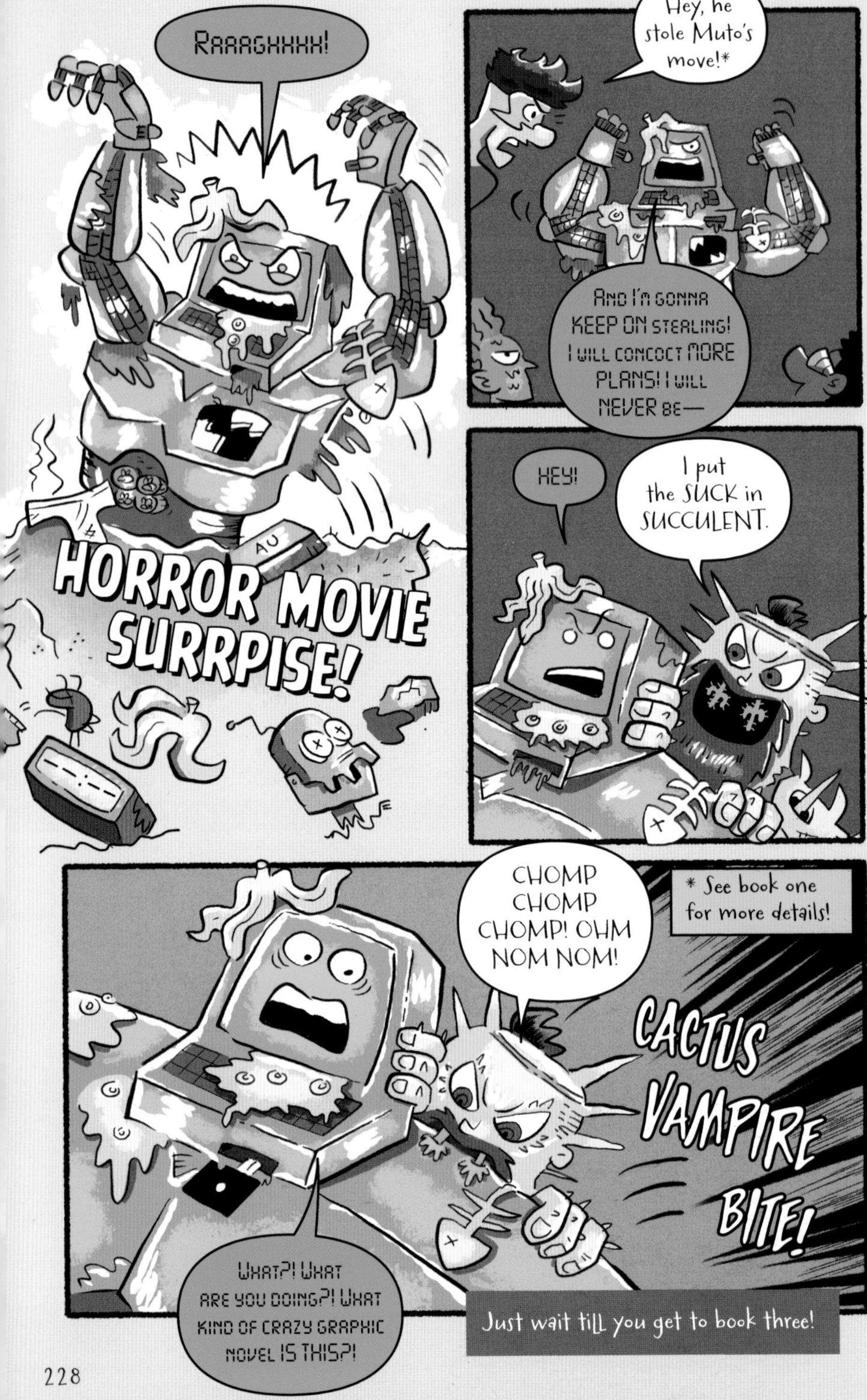

RAAAGHHHH!
Hey, he stole Muto's move!*
AND I'M GONNA KEEP ON STEALING! I WILL CONCOCT MORE PLANS! I WILL NEVER BE—
HORROR MOVIE SURRPISE!
HEY!
I put the SUCK in SUCCULENT.
CHOMP CHOMP CHOMP! OHM NOM NOM!
* See book one for more details!
CACTUS VAMPIRE BITE!
WHAT?! WHAT ARE YOU DOING?! WHAT KIND OF CRAZY GRAPHIC NOVEL IS THIS?!
Just wait till you get to book three!

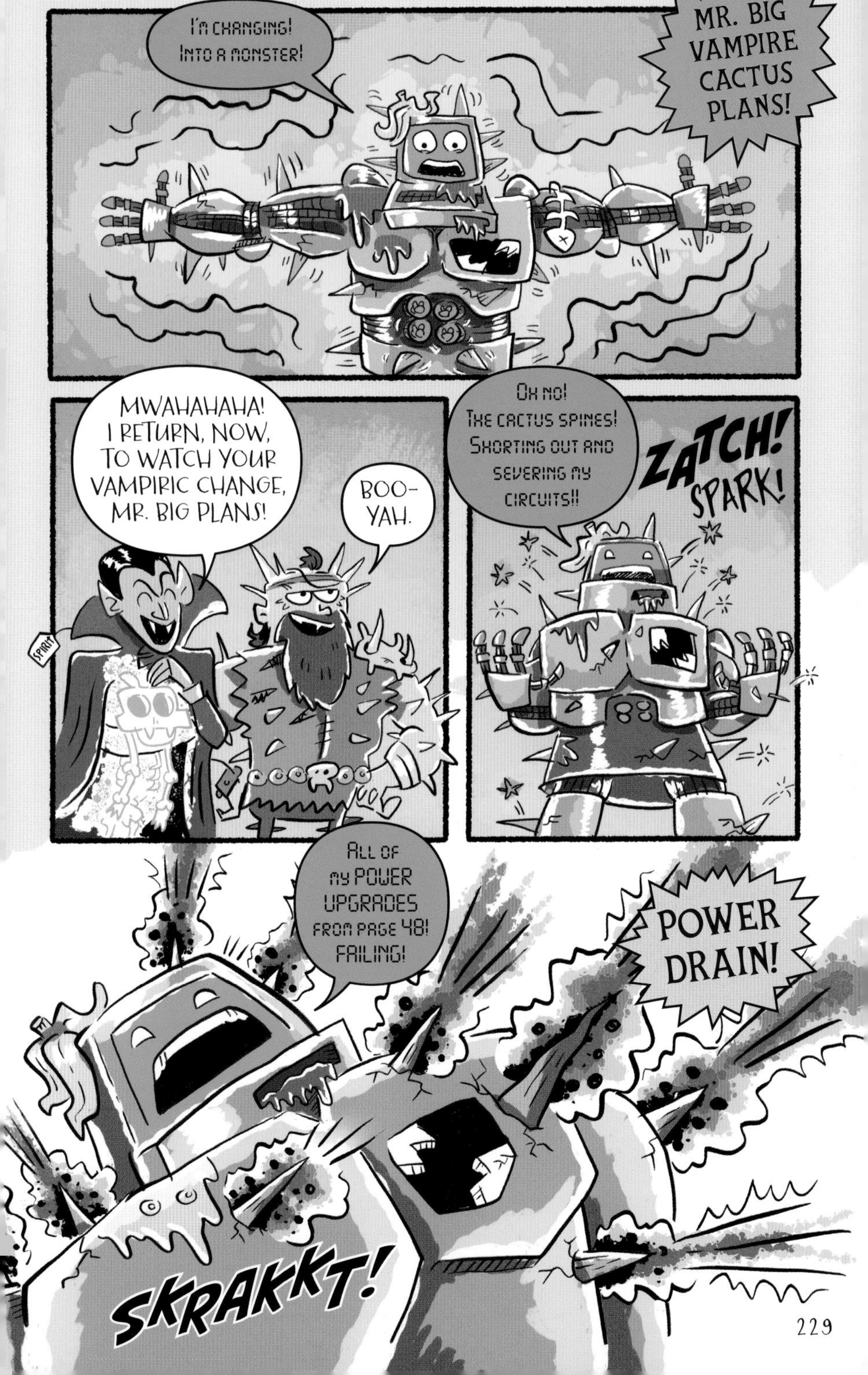
I'M CHANGING! INTO A MONSTER!
MR. BIG VAMPIRE CACTUS PLANS!
MWAHAHAHA! I RETURN, NOW, TO WATCH YOUR VAMPIRIC CHANGE, MR. BIG PLANS!
BOO-YAH.
OH NO! THE CACTUS SPINES! SHORTING OUT AND SEVERING MY CIRCUITS!!
ZATCH!
SPARK!
ALL OF MY POWER UPGRADES FROM PAGE 48! FAILING!
POWER DRAIN!
SKRAKKT!

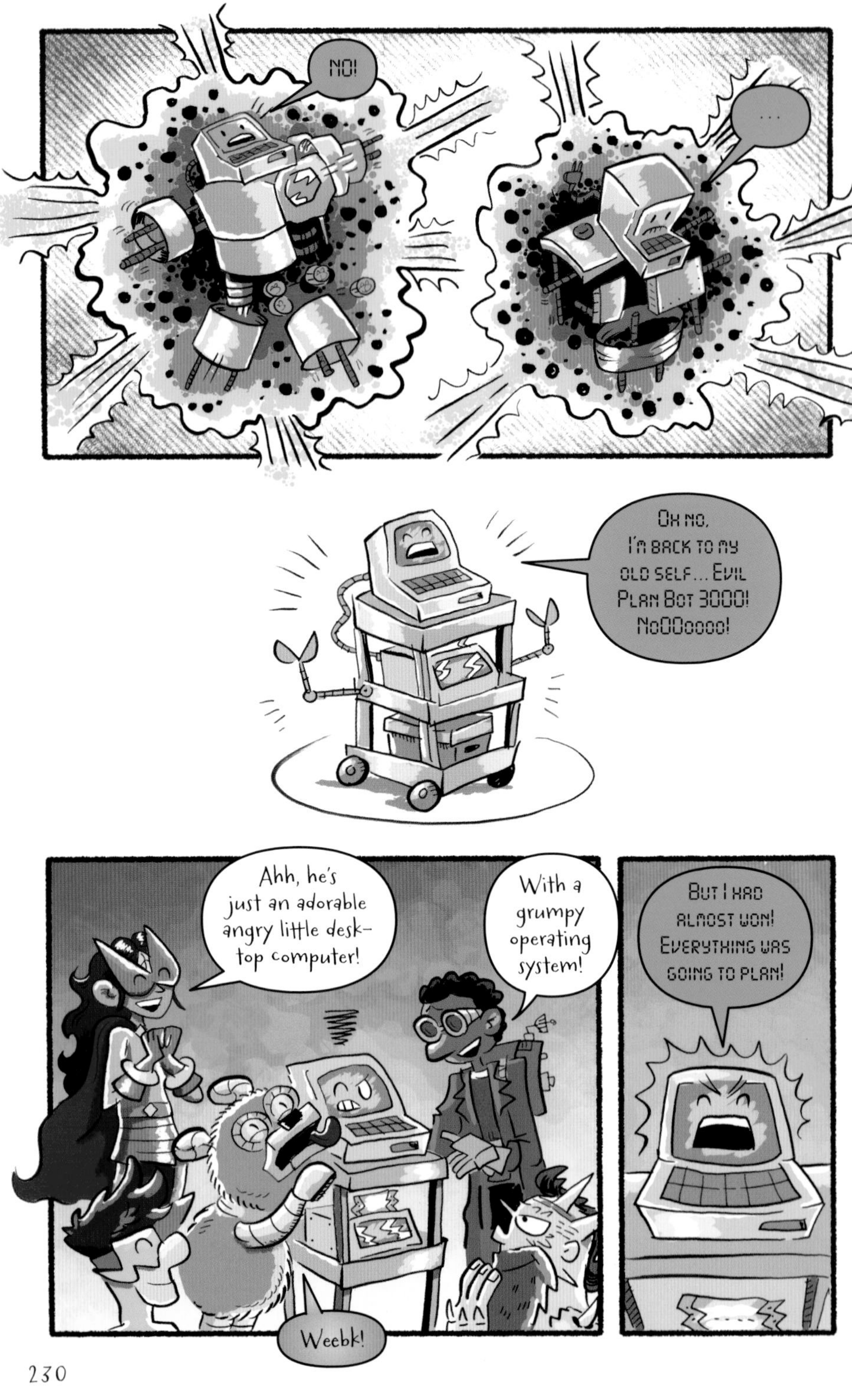
NO!
...
OH NO. I'M BACK TO MY OLD SELF... EVIL PLAN BOT 3000! NOOOoooo!
Ahh, he's just an adorable angry little desk-top computer!
With a grumpy operating system!
Weebk!
BUT I HAD ALMOST WON! EVERYTHING WAS GOING TO PLAN!

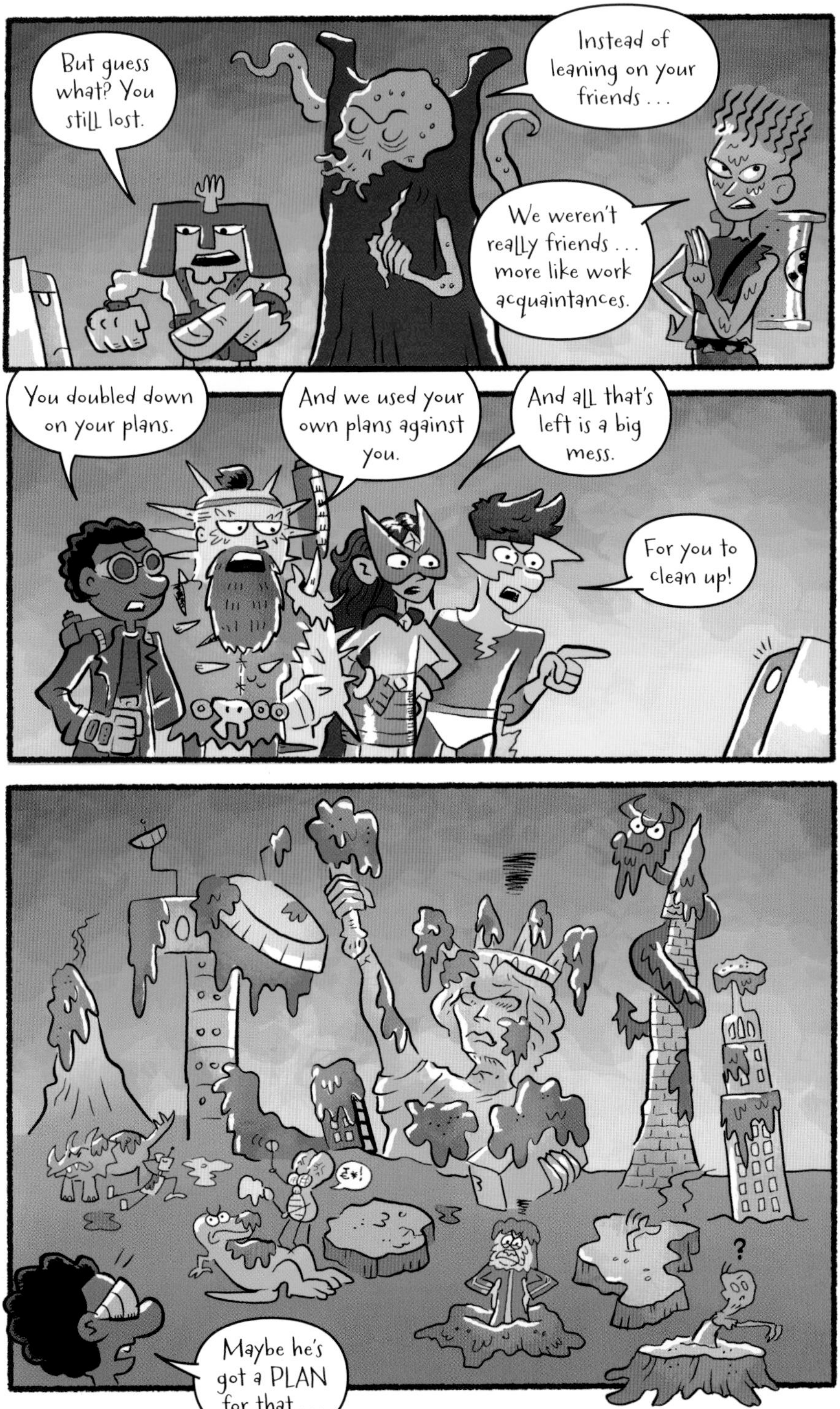

But guess what? You still lost.
Instead of leaning on your friends . . .
We weren't really friends . . . more like work acquaintances.
You doubled down on your plans.
And we used your own plans against you.
And all that's left is a big mess.
For you to clean up!
Maybe he's got a PLAN for that . . .

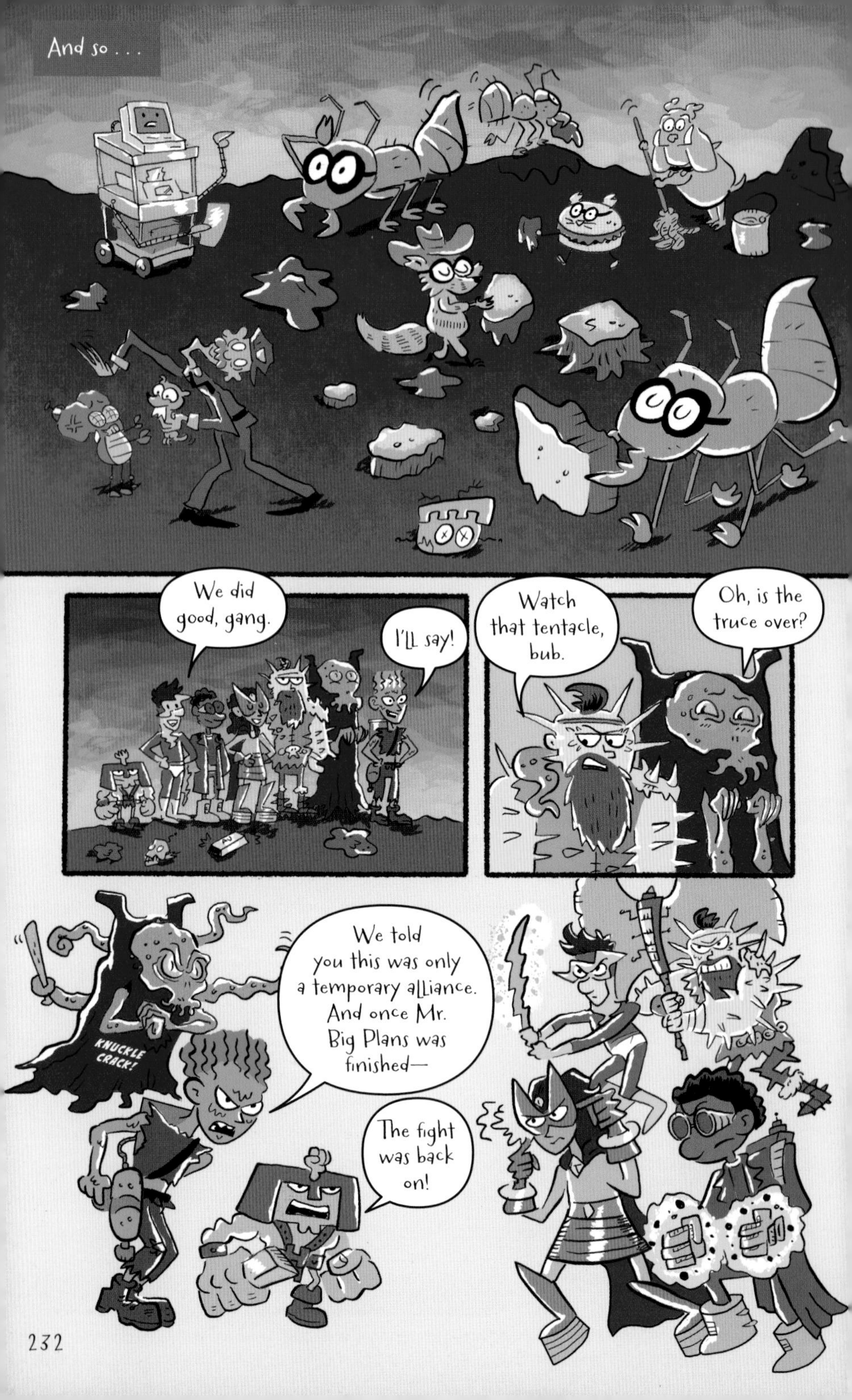
And so . . .
We did good, gang.
I'LL say!
Watch that tentacle, bub.
Oh, is the truce over?
KNUCKLE CRACK!
We told you this was only a temporary alliance. And once Mr. Big Plans was finished—
The fight was back on!

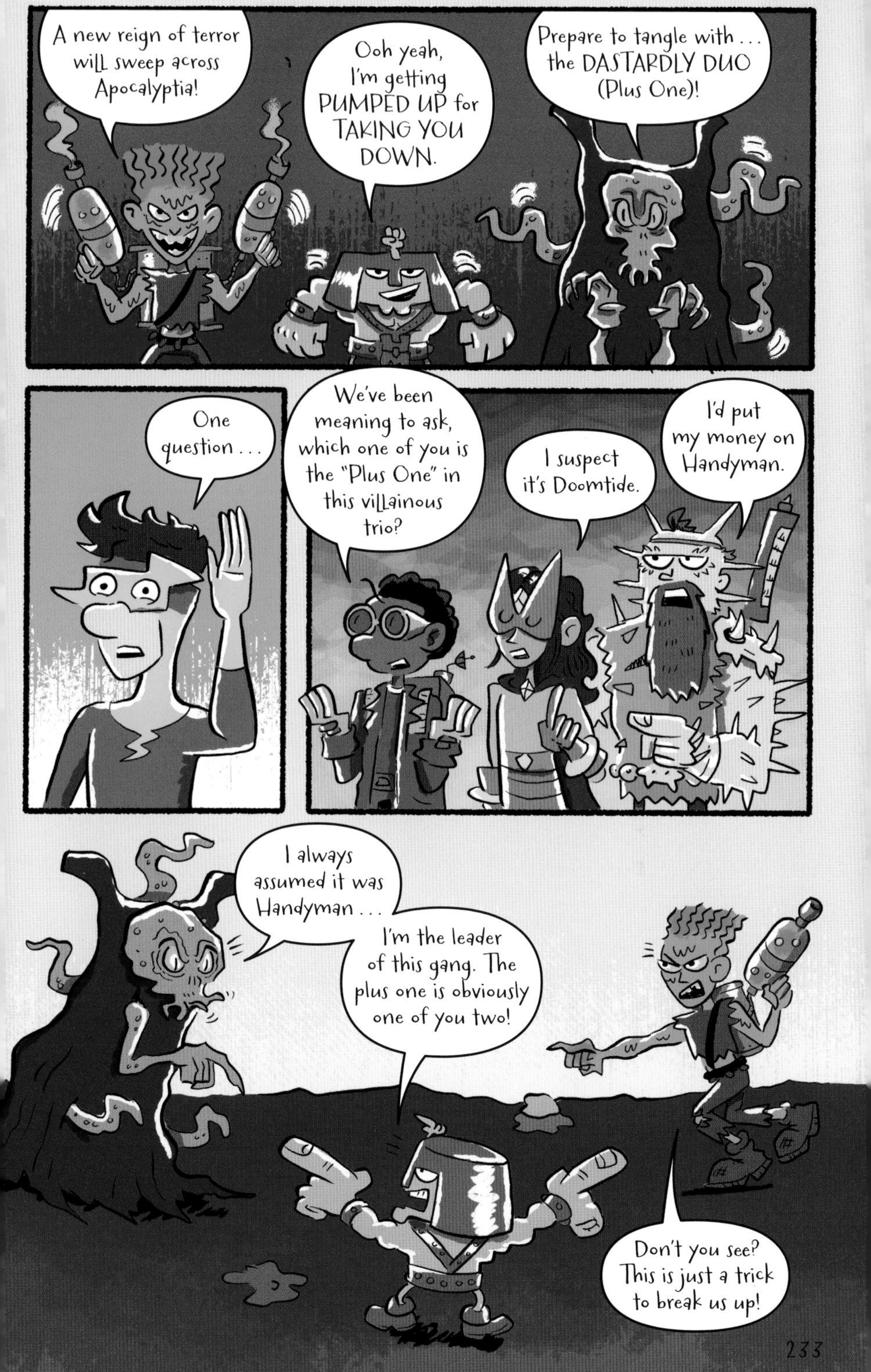
A new reign of terror will sweep across Apocalyptia!
Ooh yeah, I'm getting PUMPED UP for TAKING YOU DOWN.
Prepare to tangle with . . . the DASTARDLY DUO (Plus One)!
One question . . .
We've been meaning to ask, which one of you is the "Plus One" in this villainous trio?
I suspect it's Doomtide.
I'd put my money on Handyman.
I always assumed it was Handyman . . .
I'm the leader of this gang. The plus one is obviously one of you two!
Don't you see? This is just a trick to break us up!

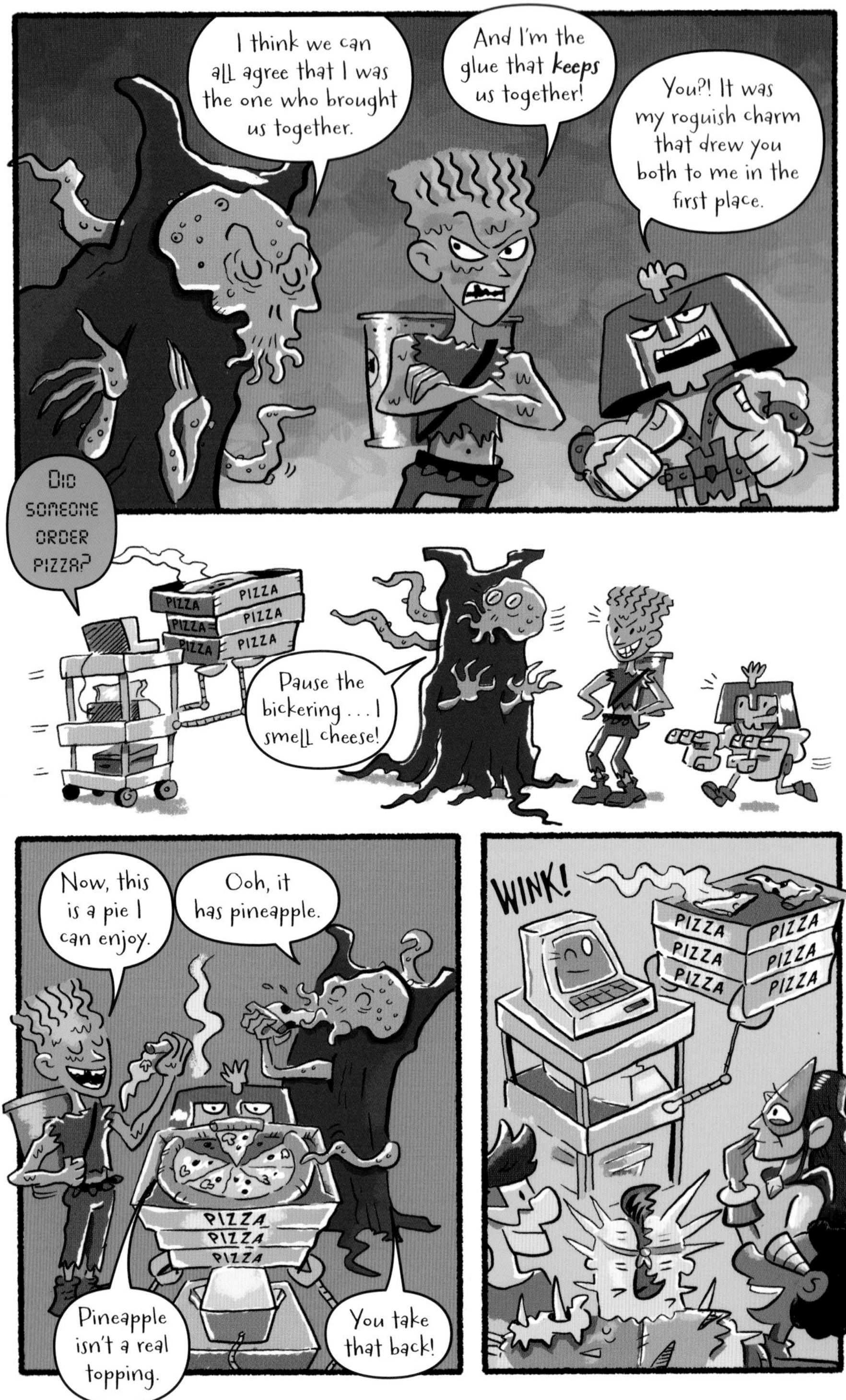
I think we can all agree that I was the one who brought us together.
And I'm the glue that **keeps** us together!
You?! It was my roguish charm that drew you both to me in the first place.
DID SOMEONE ORDER PIZZA?
PIZZA PIZZA PIZZA PIZZA PIZZA PIZZA
Pause the bickering . . . I smell cheese!
Now, this is a pie I can enjoy.
Ooh, it has pineapple.
PIZZA PIZZA PIZZA
Pineapple isn't a real topping.
You take that back!
WINK!
PIZZA PIZZA PIZZA PIZZA PIZZA PIZZA

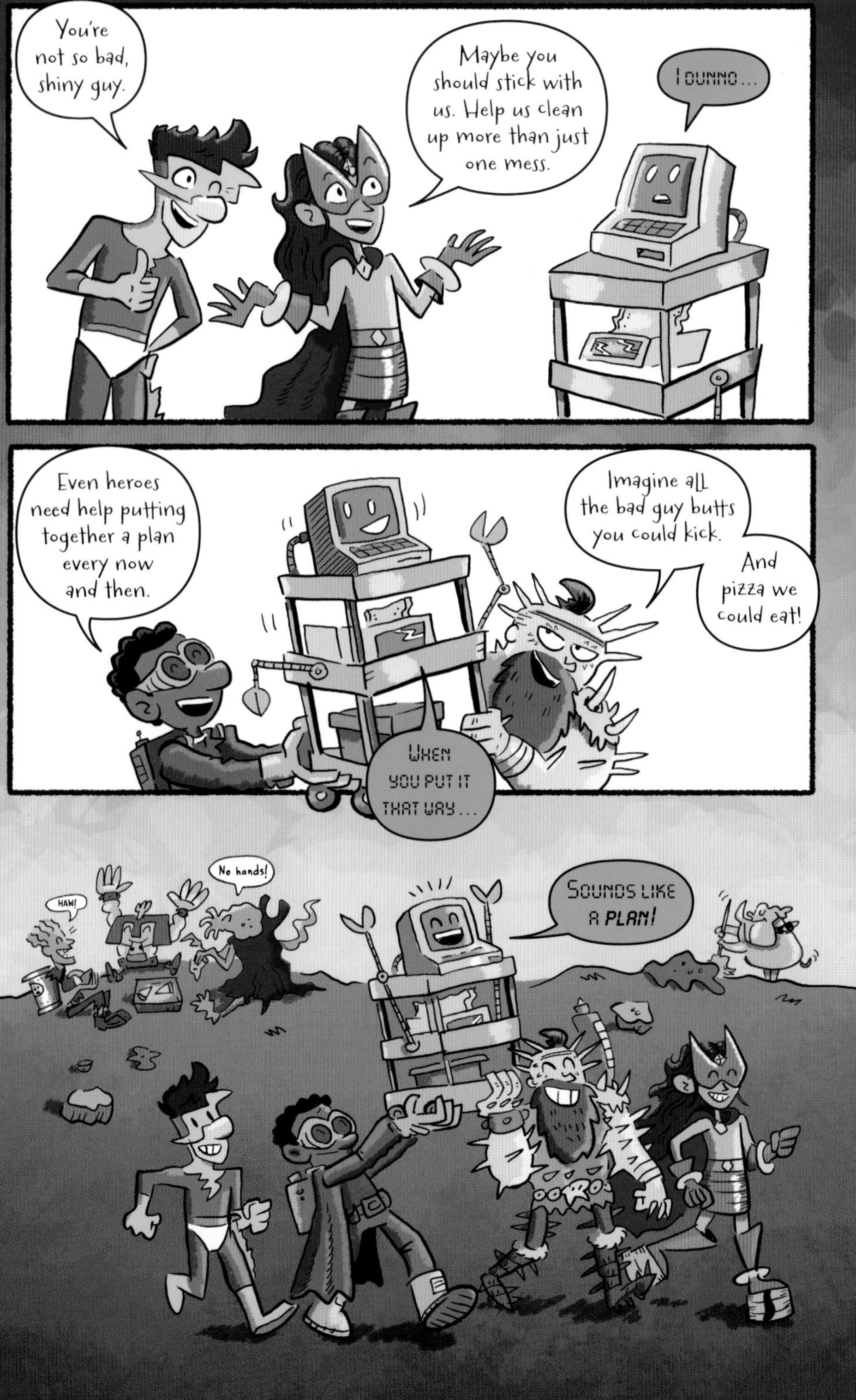
You're not so bad, shiny guy.
Maybe you should stick with us. Help us clean up more than just one mess.
I DUNNO...
Even heroes need help putting together a plan every now and then.
Imagine ALL the bad guy butts you could kick.
And pizza we could eat!
WHEN YOU PUT IT THAT WAY...
HAW!
No hands!
SOUNDS LIKE A PLAN!

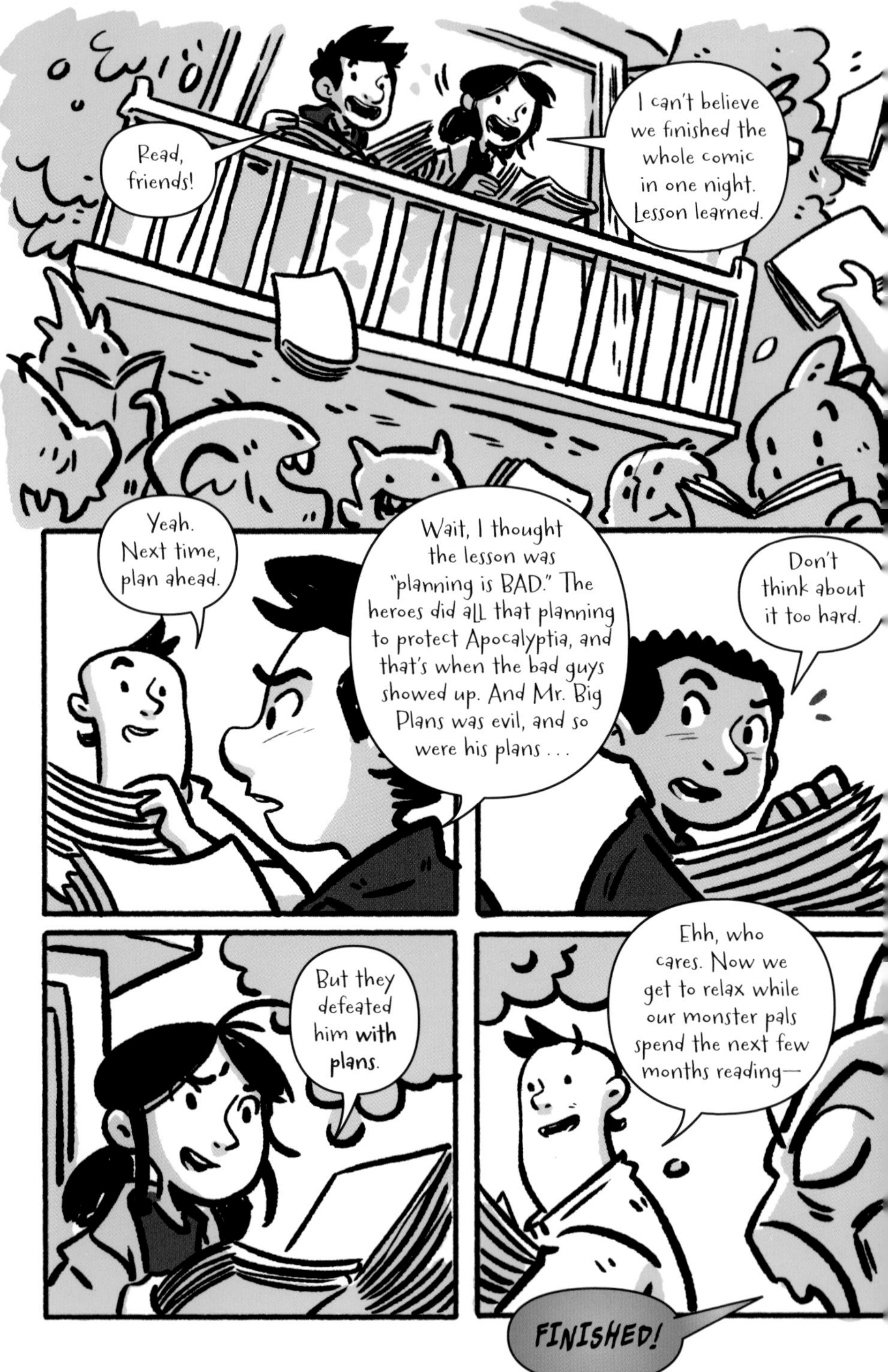
Read, friends!
I can't believe we finished the whole comic in one night. Lesson learned.
Yeah. Next time, plan ahead.
Wait, I thought the lesson was "planning is BAD." The heroes did ALL that planning to protect Apocalyptia, and that's when the bad guys showed up. And Mr. Big Plans was evil, and so were his plans . . .
Don't think about it too hard.
But they defeated him **with plans.**
Ehh, who cares. Now we get to relax while our monster pals spend the next few months reading—
FINISHED!

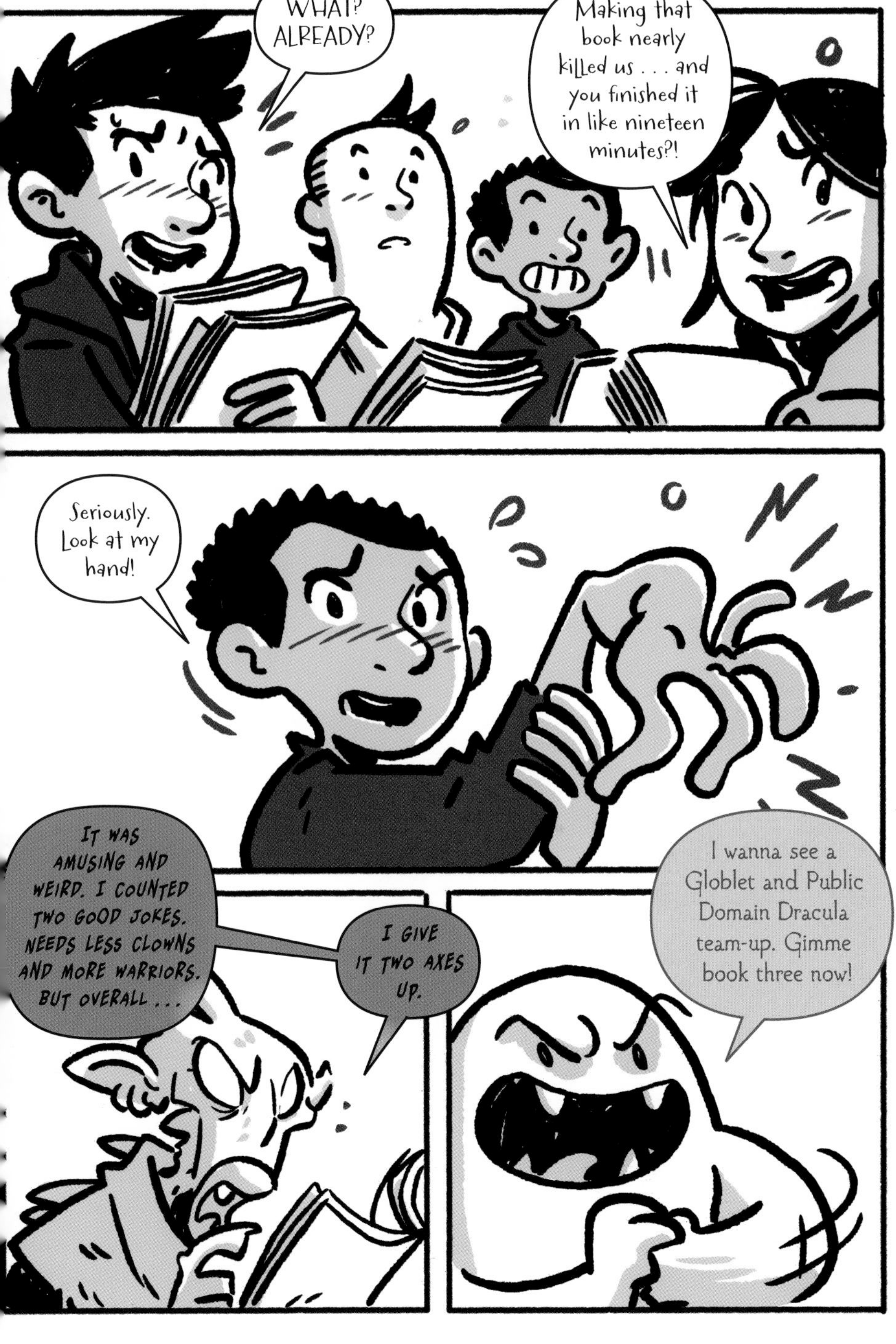
WHAT? ALREADY?
Making that book nearly killed us . . . and you finished it in like nineteen minutes?!
Seriously. Look at my hand!
IT WAS AMUSING AND WEIRD. I COUNTED TWO GOOD JOKES. NEEDS LESS CLOWNS AND MORE WARRIORS. BUT OVERALL . . .
I GIVE IT TWO AXES UP.
I wanna see a Globlet and Public Domain Dracula team-up. Gimme book three now!

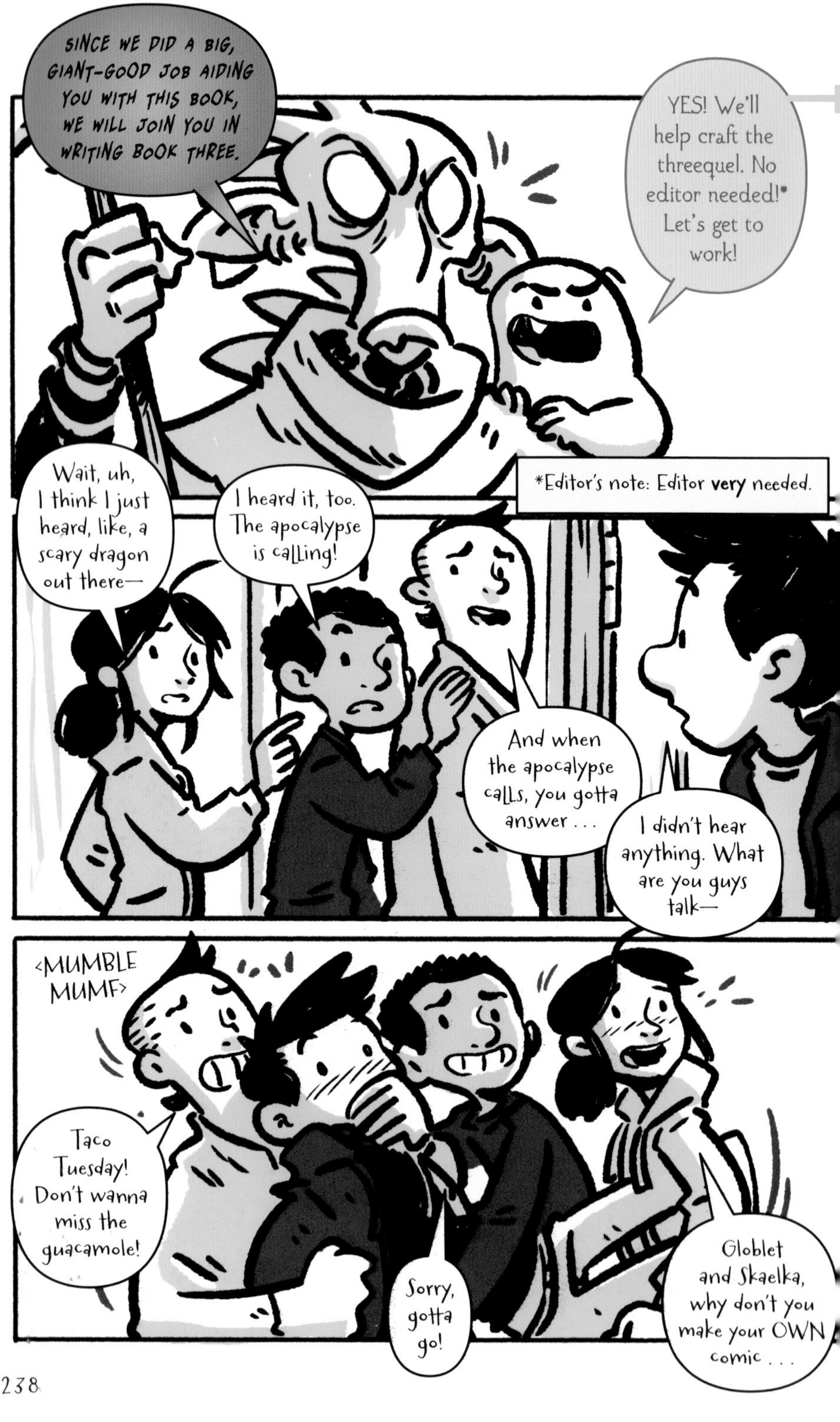
SINCE WE DID A BIG, GIANT-GOOD JOB AIDING YOU WITH THIS BOOK, WE WILL JOIN YOU IN WRITING BOOK THREE.
YES! We'll help craft the threequel. No editor needed!* Let's get to work!
*Editor's note: Editor **very** needed.
Wait, uh, I think I just heard, like, a scary dragon out there—
I heard it, too. The apocalypse is calling!
And when the apocalypse calls, you gotta answer . . .
I didn't hear anything. What are you guys talk—
<MUMBLE MUMF>
Taco Tuesday! Don't wanna miss the guacamole!
Sorry, gotta go!
Globlet and Skaelka, why don't you make your OWN comic . . .

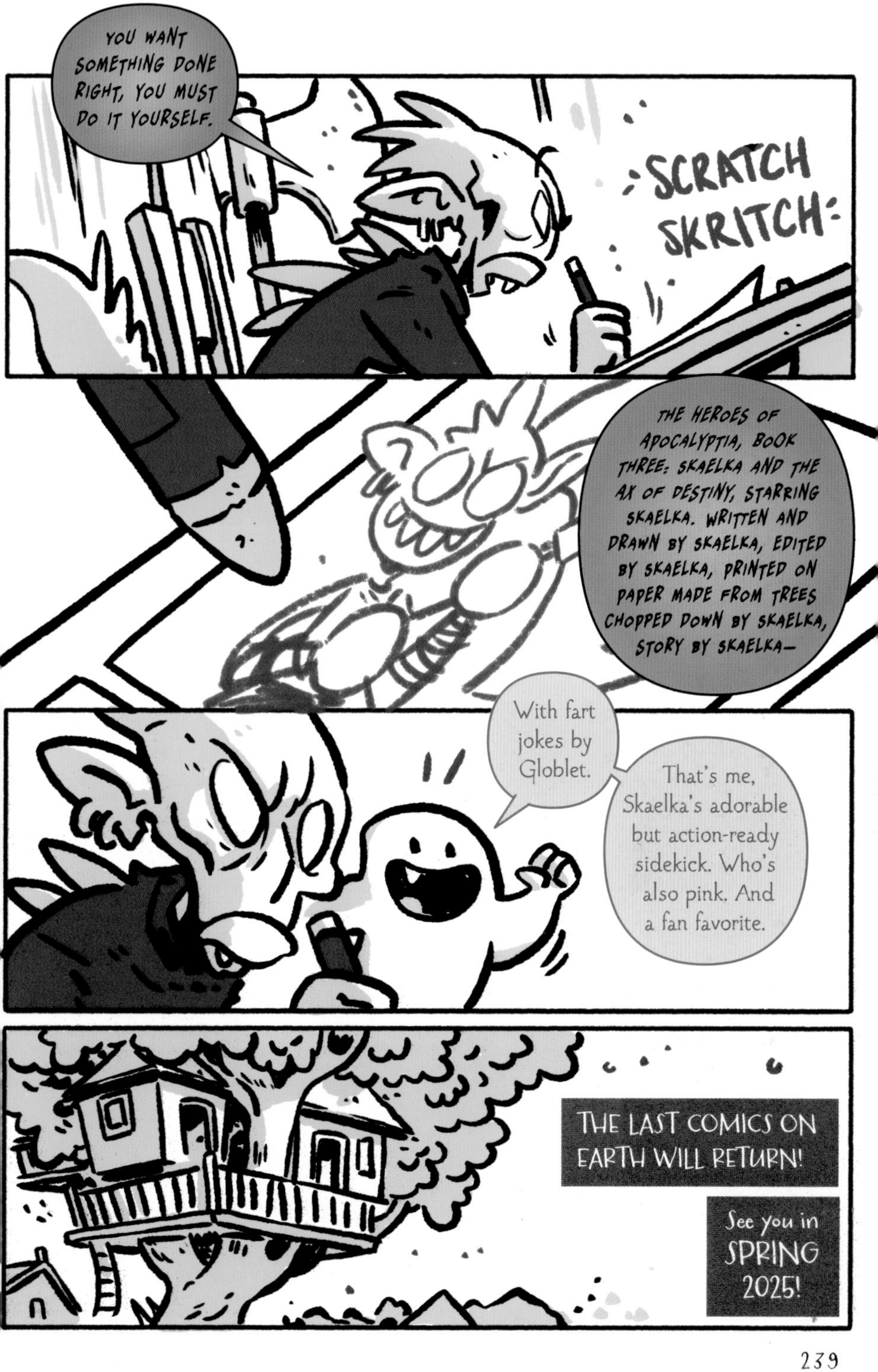
YOU WANT SOMETHING DONE RIGHT, YOU MUST DO IT YOURSELF.
SCRATCH
SKRITCH
THE HEROES OF APOCALYPTIA, BOOK THREE: SKAELKA AND THE AX OF DESTINY, STARRING SKAELKA. WRITTEN AND DRAWN BY SKAELKA, EDITED BY SKAELKA, PRINTED ON PAPER MADE FROM TREES CHOPPED DOWN BY SKAELKA, STORY BY SKAELKA—
With fart jokes by Globlet.
That's me, Skaelka's adorable but action-ready sidekick. Who's also pink. And a fan favorite.
THE LAST COMICS ON EARTH WILL RETURN!
See you in SPRING 2025!

Acknowledgments

Massive thanks to the giant-sized superhero team who helped bring this bad boy to life. A colossal THANK-YOU to Jay Cooper (*not* Jake Ooper), who made this thing about twenty-six shades of awesome. And a big "same to you" nod to Jim Hoover, who, despite my annoying last-minute changes and so many looming deadlines, has somehow served up another design masterpiece. Doug Holgate, forever and ever my post-apocalyptic partner in crime. Joe Eichelberger, you've painted Apocalyptia so bright, I gotta wear shades. Hugs and jazz hands and hat tips and MASSIVE thank-yous to Dana Leydig, Leila Sales, Tamar Brazis, Ken Wright, Elyse Marshall, Emily Romero, Christina Colangelo, Alex Garber, Lauren Festa, Carmela Iaria, Shanta Newlin, Liz Vaughan, and every other rock star in PYR marketing, publicity, and the sales booth. Virtual bear hugs and jazz hands to the legends at Atomic Cartoons for beaming Last Kids to starry-eyed kiddos globally. Dan Lazar, for every last thing, always. Haley Mancini, you are the master of last-minute, cherry-on-the-sundae jokes and gags. Andy Rogers, thanks for all the last-minute help—could not have finished this one without you. And one humongous, cartoonish, feet-lifted-off-the-floor bear hug to Josh Pruett. Writing with a buddy is the best.

—M. B.

GINORMOUS thanks to our LAST COMICS team: Upside-down Doug, Jim (the best), Mother Dana, Auntie Leila, Alphabet Chris, Color Joe, and Assistant Andy! You put the LAST COMICS in LAST COMICS! Meepu-shaped hugs to my first readers, Catie, Zach, and Amanda! Clown Apocalypse–sized gratitude to Scott, Matt, Aaron, Catie, Jennifer, Jill, Haley, Jen, and the rest of the Atomic Cartoons/Netflix *Last Kids On Earth* animated series team! Love you guys. All remaining thanks to my agent, Deborah Warren, at East/West Lit and Dan and Torie at Writers House. Hugs and kisses to you, Max; writing these books with you gets more fun and more ridiculous every time. Next book, we need more clowns. And so much gratitude and comics-love to Jay, our superhero, in every way. Thrilled that we get to make funny comics together, at least two more times! And thank you to our readers! These books ARE FOR YOU!   —J. P.

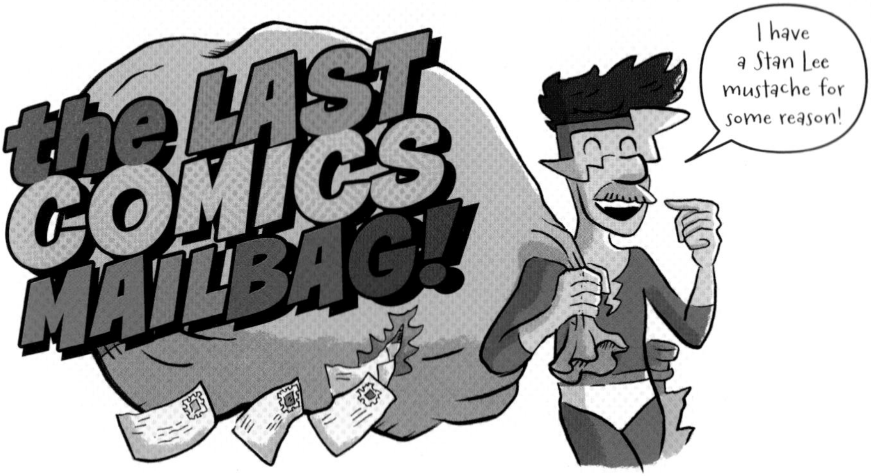
the LAST
COMICS
MAILBAG!
I have a Stan Lee mustache for some reason!

Hey there, readers! We hope you enjoyed *The Last Comics on Earth: Too Many Villains!* Did you ever think you'd see the word "plan" used that many times in *one* book? Bet ya didn't!

Some of you fantastic fans have been sending mail our way, full of questions and comments. It is only right and proper that we respond to those questions and comments. So . . . Here we go!

Max, Josh, Jay, and Doug

If you could have any of the superheroes' powers, which would you have? I would choose Boy Lightning's because I could make anything and destroy the bosses!

Jude C., age 9
Cashmere, WA

Hey, Jude! Good choice! When I was your age, I would've chosen Boy Lightning, too—because I loved baseball and I loved to draw. These days? Hmm . . . I'd probably go with Doc Baker. I love gadgets—I wish every book, movie, comic, *whatever* was crammed with gadgets. My dream gadget? A button that freezes time so I can take alllll the time I want writing the Last Comics on Earth books.

Max

Great question, Jude! I'd choose Z-Man! Sure, he's an old bag of bones and he falls apart now and then. But . . . he has detachable limbs! That means he can fetch snacks without getting off the couch. And that just so happens to be my ultimate dream in life!

Josh

My favorite character is Quint because he has a funny sense of humor like me, and I can relate to him because I also have a creative imagination. Can we see more Quint gadgets and suits soon, please?!

Stone G., age 9
Los Angeles, CA

Hi, Stone! First off, cool name . . . you must have some pretty hip parents! Yep, Quint sure is a clever dude. About five years ago, while I was writing *The Last Kids on Earth and the Midnight Blade*, I made a giant list of Quint gadgets and inventions I could use in future books. I think there were almost one hundred of them. There was a Hover Hammock, a Distractifying Disco Ball, and some special armor I'm saving for the next book. Oh, and YES. We'll do more Quint suits, too! Maybe even . . . a Stone suit?!?

Max

We have a question about Jack, June, Quint, and Dirk's superhero costumes. Did they always look like that? Or did they change after you started drawing? (We like the way they look in the book but wondered if there were other versions we never saw.)

Jack P., age 10, Dylan P., age 8,
and Donovan P., age 6
Alexandria, VA

Hey, Jack, Dylan, and Donovan! I tried a few different versions of June, Jack, and Dirk's costumes before landing on the final versions in the book. Quint's alter ego, Doc Baker, first appeared in *The Last Kids on Earth: Thrilling Tales from the Tree House*, and he didn't change much between that book and this one. Check it out!

Jay

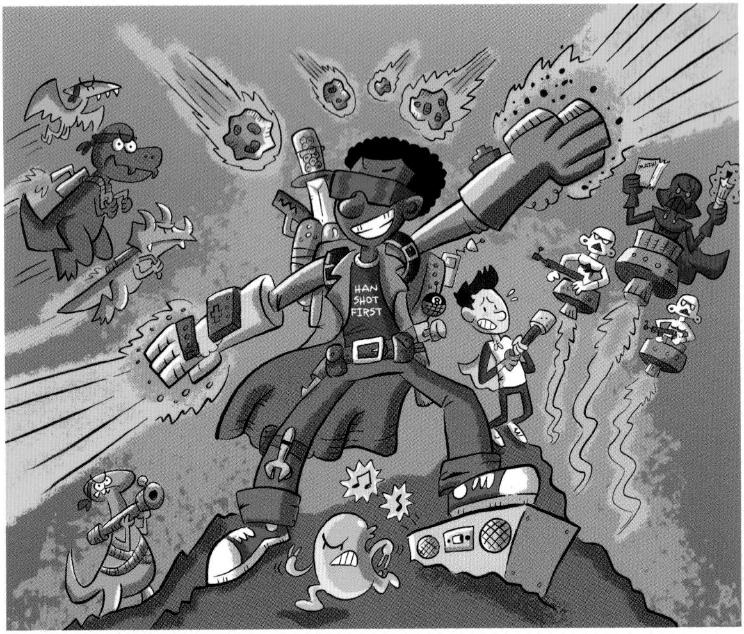
HAN SHOT FIRST

OK, Apocalyptia is a world full of *every possible apocalypse ever*, right? So do you have a favorite apocalypse? My favorite is the Cat & Dog Apocalypse, because if I lived there I could take my pets with me and we could be in charge of everything, together. I don't like the Weird Apocalypse because it looks goopy!

Luna F., age 11
Houston, TX

You're correct, Luna, the Weird Apocalypse *is* goopy. And I have bad news for you—there's going to be a <u>*lot*</u> of goopy, Weird Apocalype fun in an upcoming book. My favorite apocalypse so far is the Knock-Knock Joke Apocalypse because it's just so bizarre. Speaking of . . . I made up a knock-knock joke. Wanna hear it?

Knock, knock.

Who's there?

Meep.

Meep who?

Meepu! Yep, that's me, June's furry friend. She's doing boring stuff today, so you wanna hang out?

Max

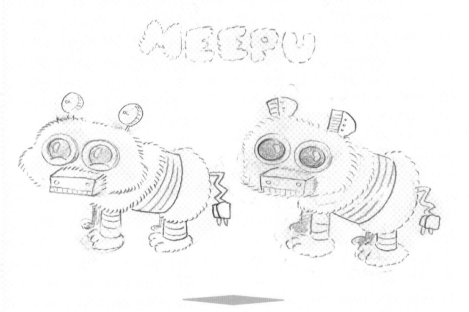

My question is do writers and illustrators have bedtimes? My bedtime is 8 p.m. but sometimes I get to stay up late if my dad is watching football. But on a normal day it's 8 p.m. and I think that's not a fair time.

Brady B., age 7
Farmville, NC

Hi, Brady, thanks for writing. I don't have a bedtime, really—but if I don't get eight hours of sleep, it's hard to draw comics or do other important stuff like go hang-gliding or run my daily half-marathon.

Jay

I don't have a bedtime. Because I don't have a bed. I sleep on my couch because sleeping in regular beds gives me all sorts of neck pain 'cause I'm old and my old neck bones just love being a pain in my neck. For real, though. True story!

Max

This question is silly, I'm a grown man. Of course I have a bedtime. It's 7:15 p.m.

Josh

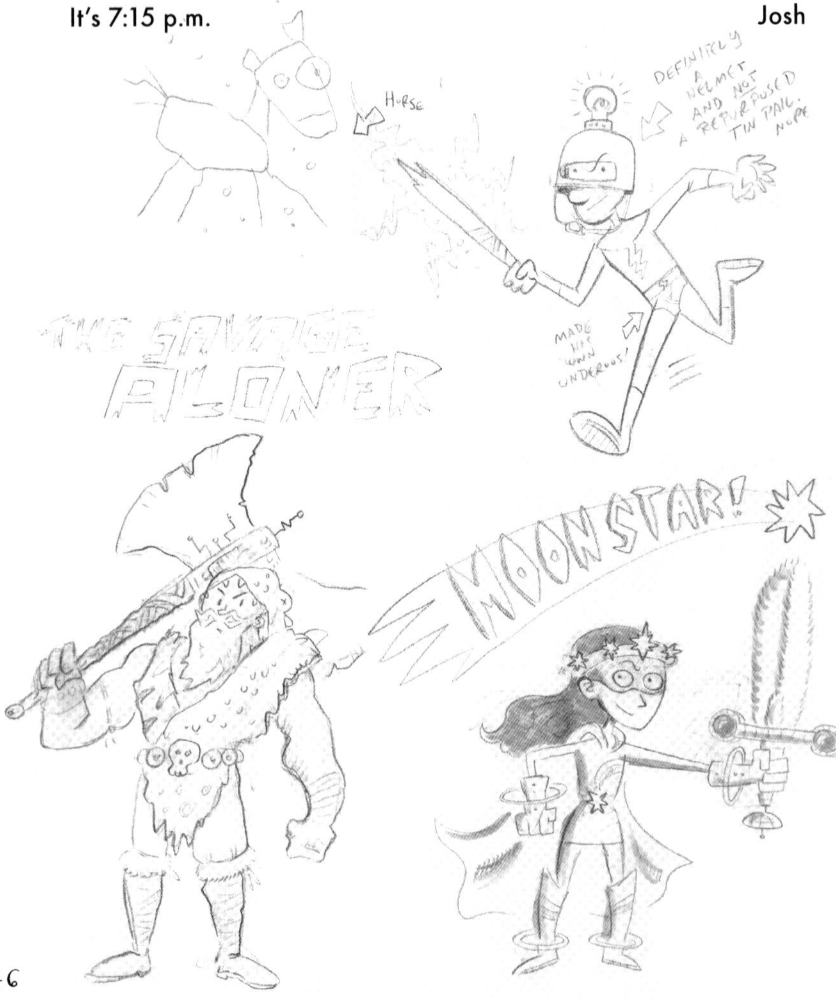
HORSE
DEFINITELY A HELMET AND NOT A REPURPOSED TIN PAIL. NOPE
MADE HIS OWN UNDEROOS!
THE SAVAGE ALONER
MOONSTAR!

I love Muto!!!! (NOT REALLY, HE'S BAD!) I mean I LOVE MUTO'S OUTFIT! Was all that stuff on his costume the illustrator's idea or was it the writers or somebody else? I need to tell you again that I LOVE MUTO and HOW DID YOU MAKE MUTO SO AWESOME???

Katie M., age 10
New York, NY

Thanks for saying all that nice stuff about Muto, Katie! You're right, he is BAD . . . but I had so much fun coming up with his design. I tried *a lot* of different ideas before landing on the final version of Muto. Take a peek at a few early Muto designs! Jay

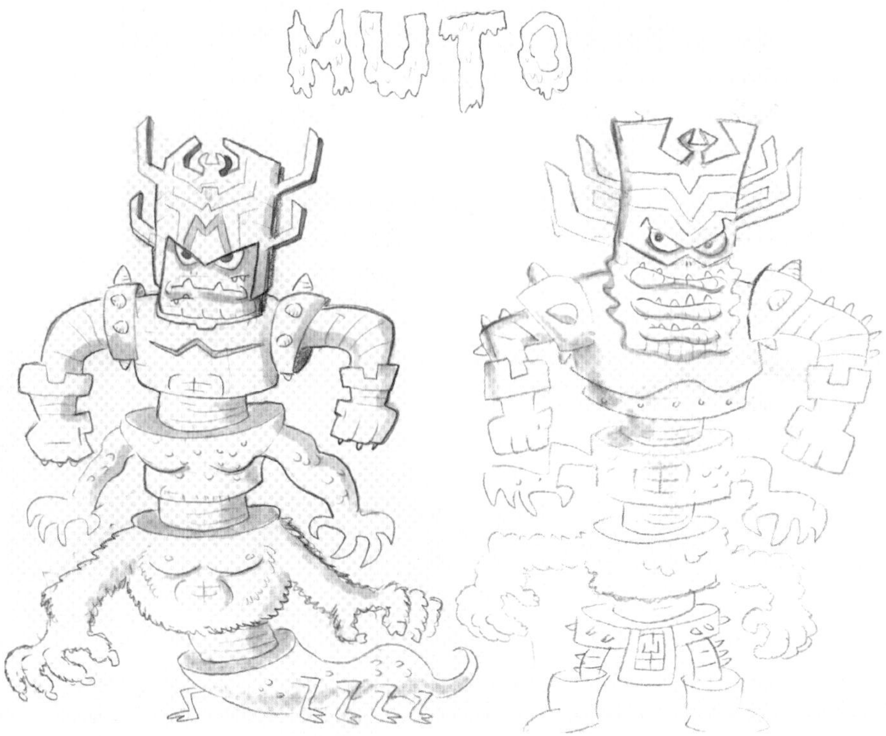
MUTO

I sent you guys a plastic bag full of nickels for buying Doc Baker's Forever Wet Toothbrush. It was part of the Bucket O' Gadgets on page 94 in the first Last Comics on Earth book (it has a #1 on the side). I never received a toothbrush or anything. I asked my sister and she said ALL of the stuff on the Doc Baker's Bucket O' Gadgets page are FAKE and not really FOR SALE. But I don't think she's being true. Help.

Ryan H., age 9
Arlington, MA

Hi, Ryan! We have bad news . . . your sister is right. None of the products featured in Quint's advertisement are real . . . yet! If and when they exist for real, we'll make sure you get the first one off the factory floor. Let us know if you'd like your nickels back. Josh probably spent them, but Max promises he'll search his couch for spare change. Until then . . . save up your nickels and buy yourself something nice!

Max & Josh

CONTACT US

Do ***YOU*** have a question, comment, or hilarious chain meme you want to share with us? Have a parent or guardian send letters to **AuthorMaxBrallier@penguinrandomhouse.com** for the chance to be featured in the next Last Comics book!

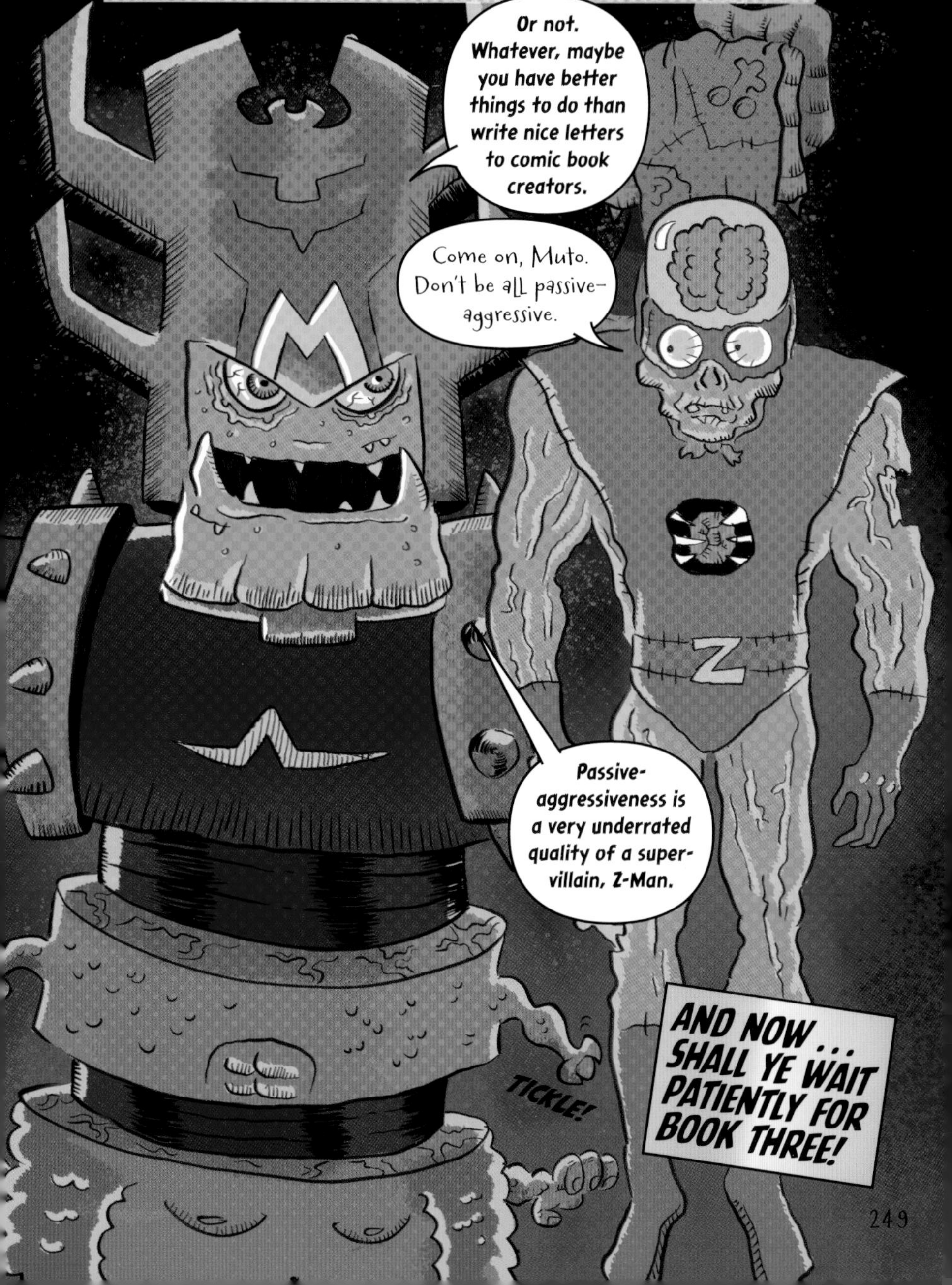

Or not. Whatever, maybe you have better things to do than write nice letters to comic book creators.
Come on, Muto. Don't be all passive-aggressive.
Passive-aggressiveness is a very underrated quality of a super-villain, Z-Man.
TICKLE!
AND NOW . . . SHALL YE WAIT PATIENTLY FOR BOOK THREE!

© Ruby Brallier

MAX BRALLIER

is a #1 *New York Times, USA Today,* and *Wall Street Journal* bestselling author. His books and series include The Last Kids on Earth, Eerie Elementary, Mister Shivers, Galactic Hot Dogs, and Can YOU Survive the Zombie Apocalypse? He is a writer and executive producer for Netflix's Emmy Award–winning adaptation of The Last Kids on Earth. Visit him at MaxBrallier.com.

JOSHUA PRUETT

is an Emmy Award–winning TV writer and the only human being on Earth to have written for both *Mystery Science Theater 3000* and *Doctor Who*. Joshua has worked in animation for over fifteen years, inflicting laughter (and monsters) on others writing on Disney's *Phineas & Ferb*, the feature film *Candace Against the Universe,* and the Emmy-winning adaptation of The Last Kids on Earth for Netflix. He is also co-author of *Shipwreckers: The Curse of the Cursed Temple of Curses, or We Nearly Died. A Lot.* with Scott Peterson. Last Comics is his first graphic novel series! Follow him @ZombieTardis.

© Guzman

JAY COOPER

has illustrated over twenty books for kids young and old, including the popular Bots series and the national bestselling *Your Guide to Not Getting Murdered in a Quaint English Village*. Jay is also an award-winning graphic designer of theatrical advertising, and has crafted art and advertising for more than one hundred Broadway shows. He lives in New Jersey with his family and a dog named Bradley Cooper. Visit him at JayCooperBooks.com and follow him at your peril: @JayCooperArt.

DOUGLAS HOLGATE

is the illustrator of the #1 *New York Times* bestselling series The Last Kids on Earth from Viking (now also an Emmy-winning Netflix animated series) and the cocreator and illustrator of the graphic novel *Clem Hetherington and the Ironwood Race* for Scholastic Graphix.

He has worked for the last twenty years making books and comics for publishers around the world from his garage in Victoria, Australia. He lives with his family and an adorable young pupper in the Australian bush on five acres surrounded by eighty-million-year-old volcanic boulders.

You can find his work at DouglasBotHolgate.com and @DouglasHolgate.

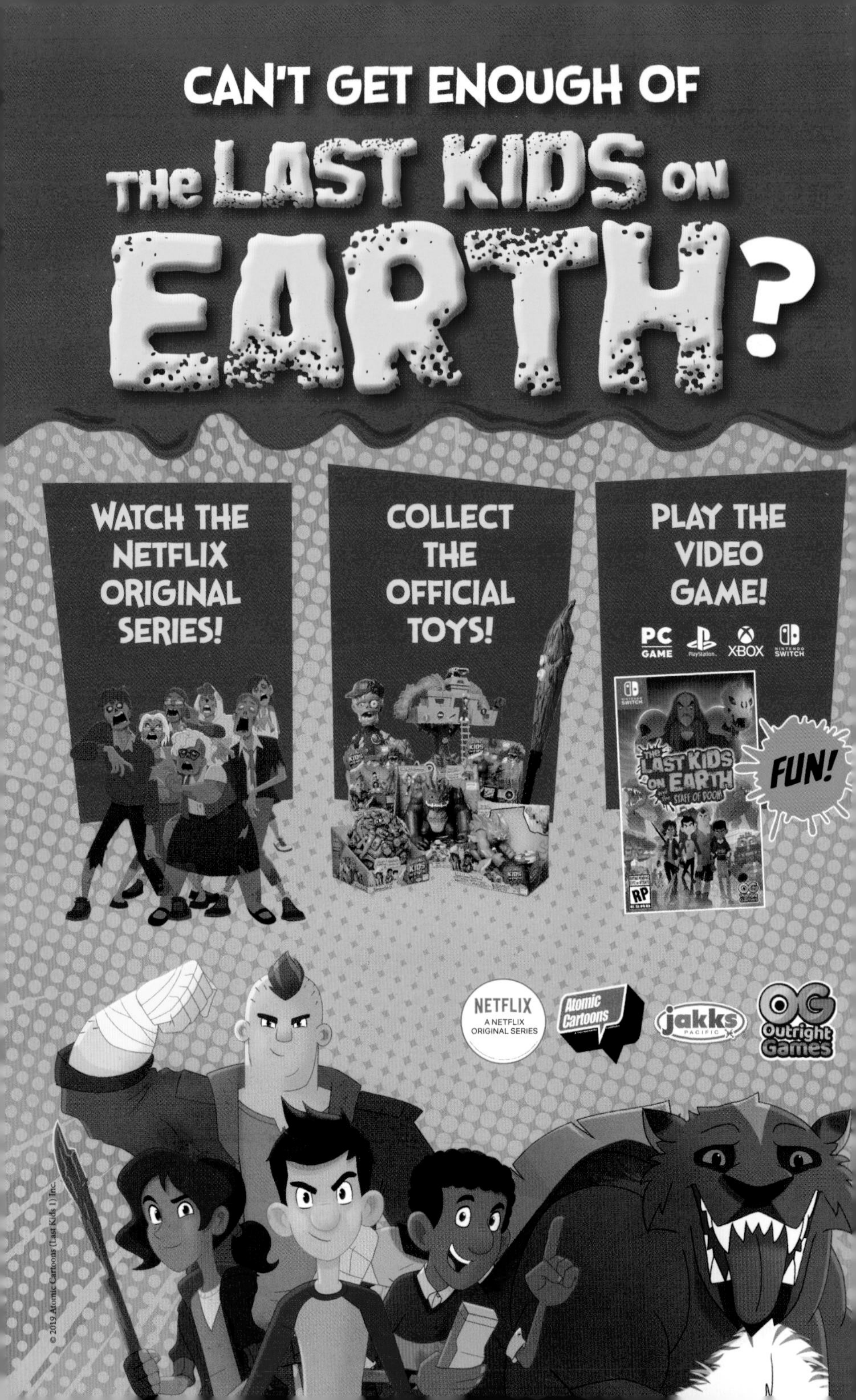
CAN'T GET ENOUGH OF
THE LAST KIDS ON EARTH?
WATCH THE NETFLIX ORIGINAL SERIES!
COLLECT THE OFFICIAL TOYS!
PLAY THE VIDEO GAME!
PC GAME
PlayStation
XBOX
NINTENDO SWITCH
THE LAST KIDS ON EARTH and the STAFF OF DOOM
FUN!
NETFLIX
A NETFLIX ORIGINAL SERIES
Atomic Cartoons
jakks PACIFIC
OG Outright Games
© 2019 Atomic Cartoons (Last Kids 1) Inc.

THE MONSTER-BATTLING FUN DOESN'T STOP HERE!

Check out all these books, people!

JOIN TODAY!

Have your parent or guardian sign up for the official Last Kids on Earth Fan Club to receive a Welcome Kit in the mail! Plus, you'll receive exclusive Last Kids news, sneak previews, and behind-the-scenes info via our e-newsletter!

VISIT TheLastKidsonEarthClub.com
TO LEARN MORE

SCAN QR CODE

TO VISIT TODAY